FOOT OF THE RAINBOW

Tony Warren

ARROW

1 3 5 7 9 10 8 6 4 2

First published in Arrow in 1994
© Tony Warren 1993

Tony Warren has asserted his right under the Copyright, Designs and
Patents Act, 1988 to be identified as the author of this work.

First published in the UK in 1993 by Century
Random House UK, 20 Vauxhall Bridge Road, London, SW1V 2SA

Random House Australia (Pty) Ltd
20 Alfred Street, Milsons Point, Sydney
New South Wales 2061, Australia

Random House New Zealand Ltd
18 Poland Road, Glenfield
Auckland 10, New Zealand

Random House South Africa (Pty) Ltd
PO Box 337, Bergvlei, South Africa

Random House UK Limited Reg No. 954009

ISBN 0 09 926391 2

900 268080

Lyrics from *Alabammy Bound*, Music by Ray Henderson and Words by
Bud Green and Bud De Sylva reproduced by permission of Keith Prowse
Music Pub Co Ltd, London WC2H OEA
© 1925, Shapiro Bernstein & Co Inc, New York Renewed
Published by joint arrangement between Shapiro Bernstein & Co Inc and
Ross Jungnickel Inc, New York
Lyrics from *The Anniversary Song* Words and Music by Saul Chaplin and
Al Jolson reproduced by permission of Campbell Connelly & Co Ltd. All
Rights Reserved.
Lyrics from *I Enjoy Being a Girl* from *Flower Drum Song* Music by Richard
Rodgers and Words by Oscar Hammerstein II reproduced by permission
of Williamson Music, owner of publication and allied rights throughout
the world.
© 1958 by Richard Rodgers and Oscar Hammerstein II
Copyright Renewed
International Copyright Secured   All Rights Reserved

Typeset by Deltatype Ltd, Ellesmere Port
Printed and bound in Great Britain by
Cox & Wyman Ltd, Reading, Berkshire

For Susan Subtle
with love

Prologue

'Mother, what was a girl from Manchester doing in the middle of a revolution?'

At six and a half, he had already abandoned both 'mummy' and 'mamma'. Rosie found herself wondering if the Californian passers-by would take little Joe for English or Italian. There were flashes of both countries in his eager, questioning glance. His elder brother, Michael, stomping on ahead of them, was very definitely a fifteen-year-old Italian man.

A bundle of paisley rags uncoiled in a shop doorway, turned into a male human being and said, 'Step closer, lady, improve your karma.'

'Michael!' called out Rosie warningly. The man in the doorway was holding out one hand for spare change, but in the other he had a baseball bat.

'What? I'm trying to experience America,' came over her son's shoulder.

At least Michael hadn't answered in Italian. He might be jet-lagged but he wasn't ratty. 'Don't stray too far ahead.'

Michael was both handsome and protective. 'Better watch yourself, Mother,' he said as he fell back into step with them. 'There seem to be a lot of hobos around.'

'Shh.' Oh dear, she was a grown-up mother in a place where she'd once been young, and she even said *Shh*, and spoke in lowered tones. 'Those aren't hobos. They're street people.'

'Those?' Disappointment and disbelief were mixed in his voice. 'But you said street people were kids who ran away to Berkeley to be free. That man's forty if he's a day.'

'Me too,' said Rosie. 'I was talking about *then*. That was the Sixties. This is now.'

Coming back to California was not working out at all the way she had planned. The last leg of the plane journey from

1

Rome had ended at San Francisco in the middle of the night. Instead of thrilling to the wonder of crossing Bay Bridge in a Yellow Cab, the boys had slept their way into Berkeley.

Her body-clock thrown out of gear, Rosie had known that sleep would be impossible. Impressing upon a half-awake Michael that she was only going down to the lobby, and leaving a note to the same effect by the telephone, Rosie went in search of the something that would tell her she was really back in the United States.

Uncommunicative night porters and decaffeinated coffee being the same the world over, she risked putting her nose outside the door for a moment. Everything she'd seen through the taxi window might just as well have been on a television screen. But, as she breathed in the night air, her sense of smell brought her to a feeling of place.

A few twists of black pepper, ground into a cedarwood chest – that's what Berkeley smelled of. It was, she remembered, the eucalyptus trees, in the hills above the university campus. And this scent brought back the very first thought Rosie had ever had in Berkeley – when is the next earthquake going to come? Only it wasn't cool to mention earthquakes in the East Bay.

Not until after the event. Did they still say 'cool'? Never mind, she was back. Her own life had been a series of personal earthquakes. But – against all odds – she was back and she was happy.

Night gave way to cool morning. This began with undisguised reproaches from her sons. 'Strikes me you've been having us on,' grumbled Little Joe.

'Just shut up,' said his brother – who then proceeded to go a lot further. What's more, he was imitating Rosie, retailing an old familiar bedtime story: 'And in the morning, across the bay, you can see San Francisco emerging from the mist. And all the skyscrapers sparkle like diamonds.' His tones became altogether more realistic: 'That's not my idea of mist. That's thick fog.'

'Yes, nothing but the beginnings of a bridge and bloody fog.' Joe was at the swearing age. He really loved strong language.

'You mustn't say *fog*.' Rosie had taken enough. 'People here call it mist. You'll get us lynched.'

'At least that would be a bit interesting.' Michael was examining his upper lip in the mirror. He already had to shave twice a week. 'When are we going to see Granny?'

'She could be rather difficult to find.' Rosie pushed him away from the mirror, jabbed some lipstick onto her wide mouth and resisted the temptation to look at herself too closely. She already knew what dark hair and blue English eyes and almost crazily high cheekbones looked like. 'Your granny hasn't got a fixed address. She's living in a Winnebago.'

'And Daddy said we know a real witch here,' piped up Little Joe.

'We do know a witch. Only I'd rather you didn't call her that to her face.' The mirror won a second glance. Perhaps the cheekbones weren't too crazy. Other people liked them but Rosie could never quite decide. She smoothed the Missoni sweater over her hips and remembered how she had thrilled to her first pair of second-hand American Levis. The figure was, thank God, still in good nick. 'We're doing nothing before we've had breakfast. Come on. I'll take you to Barry Drake's restaurant.'

That's what had brought them out onto Telegraph Avenue, once the battleground of the biggest student revolution the world had ever known. The morning mist had already lifted to reveal ordinariness. The Bank of America and Rexall Drugs and altogether too many of these shifty tramps but – yes – Barry Drake's was still where it had always been.

Rosie began to experience misgivings. This restaurant, she recalled, had also figured largely in some of the bedtime stories. Michael had always been a great one for begging, 'Tell us about when you were young.'

In her own head she could hear herself recounting, 'I wouldn't have been surprised to meet the Scarlet Pimpernel in Barry Drake's. The candle-flames always seemed out of control so that all the shadows danced down on huge long tables – with about fifty people at them. You just sat where you could. And people banged and shouted and rose to their

3

feet and made impromptu speeches. It was all supposed to be about peace, but it was the fiercest place I've ever been in.'

Rosie led her sons into Barry Drake's, only to be stopped by a waiter pointing, warningly, to a sign. It read *Please Wait for a Hostess to Seat You*. And – if and when the hostess deigned to come – it was obvious that they were going to be seated at prim tables designed to hold no more than six.

'Can't see any sign of the Scarlet Pimpernel this morning.' Michael was speaking in an infuriatingly polite voice to Joe.

'Well it's *changed*,' gulped Rosie defensively. Changed? It could have been related to any Kardomah in Oxford! Nothing lasts, she wasn't an idiot; but in her mind's eye Rosie had always expected magical Berkeley to stay the same. The whole town was a drab disappointment. Where were the people blowing soap bubbles, and the chanting Hare Krishnas, and the unlikely placards of the Jews for Jesus? What had become of those thousands of boys and girls with flowers in their hair?

'We really *did* wear flowers in our hair.' It burst out before she could stop herself.

'And the cops were "pigs",' said Michael happily. 'I always liked that part. Never mind, the Sixties were back in the Middle Ages . . .' His attention had already been redirected towards a waitress in a very short mini-skirt.

Not Joe's attention. 'Real pigs?' he asked. 'Pigs that piss bright yellow? You still haven't told us how a girl from Manchester came to be in the middle of a revolution.'

Rosie took a deep breath. 'If you promise not to say piss, in public, for twenty-four hours, I'll try to tell you.' But not the whole story, she thought to herself. Joe wasn't old enough for the whole story.

1

Strictly speaking, the village of Irlams o'th' Height is not in Manchester, it's in Salford. On a clear day – if you look downhill – you can see that geography lessons are right: cities are truly built at the foot of slopes, in the bend of a river. For four miles away, beyond the blackened factories and mill chimneys of Salford, lies all of Manchester.

The Height is not posh. In 1955 it was more a place where grown-ups could get a battery recharged, or buy fish and chips, or drink pints of Tetley's best bitter. Good bacon was considered more important, in The Height, than poshness. But the industrial village did boast one mansion.

Down a side road, past the Catholic church which looked like a big mock-Tudor shed, and beyond the caterwauling playground of the red-brick Catholic day school, stood Teapot Hall.

Anybody who was particularly interested in these things – and there weren't many – could have told you that this house was a Victorian sandstone merchant's mansion, dominated by an Italianate tower. What The Height liked about the place was the gold teapot on top of the weathervane. On even the gloomiest of days it looked cheerful, and when it caught the sun it looked magnificent.

The house was said to have been built by a tea merchant, and the tower to have been put there so he could climb up and watch his cargos sailing into Manchester, along the Ship Canal.

In those days, set amongst fields, it must have been like living on the prairie. The first intruders, edging their way towards the Hall from the main road, had been streets of Victorian working-class houses. Edwardian terraces dared to come even closer. By the 1930s a speculative builder had erected an estate of semi-detached houses whose back hedges were the very rhododendrons of Teapot Hall. But the

5

house was still mysteriously imposing and, these days, it was often referred to as 'Tattersall's'.

The Tattersall family were not tea merchants, they imported fruit. In Gran'dad Tattersall's day there had been money to burn and servants galore. Now there was just Mrs Hankey and Poor-Bertha-who-drags-a-leg and the formal gardens had been simplified into grass and gravel.

Clifford Tattersall might own the house, his wife Constance was nominally mistress of the place, but the true ruler of Teapot Hall was Nora Hankey. This forty-year-old maid-of-all-work was both plain and passionate. On election days she did not hesitate to wear a red and yellow rosette.

'I'm Labour,' she would say to anybody who would listen – which was everybody because they were all a bit scared of her. Mostly they were scared of her leaving.

'There's two classes in this world,' she would always continue, 'bosses and workers. Well, I'm not content to know my place. And my kids are going to be bigger bosses than any of you lot – so you'd better watch out!'

You watched out anyway with Mrs Hankey. Rosie Tattersall might only be eight but that was one of the first things she ever learned. The other was that being one of a pair of twins was not all that it was cracked up to be.

'Rosemary and Christopher must be such wonderful companions for one another,' people would burble.

Not true. They might have looked alike, with their straight dark hair and pale skin and rosy cheeks and blue eyes; 'Just like the blue of an old willow-pattern plate,' one of the burblers had warbled. But they were not alike at all. For a start, Christopher didn't have to wear glasses.

Oh how Rosie hated those wire-framed glasses. But she loved the world, loved people, and was always eager for new experience. Christopher was secretive and sly. His twin sister loved him but she didn't like him. Eight-year-olds are perfectly capable of thoughts as big as this. At eight, grown-ups haven't quite succeeded in telling you the standard rules of what you can and cannot think. Yes, she loved him but she didn't like him.

One of the big troubles was *THE SECRET*. Rosie, who

could already read, always thought of it in capital letters. She had caught her brother doing something. That was the way she kept it stored in her head, 'doing something'. It hadn't seemed at all important at the time, but this was not how Christopher viewed the matter.

'If you ever tell anybody, I will get up in the middle of the night and set fire to the house. You will be burned to death,' he had said.

Rosie was inclined to think he might. Just look what he'd done with a penknife to the one beautiful golden carp left in the ornamental pond. And that was only because it had refused to swim in the direction he wanted.

People who have never been one of a pair of twins can have no knowledge of how much it limits privacy. There were occasions when Christopher could get inside Rosie's head and know what she was thinking. That's why The Secret was filed under 'doing something' and not covered by a more descriptive phrase which she might accidentally blurt out.

She knew he could get inside her mind because she could do it back. What little she could extract from Christopher's head was full of pain and hurt. But when she tried to put her arms round him, he would push her away. Christopher loathed pity. His sister understood: she'd been inside – she'd sensed it.

At a more mundane level, the person who knew everything was Mrs Hankey. And she never hesitated to keep it to herself: 'Your mother was lucky to get your father – bloody lucky. She was just a girl from the offices who kept on cocking him the right look.'

Mrs Hankey was straight up and down, like Olive Oyl in Rosie's *Popeye Annual*. The little woman's mind flashed like arrows. She only needed four hours' sleep a night, and years of reading had equipped her with the right words for every occasion. She wasn't a cruel woman, she was just totally unsentimental and brutally candid: 'Your mother may think she passes for a lady in those little grey flannel tailor-mades; but I'm not kidded. Breeding will out, and she can never resist a blood-red blouse. Come on, have a mint imperial and we'll do a bit of our polishing.'

From an early age the children had been Mrs Hankey's polishing assistants. She had her own method. You applied the wax polish with one end of the cloth and buffed the surface with the other. Mrs Hankey seemed to live with one of these dusters in her hand and a tale on her lips: 'Your daddy's practically a gentleman but his father wasn't quite out of the top drawer. Everybody liked your Gran'dad Tattersall. He was a bloated capitalist, and they're bad bastards, but there was something very jaunty about him. And he was a natty dresser. Every morning he had a fresh flower in his buttonhole. It went into a little invention behind his lapel – a glass tube filled with water. If you don't polish, Christopher, I'm not telling the story . . .'

Rosie knew without looking that Christopher would resume polishing immediately. He was always looking for useful ammunition in Mrs Hankey's tales.

'And every night, your gran'dad used to remove his buttonhole and put it in the dining-room flower arrangement. Then he'd give your gran'ma a great big smacking kiss – didn't matter who was watching – he'd kiss her and he'd say, "Well, Evelyn, I've made a few bob today." He was such a chirpy little swine that you almost overlooked the fact that he'd got his cash off the workers' backs. Get some elbow-grease behind that duster, Rosie! Polish as though you mean it.'

In this instance Mrs Hankey was the boss class and she allowed herself a dramatic pause, followed by 'Just look at that dining room today! Nobody's sat down to a square meal in it for years. It's nothing but peace pamphlets and posters for a World Without War.'

The children's father was a Quaker. Between themselves they called him the woolly man because he always wore hairy tweed suits, with knitted cardigans underneath them, and grey Viyella shirts, and ties that one of the other Quakers wove on a little loom. Clifford Tattersall was tall and thin with horn-rimmed glasses. His hair was prematurely grey and his handsome face generally wore a worried expression. Mrs Hankey said that this was because he was solely occupied with world concerns.

'He's up at a very lofty level,' she would say. 'In fact, these days – if you're looking for a human relationship – you'd be better off talking to next door's dog.' But she would never fail to add that their father had once been a charmer: 'Hot stuff and no mistake! *She* soon spotted that. I sometimes think he's gone in for all this pacifism to stop himself murdering *her*.'

Rosie could feel an itch starting under one eye. But she didn't dare scratch it, for fear of getting polish on her glasses. Mrs Hankey, who had an absolute phobia about greasy lenses, would only send her off to find the window leather. The housekeeper was a bit haphazard with things like window leathers, and Teapot Hall was huge. Upstairs, there were whole corridors of rooms that hadn't been used for years.

Nora and the children were busy polishing the mahogany banisters in the entrance hall. These wound their way up to a shadowy landing hung with tapestries, like a minstrels' gallery. Their mother liked to call it the Grand Staircase.

These days, the entrance hall was used as the main living room. Constance Tattersall would gaze round all the antiques and say proudly, 'It's just like living in a British quota-quickie.' These were Grade-B movies, full of actors and actresses pretending to be ladies and gentlemen. Mrs Hankey said that it put her more in mind of a sale of settees at the Times Furnishing Company. There were certainly a lot of sofas and those tables made of brass trays with legs like rows of varnished cotton reels. The room smelled of smoke from the burning logs in the big wood and copper fireplace, and of the dried rose petals which lived in a huge blue and white Chinese bowl on the frightening oak sideboard. Frightening because it was carved with devils' heads.

Mrs Hankey put down her duster. 'I think I'm in the mood for a bit of roller-skating,' she announced.

This was not the sport practised at public rinks. First, her child labourers would go over the wooden parquet floor with a heavily waxed mop. Next, Nora Hankey would don a pair of old plimsolls to which she had sewn makeshift towelling soles. And then she would reach for a long-handled brush, its head similarly padded with Turkish towelling.

'Come on!' she would encourage the children. 'Sing the song.' It was always the same tune: one of Al Jolson's greatest hits.

> 'Oh how we danced,
> On the night we were wed,
> We vowed our true love,
> Though a word wasn't said . . .'

To these strains, pushing the brush in front of her, little Nora Hankey would waltz solemnly round the floor. She thought nothing of doing chassis and glides and skidding halts. She was amazing, and more than ever Rosie was reminded of Olive Oyl.

'Don't you ever try it,' Nora would warn them as she travelled. 'This is more dangerous than crossing Bolton Road blindfolded. But I know what I'm doing – it's the way I hold my mouth!'

Alas, today they were to be denied this performance. Just as Rosie began heading for the kitchen and the mop, her mother emerged from behind the green-baize-covered door.

Connie Tattersall was nearly as made-up as Margaret Lockwood in *The Wicked Lady* – fake beauty spot and all. And she had her squirrel coat on, which generally meant she was heading for town.

'Where's Bertha?' Connie asked snappily.

Poor Bertha-who-drags-a-leg was Mrs Hankey's hench-woman. Mostly she laid fires and washed up and peeled vegetables.

'I need her,' rapped Connie. 'Where is she?'

Oh dear, thought Rosie, not so much as a please or a thankyou; Mrs Hankey won't like that.

Mrs Hankey didn't. 'Gone to the Elite for a perm. And we all know what that means!'

Even the children knew what that meant. Women who disappeared into the Elite Hairdressing Salon for a perma-nent wave could stay strung up to the machine for hours. The experienced took sandwiches.

'So who's going to mind the twins?' Connie looked very much put out. 'D'you think I've overdone the eye shadow?'

'Yes.' Mrs Hankey was plainly getting ready to do battle.

'The bulb's gone, over my mirror,' sighed Connie. 'One way and another, everything seems to be going these days.'

Women didn't like Connie Tattersall. Rosie had known that for a long time. Men liked her; but one glance at Connie's curves, and two moments of her flouncing, seemed to set other women's mouths in a straight line. With men around she was a good sport and a lot of fun. Leave her alone with another woman and Connie turned into a wailer. 'It's your half-day, Mrs Hankey. And you know it's half-term. Who's going to look after the kiddies?'

'You're their mother.'

It's just that she's out of her depth with other women, thought Rosie. She doesn't know the rules. Constance Tattersall tried again; 'Mrs Hankey, dear . . .'

'No I wouldn't mind them. You're not the only one with a private life.'

Was Mrs Hankey giving the words *private life* some special significance?

Taking a very slightly grubby comb from her handbag, Connie crossed to a gilded Chinese mirror and began to attack her thick dark hair.

'I've dyed it . . .' she said helplessly. 'And it looks dyed. It's only a water rinse. It'll wash out.'

'I'm glad of that.' Connie might be playing for sympathy but Mrs Hankey wasn't giving an inch.

The twins' mother tried approaching the matter from another angle: 'You know what I'm like. If I take the kiddies with me I'm scared I'll lose them.'

'Then you shouldn't have had them in the first place.' Similar battles of will seemed to have gone on right through the half-term holiday. 'Except we all know why you did have them. You got yourself in the club so you could marry him. Premature twins? I, for one, was never kidded!'

Of all the adults Rosie had ever met, Nora Hankey was the only person who never moderated her conversation in front of children. But this was the most she'd ever said. It was shocking but you couldn't help being interested.

11

'Were you having us when you got married?' asked Christopher, in deep fascination.

'Now look what you've done . . .' Tears of self-pity began to roll over the mascara on Connie's lower lashes.

'I've called a spade a spade. And crocodile tears won't wash with me.'

'It was once a potent physical attraction,' sniffed Connie. 'And now we're just passing strangers.'

Her daughter recognised the words immediately. They came from 'Netta Muskett Tells a Thrilling Story Especially for Our Readers' in the last week's *Home Notes*. Rosie and Christopher would read anything they could get their hands on.

'Passing strangers, my bum!' snapped Mrs Hankey. 'Cliff Tattersall used to be as nice a lad as ever smiled. You've just worn him down. You and your carrying-on. And what's a woman, in her full flesh, doing in a separate bedroom?'

'I do happen to have anaemia,' snapped Connie. 'And you shouldn't be talking about the intimate side of marriage, not in front of the twins. They could talk, outside.'

'If you've got anaemia,' Mrs Hankey moved in for the kill, 'so has a blood-red peony. And that's what you remind me of. A bit wilting, a bit gone at the edges – but a blood-red peony. It's no good. I've had enough.' She tore off her apron. 'If I'm not allowed to speak my mind, the time has come for me to go.'

'But you are allowed,' cried Connie. 'You're a privileged servant.' Realising that this was *not* a good line to take with Nora Hankey, Connie quickly changed her tune and said weakly; 'Don't go. Just phone for a taxi. I'll take them with me.'

Going to town with their mother was something of a novelty. Connie disappeared most afternoons and generally returned – just before their father was due in – smelling like the gin decanter with the stopper out. That's when she passed round the violet-scented cachous and consumed twice as many as the children.

'Can I phone for the taxi?' asked Christopher eagerly. 'I know the number.'

'Just say taxi for Teapot Hall, straight away,' said their mother. 'And then you'd both better get washed and slip into your good reefer coats.' This rush of energy didn't last. Once again she came over vague and announced, weakly, 'Now I've gone and mislaid my new hat.'

The only telephone at Teapot Hall was kept under the stairs, inside an old sedan chair. Rosie waited for the call to finish. Telephoning might be his province, but it was generally accepted that she and Christopher only made major movements – like leaving a room – in unison.

It took Mrs Hankey to find Connie's hat, which was sitting on top of a glass dome with some stuffed weasels underneath it. Strictly speaking, it was only half a hat – like a broad Alice-band, covered in lime-green feathers.

Connie placed it on top of her dyed hair. 'Will I do?' she asked Mrs Hankey.

'Course you'll do – if you intend to be taken for a demented bridesmaid.'

Before war could break out again, Christopher emerged from inside the sedan chair and announced, 'He says he'll only come for cash. And Mr Brierley's going to bring another copy of the account with him.' This set Connie pacing, angrily up and down the parquet.

'Now I will mention it,' said Mrs Hankey. 'I wasn't going to say anything but I will. Those white court shoes of yours are squeaking. Sure sign they've not been paid for.'

Out on her own with her children, and no other grown-ups around, Connie Tattersall always turned into a different person. It was as though she was another child herself. A big tall one, who happened to have a bouncing bust. Conversations often began; 'Don't tell anybody but . . .' Today, however, she was obviously being careful in front of the driver, so they just sang 'How Much Is That Doggie in the Window?' and then she gave them barley sugar to suck.

The trip to Manchester took only ten minutes. The car stopped, as instructed, halfway up Market Street. Connie emptied the contents of her purse into her hand and passed the money over to the driver.

'Cash and tip,' she said, in a lofty, disinterested voice. 'And I'll make sure my hubby sends you a cheque to cover the account you left at the Hall.' A sudden thought seemed to have struck her for, in an altogether more interested tone of voice, she asked, 'Is that bill itemised? I mean, does it say where I've been?'

'It most certainly does. Nobody's out to do you.'

As the car began to move away Connie seemed to be thinking aloud: 'Itemised, eh? That could be dicey!' But she dismissed the thought as lightly as she discarded the tiny lime-green feather which had descended from her hat onto her good squirrel coat. 'That man's just had your mother's last six shillings – and she's moulting!'

'They were my six shillings,' said Christopher. 'You've been at my money-box again.'

Rosie felt a stab of irrational jealousy. Why was it always Christopher's money-box? Couldn't her mother sometimes swipe off her?

'I always pay it back.' The resemblance to a big child was greater than ever. 'And as often as not I slip in a bit extra.'

I wouldn't need a bit extra, thought Rosie. I'd just like to be in on it. They were standing outside Henry's. This was a department store which boasted almost permanent bargain sales. Though it was only the first week in November, their windows were already dressed for Christmas. Mechanised cardboard pixies and gnomes were wielding hammers and tugging cotton-wool beards. And a red Day-Glo poster advertised the fact that the Living Sleeping Beauty was on display in Santa's Grotto. *She's Alive – See Her Breathe*, it said.

'Can we?' asked Christopher.

'We've no money.' His mother spat on her handkerchief and wiped a smut off his cheek, quite fondly. 'It's always half-a-crown for a present. And we'd want a present each, wouldn't we? Besides, last time we tried Henry's grotto it was a bit of a swizz. The fog had got in from the street and Father Christmas was eating sandwiches out of a newspaper parcel. And he had *glasses* on.'

She sees glasses as comical, thought Rosie. She just says the first thing that comes into her head – and she's no idea

14

how much she can hurt people. When it came to specs, perhaps Henry's Father Christmas was somebody else who had no choice in the matter.

'It wouldn't hurt you to do without a present, Connie.' Christopher was always the eldest on these outings. 'And if we've got no money, how are we going to get home?'

'Shh.' Their mother's finger went to her lips. 'Connie's got a little plan.' She always encouraged them to call her by her Christian name. In fact, the twins had once overheard her telling a naval officer that she was their elder sister.

'People sing in the streets,' volunteered Rosie. 'We could always try that.'

'And I'd quite enjoy it.' As usual, their mother was game for an adventure. 'But I can't see people dipping into their pockets for a person in a fur coat. This plan of mine's going to involve just a little bit of *fibbing*.'

She was already steering them through the traffic and across Market Street. Then she led them up a narrow passageway, in the direction of a jeweller's shop with a heavy metal grille over its window.

'What are those three gold balls for?' It was one of those thoughts which Christopher and Rosie managed to voice aloud in exactly the same breath.

Connie looked caught. 'Yes, well . . . Under certain circumstances, it can mean that the shop is a pawnbroker's.'

'And are these the circumstances?' asked Christopher.

'As a matter of fact they are. Come on, let's go in. And whatever I say, don't bat so much as an eyelid.'

It was dark inside the shop, except for an illuminated glass display case marked *Unredeemed Pledges*. This was full of glittering old rings.

'Are those diamonds real?' asked Christopher.

'The prices are certainly real enough.' A distinctly nervous Connie tugged the twins towards a mahogany counter. Like something in a bank, it was divided into individual private booths. Connie rapped upon a frosted-glass window above the counter, labelled *Pledges*.

'Are we going to take the pledge?' asked Rosie. 'Do they give you money for saying you'll never touch strong drink?'

Christopher broke into one of Poor-Bertha-who-drags-a-leg's favourite temperance songs:

> 'My drink is water bright.
> Water bright, water bright . . .'

'Stop that hymn at once!' Lowering her voice, Connie added, 'He'll probably be Jewish. They generally are. You don't want to go queering our pitch with Methodist hymns.'

The window opened and an old man with a pale lemon-coloured face peered out. He had a beaky nose and shiny black eyes. Rosie thought he looked a little bit like a nice human canary.

'Good afternoon,' said Connie. She was using her posh voice. Mrs Hankey would have said she was 'putting it on'.

'Yes, good afternoon,' repeated Connie anxiously. 'I'm afraid I don't know the ropes in these matters.' Very slowly she opened her coat. She was wearing her lowest-cut lime-green chiffon blouse. The one that made her look like puddings boiling over. 'What can you offer me on these?'

Rosie was horrified. Why was her mother showing this man her front and asking him for money?

'You'll have to take them off,' he said.

'No!' said Rosie, in a desperate whisper. 'Please don't take your clothes off, Connie. We can always walk home.'

Kicking her daughter warningly on the shin, all Connie removed was a pair of antique gold clips. These had been fastening the blouse to the straps of her petticoat. 'Oh dear, I feel as though I'm floating loose without them,' she said, flashing the man a googly look.

The canary-man was only interested in the clips. Screwing something like the end of a telescope into his eye, he turned and twisted the items and examined them minutely. 'What d'you want on these?'

'I thought, perhaps, twenty-five pounds?'

'I'll give you seven.'

'But they're antiques,' gasped Connie. 'They're heir-looms.'

'Yes, and they're only continental gold. Seven pounds ten

16

shillings – take it or leave it.' The man was already drawing a huge ledger towards himself. 'Name?'

Darting her children a warning look, their mother said, 'Mrs Dorothy Caldicott. And the address is 40 Park Road, Eccles.'

Rosie felt Christopher grab her by the hand. She allowed him to lead her over to the glittering showcase. 'Such black lies!' he whispered. 'She bought those brooches in a junk shop in Pendleton for five quid. Awful, awful lies,' he sighed. 'They should be worth at least a knickerbocker glory each, in Lewis's Soda Fountain.'

With a few pounds in her purse, Connie Tattersall was a woman transformed. Life was plainly wonderful again. And she took them to the soda fountain without so much as having to be prompted. It was down in the basement of Lewis's department store. Though the shop was Manchester's own version of Selfridge's, some of the female customers in this ice-cream parlour had faces painted way beyond accepted standards of respectability. Indeed they were so heavily enamelled that, beside them, Connie Tattersall looked just a cheerful watercolour. And these women seemed to be weighing up every man who went past.

'Poor cows, it must be too cold for them outside in the arcade.' Ice cream seemed to have filled Connie with the milk of human kindness.

'What would they be doing in the arcade?' asked Rosie.

'Now that I'm not telling you.' Connie grabbed hold of a piece of angelica, which Rosie had left, and ate it herself. 'I will not have your innocence tampered with.'

'Those two men at the next table are wearing make-up too.' Christopher was watching them in total fascination. 'Listen! Did you hear that? One called the other Beryl.'

'I expect they're queries,' said Connie easily. 'You'll meet more than queries in the place we're going to. Only I don't want you going telling anybody afterwards.'

Their ice cream finished, they had a little roam round the store before emerging onto Market Street. It was getting foggy, and although it was only the middle of the afternoon the overhead street lights were already on.

'Look what I've got.' Christopher opened his hand to reveal a seashell fastened with a paper seal, with Chinese writing on it. Rosie already knew what it was. When you put them in a glass of water they opened up and magic flowers grew out of the middle. 'But you didn't have any money,' she cried. 'Did you pinch it?'

'I'm hardly in a position to tell him off.' Connie beamed indulgently. 'I nicked a lipstick myself!'

'Hold your coat across your front,' Christopher advised his mother. 'Without those brooches you can see a lot of blobby pink.'

'Pink to make the boys wink,' giggled Connie. Taking her son by the hand, she began to lead him across Market Street. The only thing Rosie could do was trudge behind them. 'And don't dawdle in traffic!' Connie snapped over her shoulder. They reached the far pavement. 'I suppose it would be too much to expect you to have a safety-pin on you, Rosie?'

'Would a little gold one do?' asked Christopher, immediately producing just such an item from the top pocket of his reefer coat. 'I saved it from when it came back from the cleaner's.'

Sometimes he's not like a boy at all, thought Rosie, not caring whether he read her mind or not. He and his mother were a gang of two. And they made Rosie feel like the enemy. If she suddenly started shouting swearwords, at the top of her voice, would they like her better and let her be in on things?

It was as though the other two were always together, laughing, whilst she was all alone on a little island for the goody-goodies. And she wasn't a goody-goody. She was as big a mix of good and bad as anybody else. But she was just as much her father's daughter as she was her mother's. And she did know right from wrong. Not much consolation on a November afternoon when shoplifting seemed to be as fashionable as fireworks.

'Where are we going now?' asked Christopher. The escapade in Lewis's had obviously charged him with a craving for further adventures.

'We're off to see a few chums of mine. It's a club at the back of Market Street. But if anybody asks at home, just say I took you for a cup of tea at Duncan and Foster's.'

'Rosie's worried about telling lies,' sniggered Christopher.

She had already felt her brother penetrate her brain. Sometimes it was like a nasty needle coming in. And Christopher knew an internal trick which she didn't. He could bring an iron shutter down, so that it was impossible for her to read him back.

'Just start crying!' Connie spoke viciously. 'Just start, that's all, and I'll smack your legs. You're not fair, Rosie. You're not a bit fair. How many kiddies get to go where I'm taking you? You could try showing a bit of gratitude.'

Connie began to study her own reflection in the window of Horne Brothers, the gents' outfitters. 'I know they say it pays to advertise but this neckline *is* a bit much . . .' Quickly she adjusted her decolletage. Not quite content with what she saw, Connie whipped a very new-looking lipstick out of her coat pocket. Briskly and skilfully she applied a whole new layer – on top of the existing colour. And in this excited moment, Connie Tattersall revealed herself as a woman who was off to meet somebody very special indeed.

'We're going to the old Coconut,' she announced.

In the 1950s Manchester was a city of clubs. There seemed to be one on every corner, and it was said that you could get a drink right round the clock. These establishments had looked as far as New York and Hollywood for their names. Tucked amidst the warehouses, in the alleyways behind Market Street, were both a Stork Club and the Coconut Grove.

'I nearly need a wee,' said Christopher.

'Well *nearly* means you can wait. You can go at the club.'

For Rosie, the afternoon was as much wreathed in mystery as it was in fog. But here, at last, was something she thought she understood. Mrs Hankey had mentioned 'the club' earlier. 'Are you going to get a new baby?' she asked.

The question seemed to throw Connie into some pleasurable soul-searching because she went quite pink and fluttery as she replied, 'It's not beyond the bounds of possibility. But not today,' she added hastily.

The Coconut Grove turned out to be in an office building, two floors up. You went down a creaking corridor with dusty bare boards. One door was labelled *Rosens – Gowns & Mantles*

(Trade Only). Another belonged to something called a milliners' sundries-man. The corridor was illuminated by a single bare electric light bulb, dangling on a long flex. And the farthest door, in the darkest shadows, just said *Members Only*. In the distance, somebody on the wireless was singing that he would like somebody else to take his hand because he was a stranger in paradise.

'Speaks to your soul, that song, doesn't it?' asked Connie, as she rapped on the door. 'It's all a bit "Knock-three-times-and-ask-for-Charlie" here.'

The whole door didn't open but a small panel, halfway down, slid back. A suspicious pair of rheumy old eyes peered out at them.

'Afternoon, Ted,' said Connie confidently. The door swung open. Ted had a face which looked as though it had been carved out of pinkish-grey lard. All his clothes were chocolate brown, except for a white tie – and he'd kept his trilby on, indoors.

'You can't bring those two in here,' he said, nodding down at the twins.

'Who says?'

'Vinnie won't like it.' The man's breath smelled of stale beer.

'Vinnie's not going to get it,' said Connie archly. 'One word out of that lousy club owner and little Connie might just start remembering where all the bones are buried.'

Connie led them into the Coconut Grove. All the windows had been painted over – so had the walls – in midnight-blue emulsion. The only light came down from grubby plastic chandeliers. It was a place waiting for something to happen. Rows of empty tables and stools lined both sides of a long narrow room which continued round a corner at the end. The bar was down at the bottom too – past a set of drums on a raised dais with a ripped sheet half thrown over them. 'Stranger in Paradise' was blaring out of an illuminated jukebox.

Connie suddenly seemed to feel the need to defend the Coconut Grove: 'You're heard of how the other half lives? Well this is it. Don't expect to find many Quakers here.'

'About bloody time too!' A woman carrying a glass had come sauntering round the bottom bend. She was plainly addressing Connie, and the place was so empty that her voice had an echo to it: 'I thought you must have run off with a black man . . .' The words turned into a raucous laugh.

Rosie knew that Christopher was as fascinated as she was by the woman's red hat. It was just like the fez which Tommy Cooper wore on television. Except the comedian's tassel had always looked black, and hers was electric blue to match the tailored gaberdine suit she was wearing.

'Why have you got a bangle round your ankle?' Christopher asked her politely.

'So men like you will ask questions about it.' Her throaty voice seemed to hint at things that were 'rude'. 'Are these the twins?' asked the woman.

'No, they're two reserves from Manchester United!' snapped Connie. 'Of course they're the bloody twins. I couldn't get shut of them.'

It wasn't flattering but Rosie was interested to note that, in this place, her mother seemed to have dropped all airs and graces. And Rosie had always liked her better without them.

'They'll be no trouble. Here . . .' Opening her purse, Connie thrust some shillings at Christopher. 'Use these for the jukebox. I'll get you pop and crisps in a minute.' Without pausing she said to the Tommy Cooper woman, 'Did you get your visa?' There seemed to be real urgency in her question.

'Visa? I got a load of American aggravation. Convictions – they wanted to know about convictions.'

'I've given you money. What are you waiting for?' Connie had rounded on the twins.

'To be introduced.' Christopher was already extending a hand. Mentally, Rosie gave him a good mark for quick thinking – this conversation was much more interesting than feeding a jukebox.

'Meet Elaine,' said their mother.

Elaine didn't bother shaking hands. Children were plainly the least of her interests. 'You know what greets you at that American Embassy? Marines with revolvers.'

'Pointed at you?' gasped Connie.

21

'No. It's the questions they point at you. Had I ever been a Communist? I ask you! But the criminal convictions bit really shook me. I kept me mouth shut but can they check? How will *you* stand?'

'Well I'm certainly not a Commie.' But Connie was looking distinctly worried. More worried still when she noticed that the twins were drinking all of this in. 'Ted!' she called to the man in the brown trilby. 'Do me a favour. Get me a couple of fizzy pops from the bar.'

'You said crisps too,' put in Christopher.

'And crisps,' she shouted. 'Now you've got money for the jukebox. Go and choose a tune.'

Reluctantly, the children headed for the machine. Silent now, it was called the Mighty Echo. 'I'm going to put the money in very slowly,' said Christopher. 'She doesn't want us to listen.'

A few feet away, Connie plainly couldn't contain herself. 'Is he here?' she asked Elaine urgently.

'Down at the end. Round the corner. He's got you a vodka martini, gathering dust on the counter.'

'I've only to think of that man,' Connie seemed to be shivering, 'and I come over all of a doo-dah. Bit different from the one I've got at home! Can you keep an eye on those two? *And just put that money in*,' she called out loudly. With this she clacked down the room on her white high heels and disappeared round the corner.

The shillings dropped in, the jukebox whirred and clicked, a record rose up and descended onto the turntable, and the air was filled with the sound of Frankie Laine singing 'Jezebel'.

Looking round, Rosie saw why the club had been named the Coconut Grove. Someone had painted palm trees, with gum, on the dark blue walls and then covered the gum with pink and green glitter dust. Rosie knew how it was done because they made Christmas cards the same way at Elm House. This was the name of the small private school where she and Christopher were pupils. The twins' navy-blue reefer coats were part of the school uniform. She found herself wondering how many other Elm House uniforms had been in a nightclub in the daytime.

22

But mostly she just worried. This worry didn't have a specific name. The word 'convictions' came into it, and what was a visa? And who were the men with guns. . . ?

'It's okay.' Christopher spoke aloud but he had been inside her head. 'I'm going to the lav. And on the way back I'll go and have a look at what's going on round the corner.'

No pop, no crisps, and no Christopher. It was fully five minutes since he'd emerged from the gentlemen's cloakroom, marched down to the end of the room and vanished. The distant laughter from around that intriguing corner sounded all that was adult. Yet nobody had seen fit to send him back. What's more, he'd taken all the jukebox shillings with him. Had they forgotten her? The twins were not, as yet, skilled at flashing one another messages over distances longer than an arm's length. Rosie got to her feet and made to follow him.

Just as she reached the corner, Elaine stepped out and blocked Rosie's path. All the child could see was electric-blue tailored gaberdine costume.

'Just you come back to the other end and sit down with Elaine.' She was carrying a bottle and a glass. 'They're out of lemonade. Your mother's sent you an old-fashioned cider instead.'

'I don't want to go back to the other end. I want Connie. I want my mummy. Why can't I be where Christopher is?'

'It's man's talk down there.' Elaine began to steer Rosie back towards the jukebox. 'Christopher's getting to know Mason Pollitt. Only you never heard me say that,' she added hastily. 'These situations are always bloody awkward.'

'What situations? And who's Mason thingy?'

'Now sit down nicely and I'll let you have a squirt of my American toilet water. When you need to know about Mason, your mummy'll tell you.'

'I want to know now. Christopher and I always do everything together.' Rosie contemplated making a bolt for the far end. But Elaine had bony knuckles, covered in diamond rings. She looked as though she'd be good at grabbing.

'You should ask your mummy to get you a nicer pair of glasses,' said her jailer. 'They make coloured ones these days.' Without pausing for breath she added, 'What d'you think about Princess Margaret?' It was the most discussed topic of the week. Princess Margaret had issued an official statement saying that she was not going to marry Group Captain Peter Townsend, who was a divorced man. 'They do say she might go into a nunnery,' sighed Elaine. 'That should put paid to all those peep-toed shoes of hers. Mind you, the royals *are* on their feet a lot so I suppose they need the ventilation.'

Rosie got to her feet and made to run down the room. She'd been right about Elaine. She *was* a good grabber. 'Now just sit down. We're having a nice little conversation. Tell me something, Rosie, don't you think ladies should be allowed to marry who they want? After all, that's what divorce is for, isn't it?'

'I don't know.' All she did know was that idle chatter had suddenly turned serious. It had got *meant*.

'You mustn't cry. Glasses only magnify tears.' But the bony grip on Rosie's shoulder suddenly relaxed as Elaine added, 'Here comes Christopher now.'

He was marching triumphantly towards them, talking as he came: 'I've got crisps *and* candy. Well, Mason called it candy. It's just a tube of American sweets. Look, the wrapper's different but they taste just like Spangles.'

'Who's Mason?' asked Rosie.

'He's a sergeant. He's got stripes and a uniform made of very thin material.'

Without having to be told, Rosie knew something else about Mason. Excitement was dancing through Christopher's mind and she was picking up on an image he was powerless to block. Mason was as black as the golliwog on a Robertson's Marmalade jar. His hair might be fuzzy but he was also as good-looking as a film star. And, somehow, Rosie also knew that he was going to use those beautiful white teeth to bite at all that was safe in her own life.

*

Fruit importers do not keep sociable hours. Clifford Tattersall was always up before dawn and on his way to town. He got to Smithfield Market in Manchester by half past six and was generally home again by four in the afternoon.

Today he had beaten Connie and the children. As they piled out of their taxi from the Coconut Grove, he was already pacing round the entrance hall.

'A penny for your thoughts, Cliff,' said Connie nervously.

Rosie surmised that her mother was probably nervous because she'd not got round to chewing her violet-scented cachous.

'You're home early. . .' Connie tried again.

'No, you're home late. Where've you been?'

The woolly man looked grey and tired and worried. But he's still very nice-looking, thought Rosie. She was glad it was Connie who was going to have to say where they'd been. Rosie loved her father and she wouldn't have enjoyed lying to him. In fact she wasn't sure she could have done it. He looked as though plenty had been done to him already.

'Where've you been?' he repeated.

'Christmas shopping,' said Connie.

He's not thick, thought Rosie. We've not got so much as a paper carrier bag between us.

'Now don't go spoiling surprises,' gurgled Connie. 'It's a little something for you. I'm going to slip it to Santa.'

'I don't believe in Father Christmas.' Clifford Tattersall was not spoiling anything. All the children in the twins' class at Elm House knew it was really your mother and father. 'I don't know what I do believe in. Not any more. Where did you get that hat?'

'This? You know me, I can never resist a bargain.'

'There are no such things as bargains. Not when we're living one jump ahead of the bailiffs.'

'Change the record, Cliff!' Connie ripped off the hat and threw it onto one of the Oriental tables.

'No! It's about time you changed your feckless ways.'

Things must be bad, it wasn't often he stood up to her like this. And it was obvious that Connie didn't like it. 'Oh I *am* going to change my ways, Clifford. There are going to be quite drastic changes round here. But I'm not sure you'll be struck on them.'

'Meaning?'

'You'll see!'

Just leave him alone, thought Rosie with considerable passion. You, you think you can go for *anybody* in glasses! You're a horrible wobbly woman who just goes out and grabs whatever she wants. And you don't care if Christopher knows things and I don't.

'Did you trouble yourself to buy anything sensible – like marmalade?' asked Connie's husband. 'I was reduced to bare toast this morning.' Immediately, Rosie picked up on a thought of Christopher's, and the Robertson's golliwog began to dance threateningly inside her own head.

'What's the matter, love?' Rosie's father was gazing down at her with concern. It was the first time anybody had been nice today and she suddenly felt near to tears.

'I don't know' was all she could manage. That, at least, was the truth.

Her father lifted her up in a great big affectionate tweed hug. 'Come on,' he said, 'let's see my favourite smile.' He gave her the beginnings of a tickle, which made Rosie start to laugh. But why was this turning his face to thunder?

'Constance? And you'd better have a good reply ready! Would you mind telling me why this child reeks of alcohol?'

'If it's awkward questions you want,' Connie was more than ready for her husband, 'what about all those copies of *Sunbathing Review* and *The Naturist* tucked away in your tallboy?'

'Have you ever seen fog like it?' They all turned round. The voice was ordinary, the question mundane. The little woman who had just come in through the double glass doors from the drive was totally unremarkable – except for the fact she dragged one leg. Bertha had finally come back from the Elite Hairdressing Salon. Very carefully she undid the grey chiffon scarf which was covering her towering hair-do.

'My God!' exclaimed Connie, in astonishment which was in no way faked. 'That hair looks as though you've got your finger in an electric light socket.'

For decades, the Tattersalls of Teapot Hall had employed living-in servants. Now they were down to one and these days she came in by the front door. Mrs Hankey lived elsewhere. Mrs Hankey had a whole private life of her own. Only Bertha lived in the attics, with the mice. She looked a bit like a bright mouse herself. A sixty-year-old human mouse with kind eyes – but her new hairstyle was wickedly Egyptian.

'They spent two hours trying to damp it down with neutraliser,' she said proudly. 'It *took* a bit too well. I was there so long I began to think I'd take root.'

Christopher suddenly rushed across the room and flung his arms round Bertha. 'I hadn't thought about you,' he said.

'Me? I'm the last person anybody need think about. If folk started thinking about me, I'd come over uncomfortable.'

'But I love you, Bertha,' said Christopher, in a panic. And then he began to cry.

'Course you love me.' Her arms were round him. 'And Bertha loves you back.' Rosie didn't mind this. It was generally accepted at Teapot Hall that the boy was the old woman's particular favourite.

'Goodness only knows what this whining's about, Christopher,' snapped his father, 'but please stop it. If Bertha's a problem, she's my problem. Though how you come to know about it has me beaten.'

They're all only interested in themselves, thought Rosie. That's why they're all sticking bits of a jigsaw in the wrong holes.

Bertha asked, in a perturbed voice, 'Why should I be a problem?'

And then Rosie thought again: it was she who had got things wrong. The fact of the matter was that they were all occupied on *different* puzzles. It made her feel uneasy. Far away in the distance, coming from under the ground, she heard the muffled rumble of a distant train. It belonged to the colliery. Coal mines ran right under Teapot Hall – hundreds of feet below them. And it suddenly seemed to Rosie that the parquet flooring was no longer the safe and solid thing they had helped Mrs Hankey polish, earlier in this day of upset and mystery.

There is no sunshine like Sunday sunshine for casting light on human character. Connie Tattersall always spent Sunday mornings in bed, surrounded by the sort of lurid newspapers that made Clifford Tattersall wince. He maintained that their very newsprint left a grubby trail across Connie's sheets. Mrs Hankey was conspicuous by her absence. The Sabbath was sacred to her famous 'private life'. Today she was known to be going to a Workers' Educational Association rally at Stockport. And Bertha had her work cut out making a big cooked breakfast for Clifford and the twins, and then making sure that the children were spick and span – in readiness for their weekly visit to the Friends' Meeting House.

Quakers don't speak of themselves as 'going to church'. Instead they attend Meeting for Worship. That particular morning, it seemed to Rosie that this was the one stable thing in a week which had been full of tensions and lacking in explanations. The week might have run her emotions ragged but at a quarter past ten – just like any other Sunday morning – the twins were outside on the top step, waiting for their father to bring the Rover round to the front door.

Quaker meetings are nothing like ordinary church services. There is no altar, no ritual, no hymns. Quakers, who refer to one another as Friends, simply sit round a bare room in silence. And if the spirit moves one of the Friends to say something, they get up from their plain wooden chairs and speak.

As they waited for the car, Christopher was trying to break a rusty fragment off the cast-iron foot-scraper. 'I wouldn't be a bit surprised if I didn't say something in the meeting this morning,' he announced importantly. Rosie could also sense mischief in his voice.

Why should he think he'd speak? The children only went into the silence of the main room for the last quarter of an hour. And she'd never heard of any child giving ministry. If Christopher rose to his feet and spoke, it wouldn't be God who moved him to do it – it would surely be his opposite number! Rosie tried not even to think the words 'the devil'. Bertha maintained that the evil one's name had only to flit into your mind for something wicked to happen.

Bertha was Primitive Methodist, and the whole journey into Manchester always seemed, to Rosie, to be lined with boxes full of people worshipping the Almighty. Scented smoke would drift out of nearby St Luke's, where mysterious internal Roman Catholic bells were already tinkling. The big bell inside the tower of the Anglican Church of St John the Evangelist had just finished tolling. Was it meant for the people in the graveyard too? Did they creep in and listen to the sermon? As the Rover passed along Broad Street at Pendleton, homesick voices were even singing hymns in Welsh. These very differences were all reassuringly familiar.

This car journey was the one time in the week when Clifford Tattersall really talked to his children. But today he was silent. And it wasn't an ordinary silence. The twins could already swim, and it seemed to Rosie that Clifford's quiet had the tense quality of somebody waiting for his turn, on the steps up to the big diving board.

From the outside, the Friends' Meeting House looked like a pillared bank, sitting at the top of a lot of steps. Toiling up these stone stairs came the Friends. Mrs Hankey had a different name for them. She called them 'fanooks'. Without being in complete agreement with the housekeeper, Rosie knew what she meant. There were more beards and sandals than was usual in Manchester in 1955, and there was a higher degree of interest in food reform and the Indian question. Equally, there were more kind eyes than you usually met in the average gang of people.

The warmest pair belonged to a rounded, untidy, straying-haired woman called Mrs Marriott, who seized a twin by either hand and took them off into a side room. Both Mrs Marriott's husband and her brother had spent the war in prison, as conscientious objectors. These men were already in the big room, where the silence was being observed. The twins would not be led in there until later.

Three other children were waiting for them in the little room at the side. They belonged to a university lecturer and always seemed to compensate for missing buttons with long words. The room had frosted windows – as though you were meant to concentrate on what you were being taught.

Rosie did just the opposite. As Mrs Marriott began to read an Old Testament story about some people called Ruth and Naomi, Rosie Tattersall reviewed the events of the past week. She seemed to have spent her time dodging round other people's secrets. There was, of course, The Secret, the one which belonged to Christopher – Teapot Hall would go up in flames if she ever revealed that. And Rosie loved Teapot Hall; loved it like a person. There was so much that was mysterious about it. Sealed attics and a cracked glass conservatory and giant wardrobes which hadn't been opened by anybody since Gran'ma Tattersall's day. Well, opened by nobody except the twins.

How many other houses had old cabin trunks, full of toys, that must have been new when Queen Victoria was on the throne? Christopher had once hauled a doll from one of these and smashed the china head and ripped open the cloth body, so that all the sawdust leaked out. Why? It was only a boy doll. What harm had it done to him?

'Rosie?' It was Mrs Marriott. 'This story's not really boring. Not if you listen properly. Just try this next bit. They're some of the most romantic words that have ever been written.'

The woman turned back to the Bible and read aloud: ' "And Ruth said, Intreat me not to leave thee, or to return from following after thee: for whither thou goest, I will go; and where thou lodgest, I will lodge: thy people shall be my people, and thy God my God. Where thou diest, will I die, and there will I be buried." What d'you think *that's* about?'

Rosie didn't have to think, she knew. 'Loving somebody.' Her answer came unhesitatingly. When you're short on love, you think about it a lot. But she wasn't going to tell Mrs Marriott that.

Crayoning came next; you were really meant to draw the story you had just heard. But Rosie hadn't listened to all of it, so she contented herself with drawing a picture of a broad-shouldered man with black hair and blue eyes. He looked like a taller, poshed-up version of Tony Curtis, the film star. This was meant to be a picture of the man who came into her head when somebody sang 'Some Day My Prince Will Come' on the wireless.

30

The blue in the crayon snapped but she'd finished it anyway. Rosie whispered to the picture, half aloud and half in her head, 'Where you go, I'll go. And when I'm dead, they'll put us both in the same grave.' She wasn't sure about this second part; it sounded a bit morbid. But the first part was everything she believed in. Mrs Marriott had just helped to put it into words. Except they came from the Bible so God had really put it into words.

'Your people will be my people.' With God on her side, she felt bold enough to say it right out loud.

Mr Perry, whose photo had been in the *Manchester Evening News* when he fasted for a peaceful solution to the troubles in Cyprus, put his head round the door. 'I think we're about ready for the children now.'

'Right, boys and girls, follow Mr Perry. I'll take up the rear . . .'

Very quietly, Mr Perry opened the door into the main meeting. There wasn't much to see. Just a plain room with a lot of people sitting on wooden chairs, round three sides of a table with a vase of flowers on it. However, one man was already on his feet and speaking. It was Clifford Tattersall. Rosie knew that when Quakers give ministry they are speaking what is in their hearts. She felt as though she'd caught her father in nothing but his underpants.

He was saying, 'I may be wrong but there seemed to be something un-Quakerly about the idea of going bankrupt. I'd got myself into this situation, so why should the Official Receiver have to solve it? So I've calculated that if I sell the house and everything, absolutely everything, I own, there should be just enough to cover my debts. And I'll be able to start again, in a smaller house, in a much more humble style.'

By now the children were in their places and Rosie's head was reeling. Could her father mean what he was saying? How could he let Teapot Hall go? It would be like selling your own dog. Not that she was allowed to have a dog. Connie said they left hairs.

Her father hadn't finished. 'Somebody much wiser than I am once said to me: "All anybody needs is a roof over their head, enough to eat and somebody to love. And if you're loved

31

back, then that's a bonus." ' He seemed about to say more, hesitated for a worried moment and then – registering his children's presence – sat down with a thud.

The room was filled with the silence. Rosie always found it to be something much more potent than just no noise. This Quaker quiet seemed to have an energy of its own. It was like a river running past you, or something distant and thrumming which was well disposed towards you. After a little while you found yourself being gathered into it. It made you a part of itself. Rosie often thought she'd like to lend the feeling to people who said they didn't believe in God. This morning, however, her own faith had taken a severe kicking.

If there was a God, why was he allowing Clifford Tattersall to shunt them all out of Teapot Hall? Still, her father had only *said* he was going to do it. Perhaps a bolt of lightning or something would come down from Heaven and stop him.

A surprise was nearer to hand. She felt a movement to her left-hand side. Her twin brother sometimes threatened to do things which never took place. Not this morning. Christopher was already on his feet – and he plainly meant to speak.

2

Christopher Tattersall was putting on a fully traditional performance. Once on their feet, older Quakers frequently closed their eyes, took deep breaths and then began to speak with some solemn phrase like 'I am reminded . . .'

Christopher let out his second deep breath, opened his eyes and began with just that: 'I am reminded . . .' Rosie knew an impressive pause would come next, and it did. But what would he add? What would be his own bit? Some demon had obviously nudged him out of his chair. What would it prompt him to say?

'I am reminded that God is a very bad man.'

Some people closed their eyes. The eyes of other Friends went worriedly to Clifford Tattersall. Just a few pairs looked straight at the small boy, who continued: 'He is very bad because of what he has done to me.'

The Secret, thought Rosie wildly. He's never going to tell The Secret? Yet half of her wished he would because, that way – once and for all – it would be out in the open. But he didn't.

Instead he continued: 'And now God's pulling my mummy away from my daddy. And I've had to spend a week being the only one who really knows about it!'

In any other setting, adults would already have seized the child and bundled him from the room. Not here. All Quakers are not pacifists but Friends – as a whole – are great believers in freedom of speech.

'In conclusion, ladies and gentlemen,' announced Christopher, and suddenly he sounded like a comedian in *Workers' Playtime* on the radio, 'in conclusion, I would like to sing a little song.

> 'I'm Alabammy bound,
> That choo-choo train won't hang around . . .'

Rosie's one fear was that he would also break into a sketchy tap dance. Before this could happen, with remarkable presence of mind Mr Perry suddenly turned to his neighbour and shook hands. When an Elder did this it was always the signal that silent worship was over. In the Friends' Meeting House, Mount Street, Manchester, this was probably the very first hour of silence which lasted only fifty-one minutes.

But it was over. Relieved adults, holding onto slips of paper, were taking it in turns to announce forthcoming meetings. And one woman roundly denounced a well-known brand of jam for being produced under un-Quakerly conditions. Friends were some of the first opponents of the slave trade and the tradition still continued.

The announcements over, people began to mill around. Mrs Marriott was brushing back her straying locks and talking urgently to Rosie's father: '. . . and the strain of all these business pressures of yours must, inevitably, have rubbed off on young minds.'

Through gritted teeth, Clifford Tattersall said something very un-Quakerly indeed. He said, 'I'd like to tan his arse.'

'But you won't!' Mrs Marriott's urgency was redoubled. 'You surely wouldn't fall into the corporal punishment trap, Cliff? Not a man who's having his children educated in the Montessori method!'

'Elm House's days are numbered too,' sighed Clifford. Would there be no end to these changes? wondered Rosie. She just wished somebody would read out the complete list, and have done with it.

The journey home was accomplished in further silence. Clifford Tattersall only broke it to say, to Christopher, 'Are you going to tell me what you meant about your mummy? You'll have to live with the consequences of your answers so think very hard before you reply.'

'Today's the day she's going to tell you anyway,' was all Christopher saw fit to answer.

As the car passed through Pendleton, people were coming out of all the churches and chapels on Broad Street. This was something which Rosie always enjoyed. She couldn't pretend that she looked forward to Meeting for Worship but –

afterwards – she was always glad she'd been. No, it was more than that. It was a feeling of having the right to belong in the sunshine – earned freedom.

Not today. All the other people in their Sunday-best looked *in* on something. And Rosie felt left outside. It was as though she was on the edge of everybody else's stories and not in one of her own. She felt cut off, behind a sheet of plate glass. It was, for all the world, like being made to wear glasses twice over.

The Rover continued on its uphill climb. By the time they got to Teapot Hall, the midday sun was shining down onto the golden teapot in a way that usually caused Bertha to say 'God's in his heaven, all's right with the world.' But everything was obviously far from right, because an agitated Bertha was dragging her stiff leg from one side of the broad top step to the other. To Rosie, she looked like somebody who'd walked a mile and found a locked public toilet.

'Don't put the car away!' called out Bertha. She always came into sharper focus when Mrs Hankey wasn't around. But this was the noisiest Rosie had ever heard her. 'Leave it there, and come and look what's standing in the middle of the hall.'

The children were the first to rattle their way through the two sets of glass-windowed doors. You couldn't miss what Bertha was talking about. Standing on the parquet, gleaming with newness, was a huge, brass-bound, crimson cabin trunk. A printed black and white label stuck on the side proclaimed that it was *Not Wanted On Voyage*.

'She even had the nerve to invite me to her farewell party!' Bertha had come up, limping and panting, behind them. She was actually leading Clifford Tattersall by the hand, as though he had reverted to being the small boy she had known in his parents' days. 'She's off to Philadelphia in the morning,' proclaimed Bertha.

'She's not,' Christopher piped up indignantly. 'She's Alabammy bound.'

'Well I knew it was *some* song. Connie was ever so full of herself. "Come to my farewell do, Bertha," she said. "We're keeping it up at the Coconut Grove." I've looked up the

35

address in the phone book, Mr Cliff. I've got it on this bit of paper for you.'

Clifford pushed the paper back at Bertha. 'Why would I want to follow her when she's obviously left for good?'

'No, she's not actually *gone*,' wittered Bertha. 'It's just the *do* this lunchtime. And then she's coming back here – for her things. She tried to give me a lot of old clothes. Well, she tried to sell me them first. Once she saw I wasn't biting, she just thrust them at me. I've left them where they fell. I wanted no part in it. Would you like a little drop of brandy, Mr Clifford?'

Clifford was pacing round the trunk. 'I'd like to know how in heaven's name she paid for this.'

'She didn't,' put in Christopher. 'She got it on your account at Affleck's.'

'There must be *twenty* steamer trunks up in the attics!' exploded Clifford. 'Yet the feckless creature has to go and land me with a bill for a new one.'

'She likes new things,' said Christopher reasonably.

Yes, and you like trouble, thought Rosie. You stand there, in your reefer coat and your red scarf – like a robin on a Christmas card – just waiting to pipe out the one song that will cause the next explosion.

It came quickly. Clifford kicked the trunk in fury, let out a loud yell, and then began to hobble round it. Bending down to rub his ankle, he lifted up an orange luggage label, tied to one of the gleaming brass handles.

'Cabin class.' He grunted. '*That* won't suit her for long!'

Bertha looked down at the unwanted scrap of paper in her hand. 'I made sure you'd be hot on her heels,' she said weakly. 'It's none of my business but she's packed two other suitcases. They're your mother's good soft-tops. She's had me washing stuff for days. Mr Clifford . . .' Her voice trailed awkwardly away.

'Carry on,' said Clifford. 'What is it you don't want to tell me?'

Bertha gulped and looked awkward. 'They're not just her own things. I know I'm not a married lady but I am a woman. And I think you should go after her and nip it in the bud.'

'No. If Mrs Tattersall wants a scene, she can have one. But

I'm going to no seedy Coconut Grove. We'll have the row here – when she gets back. I know what I *am* going to do,' he said. 'I'm going to knock some sense into a deceitful little show off.' He glowered at Christopher. 'And it's something I should have done years ago.' Cold fury had obviously wiped out pacifism, for Clifford Tattersall began to remove his thin leather trouser-belt.

'No!' screamed Christopher.

'Yes,' said Clifford. And grabbing his son by the scruff of the neck he sat down on the offending red trunk, turned the protesting child over his knee, and began to attempt to leather him. But Christopher got in first, with a quick kick at one of his father's shins. It was still Sunday but Irlams o'th' Height was changing into Bedlam.

Bright sunlight on the gilded teapot gave way to a plain grey November afternoon of scudding clouds. Dusk fell and there was still no sign of Connie. The wind began to rattle the dry elm branches in the grounds of Teapot Hall. Up in the tower, in the nursery, Christopher was still crying. This had gone on – in fits and starts – for the whole of the afternoon.

'He'd no right to do it . . .' He was sobbing this out, for what seemed to Rosie the hundredth time. 'No right at all. If he knew The Secret, he wouldn't have dared do it . . .'

'Then let me tell him,' she begged.

'No!' screamed Christopher. 'And if you ever say a word, those flames will come and burn you in your bed.'

Rosie tried to be reasonable. 'Daddy says we're going to move. If we're not here, how can you burn down Teapot Hall?'

'I don't care. I'll still know,' stormed Christopher. 'I can look into your head a million times better than you can look into mine.' Once again he was overcome with sobbing rage. As if to match his mood, the wind began to thwack against the tower, drowning out the protesting creaks of storm-tossed rhododendrons.

Doing something that was strictly forbidden, Christopher used the big nursery fireguard to haul himself up off the hearth rug. For want of anything better to do, he crossed over to the big spotted rocking horse, which stood underneath Gran'ma Tattersall's old framed print of 'The Piper of Dreams'. As Christopher climbed onto Dobbin, Rosie found herself wondering how many of their toys they would be allowed to take to some smaller house.

Up in the saddle, Christopher began to rock backwards and forwards, for comfort, in the firelight. 'It won't matter where I am in the world,' he said sternly to his sister. 'I'll still find out you've told. And I'll still *get* you.'

Half of this nastiness was just a direct result of his grief and pain. Rosie could actually feel all of this swirling towards her. But two weeping twins would be one too many. Somewhere in the distance, a dustbin lid blew off and clattered over paving stones. It most likely belonged to one of the semi-detached houses, beyond the shrubbery. Would that be the sort of house they would have to move into? No, she *wouldn't* cry. Instead, Rosie probed. 'Anyway, why should you be somewhere else in the world?' she asked.

Christopher shifted uncomfortably in the saddle. 'My bum still hurts,' he said. 'If I wasn't going away, I'd ring the NSPCC.'

It was out. He'd said it. He was going away. Before Rosie could begin to ask questions, he was saying more: 'You can be very dim at times. Bertha was talking about *my* clothes in the trunk. Mine! Can't you get it into your stupid head that we're Alabammy bound.'

Now Rosie's tears did fall. 'What about me?' she cried. 'If it's only your clothes, what's going to happen to me?'

The wind dropped for a moment, which was enough to allow them to hear the sound of a car pulling up on the gravel beneath the tower. As they rushed for the window, the car door slammed, and the ping of a taxi's meter being pushed back rose up on the night air.

'Keep the change,' said their mother, from down below. 'After all, it's only English money.' She sounded drunk. Two minds with but a single thought set two pairs of feet racing for the nursery door. 'Don't clatter,' hissed Christopher, 'or they'll only hear us and send us back up.'

The children made their way cautiously down the winding,

carpeted staircase of the tower. 'They'll be busy shouting by the time we get to the minstrels' gallery,' whispered Christopher. 'If we stay in the shadows, by the big tapestry, we should be able to get a good view.'

Noise was already rising up to greet them. When it came to a dramatic entrance, the two sets of shuddering glass doors from the garden were in the same class as trumpets. Tonight the wind seemed to want to suck them back and add even louder crashes to their usual banging.

'About bloody time too!' roared Clifford, in a voice which would have surprised them at the Friends' Meeting House.

The children had noticed, in the past, that drink sometimes turned Connie Tattersall into her own idea of a *grande dame*. She would become lofty and a mite condescending and very, very dignified. It always put Rosie in mind of Mother Goose, after she got her hands on the money.

Tonight, all Connie seemed to have laid hands on was an unopened bottle of Moët et Chandon. The dark green glass, and the gold foil, and the red seal, all looked wonderfully wicked against her pale lilac suit. As usual she had a hat on. Rosie's spectacles gave her the long-distance eyesight of an eagle. 'Look!' Rosie exclaimed. 'She's ripped her veil.'

Connie's pastel mink stole – the one dripping in fur tails – was also being worn at an angle which did not suggest sobriety. 'I've brought us a bottle of bubbly,' she was saying. It was Connie herself who had taken the twins to see *Brief Encounter*, so they knew where she'd borrowed the voice from. 'Let's try to be civilised about this thing, Cliff.'

'Who are you going off with and where are you going?'

'Champagne glasses . . .' Connie looked around vaguely. 'We need a couple of champagne saucers. Here, you're supposed to be a man, you pop it.'

As she thrust out the champagne, Clifford seized the bottle and threw it at the far wall. It exploded against the panelling with a loud bang and began to run down the portrait of Gran'dad Tattersall with his favourite trotting-pony.

'Well, well, well . . .' Connie was filled with genuine admiration. 'Only it's a bit too late for strong-arm stuff. I'm afraid I'm poised for flight.' Real interest crept into her voice as she added, 'I didn't know you had that in you.'

'Trust you to admire what I'm ashamed of.'

'It's the first sexy thing you've done in years. And, yes, everything *does* boil down to sex. Well, it does with me, anyway.' She let out a dirty snigger. 'It used to matter to you too. The first time you poked me was in your father's cold-storage warehouse. That should've told me something but it didn't. A bloody refrigerator was just about your mark! Let's have some proper light on this scene.'

Crazy firelight was already dancing round the room; the only fixed glow came from a big parchment-shaded standard lamp. As Connie swayed towards another lamp, Clifford barred her path: 'No. Electricity has to be paid for. I'm trying to save money.'

'Dear God! What's the man going to begrudge me next? We're talking about two therms of electricity, Cliff.'

'It's gas that's measured in therms.'

'Here endeth lesson number one-thousand-and-one. Have you any idea what it's been like? When I married you, everybody thought I'd gone up in the world. Everybody except you . . .' Years of bitterness had started to pour out of Connie. 'You made pretty damn sure that I didn't get too big for my boots.'

Savagely, she began to mimic him. ' "Don't you think those white court shoes are a bit common, Constance?" and "I know you weren't brought up with servants but . . ." and "I know you don't speak French *but* . . ." But, but, I'm sick of your bloody buts. It was all right when we could fuck our way out of it. Once that stopped, I felt as though I was in a finishing school for just one person. Well, I *am* finished. I'm me. I'm complete. I'm whole. You're the one with the limp dick. Oh yes,' she sneered, 'you'll switch another standard lamp on *now*, won't you? Anything except talk about these things.'

The light from the extra lamp was no friend to the proceedings, for it fell – almost accusingly – onto the big red cabin trunk. 'Where are you off to?' The stuffing seemed to be knocked out of Clifford and he asked the question weakly this time.

'America!' And even Mamie Eisenhower could not have pronounced the word in tones of more fervent satisfaction.

'Who with? You do realise I could sue this man for alienation of affection.'

'A black man, Clifford? That *would* give Smithfield Market something to talk about. I'll tell you something, sweetheart – until I'd had a black man I'd never lived. He makes me feel as though I'm lined with white satin.'

Clifford looked physically sick. 'And what about the children?' he managed to say. 'You're not just a wife, you're a mother.'

'I'll take the boy. Mason's got daughters of his own.'

And I bet they don't have to wear glasses, thought Rosie, who was still in the minstrels' gallery. Trust Connie to go and choose the twin with good eyesight! Rosie's world – which had seemed threatened – was now in fragments. And rather than face up to the terrifying possibilities ahead of her, she continued to be just part of an audience for the scene below.

Did this Mason, her father wanted to know, have money? It seemed he did. Had Connie got a visa? Two; one for herself and one for Christopher. That's where she'd been all day last Friday. And who had signed Christopher's form of consent? Connie dismissed forgery with a threatening reference to those mysterious nudist magazines.

Long past understanding any of this, Rosie began to cry. Connie might be everything that was overblown and vulgar but she was still her mother. 'She's just dumping me,' she sobbed.

'Shh . . .' hissed Christopher. 'I want to hear when we're off.'

So it seemed did Clifford: 'Your mind's plainly made up. You're packed. You're ready. When do we see the back of you? When can we have the premises fumigated?' Without so much as a breath's pause he added, in a near whisper, 'Please don't go.'

Connie might have finished with her husband but she didn't cease abusing him. 'Before you start calling me every shade of dirt, just you remember one thing. I'm me – in my own right. You, you're just your father's son! Gran'dad

41

Tattersall was six times the man you are, and everybody knows it.'

'You leave my father out of this.'

'Why? Why should I, when he was a particular friend of mine? Do you ever stop to wonder why he left me that thousand pounds? That was for the jump we never had. Oh we *thought* about it often enough. We used to discuss it on wet afternoons. "You're a well-ventilated woman, Connie," he used to say to me. "But I swore to be true to my dead wife."' Connie's boozy eyes swam with easy emotion. 'I can appreciate a one-woman man. Given half a chance, I'd have been the same myself.' Her voice took on more practical tones. 'Still, I've had the thousand nicker. The Bible says there'll be no giving and taking in marriage in Heaven. So – when I get there – I owe your dad a jump. That's only supposing your mother raises no objections.'

Clifford was looking at her in dazed disbelief. 'Spare me the muddled theology . . .'

'Because you've got the Bible cornered? It's *anything* to make me look small! I'll have you know I went to a church school. I've read my Bible.'

In a voice which only pretended to be patient, Clifford said, 'Only the Muslims believe there will be sex in Heaven.'

'Then call me Abou Ben Adhem!' roared Connie.

Up on the landing, Christopher only had to hear the name Abou Ben Adhem to add aloud, 'May his tribe increase!' Like their mother, the twins had done this poem at school. Unfortunately, Christopher said it a bit *too* aloud because Connie looked up and copped the pair of them, still huddled in the shadows.

'Listeners never hear any good of themselves,' she bawled. 'Still that's a few explanations saved. Come down, kids. It's a party!'

Christopher rushed down the stairs, reciting the words of the poem at the top of his voice.

'Abou Ben Adhem (may his tribe increase!)
Awoke one night from a deep dream of peace . . .'

Deep dream of peace? Rosie, loath to follow him, felt as

though she was living in a nightmare. And if she didn't even feel safe here, in the shadows, how would things be once she had descended that slippery polished staircase? She lingered where she was. On ground level, Christopher had got to the part in the poem where the angel was writing in a book of gold. And Connie was slopping over her son and calling him her own special angel who was off to meet Uncle Sam.

'Where's John Bull's girl?' shouted Connie. 'Come on, Rosie! Come down here and give your wicked mother a farewell kiss. Get me a gin and tonic, Cliff. And Christopher, you go and put your best outdoor coat on. Put your new shoes on too.'

Reluctantly, Rosie began to descend the stairs. The words 'new shoes' had really stabbed home. What one twin got, the other always had. 'Are there new shoes for me, as well?' she asked hopefully. It wasn't that she wanted footwear, she just wanted to be in on things.

'I'm afraid there aren't.' Connie was giving an imitation of a brisk mother. 'You see, Christopher's going on a ship and you're not. You wouldn't like it in America, Rosie. We're going where it's hot. And you know how you were at Ilfracombe.'

'But I've got a sunhat now,' was all Rosie could manage.

'No. Little girls stay with their daddies. Everybody knows that.'

'But you can't just go and split us up. We're twins.' Rosie saw this as an irrefutable argument.

Apparently she saw it wrong. 'Nobody's splitting you up. The very idea! No, you're just going to live on different sides of the world – that's all.'

'But we're twins.' She tried it again. Even as she spoke, she knew in her heart that the magic of this talisman was weakening.

A new voice startled everybody by joining in: 'You'll go the way your mother went, Connie Hicks!' It was little Bertha, on the stairs, and this was perhaps the boldest moment of her life. Immediately reverting to type, she clapped her hands over her ears and said, 'Don't think I'm listening 'cos I'm not.'

Connie literally ran across the room – it was a tottering run

– and pulled Bertha's hands down. 'My mother was a fucking angel!' she roared. 'And d'you know what's driven me out of this house as much as anything else? You and Nora Hankey. I was never good enough for the pair of you. Never!'

'Correct,' said Bertha. 'But we had to learn that. And you taught us. Even Lady didn't like you.'

Perhaps it was thoughts of Lady, a long-departed golden retriever, which brought tears to Bertha's eyes. 'I'm sorry, Mr Clifford,' she said quietly, 'I know I've spoken out of turn but I'd willingly pack for her – and that's a fact.'

'All the packing's done, Bertha.' Connie was trying to be lofty. 'Just bring the two soft-topped cases from under the stone slab in the flower room.'

'No she doesn't. Get them yourself.' Clifford was at his coldest.

'I'll need a taxi.'

'You can get that for yourself too.'

The silence that followed was almost worse than all the noise. Eventually, it was broken by Connie's clacking heels as she trailed around the house, gathering together her final bits and pieces. The only person she spoke to was Christopher: 'She could wear a sunbonnet – that's a laugh!'

Christopher was ready for off before his mother. Waiting for her, he climbed up on top of the cabin trunk where he sat swinging his legs. One of the new shoelaces wasn't properly tied and Bertha bent down, awkwardly, to fasten it.

'You was always *my* little boy . . .' was all she said. But now she was openly crying.

'I'll get Mason Pollitt to send for you,' was the boy's confident reply. His very calm was making it obvious that he must have had days in which to get used to the idea of departure. Connie now reappeared in her squirrel coat, wearing the mink stole over the top of it – like a football supporter's scarf.

'I see you're taking all your spoils with you,' said her husband bitterly.

'I'll strip off and go naked, if that's what you want,' rejoined Connie. She began to tug at her fingers. 'Here!' she said, thrusting something at Rosie. 'Don't say your mother never gave you anything.'

The child found herself looking down at a golden wedding band and Connie's big solitaire diamond engagement ring.

'Has this man got real money?' asked Clifford worriedly.

'Have you? He's got pots of it.' Connie was at her most irritatingly swanky. 'His people own a big dry-goods store. I'm not being shipped out by the military. He's sending us privately.'

Bertha was still looking worriedly at Christopher but she spoke to Connie: 'What about all those returned GI brides? They were promised the earth and they found themselves in timber shacks.'

'So he's a soldier, is he?' asked Clifford – as though grabbing for information might somehow stop his wife from leaving.

'A master-sergeant.' Was it Rosie's imagination, or was her mother already beginning to sound American?

'I cannot pretend to understand what the United States Army thinks it's still doing at Burtonwood,' sighed Clifford wretchedly.

'They're bringing joy to the women of Manchester,' was his wife's ringing reply. 'Ta-ta, Cliff, I won't give you a kiss.'

'Con, please don't go.' He looked completely drained as he fought for further words. 'Don't go. I'm *begging* you . . .'

'And fucking feeble it makes you look!' The taxi outside sounded its impatient horn again. 'You bring the two little cases, Chris. I'll manage the trunk – it's got built-in roller skates.' Turning to her husband she added, 'You never got round to carrying me over the threshold, and now I'm reduced to dragging out all my worldly goods on castors!' Suiting the deed to the word, she grabbed hold of a brass handle and began to haul the red trunk – and herself – out of their lives.

'Christopher . . .' Rosie held desperately onto her twin. 'Don't you want to say anything to me?'

'Yes. Don't you dare think this gives you any right to tell anybody The Secret. Because it doesn't. I'm taking some of the you-know-whats with me. You tell and I'll know. And even if I have to wait years, I'll come back and fix you.'

It was the same muffled quiet that you get immediately after a death. With the two noisiest elements gone from the house, the people left behind tiptoed around, as if they were in grey flannel overshoes. For two days Clifford barely emerged from his bedroom where the curtains had remained permanently drawn. Mrs Hankey maintained that he was on the edge of a nervous breakdown. She pronounced it 'breekdown'.

Ever afterwards, Rosie would associate these drawn-out days with the song 'Painting the Clouds With Sunshine'. She kept playing it, over and over again, on a wind-up gramophone – just for something to do. Even this tinny sound was muffled by a duster, which Bertha had shoved down the horn of the gramophone, so Clifford would not be disturbed. It was the only record Rosie could lay hands on. All the rest were in a cupboard that was locked. The song, sung by a tortured tenor, was all about holding back a tear to let a smile appear. But Rosie Tattersall was not smiling.

'Rosie!' Her father was at the top of the big staircase, Rosie and the gramophone at the bottom. 'Did nobody bother to tell you to get ready for going to town?' Pale and white but shaved and dressed, he was already descending the stairs.

'Did you think to bother to ask anybody?' It was Mrs Hankey. The sound of adult footsteps had brought her hurrying in from the kitchen.

Clifford looked as though he must have got dressed with his mind on other things. The top button of his cardigan was in the wrong hole, so that it hung crookedly the whole way down. The housekeeper moved in on him, indulgently: 'Come here. Let me straighten you out.'

'Would that you could,' he sighed. 'Have the men arrived? I didn't want Rosie around when they came clodhopping through.'

'Which she won't be. Not if you stir yourself and get off fast.' Mrs Hankey even straightened his tie. Clifford, rather than Rosie, could have been the one who was eight years old. 'I don't think old Mrs Tattersall'd rest easy in her grave if I didn't spoil you a bit, at a time like this. Don't think it's *you* that's getting the favours, Mr Clifford, it's her. As for that other cow . . . I'm praying for storms in the Atlantic. Nothing would please me better than to hear she'd been shipwrecked off Dogger Bank! Slip into your little tweed coat, Rosemary. It's not as though you're going to school.'

Elm House had started again, after the holidays, on Monday. But nobody had got round to taking Rosie to school. She only had to walk across and lift down the tweed coat from the hall stand, made of antlers, so she was able to listen to the rest of the grown-ups' conversation.

'Am I expected to provide these men with lunch?' asked Mrs Hankey.

'No you are not!' replied Clifford indignantly. Then he relented: 'Oh I don't know. Why should I view them as the enemy? They're only here to do a job of work.'

'Soup then,' sniffed Mrs Hankey. 'But not very *nice* soup. Just summat rough.'

'These are rough days,' sighed Clifford. 'They've already been on the phone from Smithfield Market. The same thing's been going on there since dawn.'

Struggling into her coat, Rosie finally got up the nerve to say, 'If Mummy's shipwrecked, Christopher will be too.'

'Not him,' retorted Mrs Hankey. 'The devil knows his own! That Christopher would probably float all the way to New York on a plank.'

It would be a mistake to think that the housekeeper was being unkind to Rosie. Both Mrs Hankey and Bertha had tried to keep the child busy with little things to do in the kitchen. They had even made treacle toffee. Bertha said you could foretell the future by the shapes the molten syrup made as it settled into the ice-cold water. The only definite outline Rosie had been able to perceive had been that of a monkey. They had tried to discover the significance of this in Bertha's copy of *Napoleon's Book of Dreams and Fortunes* – only to discover that Connie must have swiped the book from the kitchen shelf and borne it off to Alabama.

Rosie suddenly realised that, for the first time in her life, she was going to be alone in a car with her father. This made her feel curiously shy. And he was so used to controlling a pair of exploding twins that he seemed at a loss to know how to manage one, temporarily docile little girl.

'Do you miss Christopher?' was the best he seemed able to come out with.

It struck Rosie as a particularly dopey question. Of *course* she missed Christopher. Should she explain to Clifford that her twin was not quite gone? Not *completely*. Only that would be to allow her father inside her mind, where Christopher still lived on, in the shape of . . . *a distant high-pitched hum* was the best description she would have been able to manage. Her twin was much too far away for her to be able to 'read' him. But her own life force knew that Christopher's life force still existed. All she said to her father was: 'I could tell if he was dead – and he isn't.'

'I think I understand,' he replied, carefully. Rosie would have bet that he didn't. Rather than encourage more questions, she decided to ask one herself: 'Where are we going?'

'Down to the firm.'

In the child's mind *THE FIRM* was in the same size letters as Christopher's secret. Edwin Tattersall & Son, Wholesale Fruit Merchants (Manchester) Limited, had been the brain-child of Rosie's great-grandfather. Except in those days it had been called Muirhead's and belonged to somebody else. The name Tattersall was not blazoned across the front of the offices until the 1880s. These offices in Smithfield Market in Manchester were up on legs, like railway signal boxes, made of pale golden varnished wood. Tattersall's stood on a paved square, on the edge of a cobbled street, under a great Victorian steel and glass span, in the style of the Crystal Palace.

In that wholesale fruit and vegetable market, space was not reckoned by the foot but by the inch. Even the gap between the stilt-like legs of the offices earned its living by being piled, eight foot high, with crates of perishable produce.

Not today. There wasn't so much as a box of apples in sight. The Tattersalls always said, 'You can't miss our stall. We're the one with the flashing neon fruit bowl, on the

Wholesale Square.' The sign was not lit up – the bobbing pineapple and the dancing tangerines were standing still. The rest of the market was ringing with activity; but no railway carts drawn by dray horses were unloading at Tattersall's. No busy little vans, from outlying grocers' shops, were carrying fruit away. For the first time in her life, Rosie could actually see the flagstoned floor. Tattersall's was looking like something that was over.

Over but covered with a rash of square spots. Even the huge sales till, all brass and scrollwork and embossed with copper bunches of grapes, had been dabbed with one of the numbered adhesive stickers. A veritable eruption of these numbers seemed to have attacked every portable object. There was even one on the neon fruit bowl.

The only thing that was as usual was Little Cyril, the head salesman. He was still standing at the bottom of the stairs which led up to the empty office aloft. Normally he was full of market wisecracks and uniformed in a white warehouse coat. Today he was just a sad-looking man in a dark suit and a black homburg hat.

Little Cyril (never to be confused with Big Cyril who ran the flower side) generally had a bit of something in the toffee line in his pocket for Rosie. That too had changed. This morning, all his worried attentions were directed towards Clifford Tattersall. 'Proberts, in the far corner, have offered me a job. It's give-or-take the same money,' he said. 'At least that's me suited. And most of the other lads are getting snapped up. But what about you, Guvnor? Who hires bosses?'

'Nobody. They start again. Only there's going to be nothing left to start with. The fault's nobody's but my own – I should have built up the foreign side again, after the war.'

'Why is everything covered in spots?' asked Rosie.

'For the auctioneer.' Cyril seemed to think this explained everything. It didn't. Not to an eight-year-old. It took her father to say 'Everything's going to be sold' before she understood.

'Even the neon fruit bowl?'

Clifford nodded.

'But it's got our name on it. How can you let somebody buy our name?'

Little Cyril looked uncomfortable. 'Have you got a money-box?' he asked Rosie. 'Here.' He dug in his coat pocket and thrust a loose ten-shilling note in her hand. It was the first time he'd ever offered her money.

'There was no need for that, Cyril.' Her father spoke gruffly and his eyes looked as though the last thing they wanted to do was meet anybody else's. 'So everything's under control, is it? Just thought I'd have a last look.'

Rosie could tell – by the haunted way he was glancing around – that Clifford was suddenly anxious to be off. Yet still he lingered on, like somebody who knows he's got to say goodbye but doesn't want to do it. Unexpected November sunlight was pouring through the vaulted glass roof. The echoes inside the market were much the same as in a railway station. But the smell was different – that sickly-sweet smell of too many apples and of discarded oranges in the gutters. And the sharp freshness of new wood from tens of thousands of crates. None at Tattersall's. And a whiff of fish, drifting in from the next market, down on Shudehill. ·

'I never thought I'd miss the pong,' said Clifford, 'but I will. I'll be in touch from London, Cyril.'

'Are we going to London?' asked Rosie eagerly. He didn't answer her and a little thought suddenly grew big. 'You're not going to put me in an orphanage, are you?' she asked fearfully.

'I'll be getting along too,' said Little Cyril quickly. 'I'll go down and have one in the Turk's Head. Fancy a last pint, Guvnor?'

'Fraid not. There's her.' Clifford nodded down at his daughter. 'Sorry.'

Cyril was shifting his weight from one foot to the other. It was as though he seemed to feel that the occasion demanded something more. 'I was a lad of thirteen when I came to Tattersall's,' he said respectfully. 'I can just about remember your grandfather, Mr Clifford. He always wore a big diamond ring.' Cyril laughed. 'They used to say he got it cheap, off old man Muirhead, when he snatched the firm from over his head.'

Rosie's father looked round the dismantled stall. 'Rags to rags in three generations, eh? The old Manchester story!'

'Abyssinia,' said Cyril, mysteriously.

Obviously it wasn't a mystery to Rosie's father because he called after the departing employee, 'Yes, and I'll be seeing you too, Cyril.'

'What happened to the diamond ring?' asked Rosie.

'You've got it. It's the one your mother gave you on Sunday. Trust Connie to be the only person who managed to pull something out of the wreckage! Come on, Rosie, give me your hand. We've got to walk through the market to the car. And we're going to do it with our heads held high.'

Rose could see people from nearby stalls watching them, covertly, as they went. Eventually, one man called out, 'Chin up, Cliff!' Then similar cries began to come from all sides. 'Good luck.' 'Yes, chin up!' 'Don't let them grind you down.'

Her father's hand was nice and dry and warm, but she could feel it shaking as she held it. Rosie wanted to say something to cheer him up. 'Daddy, there's a place on Market Street – with three gold balls – where you can sell things. Perhaps they'd give us a lot of money for the ring and everything would be all right?'

Her father didn't seem inclined to answer. Suddenly there was no longer glass between them and the sky. They were out on Swan Street and the smell of fish was much stronger. Men from the Corporation Cleansing Department were already hosing down the cobblestones with a strong solution of bleach.

'Yes, I should have built up the foreign side,' reiterated Clifford. It was a thought which must have been running through his mind since they left the stall. 'I'll not be back.'

'Morning, Mr Tattersall.' Two people said it – women in black – nuns. Rosie had been down to the firm often enough to know that these were the Little Sisters of the Poor. They were Smithfield Market fixtures, and they always seemed to greet people with one hand held out. Today was no exception. Clifford sighed, fished in his pocket and gave the old one a shilling.

'*And* he's broke,' said Rosie with considerable pride.

'We'll pray for you, Mr Tattersall.' The elder of the pair had awful wire-framed glasses, just like Rosie's. She also had

all-seeing eyes. 'We were sorry to hear about your troubles.'
The nuns were always privy to the latest Shudehill gossip.

'Pray for the child,' said Clifford. 'I'll get by. She's the one
with an uncertain future.'

'And that can be an adventure in itself,' put in the younger
nun, the pretty one – she was Irish. And the men of Smithfield
Market always said she was wasted. 'An uncertain future can
lead to awful big things.'

'What's your name, child?' asked the plain one in specs.
'God and his Holy Mother like us to be very specific in these
matters.'

'Rosemary Tattersall.'

The pretty one burst in again with, 'Well I'll pray you don't
have a dull life, Rosemary.' She seemed full of urgent
friendliness.

'Yes, and I'll pray for a safety-brake on that flapping tongue
of yours, Sister.' Her bespectacled colleague was already
heading towards a man with a heavy gold watch-chain
stretched across a prosperous belly. When it came to credit
rating, the Little Sisters of the Poor were more skilled than
any manager of a Smithfield bank.

The restaurant wouldn't have Rosie and Clifford. It was on
Market Street, down a long tiled corridor, with a sign that just
said *The Chop House*.

A great big uniformed waitress, with a bust that stuck out
like the royal box at the Manchester Palace Theatre, and a
starched white cap on top of a lot of dyed-red hair, barred
their way with: 'You should know better than to try and bring
her in here, Mr Tattersall. It's strictly gentlemen only.' Her
tones were very stern and bossy. 'That little girl's *female*.'

The place smelt of roasting joints of meat. Because she
obviously wasn't supposed to be there, Rosie immediately
found the restaurant highly intriguing. There were more of
the elaborate tiles in burgundy and green and not so much as
a chink of daylight. The room was dimly lit by hanging bronze
electroliers. Exciting flaming things were happening at some
of the white damask-covered tables, where crombie-
overcoated men in homburgs and Anthony Eden hats were

chomping on big midday dinners. Perhaps the fact that her father always went bareheaded had marked him down for failure? It might be an idea to sell the ring and get him a trilby. What was it the posters said? '*If You Want to Get Ahead Get a Hat!*'

'She's only a very *little* female.' Clifford was still trying to argue with the waitress. He should have known better.

'And what if she wants to go somewhere? What if she's taken short? We haven't got the facilities.'

'I went before I came,' volunteered Rosie.

'Would this be Connie's kiddie?' asked the waitress, in more human tones.

'Yes.'

Rosie felt that the woman was looking down at her with too much interest. 'I knew your mother when she was still doing it for dolly mixtures.'

'Honestly, Ethel!' said Clifford reproachfully.

'That's what I *mean*,' she cried. 'Even my own conversation's not for mixed company. It's been ruined by business gentlemen.' Once again she became more human: 'I'm sorry to hear that Tattersall's is going down the Swanee, Mr Cliff. But three cheers for the fact that Connie's sugared off to America!'

'How did you know that?' he stammered.

'Know?' She looked amazed. 'You men are much bigger gossips than any women. This chop house has been buzzing with nothing else since Monday. And I think it's very brave of you to go off to Covent Garden with nothing definite in view.' Again she switched her attention to Rosie: 'How d'you think you'll take to London?'

London. There it was again. But before Rosie could say anything, Clifford cut in with, 'If you can't feed us, we'd better look elsewhere. Ta-ta, Ethel.' With this he began to steer Rosie back up the corridor. As they got out onto the pavement, Rosie refused to be steered any further.

'You're not taking me with you, are you?'

'I wonder if that shop opposite has a cafeteria?'

It was Henry's, the shop with the permanent bargain sale where everything was Empire Made. Rosie wouldn't have cared if it had been Kendal Milne and Company – Manchester's own version of Harrods. All she wanted to know was where she stood. 'You're not taking me with you,' she repeated. 'And when I asked you about an orphanage, you never answered me.' By now Rosie was shouting, loudly. 'You didn't and you can't say you did.'

Clifford tried to control the situation by lowering his own voice: 'How do I put you in an orphanage when you're not an orphan?'

'I'm not an anything,' wept Rosie, 'I'm just in the way. I want my mummy back,' she wailed.

'Rosie, please . . . people are staring.'

'I don't care. And anyway, people stared at you in that place that wouldn't let us in.'

This was true. Clifford had drawn a lot of pitying, complacent glances from the chewing men in the chop house. It was equally true that Rosie was missing her mother. Connie wasn't just everything that was awful. There was also a big, generous, daft, friendly side to her. A side which bought knickerbocker glories and blew raspberries in the face of convention.

'I want my mummy and I want Christopher.'

'Well they didn't want you.'

'You shouldn't have said that.' Clifford had voiced aloud the one thought she had been trying to push aside for days. Rosie was hurt to the quick. 'Why did you have to go and *say* it?' she wailed. 'Anyway, you don't want me either – I can tell.' Once again the tears began to roll down her face, and people were pausing and pretending to look in shop windows, just so they could hear what was going on.

'What are you going to do with me?' asked Rosie, in a frightened voice.

A woman, who had been edging nearer, now decided to join in the conversation: 'Excuse me, dear,' she said to Rosie, 'but do you *know* this man?'

'He's my daddy!' shrieked the child.

'I'm awfully sorry,' the woman was suddenly trying to talk a bit posher for Clifford's benefit, 'but you hear such awful things about kiddies and strangers . . .'

Clifford bent down, picked up his daughter and began to carry her through the traffic: 'What are you going to do with me?' she repeated brokenly.

'Arrangements have been made,' was the tight reply. 'But this is neither the time nor the place to begin to explain. The first thing I'm going to do is get some food inside you.'

'I'm not hungry.' He was now carrying her through the ground floor of Henry's. It began at the Glove Department, went past Ladies' Jumpers and then you came to a wrought-iron and marble staircase, like something in a small cinema. Even Rosie – up aloft in her father's arms – could tell that Clifford looked out of place. A sign at the foot of the stairs said *Why Not Try a Tasty Snack in Our Inexpensive Luncheonette?*

'I'm not hungry,' repeated Rosie stubbornly. But this didn't stop Clifford carrying her down to the basement snack bar. It was self-service.

'Would you please try not to draw any more attention to us? Just trust me, Rosie. I'll tell you in my own good time.' He looked perturbed. 'I think I'll give you half an aspirin when I get you home. Food: what would you like?'

Was it only a week since she had sat in just such another snack bar with her mother and her twin? 'I don't want anything.' He made her have a meat and potato pie – and all it did was get big in her mouth.

'I'm not an ogre, Rosie – don't think you have to force that pie down if you're not enjoying it.' Clifford seemed to be looking around for further inspiration. His eyes lighted on another sign. *Visit Santa Claus in His Grotto. See Also the Living, Breathing, Sleeping Beauty.* 'Let's go and see Father Christmas,' he said.

'I don't believe in him. It's only you and Mummy.' The tears – which had stopped – started again.

'Oh God!' said Clifford helplessly. 'Let's go and see him anyway.'

Henry's grottos had a tawdry magic of their own. The store did not employ a particularly sophisticated display staff and, at Christmas, this was all to the good. The winding, tunnel-like series of caves which they had erected was made of painstakingly crumpled cardboard, sprayed dark green and covered with spangles and glitter dust. It could have been the work of a sophisticated child. All the nodding pixies and elves in the spotlit tableaux had a curiously home-made quality to them. It made you feel as though you could go home and get out scissors and Seccotine and start making something similar yourself.

But who would you have got to be the living, breathing, grown-up Sleeping Beauty? The big blonde woman was lying under a pink spotlight, on a single divan bed with a white, button-studded, plastic headboard. A Day-Glo sign said that similar bedheads were available – at four pounds, nineteen shillings and sixpence – from the Occasional Furniture Department on the second floor.

'What a rude nightdress,' whispered Rosie, entranced. 'You can see the ends of her titties sticking through it.'

The woman opened her eyes and looked straight at Clifford Tattersall – who was staring at her much more hungrily than he had ever done at his meat and potato pie.

'We're just off to see Santa,' he said hastily to the Sleeping Beauty, and he tugged Rosie through a cardboard Gothic arch decorated with real snails' shells, painted silver.

Father Christmas was sitting against a bright green velveteen curtain with a sack at his feet. There was no fairy – there was a photographer instead. 'Present or photo?' asked the man in the cotton-wool beard and the red costume, which was nice and new this year.

'Er . . . just the present.' Awkwardly, Clifford held out the half-crown ticket he had bought for Rosie at the entrance to the grotto. Santa fished in his sack and produced a small children's puzzle. It was a thick cardboard box with a glass top and a bead of quicksilver inside, which was meant to find its way across a gaudy Crazy Golf course. Rosie was very pleased to have this but wondered if she would be allowed to keep it. Grown-ups always worried that children might prise open these puzzles and swallow the mercury.

'Thank you.'

'Come and sit on my knee, little lady, and tell me what you want for Christmas.'

'I don't believe in him.' Rosie looked questioningly at her father. 'Have I *got* to sit on his knee?'

'No, stay where you are if that's how you feel. Just tell the man what you want for Christmas.'

Rosie hesitated. She knew exactly what she wanted – but she didn't like to say it aloud. 'What I want, I can't have.'

Father Christmas leaned foward. 'How will I know till you tell me?'

Rosie took a deep breath: 'I want my daddy to get my mummy to come back to us. And she has to bring Christopher.'

'Dear God, this can be a tragic job,' sighed Santa Claus. 'I'm really a stand-up comic. Wife left you?' he asked Clifford, very man-to-man. 'Mine's hopped it too. She just left the dinner in the oven, a note on the washstand, and went off with a man who demonstrates potato peelers. Probably a very similar situation to your own, sir. I'm left holding a small daughter too. What do you do with them?'

Surprisingly, Clifford seemed glad of somebody to talk to. 'I think I've got the right answer,' he said, 'but I'm not one hundred per cent sure. I hope you soon find the solution to your own problems. Say goodbye, Rosie.'

She was suddenly struck by a horrific thought: 'Goodbye? You're not just going to leave me here in a cardboard grotto, are you?'

'No. I'm not leaving you anywhere.' Suddenly he looked awkward. His love of the truth had plainly risen to the surface again and he added, 'Well, not at this precise moment anyway.'

The rash of numbered paper spots had spread to Teapot Hall. As Rosie climbed out of the car, clutching Father Christmas's mercury puzzle, she saw that there was now a little number on each of the garden benches at either side of the front door. The inner glass doors rattled open and Mrs Hankey emerged into a dying November sunlight.

'I'm scared of standing still,' she said to Clifford, 'in case somebody comes up and slaps a number on me too. The men the auctioneer sent are miserable bastards in gaberdine macs.

One of them's been here before; we knew him as an unreliable window cleaner. I'm afraid I've had to put a stop to cracks about *The Fall of the House of Usher*. It's not as if we owe *them* money!' After years of protestations to the contrary, Mrs Hankey suddenly seemed to have taken on the role of the last of the loyal family retainers.

Not quite the last. The sad little procession trooped into the house to find Bertha – in her best coat and her grey chiffon headscarf – sitting on one of the sofas. Her stiff leg was sticking straight out in front of her. 'I had to put me bits and pieces in something, Mr Clifford,' she said, 'so I used this old wicker laundry basket. They went out of business years ago and it's not as if it would have fetched much.' She had plainly been crying.

'Where are you going, Bertha?' asked Rosie, looking around in horrified wonder. Things which had stood in the same place forever had been moved into random heaps. The coat stand, made of antlers, was now marked *Lot 376* – which plainly included the elephant's-foot umbrella stand and an upended row of knobby mahogany hat pegs. Things from far corners, which had been loved and polished for years, were now out of the shadows with all their blemishes on view.

Even the rugs had been rolled up and leaned against the walls. And all the curtains had been taken down and piled into folded heaps, like the mattresses in 'The Princess and the Pea'. Rosie found herself wondering whether the very bedsteads had been unbolted. And if Bertha was packed and ready for off, where was she meant to spend the night herself? A situation which had been full of threats was now turning into something downright frightening.

She repeated her question: 'Bertha, where are you going?'

'To my Cousin Mercy's on Brindle Heath. *Please* don't make me go in your car, Mr Clifford. Take the luggage but not me. I'll make my own way – on the bus. It's just that I don't want to get there and have everybody laughing at me . . .'

'Why should they laugh?' asked Clifford.

'It's me leg. Let me go on the bus. All the conductors know me. I can manage buses. If I go in a motor car, me leg has to stick out – through the window. Don't make me go in that car,' she sobbed. 'I'm sorry to be a nuisance.'

Panic began to rise inside Rosie. If her father was off to London, and Bertha was going to Brindle Heath, was she going to be left alone in this new, uncurtained, frightening, topsy-turvy Teapot Hall?

'What's going to happen to *me*?' she shouted.

Mrs Hankey turned a cold eye on Clifford Tattersall. 'Don't say you haven't had the courage to tell her?' she asked. And she asked it in tones of hostile contempt.

3

'Mrs Hankey's? How can I live at Mrs Hankey's?' wailed
Rosie. 'That's her private life. You always called it her *sacred*
private life. She won't want me in it.'

'Well there's gratitude,' bridled Mrs Hankey.

'She's being paid to have you.' Clifford had assumed a
maddeningly 'patient' voice.

'And not being overpaid, either.' Mrs Hankey had taken
exception. 'Not being overpaid by a long chalk. Only
accepting what's due. And that to be done as a favour.'

It all seemed so settled, so set. Feeling as though she was
already as good as out of the door, Rosie began to sort
feverishly through her mind for something – anything –
which would keep her at Teapot Hall.

The stamps! 'I can't go,' she said with a flood of relief, 'I've
sent for some foreign stamps. They're coming from a place
that advertises in the *Children's Newspaper.*'

'What's that got to do with anything?' asked her father.

'They're coming *on approval*,' explained Rosie urgently.
'It's this place called Stanley Gibbons. They send them for
nothing; if you don't like what you get, you're on your honour
to send them back.'

'I'll deal with that.' This pronouncement made, Clifford
plainly regarded the matter as closed.

Rosie didn't. 'I don't want to go getting a bad name at
Stanley Gibbons,' she said worriedly.

Her father now turned to Mrs Hankey. 'Have you got her
things together?'

'All her clothes and her teddy and her golliwog.'

'What about my dolls?' asked Rosie, panic rising in her
voice.

'You can only bring Sylvia.' Mrs Hankey was at her firmest.
'It wouldn't be right if she brought more, Mr Clifford. She

can have just the same as my little girl's got – that way there'll be no jealousy.'

Rosie couldn't believe what she was hearing. 'I've looked after them as carefully as real babies. Some of those dolls belonged to my gran'ma.'

It didn't matter what Rosie said, all Mrs Hankey's replies were addressed to Clifford. 'The auctioneer said that job lots of the wax dollies could fetch quite good prices.'

'He's not stuck numbers on their *faces*, has he?' gasped Rosie. 'Daddy, please don't let them stick numbers on their faces – they'll *mind*!' Her troubled head was now filled with awful visions of Betty with *37* on her forehead. And of other stickers on Black Jemima and Mrs Potter and Winkum with the patched jacket . . .

'She can bring five books,' Mrs Hankey was still laying down the law. 'Our Hazel's got five books and I don't want any animosity.'

Five books? The childrens' bookshelves at Teapot Hall dated back to the turn of the century. They were practically a library in themselves. There was everything from the *Childrens' Encyclopaedia* to complete bound sets of E. Nesbit and of Biggles.

'Five books, the Bible and a Complete Shakespeare,' put in her father. He sounded curiously like Roy Plomley on *Desert Island Discs*. 'Your little girl can share the last two.'

'I've nothing against God,' Mrs Hankey sounded as though she was discussing a brand of soap powder, 'but I'm not absolutely convinced that the old gentleman exists. It's to be firmly understood that I won't stand for some bit of a child preaching God under my roof. Go and choose five from upstairs, Rosie. Your daddy can get the other two from his study. Could I ask you to make it a *thin* Shakespeare, Mr Clifford. We've barely room in our house for so much as an extra pamphlet.'

Bertha shifted her leg into a more comfortable position. 'D'you want me to come upstairs with you, love?' she asked Rosie. She made it sound as though the child was going to view a corpse. And in a way she was.

Rosie chose to climb the stairs, for the last time, on her

61

own. As she walked along the minstrels' gallery – mentally selecting just five books – she could hear men talking in the distance. She padded up the winding tower staircase and the voices got nearer. As she walked down the nursery landing, a man in a long beige raincoat, carrying a notepad, emerged from her bedroom. 'Come to view the wreckage?' he asked, not unkindly.

She recognised him as the one-time window cleaner. 'I'm trying not to look,' she said.

'All good things must come to an end.' He used a pencil to make a satisfied tick on his list. 'Still, it wasn't your fault the mean sods never tipped me at Christmas.'

Rosie hurried past him and opened the day nursery door. Dobbin, the rocking horse, bore an extra spot – one with a number on it. Rosie was heading for the big bookcase when she caught sight of the dolls. Dolls? The word wasn't strong enough, they were her *friends*. And these friends were now tied together, in bundles of six. Tied with cruel brown twine that must surely have been cutting into them. 'I'm sorry,' she sobbed, 'I don't get a say in things any more. It wasn't me. *Honestly* it wasn't me.'

To untie the poor creatures might only give them false hope. Wiping tears aside with the back of her hand, Rosie continued towards the bookshelves. At least the books had been left in place – for the moment. She knew exactly where each of the ones she wanted would be. But she needed a chair to reach the top shelf. There was still one left silhouetted against the window. It was the one which had *Boys and Girls Come Out to Play* engraved across the top of the backrest, in pokerwork.

A rattling, cawing noise was coming from the garden. The Teapot Hall magpie was dive-bombing a worm, near the lead sundial in the sunken garden. It was always called the Italian garden because the trees round the edge were sad cypresses.

One magpie was always supposed to be 'one for sorrow'. There had once been a time when the garden had boasted 'two for joy'. But a cat had got the magpie's wife – and he'd stayed by her corpse, making hoarse crying noises, for days. There were weeks on end when the bird seemed to disappear.

But he always came back to be the only inhabitant of the empty ramshackle nest.

Avoiding the dolls' eyes, Rosie looked round the room for the last time. Adults might say that Teapot Hall was an architectural joke but she didn't find it funny – she loved it. And now she was having to go. Idly, she opened the little cupboard that had always been Christopher's special secret place.

Of course it was nothing to do with The Secret. No cupboard could contain that. He had left behind some home-made peg dolls with crepe paper clothes drawing-pinned to their wooden bodies. And something else too – something which had gone missing many months ago. Christopher had also left behind the spare front door key.

Rosie seized the intricately chased iron key and showed it to the room. She felt like Gran'ma Tattersall's engraving of a High Church priest with a communion chalice. 'I'm keeping this,' she murmured to the walls and the fireplace. 'I'm keeping it. And one day, I'll buy all of Teapot Hall back again.' She actually called out loud, through the window, to the magpie: 'You look after the house for me. Dive-bomb anybody else who wants it!'

As Rosie began to carry the books downstairs, the idea of the big key, in her knickers' pocket, made her feel better. They could turn her out of Teapot Hall but she knew how to get back in.

She descended to the ground floor to find her father, sitting like a disconsolate visitor, on a chair that was famous for being the hardest in the house. 'Bertha's gone on the bus,' he said morosely. 'I'm going to drop off her things later. She slipped away while you were upstairs because she couldn't bring herself to say goodbye to you. But you're to go and see her – at her cousin's – whenever you like. You'll enjoy that, won't you?'

Rosie nodded. Cousin Mercy was blind and had a Braille watch and an upright piano.

A nod was obviously less than Clifford had wanted. Attempting to return himself into Rosie's favours he said,

'Perhaps you'd like to look round this room and choose a memento?'

'Only this room? All the dolls upstairs are tied together like firewood.'

'We've already been into the question of dolls with Mrs Hankey. You'll have to settle for something else.'

If Rosie couldn't have her doll family she didn't really care; except she did. Her eyes suddenly lighted on a framed drawing of Teapot Hall, done in sepia ink. 'Could I have that?'

Her father looked dubious. 'It's always been thought to be rather good. Couldn't you settle for something different? I shouldn't think Mrs Hankey's got the wall space for pictures.'

What would Mrs Hankey have room for? Certainly not the big scraps screen, nor the stuffed weasels under the glass dome where Connie once placed her hat. The camera, which stood next to it, had the words *Zeiss-Ikon – Box Tengor* printed above its lens in white lettering.

'Has the little box camera got a film in it?' asked Rosie.

'Now you mention it, I think it has. It's one we didn't finish off – at Ilfracombe.'

Trust him to go and mention Ilfracombe! But if Rosie couldn't have the drawing of the house, she would settle for the camera. She could use it to take her own photograph of Teapot Hall. But not today because it was already starting to go dark.

Mrs Hankey, buttoned into her outdoor coat, came banging through from the kitchen. 'That's the gas switched off at the mains,' she announced. 'Save me getting a chair, Mr Clifford. You reach up and do the electric. It's in that oak box with the little brass sneck on it, between the two sets of doors.'

'I've lived here all my life and this is going to be the first time I've ever touched that box,' said Clifford, in a voice of wonder.

'Cushioned from reality, that's what you lot have been,' grunted Mrs Hankey. 'Well, them days are over.'

'Ready?' Clifford walked across the room, reached up, undid the oak cover, pulled on a switch and extinguished the lights of Tattersall's Teapot Hall.

Saracen Street wasn't far away. It was still in Irlams o'th' Height. To the unaccustomed eye, all Lancashire streets of terraced houses look the same. It is true that they are mostly built of red brick. And that they are all topped off with purple slate roofs. Beyond this, the differences are as varied as liquorice allsorts. The terraced houses in Saracen Street certainly opened directly onto the flagstone pavement; but they also had bay windows – which put them one point up on their neighbours in the street which ran behind them. Unlike that neighbouring street, they didn't have cellars. This was considered half a point down. Only half a point, because 'damp' came into the equation.

Totally unaware of these subtle social nuances, Rosie sat next to her father in the front passenger seat of the Rover as it bumped over the paving setts of Saracen Street. Mrs Hankey was in the back of the car with Bertha's wicker basket and Rosie's belongings loose in her arms.

'Number seven, isn't it?' asked Clifford. Cheeky kids, playing under the street light, were already gathering round the car as it began to slow down. One actually had his head shoved through the window. He had cropped blond hair and wicked green eyes. 'Mister,' he yelled in a surprisingly husky voice for such a small boy. 'D'you want to give me a shilling so some kids won't kick your car?'

In the back of the car, Mrs Hankey cleared her throat meaningfully. This noise must have held some special significance for the boy because he cried out, 'Flipping heck! It's me mam!' and his head disappeared.

'Our Colin,' said Mrs Hankey, grimly. 'Colin by name but all the other kids call him Zav.'

'I can't have seen him since he was two.' Clifford had brought the car to a complete standstill outside number seven. 'He's plainly turned into a most enterprising young man.'

'He's that all right. I've never made any secret of the fact that my children are going to be bosses, Mr Clifford. And that's the last time I'm ever going to call you *that*. Them days are over. If you come to visit Rosie, you'll be plain Cliff in my house. I'll carry her things into number seven. But that's the end of my days of waiting hand and foot on you lot. Come on, Rosie, get out.'

Cars were few and far between in Saracen Street, and the unaccustomed sound of one stopping had brought a man out onto the doorstep. A middle-aged version of the blond boy, he was wearing a sleeveless singlet and old trousers and bare feet and tattoos. As Mrs Hankey pushed Rosie's belongings into his muscular arms, she said, 'And I can do without any acid comments from you, Tippler.'

Rosie knew very little about Mrs Hankey's closely guarded private life, but Bertha had told her about Tippler Hankey. He didn't get this nickname because he drank. It was because he used to knock men over – for money. Tippler's time as a fairground boxer had long since come to an end. Bertha had always maintained that, these days, he wouldn't so much as say boo to a goose. Yet Mrs Hankey was still warning him, 'We want nothing that leads to bloodshed.'

Standing hesitantly on the pavement, Rosie wondered why her father hadn't moved from the wheel of his car. 'Aren't you coming in too?' she asked, suddenly scared.

'No. I'm going to take the car down to Chester Road. A dealer said he'd see what he could offer me.'

'Does that mean he'll keep it?' When her father nodded, Rosie burst out with, 'How will you get back here? On the bus?'

'He's not coming back, Rosemary. Not today anyway.' Mrs Hankey was at her most brisk. 'I thought that was understood.'

Panic welled inside Rosie and her voice rose to match it: 'No, it *wasn't* understood. I didn't know he was going now. Not this exact minute.'

'Come on,' her father leant across the steering wheel towards the open passenger window, 'give me a nice kiss.'

'He's going to drive away and leave me . . .' shouted Rosie. 'No, you can't. I won't let you.'

'Cancel the kisses and get that engine started,' hissed Mrs Hankey. 'And you,' she said coldly to Rosie, 'get inside.'

'I do love you . . .' called Clifford awkwardly, through the window. But the car was already beginning to move away from the kerb.

'No!' shouted Rosie, making to run after it.

In the ensuing hullabaloo, Tippler dropped all of Rosie's belongings – her pencil box made the worst clatter – and Mrs Hankey grabbed hold of the child.

'I'll kick!' warned Rosie furiously.

'You do and you'll pay for it with a warm backside. You little madam! You're nothing else.'

'She's upset,' said Tippler, reasonably.

'Yes, and half the street's watching. Seen enough?' she yelled at a big woman who had emerged from the house next door. 'Got a good enough story to take down to the pub?'

'I only go out for the company,' muttered the woman. And with this she went back in and slammed the door.

'I just hope you're pleased with yourself,' Mrs Hankey had rounded on Rosie. 'You're not so much as through the front door before there's trouble with the neighbours.'

The Hankey boy had been watching all of this with intense interest. Now he spoke. His voice was so deep as to be almost a croak. 'You never mentioned her wearing glasses,' he said. 'You never told us she was a specky four-eyes.'

That did it. The kick that Rosie had not been allowed to deliver now landed on the blond boy's shins.

'She's a woman, Zav,' warned his father seriously. 'And we don't hit women in this house.'

'No, but we can hate them,' said the small boy darkly.

'For God's sake let's go in.' Mrs Hankey was glancing round the lamplit street. 'There's a face at practically every window.'

This was the first time Rosie had ever crossed the Hankey threshold. But she had been in other terraced houses with Bertha, so she knew that the long creaking corridor from the street was called the lobby. And that the first door would lead into a front room, known as the parlour. Rosie plainly wasn't regarded as 'company' because Mrs Hankey frogmarched her past this parlour and into the kitchen.

The room was dominated by a huge black-leaded kitchen range. It was like something out of a Christmas pantomime

67

with a coal fire blazing behind bars in the middle. It also boasted highly polished black doors, and built-in hobs with shining pans stacked on them. A sooty-bottomed kettle sat on the fire.

'If all this upset's made you want to go somewhere . . .' said Mrs Hankey, '. . . you'll find it down the yard.'

Through a cream lace curtain hanging at the window Rosie could just about discern the outline of a collection of wooden mangles and zinc washing tubs. Electric light was falling onto them from the uncurtained scullery window. There was enough illumination to see that the brick-walled yard was whitewashed; and that it had a tall, solid-looking bolted gate.

Mrs Hankey must have been following the direction of Rosie's gaze. 'And don't think you can pull back the bolt and make a dash for freedom because you can't. It's too high up.'

'You want to watch out for this spitfire,' said Zav. He was speaking to a blonde girl of about Rosie's age but smaller, who was sitting at the kitchen table unconcernedly crayoning a colouring book. 'She's drawn blood already,' he added even more darkly. 'And all I did was to mention her glasses.'

'Rosemary!' exclaimed Mrs Hankey warningly. She never called her 'Rosie' again. From that moment on, it was always Rosemary, pronounced as two words – Rose-Mary.

'Why is that girl wearing one of my dresses?' asked the child from Teapot Hall.

'One of your last-year's dresses,' Mrs Hankey corrected her. 'And she's not "that girl". She's our Hazel. And I wouldn't recommend you to fall out with her because you'll soon be sharing the same bed.'

'I always liked that dress,' said Rosie quietly. Sharing the same bed? This new thought had only just struck home.

Mrs Hankey was not best pleased. 'Your mummy gave that dress to me – to do what I wanted with. I trust you believe that? Or perhaps we'd be better off having this argument down at the police station? While we're there, I could put in a request to have you transferred to a home for unruly girls.'

'Would I have to share a bed with strangers *there*?' asked Rosie in a very small voice. The idea was really worrying her. 'When's Daddy coming back?'

'When you've settled in. So you'd better put your mind to it.'

This whole conversation had been accompanied by the sound of fierce barking from the yard and scrabbling noises at the back door. 'Let that dog in or we'll have no paint.' Mrs Hankey was talking to Colin. 'No paint and no peace. Not that we've had much of that since milady graced us with her presence.'

The back door was in the scullery. As Colin opened it with a shuddering rattle, a small, bright ginger animal hurtled into the room. With pointed ears and brightly interested eyes, it looked like a cross between a dog and a fox. That or some angry baby animal in a television documentary about the African jungle. This indignant creature was plainly very near to the wild.

'Settle down, Trixie!' roared Mrs Hankey. 'Show us what a good girl you can be.'

This was plainly the last thing Trixie intended doing. First she shot round Rosie in a clockwise direction, and then she tore back – widdershins. Rosie was more interested than scared. Interest turned to delight as the bright ginger animal carefully positioned itself at her feet, rolled onto its back and revealed a blonde undercarriage. From the way Trixie's tail was wagging, she plainly wanted to be friends.

'She *likes* me,' said Rosie in astonishment. 'At long last somebody likes me.' As she bent down to scratch the animal's tummy she was very near to tears.

Colin, the Zav boy, crouched down too. He put his face right up to Rosie's. 'Don't you talk posh?' he asked in a menacing croak. 'Still, our Trixie's never wrong. There must be a bit of something to you.'

'There you are then!' Tippler Hankey was obviously something of a peacemaker.

Colin got back to his feet. 'But she shouldn't have kicked me. Not out in the street. Other lads could have seen it.'

'I *think* I'm sorry,' said Rosie, carefully.

'Not good enough,' rasped Zav. And picking up the animal, he carried it out of the room.

*

69

Sharing a bed with somebody, when she'd never done it before, was proving an unnerving experience. Whichever way Rosie turned, bits of her – like hips and knees – couldn't help but accidentally touch. She could, of course, have moved right to the edge of the bed. But she didn't want Mrs Hankey's daughter to think she was being standoffish. As yet, Rosie had formed no concrete opinion of Hazel Hankey; she seemed a dreamy faraway child – not somebody whom it would be easy to get to know. And here they were, under the very same sheets and blankets! Their feet were even meant to be on the same hot-water bottle, but Rosie had drawn the line at that.

Hazel, already asleep, was a heavy breather. The pair of them were lying on an all-embracing feather mattress. It was a bit like trying to settle down amidst swans. This feathery idea struck Rosie as more eerie than romantic.

Hazel murmured in her sleep and then shifted onto her back. The heavy breathing turned into a light snore. But she's really quite pretty – in a pink and white and blonde way – thought Rosie. No, she corrected herself, very pretty.

The snoring increased and sleep refused to come. There had been attics at Teapot Hall but they were nothing like this one – it didn't even have a door. Instead, the stairs just rose up through a gap in the bare floorboards. There was, to be fair to Mrs Hankey, a neat strip of carpet at either side of the bed. No wardrobe though; just a curtain on a string across a recess, to one side of the fireplace.

Pushing aside the thought that the house smelt faintly of the ghost of teatime's smoked haddock and of cheap carbolic soap, Rosie meditated on the fact that everything was almost frighteningly clean.

. . . Ratlike scutterings started and stopped on the wooden staircase. Then they started again.

Rosie let out a little scream and Hazel sat up with a start. 'What's up?' she asked sleepily.

As politely as she could, Rosie said, 'I think it's rats.' Immediately there were two more furtive scuttles.

'Is it heck rats!' yawned Hazel scornfully. 'It's our Trixie. She wants to come up and play teddy-bears. Don't let her in

70

or she'll boss the whole bed.' With this she turned over and went back to sleep.

Cold white moonlight shone through the attic window. But at least the snoring had stopped. The scuttering hadn't. Trixie's head now came into view, over the top of the stairs. The glance was interested, questioning, *determined*. As the rest of her body appeared, Trixie was obviously doing a small dog's version of walking on tiptoe.

Hazel stirred again. 'Make her go downstairs,' she murmured.

The little terrier froze in her tracks. But her tail was wagging and she seemed to understand what Rosie had in mind. The pair of them waited for Hazel to resume her imitation of a distant chain saw . . . and then Rosie patted the washed-out candlewick bedspread encouragingly. Trixie was up on the bed faster than a flue-brush goes up a chimney. But it soon became obvious that she wasn't in the exact position of her choice.

She began turning round discontentedly and nudging Rosie with her cold black pointed nose. The more you looked at Trixie, the more extraordinary she seemed. Her little legs were no thicker than sticks of celery. Not that Rosie had ever seen such a thing as bright orange celery. The foxlike animal had one set of bristling whiskers above some more – which wept down into a fine divided beard like Fu Manchu. 'I bet people have laughed at *you* too,' whispered Rosie.

Remembering something Hazel had said, Rosie held back the bedclothes and the animal dived under them. Teddy-bear? Trixie actually snuggled her head under Rosie's chin, put her paws over the bedspread, and then let out a deep sigh. A pair of dark brown eyes looked up into Rosie's face. The girl was plainly not responding in the desired manner.

Again the dog let out another pointed sigh. Rosie copied her. She felt a tail wagging against her. Another sigh from the dog brought another imitation from Rosie. Yet another deep, deep sigh . . . It was the strangest thing, but Rosie felt as though she was being taken care of – being taken over. It was like magic. And of course she *was* being cared for.

Trixie Hankey was lulling Rosie off to sleep with exactly the same method she would have used on any other unhappy puppy.

'Where are your glasses?' asked Hazel, as the pair of them carried their satchels down Saracen Street.

'Oh I don't *always* have to wear them.' Rosie crossed her fingers to cover this airy lie. She was on her way to crossing the next hurdle – a new school. And she was blowed if she was going to face it disadvantaged by spectacles. Effort had already gone into this plan. Straight after breakfast, while Mrs Hankey was occupied in the scullery with a face flannel and Zav's neck, Rosie had nipped into the deserted parlour and hidden her glasses in the meter cupboard.

At Elm House, most of the pupils had been delivered to the front door by motor car. Either that or led there by hand. Things were plainly very different at the council junior school. Hordes of unaccompanied children were streaming towards it from all directions. The school was in a single-storey, dirty red-brick building, behind a high wall, with broken glass stuck into the cement on top of it. Outside the main gate, older boys fought for a last swing on two big lamp posts. Gangs of girls, sailing confidently across the yard, were screeching and shouting in a manner that would have been very much frowned down upon at Rosie's little private school.

There didn't seem to be any kind of morning assembly. You just went to your own classroom and it started. Rosie was relieved to find that she was already expected. 'Miss Swaine told me yesterday to bring you into our classroom,' explained Hazel.

'Is she the teacher?'

'No, Swaine-Swine's the headmistress. Olive Bucket's our teacher. She's got a deadly arm with chalk.'

This woman was already standing behind her desk. Without her glasses, Rosie could see things perfectly clearly –as long as they were at a distance. There was certainly something coldly distant about this teacher. She had thin, faded blonde hair and watery blue eyes and a nose that was pinker than the rest of her face. 'Are you Rosemary Tattersall?' she asked.

'Yes, Miss Bucket,' replied Rosie politely. She wondered why Hazel was giggling.

The woman treated Hazel to a freezing glance and then transferred it to Rosie. 'My name is Miss Buckley,' she said. 'Sit down at the desk with Hazel.'

Like many Lancashire schools, this one had begun under the auspices of the Church of England and still maintained a tenuous connection with it. The day began with an un-accompanied rendition of 'All Things Bright and Beautiful'. The classroom was only divided from the one next door by a shivering wood and glass partition. The class on the other side of it was singing 'Jesus Bids Us Shine'.

There was nothing bright and beautiful about the class-room. It had varnished rafters and cream and brown paintwork and the windows were positioned so high up that all you could see was that frightening broken glass, on the top of the walls. '. . . *Amen*,' they sang. And then everybody made scraping noises with their chairs as they sat down.

'Rosemary Tattersall, come up here. Have you ever seen a book like this one?'

Indeed she had. As Rosie advanced to the front of the class she could just about see that it was a Beacon Reader. How old did Miss Buckley think she was? A Beacon Reader? It was almost an insult.

'Read!'

Rosie took the book. Now she was nearer to it, her eyes couldn't be sure which volume she had been handed. But if that was a house on the cover – and she was almost certain it was – then this was the book for absolute beginners. Book One! Taught in a small class and given a lot of individual attention, Rosie had been reading her way through popular childrens' classics for three years.

She opened the book. The words in front of her swam into a blur. She certainly wouldn't be able to read them but she was pretty sure she could remember. She began to recite: ' "I am Old Lob. I am Mr Dan. I am . . ." ' Who came next?

There was the farmer – she'd done him. And she'd done his dog too. So who came next. . . ?

'That's not what we call reading.' Miss Buckley's voice was close to a sneer. 'Not in *my* classroom. I'm afraid I don't have anything easier than that book. I think you'll have to go down to the infants and begin again with your alphabet and flash cards.'

The door opened and in came another woman. All the children scraped back their chairs, got to their feet and chorused, '*Good morning, Miss Swaine.*'

'Good morning, children. And this must be my first chance to say good morning to Rosemary.'

As the headmistress started advancing towards her, Rosie was able to make out kind eyes and (because she didn't want to stare too long into the woman's face) hand-knitted stockings. As Miss Swaine got nearer, Rosie looked up again to see her turn into a grey-haired tweed-suited blur.

'So you're Connie Hicks's little girl?' The voice belonging to this hazy outline was not unkind.

Before Rosie got a chance to answer, Miss Buckley seized hold of the conversation again. In a spiteful mutter she said to the headmistress, 'If she's her mother's daughter, we might have to think about segregating the bigger boys at playtime.' She then went into more covert mumbling about the shocking fees at Elm House and the disgraceful results of their teaching. This reached its climax with, 'It's just possible the child may be *retarded.*'

An indignant Rosie caught a pleasant whiff of Atkinson's Lavender Water as the rounded tweed outline of the headmistress turned towards her. 'Rosemary, have you ever had your eyes tested?'

Rosie was saved from answering by the sound of a peremptory knock on the frosted glass of the classroom door.

'There's no need to break my good window,' bawled Miss Buckley. 'Come in whoever you are – and have the grace to do it quietly.'

She was shouting at the wrong person. The door opened abruptly and Nora Hankey stomped into the classroom. Although Mrs Hankey had thrown on her shopping coat, she had neglected to change out of her carpet slippers. In one hand she was carrying an all too familiar brown leather spectacle case.

As the visitor walked up to the desk, a glower directed at Rosie turned into an out-of-focus smudge. 'Something got left behind,' the angry presence announced. 'One pair of glasses!' Rosie felt them being pushed into her left hand.

'The child never said a word . . .' Miss Buckley was addressing this protest to the headmistress.

'Was she offered the opportunity?'

As Rosie pulled the horrible wire sides of the glasses round her ears, and all the other children giggled, the head-mistress's face swam into sharp focus. It was a kind face, plain and clever. 'Come and see me in my office at four o'clock,' said Miss Swaine. 'There's nothing to fear.' Her attention was now directed at the classroom at large. 'I don't know what you're finding so funny. You'll all come to false teeth and glasses in the end – everybody does.'

A hand shot up: 'Has the new girl got false teeth, miss?' It was a big beefy girl with red hair and so many freckles that in some places they joined up into light brown blobs.

'This is Bernadette Barrett,' said Miss Swaine calmly to Rosie. 'She is a bully. They are to be pitied.' Turning to Nora Hankey she asked, 'Would you mind if I introduced you to the children? This is as good an opportunity as any other. Children, this is Mrs Hankey – Hazel's mother. From next Monday onwards, she is coming to be one of our dinner ladies.'

Bernadette Barrett made vomiting noises. Mrs Hankey quelled these with one look.

'Just the woman we need,' breathed Miss Swaine to Miss Buckley. 'Bernadette Barrett, see me at four o'clock.' With this, the headmistress steered the new dinner lady out of the room.

A new day at a new school is always a disjointed experience, and in this particular classroom there seemed to be more visitors than lessons. The next arrival was the vicar. Nowadays the school was run by the education committee of the local council but it still retained this last parish connection.

The vicar seized upon the new arrival with glee. He recognised her as one of the Tattersalls of Teapot Hall, knew that they were Quakers, and insisted upon telling the children all about that religious sect. He'd just got to a bit about one Quaker being left to rot for years in Lancaster jail when something hit the side of Rosemary's face with a splat. She lifted up her hand and pulled down a pellet of chewed-up paper which had been sticking to her cheek.

As she peered round the classroom she saw that Bernadette Barrett was both smiling in triumph and bending back a plastic ruler – ready to take aim again. Rosie turned her head back towards the vicar. Splat! Bernadette had scored another direct hit.

'She's great at rounders too,' murmured Hazel in a voice that suggested she had been recalled from a dream.

The next lesson was geography. The textbooks were handed out from the front. It was a case of 'Take one and pass the rest behind.' The book Rosie got had the words *Olive Bucket Farts Bright Blue* written across a picture of the Amazon rain forest. It was all very different from Elm House.

The textbooks were not the only thing that was being passed from hand to hand. A folded paper note was also surreptitiously doing the rounds. When it reached Hazel Hankey, she handed it to Rosie with a mutter of, 'It's for you.'

'Me?'

'Hush! Don't let her catch you reading it.'

Rosie unfolded the note. It was written on a lined page ripped from an exercise book. All it said was, 'You are posh. We are going to scrag you. Watch out.'

The school playground was sharply divided by a line down the middle. Girls kept to one side and boys to the other. You couldn't see this line. Nobody had painted it on the flagstones. The children just drew it with their own territorial behaviour, though the fact that the brick-built boys' and girls' lavatories were at different ends of the yard must have originally helped to set the limits.

There can be a cruel, ringing cry to the sound of a council school at play. The toys were harmless enough. In the 1950s children still played games in seasons. Hopscotch in the spring gave way to skipping ropes in summer, and this November there had been a sudden upsurge of wooden tops and whips.

Here again the sexes were sharply divided. The girls chalked coloured circles onto the flat surface of carrot-shaped tops. If you tried altering this tradition into a pattern of squares or diagonals, when the tops were whipped into action the design would simply whirl into grey. Done the proper way, you got dancing circular rainbows.

Boys scorned such frippery. Their tops, known as window-breakers, were shaped like a button mushroom whose long stalk had been put through a pencil sharpener. Made of varnished wood, and already stained with red and blue rings by the Japanese manufacturer, they spun and bobbed on metal points with a ferocity that was said to be capable of blinding. Young males replaced the string in their whips with a leather bootlace.

Rosie found their cracking noises both cruel and full of menace. As they whipped, the boys shouted and the girls screamed; and all of this echoed round the bleak quadrangle with the savage broken glass on top of its walls.

Rosie was already scared. Who were the people who were after her? It had to be more than one because they had said 'We'. *We are going to scrag you . . .* ' the words were going round and round in her brain. One of the worst things about juvenile bullying is the waiting. Threats are not always carried out but the dreadful waiting causes its own brand of pain.

Had Bernadette Barrett written the note? She was heavily occupied in belabouring a top. It wasn't carrot-shaped like the rest. It was the kind known as a turnip: squat and stubby –very like the girl who was whipping it.

'She used to go to the Catholic school,' said Hazel, 'but her mother beat up the priest – so now she has to come here. There's Barretts right through the school now. All the rest are boys. You should see the nit nurse examining them.'

Bernadette rose up from her top. Blue chalk had rubbed off

77

onto one of her knees. To Rosie, it looked like woad on an Ancient Briton.

Noticing that the new girl was watching her, Bernadette licked a finger and solemnly drew it across her own throat.

'That means you're dead,' said Hazel calmly.

'But I'm not!'

'No, but you soon will be. Do you want to go to the toilet?'

This was something which had already given Rosie much cause for thought. In truth she was dying to go. Her great fear was that once inside that sinister brick building at the end of the yard the mysterious 'They' might materialise and *get* her.

'Come on,' said Hazel, 'I'm going anyway. I'm sorry to say this, Rosemary, but you do make me feel noticeable. The whole school's talking about you.'

'What will they do to me?' asked Rosie, following her and more worried than ever.

'They'll probably give you Chinese burns, for start.'

'What are those?'

'If I stopped and showed you, they'd definitely give you them. Just talk about film stars, then they'll think you're not scared. Did you ever see Elizabeth Taylor in anything?' she asked loudly.

'No,' said Rosie, who felt as though she was walking to the gallows. 'No, I didn't.'

'I think they must have dyed her eyeballs. They're bright mauve.'

Thinking to be helpful, Rosie said: 'It's not pronounced "morve", you should say "mowve".'

In her languorous, nonjudgemental voice Hazel announced, 'I can see why people think they want to murder you.'

The smell inside the lavatory building was . . . Rosie didn't know a word for it. It stank. But that wasn't strong enough. It hummed, it buzzed, it was an odour that was almost patterned.

'Me mother says there's still some of her own down there.' Hazel had noticed Rosie wrinkling her nose. This moment had got to be the farthest Rosie would ever feel from the safety of Elm House. Or so she thought . . .

'*Got her!*' The cry came from the door to the playground. 'Let's duck her down the toilets.'

'Yes, and pull the chain.'

Bernadette Barrett, surrounded by some juvenile hench-women, was blocking out the daylight. 'Or we could hang her,' she proposed. 'And then say that Daddy Brannigan must have got in.'

'Who's Daddy Brannigan?' asked Rosie in a shaking voice, attempting to placate them by just saying something.

'He gives girls toffees and then he does them,' smiled Bernadette. 'He'll be the one blamed for your murder.'

'Get in a cubicle and bolt the door,' hissed Hazel. She sounded really scared. 'I'm going for help.'

Rosie scrambled to do as she was told. New light came through a grimy pane of glass, high up in the rafters. And Rosie could just make out the words *Norma Coxon goes in the bushes with anybody* on the back of the door.

On the other side of it, the Barrett girl and her gang had plainly transferred their attentions to Hazel. But from the sound of it, Tippler Hankey's daughter was managing to fight her way through them. And then – yes – she'd definitely got away.

A moment's silence was followed by some loud 'shushes'. Next came muffled footsteps – several sets of them – and more silence. It seemed to go on for ages and was only broken once, by a nasty giggle. Suddenly, a tremendous kick shook the door and Bernadette Barrett yelled, 'You can't stop in there forever. Come on, girls, let's get over the top!'

What had been fear was now replaced by blind un-reasoning panic. Rosie began to scream. She even surprised herself by the volume of noise. She hadn't known she could make anything like it. But surely somebody would hear it and come?

Where had all the kind people in the world gone to? 'Daddy, Bertha . . . Just somebody come.' She was beyond caring who heard her. 'Please come. I've hardly cried at all and everything awful's been happening to me. I can't help crying this time. I'm sorry,' she sobbed, 'but I just can't help it.'

79

Suddenly there were screams on the other side of the door. They were screams of young female excitement and cries of 'There's a boy in the girls' lavvies!' and 'You could go to prison for this,' and 'He wants to see girls with their knickers down.'

Silence fell eventually. Through it rang a deep croaking voice. 'Come on out, Rosemary.' It was Zav Hankey. 'Open the door,' he called. 'They won't do anything to you now. Not with me here.'

'My brothers will splatter you, Zav Hankey!' This was Bernadette talking. Rosie decided to stay where she was.

'They couldn't,' said Zav. And he said it with absolute certainty.

Just as Rosie was beginning to unbolt the door, another, younger, more distant female voice joined in: 'Honestly, there *is* a boy in the girls' toilets, Miss Buckley. He walked straight in through the door.'

'Is that Colin Hankey? I might have known it!' Miss Buckley sounded furious. 'Do you know where little boys who spy on ladies' powder rooms end up? They end up in Strangeways Prison.'

'For stopping a murder?' asked Zav indignantly. 'I think you'll find you're wrong there.'

'And I think there's something altogether too cocksure about you. You will see Miss Swaine at hometime this afternoon. Who's behind that door?' she called out.

Reluctantly, Rosie opened it.

'Well, if it isn't our poor little rich girl! I can see that I'm going to have to keep a very close eye on you, Rosemary Tattersall. People aren't paid to carry you around in *this* school.'

At four o'clock Rosie found quite a queue waiting on the bench outside the headmistress's office. Zav was there, and Bernadette Barrett, and a small boy in a torn jersey who was wearing an expression of deepest guilt. This child was clutching an atlas which had got ripped in two. He was the first to be summoned into Miss Swaine's presence.

'All the rest's *your* fault,' Bernadette Barrett said to Rosie.

80

Zav just glared straight ahead. You could hear the head-mistress's voice mumbling angrily from inside her office. 'All the girls in our class have got crushes on you, Zav,' continued Bernadette. 'Except me,' she added hastily.

In that moment, Rosie knew that Bernadette was possessed of the biggest crush of all. This in no way prepared her for what the Barrett girl was to say next.

'She *loves* you.' Bernadette was pointing at Rosie. 'You came and rescued her and now she loves you. Look, you can tell she does, she's going red!'

The office door opened and the boy who had gone in with the atlas emerged without it. Miss Swaine loomed behind him, emitting wafts of Devon violets. 'Come in, Bernadette Barrett,' she said sternly.

As Bernadette followed Miss Swaine through the door, Rosie said to Zav, 'It's like "Ten Green Bottles". What I mean is . . .'

'I know what you mean and I'm not talking to you.'

Why had he too gone bright red? He'd nothing to worry about. She didn't love him. She was beginning to *like* him, and it was certainly true that he had come to her rescue – but she knew what the man she loved would be like. He would be that man with dark hair and blue eyes, the one she'd drawn at Quakers. There was no way she could entertain romantic thoughts about a blond like Zav, even if he did have wonderfully wicked green eyes.

Was it only last Sunday that Mrs Marriott had read them the Bible story? The one about Ruth and Naomi and about thy country being my country and thy people being my people. That's how she wanted to feel about the boy she loved. She certainly didn't feel that way about Zav Hankey.

This silence was awful. Just for something to break it, Rosie began to sing quietly:

> 'Ten green bottles, hanging on the wall,
> Ten green bottles, hanging on the wall . . .'

'And if one green bottle should accidentally fall, there'd be nine green bottles hanging on the wall,' snapped Zav in a voice which left no doubt that he was Nora Hankey's son.

81

'You're very chirpy for somebody who's waiting to see Swaine-Swine. But you're not going to get the cane.'

'Are you?' Rosie was horrified. 'Anyway, I thought you weren't talking to me.'

'I'm only talking long enough to tell you to shut up.'

Silence fell again. Zav eventually broke it with: 'Don't think I'm saying more because I'm not.'

'See if I care!' Why had he gone red again?

To pass the time, Rosie began to count glazed tiles on the wall at the side of the door. When she'd got to one hundred and twenty-three, the door opened and Bernadette Barrett emerged red-eyed. 'She wants you next,' she said to Zav. With this, Bernadette headed straight down the corridor without giving Rosie so much as a glance.

Left to herself, Rosie stopped counting the tiles and wondered whether she ought to be feeling more nervous. Miss Swaine had said there was nothing to worry about. Still, that was before she knew Miss Swaine owned a cane. They hadn't believed in corporal punishment at Elm House but, from reading an easy version of *Tom Brown's Schooldays*, Rosie knew that canes were meant to swish.

She listened out for this noise apprehensively but all she could hear was a more distant mumbling from Miss Swaine interspersed with some indignant squawaks from Zav. Still, it didn't sound as though he was being beaten. This was an awful place and it smelt of stale school dinners.

Once again the door creaked open and Zav came out. Jerking his head over his shoulder he indicated that Rosie was to go in.

A coke fire was burning sulphurously in a little tiled grate but above it was a picture that was as familiar as being tucked up in bed at Teapot Hall. 'The Piper of Dreams!' exclaimed Rosie with something approaching joy. It was like finding an old friend; but this was a bigger version of the print on the nursery wall. There he was, the strange elfin boy in a hat with a peacock's feather, sitting against a tree trunk, playing a reed pipe. And all around his head were sprites, like music.

'I brought him from home,' smiled Miss Swaine. 'I've had him since I was your age. D'you know who he suddenly reminds me of? He reminds me of that boy who's just walked out of the door.'

'Zav Hankey?' asked Rosie, incredulously. 'Why should Zav be like the piper?'

'Because there's a great deal more to him than meets the eye. He will go far,' Miss Swaine pronounced solemnly. Looking more cheerful she added, 'But we've all got a long way to go – even Bernadette Barrett. You've got a choice there, Rosemary. You can either make a friend or make an enemy.'

'But she hates me!'

'She's certainly used you badly. But she didn't understand. That's all there was to it – she didn't understand. The slate's wiped clean now. It's up to you to start again.'

'With her?' Rosie couldn't believe her ears.

'It's not long since she came here and she's out to forge a reputation. Her life has been awful. That's all I'm telling you and it should be all I need to tell you.'

'D'you think?' asked Rosemary, dubiously.

'Yes I do think. Now then, your reading – tell me what you're reading at home.'

'I don't live at home, I live at Mrs Hankey's, and I was only allowed to take five books.'

'Which ones did you choose?'

'*Five Children and It* and *What Katy Did* and one "William" book and two by Noel Streatfeild.'

'I *love* William.' Miss Swaine was all enthusiasm. 'Have you read *What Katy Did Next?*'

Rosie was astonished. How could a woman who talked like a saintly poem by Patience Strong love 'William' books? But Rosie hadn't read *What Katy Did Next* and she said so – in case there was any chance of getting her hands on it.

'If you promise to look after the book, I'll lend you my own copy. I want you to tell me something. I've talked to both your father and to Mrs Hankey so I know you've been through a big upheaval. How do you *feel?*'

Rosie just resisted the temptation to say 'With my brain, how d'you *think* I feel?' Having speedily decided that she liked Miss Swaine, she decided to tell her the truth. 'I'm behind a pane of glass,' she said, 'and everybody else is on the other side. They're all in it and I'm just watching.'

'You may find this hard to believe,' smiled the head-mistress, 'but you're an extremely lucky girl.'

'Why?' gasped Rosie.

'Because I'm forever talking to young people who have no idea of what they want from life. You already *know*. You want to get to the other side of that pane of glass.'

'But how do I do it?' asked Rosie urgently.

Miss Swaine assumed a faintly pious expression. 'That, my dear, will be the great adventure.'

Rosie dared to ask it: 'Have you ever read poems by Patience Strong?'

'Yes. And for my money they're rather piffle. All except that one about the wood. That has magic.'

This was so exactly how Rosie felt that she dared to ask another question: 'So getting there's going to be an adventure?' Her tones were still somewhere near disbelieving.

'You may not believe it, but you are *blessed*.'

More Wayside Thoughts from Patience Strong! Bertha had often read aloud similar things from a fourpenny magazine. But everything had suddenly started to feel better. 'And I must say you smell very nice, Miss Swaine,' said Rosie.

'One does one's best to overcome the coke fumes. That's what life's about really.'

'*You* could write little poems for *Home Notes*,' said Rosie. As she got up to go, she suddenly found herself feeling a lot better.

A large poster on a brick wall at the end of Saracen Street announced *Friday Night Is Amami Night*. This advertised a well-known brand of shampoo. At number seven, they didn't just wash their hair on Friday evenings – they washed every inch of themselves. And they did it very publicly.

Steam: there were pans on the hobs, and a kettle on the fire, and more steaming pans on the gas cooker in the scullery, where a small copper boiler was beginning to dance on brass feet as yet more water was heated up for the

Hankeys' weekly ablutions. Windows, mirrors and even Tippler's reading glasses were misted up with steam.

Tippler had already carried in the long narrow tin bath from the yard. Now he was sitting in the rocking chair at the kitchen table, playing a game of patience. Wearing nothing but a pair of full-length woollen long johns – with an embarrassingly noticeable rubber-buttoned fly – he was a sight to behold. You could read his tattoos. *For King and Country* stretched right across his chest, with British bulldogs at either end of the tasselled banner. *Mam and Dad* were inside a heart on one forearm, and the word *Nora* was encircled by a flight of bluebirds on the other.

'Are there any more words on your back?' Rosie asked Tippler.

She had already found him to be the most approachable person in the household.

'Just the Union Jack. But it flaps.'

'How?'

'Watch!' Tippler rose to his feet, turned his back to Rosie and revealed a wide expanse of indelible red and blue flag. As he flexed his shoulder blades, the tattoo did indeed jump up and down.

The door from the lobby burst open and Zav dived into the room as naked as Tom in *The Water-Babies*. He was hotly pursued by Mrs Hankey and a dancing, barking Trixie.

'Rosemary wasn't meant to see that part of you, Colin,' stormed Mrs Hankey.

'Christopher had one too,' said Rosie calmly, and then added in tones of polite interest, 'But his didn't have a wrinkly end.'

'Don't talk so common,' rapped out Mrs Hankey. 'We don't dwell on dickies in this house. Help me get the clothes maiden round the fire . . .' This was the Lancashire word for a clothes horse. 'And we'll need some sheets from the bottom drawer of the dresser.'

Rosie proceeded to help Mrs Hankey build a privacy cubicle around the tin bath in front of the fire. Tippler began to pour in the water. 'Where's me bath salts?' he asked.

'You're a bloody Jessie!' growled his wife.

'If you were a man, I'd knock you down for that,' Tippler growled back. But he was grinning. 'Our Hazel got them for my birthday and I don't want her feelings hurt.'

Marching over to the dresser, Mrs Hankey opened one of the fretwork doors and produced a glass jar of petunia-coloured gravel labelled *British Home Stores – Exquisite*. 'Trouble with our Hazel is she's got your brains, Tippler. Zav! Will you please put something round that middle of yours. A towel, you daft clod – not the dog rug!' Turning to Rosie she added, 'Zav's got his father's muscles and my grey matter – he will go far.'

Rosie found herself impressed. 'You're the second person who's said that today.'

An anguished howl went up from behind the screen of sheets. 'I wouldn't care,' shouted Tippler, 'I only put a bloody toe in.'

'Get your dad a kettle of cold.' Mrs Hankey was addressing Zav. Scented fumes began to rise up from behind the sheeted screen. Rosie found herself reminded of a record they sometimes played on *Housewives' Choice* – 'In a Persian Market Place' it was called. These thoughts were interrupted by a distant banging on the knocker of the front door.

'Teddy Ashworth's dead!' cried Mrs Hankey. 'They say the new rent man's a lady. We can't have her walking into a nudist colony. Rosemary, take that rent book off the dresser. You'll find a little pile of money on top of it. Give it the woman and make sure she initials my book.'

Rosie counted the change as she carried it up the hall. It amounted to nineteen shillings and fourpence. The woman on the doorstep had nosiness pouring from behind rimless glasses. 'Aren't you the little girl from Teapot Hall?' she asked.

'I used to be,' said Rosie, 'but now I'm turning into somebody else.' And there was no self-pity in this statement.

Tippler and Zav had their baths first and then the water was changed and it turned into Ladies' Night. With the males banished to sit in front of the gas fire in the parlour, Mrs Hankey started to remove all her clothes. Just as Rosie was thinking that the resemblance to Olive Oyl was at its most striking, Nora Hankey climbed out of the last garment of all.

Rosie let out an astonished shriek: 'Poor Mrs Hankey! How awful! I'd no idea . . .'

'No idea what?'

'That you'd got a little beard between your legs.'

'Don't be so personal,' retorted Mrs Hankey. 'All ladies have these.'

'*All* ladies?' gasped Rosie. 'When will I get mine?'

'I don't know what they taught them at that private school,' yawned Hazel. It sounded like something she'd heard somebody else say, earlier.

Lowering herself into the tin bath, Mrs Hankey had obviously decided to change the subject: 'Rosemary, you said that somebody else had said that our Zav had far to go. . . ?'

'I thought we were supposed to call him Colin,' put in Hazel.

'We are but the other's catching. Who said it, Rosemary?'

'Miss Swaine. She said he was like the Piper of Dreams.'

'Hmph,' snorted Mrs Hankey, soaping her shanks, 'he's like somebody who's keeping something from his own mother. Ten to one it's mischief. There's something going on in this house that I don't know about. A mother can sense these things but I'll get to the bottom of . . .'

The door opened suddenly and Tippler's head came round it. Nora flung her bony arms across her chest and let out a terrible cry of *'Out'*!

Tippler's head disappeared.

'That was a near thing,' breathed Nora. 'We forgot to pull the clothes maiden round me. He nearly saw me with nothing on.'

'Has he never?' Rosie asked in wonder.

'Never.' Mrs Hankey was at her proudest. 'Never in the memory of God. Saracen Street has much stricter rules than Teapot Hall.' With this she removed her false teeth and reached out to place them in a teacup of bleach, which was waiting on the floor. Intimate conversation was plainly at an end.

*

You could see Teapot Hall on the skyline – that was the worst thing about the daily walk to the new school. Glimpsed through the skeletons of late autumn trees, the sandstone tower managed to look curiously forlorn and abandoned. And Rosie would attempt to flash a message to the house – in the same way she had once flashed them to Christopher: 'I still love you and I'll buy you back' was what she wanted Teapot Hall to know.

Although she still had the front door key, Rosie had never returned. Some instinct seemed to be telling her that – before she did – she would have to get strong. Strong inside. She was already improving. Yesterday had proved that. It had been Sunday morning and Mrs Marriott, from Quakers, had turned up at Saracen Street and proposed taking Rosie to the Friends' Meeting House.

'Will my daddy be there?' asked Rosie hopefully.

'No. He's in London. Do come anyway.'

Rosie refused. '*She* used to go there,' she explained as politely as she could. 'I'm not her any more.'

Good Quakers don't fly off the handle. 'God's still the same,' said Mrs Marriott carefully.

'It's nothing to do with God. It's to do with Daddy ditching me.'

Mrs Marriott seemed reluctant to leave it at that: 'Your father particularly asked me to offer you this opportunity.' Suddenly assuming the humble face of somebody who was about to give ministry, she added, 'Everything's to do with God . . .'

'Not on my doorstep!' Mrs Hankey had erupted into view. 'The child must do as she sees fit. I'll thank you to keep the opium of the masses off my front step. There's no God in Soviet Russia.'

'Yes and look where it's got them!' countered Mrs Marriott.

Rosie had quite admired the Quaker's steadfast answer, but nothing would have got her back to Mount Street. It belonged in the past, like the things in the private drawer Mrs Hankey had allocated her – the five books, the box camera, her mother's rings and the key to Teapot Hall. But those were parts of the past that she still wanted. Rosie knew that Nora Hankey would no more dream of going into that drawer than she would think of going into somebody else's purse. It was private. And private was sacred in Saracen Street. No, going off to Quakers would only have got her labelled odd and different.

All that had happened yesterday. Boys ricocheting round the school gates didn't frighten her half as much today. Rosie found herself wondering whether Mrs Hankey would be nervous later on in the morning when she arrived to take up the post of new dinner lady.

There was even beginning to be familiarity in school routine. The morning hymn was followed by sums, then a bit of history, then playtime. The idea of this break in the school yard presented Rosie with some mild foreboding but, in the event, Bernadette Barrett and her hoydens kept their distance. And Hazel introduced Rosie to a girl called Audrey something whose auntie had once cut out a frock for Ruby Murray.

Straight after playtime came reading. When it was Rosie's turn, she pretended to stumble over a few hard words so the rest of the class wouldn't think she was a clever-guts. The combination of glasses and a reputation for cleverness would be too like somebody in *Beano* – a comic greatly favoured in the Hankey household. Rosie had already learned it didn't do to mention such middle-class publications as *Sunny Stories* and *Chicks' Own*. It wasn't that she was being disloyal to her past. She was simply beginning to learn how to erect defences.

The next lesson saw Miss Buckley replaced by the headmistress. She was there to teach them something Rosie had never learned at Elm House – current affairs.

Somebody called Donald Campbell had just set a new waterspeed record in his *Bluebird* speedboat. One of the boys had brought a model of it, made by Meccano, so everybody could see what it looked like.

Miss Swaine then began to talk about something called the Clean Air Bill. Men in Parliament were going to stop smog. The headmistress produced an architect's drawing of

Manchester Town Hall. The building wasn't black like today, instead it was pale golden.

'And that's how it will be again,' the headmistress promised them. 'Ours will be a beautiful city. And if we're to believe everything we're told, the air will smell like champagne.'

As a big discussion started about buildings being cleaned with chemicals, Rosie reflected that the air in the classroom was beginning to smell of school dinners. The van had obviously arrived from the cooking depot and wafts of council-school gravy were on the air.

These dinners were served in the hall. That's where Rosie got her first glimpse of Mrs Hankey, doling out boiled mince with a soup ladle onto thick white pot plates. She looked alien and official, in a white overall and a white net mobcap, like a coarse hairnet, which ended low on her forehead, almost covering her eyebrows.

Rosie forced down the main course and took her plate back for pudding. At this school you didn't get a separate plate for each course. The ladle was no longer in evidence. Instead, Mrs Hankey and the other dinner lady were each using one of their own hands to dive into a big enamelled bowl of rice pudding. You got a slop each. Rosie did her best to appear blasé and experienced; the previous Friday she had been appalled to watch semolina given the same treatment.

'What a thing to do to Chinese wallop!' It was Bernadette Barrett, ahead of Rosie in the queue. Her criticism was directed at Mrs Hankey. 'Know what you are? You're a dirty cow, that's what you are!'

Rosie's temper soared in a flash. 'That's no way to speak to my Mrs Hankey,' she shouted. Leaning quickly across the counter, and turning her own hand into a scoop, she filled it with stinging hot rice pudding, which she *threw* at Bernadette Barrett.

Her spattered enemy let out a piercing shriek.

Miss Buckley was up from the teachers' table in seconds. As she tore towards Rosie she bawled, 'Well, somebody's certainly turned into a slum child in record time!'

'Oh no she hasn't,' said a husky familiar voice. Only now did Rosie realise that Zav was behind her in the halted pudding queue. 'She's not turned into a slum child at all,' he said. 'She's turned into an honorary Hankey.' From the fervent way Zav shook her pudding-wet hand, he could have been granting Rosie the freedom of Irlams o'th' Height.

4

'I will not have it!' This afternoon, Miss Swaine's annoyance was as evident as the pungent coke fumes in her study. 'The pair of you seem to think that this whole school is being run for the benefit of two little hobbledehoys.'

Bernadette glowered. Rosie felt highly indignant. What about loyalty? She was, after all, living under Mrs Hankey's roof. Surely she wasn't expected to just stand by and do nothing whilst Bernadette shouted swearwords at her friend?

Miss Swaine had not even paused for breath: 'If you did but know it, the pair of you have much more in common than you realise.'

'I've nothing in common with her,' snarled Bernadette, a vivid flush spreading amongst her freckles. 'She's posh and she thinks I'm dog-dirt.'

'Rosemary, what *do* you think of Bernadette?' The headmistress was in like a knife. 'Come on, let's have it out in the open.'

'She'll only say I'm telling tales . . .'

'That's what we're here for. Nobody's going home until some tales have been told. What do you think of Bernadette Barrett?'

The best Rosie could manage was, 'She goes for me. I've done nothing and she goes for me . . .'

'Who flung Chinese wallop?' Bernadette was shouting again.

Rosie was startled to see that her enemy was also crying. She was blowed if she was going to start weeping too, but the temptation was certainly there. Tears were nearly rising to the surface.

'She thinks she's it,' snuffled Bernadette.

'Bernadette,' Miss Swaine was very much in control of the situation, 'have you got a handkerchief?'

'No. You can look down your nose at me for that, too,' she sniffed at Rosie.

'Here, take this.' Miss Swaine handed the ginger-haired girl a handkerchief in beautifully ironed white cambric. 'Blow your nose. We're going to play a game. It's called the truth game. Anybody is allowed to ask anybody anything. But we all have to promise we won't tell anybody else. Not one word to anybody. Those are the rules.'

'Anything?' asked Bernadette in astonishment. 'I swear by Jesus and his Holy Mother I'll never tell another soul.' Without pausing she added, 'How old are you, Miss Swaine?'

'Fifty-seven.'

'Gerraway! I'd have given you fifty. How old's Miss Buckley?'

'Miss Buckley is not taking part in this exercise. Do you promise too, Rosemary?'

Rosemary could hardly believe what was happening. 'Yes . . . I promise.'

'Get the Bible out,' insisted Bernadette. 'Make her really swear.'

'Her promise will be quite good enough, thank you.'

'I'll never understand Protestants,' sighed Bernadette.

'Right, Bernadette, no, I don't want the handkerchief back, thank you. You may keep it. You may also tell us why you are at this school and not at the Catholic one, where you began.'

Bernadette, who had become quite cheerful, suddenly turned unhappy and uncomfortable again. 'Because me mother bashed up the priest.'

'Why?' Suddenly, Miss Swaine could have been wearing a barrister's wig.

'Because he told her off.'

'Why?'

'Because I'd bashed up some kids for calling her names. And if you ask me "why?" again, I'll splatter you. Why have you never been married?'

'Because nobody ever asked me.' Miss Swaine was unabashed. 'What were these children saying about your mother?'

'That she lives with a man who's not her husband.'

The headmistress looked very serious. 'We are all of us agreed that none of this conversation will ever go beyond these four walls . . .'

Bernadette jerked her head in Rosie's direction. 'We've got nothing on her yet. Have you ever been kissed by a man, Miss Swaine?'

Miss Swaine nodded briskly. 'By two men: my father and my brother. Rosemary, your turn. Where's your mother?'

'She ran off with a black man.'

'Fucking hell fire!' exploded Bernadette, in something precious close to admiration. 'Even mine never managed that much.'

'We can do without the swearing,' interjected Miss Swaine.

This was just long enough for Bernadette to pause and think and return to a former attitude: 'Tattersalls can do what they like. Everybody knows they're stinking rich.'

'But we're not!' piped up Rosie indignantly. 'All the money's gone. And now I have to live at Mrs Hankey's.'

'That's nothing,' boasted Bernadette. 'There's no room left at our house so they've put me to sleep at Biddie Costigan's – and everybody says she's batty.'

Miss Swaine's voice rose above these exchanges: 'And the pair of you have nothing in common?'

Bernadette was not prepared to leave it at that: 'She's not got red hair and freckles.'

Rosie countered with, 'You don't have to wear glasses.'

The silence that followed these exchanges was broken by just one word from the remarkable Miss Swaine. 'Precisely,' she said. And then she repeated it: 'Precisely. It looks to me as though your quarrel's over. And so is this game. Think twice before you play it again in the future. If you don't *need* to play the truth game it can often end in tears.'

When Tippler Hankey heard about the flinging of the rice pudding, his prizefighter's glee knew no bounds. 'Well done, little un!' he kept on exclaiming. 'By Jove, yes, bloody well done!'

94

'Less of the bloodies please, Tippler.' Mrs Hankey was serving up a delicious Lancashire hotpot – a brownstone casserole filled with neck-end chops and onions in gravy, topped off with a golden layer of scalloped potato crust. 'If you want to make yourself useful, you can get me the pickled red cabbage.'

'Rosie's the one who's proved herself useful,' protested her husband, as he made his way to the big cupboard at the side of the open fireplace. 'She's shown she's got the killer instinct.' As usual, he had chosen to eat in vest, pants and tattoos. 'After tea, p'raps we should move the furniture back and I'll teach her a bit of jujitsu. Lady wrestlers are quite the coming thing!'

Was he serious? You could never tell with Mr Hankey. Sometimes he reminded Rosie of a little boy who had never quite grown up.

Mrs Hankey was plainly of the same opinion. 'See that man there?' She was speaking to Rosie but pointing at her husband. 'D' you know what his first prize-money was? Two racing pigeons! He got them off a gypsy referee, and both birds had flown home by midnight.'

'Great days!' Tippler opened the pickle jar and managed to spill crimson vinegar down the front of his singlet. 'But our Zav's the one who's going to pick up the real prize-money.'

'Over my dead body!' snorted his wife. 'There's enough brain damage in this family with you. Zav's meant for big things. You've only got to look at his school reports. Top in everything except scripture.'

'What sort of big things?' asked Hazel, munching.

'Time will tell.' Mrs Hankey, who had been shaking out a great cloud of pepper, emitted a loud sneeze then added, 'He's in a position to pick and choose. Come to that, Hazel, what do you propose doing with your life?'

'That's easy. I'm going to marry a rich husband who'll buy me everything I want.'

'You're certainly beautiful enough,' beamed her proud father.

Her outraged mother's mouth had been opening and shutting like a goldfish's. Now it formed words: 'Marry a rich man? That's one of the most shocking things I've ever heard said in this house. To think that a daughter of mine would consider selling herself into bondage! I thought I'd brought you up better than that.'

Hazel was unperturbed. 'I don't care. It's what I'd like.'

'To be nothing but a bloody ornament?' Her mother began chewing furiously.

Tippler turned his attentions towards their son. 'What *do* you fancy after school?'

It was Mrs Hankey who did the answering. 'University. What d'you think he fancies?' With this she removed her bottom denture and glared at it. 'Either these teeth have lost their cutting edge or that butcher's worked mutton on me, instead of lamb.'

Zav swallowed a mouthful of hotpot and announced, 'I'm going to be a world-famous singer.'

'You're *what*?' If he'd said he was going to be a mass murderer Mrs Hankey could not have sounded more outraged. 'Singer? You've got the voice of a foghorn!'

'I don't care.' He was totally unabashed. 'I'll make it into a famous foghorn.'

'This has got to be one of the worst meals of my life,' groaned Mrs Hankey.

'Give over, it's quite tasty,' beamed Tippler. Even Rosie could tell that he was teasing.

Mrs Hankey fell for it. 'I'm not talking about food, though I'll have that thieving butcher. I'm talking about ambition. What's the easy road out of Irlams o'th' Height?' she demanded like a soapbox orator. 'I'll tell you what it is – either going on the stage or marrying a rich husband. Of course there is one other,' she continued inexorably, 'prizefighting. And where did that get you?'

'Don't bring me into this.' Tippler looked alarmed.

'You are in it whether you like it or not. It landed you with a little light job at a dyeworks. And you only got that because Mrs Horsefall remembered you jiggling up and down in baggy boxing shorts. "Well done thou good and faithful servant!" ' She spat out the quotation with contempt and returned to her own fight. 'Is it wrong of me to want better for my kids? But it seems that the apple doesn't fall very far from the tree.' From the glower she gave him, Tippler Hankey was plainly the tree in question.

This malign look was now transferred to her son. 'A singer!' She spat the word out in tones of deepest scorn. 'Still, I suppose it could have been worse. I suppose he could've wanted to be a singing waiter.'

Mrs Hankey rose to her feet. 'Whatever happened to ambition?' she cried to the world at large. 'Teapot Hall didn't sell,' she added in altogether more mundane tones, as she reached over the dresser for the Daddy's Sauce bottle. 'The contents were all snapped up but they couldn't get anybody to bite on the building. That fool of a Bertha had to drag her stiff leg to the auction. Landed back here in tears. "End of an era," she kept saying, "end of an era . . ." Not much hope for the next era,' she glared at her son, 'if all it wants to do is go on the stage.'

Zav remained calm. 'I'm not going on the stage. I'm going to be a recording artist.'

'He's very up to date,' said Tippler proudly. 'He's forward-looking – you've got to grant him that.'

'I'll grant him a first-class education – that's what I'll grant him. I'll grant him the right to pick and choose. And he's not going to be no tuppenny jazz singer!'

'No, I'm going to be a million-pound one,' beamed Zav.

From the first mention of the words 'Teapot Hall', Rosie had lost interest in thoughts of the Hankeys' ambitions. Nobody wanted to buy the house she loved. Half of her was glad. It meant that the Hall still belonged to her own family. But she thought of the house as a living entity. If nobody wanted it, the poor thing must be feeling very neglected.

She was nevertheless feeling better. It had been a good day. Zav had called her an honorary Hankey and Bernadette Barrett was no longer the enemy – she was just a girl with her own tragedy and red hair and too many muscles. These minor thoughts were being swamped by a bigger and more daring one. Yes, she was feeling tough enough; she dared do it. It was just a matter of timing. She would choose her moment, and take the key from her private drawer and go back to visit Teapot Hall.

Trixie, the dog, suddenly emerged from under the table and headed for the back door.

'If she's been out once, she's been out twenty times,' said Mrs Hankey. 'And she keeps barking at the old coalhole.'

'Probably a dead rat in it,' observed Tippler.

'There's no key to the padlock, I do know that.' Mrs Hankey, nearest the door, got up to open it. 'I've not clapped eyes on that key since we got the zinc bunker.'

It had stopped being the rice-pudding day and turned into the day of the keys. Mrs Hankey might not know where this one was but somebody else did. Behind his mother's back, Zav treated Rosie to an extremely companionable wink. So Mrs Hankey was right. She had been saying for days that Zav was up to something.

November being the season of dark nights, Rosie could not put her plan into execution until the following Saturday morning. The early light was thin and watery but she supposed there would be enough of it to take a photograph. Rosie descended the creaking stairs of number seven with the iron key hidden in her pocket and the Zeiss-Ikon camera slung round her neck.

'Mrs Hankey, do films go off? This one's been in the camera since Ilfracombe.' She could even say that place-name without feeling pain. Things *must* be getting better!

'Search me! I haven't had me photo took since they used to put your head in a clamp. Sid Molyneux would be able to tell you. Knows all there is to know about cameras. He's the dispenser at Gledhill's the chemists. If you're going over to the other side of Bolton Road, be sure and use the venetian crossing.'

She meant 'zebra' but Rosie understood. Mrs Hankey had a way of rechristening objects that was all her own. Sometimes they were better than the real thing, reflected Rosie, as the traffic halted whilst she crossed over the black and white stripes. There was a definite holiday air to Irlams o'th' Height this Saturday morning. More and more people were starting to work a five-day week, and it seemed to have freed them to smile. For the first time in weeks the child actually felt glad to be alive. And next week the whole school was going to the circus.

Gledhill's was an old-fashioned pharmacy. Two huge and mysterious bottles, one filled with red liquid and the other green, dominated its window display. Two more of these stoppered glass receptacles, this time in lavender and blue, sat on top of the oak partition which divided the interior of the shop from the dispensary. Shelves of patent medicine bottles made three-dimensional wallpaper from floor to ceiling. And behind the glass-topped counter stood a dapper little man in a long white coat.

'Can I be of service?' he asked. He was just a bit taller than the brass weighing machine (*Know Your Weight – One Penny*). Despite the fact that his sandy hair was sharply brilliantined and that he had teeth like Bugs Bunny, there seemed something remarkably eager and helpful about him.

'I'm sorry,' said Rosie. 'I was just having a nice sniff. Isn't the chemist-shop smell beautiful?'

'Remind me!' he said. 'Tell me what it smells of. You get a bit used to it when you work here.'

'Tar and Pine Cough Mixture and Patent Chloroform Throat Tablets and just a whiff of scented soap. It's beautiful. You could bottle it and sell it as perfume.'

The man beamed happily. 'That's a remarkably handsome camera you've got there. One of the best box cameras ever made, the Zeiss-Ikon.' The man reached out a hand as though this enthusiasm wouldn't be satisfied until he'd touched it. 'May I?'

Rosie had no objections. Actually it made things easier. It wasn't as though she was planning on buying anything. 'The film's been in since last summer. Will it be all right? I was told to ask for Mr Molyneux.'

'You've found him.'

'Do you *really* know everything there is to know about cameras?' asked Rosie in awe.

'I certainly know that this lens could do with a rub,' smiled her new acquaintance. 'I'll just nip it in the back and do it for you. Want to see some pictures while you're waiting?' He slid a big yellow envelope marked *Kodak* across the counter.

'They're a few of my own. Hold the prints by the edges,' he took hold of one and demonstrated '. . . like that. That way you won't get fingermarks on them.' Though Rosie didn't know it, this was to be the first of a thousand lessons. An important figure had just come into her life.

For the moment Sid Molyneux disappeared behind the forbidding oak partition. Half of his photographs were of a wedding group. The poor bride was wearing a windswept veil and – horror of horrors – horn-rimmed glasses. Rosie vowed that she would rather be led down the aisle by a guide dog than get married in specs. Perhaps she could put Trixie into some sort of bridesmaid's frock? Rosie reflected that the mysterious barking, whenever the little dog went into the yard, had stopped as suddenly as it had started.

The rest of the photographs were of people with pint pots in their hands, standing round a piano. Some of them showed women holding onto daintier glasses. All the pictures featured a different person looking nervous – because they'd got a big white parrot sitting on their shoulder.

'My feathered friend's called Eustace.' Mr Molyneux had returned with her camera. 'I take him round the pubs at weekends. It helps drum up business.'

'But I thought you were a chemist?'

'So does the boss – until he wants his precious baby photos taking.' Mr Molyneux's own baby-blue eyes shone with cheerful fanaticism. 'No, this job's just a means to an end. I don't have a wife, I'm wedded to the camera.'

Rosie wasn't sure what he meant. But she knew he wasn't talking down to her. She could have been his own age. She liked that.

'I've cleaned the lens and you've got four exposures left,' he said. 'That means four pictures to go.'

Rosie was glad of this bit of technical explanation. She needed more. 'When I've taken them, how much will it cost to turn the film into real photographs?'

'Developing and printing? For you, nixey-plonk. Nothing.'

'But why. . . ?'

Mr Molyneux looked half-embarrassed. 'One good turn

deserves another. I used to deliver your Gran'dad Tattersall's newspapers. He gave me my very first camera.'

'How did you know who I was?' asked Rosie in amazement.

'Everybody knows everybody else in The Height.'

'I didn't know you,' she pointed out reasonably.

'You do now,' he said.

She did. And what's more she felt better for knowing him. As Rosie stepped out of the dark chemist's shop and into the sunshine, she became aware that Mr Molyneux's enthusiasm was catching. It left her feeling that this Saturday morning was filled with infinite promise. This realisation had an odd effect upon Rosie; she found herself looking at Irlams o'th' Height as though she'd never seen it before.

People maintained that you could spend your whole life in The Height without having to travel the four miles into Manchester for anything. Only yesterday Tippler Hankey had said, 'You can get a suit of clothes at Davies's and a wooden wardrobe at Albert Johnson's.' These were both larger double-fronted establishments, but the rest of the shops were more pokey and had names like The Beehive, which sold knitting wool, and the Misses Baldwin – whose shopfront proclaimed them to be *Specialists in High Class Outerwear & Ladies' Millinery.*

As Rosie walked towards Teapot Hall with the box camera slung over her shoulder (Mr Molyneux had kindly adjusted the length of the strap) she tried to think of something you couldn't get – and failed. Everything was here from dressed tripe to treacle toffee. Some of the older shops didn't open out onto the pavements but onto strips of knobby cobblestones instead. In Rosie's present cheerful mood, the grimy industrial village was beginning to seem like a Lancashire version of Toytown.

So why did she feel she was being followed? As she jerked her head round, somebody, moving faster, disappeared through the doorway of Wheatley's, the sweetshop and temperance bar. Rosie carried on towards the venetian crossing and reflected that Mrs Hankey's funny names for things had a way of sticking. Again she turned as she sensed the same somebody behind her.

'Can't dodge in that shop,' grinned Zav. 'It's full of fat women and pink corsets.'

Rosie ought to have guessed it was him. Ever since the rice-pudding incident Zav had turned into her shadow's shadow. 'What do you want?'

'Nothing.' Then he added airily, 'I'm just out and about. Where you off?'

'Teapot Hall. I'm going to take a photograph.'

Zav looked momentarily alarmed then said, 'Take one of somewhere else. I'd give Teapot Hall a miss if I was you.'

Who did he think he was? 'I'm not you and that's where I'm going.'

They were over the striped pedestrian crossing and he was still bounding along at her side. Zav had so much energy that he covered about three times as much ground as anybody else. Straight lines seemed to bore him, so instead of walking he leapt and darted. 'If you've absolutely got to go there, I think I'd better tell you a secret.'

'Please don't.' And if that had come out too primly, Rosie didn't care. She owned more than her fair share of curiosity, but experience had taught her to be wary of other people's secrets. Her mother had frequently weighed her down with the things. And the threats attached to her twin brother's big secret still haunted her dreams.

'You're not very friendly.' Zav sounded a bit hurt. How could she explain to him that – just for this Saturday morning – she had stopped being the Hankeys' lodger? That the sun was shining down on Rosie Tattersall in her own right.

It seemed she didn't have to. 'Are you like a princess going back to her old castle?' asked Zav.

Put like that, it all sounded very far-fetched. 'One of your garters has broken,' she said.

'I know. I don't mind. I just let that sock hang down. Don't take a picture of the house, take one of me instead.'

'I can't. I've only got four thingies left.' *Now* would he go away?

It seemed he wouldn't. 'You could take two of me, two of the house – and then I'd buy you a film for your trouble.' This idea had been conceived and delivered in one flash.

Rosie was beginning to see what Miss Swaine meant about Zav Hankey. 'What d'you want the picture for?'

The answer came without any hesitation: 'For when I'm famous. Then they'll be able to see what I was like when I was just ordinary.'

'With your sock hanging down?'

'You could cut that off,' he pointed out reasonably. 'And you could take a whole lot more pictures with the new film I'm going to buy you.'

'All right,' conceded Rosie, who liked a bargain. She was, after all, a merchant's daughter. 'But I'm not taking you outside Teapot Hall.'

'You *have* to,' he said urgently. 'And then, when the picture's in the papers, it'll say underneath: "Millionaire Zav Hankey outside the house where his mother was a lowly servant." '

'She was the boss of the whole place!' retorted Rosie indignantly.

'The other's a better story. I know what I'm doing. I think about these things a lot. What do you think about?' he enquired interestedly.

On her walk through The Height, Rosie had been considering her own status. Did she count as an orphan? With both parents gone she certainly felt like one. 'I think about who I am,' was all she said to Zav.

'Who you are? That's easy. Me mother says it every day but she doesn't let you hear.'

'What does she say? Who *am* I?'

'She says you're a gutsy little madam. She says you're definitely Gran'dad Tattersall's granddaughter.'

Rosie suddenly felt as though the unexpected November sun was shining for her and for her alone. She had a new identity. Gran'dad Tattersall had always been regarded as everything that was adventurous. And a world expert had said that she was definitely his granddaughter. 'I'll take your picture, Zav,' she said happily. 'And you don't have to bother buying me a new film.'

'You'll take two and I *will* buy it.'

'Okay.' Deals, bargains – she was her grandfather's

descendant and these were in her bones and in her blood. The sentimental streak, which wanted to give Zav a present for saying something that made her happy, must have reached her from her mother. Connie wasn't *bad*, she was just sloppy. And her father was more like fog than a person. None of this mattered any more. She was Rosie Tattersall in her own right. And the golden teapot seemed to be gleaming in recognition of that fact.

'Stand on the front doorstep, Zav. Spread out your hands.'

'Why? Why spread them out?'

'To show them the house.' She was already looking in the viewfinder. 'It's a picture of both of you.' She'd learned how to use the camera on that hot holiday in Ilfracombe. She pressed the shutter – *click*. The word 'Ilfracombe' had lost its power to hurt her.

'Stay where you are, Zav,' she called out. 'I'm going to take another. Laugh! Think of Olive Bucket finding you in the girls' toilets.'

Zav laughed involuntarily. As the shutter caught the moment, Rosie felt a feeling of triumph. This was easier than crayons or paints and brushes. It was still making a picture but you did it with real things. And it gave you this wonderful feeling of being in control. 'Okay, you can be serious now . . .' She took another picture of him. And then she stepped back and took just one of the house.

The sandstone mansion was already showing signs of dereliction. Somebody had thrown a stone through an upstairs window and smashed the glass. Over the front door a large sign said *For Sale or Might Consider Letting*. Underneath was the name of an estate agent who described himself as 'superior' and had offices in Bexley Square, Salford.

'I'll get it back,' she said matter-of-factly. 'One day I'll buy it for myself.'

'I was going to have it,' said Zav. 'For me.'

'You can't. It's mine.'

He paused, thought for a moment and then nodded firmly. 'Fair do's,' he said, sounding like Tippler. 'But would you let me come and stay? Only once.' Suddenly he was looking embarrassed. 'You don't have to if you don't want.'

'I do want. Let's go and choose which room you'll have.' In her enthusiasm, without thinking what she was doing, Rosie had produced the iron key.

'We shouldn't go in . . .' Zav was suddenly worried.

'That's the first time I've ever known you scared.'

'I'm not scared.' He was furious. 'Just you take that back!'

'Shut up. I'm opening the door.'

'No.' He seemed panicked. 'Please don't do that. You mustn't go inside. You might not like what you find.'

Rosie was struck by a sudden thought. 'Was it you who broke that upstairs window?' she demanded sternly.

'No. He did it. He threw an old shoe-tree. I couldn't stop him.'

'Who threw an old shoe-tree?' asked Rosie indignantly.

Zav had gone bright red. 'A friend of mine. He's sort of living here.'

Rosie was already concentrating on the key. Getting it in the lock was easy enough, but turning it was quite another matter.

'Let me,' Zav reached out a hand.

Rosie pushed it away. 'You've done quite enough already. Lending out other people's property!' She even managed to throw in a tutting noise that would have been worthy of his mother. The key simply refused to turn. 'Go on then, you try. But I bet you can't do it.'

'I can do anything I set me mind to,' said Zav. The door was open in a moment. Rosie suddenly felt nervous. The house had always been like a person to her. Would it be fair to just roll in – when the place was down on its luck?

These thoughts were too half-formed and private for public consumption so what she said aloud was, 'I hope you haven't gone and let a tramp in.'

Zav just grinned.

The last Tattersall in Irlams o'th' Height led the way over the threshold and through the rattling inner doors. Bereft of furniture, the entrance hall looked huge. The bare walls seemed stencilled with a new design, left by the pale patches where pictures had once hung. There was still a solitary battered portrait hanging crookedly on a far wall. And somebody had left something knitted and woollen hanging on the carved wooden pineapple atop the bottom newel post. As Rosie got closer she realised that it had once belonged to Winkum the doll – it was his patched jacket. Still, if somebody had taken it off it meant that at least the dolls must have been untied. It was all too much . . .

'Don't cry,' said Zav. 'You're going to get it all back. Well, that's what you told me.'

'I can't get Winkum back.' Her voice came out sounding choked.

'Who's he?'

'He smelled of old mothballs and you could cuddle him . . .' Rosie couldn't help it, she was really sobbing. 'And now strangers have got him and they didn't even bother taking his coat. Gran'ma Tattersall mended that coat . . .'

'Is this your gran'dad?' Zav had walked across the room and was looking up at the damaged picture. It was Gran'dad Tattersall with his trotting-pony. The top of the frame was smashed and the whole thing was still covered with sticky-looking marks where Connie's rejected champagne had run down the varnish.

'Yes,' sobbed Rosie, 'and my mummy owes him a jump in Heaven.' She walked across the room and looked up at her grandfather.

'What sort of a jump?' asked Zav.

'I don't know.' Rosie wiped away her tears and her grandfather looked out at her from the picture that must have been too knocked about to interest anybody at the auction. Though it was a jolly face, it also looked full of determination. He didn't look like a man who would have much time for tears.

'I'm worried about who might be living in our house,' she said to the picture. In truth, this was a bit of an act for Zav's benefit. What she was really thinking was that her grandfather would not approve of a Hankey knowing that a Tattersall was feeling sorry for herself because beautiful Teapot Hall had fallen on bad times.

'It's nobody awful in the house,' Zav croaked indignantly. 'Give me credit! I wouldn't just bring anybody here. Our family have worked for yours for years.'

'Is this revenge?' asked Rosie sternly. Her vivid imagination was already conjuring up visions of a wild gypsy tramp in a red and white spotted neckerchief, with string tied round the knees of his trousers. Yet something strange was happening. This vision was now misting into the black-haired man with blue eyes whom she had drawn, in crayons, at the Friends' Meeting House ('Thy people shall be as my people'). 'What's he like?' she asked, trying to keep too much interest out of her voice. And she quite startled herself because – as she asked this question – she had sounded more than a bit like her own mother.

'Well . . .' Even as Zav was considering his answer, the air was filled with a distant pounding noise. It sounded like somebody dancing an angry jig – somebody in felt boots.

'He's heard us!' cried Zav in delight. 'Hang on, lad, we're coming.' Zav actually seized hold of Rosie's hand and began tugging her in the direction of the green baize door. His hand felt nice and dry and warm and confident. Instead of going through the door into the kitchens, he paused outside the one next to it. This sealed off the flower room, with its stone sink and barred windows.

'Close your eyes,' he said, letting go of her hand.

She hesitated. 'Is anything awful going to happen?'

'No. Something magic. Just close them till I tell you and then you'll see.'

Rosie obeyed. She heard the door opening, then a lot more dancing, then Zav saying 'Shush.' This was followed by some smacking, kissing noises. 'Open your eyes,' called out Zav.

In his arms he was holding a baby chimpanzee. 'I call him Jesus,' he said huskily, 'because he's so beautiful.'

The animal was the size of a two-year-old boy. As Rosie stretched out her hand to touch it, the little chimp leapt from Zav's arms and tore into the entrance hall. In a moment it was up the stairs, along the minstrels' gallery, back down again, and swinging round and round at arm's length from the pineapple knob.

'I thought your family didn't believe in Jesus Christ,' said Rosie. It goes without saying that she found the baby chimp enchanting.

'Nobody tells me what to believe in. Anyway, it's just a name.'

'How can we call out *Jesus* in the street?' Rosie was already embracing a future that was full of the little animal. 'Where did his nappy come from?'

'Bolshuss Baggott keeps nicking them off clotheslines.'

'Bolshuss?' Could he mean Peter Baggott? 'It sounds rude.'

'It's just a nickname. We've all got them now. There's Bolshuss and Lenin and Nadger. It was Nadger's dad who came home drunk with Jesus. His mother nearly had a fit.'

The young chimpanzee was now making all of its hair stand on end – like a comedian's fright-wig. 'Is he all right?' asked Rosie.

'He's just showing off because you're new.' As if on cue, the animal headed for the green baize door. He was through it in one agile bound. The children followed him. The only noticeable things about the old butler's pantry were cold emptiness and a dripping brass tap.

'That water's meant to be off,' said Rosie worriedly.

Zav went into one of his crimson blushes. 'We needed facilities,' he explained. The blush even extended beyond his blond, cropped hairline. As Rosie gazed at this she sensed that somebody was looking at her. It was the monkey. His eyes were just like a human being's, except that the whites were brown. This gave extra glitter to an expression that was as friendly and intelligent as Zav's.

'I've nothing to give it to eat,' she said. She felt downright inhospitable.

'That's all right. We go round robbing bins.'

'Bins?' Rosie was appalled. 'Who's we?'

'Me and the rest of the skiffle group.'

'What's that?'

'Something I don't want me mother to know about. We do it in Nadger's front room.'

This was news to Rosie. Though, when she thought about it, she knew what a skiffle group was. They made music out of makeshift instruments like washboards and thimbles, and tea chests with a broom handle poked through the middle and a twine string for strumming.

'Me mother's dead set against me recording career.' All of Zav's *my*'s came out as *me*'s. A lot of people did this in The Height but there were no half measures to Zav Hankey and he did it the most.

'I bet your mother will be dead set against monkeys too!'

'He's a chimp. Anyway, she need never find out.'

'Mrs Hankey?' asked Rosie incredulously. 'You can't keep anything hidden from Mrs Hankey for long.'

The little chimp suddenly decided to use Zav as a ladder. It ended up on his shoulders. With surprisingly sensitive fingers, the animal began to search through the stubble on Zav's scalp – just as though Zav was another chimpanzee.

What was that noise? It could only be an iron key grating in a lock. The side door of Teapot Hall led straight from the garden into the butler's pantry. When Rosie said you couldn't keep anything from Zav's mother for long she had spoken a piece of predictive truth. Nora Hankey was already over the doorstep and glaring at the chimp, which was still rooting through Zav's cropped hair.

'Got your own nit nurse?' she said to her son.

The voice of a newcomer turned the chimp into a rocket. Within seconds he was up by the ceiling and flying along an empty platerack. In the process he managed to bring down an abandoned aluminium egg-poacher. This fell into separate parts at Mrs Hankey's feet with a series of clatters.

For once Zav sounded alarmed: 'I didn't expect to see you here . . .'

'I could say the same thing. Somebody's got to keep the place aired. Come here you,' she said to the amimal. Surprisingly it did. It leapt down onto the wooden draining board and fixed her with a knowing, hurt gaze. 'So this is the monkey Ben Nelson bought in a pub on Salford docks.'

'However did you know?' gasped Zav.

'Me? I know everything. I've got eyes in me bum, and you'd do well to remember it!'

But mother and son were not really fighting. Rosie was finding something almost enviably conspiratorial about the way Mrs Hankey seemed to be joining in Zav's monkey-tricks.

'I can keep him, can't I?' he asked.

'I suppose,' sniffed his mother. But it was only a token sniff. 'At my time of life, the last thing I expected to be doing was boiling nappies again.'

'I'm potty-training him,' explained Zav earnestly.

'It's just to be hoped he's quicker at it than you were. Answer me something, Zav Hankey: that animal spent two days in our coalhole, didn't he?'

Zav looked astounded. 'However did you know?'

'Our Trixie told me.'

By this time Rosie was almost inclined to believe her. She found herself full of admiration for the way Zav had caught the expression in his mother's eyes when she first saw the chimp and turned it to his own advantage. So why hadn't he just turned up on the doorstep at Saracen Street with this animal orphan? Because he was his mother's son and both of them dearly loved a bit of drama – that was why. Rosie was coming to realise something that Zav must always have known: Mrs Hankey was only capable of being generous when it wasn't expected of her.

Jesus's entry into Saracen Street was almost as triumphal as Palm Sunday in Jerusalem, but the first thing that had to change was his name.

'People would think we were swearing,' said Tippler. 'How about Jesus' dad's name? How about Joe?'

And that's what came to pass. It was Trixie, the dog, who landed the chimpanzee with his surname. Theirs was not a happy animal alliance. For years she had been queen of everybody's hearts. Suddenly she had a dazzling rival. What's more, he was capable of infinitely greater naughtiness than she was; he had the added advantage of Fingers.

Joe Fingers – that's what they called him; and he soon had to have a cage. Not for everyday purposes; just for nights and for when the family went out. The materials were not precisely stolen, more acquired. All the components came from the dyeworks, and everything left that building under somebody's overcoat. Tippler's friends were much taken with Joe

Fingers. Let's be honest – the items for the cage *were* stolen. But that kind of theft was considered 'sport' at the dyeworks. 'Nothing too hot or too heavy' was its employees' proud boast. To this end they smuggled out everything from iron bars to floorboards; and such was Joe Fingers' high standing in the household that his new home was built in Mrs Hankey's holy of holies – it was built in the front parlour.

Shy Tippler was heard to observe proudly, 'A monkey gives a man a certain standing in the street.' Zoologically he was a chimpanzee, at number seven Saracen Street Joe Fingers was 'Our Monkey'. But all the scripture in Rosie's Quaker background left her worried. She couldn't help remembering that the 'Hosannas' of Palm Sunday had paved the way for the more dramatic events of Good Friday.

The next thing that happened was magical. But it didn't happen until the following Saturday. That's when Rosie took her film to Mr Molyneux, at Gledhill's, to be developed.

It was magic wrapped up in a lot of mechanical processes. 'We shut at four o'clock,' he said. 'If you come back then, you can come into the darkroom and watch me processing.'

This inner sanctum was at the other side of the forbidding oak partition, the one hung with framed chemist's diplomas. First you came to the dispensary where Gledhills still made some of their own tablets. Mr Molyneux showed her the moulds – they looked like dolls' baking tins. There was the usual chemist's shop smell in this part.

Sid Molyneux led her to a door marked *Do Not Enter When Red Light Is On* and pushed it open. The smells changed completely. They were still chemical but there was something acrid yet exciting about them. Had Rosie but known it she was breathing in her very future. These were the smells of photography.

'The developing tank's ready but I have to put the light out while I remove the film. If you find it scary, we'll whistle.'

'I'm not a very good whistler,' admitted Rosie. 'Could we sing instead?'

They settled for a chorus of 'I'll Be Loving You Always'. In the darkness, Sid added to the noise by making mysterious little engineering sounds like ratchets turning, and then some clatters and a few clicks. These were followed by a very determined screwing sound.

The red light went back on again. Mr Molyneux had one hand on a black Bakelite cylinder. In the other he was holding a thermometer. He wiped this on a cloth. 'I'm just going to check the temperature of the developer. You tend to need it a bit warmer in winter.'

It all got mechanical and mysterious again with liquid developer being poured into the black object. Once that was right, this little tank was treated to a lot of banging and inverting; 'That's to get the bubbles out,' he explained. 'I've got the timer on for six minutes. What shall we talk about while we wait?'

Rosie's reply came unhesitatingly: 'Gran'dad Tattersall. Tell me what he was like.'

'A diamond. You can say that about a lot of people but it fitted him to the ground. He was a fiery little man. Always wore Anazora Viola haircream and cloth-topped boots.'

'And the buttonhole,' said Rosie happily. She was enjoying this.

'And the flower in the buttonhole,' agreed Sid. 'Practically his trademark, that flower was. He used to hand me down his old suits. I once found a gold cigar-cutter in a waistcoat pocket. Gave it back, of course. And got a white fiver for me pains. Loved grand opera your gran'dad did. *Loved* it! When Caruso came to Manchester he always made a point of dropping in at Teapot Hall. Before my time of course . . .'

Once again Sid juggled the developing tank upside down and gave it another thump on the benchtop. 'He loved the music hall too. I used to caddy for him, on Swinton Park Golf Links, when he went out for a round with George Formby. They tried to get your gran'dad to put money into Manchester Film Studios. They didn't succeed. He said he only understood fruit. It was possible to lead Ned Tattersall but he wouldn't be driven.'

'Mrs Hankey says I'm just like him.'

'Can you dance the Highland Fling?' demanded Mr Molyneux sternly.

'Yes,' gasped Rosie. She had acquired this accomplishment at Elm House. 'I won a silver egg cup for it.'

'Would you stop a dog fight?'

'If I had to.' It was no less than the truth. 'Was Gran'dad Tattersall good at that?'

'I've seen him separate mad greyhounds.' Sid Molyneux narrowed his eyes and gazed deeply into Rosie's as he asked his final question: 'Can you tell me – to a farthing – how much you've got in your pocket?'

'Four and sevenpence ha'penny.' The answer came out promptly; her father sent her a five-shilling postal order every fortnight.

'Well that's it then,' decreed Sid. 'That's settled. You're definitely a chip off the old block. If you do as well as him you'll do all right. He was a rum little bugger but he left the world a better place than he found it.'

Stage by stage, Mr Molyneux now proceeded to give her a lesson in developing and printing. Others might have found the process boring; Rosie was enthralled. Eventually, a strip of film emerged from the drying cabinet on a wooden clothes peg. Under the red light's glow Sid put this into a machine like a magic lantern, which briefly projected shadowy images onto a sheet of photographic paper.

They moved back to the workbench where the paper was immersed in an enamelled tank of fluid. Rocking it gently, Sid Molyneux said in a voice other people might have saved for something holy: 'All these years and I still find this moment magic. If you watch you'll see. The darks come in first . . .'

What did he mean? And then Rosie *saw* . . . Shapes were beginning to form on the paper. At first they were like fragments of a jigsaw puzzle and then they began to turn into something specific. The strip of paper was becoming a series of photographs of the Rosie Tattersall of last year. Sunhat, shrimping net, Christopher at her side . . . She was back in the world of Aertex shirts and Clark's sandals.

Here was her father in shirtsleeves, wielding a half-sized cricket bat. There was Connie shaking sand out of a high-heeled shoe; her rhinestone bracelet hadn't half caught the sunlight. It was Ilfracombe and cream teas and the Rover with

113

the windows wound down. One picture had been taken outside W. H. Smith's. Rosie and Christopher could be seen going into the shop to spend their birthday book tokens.

Rosie wondered whether she should be feeling sad. In truth she just felt blank and more than ever behind her plate-glass window. All she could remember about that outing was the delicious smell of new books – W. H. Smith's had always been a highlight of a seaside holiday. The smell inside her imagination was now replaced by the reality of vinegary fumes rising from a second enamelled tray.

'Hypo fixer,' explained Mr Molyneux as he transferred the strip into this solution and began rocking the container. Most people would have found this new odour distasteful. Not Rosie. The smell went with the process and she knew – beyond any shadow of doubt – that photography was going to play a big part in her future.

'You're like Merlin,' she said admiringly to Mr Molyneux.

'Anybody can do it, once they know how. And now you do. By heaven, this little lad couldn't stop a pig in an entry!' It was Zav Hankey on the two pictures before the final shot of Teapot Hall.

Mr Molyneux had exaggerated but Rosie was forced to admit that Zav was just a little bit bow-legged. 'I'd never noticed before,' she said.

'You can't deceive the camera. Mind you, it'll stand him in good stead with the ladies. Women go for it. They'd deny it, if you asked them, but it's a thing I've noticed over and over again. Look at all those cowboy film stars! Look at Prince Philip. That little lad's going to have huge success with women.'

'Huge success with women,' screeched a parrot's voice.

'He's out on the back step in his cage,' said Mr Molyneux. 'He knows I've promised him cuttlefish.'

'*Huge success with women*,' screeched the parrot again.

Mr Molyneux's kind eyes became suddenly thoughtful. 'I'm looking for a woman,' he murmured. 'It's for rather an unusual purpose.' He seemed to feel as though he'd said too much because he added, 'Please don't say I said anything about that to Mrs Hankey. She might not let you come here again, if she knew.'

'Knew what?' Rosie had only been half listening. Most of her attention was centred on the picture of Teapot Hall where a small face could be seen peering through the old flower-room window. The face belonged to Joe Fingers.

'In fact she definitely wouldn't let you come here . . .' Mr Molyneux was now looking downright guilty.

'Fire!' One moment all the homegoing children were busy discussing tomorrow's visit to the circus, the next this single cry wiped circuses to nothing. 'Fire!' 'Fire! Fire!' The cry was taken up on all sides as the urgent sound of the fire engine's bell sent a hundred pairs of feet running towards the school gate. Bernadette Barrett even went so far as to grab Rosie's hand. It was as though this new excitement was turning guarded friendliness into intimacy.

In the midst of the teeming children, Rosie caught a glimpse of Zav, haring ahead with his skiffle group, Bolshuss Baggott and Nadger Nelson and Little Lenin – whose parents were poor and sent him to school in sparking clogs. Today you could see how the footwear got its name. As the boys tore up the street after the fire engine Lenin's clog-irons were striking the pavement fast enough to let off little flashes of lightning.

The fire engine turned the corner. Its young pursuers followed to a thundering extent that had dog-walking old ladies dashing indignantly into doorholes for safety. It was a grey gloomy afternoon. By contrast the scarlet and gold of the fire engine looked splendidly dashing. The men had obviously mounted it in a hurry because as it went past some of them had still been doing up their tunics.

'Run!' implored Bernadette, whose prowess at rounders included the fastest pair of legs in the whole school. As they thundered along Claremont Road, Rosie was just about managing to keep up. 'Can't smell smoke!' bawled Bernadette over her shoulder.

Panting up behind, Rosie was getting the beginnings of a stitch in her side. 'I'll have to stop . . .' she gasped. But the fire engine was already at a standstill. And it had stopped outside the Hankeys'.

'Look!' Bernadette was pointing upwards.

Rosie was more concerned with what was going on in the house, where she could hear Trixie barking her head off. 'I've got a key.' She was desperately looking round for Zav.

'You don't need a key, you need a ladder. Look!'

Up on the rooftop, next to the chimney stack, sat Joe Fingers. He didn't stay still for long. In a moment he was on his feet and dancing nimbly round a jagged hole in the roofing, where a lot of slates had been poked out. Some of them had fallen as far as the iron guttering. The sound of all the children shouting, and the noise of the fire bell, was making him chattering-angry.

'Don't!' yelled Rosie. 'Joe, please. *No!*'

She was too late. In a matter of a split second, a purple slate had been flung down and was smashing onto a fireman's brass helmet. And that was just the first of a furious shower. Sweet Joe Fingers had turned into a little demon.

'Stand back!' yelled the head fireman. 'Everybody onto the far pavement.' As he shouted he dodged a slate, meant for himself. Emboldened by all the attention, Joe had now laddered it up the chimney stack where he was attempting to wrench off the television aerial. In the process he accidentally dislodged a rickety old red clay chimneypot. As it rolled towards the watchers beneath, it seemed to get bigger with every turn, and then its weight proved too much for a front section of the roof – which gave way beneath it. The big clay object disappeared into the house with a destructive-sounding crash. This was only topped by cries from the crowd and redoubled crashes from within.

A small figure detached himself from the onlookers on the far pavement and headed for the front door of number seven. Key in hand, it was Zav Hankey.

'I'm going in,' he called out to the visibly nervous firemen.

'You're not,' shouted the head one. 'And *you* can come back too.' This was to Rosie who had hurried across to join Zav.

'That monkey's a member of our family,' she called back

116

indignantly over her shoulder; she was surprised to see that Bernadette Barrett was behind her.

'You stick up for your rights,' said the freckled redhead firmly. 'I'll knee anybody who tries to stop you.'

Nervously adjusting his helmet, the boss fireman rushed towards them. 'Nobody goes in there till I say so. That place is a potential deathtrap.' He had raised his voice enough for people on the far pavement to hear. One of them now rolled importantly towards them.

'I'm allowed on this side of the road,' she said to the fireman. 'I'm Mrs Jelly from next door.' It was the woman who had been too interested on the night of Rosie's original arrival in Saracen Street.

She was known in the neighbourhood as Pathé Gazette – 'The Eyes and Ears of the World'. These piggy eyes were now raised nervously upwards. 'If he lobs anything from their roof onto mine, am I covered?' she asked the fireman.

'All depends on your insurance.'

Mrs Jelly nodded down at Zav and Rosie as though they had no powers of comprehension. 'Hankeys have only got barest of cover,' she said with grim delight.

'How do *you* know?' asked an outraged Zav.

'If you want to keep secrets, you want to learn to lower your voices. Those walls are like paper. This little lot's going to cost your dadda plenty.' Above them, Joe was plainly up to something entertaining because the children across the road all burst out laughing. 'And it's not as though Mr Hankey's on a big wage,' said Mrs Jelly, with every evidence of satisfaction.

'Didn't your Spirella corsets cost a lot of money?' asked Zav angrily. 'We can hear things from our side too.'

Word of the monkey business in Saracen Street had plainly spread through The Height. Mrs Hankey now panted into view from the direction of the main road. Hazel, weeping lavishly, seized this as an opportunity to join the group by the front door.

'Okay, that's enough. That's it,' said the fireman. 'Put that key away, missus,' he called to Nora Hankey.

'That *is* my dog in there, barking her little head off . . .'

'I wouldn't care,' sighed the woman from the next door.

117

'I was trying to sleep off a headache. Certainly it's your dog, but it's also your monkey that's ripping everybody's roofs to bits.'

'Sod off, Mrs Jelly!' were the last words Nora managed, before several firemen – on a nod from the leading officer – forcibly swept her, and the rest of the group, back across the road. The whole street was out. Somebody had even put Mrs Mitchell, who had a tubercular hip, onto a chair at her front door.

'The way I look at it, we'll have to go up and get him,' said the leading fireman. 'He doesn't seem as though he's going to respond to entreaties.'

'You'd be wasting your time,' protested Nora Hankey. 'In this state he'll only go to Zav. What started this?' she asked her son.

'Don't know. Couldn't I go up through the attic?'

The fire officer shook his head dubiously. 'One heavy pot's gone down already. It could be the whole chimney stack next.'

'It *is* just one baby chimpanzee,' said Mrs Hankey, caustically.

'Yes, but it looks as though demonic forces have got inside him.' Mrs Jelly had a sister-in-law who was a fervent Pentecostalist.

Gazing upwards, Hazel suddenly let out a horrified wail of, 'Look how he's showing us up now! He's waving his nappy and weeing with his widgey.' When she came out of her usual pretty dazes, Hazel was capable of being as dramatic as the rest of her family. 'Cover yourself up!' she called out. More slates came slithering down in reply.

'We'll soon be stripped to the rafters,' gasped Mrs Hankey. 'If you're in charge, all I can say is you'd better crank your ladder up. Get our Zav to chimneypot level.'

'I'm afraid I couldn't accept that responsibility.' Up went the ladder with a lone fireman on the raised platform. Joe Fingers plainly viewed him as a coconut shy. The slates Joe lobbed missed their mark, but the ladder came down quicker than it went up.

'We'll have to try a hose,' said the man in charge.

Mrs Hankey was outraged. 'Over my dead body. And I'm in big with the Mayor.'

118

'We call him Uncle Stanley,' Hazel piped up proudly. 'Me mam's photo's been in the *Salford City Reporter* with him.'

'Crank Zav up,' repeated Mrs Hankey. Suddenly she seemed to be the one in charge. 'Something's frightened that animal into naughtiness. He worships my son. I'll be responsible. You can have me up in court if anything goes wrong.'

Official authority wasn't giving in that easily. 'I think I'd better slip to the phone box and ring down to the station . . .'

'I'll go up with the little lad,' volunteered a young fireman who still hadn't done up his tunic.

'Hold Zav in front of you, like a white flag,' instructed Mrs Hankey. 'You'll come to no harm.'

So that was decided upon. The whole street fell silent as the ladder went up again with Zav and the young fireman on the projecting platform.

'Hold onto the rail, love,' called Mrs Hankey, gazing upwards.

Suddenly seized by an inspired thought, Rosie shouted something up too: 'Sing to him, Zav. He likes it when you sing.'

Zav began to sing:

> 'Yes Jesus loves me,
> Yes Jesus loves me,
> Yes Jesus loves me,
> The Bible tells me so!'

At the repeated sound of his old Biblical name, Joe Fingers danced happily towards the gutter of the roof.

'Come on, lad,' called Zav gruffly. And with one cheerful leap the small animal was safely in his owner's arms.

As the crowd roared its approval, Zav bowed to them from up on high, flashing his teeth as he laughed and hugged the monkey triumphantly. And in that moment Rosie suddenly saw with absolute clarity that, one day, Zav Hankey could not help but become a great big star.

Joe Fingers, back in his cage, was in darkest disgrace. How

119

he'd got out in the first place remained a mystery. But there could be no denying the magnitude of his crimes. Not only had he wreaked havoc from the roof ridge; he had also lured poor little Trixie into the gas meter cupboard – and locked her in.

'No wonder her barking sounded muffled,' said Mrs Hankey indignantly. 'She must have felt like a miner's canary.'

The rent woman, the nosy one in rimless glasses, was refusing to take a sympathetic attitude. 'If it had been an Act of God,' she said, 'our own insurance would have covered it. As things stand, you're liable.'

'I wouldn't care but the little devil's done for the television picture too . . .' Tippler was pointing to the ten-inch black and white set, where Hughie Green could be seen whirling round like a dervish in a snowstorm.

'That's your problem,' sniffed the landlord's representative. 'And I'm not at all sure you should be having a monkey here.'

Mrs Hankey seized the rent book from the dresser and slapped it onto the kitchen table. 'Is there anything printed inside that rent book as mentions monkeys?'

The woman looked nervous. 'I couldn't say without looking.'

'Well I can recite what's printed inside that front cover. Know it by heart. If this was Russia, the state would be providing us workers with accommodation. I bet they can keep dancing bears in Moscow, if they want to.' But this was just for show. 'He'll get his roof back,' she muttered miserably. 'We'll find the cash from somewhere. Bang goes next year's holiday at Butlin's – that's for certain.'

'What about me Butlin's talent contest?' moaned Zav. 'The prize-money was going to buy me a guitar.'

'You should've thought about that before you went and turned us into a Wild West show. He'll get his roof back.' She repeated in dismissive tones.

The rent woman refused to budge. 'It'll have to be done to standard,' she insisted.

Tippler suddenly stood up. 'Were you born heartless?' he

asked. 'Can't you see the wife's stunned? But she's got a nasty paddy too. If I was you, I'd get out while the going was good. I'd sling my blasted hook! If you don't mind me saying . . .' He added the last bit in tones that were more familiar than his sudden fierce defence of his wife.

But it had obviously moved Nora Hankey. 'We'll manage, love,' she said to him, 'we'll manage.' And then she started to snigger: 'Did you know that one of those slates just missed Lily Jelly?'

The rent woman went and the day of reckoning was really upon the household. 'It'll come to hundreds, bound to,' said Mrs Hankey. 'Just let the fire brigade try charging, that's all. Those ladders are public property, and our Zav did all the real work. Still, that monkey's got to go.'

'You don't mean it? You *couldn't*!' Zav had already gone white. Now he turned bright red. 'You'd never think of getting shut of him!'

'You watch me!' His mother was wearing an expression that left no room for argument. 'I've already been to the phone box. The arrangements are made. On Monday afternoon, I'm taking Mr Joe Fingers to Belle Vue Zoo.'

The expected thrill of the next night's circus had turned to ashes. For a start it was in the one place which no child in the Hankey household wanted to think about. The circus took place in the King's Hall, and the King's Hall was part of Belle Vue Zoo and Pleasure Gardens.

Alone in the spotlight, the ringmaster in his scarlet coat and black top hat was intoning into a crackling hand microphone: 'In a few moments, those patrons who are of a nervous disposition will be asked to close their eyes. The St John's Ambulance Brigade are in kind attendance but we do not want their resources to be overstretched . . .' This ringmaster, George Lockhart, was a Manchester legend who had a port-wine voice, like a floorwalker in a superior gents' outfitters; the kind of voice that says, 'I thenk yew.' But he was a dab hand at building suspense.

'Belle Vue International Circus has never spared any expense in bringing its patrons rare and exotic animals from

121

the four corners of the globe. Tonight, we proudly present a human being who is so unusual that he can only walk in our pleasure gardens under the cover of darkness. A living work of art, the world's most tattooed man . . .' The circus orchestra began fighting its way through a bit of eerie Wagner as the ringmaster's voice rose to a crescendo with: 'The nervous should close their eyes *now*. The rest of you, be prepared to blink in amazement. My lords, ladies and gentlemen, we give you – the Great Omi!'

The spotlight flashed off, and when it flashed on again you didn't get much more than a blink for your money. The man standing there was holding open a scarlet satin cape to reveal that he was indeed completely tattooed – in crimson and blue-black – from the top of his shaved skull to the tips of his toes. You just had time to realise that he was also wearing a pair of discreet bathing drawers before the cloak was closed, the lights went up to full, and the Great Omi sloped off through the star-spangled curtains at the back of the ring. Within moments he was back, carrying a stack of signed photographs of himself. These were presumably for sale. But the music had changed to 'Temptation', the interval had arrived – and Rosie knew she had strict orders to fulfil.

Other schools generally went to the circus on a Monday or a Thursday, when the King's Hall was liable to be only half-full and seats were reduced for party bookings. Not Rosie's new school. Mr Lingard had been a benefactor since the days when the school was run by the Church, and this former colliery-owner did things in style. A de luxe charabanc for transport, slap-up seats on a Saturday night, a little box of quite good chocolates for each of the children, and even a docket which you could exchange for an ice cream in the interval.

Rosie was about to forgo this last pleasure. Zav had a plan. He, of course, was sitting with the big boys. But Rosie was under orders to meet him, outside the King's Hall, the moment the interval began.

'It says you can have either an ice-cream or a Koola-Fruita lolly,' said Bernadette Barrett who had been studying the fine print on the docket.

'Have both.' Rosie thrust her own bit of buff paper at Bernadette, who had joined the queue in the foyer. Without offering any further explanation, Rosie headed for one of the glass doors and pushed on the iron emergency bar, which sent it rattling open into the darkness where lions roared in the distance, and caged birds screeched, and buses swished through the rain on distant Hyde Road.

Zav was already waiting for her in the shadows. 'I hate zoos,' he said. The circus was surrounded by one. Belle Vue was one of the last of the great Victorian pleasure gardens; it boasted a fairground, an ornamental lake, an open-air dance floor and mammoth firework displays. Tonight it just seemed full of dismal, rain-splattered darkness.

'We've got to go and inspect Monkey Mountain.' Zav was already striding ahead. 'See if it'll do for him. I know the way, I've been before. I didn't like it then.'

The night air was suddenly rent by a terrible strangulated cry.

'Peacocks.' Zav knew a lot about animals. 'They can't be struck on this place, either. Did you know that Belle Vue's still got a bear pit? A cruel iron thing.'

'I thought they'd stopped using it?'

'I don't care. It's still a cruel zoo. It dates back to the dark ages.'

As the children hurried through the rain, grown-ups were streaming into a building called the Tudor Ballroom. The price of admission to this, or to the circus, gave patrons the right to roam the pleasure grounds at will. Rosie still felt nervous. Bernadette, who loathed authority, wouldn't comment on her absence, but Olive Bucket might notice that she wasn't in the ice-cream queue. Perhaps she'd just assume she was taking a long time to spend a penny. Just as Rosie began to relax, she was horrendously startled by a clattering, roaring, arriving-and-departing noise. One minute it roared in, the next it was gone.

'The Bobs.' Zav was pointing upwards, in explanation, to the wooden framework of an enormous fairground big dipper. 'It's no place to bring up young monkeys.'

They had reached Monkey Mountain – a big slab of rock

123

with a water-filled moat around it. The children looked in vain for signs of any animals. 'They must have taken them in for the night.' Zav sounded even more worried than before. 'He likes to sit in front of the fire at night. I bet they've not got those sort of comforts here.'

Rosie suddenly noticed a curved metal span, like the arch of a small railway station. 'Is that another monkey place?' she wondered aloud. It was covered with wire netting, and a bleak-looking shed stood in the middle.

'Another monkey prison, more like.' Zav's voice cracked. Rosie didn't dare look at him because she was almost certain that he was crying. Once again the big dipper swooped and roared remorselessly. This time it was on a steeper bend and some of the passengers were screaming.

'You've no chance against them,' said Zav. 'I was daft to think you had.'

'No chance against who?'

'Grown-ups. They'll put him in a cage and people'll poke daft things through the bars. And he won't have the sense not to eat them. I'm thinking of dressing him up as a baby and leaving home. D'you want to come with us?'

'Where would we go?'

'I don't know.'

The trail back to the King's Hall – past buildings full of captive animals – was a dismal, silent one. The only thing Zav said was, 'What we really need is friends in high places.'

The door they had left open had clanged shut so they had to motion to Bernadette through the glass to let them back in. 'Hurry up,' she said as she pushed down the iron bar. 'We're watching people having their photos took. The man's got a parrot and a monkey.'

Hearts really can sing – and Rosie's did just that. She had suddenly been struck by a wonderful saviour of a thought. 'I've got a friend in a high place! Well, highish. Joe Fingers needn't go behind bars. Sid Molyneux's already got a parrot. He's dead envious of another photographer with a monkey. Mr Molyneux will have him!'

'Will he be good to him?' asked Zav sternly.

'Well he was good to me . . . nobody's been as good for years. And he wasn't even paid.'

'Rosie,' said Zav. 'I will love you forever.' Not caring who was listening, and there were big boys around, he continued, 'Forever and ever and ever.'

'Please don't.' Rosie was deadly serious and much alarmed. There was nobody she *liked* more than Zav. But he in no way matched up to her long-cherished vision of the broad-shouldered man with black hair and blue eyes. She felt obliged to say it again: '*Don't*, Zav! Don't love me.'

'It's too late now.' He was smiling like the sun coming out. 'I already do. It's all settled.'

5

The 1960s, as popularly remembered, did not begin in Irlams o'th' Height until well into the decade. And yet, when Rosie came to look back, in later life, she realised that the signs had been there from the very beginning. With hindsight, she recognised the stirrings, the rumblings. Mary Quant and Vidal Sassoon had yet to exert one whit of influence on Bolton Road. But at number seven Saracen Street the sounds of skiffle had given way to rock 'n' roll.

The group no longer rehearsed in Nadger Nelson's front room. And they had a new name – Zav and the Hankeys.

The only David Bailey they'd heard of in The Height was a bus driver from Bank Lane; the revolutionary photographer didn't mean a light. But Rosie had maintained her photographic interests. At the age of fourteen she already had a Saturday job. She worked for Mr Molyneux in Gledhill's darkroom where she washed and dried prints and guillotined them to size.

The children were being educated variously. A true Socialist, Nora Hankey had studied all the state educational opportunities; scholarships were expected and won. Zav was roaring ahead at Salford Grammar School. Rosie had limped along at Pendleton High School for two unhappy years. There was nothing wrong with her work but there were girls at the school who had been with her at Elm House – and oh how noisily they pitied her! You could buy the uniform at two shops, and Nora Hankey had settled for the cheaper one – whose buttons always cracked at the dry-cleaner's. Rival establishments spoke of Pendleton High School as 'Pigs' Home for Snobs'.

Nora was not at all satisfied that this was the right place for Rosie. Clifford Tattersall hardly entered into things these days; he just sent a monthly cheque. His daughter could draw well and her interest in photography practically amounted to a passion. Mrs Hankey took on the Education Committee single-handed and managed to arrange a transfer to the Junior Art School, where snobbery didn't enter into things and you were only as good as your talent.

She was having less success with her own daughter. 'That silly little Hazel only worships at the false shrines of beauty and money.' With her enormous green eyes and great tumble of golden hair and the beginnings of a sensational figure, Hazel's sole ambition was to be a model girl. She was presently at a council school called Tootal Road, but she only talked to boys from the Grammar School.

Mrs Hankey was not neglecting her own education. Esperanto, that was her latest craze. Every Thursday evening she would toddle off to the Adult Education Institute, by Lower Mosely Street bus station in Manchester, and learn more of this new international language. She viewed this as her personal contribution towards Utopia. The revolution had failed to materialise so she was now in the vanguard of planet citizens.

'Mi boligos la akvon,' she said as she put on the kettle. The rest of the household were meant to understand that she was boiling water, and to reply in similar Esperanto. Tippler was somewhat limited by the fact that he could only count to five ('Uno, du, tri, kvar, kvin . . .') before he got stuck. He had, however, managed to acquire one full sentence: 'Cu ni dancu?'

It meant 'Shall we dance?' and he used it on every possible occasion.

Zav was forever grabbing hold of his mother's textbook and turning phrases into charades. 'La fantoma estas apcronta,' he declared impressively. And then flung open the lobby door to admit Trixie, draped in a white cotton tea towel. 'That meant, "the ghost is about to appear," ' he added innocently.

'I hope some homework's about to appear,' snapped Mrs Hankey.

'I can do all the studying I need with me *Bert Weedon Guitar Manual*. You can't say I don't get through school exams because I do.' It was getting harder to argue with Zav. At almost sixteen, he looked fully twenty. Well over six foot tall,

127

all the early promise of muscularity was rapidly being fulfilled. Grown-up women neighbours had already started giving him the kind of hungry looks that caused Mrs Hankey to snap, 'You're wasting your time on a little lad.'

But he wasn't a little lad. And his heart belonged to his second-hand guitar, and his Dansette record player, and to his big Grundig tape recorder.

And to me, thought Rosie guiltily. And, oh dear, how I wish it didn't!

'Have you developed me pictures?' Zav asked her.

Developed them? She had hardly liked taking the things. Zav had known exactly what he'd wanted. Carrying his guitar into Light Oaks Park, he had borne it up onto the bandstand, where he had unconcernedly stripped off his shirt.

'Just get the sunlight to catch a nipple,' he instructed her.

'Why?' Rosie's old box camera had now been replaced by a battered Rolleiflex, a present from Mr Molyneux. 'What effect am I supposed to be aiming for?'

'Sex!' His teasing laugh revealed a flash of those white teeth. 'Pure commercial sex. I'm going to be England's Elvis. Except I'm going to be more than that. I'm going to be America's Zav Hankey. You get this picture right and all the rest will follow.'

Seeing Zav through the viewfinder, Rosie began to understand what women saw in him. With a camera in her hand Rosie ceased being a child and turned into a woman herself. But not one who fancied Zav Hankey. Still, the artist in her was forced to admire the shapes his body was suggesting to the lens. He was sex, he was energy, she could have been photographing Pan.

Instinctively, Rosie began to tune into the picture he wanted. 'But the weather's too warm for it,' she said. 'Nipples only stick out when it's cold.'

An ice-cream van's bell sounded in the distance. 'Run and get an ice lolly,' he begged her. 'We'll rub me chest with that.' She made him go and get the lolly himself; but that was how the pair of them arrived at a picture which was to become part of pop history.

All of that was in the future. Now, in his mother's back

kitchen, Zav was repeating, 'Have you developed me pictures?'

'Yes, but I haven't printed them. They're at Gledhill's. Mr Molyneux's expecting me after tea. We've got a whole load of pub pictures to process.'

'What d'you want these pictures for?' Mrs Hankey asked Zav in the kind of tones that suggested she'd be mentioning O levels next.

'Something,' was his evasive reply.

'That's no answer. You seem to have forgotten the meaning of the word homework. All you seem interested in is recording those songs. One day I swear I'll take that Grundig to the tip.'

This was just talk and Zav knew it. 'I've got plans,' was all he chose to reply.

'I trust they include university?'

He was saved from replying by the fact that the door from the lobby opened and Hazel entered, her face plastered in make-up. 'Cu mi estas bela?' she asked her mother.

'Beautiful?' snapped Mrs Hankey. 'You look a downright fivirino.' Turning to Rosie she added, 'When they taught us that word, the person who sprang to mind was your mother.' Nothing beyond postcards had been heard of Connie for years. 'There was a fivirino if ever I met one!'

But from the way Tippler Hankey was beaming, he plainly thought that Hazel was very beautiful indeed. Spreading his arms wide in invitation, he uttered his only phrase in Esperanto: 'Cu ni dancu?' And the pair of them waltzed fetchingly round the kitchen whilst Trixie (the hundo) barked her little head off.

The red light was on in the darkroom. Mr Molyneux was sorting through a pile of prints. These had just come off the dryer. They were of Joe Fingers and Eustace the parrot, with people in pubs. 'And is my photographic composition to your new high standards?' he asked Rosie tartly.

She knew he wasn't really serious. In the six years since they'd met he had turned into a cross between a favourite uncle and a fellow conspirator. It was only recently that

Freddie Click-Click had come between them. This was a photographer who appeared once a week on BBC children's television. The man had a jaunty personality and spotted bow ties to match. He specialised in handing out advice to young photographers. Mr Molyneux considered some of this to be much too high-flown.

Not that he'd ever seen Freddie Click-Click. Sid was always working at Gledhill's when the personality photographer came onto the screen. But Rosie frequently showed evidence of the Click-Click influence in her own pictures.

'Good God!' These days Mr Molyneux was no longer tall enough to look over Rosie's shoulder, so he was peering round her at the photographs in the farthest tank. These were being subjected to regulated swills of water. 'We used to have a name in the trade for pictures like that. We used to call them "a bit under the arm". I presume the young gentleman *was* wearing his trousers? I must say you've left me wondering.'

It was the picture of Zav on the bandstand. More by good luck than by skilled technique, the picture had emerged exactly as Zav wanted. Bare flesh, a flash of guitar strings, the aroused nipple – they were all there. Yet Molyneux was right. The picture was so sexual it could have caused the washing waters to ripple of their own accord.

Sid Molyneux cleared his throat nervously. 'Rosie, I was once foolish enough to tell you that I was looking for a woman – for a certain purpose. I shouldn't have done it. I was daydreaming aloud. Fortunately you were too little to understand at the time . . .'

But she had never forgotten it. It had struck her as a bit eerie – like puzzling Tampax or packets of Rendell's Foaming Pessaries in Gledhill's shop. Mind you, he'd had no hesitation in explaining – in a frank and comfortable way – what those were about. But she had never liked to question him about the 'woman for a certain purpose'.

'I've found her.' Mr Molyneux was all eager excitement. 'This photograph of yours has freed me to explain. For years I've wanted to photograph a lady in the nuddy.'

'The what?' Rosie genuinely didn't understand.

'The buff. Nude. Me and two other lads from the camera club are desperate . . .' Mr Molyneux paused impressively and then said, 'Beryl Meeson has kindly consented to do it.'

'Oh. Who's she?'

'You *must* remember Beryl! She kept getting funny exposures. They were photos of the Church Lads Brigade. It turned out to be a faulty flash attachment.'

'And you're going to take pictures of her with nothing on?' Rosie was in no way shocked. She was used to the senior art students going off to life classes on Tuesdays and Thursdays. But she was very fond of Mr Molyneux so she was worried for him. 'You want to watch it. I bet this Beryl will want something in return.'

'She demands quite a high price.' Mr Molyneux looked half-embarrassed and half-proud. 'She wants Holy Matrimony. And it has to be in a church.' The year might be 1961 but Irlams o'th' Height had in no way started to swing.

'Has she met Eustace and Joe Fingers?' demanded Rosie, quite sternly. Mr Molyneux had no mother to guide him so she felt herself responsible.

'Oh yes. We all went to Peter Pan's Playground at Southport on Sunday. Actually, I could have picked up quite a bit of casual business, but one of their regular photographers cut up nasty. Beryl handled the situation magnificently. While I got the car started, she threatened him with a Thermos. That held him back!'

Rosie removed her prints from the chugging waters. 'I bet the other lads from the photographic club are dead jealous. Where are they going to find life models?'

Mr Molyneux looked a bit embarrassed again. 'Actually, she's going to let three of us take pictures.'

'When you're the one who's going to marry her?' Rosie's sense of fair play was outraged.

'But we've been like the Three Musketeers.' Mr Molyneux was all fervent explanation. 'For years we've done nothing but take photographs of swelling hillsides – while we dreamed of the real thing . . . I couldn't deny them. Besides, Beryl and I are going in for a semi-detached on the Ravensdale Estate.

The lads are going to help us with the deposit. Just a loan,' he added hastily. 'But interest-free.'

'I hope you've seen her with her clothes off,' said Rosie. 'Say you went to all that trouble and she turned out droopy?' She could see by his face that he had not been accorded this privilege. 'You get a good look first,' she insisted.

'It might strike Beryl as a bit commercial.'

Beryl had already struck Rosie as a lot commercial. 'I'd definitely want to see the goods before I bought. Why don't you lend her a camera and get her to take her own pictures in a full-length mirror?'

'I couldn't do that. I wouldn't have the nerve.' Mr Molyneux was looking at Rosie in amused admiration. 'For the last few minutes you've been sounding just like your gran'dad. He'll never be dead while you're alive! You've got merchant blood in you. What if you're right and she *is* droopy?'

Rosie had already been through that thought process. 'She'll still be nice company for you.'

'She will.' He was happy again so there was obviously more to this relationship than Beryl Meeson's bust. Or was there? 'She looks a treat in her swimming cossy,' he said thoughtfully. 'So if the worst comes to the worst, I can do her part-draped. There's a definite market for professional figure studies. There's *Lilliput* magazine and *Health and Efficiency* . . .'

'My father used to keep that hidden at the top of his wardrobe.'

'I'm not sure you should be telling me that.'

'After what you've just told me?'

'Aren't we daft?' beamed Mr Molyneux. 'We're a real daft pair, you and me.'

He often took pleasure in saying this, after they'd had a serious conversation. There was familiarity and safety in 'Aren't we a daft pair?' Now he returned to the subject of Rosie's father. 'When did you last see him?'

'On that awful holiday in London.' Clifford Tattersall had given Rosie a week at the Penn Club, a Quaker establishment near the British Museum. It had been a week of worthiness, full of dispirited expeditions and evasive conversations. It was as though something had died inside Clifford Tattersall and this left Rosie with nothing to latch onto. The only conversation she really remembered had been about his hair.

'Why have you dyed it, Daddy?'

Clifford had sighed as he replied: 'It's just a token gesture to a young man's world.' They went in the cheap seats everywhere and always seemed to be walking through fine rain to one bus stop further along the route – to save the ha'penny. It had all seemed a very far cry from the warm luxuries of Teapot Hall. That was a building which was still standing empty.

Mr Molyneux recalled her to Gledhill's darkroom and today by asking a question about her mother: 'Has Mrs Connie ever married again?'

'Once for certain but we think she's left him. Postcards don't tell you much.'

'Christopher must be nearly a man.'

Whatever Christopher was, he was alive. That much Rosie did know. The distant hum inside her head – the one that proved his living existence – was still there. However, with all the bodily changes that had happened when her periods started, this ability to register him at a distance had got dimmer.

She carried the big wet glossy prints of Zav over to the drycr. Mr Molyneux followed. As Rosie spread out the pictures he began studying one of them through narrowed professional eyes. 'All I can say is, if Freddie Click-Click taught you how to do this, I take my hat off to him. It's nothing short of remarkable.'

'Zav knew exactly what he wanted.'

'The camera loves him,' said Mr Molyneux. 'Absolutely loves him. I'll tell you something else; from the look in his eye, that lad was in love with whoever took the photograph.'

'It was me. You know it was me.' Rosie didn't even want to think about it.

'I certainly do know. And I know something else – you want to watch yourself with Zav Hankey!'

*

133

Suddenly, Bolshuss Baggott was out of the group. One minute he was bashing away on a set of antique drums which had formerly graced the orchestra pit of Salford Hippodrome, the next he was gone.

'The chemistry wasn't right,' was the only explanation Zav offered. This was the first time anybody had heard that expression in Saracen Street. The Sixties might not have come into their own but the potion was bubbling away under the surface. And faint whiffs of the fumes were beginning to drift up to Irlams o'th' Height. Yet come to think of it, they were quite strong fumes. Pop groups in search of a drummer were just as symptomatic of the period as you could get. It was just that nobody had started thinking of it as a period. It was simply happening.

Stray young men began to turn up on the Hankeys' doorstep; some on bikes, some disgorged from the back of vans whose handles were held together by string. Few working-class people owned telephones so messages were passed via a teenage bush telegraph. And the word was out that Zav Hankey needed a drummer.

Most of the lads who turned up were throbbing with ambition but minus a set of drums. One boy called Nigel owned as splendid a collection as anybody could dream of. But he came from the dainty Ravensdale Estate. And Zav dismissed him as 'a right Burton's blazer. There's nothing animal about him. He's not *sly* enough. Can't imagine him smashing up a benzedrine inhaler and eating the middle!' Zav and his friends had started doing this for kicks. The amphetamine-soaked paper gave them extra, artificial, energy. They didn't know what they were doing. They had no idea of what was starting.

'My brother does that too,' sighed Bernadette Barrett. In a heavy Junoesque way she had become almost attractive. These days people were actually dyeing their hair Bernadette's shade of red. And she was short of neither brains nor ambition. What's more, when eventually given the opportunity, she had proved herself a steadfast friend. Even Mrs Hankey had begun to approve of the girl who had once criticized her handling of rice pudding. Bernadette was seizing hold of everything Pendleton High School had to offer; her great aim was to go on to the London School of Economics. And then she wanted to go into politics.

'She'll keep the red flag flying,' said Mrs Hankey. 'If it's left to Bernadette, we could still see barricades in the streets.' Although Mrs Hankey had stopped saying 'Come the day', she had never quite relinquished her revolutionary ambitions. Keir Hardie's picture still glowered down on the front parlour.

Bernadette's family were not precisely Irish. In truth they were settled tinkers who had abandoned their caravans for council houses on the farthest reaches of The Height. Not that Bernadette lived in her mother's overflowing household. She was still lodged with Biddie Costigan who was an unofficial squatter in a converted railway carriage, down by the corporation tip.

This ramshackle dwelling was not very clean but it was tremendously Catholic; you could hardly turn round for holy statues. The windows were hung with old lace curtains, the place was heated by a small black cast-iron stove with a flue-pipe that went straight through the railway carriage roof. All the beds were bunks which were supposed to stow away into the walls, but they were used as seats and you often had to make a bed before you could sit down. Sometimes when Rosie called there would be somebody *in* bed – even at midday. This was always the wickedest of Bernadette's brothers – the one who ate the paper from inside inhalers. Already exotically named after one of the English martyrs, by common schoolboy consent he had acquired a new surname. He was Cuthbert Mayne Mongoose.

Nobody visiting Biddie's shanty for the first time took much notice of the juvenile lodgers. Mrs Costigan was too vivid a personality in her own right for that. It would be impossible to overstate Biddie Costigan's Catholicism. The white-haired woman with the naughty black eyes remembered devotions which even the Pope had forgotten: plenary indulgences, debatable votive offerings, rare saints for weird causes – state your need and Biddie Costigan would come up with the Catholic answer.

Yet there was a core of childlike simplicity to Biddie's faith. She only had short legs and they were a bit bandy, but that didn't stop her roaming for miles. She was always followed by a retired racing greyhound, who shivered a lot, and she always carried a baker's loaf. As she progressed past the tip and towards the slag heaps, she was often surrounded by flights of birds, for she was permanently, and gently, ripping the loaf apart and scattering it before her.

' "Feed ye my sparrows," that's what he said and that's what he meant.' This was her constant explanation – Biddie was more than a bit repetitive. When the loaf ran out she would call into a corner shop and buy another. As she tried to barter for one that was a day old, she didn't sound Manchester and she didn't sound Irish; she sounded a wanderer. And that's what she was. She'd seen a lot of trouble so she understood it in others. That's why the greyhound and the Barrett kids loved her.

Children who didn't know her could be cruel. They would throw stones at her and shout names and pretend to attack the timid greyhound – they liked to watch it shiver. Had they given Biddie Costigan even half a chance they would have discovered that she could look into them, that she could *read* them – and that this could be very useful.

One of the first things Mrs Costigan ever said to Rosie was: 'You hate those glasses, don't you? Well, *don't*. They're just there to do a job of work. What you'll have to do is save up. They've discovered a new invention. They're like little glass windows that you slot into your own eyes. No frames, nothing. Can't tell you've got them in.' With even deeper perspicacity she added, 'It's about time somebody told you that you're beautiful. There's the mirror. Have a look.'

But without her specs Rosie could only see a blur. And with them on, she couldn't see herself for the glasses. She was just specs perched on a nose. And she wasn't at all sure that *that* wasn't too big.

Mrs Costigan had rescued many treasures from the corporation tip. Opening a book of Giotto drawings, she pointed to a similar nose on a Renaissance woman. 'Never let

136

me hear you say again that you could use your nose to spike waste paper. That nose is *classical*!'

Rosie was only half convinced of this but Biddie had filled her with a new ambition. Just as soon as was humanly possible she was going to get herself a pair of contact lenses. Whenever she approached opticians they always said the same thing: 'Go home and come back with your mother.' There would have been no point in appealing to Mrs Hankey to act as a substitute; she viewed vanity in the same light as capitalism.

The first time Rosie ever remembered seeing Bernadette's elder brother, Mongoose, he was running along the spikes of the pointed railings that ran round the graveyard. On the very tips of the points, in plimsolls, fast as a rat. Mongoose was a loner. Though other children viewed him as an outsider, nobody dared throw stones at him. He was dark and broad-shouldered; but he was not the man of Rosie's dreams. He wasn't tall enough and his eyes weren't blue. It was hard to say whether they were green or yellow. And then there was the peculiar black woolly bob hat. Bernadette maintained that her brother even wore it in his bunk-bed.

This was the young man who turned up at Saracen Street and explained to Zav that he hadn't got a set of drums but he was quite sure he owned the ability to nick whatever was required. He also claimed to have *rhythm*, and set out to prove it by rat-a-tatting with anything he could lift up and make vibrate.

'Mongoose?' said Zav when he'd gone. 'He's more like a mad ferret!'

'You'll look like Revnell and West.' His mother was talking about a variety act where one partner was very tall and the other diminutive.

Zav dismissed this with, 'He'll be behind me. He's only going to be supporting – with Nadger and Lenin.'

'Without drums?' scoffed Mrs Hankey. She was not privy to Mongoose's criminal intentions. 'What's he going to bang on? Empty cake tins?'

'He'll find drums.' Zav seemed instinctively confident. 'And when he's found them he'll batter hell out of them. He's a subtle bugger. Did you notice all those sexy sounds he was managing to make with the end of a knife blade?' Suddenly he rounded on Rosie: 'Do you think he's sexy?'

Was she being asked as herself, or as a representative member of female audiences? Nowadays Zav's streak of jealousy was six foot two inches tall. But he wouldn't mind Mongoose appealing to *audiences*. He'd want that.

'Girls will like him,' she said.

'I'm not talking about girls, I'm talking about you.'

'Well I'm a girl . . .' It came out awkwardly.

Zav's reply didn't: 'And you fancy him?'

'No.' That was firm enough.

'Good.' Zav walked out of the room and Rosie could have wished that he had not left her, on her own, with his mother.

'You're going to have to watch yourself.' Once again Nora Hankey was demonstrating just how remarkable she could be. Whilst remaining the most loyal of mothers, she was capable of soaring to eagle-heights and taking the overall view. 'He's more than a bit smitten on you.' Rosie decided that if she said nothing the conversation would end there. She was wrong.

'I know you're only fourteen. And I'm pretty sure you don't feel you're too good for him . . .'

'I don't.' This was the truth. 'I love Zav. But not like that.'

'And there's no bigger problem on earth than two people who can't agree on the definition of love.' The Workers' Educational Association had improved Nora Hankey's vocabulary but the ideas inside her head were still highly personal. 'He sees it as love. Doesn't realise it's only Nature telling him to breed.'

'Well I'm sorry,' said Rosie politely, and only hoping that it hadn't come out as prim, 'but I'm not going to breed with him.'

'I'll tell you what you *are* going to do. You're going to wash your mouth out with soap for saying such a vulgar thing.' You never quite knew where you were with Mrs Hankey for now she continued with, 'Sex is a funny thing. The first time Tippler put his hand on my arm I started rippling in the nether regions.'

'Really rippling?' asked Rosie, fascinated.

138

Nora nodded. 'And fool me went home and said to me mother, "What's wrong with you when you feel as though you've got a butterfly in your doo-dah?" She didn't let me out of her sight for a fortnight. Tippler was barred from the house.'

Rosie was really worried. 'I've never felt like that.'

'You will. And that's when the trouble starts. I don't believe in wrapping up the facts of life. Man is an animal, Rosemary. So never let that damn fool of a son of mine catch you half-dressed. They get these urges. It wouldn't be fair on him.'

Rosie, who was wearing a short-sleeved cotton frock, went straight upstairs and got her cardigan.

These were the months when Zav wrote the first of the songs. Irreverant, sometimes almost surreal, they were full of personal references. Everything was grist to his creative mill. Some of the songs were passionate beyond his experience, yet even when he was singing of true love he specialised in great teases:

'How I love you, Lily Jelly,
Let us fly to Light Oaks Park,
We could make it by the bandstand,
We could brighten up the dark.'

Nora was horrified. 'I just hope next door can't hear you through the wall.'

'The whole world's going to hear me.'

'I'm not worried about the whole world, I'm worried about Mrs Jelly.'

But Zav was already into his next song, 'So Lonely the Great Omi'. And from that he swung into 'Olive Bucket You'll Get Yours!' Forty miles down the East Lancashire Road two boys called McCartney and Lennon were turning their own experiences into more songs. As pretty Donovan roamed the south of England with Gypsy Dave, he too was putting words against chords. It was stirring. It had started. It was moving in New York, where people suddenly found themselves beyond ignoring Paul Simon and Art Garfunkel. In northern California it was with Country Joe, unless you were looking through the sunlight onto the next ridge: The

139

Grateful Dead stood there. Dozens of these talents were beginning to shimmer in seeming isolation. Out towards Los Angeles a girl called Elliot changed her name to Mama Cass, because she'd found a Papa and two more members of one of the new extended families. The dozens of embryo talents metamorphosed into hundreds. Everything was suddenly shifting around and starting to come together. It didn't have a name yet. They just called it *now*. But even in Saracen Street the young were beginning to realise that now was a special time to be alive.

Middle-aged Mr Molyneux had so many dreams invested in Beryl Meeson that Rosie was scared of meeting her.

'I want you to like Beryl,' he said. 'After all, you're my only family.'

This statement startled Rosie. She knew that prior to Beryl he'd been alone in the world. But Mr Molyneux was fully adult so she'd never thought of his 'alone' as being of the same kind as her own. On the face of it, Rosie shouldn't have been lonely at the Hankeys'. But the face of things doesn't reach to the inside. That's where she felt solitary. That's where she realised that the rest of the household was related; and she could never quite push aside the thought that the Hankeys were *paid* to have her. But the idea of being Sid Molyneux's 'only family' struck her as being a bit . . . sloppy. That was before she paused and realised that the friendly little man had also chosen Eustace and Joe Fingers. And if Gran'dad Tattersall hadn't been Sid's hero . . . That settled it: if Sid felt the need for a family the least she could do was oblige him. But, oh dear, it was going to make it harder than ever to meet Beryl.

'We could all go to tea at a café in town,' proposed Mr Molyneux. 'Except I've only got Sundays and not much is open. I'd suggest Blackpool but there's the parking to consider.'

Was he as hesitant as Rosie was herself? 'Do you want me to meet her or don't you?' she asked.

'I want you to *like* her,' he repeated.

'What if I think she's awful?' Perhaps they *were* semirelated: he certainly allowed her to speak familiarly enough. 'I just want to make sure you're not getting a dud. Can she cook?'

He didn't know. Sid set up two separate meetings and cancelled both at the last minute. 'She's as nervous as you are,' he explained.

'What's she got to hide?'

'What she's got she can't hide.' He grinned. But it was only 'all pals together' – there was nothing rude about it.

When Gledhill's had a big rush on, they sometimes processed prints on Friday evenings. These days Rosie was allowed to have her own key to the side door of the shop, so as not to bring Mr Molyneux out of the darkroom. As she let herself in, she saw that the warning light was on, outside the inner sanctum. She could hear muffled laughter coming from inside. She recognised Sid's guffaws but the other voice was female. Not wishing to be caught eavesdropping, Rosie rapped firmly on the door and then called out, 'It's only me.'

There was immediate silence. After a few moments the door opened and Sid peered out. 'You can put the big light on now, Beryl,' he muttered over his shoulder.

The first thing Rosie saw when she walked into the darkroom were some huge glossy prints on the dryer. They were of a jolly-looking woman with a bust the size of two melons. She was stark naked except for a strategically held fan.

'We got the engagement ring on early closing day,' said Mr Molyneux proudly. 'She doesn't droop, you can see for yourself.'

'What an introduction!' The voice belonged to a woman who could only be the photographic model. Her French scent was more expensive than her coat, a big tweed stroller with a nylon fur collar. But there was something generous and expansive about her smile. 'You must be his famous Rosie.' She had strong teeth and brown eyes and dark hair. The woman was little more than a girl and in some ways she looked like a younger version of Connie Tattersall. But Connie had never been motherly and Beryl was; it shone out of her. For the moment she was still preoccupied with the photographs.

141

'Don't show her the back view, Sid,' she protested, 'you can see where my panty-girdle left a mark.'

For a woman with such a big bust Beryl had a very small waist and a neatly rounded bottom. 'I suppose we should have waited till we got married,' she said solemnly. 'But once I'd got that engagement ring on, I felt I couldn't deny him. He had me posing for two hours. I think I'd still be at it if I hadn't caught my derrière on his little paraffin heater. He wanted to rub it with Acriflavine but I said to him, "There *are* limits. I'll rub my own bottom, thank you." '

She was every bit as likeable as Sid. But Rosie soon learned that Beryl was so obsessed with her own bust that she seemed to feel obliged to bring it into the conversation like a shy relative. As Sid went out to put on the kettle she began to confide in Rosie, who was still looking at the pictures. 'This bosom of mine has been nothing but a curse. It's always made me seem what I'm not. I know you're artistic so you won't be shocked. Most men just want to maul my front. Sid's the first person who's ever had a respectful use for it. You're getting quite a nice one yourself.'

Rosie was still at an age where she found her new figure embarrassing enough to want to change the subject. 'May I see the ring?'

It was two rounded diamonds. 'We're having a spring wedding,' breathed Beryl. 'And Sid wants you to be brides-maid.'

'No.' It came out as rude and that wasn't what she'd intended. Rosie tried again. 'I'm sorry but I can't be.'

Kind Beryl looked as though she'd been smacked in the face. 'They're only art studies,' she said quietly.

Rosie felt dreadful. 'It's not that. Please don't think that. It's me.'

'Have you got a little bit of a crush on him?' asked the new fiancée gently.

'No.' Inside her own head, Rosie was darting around for any explanation other than the truth.

'You could tell me. God knows I'd understand. I think he's nice enough to eat.'

'It isn't that, honestly.'

142

Sid came back into the room beaming. Beryl wiped out his smile with, 'She doesn't want to be a bridesmaid.'

How could she explain? It would sound silly. For years they had been processing wedding groups where some poor bridesmaid had spoiled the picture by wearing glasses. Other people might not view it that way, but Rosie did. And she didn't want to be that bridesmaid. She didn't want to be pitied. The engaged couple were looking at her with a mixture of bewilderment and rejection. She knew they had only meant to please, that they deserved better than this.

'We'd have paid for the frock,' said Sid in a hurt voice.

It was no good. She was going to *have* to explain: 'I don't want to show you up by wearing glasses.'

'Is that all it is?' asked Sid.

'Show you up' had come out as curiously Saracen Street. 'Spectacles may seem nothing to you . . .'

As Sid said 'Shut up!' tears began to roll down Rosie's face. He ignored these and carried on talking. 'Shut up and listen. For years I've only paid you half of what you're really worth. Want to know where the rest is? In National Savings Certificates, in your name. And do you know what I've been saving it for? You should do. You've been hankering after them for long enough. Those bloody contact lenses!'

Now Rosie was really crying. Unexpected kindness was the one thing guaranteed to make her weep. But things weren't as easy as he seemed to think. 'You have to go to the opticians with your mother,' she sobbed, 'I don't even know where mine is.'

'That one's easy,' exclaimed Beryl joyfully. 'I'll crack on I'm your mum. What if they *do* think I had you at twelve? Please stop crying or I'll start as well. Oh dear, poor little thing, it's no good, I'm gone . . .' Big tears began to roll down Beryl's cheeks. But this set them all laughing and everything was suddenly as merry as a marriage bell.

'Fancy you swearing, Sid,' sniffed Beryl half admiringly. 'I didn't know you had a "bloody" in you. I knew a lady who had contact lenses,' she added. 'She could tap her eyeballs with a teaspoon.'

Rosie refused to be put off. 'Is the money really there and mine and saved up?'

'It's had your name on it for years.'

Rosie's next line was out almost before he'd finished speaking: 'When can we go and get them?'

'Tomorrow,' said Beryl decisively. 'We'll go to the opticians tomorrow. I was going into town – to Etams – anyway. This bosom of mine is very heavy on brassieres.' There was a lot that was absolutely splendid about Beryl Meeson but it had to be admitted all roads led back to her bust.

Now began the autumn evenings when it seemed as though half The Height was reaching for their coats and heading for the Hankeys' front door. The first to arrive was Little Lenin's mother. A dim, bewildered woman, she was the kind of creature Mrs Hankey described as 'a poor soul'.

And Lenin's mother was a soul in torment. 'I had such high hopes for that boy,' she sighed, 'and now he does nothing but dance to your Zav's tune. I never see him. And when he *is* in, it's nothing but Radio Luxembourg on at full blast. He's meant to be a sixth-former and he never so much as opens a book. No wonder they've took away their prefects' badges – it's nothing but music, music, music.'

Nadger Nelson's parents arrived to voice similar complaints. 'It's these gigs they go on,' grumbled Ben Nelson. 'They're getting further and further afield. Last weekend it was two ballrooms on Merseyside!'

'*And* he came back with a love-bite,' said Mrs Nelson, in tones that suggested Nora Hankey was somehow responsible.

When Biddie Costigan turned up, it wasn't so much what she said as what she did. She arrived at the front door in a van driven by an undoubted gypsy who proceeded to help her unload Mongoose's set of drums onto the pavement. 'I've nothing against what they're doing,' beamed Biddie, 'but I reckon it's your turn to stomach the noise. I've had enough. Zav takes the lion's share of the profits so you can have the aggravation.'

'Zav writes the songs.' Nora Hankey wasn't turning into Shirley Temple's mother, but nobody was allowed to criticise her son. Especially not a Catholic tinker from out of a shanty of a railway carriage.

Rosie watched all of this going on through her new contact lenses. At first they had felt a second cousin to grit in her eye. That soon passed and the only problem left was a dread of smoke-filled rooms; smoke made her eyes smart. It had also to be admitted that when she took them out in the evening it was as great a relief as removing tight shoes. Sometimes she even swapped back to her glasses. But choice entered into it now. And she didn't mind one bit being a girl who *chose* to be seen in specs.

The person she finally allowed herself to examine in the mirror – through her new lenses – came as a surprise. There was no mistaking her inheritance of Connie's fine complexion and Clifford's amused eyes. His eyes had sparkled like that when the twins were little. But the thing Rosie was awed to discover was that Biddie Costigan had been right: the girl in the looking glass was well on the way to being beautiful.

If this should have released her from behind her private pane of glass, it didn't. Self-pity didn't enter into it. Anybody orphaned who has ever been a long-term paying guest will understand exactly how Rosie felt. In her own mind she was still in this world on polite sufferance.

That autumn, the most exciting caller of all was first heralded by loud cries from children in the street. Nora sent Tippler into the parlour to peer through the lace curtains to see what was going on.

He returned with, 'There's a Rolls-Royce outside Jellys'. They must have come up on the pools.' Now came a knock at their own front door. This time Mrs Hankey didn't send Tippler – she went herself. And Rosie couldn't resist following her.

Big Lily Jelly was on the front doorstep and she was pink with excitement. 'This gentleman mistook me for you . . .'

'Then he must want his bumps feeling.' Nora was refusing to be impressed.

Children were already swarming over the bonnet of the limousine and a uniformed chauffeur had emerged from the car and was attempting to swat them off with a kid glove. The man standing on the doorstep took no notice of this. Saracen Street had a word for the supremely well-dressed. It was 'immaculate'. And that's what this man was – sleek and immaculate.

Yet he's not as upper-class as he'd like us to believe, thought Rosie. The clipped black hair, the dark overcoat like a second skin, the carefully knotted spotted foulard scarf – all of these looked purest Mayfair. But when the man spoke he had a marked cockney accent. 'I'm Danny Cahn,' he announced.

'Would you mind asking your chauffeur not to say "fuck"?' asked an unblinking Mrs Hankey.

'Don't say fuck,' Mr Cahn said without so much as removing his own eyes from Nora.

He's trying to charm her, thought Rosie. He's out to woo and win her with those dark spaniel's eyes. And he's chosen the wrong one.

Or had he? 'Thank you,' said the fierce little woman, 'you'd better come in. That will be all, Mrs Jelly, ta.' Company manners were definitely the order of the day and as they reached the kitchen Tippler was already struggling into an unaccustomed shirt.

'This is Mr Cahn.' Nora nudged Trixie off the best armchair and indicated that he should sit down. There was no servility in this, just basic Saracen Street politeness. Mr Cahn remained on his feet and began to shake hands with Tippler.

'Any connection with Genghis Khan?' asked Tippler too innocently.

His wife shot him a warning glance as she said, 'There used to be a Cahn's raincoat factory at the back of Cheetham Hill.'

'Cousins of mine.' Danny Cahn smiled easily.

'Now I *am* impressed.' When Nora said this Rosie could hardly believe her ears. But Mrs Hankey went on to elucidate: 'Cahn's were one of the first raincoat factories to welcome in the unions.'

Dapper Danny was obviously a man who knew how to capitalise on a stray hint. 'We are, after all, in the city of Friedrich Engels,' he said impressively. 'Whenever I'm near my cousin's factory, I like to feel I'm treading where Engels trod. I believe Karl Marx was up here for a short time too?'

The whole of this conversation had been accompanied by

146

splashing ablution noises from the back kitchen; Zav was always a noisy washer and he could also be heard singing 'The Great Omi' through the closed door.

Danny indicated this door with a thumb. 'That sounds remarkably like the young man I've come all this way to see.' The door opened and Zav walked in wearing nothing but lean muscles and a pair of clean but shrunken underpants. There was nothing shrunken about their bouncing contents. Cahn's eyes flickered – almost imperceptibly – towards Zav's middle. But it was perceptible enough for Mrs Hankey to dart her husband a significant look. Tippler returned this with a slow wink.

'Cover yourself up,' said Zav's mother sharply.

But her son had registered the Jewish visitor. 'I don't believe it!' he exclaimed. 'Who'd ever dream that Danny Cahn would walk down that old strip of carpet in our front lobby! Did you get me tape?'

'And the picture,' smiled Danny.

'Was it that photo that Rosemary took? The one that always makes me feel uncomfortable?' asked Nora Hankey belligerently. 'Do as you're told, Zav. Get some clothes on.'

Zav reached back into the scullery for a pair of Levis. 'What did you think of the songs?' he asked.

'I smelt gold.' Danny was still smiling. 'I've had my spies out watching you. I got good reports back. That's why I'm here.' Now he turned the beam of his attention onto Nora Hankey: 'I've come to make him a star.'

'Well you've come to the wrong shop. He's going to university.'

'A very creditable statement. You and my own mother would seem to be two of a kind. But I resisted higher education and I've not done badly. That car outside's paid for *and* I've got a Jag as well.'

'And where's your culture?' snorted Nora.

'On my bedroom wall. Two original Picassos. Where's yours?' He wasn't scared of her, though he did correct himself: 'No. That was wrong of me. I know where it is. It's invested in your son. But there are more ways of breaking an egg than hitting it with a big stick. Pop music has bought me a

147

penthouse in Holland Park. And believe you me, when you come from down the City Road, that's class!'

'Big talk's cheap enough,' snapped Nora.

'I've come to talk big action.'

Nora rounded on Zav. 'A shirt wouldn't come amiss, either.'

'Me dad's got mine on. He must have snatched it off the chair when the knock came.'

Danny Cahn picked one of Trixie's hairs off the sleeve of his dark cashmere overcoat. 'Zav could soon be in the realm of silk shirts.'

Nora remained belligerent. 'Who are you and what's your game?'

'He's only one of the biggest managers in England,' gasped Zav.

'And not unknown in the United States of America.' Danny was still behaving like a man in charge of the situation. 'Are you this young genius's girlfriend?' he asked Rosie.

It was Nora who answered: 'No she's not. She's just the lodger. And don't you go filling my son up with daft ideas. Some genius!' she snorted. 'He's barely got the sense to come in out of the rain. You seem very full of your own importance, Mr Cahn. You turn up here, unasked; you talk about turning him into some kind of ten-minute wonder . . .'

'I'm talking long-term contract.'

'Then state your terms,' rapped out Nora. 'Not that you'll win me over.'

Danny Cahn finally sat down. This inevitably put him at risk of further doghair but he didn't seem to mind. The plan he began to unfold was like nothing that had ever been heard in any back kitchen in Saracen Street. Zav might have dreamed of it, but here was the proposed reality of recording deals and television appearances and nationwide tours in first-class venues. Cahn had worked proven magic for other boys and now he was drawing back a veil to show them his idea of the transformed, polished version of Zav and the Hankeys.

'We can't be expected to speak for the other lads' parents,' interjected Nora.

'Nobody's asking you to do that. Quite frankly, the other boys are disposable.'

'No.' Zav was adamant. 'I want them. They're part of how I'm doing it.'

'Then you shall have them.' Danny Cahn lit a cork-tipped cigarette and Tippler reached quickly for an ashtray for him.

For some reason this seemed to infuriate Nora. 'Who are you to say what my son can and can't have? Who d'you think he is – "Popo the Puppet"?'

'I'm someone who can't bear to see talent going to waste.'

'Yes, and I think you're someone who'd try and manipulate a herd of wild elephants. Well you're not manipulating me. This family needs to discuss this matter in private.'

'I've come a long way . . .'

'Then you'll probably be glad of a nice little sit-down in my front parlour. Here's the *Daily Herald*. The parlour's down the lobby on the right. And make sure you shut the door.'

'I'll show you the way.' Zav was all eagerness.

'You'll do nothing of the kind.' His mother headed him off. 'You're needed here.'

'Don't sit on the settee,' Tippler called after the departing figure, 'that old Rexine's a bugger. The cold strikes right through.' The door to the lobby closed and then they heard the parlour door being opened. Only when that too had rattled shut did anybody speak.

'He's a poof,' said Nora Hankey. 'Did you see where his eyes went?'

'He was only looking,' pointed out Tippler reasonably. 'Zav's big-built. Other fellers wonder how their own would size up against it.'

'Don't talk so vulgar,' snorted Mrs Hankey. 'Will it stop at looking, that's what worries me. He'll have to be spoken to. And that's only if we let you do it,' she added, turning to Zav. 'This is what comes of sending suggestive pictures of yourself through the post.'

'But you're not going to let me miss this chance? You couldn't.'

'I don't suppose I could.' She said it almost sadly. 'No, I don't suppose I could.' Suddenly she was fierce again: 'But we're the ones who have to sign. You're under age. You heard him say that. Answer me honestly, Zav, how important is he?'

'He's massive. He's in the first four and it's hard to say who's top.'

'Flaunting your body . . .' But the fight had gone out of her. 'Well, nobody's going to be able to say that I stood between you and your big chance. Kids! You offer them every opportunity and they still go their own sweet way. Get him back in. You fetch him, Rosie. But he will *have* to be spoken to.'

The route to the parlour was all creaking floorboards. 'They've finished talking. Could you come back in?'

'Why haven't you got a Lancashire accent?' he asked.

'Because I'm an outsider.' Nora Hankey's 'just the lodger' was still stinging.

The Hankey family were grouped round the kitchen in awkward silence. 'I think Father's got something to say to you.' Nora nudged her husband significantly.

'Me?' Tippler's voice came out in something like a squeak. 'What have I got to say?'

Nora's eyes went impatiently to the ceiling. 'If you want a thing doing, do it yourself!' She transferred her gaze to Danny Cahn. 'We know what you are and we've nothing against them. I knew one before, nice lad – went under the name of Gloria. All I'm saying is, when it comes to our Zav, you've got to keep your hands to yourself. Understood?'

Danny Cahn was not one whit abashed. 'He's not my type,' he replied in tones which sounded absolutely honest.

'Do you lads still get in the Fitzroy Tavern in London?' asked Tippler cheerfully.

Nora looked, to say the least of it, startled. 'And what would you know about such places?'

'I bet he was in the navy,' beamed Danny. 'All the old matelots know the Fitzroy.'

Nora wasn't beaming. 'And you went in a place like that?' she asked her husband.

'Never for anything more than a pint of mixed.'

His wife looked marginally mollified. 'I'm very glad to hear it. Mind you, Lily Jelly says she only goes out for the conversation.'

150

'Is there a real Lily Jelly?' asked Danny eagerly. 'I really loved that song on the tape.'

'I told you those words would only lead to trouble.' Nora picked up the fly-swatter and landed Zav one. But it was quite an affectionate swipe. She had no idea of the merry-go-round that Danny Cahn was about to set in motion. Even Danny Cahn had no idea of the size of that.

As Zav's cropped hair grew so did the successes. By the time it had bushed out into a curly blond Afro style he was already a regular on *Top of the Pops* and *Ready, Steady, Go*. And the name Lily Jelly was known the length and breadth of Britain.

'Yes I'll find you, Lily Jelly,
And I'll bring you to my side.
By the bandstand, past the nettles,
We will ride, ride, ride.'

'I could sue you know,' said the next-door neighbour. 'Half the Wagon and Horses are encouraging me to get legal aid. People keep saying it's funny how a little lad could have got feelings for an older woman. I don't agree. I think he did it for revenge, because I never let him have that ball back.' But she was more flattered by the attention than she was annoyed. Lily Jelly was having a genuine Sixties experience – she was being famous for fifteen minutes – and she was loving it. She even enjoyed throwing a bucket of cold water over an in-depth reporter from the *New Musical Express*.

Soon Zav and the Hankeys had their own fan club. Their very first long-playing record, *Hankey-Panky*, shot straight to the top of the charts; and in next to no time the boys were crossing the Atlantic to appear on the *Ed Sullivan Show*. Just who, Rosie wondered, did American audiences imagine Olive Bucket was? They could have no doubts about the Great Omi – the sleeve of this album featured a picture of the group standing against a blown-up reproduction of his tattooed face.

As Rosie turned the pages of their fan magazine she marvelled at Danny Cahn's skill. Zav was being sold as distilled sex appeal. Mongoose was mischief in a woolly bob

151

hat. Little Lenin (now nearly six foot tall) had been packaged as a gangling clown, whilst Nadger Nelson, who had always struck Rosie as being as dull as his sandy hair, was presented to the world as 'sensitive'. He was the one who was supposed to be buying his parents a new house. It wasn't true but it looked good in print.

Irlams o'th' Height was not overimpressed. It never is. When the boys came home on a flying visit they went everywhere by taxi – which had always been considered suspect in the village. 'The higher they climb, the further they'll fall,' was the general opinion.

'But they can't smell the air up here,' said Zav. 'It is fucking beautiful!' He said that word a lot these days. But he only dared do it once in front of his mother. Out came the carbolic soap and, star or no star, he was led, protesting, to wash his mouth out at the kitchen sink.

But Nora was proud of him. Fiercely proud. When Zav interpolated a chorus of 'The Red Flag' into one of his songs, people wrote letters to the BBC and to *The Times*. What, they asked, was the youth of this country coming to? In the end, that track was only allowed to be played on commercial radio and pirate stations – but the first time she heard it on the wireless Nora Hankey wept with pride. 'If he's still remembering the people's flag,' she said, 'he's not gone far wrong.' Of course all he got to his face was: 'Still doing the barber out of an honest living?'

The banned song caused if anything more of a furore in America. There was even talk of Zav's visa being revoked. Danny Cahn handled that. Danny handled everything. Other managers of that period worked their groups into the ground and then moved on to exploit other new talent. Danny had his eyes set on long-term international success. If Zav was to achieve this, Cahn knew that he had to be free to return – from time to time – to the source of his material. Zav had to be able to recharge his batteries and write new songs: and he did that best in the north of England.

'It's good to be home,' said Zav. 'It's good to know I'll be sleeping on that old flock mattress again.'

If this remark should have pleased Nora Hankey, it didn't.

152

Rosie wondered whether this had anything to do with the cheque. Hazel Hankey had just finished a course in shorthand and typing; and now Zav had written out a cheque in favour of a woman called Sheelah Wilson who ran Manchester's biggest model agency.

'What does she want to go and learn modelling for?' demanded Nora fiercely. 'She's vain enough as it is.'

Hazel had plenty to be vain about. At sixteen the natural blonde hair was piled on top of her head in a style which resembled a beehive. The fringe beneath framed a pair of huge, lazy green eyes. Men in two-tone cars had started waiting at the corner for Hazel Hankey.

'Modelling?' snorted Nora. 'The girl's in a permanent daze! One of these fine mornings I swear she'll fall off those high heels she wears. She'll make a nice model with a ricked ankle. Wake up, Hazel, I'm trying to talk to you!' These days Mrs Hankey was forever comparing her own daughter unfavourably with Bernadette Barrett. At the last election Bernadette had spent a whole week leafleting houses. 'She's going to be the next Ellen Wilkinson,' said Mrs Hankey with pride. Red Ellen, a former Member of Parliament who died in office, was a Manchester legend. Politics still took precedence over pop music in Saracen Street. And politics left Rosie cold. Odd sly remarks of Nora's had her wondering whether she was viewed as a Conservative spy. The only time she ventured to say she had yet to form any political sympathies, Nora countered with a speech about people having died in order to give women the vote. You couldn't win.

'I've got to go and see a man about a box,' said Zav. 'D'you want to come with me?' he asked Rosie.

'What sort of box?' Mrs Hankey might have been in like a gimlet but these days Zav was made of hard wood. All she got in reply to her question was a sly wink.

'You get more like your father every day! Go with him, Rosemary, do me a favour. If you say you'll go he'll get out from under my feet. I don't think I've so much as shaken a rug since he landed in from Paris.'

As the two young people got out into the lobby, Zav said to

Rosie, 'Have you still got the key to Teapot Hall? Can you bring it?'

Minutes later the pair of them were swinging round the corner of Swinton Park Road where the outline of Teapot Hall stood on the skyline. 'Are we really going to see a man about a box?' asked Rosie.

'Two boxes. I'm going to start making time capsules.'

Rosie suddenly found herself thinking about Beryl Meeson who was Beryl Molyneux these days. The photographer's new wife said of Joe Fingers, 'I could only say this to another woman but he's getting to be a big lad. He's very conscious of the fact I'm female. I always feel I've got to watch my back.' Rosie felt the same way about Zav Hankey.

'I'm going to make a box for my life up till now,' he explained, 'and then a time capsule for each year.'

'What will you put in them?'

'The first one's going to have my birth certificate and school reports, and photos of Trixie and Joe Fingers, and me old *Bert Weedon Guitar Manual* . . .'

'Why do we need to go to Teapot Hall?' She hadn't so much as been up the drive in two years. This was not lack of love – decrepitude had made the place hard to visit. In her own mind there was a half-formed idea that, one day, she would somehow make enough money to be able to offer her father a minimal sum for the bricks and mortar. And then she'd make some more money and restore the house. 'What's Teapot Hall got to do with your time capsules?' she asked.

'That's where I first saw you.' His tone suggested she shouldn't be needing a explanation. 'I saw you through the hawthorn hedge and I'd like a souvenir from inside.'

'Oh,' was what she said aloud. But 'Oh dear. . .' was what Rosie was really thinking. Would he never let go of the idea that they were made for one another? Whenever he said things like this she found herself widening the gap between them: physically making the space a few inches wider. There could be no denying it was very like Beryl Molyneux and the chimpanzee.

As they reached the Roman Catholic church, its front door was pushed open and Biddie Costigan emerged on a whiff of stale incense. She was all beaming smiles and bandy legs. 'I've just been burning a candle for the new album,' she said. 'I see that it's sticking a bit in Scandinavia.' Biddie read all the musical trade papers. She had them delivered. The newly rich Mongoose was generous with her so, these days, she had the bread for the birds delivered. Biddie tore a crust from her loaf and broke it into bits. 'I'll never take to the name Bert Mongoose,' she said, wrinkling her nose. 'Why can't the papers call him Cuthbert? Is it true you've all started smoking drugs?' Biddie never wrapped anything up. 'I've lit a candle for that too.'

Fame hadn't taken away Zav's ability to blush. 'You don't want to believe everything you read in the tabloids,' he stammered.

'I've already questioned Mr Cahn about it,' she said. 'Told him that the Jews and the gypsies should stick together this time. It strikes me you lot use pot like your daddas used mild ale. Only pigeons get crust . . .' This was said sternly to a sparrow. The usual flight of birds had begun to flutter round her. 'They wait for me on the gate while I'm in church,' she explained. 'Know what the words on the gate mean?' She was pointing at the inscription, *Porta Caeli*.

'The door of Heaven.' Zav had done Latin at Salford Grammar.

Biddie's naughty little black eyes narrowed as she gazed at Rosie and Zav. 'You make a nice pair,' she said.

'But we're *not*!' It was out before Rosie could stop herself.

'That's not how he sees it,' said Biddie. 'And you know how stubborn he can be. You'll find you're dealing with a lad who's already moved one set of mountains.' A handful of bread went up into the air, the birds spread round her like a fluttering fan, and Biddie Costigan began to roll towards the main road. The noise of flapping wings half obliterated her final utterance but it sounded something like, '. . . big changes on the corner.'

What corner and what big changes? Rosie wanted to think about anything that wasn't to do with her relationship with Zav. But Zav was the kind who could even grab hold of wreckage and turn it to his own advantage. 'I get hundreds of letters from girls every week. Cahn's got a woman in the office who does nothing but send out photos. You should see some of the things those kids write. Their mothers'd die if they read them. I could have me pick. It's the same after every single show. But it's not what I want. I only want . . .'

'No!' Rosie was almost shouting. 'Don't be fool enough to say it.' Now she found herself struggling for words. 'What we've got is good. It's special. Why try and turn it into something else?'

'What have we got? You name it.'

She couldn't. It was all too dangerous. He was not her brother and he was more than her friend.

'What's wrong with me?' he persisted.

'Nothing. It's not you, it's me.' The dream she had dreamed all those years ago in the Friends' Meeting House – dark hair, blue eyes, broad shoulders – had never left her. If innermost dreams can't be unreasonable, what can? Anyway, she thought, who says it's unreasonable – it's just me.

'You're not a lesbian, are you?'

'No.' She knew what the word meant. She was in the Senior Art School now and stories had circulated about a girl called Phil who had a duck's-arse haircut and always wore trousers. 'No, I'm not a lesbian.'

'Nadger Nelson likes boys.' Zav stated this very matter-of-factly. Perhaps he was glad to change the subject. 'We didn't find out till Hamburg. You should see some of the trans-vestites there – they'd blow your mind!'

'Is that what he goes for?' Rosie too was glad to talk about something – anything – else.

'No. He likes men. They've got to look as normal as possible or he isn't interested.'

'Did Danny Cahn start him off?'

'He didn't need starting off. It's just how he is. Whatever lights your candle – that's what I always say.' Youth was moving into the much-heralded Age of Aquarius. 'You don't half have to watch yourself with those cross-dressers in Germany. They're brilliant at making you feel a real he-man.'

'Zav!' Rosie was only pretending to be shocked in order to keep the conversation away from his passion for her.

'I never did anything,' he said. 'But you can see how people

156

could fall for it. Some of them are sensational-looking, real boobs and the lot. It's a bit eerie.'

Teapot Hall was looking eerie too. Early winter afternoon mist was hanging over the top of the tower and a yellowing poster on the front door said *Beware: It Is Dangerous to Enter These Premises*.

'Big house for one family,' observed Zav, as Rosie struggled with the key. She was glad he didn't offer to do it for her. The house was hers in everything but name. Just don't let him offer to buy it for me, she prayed inwardly. If he did she might have to let him, and that would mean faking loving him – and she couldn't do that.

The key turned in the lock. The glass in the two sets of inner doors had been wantonly smashed since her last visit, broken smithereens carpeted the entrance hall; glass and abandoned V.P. wine bottles and the casings from old fireworks and an empty purple and white Durex packet.

'You've got mail.' In the gloom, Zav held out something he had found behind the door. The damp picture postcard was of Marilyn Monroe. The stamp was American. The postmark was December 1963. It must have been lying there for nearly a year; posted in somewhere called Cheyenne, Wyoming, and written by Christopher. Her twin brother's handwriting had turned American. The message read, 'Will this ever find you? I am a bit blue but full of hope. What I was expecting never happened. Can you wonder? But there are ways of making it happen. Enough said. Chris.'

'What does it mean?' Zav had been unashamedly reading the message over her shoulder.

'It's The Secret.' It was out aloud before she realised what she was saying. 'It's Christopher's secret, not mine. I can't explain.' Rosie was listening for the buzz inside her head. Though it was down to a minuscule thrum, it meant that Christopher was still alive somewhere. And the postcard showed that he was still obsessed with that mysterious business which had haunted their early childhood.

Zav had the sense not to pry. He knew about bonds between brothers and sisters. 'I'm bothered about our Hazel,' he said. 'I wouldn't say it to anybody else but she's getting a bit too keen on brand labels and luxury. If she's not careful she'll end up a snob.'

From outside the house there came a clattering noise, like iron poles hitting the ground. It sounded like a game of cast-iron spillikins. Zav rushed for the front door, closely followed by Rosie, who was glad to leave behind the stale urine-laden atmosphere of the abandoned house. Out on the front drive, workmen were throwing scaffolding from a lorry onto the ground.

'Hey you!' shouted one who seemed to be in charge.

'Is that us you think you're bawling at?' Zav was bristling dangerously.

'You've just come out of private property,' said the man. There were three of them altogether, and the youngest muttered something about Zav Hankey getting his end away.

Zav was on him in a second, thumping and pounding. 'You'll pigging take that back,' he stormed. 'Bastard loose-mouth!' It took the other two workmen to drag him off. As he kicked and struggled with them he shouted, 'This young woman's family own the property.'

'Oh no they don't,' said the foreman. 'It's been bought by the Local Health. It's going to be turned into a nurses' home.'

Zav had only brought Rosie to Manchester to cheer her up. He had even risked getting on a 77 bus; but homegoing schoolgirls spotted the star and kept trying to make him kiss them, so at Pendleton they had swapped into a taxi.

'Think of the Health Authority as caretakers,' Zav said to Rosie in the cab. 'Anything's got to be better than the place being used as a public convenience.'

'But they'll change it,' was all she could manage to reply. Her head was full of rotating visions of blocked-up fireplaces and a modern central heating system – she had even managed to grow a red-brick annexe in the grounds. 'They'll alter it and it won't be Tattersall's any more.'

'It's years since I heard anybody call it that.'

'I've never stopped thinking of it as ours. Never . . .' She was crying now. 'Even when rooks got in and those tramps started a fire. I just thought that one day I could go to Daddy and say, "Here's the money, I want it for my own." '

'It wasn't a very realistic thought.'

That did it. Rosie began shouting. 'Did you ever think realistically? No, you didn't. But you made it all come true. Why should you be the only one? Why shouldn't I be able to make my things come true?'

His arms were suddenly round her. 'Shh,' he said. 'If you believe enough, it'll turn out right in the end. That's all I did – I believed.' Half of her was marginally comforted. But as the cab swung round the bend near Salford Station, throwing them even closer together, a warning voice inside was telling Rosie that Zav was getting more out of this unaccustomed proximity than she was.

The taxi driver slid back his glass partition. 'Do you want me to take the pair of you to a hotel, mate?' he asked Zav.

The pause before Zav answered was only fractional. 'No I do *not*. This whole town seems to have sex on the brain.'

'P'raps we're all influenced by your records,' grinned the driver. 'Look what you wanted to do to Lily Jelly!'

Zav let go of Rosie and said, 'Just take us to one of those coffee bars at the back of Deansgate.' There was a whole crop of them. They were relatively new. 'Not the Mokarlo, it's too piss-elegant.'

'And you certainly wouldn't want the Pansybar, Zav,' laughed the driver. That was the unofficial name of an establishment properly called the Zanzibar. The cab nosed its way up an alley, near to the Hidden Gem Church, and disgorged them outside somewhere brand-new. It was called Vesuvius. 'This town's beginning to catch up with the times,' said Zav, as they piled down a wooden staircase and into a basement with a stone-flagged floor.

The décor featured papier-mâché palm trees against murals of erupting volcanos. That's what the management had provided. The customers had added stripes: black, magenta and duck-egg blue ones on the scarves of students from Salford Tech; blue, green and white ones belonged to people at Manchester University.

A lot of the boys had begun to grow their hair and had

already acquired the cool attitude that went with this look. Although Zav was drawing sidelong glances, he could expect to go unpestered.

'Cappuccino?' he said to Rosie. 'Rosie, I'm talking to you.'

But there was absolutely no chance of her hearing him. None. In her head she was hearing that piece from the Bible: 'Intreat me not to leave thee and forsake me not . . .' Standing by the cash register, paying his bill, stood the man she had drawn, all those years ago, in the Friends' Meeting House. '. . . thy people shall be my people, and thy God my God.' Black hair, broad shoulders and blue eyes – he wasn't crayon scribble, he was flesh and blood. And he was alive and he was here in Manchester.

6

That was the winter when a dream turned into an obsession. One glimpse – before he disappeared up the stairs and into the street – that had been enough to throw her whole life into focus. She had to find him again. If the childhood fantasy had grown out of a quotation from the Book of Ruth, Rosie took the text for her search from the Song of Solomon: 'I will rise, and go about the city in the streets, and in the broad ways I will seek him whom my soul loveth.' All this on the strength of a single glance at a man by a cash register? Yes. Unhesitatingly yes.

The only person who was privy to the details of Rosie's search was Bernadette Barrett. Biddie's shanty was no place for serious study, so Mrs Hankey had encouraged the young Socialist to bring her books up to Saracen Street, where she could do her homework in peace, in the front parlour.

'Trust me to have to go and borrow a kid from down by the tip to live out my dreams,' she said. 'What if the gas fire does set me back a few bob a week? It's a small price to pay for helping to put a woman in Downing Street.'

Not much homework was being done this evening. Rosie, whom life had taught to be secretive, was discovering that the only relief to be had from the pain of this heady new passion was in talking about it. More precisely, in talking about him. He even had a capital 'H' inside her head. Whenever she thought about him during the day, she allowed herself to draw a big 'H' on the edge of the page of her rough sketch pad. Seventy-four such letters was her record to date. In the pottery class she even incised a clay vase with a border of Hs in scraffito work. In lettering lessons she chose to make garlands of the words Him, Him, Him, – until her teacher asked whether she had perhaps embraced religion?

'Oh yes,' she answered fervently. 'But it's a religion all of my own.'

161

People in this state are impossible to be around, and Bernadette was getting nowhere with the Tolpuddle Martyrs that evening. 'I'll let you talk about him for three more minutes,' she said firmly, 'and then I've got to write five hundred words on outside attitudes to oppression.'

But what was there left for Rosie to say? 'It's a bit like that old song. "I did but see him passing by and yet I'll love him till I die."'

'You're barmy,' said Bernadette. 'You need a Fenning's Cooling Powder or something. One glance at this man. . .'

'That's all it took,' said Rosie happily. 'And I have to be quite honest, the first and second things I noticed about him were his bottom. Two neat handfuls. And that was before he turned round and I actually recognised him. The bottom came as a bonus. He's got the lot!' She hoped she didn't sound smug. Not that she felt smug; she felt ripped into bits. Some of them were warm glowing bits and others made her squirm with embarrassment. But if she was behaving ridiculously she didn't care – except she did. It was all wonderfully painful. But how to explain? 'It's just that I *recognised* him,' she said defensively. Her spirits suddenly soared again as she added, 'And I'm pretty sure I had the same effect on him.'

'Well he's certainly not going to any great trouble to find you again!'

'How do you know?' cried Rosie. 'We could both be searching Manchester from end to end, and just managing to miss one another. If only he'd worn a *scarf*! At least I'd know whether he's at the university or at Salford Tech. Still, the fact that he didn't proves that he's bigger than the bad weather.'

'Or that his wife was washing it at the time.' Bernadette began sharpening a pencil in the manner of a young woman who had almost had enough. 'Anyway, Salford's a university too, these days.'

'How could he afford a wife on a student grant?'

'How d'you know he was a student?'

'It was the most intelligent face I've ever seen.'

Bernadette remained unconvinced. 'Shop assistants from

Kendal's go into Vesuvius. When you *do* walk into him, the first thing he'll probably say will be, "Cash or account, madam?"'

'I wouldn't care. Anyway, he couldn't be working at Kendal's, he was in an open-neck shirt.'

'And I expect you counted the hairs on his chest.'

'What hairs? There weren't any. Stop it!'

'No, you stop it. I've got work to do. No man's going to secure my future for me.'

'Oh he won't secure my future,' said Rosie, away in her dream. 'Our careers will grow together. Me with my photography. Him with whatever it is.'

'Would you still love him if he was a binman?'

'In handmade Italian loafers? Talk sense!' Rosie drifted out of the parlour and creaked down the lobby towards the kitchen where she could hear Hazel getting it in the ear from Nora Hankey.

When Hazel had finished her modelling course, her mother had been of the opinion that it would lead to a job. Nine to five, Monday to Friday. Sheelah Wilson preferred her girls to work on a freelance basis. A set of photographs had to be taken and circulated to other photographers, who rang in to the agency and booked girls on an hourly basis. These Wilson girls also seemed to attend endless auditions for fashion parades. It was true that models from this Manchester agency worked all over the world. But when it came to earnings it was a case of either feast or famine. A whole lot of well-paid jobs in a lump and then nothing for weeks on end.

This method of earning a living offended Nora's work ethic, so she had taken herself to town and confronted the redoubtable Miss Wilson in her all-white lair. Rosie had accompanied her landlady on this brave outing, and had listened fascinated as voices rose to an extent which set the crystal chandeliers a-tinkling.

Nora did not pull her punches. 'You do realise you're peddling flesh, don't you?'

'Certainly,' said Miss Wilson. She pronounced it 'Sortainly'. She had quite the poshest voice in the Barton

163

Arcade and, with her enormous eyes, looked like a startled roe deer – but blonde. In her time, this former model had taken on Balenciaga, and won. But she'd never been confronted by a Mrs Hankey before.

'Our Hazel's got a hundred and eight guineas outstanding on photographic jobs.'

'My dear, don't I know it! And seventy-five of that's from one big catalogue session. I simply can't get the money out of them.'

'I could,' said Nora.

The huge eyes narrowed appreciatively. 'I'll bet you could. Mrs Hankey: you and I might be able to do one another a bit of good. How would you like a little job – debt collecting? I'm afraid it would have to go through the books. I don't believe in swindling the system.'

Had Sheelah Wilson but known it, she could not have said anything more calculated to impress. Nora believed that Socialism went hand in hand with social responsibility. 'I'm afraid I'm a retired person,' said the woman from Irlams o'th' Height. 'But what you *could* do is get our Hazel a proper job.'

'Doing what?'

'Modelling.' It came out as 'mogelling' because that was how Nora always pronounced it. 'Isn't there some way it can be done on a regular basis?'

'There's *wholesale*.' The fastidious Miss Wilson could have been talking about soiled knickers. 'There's nothing more nine to five than wholesale.'

'That'll do,' nodded Nora. 'Does it come with a wage packet at the end of the week?'

'A rather small one and flat feet and bunions. My dear, they have to put the clothes back on hangers and stow them on rails. You'd never want that for your daughter.'

'Try me! It'd be a sight better for her than sitting round the Kardomah with that Lorraine – the pair of them painted up like Red Indians. You get her into wholesale and I'll collect a few debts for you as a favour. It'll make a nice little hobby for me.'

And that's what happened. Nora proved a dab hand at

culling in the money and Miss Wilson – good as her word – got Hazel a job at Mamavin Fashions. It was in the same building as the old Coconut Grove Club. An unlikely friendship grew up between Mrs Hankey and Sheelah (by now they were 'Nora' and 'Sheelah') and they could sometimes be seen sipping coffee, and examining cheques, in the sedate setting of Sisson's Tearooms in St Ann's Square.

All of this had started before Christmas. Now it was March. As Rosie came from the lobby into the kitchen Hazel was sitting in the rocking chair, painting her toenails. Her mother was just putting mint sauce onto a cold lamb sandwich, intended for Bernadette in the front room. Mrs Hankey was of the school which believes that brain work needs feeding.

'D'you know that Sheelah thinks we're Communists?' she said. 'We had a funny afternoon. She tried to force me to buy a little black dress and I gave her a lecture on the National Health Service. She'll think twice before she goes into a ropy private nursing home again. She wanted to know how you were coping with the spring rush at Mamavin's.'

Hazel had a quick inhale of the nail-varnish bottle and then screwed the top back on, 'I'm sick of Mr Vincent and I'm sick of his mother. I've walked out.'

Nora slapped the sandwich onto a plate in a fury. 'A personal friend of mine is good enough to go to the trouble of getting you a job and. . .'

'I've walked into something else.' Hazel was calmly unabashed. 'I've already been doing it for two days.'

'What sort of something?' This came from Tippler who was down on his hands and knees doing something mysterious with an oil can and one of the oven doors.

'I'm a promotions girl.'

'Meaning?' asked Mrs Hankey dangerously.

Hazel remained calm. 'It's dead mod. You wouldn't understand.'

'Try me. Go on, try me. And I just trust this job doesn't involve standing in Lewis's Arcade saying "Good afternoon, sir" to lonely gentlemen!'

Hazel giggled. 'You're not far wide of the mark. I go to

165

town and I go to these offices and that's where we have to change. This week it's a red and grey mini. Just like one of Jackie Kennedy's, with shiny white plastic boots. They come right up to the middle of your thighs.'

The oven door went to with a clang. Tippler rose to his feet. 'And what do you do in this get-up?' he asked worriedly.

But Hazel wasn't worried. 'Me and Lorraine have to go to the station. And when the trains come in, we go up to businessmen and say, "Excuse me, sir, do you smoke?" If they say yes, we hand them a packet of three. It's a new brand of filter tips called Yorks. Would you like some, Dad? I've got dozens in my modelling case.'

Nora Hankey had gone even paler than usual. 'And what if these men say "No I don't smoke but how would you like to come jitterbugging instead?"'

'We're trained to handle that.' Hazel was now rubbing Johnson's Baby Lotion into her long sleek legs. 'Do you need the ironing board for anything, Mam? I want to have a go at ironing my hair.'

These days Hazel wore her hair like a medieval pageboy. It hung straight and shining to her shoulders. But her mother was interested in neither hair nor ironing boards. 'That job stops now,' she proclaimed adamantly.

Hazel refused to be riled. 'It pays a bomb. I'll give you extra money for my keep. The cigarette job finishes tomorrow and then we're off to Rochdale Co-op. It's a little green uniform. We're doing Batchelor's packet soups; the secret's in the whisking – you do it in a tin pan.'

'You're nothing but a demonstrator,' snapped Nora Hankey.

'I know it might look like that now. But when the Motor Show comes, we'll all be going to London to sit on cars, in bikinis. Fords particularly asked for Manchester girls because the buyers like the accent. You serve them cocktails.'

Nora shook her head. 'Somebody else does – not you.'

'If you don't let me I'll leave home.' There was no threat

in this. It was a calm statement of fact. 'I'll leave home and go in a furnished flat with Lorraine.'

Nora's mouth went into a tight line and then she said, 'Do you know what Sheelah Wilson says about Lorraine?'

'No, but I know what Lorraine says about Sheelah Wilson!' The phone rang and Trixie started barking. The telephone was still newly enough installed for a call to be an event.

Mrs Hankey was obviously much thrown by the conversation with her daughter, and had yet to get used to the idea of a telephone of her own. 'Teapot Hall,' she said, automatically, into the receiver. 'And just you stop laughing at your mother, Zav. How are you? He's in San Francisco again,' she said to the rest of the room. 'What's the weather like? That's nice. Zav, I'm glad you're on. I want you to talk some sense into your sister. It seems the mogelling's gone out of the window. She's turned into a kind of geisha girl for advertising. Here. . .' Nora pushed the receiver into Hazel's hand. 'And just remember it's a pound a minute.'

'Hiya, Zav. Would you bring me back a pair of Levi hipsters? Get me men's, they're better cut round the bum. . .I'm being a promotions girl. . .Yeah, dead happy.' There was another pause whilst Zav was obviously talking some more and then Hazel laughed and said, 'I expect we'll welcome her into the Sixties in about nineteen eighty-two.' When Hazel smiled she turned into a different person. 'Who? Yeah, hang on. He wants you.' This was to Rosie.

'How's San Francisco?' she asked.

There was a tiny echoing pause before his voice came through with a sucking sound: 'Magic. Actually I'm across the bay. I'm in Berkeley. We're doing a free concert on the campus. Berkeley is something else! It's the city at the foot of the rainbow and I'm *very* mellow.'

'What does that mean?'

'You'd have to be here to understand. Everybody should come here.' He sounded different, more relaxed, almost languorous. 'Listen, man. . .'

'I'm a woman not a man.'

'I'm very glad to hear it. Danny's had an idea. You know

the old picture you took of me with my shirt off – the one on the bandstand. You can't move for it here. It's on everything from posters to tee shirts. We're being ripped off left, right and centre. Danny wants you to have a go at shooting a new image.'

'Me?' Rosie could hardly believe what she was hearing. 'Why me when you've been done by Bailey and Richard Avedon?'

'Because you did the one that worked. We're in England through April. He thought you could come on tour with us. Catch some shots as we go. On the bus, Rosie, on the road. . .'

'I thought you went by limo these days?'

'Gave it up. Too lonely. You know me, I'm just a humble Irlams o'th' Height boy at heart.'

'Your mother says to remind you it's a pound a minute.'

'*Cashbox* keeps trying to convince me I'm a millionaire. Can I tell Danny that we'll catch you at the beginning of April?'

'You sound very American.'

'I'm international, Rosie. And I'm offering you the chance to be the same.'

At this point Nora snatched the receiver, bawled 'Goodbye,' and replaced it on its cradle. But the cult of youth was under way. The younger generation were winning through on every creative front. And even Nora Hankey was powerless to prevent that.

The Sixties were full of songs about people being 'on the road'. This phrase was a throwback to the Beat poets of ten years earlier. The updated reality could mean anything from prolonged hitchhiking to a pop group playing a tour of one-night stands. They didn't just do this at the beginning of their careers; they went on long tours, over and over again, to reinforce chart popularity with the energising magic of a personal appearance. And all the audiences did was *scream*.

Zav was supported by three other groups who played the first half of each show. These were rising young talents from Danny Cahn's stable. For all the notice the mostly female

168

audiences took of them, they might just as well have stayed at home. 'Zav, Zav, we want Zav.' 'Panky-Hankey, Hankey-Panky.' 'Zav Zav Zav Zav Zav. . .'

'And if the seats aren't damp when we've finished, we've failed,' said Mongoose.

Zav threw him a warning look. He didn't approve of talk like that in front of Rosie. The show was over for that night. They were backstage in a dressing room at the ABC Cinema in Norwich. The hotel where they were meant to be spending the night had just sent a message to say that their premises were a Grade Two listed building so they regretted that they couldn't accommodate the boys.

'What's that got to do with having us?' asked Rosie.

'It's the fans,' explained Dave, the road manager. 'They rip bits off the building for souvenirs. I wouldn't care but I booked the whole deal in my name. Word must have spread. These hotels are getting as cunning as us. I've used Rosie's name for Cardiff,' he added to Zav. 'Two suites, nine double bedrooms, room service galore – and we still have to travel incognito!'

'And how are we supposed to get out of here alive?' asked Mongoose. Normally they ran straight from the stage into cars, already waiting at the stage door to take them to the hotel. There was rarely time to check in until after the show.

Cries of 'Zav Zav Zav' rose up again from ground level. 'And that's not going to stop till somebody puts their head out of the window. You do it, Dave, you're nearer,' said the object of all the waiting fans' interest.

'I'm busy autographing your pictures.' Dave, a hulking great lad from Salford, was long past being impressed by fame.

Zav who was busy cleaning his teeth said, 'You put your head out, Nadger.'

'Put your own fucking head out, I'm eating a cheese-burger.'

Zav walked across to the frosted window and threw open the Thirties metal frame. A concerted scream rose up through the night. Zav waved dutifully to the crowd below and slammed the window shut. 'Any head would have

169

done,' he said. 'All they need is a blob against the electric light.'

'Won't it just make them scream more?' asked Rosie.

'You'd think it would but it doesn't.' Nadger slung the remains of his cheeseburger into a wastepaper basket. 'You get a pause while they talk about it amongst themselves.'

Rosie immediately saw the sense of this. A second glimpse of the man she saw in Vesuvius would have sent her straight off to discuss the matter with Bernadette. But there had been no second glance.

'I don't care whether the hotel will have us or not,' said Nadger. 'Somebody's got to get me there. I've got a heavy date lined up in the bar.'

'One day you'll find the police waiting for you,' said Cliff. Homosexuality was still illegal in England.

'A handsome copper? Yes please!' Nadger began to remove his stage make-up. He was the only one who bothered to do anything round the eyes. Zav and the rest of the group just slapped on a bit of suntan pancake and left it at that.

'I'm supposed to be connecting with a guy at the hotel.' Mongoose looked worried.

'Not another bent chemist?' asked Zav. 'Not more of those bloody purple hearts? Speed kills. It definitely kills. You see that written up on half the walls in California.'

'What's speed?' asked Rosie.

'Pep pills.' Lenin had looked up from reading his *Beano* comic. 'I've still got some dexies left,' he said to Mongoose. 'You can have a few if you want.' This was one of the meanings of getting by with a little help from your friends.

'I'm seriously thinking of saying drugs are out,' announced Zav.

The road manager's eyes went immediately to the dressing-room door. 'Keep your voice down.'

Mongoose marched straight up to Zav. 'You're thinking of banning drugs? *You* are? Just who d'you think you are – King Dick?'

'I'm somebody who could go solo tomorrow. And less of the King Dicks. I've still not forgotten that photograph.'

'I didn't mind,' said Rosie hastily. 'Honestly. I just wanted to see the quality.' Mongoose sniggered and Zav dealt him a swipe which sent the the famous bob hat flying across the room.

The photograph in question had been taken at a motorway service station. The sign had read *Your Own Photo Delivered in Four Minutes*. These machines were something new. Mongoose had gone into the booth, climbed up on the seat, drawn the curtains and unzipped his pants. The resulting photographs resembled a small orchid on a black velvet cushion. In the fourth shot the stamen had been more prominent. But all Rosie had been interested in was the quality of the print.

The photographs that Rosie was supposed to be taking on this tour were not coming easily. The camera went everywhere with her, but the results were no better and no worse than any other competent photographer could have achieved. Rosie found herself haunted by one question; had that famous early image been a lucky fluke? This thought put her talents in chains – sometimes she was so afraid of failure that she couldn't bring herself to take the cover off the camera's lens.

Where were they all going to sleep that night? No room at the inn was nothing new on this tour. Worried hotels had started cancelling all along the way. When this happened, the standby routine involved packing everybody onto the single-decker bus and driving on – through the night – towards their next date.

The coach was like a long narrow tube of subdued light, speeding through the darkened countryside. Motels were as yet unheard of in England. Rosie was the only girl on the bus. Big Dave had assigned her a whole seat to herself, behind Zav, with the suggestion that she should stretch out and try to get some sleep. 'Get your head down,' he'd said. Rosie found herself wondering why she found the expression distasteful. It sounded like something long-distance lorry drivers did, in ramshackle places with signs outside saying *Good Pull-Up for Drivers*. Would even these places welcome them? And say they did, what would the sheets be like?

Somebody at the front of the coach was playing 'Unchained Melody' on a guitar. The tune was being picked out delicately, carefully, even ironically. She heard Zav saying to Dave, 'There's always some talented sod in the next dressing room, just waiting to grab the crown.'

What were the words of this song? Something about lonely rivers crying 'Wait for me, wait for me. . .' Rosie found herself wondering whether the man from Vesuvius was waiting, somewhere, for her. Wasn't a quarter to three in the morning supposed to be the hour when terminal patients in hospitals were said to be most likely to give up the ghost?

The coach had sped into an area lit by street lamps and Rosie decided to stretch her legs. Walks down the central aisle of the charabanc were the social highlights of the journey. The bus was only part-full so it was often possible to sit down and talk.

Lenin was reading another comic, *Dandy* this time. Rosie watched him pass a flat half-bottle of whisky to Nadger Nelson, who dribbled some into his can of Coca-Cola. Nadger had a black and white pocket-sized book on his knee; *Man Alive* it was called. He seemed very relaxed about being seen with soft-core pornography. 'I quite fancy this one,' he said to Rosie. He was pointing to a picture of a body-builder in a Roman helmet and a posing pouch. 'In Sweden you can get them without the white bags over their thingies.' He wiped the neck of the whisky bottle with a paper handkerchief and offered it to Rosie.

She shook her head and moved further down the aisle. The bus jolted and she suddenly found herself pitched next to Mongoose. 'Sorry,' she apologised and made to rise.

'Don't be,' he said, pulling her down again, 'I'm bored out of my skull.' The whisky bottle was now passed over the back of the seat and Mongoose took a deep swig. He too offered it to Rosie.

'No thanks, but have you got any Imps?' She and Mongoose shared a passion for these tiny, hard black

172

liquorice pellets. Mongoose pulled his Imps tin from out of his embroidered Afghan coat pocket. The boys had all brought these Indian coats back from California. 'I'm out of blackies but I've got something else. Open your mouth. . .' He dropped a couple of small yellow tablets – each the size of an Imp – onto her tongue.

She had thought they were miniature dolly mixtures but the taste was too bitter for that. Not wanting to spit them on the floor she swallowed them instead. 'Mongoose, they tasted vile. Whatever were they?'

'Just something to see you through the night.' A flash of mischief sparkled in his eyes. And just as quickly it was gone. 'D'you think our Bernadette's going to make anything of herself?'

'I'm certain of it.' The tablet had left a brackish afterglow in her mouth. 'Come on, Mongoose, what were those things?'

His reply, when it came, was relaxed and easy. 'They just give you a bit of zip. Like black coffee, but you don't have to keep on drinking the stuff.'

Rosie began to feel reassured. Her search round coffee bars, for the Vesuvian, had got her well used to espresso. She and Mongoose fell into desultory conversation about Bernadette's addiction to politics. But the conversation didn't stay lethargic for long; it was soon followed by a much livelier discussion about Biddie Costigan. Did Mongoose really believe that the old woman's prayers to certain specific saints, for difficult causes, worked?

'All I can say is St Jude got *Hankey Panky* from nowhere to number one in Sweden. And St Jude's meant to be the patron saint of lost causes.'

It was the words 'nowhere to number one' that had the dynamic effect upon Rosie. Suddenly she wanted her camera in her hands and she wanted to take pictures. Here and now. In one flash she'd seen what had to be done. The real Zav was the man who travelled through the night. This was the image that would take her new pictures to the top. Rising to her feet, Rosie darted back up the aisle and fished

173

her Rolleiflex out of her totebag on the overhead luggage rack.

'Are you asleep or are you just dozing?' she hissed over the top of the seat in front.

'I'm playing around with the words of a new song, in my head,' was Zav's mumbled reply.

Rosie was back into the aisle in a moment and already adjusting her camera. 'The bandstand picture was great,' she said excitedly, 'but it was all too much on a plate. They got to see the lot. Unbutton your shirt to just one before the waist but don't pull it apart and don't make it look posed. Zav, no, don't lick your lips. Keep on feeling dreamy. Now, just slide that hand inside your shirt and idly smooth it up and down your chest. *Yes*! And again. Now lower your head a fraction, bring your eyes to camera, and think about sex.'

He looked rumpled, he looked tousled. It was hard to tell whether the man in the viewfinder was just thinking of getting into bed or getting out of it. But one thing Rosie did know, Zav looked like the spirit of *now* – and a million of his fans would find that infinitely desirable. Not Rosie. To her it was just a job of work. 'Okay, you can button yourself up again.'

'What brought that on?' Zav asked. He was now fully awake and highly curious.

'I didn't think I could do it but I did.' Rosie flopped down happily beside him. The only trouble was she didn't want to stay flopped down. She was absolutely charged with energy and she couldn't stop biting her lower lip. 'I think those little yellow tablets might have helped.'

'What tablets? Jesus, the pupils of your eyes are pinpoints! You've been on speed. Who slipped you that?' Ignoring the fact that they were on a bumpy bit of road, he got up, pulled Rosie to her feet and began to propel her down the aisle.

'Was it these two?' They had got as far as Nadger and Lenin.

'No,' protested Rosie. 'They were just reading.'

'And such brilliantly intelligent material,' he snarled. 'A comic and a wank book!'

'Lighten up,' said Lenin. 'We're your friend, not your enemy.'

'They learned to talk that shit in San Francisco,' glowered Zav. 'And they rode the whole way to California on my back. Did Dave give you that pill? Answer me. Because if he did, this is where he gets off the bus.'

'No, it wasn't Dave.' Rosie was getting scared.

'Who was it?'

'I'm not telling you.'

'You don't have to. I've just remembered who scored some dexies in the dressing room. Right, piss-face!' They had reached Mongoose. 'Did you give Rosie speed?'

'It was only prescription stuff.'

'Whose prescription? Certainly not yours. Know what you are? You're *nothing* in a daft hat! I could find half a dozen session guys who would riff you out of the studio.' Mongoose made to rise, Zav pushed him back into his seat. 'You've just done it on your own doorstep, Mongoose. You're out! And the wanker and Dumbo go with you. I won't let Danny down. I'll play the last bit of the tour. But after that you'd better start learning "Thanks for the Memory". I'm going solo.'

As she twisted and turned – sleeplessly – on a noisily sprung mattress in a Welsh hotel bedroom, Rosie Tattersall began to have some understanding of a currently fashionable word. Wrecked. That's how she felt – wrecked. And her eyes were refusing to stop tracing the outline of the geometric design on the purple and orange wallpaper. Triangle, circle, cube. Triangle, circle, cube. Triangle. . .

Even after the noisy exchanges on the bus had subsided, she had clung to the belief that Mongoose's magic tablet had been a miraculous way of unleashing talent. That it might be an idea to get hold of some more. First she would try to sleep in the uncomfortable seat, and then she would give the matter some thought. But relaxing had proved to be an impossibility. Though Rosie ached with fatigue, her brain had continued to race. As the bus reached a motorway she wasn't just biting her bottom lip, she was grinding her teeth as well.

'Zav,' she said, 'everything's going faster and faster in my head and I can hear my own heart beating. I don't think I like it.'

'P'raps we should give her a downer,' suggested a worried Dave. 'Some people just can't take speed. A red and green sleeper should balance things out.'

'We give her nothing,' said Zav. 'Nothing at all. The amount she's taken won't kill her. She's better off learning the hard way. What gets me is that *choice* didn't come into it. . .' He looked more than a little concerned. 'D'you feel okay, love?'

'I feel as though I'd like to do ten different things at once. I'm tired out but I'm still bursting with crazy energy. And I'm desperate for another wee.'

In all, they'd had to stop the coach seven times for her. Amphetamines force liquid out of some people and Rosie was proving to be one of them. These same people often find that the initial rush of euphoria is replaced by all-enveloping gloom. This had started to take control of her even before they reached the Welsh border. Plate glass, she thought, plate glass, plate glass. I have spent half my life behind this window. Why am I always on the outside looking in? People must think I'm as cold as my own camera. And I don't *want* to be cold.

The bus journey had seemed never-ending. Just as she was beginning to give up hope of it ever happening, a grey dawn broke and they rolled into Cardiff. And now Rosie was clanging around on this awful hotel mattress. Her sense of hearing felt peculiarly heightened, the inside of her mouth could have been lined with suede; that personal sheet of thick glass had never felt so murky. And the curtains in this room were too thin, they let in the light. Oh no! The design on the curtains was the same eerily absorbing one as on the wallpaper. Circle, triangle, cube. Circle. . .She only stopped counting them when her bladder pushed her yet again to the bathroom. If this was drugs, they could keep them.

As Rosie sat on the loo, she tried to comfort herself with the thought that there were only two concerts to go. One here and one in Bristol. And after that they were bound for London. This carrot had been held before them throughout the whole grinding tour. Danny had vowed that their break in London would be purest pleasure: 'I'm going to show you a good time' – that had been Danny Cahn's promise. But he had reckoned without Zav's inherited fighter's instinct.

The two young people from Saracen Street were in Danny's top-floor flat. Five floors below, outside on the pavement, a small army of reporters and photographers were awaiting further developments.

'At least it makes a change from screaming girls,' said Zav. He sounded somewhat indistinct – his upper lip was still swollen.

Rosie, not even wanting to think about the horrors of the unexpected fight, was still peering through the slats of the venetian blinds. 'There are girls down there as well. Plenty of them. Two have just arrived with a banner, but I can't quite make out the words.'

'That settles it; you can't go out and have your hair done, Rosie.' Danny had come in with a tray of coffee. In a crisis he was a tremendous mother hen. And this was definitely a crisis. 'Those girls will have seen you described as his constant companion in the *Daily Mirror*. One lot of blood-shed's enough. I don't want a stabbing incident on my own front doorstep. Some of those fans are rabidly in love with him.'

The phone, which had never been still all morning, rang yet again. Almost immediately, the bell of a second telephone began shrilling. The tray went down onto a smoked-glass and chrome table. 'If that's New York, about Zav, I'll get straight back to them,' Danny called out to an invisible secretary. 'And keep the conversation very positive,' he added. 'Smile while you're talking!' Sinking down onto a white leather sofa he sighed. 'I may never smile again. And it'll take a lot to get me back to Bristol.'

This was where the fight had taken place. 'Would you please straighten my Andy Warhol, Rosie? It's hanging crooked. Brian Epstein keeps trying to tell me it's a fake. Would I have a fake? Zav, go and put some more ice on that black eye.'

177

Zav stayed where he was. 'I wonder if they had to put Lenin's nose in splints?'

Rosie was straightening the big picture of an electric chair. 'You *could* have a fake,' she pointed out reasonably. 'After all, you always told us this penthouse was in Holland Park. The address is Kensington High Street.'

'Don't be so picky. It's still in the W8 postal district. Princess Margaret still lives next door. And, oh Christ, she's somebody else who's supposed to be meeting Zav and the Hankeys next week.'

'She'll just have to meet me on my own,' said Zav.

Danny began to pour the coffee. 'After today's headlines she'll probably be terrified. They make you sound so volatile.'

'I am volatile.'

'Yes, dear, but was there any need to cut such a swathe? Did you really have to send all three of them flying?'

'When they were pissed? If I'd warned them about whisky and Coke once, I'd warned them twenty times. They were nothing but bloody amateurs. They were just playing at it. They were pissed onstage.'

Danny sniffed irritably. 'There was still no need to chuck Mongoose into the audience. He'll sue, you know. Just see if he doesn't.'

'And did *you* know that he tried to grope Rosie, on the side of the stage?'

She could feel herself going scarlet. 'You said you wouldn't say anything.'

'That was before everybody turned me into the villain. I'm just saying what I saw. Other people saw it too. I'm sorry, Rosie.'

'Don't be sorry, children – either of you. I'm not.' Danny looked relieved and delighted. 'Somebody crack open a bottle of champagne!' he called through the open door. 'If he tried to feel up Rosie, we're out of the wood and through the trees. All it needs is a sworn affidavit. Trouble was bound to come one day. I knew it. That's why I made sure their contracts weren't worth the paper they're written on.'

Zav looked Danny straight in the eye. 'P'raps I ought to be taking legal advice on the strength of *my* contract.'

Danny waved away the thought with a well-manicured hand. 'Any lawyer in the land would tell you that yours is rock solid. I happen to love you. And your talent. The other three were tats.'

Zav pulled a packet of Rizla cigarette papers from his blue jeans pocket. 'Tats is the right word for them. How was I ever going to be able to go and meet Elvis with that lot stringing along behind me?'

'Aren't you the naive one?' asked Danny. 'And Elvis hasn't got tats of his own?' He watched Zav extract three cigarette papers from the packet, lick the gum on one and begin sticking it to another. 'You wouldn't by any chance be thinking of rolling a joint?'

Rosie's sense of fair play was outraged. 'Zav! I thought you were against drugs? I thought that was meant to be the biggest argument against Mongoose.'

'I'm against speed.' He stuck the remaining paper down the side of the other two. 'Speed's chemical, hash is natural. It doesn't do any harm.'

'Until they find it does,' said Danny. 'I sometimes think I should go away and hide in a corner – I'm so out of touch with the times!'

'You wouldn't be on your own,' sighed Rosie, 'I'd be there with you. Is there something wrong with us?'

'No, dear, they're all rolling joints to be unusual. That's what *they* think. The truth is they're just being conventional in a different way.'

More than ever, Rosie seemed to be dividing herself from the rest of her generation. But she had never liked the idea of drugs. And after her recent experience she certainly wasn't going to change to please the fads of the year of 1964.

'How old are you, Rosie?' asked Danny.

'Seventeen.'

'Never been kissed, kicked or run over! And I thought *you'd* been in a bloody accident!' This was directed at Hamish, the chauffeur, who had come through the door bearing a large, greasy brown paper bag and a big yellow Kodak envelope. Hamish was *called* the chauffeur; though this tough young Glaswegian lived in the flat, however hard you counted the bedrooms it was impossible to work out where he slept. Rosie had drawn her own conclusions.

'Two hours to get three salt-beef sandwiches!' exclaimed Danny. 'We could have *walked* to the Nosh Bar in Windmill Street in the time.'

'Lex Car Park was full,' grunted Hamish, 'and I had to pick up Rosie's pictures as well.'

As he handed over the envelope she noticed, for the first time, the enormous size of Hamish's hands. Girls at the art school maintained that if you measured from the back of the middle of the hand to the end of the longest finger. . .Never mind that. The pictures from the tour were back.

The black and white ones were in sheets of contacts. Dozens of miniature prints – one of each shot she had taken. As Rosie scanned through them, she relived the creative doldrums of that journey from one ABC Cinema to the next and the next and the next. The pictures were boring, pedestrian; they looked like cheap imitations of a dozen other photographers. She turned to the final sheet. Over her shoulder, Zav let out a thrilled whistle.

'You've done it,' he shouted. 'Danny, quick, look! She's absolutely hit it.' These were the pictures taken on the bus.

Danny was all excitement. 'Talk about come-to-bed eyes! These shots would get us locked up in the Bible Belt. May she have done some in colour, please God.'

Infected by their excitement, Rosie broke the Sellotape on a long narrow cardboard box which was attached to the envelope. Her hands were actually shaking as she began to pull out her colour slides in their little cardboard mounts. 'Dull, dull, dull. . .*Yes!*'

'That one's going to be as famous as the bandstand picture,' breathed Danny.

'And not one single member of the fucking backing group in sight!' laughed Zav. He must have noticed Rosie's face. 'What's the matter? You look ready to cry. They're brilliant. *You're* brilliant. . .'

She shook her head. 'No I'm not. That pep pill took them, not me.'

'Pills can't put talent there when it's not inside you,' protested Danny.

'No, but it unlocked it.' Rosie had rarely felt more mixed-up and miserable in her life.

'You'll unlock it again.' There was a kind side to Danny. 'You will, I promise.'

Rosie was not convinced.

But Danny was overjoyed. 'These pictures have even stopped me thinking about Brian Epstein's bloody Beatles. They've given me twenty seconds' relief. And that takes some doing in this year of Our Lord. Well, *your* Lord, I suppose I should say. Hamish, go and answer that doorbell. And find out what happened to the champagne.'

'I'll go.' Rosie didn't want to look at the pictures; didn't want to be part of any further discussion. If you had to take pills, to be in tune with the times, then she didn't know what she was going to do.

Out in the hall there were two locks on the door, to match Danny's double phobias about fans and burglars. Finally she managed to get them both to stay open at the same time, and pulled back the door.

Hazel Hankey was standing outside in the corridor, with Trixie in her arms. 'She didn't like the lift,' said Hazel. 'I think she's going to be sick. I might have to be sick too. I do it a lot these days. Rosie, I'm pregnant.'

Whole new patterns of speech were beginning to emerge. You had to be 'with it' to fit in with the Sixties. That afternoon Zav Hankey was definitely without it. He had lost his cool to an extent which had him sounding exactly like a male version of his own mother. 'Who's the father?' he stormed at his sister. 'You tell me and I'll go and kill him.'

'It was only that I wanted to see the inside of the Midland Hotel,' said Hazel – as if this explained everything.

'Who took you there?' demanded her brother. 'Who's the father?'

'It's not as easy as that,' sighed Hazel, 'I wanted to see the inside of the Grand Hotel too.'

'How late are you?' asked Rosie.

'Two months and two days. And you know me, I'm always regular as clockwork. Aren't the department-store windows wonderful in London? If this is Kensington, that shop called Bus Stop must be somewhere near. Fancy trying a few things on?' she asked Rosie.

'Hazel, you are pregnant!' roared her brother.

Trixie began to bark fiercely and Danny fed her a bit of salt beef from inside one of the uneaten sandwiches.

'Does me mother know?' demanded Zav.

'She found out, for sure, this morning. I think she's had her eagle eye on the Tampax box. She wasn't very helpful. She said I'd made my bed and I must lie on it.' For the first time Hazel showed some emotion. 'I don't think I *want* to lie on it,' she wailed miserably.

'Danny, what do we do?' Zav was looking at him with absolute trust. Danny could fix anything. Rosie finally understood their relationship. It was love. But not the kind that would get them into the *News of the World*. The Jewish homosexual had turned into Zav Hankey's surrogate father.

'I need to think and I need to make a couple of phone calls.' Danny Cahn walked out of the room.

As brother and sister bickered and argued, Rosie considered this new idea of Danny as a father figure. Did it make Zav disloyal to Tippler? Not really. Mrs Hankey had always been the real mother and father of that household. Tippler had been more like one of Zav's mates. Odd to think that throughout all that joking friendliness his son must have felt that he was minus a tough father. And Danny was tough. He could make things happen. He was Father Christmas – he could make dreams come true. But what was he planning on the telephone? For the first time since Hazel arrived, Rosie allowed herself to examine the word 'abortion'.

Zav must have been doing the same thing. 'It's murder. You know that, don't you? It's alive and it's inside you and you want to do it to death.'

For once Hazel got heated. 'Don't jump to conclusions. Anyway, I bet you wouldn't talk so clever if it was a girlfriend of yours.'

Zav went bright red, opened his mouth to speak, and then closed it.

His sister was in like a knife. 'What were you just going to say?'

'Nothing.'

'You were. I know you. I'll only nag till you tell me. Come on, Zav, why have you flushed up?'

'Because I've got a baby.'

'Where?' It was Rosie. She was amazed.

'In California.'

'Who's the mother?' asked Hazel. Zav didn't answer. 'Well, how old is it?'

'Two months. He's called Moondog. He's magic.'

Rosie was startled to encounter a feeling of loss; she had always considered Zav to be totally committed to her. And now he was a father. And he must have got up to something to make a baby. It wasn't that she wanted him herself; but she felt as though she had suddenly lost a special role in his life. She also found herself wondering how the expression 'a dog in a manger' had come about.

Zav could have been reading her mind. 'It was only sex,' he said. 'But it was good sex and he's a cracking little boy. He's with his mother in Walnut Creek. You needn't worry. I pay for their upkeep.'

Danny marched back into the room. 'Right! You've got an appointment with a psychiatrist, in Upper Wimpole Street, at five o'clock.'

'A psychiatrist? I'm pregnant not batty.'

'Yes, but you've got to remember to *act* batty. Now listen, you have to keep on telling him – if you're forced to have this baby, you'll kill yourself. In fact you could even go over to the window and threaten to throw yourself out. You might not feel like that but you have to put on an act. He'll know it's an act but he can't sign the consent form until you've gone through with it.'

'If you kept the baby, I'd adopt it,' said Zav. 'It'd make nice company for mine.'

'Yes, and it would ruin my figure. Some hopes you've got there!'

183

'They're trying to get you a bed in the nursing home for tonight. The surgeon's the psychiatrist's cousin. He's a Harley Street wallah. He does them after hours.'

Rosie suddenly felt sick.

'Now can we go to Bus Stop?' asked Hazel, who suddenly seemed better. 'I've read all about it. They were the first shop to have a communal changing room.'

'You'd be better off buying yourself a nightdress and a toothbrush,' said Danny. 'Is that dog your only luggage?'

The conversation about nursing-home necessities flew backwards and forwards. Eventually, Danny led them to a front window and pointed out a department store, directly opposite to the block of flats, called Derry and Toms. He then rang down to see whether the porter would let them out through his back door but the man was out.

'Needs must when the devil drives,' said Danny. 'You'll have to use the front. Just march through the reporters with your heads down and your mouths shut.'

As they emerged from the mansion block, the first thing the girls saw was a home-made banner: *We Still Love Mongoose*. It was being held up by two teenaged fans. You could see where the expression 'dolly bird' came from. In their skimpy dresses and long false eyelashes, these girls looked like Barbie's brunette sisters. There were almost as many fans as there were reporters. 'You're the girl from the tour, aren't you?' asked a man who knew how to make use of a pair of dark eyes. 'Is it true that Zav's going solo?'

Hazel, preoccupied, came out of her usual daze and said to Rosie, 'Fancy Zav naming his little boy Moondog.' A dozen pens began writing on a dozen shorthand notepads. Rosie found herself wondering how Danny would take this in his stride. Hazel's quote had already started a chorus of shouted questions which could only lead to further headlines. But headlines sold records. And these days Danny was spending more and more time worrying about the threat of 'Brian Epstein and his bloody Beatles'. They were said to be going to change everything. And other singers were going out of fashion – overnight.

*

184

Though Hazel had never visited London before, she knew all about the shops: 'I've been studying the advertisements ever since I was in the juniors. I made the taxi from Euston Station bring me along Knightsbridge. When we went past Harvey Nichols I understood how religious people must feel in Jerusalem.'

Derry and Toms was less to her taste: 'It's a bit too safe and old-fashioned,' was Hazel's opinion. 'The sort of shop where the Queen Mother might buy her winter vests. Ye Gods, look at that nightgown! It's a posh version of something off Mrs Jelly's clothesline. Have you anything that isn't flannelette?' she asked the elderly woman assistant behind the counter, who was all in black with a serrated hairstyle.

'Pure silk, Sea Island cotton or Tana lawn?' The assistant threw in 'madam' as an afterthought.

'D'you think it'll get blood on it?' Hazel asked Rosie.

This was the moment they noticed that they were not alone. A photographer's flashbulb exploded. The woman who stepped out from behind him should never have worn a mini-skirt. But Rosie stopped thinking about spindly shanks when she saw that the skinny creature was carrying a notebook. 'La fantoma estas aperonta,' she said out of the side of her mouth to Hazel. The had been using this bit of Esperanto for years – as a private warning of imminent danger.

'Would you like to say any more about Zav's little baby?' The thin woman smiled at Hazel like a crocodile.

Rosie answered for her. 'No she wouldn't.'

'Is this nightdress for any special occasion?' put in the photographer.

'Does your union allow him to ask the questions?' Nora Hankey's daughter was talking to the reporter. 'I'd have thought his job was just to take the pictures.' To her horror, Rosie saw that Hazel was already tidying her fringe with her fingers. 'I've not really got enough eye-liner on for photographic,' she muttered to Rosie.

'What's the nightdress for?' The reporter had taken over the question.

'She's having her appendix out,' said Rosie quickly.

'Oh yes?' There were years of saloon-bar knowledge in the scrawny woman's eyes. 'Tell me the old, old story! Is this one Zav's too?'

'I *am* his sister!' Hazel was all indignation.

'I always think these are nice for the hospital or the nursing home.' The shop assistant was spreading something plain and white and demure onto the counter.

'We'll take one.' Rosie produced the wad of money which Danny had provided. 'One in medium. No, two, she might need to change.'

'Was this what the fight in Cardiff was about?' asked the woman reporter. 'Do any of the other boys enter into this?'

Rosie began to realise that some of the other customers were not the real thing. Another photographer's flash proved that. They had been systematically tailed and now their pursuers were moving in on them.

'Mrs Dando!' called out the woman assistant, to a well-corseted dowager of a senior saleslady who was draping a jabot on a chromium stand. 'Could I have you for a moment? I'm a bit out of my depth here.'

'No you're not,' said Rosie. 'Just give us two nighties, like I told you. Here's the money. Wrap them up quickly.'

More flashes went off.

'Gentlemen, *please*!' Mrs Dando stepped forward reproachfully. 'Kindly remember where you are. This is *not* St Tropez.' She seemed quite pleased with her own bit of sophistication.

'With any luck they'll chuck them out,' said a young reporter with mutton-chop sideburns and a ballpoint pen held at the ready.

'The one in tight trousers with the microphone isn't bad-looking,' murmured Hazel interestedly. 'Do you think they make real money?'

The nightdresses cost a small fortune. And the assistant wasted time by wrapping them in tissue paper before putting them into a box, which finally went into a carrier bag. Then there was another wait for change. Throughout all of this, flashes were going off and reporters were unsuccessfully bombarding Hazel and Rosie with questions.

'I'm afraid I'm going to have to ask you all to leave,' said Mrs Dando self-importantly.

'Would you mind pointing towards that exit sign and looking stern?' asked a photographer.

'I'm pointing at nothing,' snapped Mrs Dando. 'You come in here, you turn my lingerie department into an Arab bazaar. . .' Her sophistication went to the four winds. 'I'm blowing the whistle on you.' One reporter attempted to lay a calming hand upon her arm. 'That's assault!' she cried. 'You're a witness, Miss Latimer. That man laid hands on me. Phone upstairs; we need the store detective here.'

The other members of the press seemed greatly interested in watching a rival discomfited. 'No offence meant,' he protested.

'Well, plenty's been taken. My own husband would think twice before he did that. Make that call, Miss Latimer. Say we need a man down here. . .'

Under cover of all this Hazel hissed at Rosie: 'Rush for the lift while the door's still open.' Hazel began running and Rosie grabbed the carrier and followed. As they got inside the metal-lined cabin a uniformed lift attendant said calmly, 'Going up.'

'I think I'm going to be sick again.' Hazel looked awful. 'There's bound to be a Ladies in the roof-garden restaurant.'

'How d'you know about that?'

'I've read everything there is to be read about London shops. It's famous.' The lift delivered them into the open air. What on earth was this huge formal garden doing on top of a Kensington department store? And however had they got all the soil up here? Amidst the palm trees and the peacocks there was also a telephone box.

As Rosie pressed button A and her four pennies dropped with a clang, she was overjoyed to find that Danny had answered the phone himself. 'Help!' she said. 'We're trapped at the top of that shop and half of Fleet Street's on our trail.'

Danny was more than used to such emergencies. 'They've managed to dodge up here too. You must have left the front door open. Listen, forget the apologies, just get in a taxi and drive up to the Piccadilly door of the Ritz Hotel. Walk straight in.'

'Are we grand enough?' gasped Rosie.

'My dear child, you've got style enough for three people. Your great charm is that you don't know it. The Ritz don't encourage reporters. I'll be waiting for you in the Palmery. It's bang opposite that entrance. I'll have Hamish waiting at the other one in the Rolls. And get a move on, Rosie. She's due on that psychiatrist's couch in three-quarters of an hour.'

Rosie could see Hazel drifting out of the ladies' cloakroom. In the same moment she also spotted a rabble of reporters streaming out of the lift and peering round.

'Bye, Danny.' He had brought sanity to bear on the proceedings and she suddenly felt able to cope. Was he, she wondered, turning into her own unlikely father figure? Marching straight up to Hazel (who had not neglected the opportunity to apply more eye-liner) Rosie said, 'Not one word. We're surrounded but we're okay. We're under orders. All we've got to do is find a taxi and then Daddy Dan takes over.'

This was easier said than done. Oddly enough it was a reporter who finally managed to hail one. He seemed to be under the impression that he was coming with them. In fact they even had to slam the taxi door on him. Rosie sank back in her seat with a sigh of relief. 'The Ritz Hotel,' she said to the driver.

These words had Hazel thrilled to bits. 'It's about as elite as you can get,' she said in her new guidebook manner. 'Mind you, the Connaught's supposed to be just that little bit more exclusive. I'm surprised Danny doesn't know about the Connaught.'

Rosie could cheerfully have smacked her. Instead she looked round to see whether the reporters had managed to trail them. At long last Hazel had shut up. After a couple of minutes the taxi slowed down at the point where the road they were on joined up with another. A street sign on a wall said *Knightsbridge*.

'The Scotch House is supposed to be very good for woollens,' yawned Hazel, as she peered out of the taxi towards a shop on the corner.

Attempting to show a shred of polite interest, Rosie's eyes followed the direction of Hazel's pointing finger. She vaguely registered a window full of lengths of tartan and cashmere jumpers. And then she sat up with a start. This had nothing to do with the shop window and everything to do with the figure standing in front of it.

Dark hair, broad shoulders, blue eyes gazing down into an opened newspaper. It was the man from Vesuvius. With a sickening lurch, the taxi passed through the traffic lights and began to travel towards Hyde Park Corner. Rosie turned round to look through the smoked-glass rear window. The tall, lean and infinitely desirable figure had already tucked his newspaper under his arm and begun walking in the opposite direction.

There is a certain anonymous kind of waiting room which always seems to have beige walls, string-coloured curtains, matching tweed armchairs – and a pile of *National Geographic* magazines on a glass-topped table.

And you're always on your own in it feeling apprehensive, thought Rosie; and there's generally the hum of distant traffic in the background. She had bought her own reading matter from the bookstall on nearby Marylebone Station. A copy of *Queen*, a magazine much favoured by Hazel. She had also bought a bunch of grapes with money provided by Danny Cahn.

By now it was late evening and this was the second waiting room of the day. The one at the psychiatrist's had been more like a gentlemen's club, with only the faintest of whiffs of antiseptic. The smell here was much more medical. Rosie's stomach lurched; not just medical – *surgical*. Whatever were they doing to Hazel?

They were aborting a baby, that's what they were doing. And when you realised that it was going on in this very building, the idea took on a reality which hardly bore thinking about. Rosie's gynaecological knowledge was

189

minimal; would it be alive when it came out? And if it was, what would they do with it?

Just for something else to think about, Rosie began to flick through the magazine. It was strong on fashion and lifestyle but a surprising number of people bought *Queen* simply to see what Celeste had to say. This elderly American was one of the best astrologers of the day. She had completely changed the style of glossy magazine predictions by presuming that her readers would be interested in more than vague prophecies. Celeste delineated what was going on in the heavens and then went on to suggest how the planets would influence people's lives.

Rosie's finger traced its way down to her own birthsign, Gemini: 'The gentle influence of Venus is liable to be overshadowed by the delaying tactics of stern Saturn. Those in the throes of a romantic obsession should expect little more than hints, suggestions, and the odd tantalising glimpse of the gift of love which Venus will continue to attempt to bestow.' Well, that figured! She'd certainly glimpsed him. Rosie chose to cling onto this bit rather than the part which went on about delays, frustrations, and somebody with an interest in the occult.

The waiting-room door opened and a figure from a Renaissance painting walked in. It was big blond Zav, in a huge suede jerkin and skin-tight jeans. As he flung himself down into an armchair, Rosie stared in fascination at the front of his jacket. 'Zav, has my eyesight gone funny or is your chest moving around?'

'I've got Trixie in here.' He pulled down the zip fastener and a pointed nose and pair of bright eyes emerged. More than ever, Trixie looked like a dog crossed with a fox. 'She's going a bit grey round the snout these days,' said Zav. 'I feel as though I'm going grey myself. There's pandemonium back at the flat. Any news of Hazel?'

Rosie shook her head. 'A nurse came in and offered me a glass of Ribena. Wasn't it a funny thing to suggest?'

'I expect the patients leave bottles of the stuff behind.' Zav looked round the room distastefully. His eyes were also filled with something close to panic. 'That shit of a

Mongoose had a girl in one of these places. It must have been scruffier than this – it was a fifty-pound job. In and out the same afternoon. She said they hadn't changed the sheets from the last one. She went funny afterwards.' What he really wanted to say now came out: 'How do they do it, Rosie? What do they do?'

She wasn't used to seeing Zav looking helpless. 'I don't really know. I think it's like a curette. This place is meant to be above-board so it won't be knitting needles or anything awful like that.'

Zav looked unconvinced. 'It was funny-peculiar she went. He got shut of her. That fucking Mongoose has never been anything but a grade-two opportunist. Have you seen the *Evening Standard*?'

'No.'

'He's been pouring his broken heart out to Maureen Cleave.' This young pop columnist was a force to be reckoned with.

'Does she take his side?'

'Maureen's cleverer than that. She's just printed all he has to say and then she goes on to ask me open questions. Have I got a massive ego? Did I take more than my fair share of the profits?'

'Why don't you just ring her up and tell her?' It seemed perfectly simple to Rosie.

'That's what she hopes I'll do. She can't understand why Danny won't let me talk to her. I like Maureen. We're friends. He's scared that she's got a whiff of his big plan.'

'What big plan?'

A guarded look came into Zav's eyes and instead of replying to the question he said, 'Of *course* I've got a big ego. How else would I have carried that load of leeches?' Without so much as a pause for breath he added, wildly, 'Will they have given her an anaesthetic?'

The door opened and a nurse walked in carrying a copy of the *Evening Standard*. As she placed it on top of the *National Geographic* magazines, Zav rose to his feet and all but shouted, 'What are they doing to her?'

191

'Shh.' The nurse lifted a finger to her lips. 'You mustn't wake the babies.'

Zav looked dazed. 'What babies?'

She was only young and just missed being pretty. 'This *is* a nursing home. Ladies come here to have babies.'

'So you do let some of them live?'

At this the nurse threw him a chilly look. 'I *thought* I wanted your autograph,' she said reproachfully.

'Well you wouldn't have got it,' scowled Zav. 'Is she okay?'

The girl chose to address her reply to Rosie. 'We're just tidying her up. I'll come back and take you through in a few minutes.' Throwing another cold glance at Zav she left the room, only to reappear immediately with disbelief written all over her face. 'That *is* a dog's nose!' She was pointing accusingly at Zav's jerkin.

'That's right.'

'It shouldn't be here. It's absolutely against the rules. You certainly can't take it in to see the patient.'

'We've had this dog since I was eight,' said Zav. 'I grabbed it off a woman in the same line of business as yourself. She was trying to flush it down a toilet.'

'We'll see what Sister has to say about this.'

'You give Sister a message from me. The dog stays. If it goes, I go with it – and your bill doesn't get paid.'

But the nurse was ready with her own answer. 'No wonder Mongoose walked out on you,' she snapped. And with a triumphant glance at the *Evening Standard* she marched out of the room.

Zav shook his head. 'That's not how Maureen Cleave painted it but half the others did. Mongoose is claiming it as some kind of march to freedom.' Zav had gone white. 'What did she mean by "just tidying her up"? Will it be messy?'

'I don't know. I'd tell you if I did but I don't. Zav, do you think we should tie Trixie to this radiator before we go in?'

Zav unzipped his jerkin and lifted the terrier down to the ground. 'I only brought her to cheer Hazel up. No. She goes in with us. What harm can she do?'

Rosie decided to change the subject: 'What's Danny's big secret?'

Zav began pacing up and down in a manner which brought expectant fathers to mind. But he must have stopped thinking about his sister because he suddenly halted, swung round on Rosie and asked, 'In a million years, would you ever marry me?'

'No.'

'Then you'll just have to wait and see what Danny's up to. You can find out with the rest.'

Could they have been hearing one another properly? Had she just been offered – and refused – a proposal of marriage? She supposed she had. As Zav rustled through the pages of the *Evening Standard*, Rosie found her initial embarrassment replaced by mild fury. He knew her feelings towards him; how *dare* he place her in such an invidious position? But this high-minded attitude only lasted for seconds. This was Zav she was dealing with. Though she wasn't in love with him, he was her closest friend on earth.

'Am I meant to offer you some explanation?' she ventured.

'Not if you have to sound like somebody out of *Pride and Prejudice*.'

'You're much nicer than that awful curate was.'

'But not nice enough.'

'If I told you the whole story you'd think I was mad. There's only one person I want, in that way. I don't even know him. I've only ever caught two glimpses.' She pointed to the copy of *Queen* on the arm of her chair. 'Celeste says that Venus is on my side.'

'Does that mean you're meant to live happily ever after? Whoever he is he'd better watch his back, that's all I can say. One wrong move and I'll kill him!'

Rosie's natural instinct was to go across and put her arms round Zav – he looked so miserable. But that kind of proximity could lead to trouble. It wouldn't be fair. But what *was* she to do? She was saved from further awkward conjecture by the arrival of another nurse.

This one was much older in heavily tailored navy blue. Her voice was as starched as her coarse lace cap: 'I am Sister Pearson and I would like it to be known that I am absolutely against that dog.'

From the floor, Trixie began to emit a warning growl. The little terrier's lip was turned back in a way which had often sent cats flying over the yard wall. Zav stroked her reassuringly. 'Sounds as though the feeling's mutual,' he said to the stony sister. 'Where's our Hazel?'

'Follow me.' Sister Pearson's skirt was a bit tight around the bottom for a woman who was trying to express righteous indignation with her back.

Hazel was sitting up in bed in one of the Derry and Toms nightdresses. You could still see the fold marks where it had come out of the box. 'They've done it,' she said blankly.

'She's a little bit sedated.' In the presence of a patient, Sister Pearson was an altogether more pleasant person.

'I didn't think I wanted it. . .' Hazel was still staring at nothing. She looked very young. They must have made her scrub all the make-up off before they operated. But Rosie suddenly realised that – in terms of experience of adult life – the girl in the nightdress was much older than herself. 'What a surprise, eh?' murmured Hazel. 'What a turn-up for the flipping book. You think you know yourself and then it turns out you don't. I was having a little baby. . .' This last word turned into a sob.

Zav went across and put his arms round her. And he's a father himself, thought Rosie. I'm the one who knows absolutely nothing. She too wanted to put her arms round Hazel. But that might mean touching Zav. So if she touched Zav, she touched Zav – Rosie rushed for the bed and became part of an untidy unhappy hug.

'This grieving process is entirely natural,' said Sister Pearson. 'It's something which is to be encouraged. You have a nice cry, Miss Hankey.' With this she straightened a dressing-table cover and walked out of the room.

The hug separated into three isolated people. Hazel fished out a handkerchief and blew her nose. 'Have you ever noticed, when somebody tells you to have a good cry, you don't want one any more.'

All this emotion had squashed the grapes. 'Danny sent them,' explained Rosie. 'And I brought you a copy of *Queen*.'

'I want a copy of *Autosport* too,' said the girl in the bed.

'What was it?' asked Zav.

'Come again?' Hazel looked puzzled.

'Was it a boy or was it a girl?'

'How can I be expected to know what it bloody was?' shouted Hazel. 'I was out for the count.' She stopped shouting and repeated, 'I thought I didn't want it,' in exactly the same voice she had used before. It was as though somebody else, another Hazel, was emerging from deep inside her.

This obviously embarrassed her brother. 'What d'you want *Autosport* for, anyway? Sit, Trixie!'

'Everybody thinks I'm dim,' said Hazel. 'Well I'm not!'

'Course you're not dim,' Rosie reassured her. 'You've astonished me today, with how much you know about London.'

'Yes, and I'm going to learn everything there is to learn about motor racing.' Hazel patted the bed and Trixie jumped up; this took two attempts because the hospital bed was higher than the one in the attic at Saracen Street.

'Why the sudden interest in motor racing?' asked Zav.

'Because I'm going to start going to Oulton Park on Sundays. It's a racing place out in Cheshire. Lorraine says all the men are loaded. It's not as though I want much. I only want a rich husband who'll buy me nice things. D'you want to play teddy-bears?' she asked Trixie, as she pulled back the bedclothes encouragingly.

The little dog immediately picked her way across the sheets and snuggled into the crook of Hazel's arm. Trixie's eyes were full of love and Hazel suddenly held her close. The dog could have been a baby – the one she wasn't supposed to have wanted.

A difficult situation had arisen but Mrs Hankey was facing it with equanimity. 'Mongoose and Zav may be daggers drawn,' she said to Bernadette, 'but we're not going to let it come between you and me. There's a crying need for women in the government so just you get in that front parlour and do your maths homework.'

'Will it interrupt you if I do a bit at the drawing board?'

Rosie asked her friend. These days the front parlour was a cross between a study and a studio.

'It makes a change to see *you* with your nose in a library book.' Mrs Hankey was talking to Hazel, who was sitting in the rocking chair reading a biography of Stirling Moss – the champion racing driver.

'I'm going into town in a few minutes,' yawned Hazel. 'I'm going to get a bikini wax.'

Her mother looked outraged. 'I'm all for women having the freedom to do what they want with their own bodies. But don't you think you've done enough to it for one week? You could still haemorrhage.'

'It's my brain that thinks it's going to haemorrhage.' At Hazel's feet, Trixie let out a little bark; she seemed to have been permanently stationed in this position since their return from London. 'God how I hate men! From now on, I'm the one who's going to be taking them for a ride.'

'I'll never change you so I've given up trying,' sighed Nora. 'But don't let your father hear you talking like that or it'll break his heart.' Tippler didn't even know about the abortion. Hazel's brief pregnancy had been written off as 'a false alarm'. And neither of the Hankeys knew that Zav had turned them into grandparents.

Rosie and Bernadette drifted into the parlour. The front room was quite transformed; everything that could be painted was now white, even the fireplace. A drawing board stood under the window which was covered in their pride and joy, a pleated paper blind – a donation from Zav. There was a big blue poster on the chimney breast. It was for a Hankeys concert at Winterland in San Francisco; the lettering was printed over Rosie's original bandstand picture.

She had also made the glazed ceramic pots which stood in the fireplace, and the terracotta figure of a male nude that was lying face down on the mantelpiece. It goes without saying that this was a representation of the man from Vesuvius. Bernadette pointed towards the clay statuette as she settled down at the old treadle sewing machine, which they had converted into a white-glossed desk. 'Listen, I've been thinking about him. . .'

'Celeste was certainly right about tantalising glimpses,' sighed Rosie. 'The more I think about it, the more certain I am that he was ahead of us – at the ticket barrier – coming off the London train.'

'If he's sometimes in London and sometimes in Manchester, I think I might just have had a sudden inspiration.' Bernadette paused impressively, looking thoughtful.

'Quick, tell!' pleaded Rosie.

'It's only a theory but they have offices in both places and he definitely sounds the right type – I think I might just know where he works.'

When Granada Television built their huge studios on Quay Street, they didn't just change the Manchester skyline, they also attracted an exciting infusion of creative talent into the city. It was as though a bunch of glamorous pirates had suddenly scrambled out of the River Irwell and gone into business on its banks. By 1964 they were no longer regarded as newcomers and they were shipping television programmes round the world.

Entry Prohibited Except on Business: these words were inscribed on an iron bar across a private road which led into the television company's car park. But Rosie was on foot so she went up to the glass and timber shed of a lodge and rapped on the window. 'I've got an appointment with Mr McGoldrick in the graphics department,' she said to the commissionaire.

She found herself obliged to wait on the pavement for a few moments, while he made a telephone enquiry. She could already see a sign that read *Graphics Dept*. It was on the side of a two-storey building. This looked like stables big enough for carthorses. And that's what they were: the Granada architect had taken existing Victorian railway buildings and incorporated them into a modern studio complex.

A man was walking down a cast-iron staircase on the front of this stable block carrying a grey and white geographical globe with the words *World in Action* painted round it. Rosie had seen this same item a dozen times on television – and only an iron bar divided her from the excitements of the world where it belonged.

'You can go in. It's up there.' The commissionaire indicated that Rosie should pass through a little gap at the side of the barrier. She was in the sort of nervous mood where she was reading signs and symbols into everything. It seemed as though she was slipping into this place sideways. If the uniformed attendant had pressed the button which raised the barrier, she would have felt she was in with more chance of getting a job. And that meant more chance of seeing Him. Bernadette had decided that the man from Vesuvius must work at Granada Television.

Cheek, that's what had got Rosie here, sheer unadulterated cheek. She had sent the head of the graphics department some random samples of her work together with a request for a job – any job. The samples had gone off in a portfolio and the price of the postage had been crippling.

'I don't normally see people who just write to me out of the blue. . .' Max McGoldrick had her folio open and was leafing through the mounted designs. 'What interested me was your combination of graphics and photography. Why is this picture of Zav Hankey in here?' It was the bandstand shot.

'I took it.'

'Well, he *does* come from Irlams o'th' Height. . .' Mr McGoldrick sounded as though he was trying to convince himself of the authenticity of this claim. He was a gentle-looking man with brown eyes and a beard to match.

He doesn't believe me, thought Rosie. She pulled open her totebag and took out her purse. 'There you are. There's another picture of us, together. But I can't pretend to have taken that.' It was one of the 'four for two shillings' pictures, taken in the motorway booth on the tour.

'How do you know him?'

'We were brought up together.' As she delivered this standard answer, Rosie was looking round the huge airy studio where sections of roofing slate had been replaced by sheets of glass.

McGoldrick was still examining the bandstand picture.

'This is a *very* famous image.' Rosie just nodded; did he think he was telling her something she didn't know? He continued with, 'I'd have thought you would have been besieged with offers to take more?'

'I've just done some. His manager's got all the negatives. I'm still at art school but I need a job.' Her roving gaze round the studio had left her slightly disappointed. If the man from Vesuvius worked at Granada it certainly wasn't in this department.

McGoldrick was looking at Rosie's covering letter. 'I see from this that you're now in your first year in the seniors. Why don't you want to finish your course?'

'It's a general design course, I want to concentrate on photography. The best schools for that are in London. I have to make money to get there.' These were not slick lies, they were the truth. But one glimpse of her dream figure would have meant that his country would be as her country – and London could go hang itself!

'Don't you know about student grants?'

Of course she knew about grants. How much you got depended on how much your father earned. Clifford was said to be making money again but he was still recouping his losses from the Fifties. The education authorities could hardly be expected to take this into consideration. 'I don't qualify,' was all she said aloud.

Max McGoldrick was still looking dubious. 'The only vacancy I've got calls for little more than a dogsbody.'

'That's me,' said Rosie cheerfully.

Once again he picked up the picture of Zav. 'The girl who took this couldn't be blamed for being a bit of a prima donna.'

'You don't know the girl,' laughed Rosie. She just resisted using the word 'fluke'. She was, after all, trying to sell herself. Was she being a bit too 'take it or leave it'?

But it seemed she had already succeeded. 'Come in Monday morning at half past nine. I'll take you through to Personnel before you start. They'll talk money and National Insurance cards with you. . .' Again he seemed to hesitate. 'There'll be times when I really will expect you to push round a broom.'

Rosie tried to reassure him with a smile. 'You may not realise it but you're looking at Cinderella,' she said.

'Well I'm a sucker for a happy ending,' he replied cheerfully. 'I love this shot of the tattooed man with the little dog.'

'Do you like dogs?' asked Rosie. She knew where she was in a place like this. And there were men like Max McGoldrick teaching at the art school. She could be happy here.

'I love dogs,' he said, 'I've got three.'

'Well, you can be sure I won't mind pushing a brush for somebody who loves dogs.' Life might have handed her a strange deal but adversity had bred quick wits. But had that bit about dogs been too like sucking up? Anyway the interview was over and Rosie had even surprised herself at how well she had coped. She couldn't help but wonder whether Gran'dad Tattersall was beaming down on the proceedings.

A breeze was blowing but the sun was shining as she walked along Deansgate. The lunchtime editions of the *Manchester Evening News* were already out on the streets. Rosie had just decided that she would celebrate her new job with a trip to Vesuvius when she noticed a familiar name on one of the newsvendor's flapping posters: *ZAV – NEW DEVELOPMENTS*.

She grabbed a paper and paid for it – but the story wasn't on the front page. And when she tried to open the newspaper the wind danced into the pages and caused them to flap wildly. Already encumbered with a portfolio and a totebag, Rosie decided to hurry to the coffee bar and read the story there. But curiosity got the better of her and she had one more attempt in a shop doorway. The wind still won; she would just have to wait until she got downstairs in Vesuvius.

It wasn't quite midday so the place was relatively empty. Rosie dived through the papier-mâché palm trees to a vacant seat, dropped her bag and her folio onto the ground and began to scrabble through the newspaper. Her search was halted by the sudden sight of a dreadful press photograph of Zav with Danny Cahn. The picture made the pair of them look downright furtive and the headline above it read *ZAV TO BECOME A YANKEE CITIZEN?* That was the moment she got the distinct feeling that somebody was watching her.

Well, they could stay watching. She needed to see what the *Evening News* had to say for itself: 'Stunned fans have been gathering outside pop-supremo Danny Cahn's London flat amidst rumours that Cahn is to close his London office to concentrate on extensive Stateside interests. He is thought to be planning to take his most famous client, Manchester-born Zav Hankey, with him. Teenage girls wept. . .' It was no use, the feeling of some-body staring was burning into her. She would have to look up. She could actually *feel* the direction the eyes were coming from. Rosie turned towards them.

It was Him. And God he was beautiful. He wasn't just staring, he had one of the new indelible felt-tipped pens in his hand and it was glance, draw, glance, draw. He was sketching her. And he was doing it directly onto the metal table top.

She looked down again at the newspaper. A full minute must have passed before she realised that all she'd been doing was reading one line, 'The past seven days have been troubled ones for Zav,' over and over again. For many months her whole aim in life had been to find this man. But practical plans had never stretched beyond that. . .It was no use; she would have to look up again, to be sure he was still there.

He had chosen this moment to rise to his feet. Was he coming over? No. Raising an amused eyebrow, he simply pointed down to the table top with a long tapering fore-finger. Even as she was thinking that this was the first time she had really registered his hands, he had already crossed to the cash desk where he slammed down a ten-shilling note. This done – without waiting for change – he marched purposefully up the stairs and disappeared into the sunlit street. The last she saw of him was his feet (brogues today) passing the top of the cellar window.

The girl behind the cash desk had hardly slipped his change into the saucer for staff gratuities before Rosie was also on her feet and crossing the room. Perhaps he'd scrawled a message on the table top? The place was suddenly filling up and she felt she had to get there quickly, before somebody else sat down.

The message was in both words and a picture. She could hardly believe what she was seeing. How had he *dared*? And what if somebody else was to see it? And indelible ink would not wash off. Her cheeks burning with thrilled indignation, Rosie reached a quick decision; there was only one solution to this problem – she would have to pinch the table.

7

The words on the table top said *Absolute Commitment Offered and Expected*. These were followed by a telephone number. But all of this was written underneath the drawing. Oh that drawing! How had he known what she looked like naked? Yet the artist in Rosie was forced to admit that the picture was not lascivious, the man had not been drooling as he did it. The likeness had been drawn with great tenderness; with something which even approached love.

Rosie thrilled to this and then went cold inside; when Hazel Hankey had gone into Manchester for her bikini wax, she had seriously thought of doing the same thing. How had this man known the exact outline of that dark patch? The blush began to burn again and Rosie – terrified that somebody else would see this piece of artwork – wondered whether to sit on the table.

Instead, she dived across the room and grabbed her things. Returning quickly, she placed the portfolio on top of the drawing. But the very first thought had been the best one. Somehow she was going to have to steal this piece of furniture.

A waitress with a cloth in her hand had been coming nearer and nearer. Now she approched Rosie's corner. 'Could I just empty that ashtray?'

'Yes.' Was the cloth for mopping table tops? Rosie straightened the portfolio nervously.

'Aren't you the girl who once came in here with Zav Hankey?' asked the waitress. With her Dutch-doll haircut and her striped fisherman's jersey, she could easily have been a student herself.

'Yes. Months ago.'

'Could I just mop your table?'

'Couldn't you leave it?'

'I think Zav's to dream about. I *can't* leave it. The owner comes round checking after me. He's a pig. I wanted to write to Zav for a photograph but I didn't know where to send the letter.'

Rosie kept her hands on the portfolio. 'I'll *give* you a photo of Zav,' she said. 'Now. This very minute. I've got one in my folder. But if I do, you'll have to help me.'

'In what way?'

'First of all, could you have a go at rubbing this drawing off?' Reluctantly, Rosie slid back the portfolio.

'Oh my God!' The girl rubbed diligently but the damp cloth just added a high gleam to the nude. Rosie had already undone the tapes on the folder and now she extracted the big bandstand picture.

'It's my favourite,' gasped the girl.

Even in the midst of her panic Rosie failed to resist the temptation of saying, 'I took it.'

'And did you do that drawing too?'

'No I did not. But I've got to take it with me. Can you help?'

The white folding table was clanking around in the back of the taxi. You couldn't see the drawing because Rosie had buttoned her cardigan right round the metal top.

'What number Saracen Street?' asked the driver. They were already in Irlams o'th' Height.

'Seven.' They drove on in a silence that was only broken by the rattle of the piece of stolen furniture. Both the waitress and the cashier had helped her get it out of Vesuvius. Zav's name spelt magic in Manchester and Rosie had been obliged to promise to return with yet another copy of the photograph.

'If the artist had missed your pubic hair out, it would have been different.' That was how the cashier had squared the deal with her own conscience. 'We couldn't have people putting their cappuccino on that! We'll tell the owner that engineering students took it. We'll say it's part of Rag Week.'

In the back of the taxi the table gave another lurch. 'A lot of cabbies wouldn't have picked you up with that.' This driver was sucking on a stinking pipe. 'We're not meant to be light haulage merchants.'

As the car turned off Bolton Road and swung round the

corner, Rosie saw that a small crowd was gathered on the pavement, outside Hankeys'. Some of them had cameras, which could only mean one thing – reporters.

Rosie leant forward. 'Drive straight on to the end of the street, go left and pull up,' she instructed the driver. Still sucking on his pipe until it made bubbling noises, he nevertheless slowed down to see what was going on at number seven. Rosie slunk down in the back of the cab. She thought she heard somebody say, 'It's that girl,' but she couldn't be sure.

'Where to now?' The surly driver had got them to the end of the street.

'I'm just getting out for a second. I want to see if there are any more of them down the back entry.' The Hankeys' tour had left Rosie experienced in these matters.

Yes, there were two more stationed outside the yard gate. Perhaps Zav was inside or maybe they just wanted a comment on his imminent departure for America. Whatever they wanted, any hopes of sneaking in the table were plainly out of the question. Rosie got back in the cab. 'Let me think for a minute,' she said to the driver.

'It'll have to be a short minute,' he replied. 'I'm picking up a regular at one o'clock, outside Cheetham Assembly Rooms. Would you mind hurrying up and paying me off?'

'Couldn't you just take me a bit further?' pleaded Rosie. She did not fancy the idea of being left in the middle of Claremont Road, holding onto a cardigan-clad table.

'Where?' He was plainly ready to get nasty.

Where indeed? Light Oaks Park? What use would that be. . .?

'Hurry up. Time's money to me.'

A pigeon landing on the pavement gave Rosie a sudden idea. 'Take me down to the tip,' she said. 'Cut straight through and you'll come to a railway carriage turned into a house. It's not far. It's downhill all the way.' Not that dumping the thing on the tip would be any use. It was often crawling with people foraging for junk. But Biddie Costigan was unshockable. Biddie would know what to do.

'I'm not sure my springs are up to this,' grumbled the driver as they passed under the iron railway arch and began to bounce along a dirt road. The clanking inside the back of the cab had increased alarmingly with each bump. 'No, this is as far as I go. You'll have to get out.'

Rosie paid him off and manhandled the table a further hundred yards. The weather had turned gloomy. Great heaps of cindery rubbish were piled up on either side of her. The air was sickly-sweet with the scent of decay. Amidst the torn cardboard boxes and old mattresses and bicycle wheels and brown banana skins, there seemed to be an unlikely preponderance of damp tea leaves. A skinny, fiercely barking dog rushed towards her. But it was only Sailor, Biddie's greyhound.

Why on earth had she said to the man at Granada that she would be happy pushing a broom around for somebody who loved dogs? It must have sounded sucking-up and idiotic. This was the moment that Rosie slipped on something slimy. Her feet went from under her and the table landed on Biddie's doorstep with a crash.

The door opened immediately and Biddie gazed down at the piece of furniture which, by now, seemed to have been haunting Rosie's life forever. 'Just what I always wanted,' the little old woman exclaimed with joy. 'I've been searching the tip for an item like that for years.'

'You haven't seen it with its cardigan off!'

Biddie had already begun to pick up the table and now she undid the woollen covering. 'What a beautiful resemblance!'

'He never actually saw me like that.' Rosie was suddenly full of revived indignation.

'No, but it's how he'd like to see you.' Biddie never needed things explaining to her. 'And Gabriel's message is certainly honourable enough.'

Rosie was at a loss to understand what the old woman meant. 'Who's Gabriel?'

'The man who did it. Look! Worked in the shadows, down by the side of the thigh – Gabriel Bonarto. Sounds like an Eyetie to me. What a good job Mongoose had me put on the phone, you can give this artist a tinkle. Gabriel Bonarto. . .it has the ring of a good angel to it.'

'But he did *that*!' exclaimed Rosie, as though Biddie had missed the whole point.

'Of course he did. He's a man. That's what they're like – if they're honest. And Gabriel's a good Catholic name.' Biddie was already putting on the kettle. 'He'll probably expect you to convert for him.'

'With what he's got in mind?' In truth she was already trying the name Rosie Bonarto for size. And if thy country was going to be as my country, would they have to live in Italy? This was madness! She'd drawn somebody when she was eight; and now she was nearly eighteen and the man had walked off the page and into her life.

'Gabriel Bonarto.' She listened to herself saying it out loud. And as she said the words the odd thing was that she felt as though she could have spoken them a thousand times before. They were entirely familiar. And another odd thing was happening. Well, almost happening. For the first time since her childhood she glimpsed the possibility of emerging from behind her pane of glass. Hope was something quite new in Rosie's life. It was so new it was dazzling.

Tattersall caution cut across this with the thought that a total stranger had had the nerve to draw her with nothing on. Well, you missed my mole, she thought triumphantly. You missed that so you couldn't have had *real* X-ray eyes. The only thing was, she was imagining herself revealing the mole to him; and it was on her left breast. This was terrible!

'Where's that phone?' Biddie was following the trail of a long telephone lead; she finally located the instrument under a tea cosy which represented a crinoline lady with a pot head and body and a knitted skirt. Rain was now battering onto the tin roof of the shanty. But there was a fire burning in the cast-iron stove and the converted railway carriage felt wonderfully safe and secure. It was a grown-up version of a child's den in the bushes in Light Oaks Park. Dens were always best when it was raining.

Biddie held out the telephone. 'Come on. Nothing ventured, nothing gained.'

Rosie was suddenly filled with apprehension. One telephone call could take her from all this cosy security into. . .into what? Whole months of her life must have gone into dreaming about this man. Now he had shown her the outline of some dream of his own. It was too bold, too stated, too masculine. . .

'You did want a man.' Biddie was as usual reading the very air. 'You wanted a man and that's what they're like.'

Rosie dialled the number. The exchange was RUS for Rusholme.

'Lots of furnished rooms in Rusholme,' said Biddie. 'There's Indians there and black men in spiv suits.'

Rusholme was 'the other side of town' to Rosie. The very phrase was still wrapped in childhood mystery. It ranked with 'two buses to get there'. Click. She'd connected but the line was ringing engaged. She held out the receiver so Biddie could hear the tone.

The twinkling old woman handed her a consolation prize of a wrapped caramel toffee. 'He's probably phoning round the lads to say he's found his dream princess. Try again in a minute.'

Rosie replaced the receiver. 'He's never struck me as being the kind who runs in a pack. Whenever I've seen him he's been on his own.'

Biddie suddenly looked both thoughtful and sad.

'What's the matter?' asked Rosie. 'Biddie, what is it?'

'You could have been describing Mongoose. Always on his own. I've had him since he was eight. He never had a friend in the world till Zav came along.'

In all the Gabriel Bonarto excitement, Rosie had forgotten that she hadn't seen Biddie since the Hankeys' break-up. 'They couldn't have gone on the way they were, Biddie. I was there, I saw. It was one row after another.'

'He's not a bad lad.' Biddie was suddenly being a bit too busy with the kettle. 'His card was marked before he started. It's in his blood. His father drank himself into a tramps' hostel. And Cuthbert Mayne Mongoose is doing it the modern way. In the last six months he's been through more pills than Gledhill's the chemists. . .' Enamelled teapot in hand, Biddie looked tired and out of her depth. 'It doesn't stop at pills.' She began to pour the boiling water. 'Does Zav still make those boxes – the time capsules?'

'I think so.'

'I want you to give him something.' Biddie put the crinoline lady over the teapot and began to roll across the shanty on her bandy legs. With some difficulty she bent down and pulled open a wheezing drawer, underneath one of the bunk-beds. Throwing aside an old dog collar and a faded flag with a harp on it, she finally came to what she wanted. It was a St Bruno tobacco tin. 'I know Zav,' she muttered. 'He's got a conscience. Sooner or later he's going to start wondering whether he was the one who sent Mongoose down the rocky road. I want you to give him this tin for his time capsule. That way he'll always know that it started before the row.'

'Know that what started?'

'Open the box but mind your fingers.'

The tin was dented, its paintwork scratched. Rosie prised off the lid. The only time she'd seen anything similar to the contents had been at the dentist's. Inside the tin lay the barrel of a hypodermic, two rusty surgical needles and a blackened teaspoon.

'Zav did the right thing.' There were tears in Biddie's eyes.

'But we can't just steal this. . .'

'We can. Mongoose thinks it's gone. I took it off him. And much good it did me! He's got a brand-new one now. One with a bright shiny needle. He was the last person on earth who needed to come into money. Cuthbert was always one on his own, and now he's got this for company.'

In that moment Rosie stopped hating Mongoose. She even stopped disliking him. But her heart was going out to Biddie. 'Surely there's something we can do to help him?'

'He doesn't think he needs help. The way he tells it, it's all under control. "Joy popping", that's what he calls it. Some joy! Try your phone number again.'

This time Rosie got the normal ringing tone, and it rang for a long time. Click. Somebody had picked up the receiver. For the first time in its life, Rosie's heart missed a beat.

'Yes?' It was a woman's voice.

Completely thrown, Rosie's first inclination was to put

down the telephone. But after a moment's hesitation she managed, 'Is Gabriel Bonarto there?'

'No. He's out.' The female voice sounded deep and throaty and mildly indignant. 'And if you're thinking of ringing back, would you please leave it for two hours? I'm painting his room for him and the phone's behind a mountain of furniture. Who is it?'

'Oh you wouldn't know me.' Why was she sounding guilty?

'Any message?'

Another woman had answered, that's why she was sounding guilty. 'No. Yes. . .just say that the girl from Vesuvius rang.' Suddenly she decided to ask the daring question that was uppermost in her mind. 'Is that Mrs Bonarto?'

'The day I become Mrs Bonarto, pigs will have flown!' Rosie found herself listening to the dialling tone – the woman at the other end must have slammed down the receiver.

'I don't think she was very pleased with me,' Rosie said ruefully to Biddie. 'Still, she's not his wife.' In truth she was feeling much more than rueful, the emotion she felt was ridiculously strong for one simple telephone call to Rusholme – she felt betrayed. But it wasn't such a simple call. It was the culmination of years of yearning. Rosie felt as though her dream figure – who was suddenly a reality – had actually allowed her to be hit in the face. There was another woman. 'I won't be ringing again,' she declared defiantly.

'But that's not the end of it,' said Biddie. And she said it with absolute certainty. 'Drink your tea. When this rain slackens off, I'll nip up to St Luke's and light a candle for you both.'

'When he's got another woman doing his painting and decorating?'

'You said yourself she's not his wife. I'm looking for a victory for Holy Mother Church here. We'll make a good Catholic of you yet. "I saw Rosie Bonarto at Benediction. . ." I can just hear meself saying it.'

'Stop it!' cried Rosie. 'I don't even want to think about it.' But she did want to think about it. She wanted this cup of tea to hurry up and cool down so that she could drink it, and then she would go and walk through the rain and think and think and think.

They were still known as 'the rabbit hills' though a wild rabbit hadn't been seen in Irlams o'th' Height for years. These days, the slopes were just a couple of gritty promontories at the back of the graveyard. Rosie looked down into the Irwell Valley, which was all descending rooftops, and blackened grass, and goods trains shunting across an intricate network of railway lines. Should she carry on towards the giant egg cups of Agecroft Power Station? No, it was altogether too damp for a walk in that direction; in fact the whole notion of a solitary romantic wander was rapidly coming unstuck.

Not that it was really raining. It's just fine Lancashire drizzle, thought Rosie. The kind you can never capture in a photograph. Point a camera at it and all you end up with is vapour on the lens. She had already begun to walk past the terraced houses of St John's Street but the idea of passing the monumental mason's yard at the top lowered her spirits even further. Instead she turned into the graveyard; if she was going to be depressed she might as well go the whole hog.

A woman bending over a grave straightened up. It was Beryl, Mr Molyneux's wife. 'I thought I'd bring Mother a few daffs,' she said. 'They were a shocking price and the green's gone all floppy on me.'

There weren't quite enough flowers to fill the marble vase which was engraved *Mum*. The inscription on the gravestone read: *Sacred to the Memory of Elsie Meeson, Died 1948.* '*O for the Touch of a Vanish'd Hand and the Sound of a Voice That Is Still.*'

'She'd go mad if she knew I'd got the daffodils from Stott's,' said Beryl. 'She always said flowers from Stott's was throwing good money after bad. Still, I miss you, love.' Beryl was talking to the headstone. 'D'you miss yours?' she asked Rosie.

'She's not strictly dead.'

'Mind you, there's nothing wrong with Stott's vegetables,' said Beryl. 'How old were you when she hopped it?'

'Eight.'

'I was ten when mine passed away. It leaves you with nobody to tell you things. Are you walking up to your gran'dad's plot?'

'I wasn't but I will.'

They began to squelch their way up the damp path. The Tattersall family grave was right up against the church. Beryl was better dressed for the weather than Rosie, in a tightly belted white raincoat. 'Is that cardigan of yours *meant* to be as baggy as that?' she asked.

'It's had a stretching sort of morning.'

'Listen!' Beryl suddenly sounded much less graveyardly. 'We've just had a bit of excitement in the shop. Your Zav's been in with his Jewish manager. I was helping out behind the counter but Mr Gledhill let me slip off with them. Zav wanted to say goodbye to Joe Fingers.'

'So they really are off to America?' Rosie had stopped believing in what she read in the newspapers.

Beryl nodded. 'He wanted to see Joe first and then he's going to face up to his mother.' She paused by a gravestone which resembled a harp with broken strings. 'I'm afraid I had to say two very terrible words to Zav.'

'What sort of words?'

Beryl looked deeply ashamed. 'Chester Zoo. You're going to get wet through, Rosie. Let me put this umbrella up. It's only a little stubby but it does the job. You see, Rosie,' she continued seriously, 'Joe Fingers has developed *habits*.' The very word seemed to set her moving along the path more quickly and her umbrella poked its way into some overhead branches, which brought more water onto them than it kept off.

'What kind of habits?'

'It's my front,' sighed Beryl. 'He's absolutely fascinated by it. At first he just used to stare at my bosoms. But now it's got so he wants to reach out and weigh them up and down, *thoughtfully*. You'd think he was judging prize melons. Don't imagine it gets him excited,' she added hastily, 'because it doesn't. We would never have allowed anything like that. It's just a funny little habit he's got into.'

Rosie was saved from laughing out loud by the fact that she

was now in charge of the umbrella and more overhead branches needed negotiating.

'It doesn't end there,' said Beryl solemnly. 'He tried the same routine on the postwoman. She cut up quite nasty. It was probably my fault for using the word "spinster".'

'So he's got to go to Chester Zoo?'

'Unless Zav can get him into America. Danny's going to get on to the embassy. Oh I will miss the little bugger!' In Irlams o'th' Height this word was often used as a term of considerable affection. 'Zav must know I'm genuinely fond of Joe. Look how I had him dressed as a pageboy at the wedding.'

They had reached the Tattersall family grave. Although this edifice had only been erected in the 1940s, its style was reminiscent of an earlier era. The tomb resembled a dark orange marble table with four lion cubs for legs. At first glance the whole thing looked as though it had been carved out of glazed potted meat. It could easily have been the memorial of a successful circus proprietor. There had been nothing of the Quaker about Clifford Tattersall's father.

'"*Onward and Upward*".' Beryl was reading the inscription. 'How lovely to be so sure of Heaven.'

'Actually, it was the motto of the business,' said Edwin's granddaughter. 'He had it in lights, round the clock on the stall. It was engraved on the silver soup tureen too.' She suddenly found herself remembering that awful day when everything was sold.

'And now Teapot Hall's full of nurses,' sighed Beryl. 'How are the mighty fallen, eh? Oh dear, was that awful of me? Something does worry me, Rosie. Not just today, it's been in my mind for a while. You've no mother to guide you, and I shouldn't think Mrs Hankey's much help with the intimate side of life.' Beryl was going prettily pink underneath the beige umbrella. 'If you ever wanted to know anything about *anything*. . .well I just hope you'd ask.'

Why not ask, why not? There was nobody to hear them. Not unless you counted Gran'dad Tattersall. Anyway, by all accounts, he'd been a sport. 'Is it all it's cracked up to be?' Oh dear, Gran'ma was under the marble table, too.

'What?'

She'd started now. 'Sex.'

'Sid always says it's as good as taking off in an aeroplane.'

'Yes, but that's a man. But what does it do for you?'

Beryl thought seriously for a moment. 'When we get it right, it makes me feel complete. It's all curves, there's no square lines, it's lovely. Mind you, I'm lucky – Sid's always had the *interest*.' Beryl began to choose her words carefully. 'Strictly between you and me, the photography should have given me the clue. He did want to take the pictures for art's sake but he liked the sexy side.'

'What about those friends of his?' asked Rosie, alarmed. 'The Three Musketeers. Did they like the sexy side too?'

Beryl shook her head. 'We decided against letting them in on it. It was too special. We got the rest of the deposit from Barclays Bank instead. Have you got a man in the offing, Rosie?'

'Yes.' She hoped Beryl wouldn't ask too much more. 'At least I think I have.'

'Well, you make sure he's got the interest – that's my advice to you. I go to coffee mornings, and some of the complaints I hear against husbands are tragic. Would you believe that there are men who stop up half the night with a pretend hobby – just to get out of doing it?'

Rosie thought of the drawing on the table top. 'I think this one could definitely be said to have the interest,' she assured Beryl.

'Well then, onward and upward! Whatever am I saying?' cried the chemist's wife. The prettily pink face had turned to scarlet. 'Listen, Rosie, I know everything's speeding up and people are doing it before marriage. Whatever you do, take precautions. Don't just let him go spurting inside you, willy-nilly. Oh dear, I've said more than I should. . .'

'No you haven't. I promise you, you haven't. You've only talked the sort of sense I needed to hear.'

'Well if there's anything else. . .'

'Yes, there is. Could you give me three pennies for a thruppenny bit? I need to make a phone call.' There was no longer any need for the umbrella. The rain had stopped and the sun was coming out from behind the clouds above the

214

power station. This view might have looked like a National Savings poster, but there could be no denying that, amidst the graves, it was wonderfully good to be alive.

When Nora Hankey wanted to describe domestic chaos she always said, 'This house is like Muldoon's picnic.' That rainy and sunlit Monday afternoon, Mr Muldoon himself should have been in special attendance to supervise the proceedings – except there wouldn't have been room for him. The press were still outside on the pavement, where Danny Cahn's Rolls-Royce was now parked at the kerb. And when Rosie came in from the street she found the kitchen blue with cigarette smoke and crammed with problems.

Poor Tippler's was the most noticeable. This was the day he'd elected to have all his teeth out, and he was sitting in the rocking chair with a caved-in face and a woebegone expression. Danny was in the best armchair, Hamish in the one that crippled your bottom, and Zav and his mother were pacing round one another like caged lions. Hazel had retreated out of harm's way onto a cushion on the floor, under the table with Trixie. The air was so charged with tension that Rosie stopped thinking about the calls she'd just attempted to make to Rusholme. She'd tried ringing the number, without success, from both of The Height phone boxes. But here was bigger drama.

'Am I a gran'ma or aren't I?' bawled Mrs Hankey.

'You are.' Zav spoke tightly. 'I've already told you.'

'No. Let's have it right.' Olive Oyl could have been about to throw Popeye through the window. 'The first I heard was from a lady reporter who asked me to confirm a rumour. How long have these rumours been buzzing round?'

'Ever since our Hazel opened her big gob in London.'

'You're all too bloody fertile for me!' snapped Mrs Hankey.

'What ish it?' asked Tippler, indistinctly, from his rocking chair. 'Ish it a boy?'

'Yes, and he's a belter,' grinned Zav.

'Thatsh nice.'

215

This was too much for Mrs Hankey. 'What's nice about everybody on earth knowing before we did? What's nice about that?' She rounded on Rosie. 'Did you know?'

'Er. . .yes.'

'You see!' Nora was ablaze with triumph. 'An outsider knew before the grandmother did. I'm surprised you didn't just leave me to read it in the paper. And what's all this those reporters are saying about you swanning off to America?'

'We're here to put our cards on the table,' said Danny Cahn.

'I always said you'd turn into a bloody puppet master.'

Danny looked hurt. 'I thought I was a friend.'

'Friend? Do you know the meaning of the word? Some friend! All you've tried to do is replace his father.'

She never misses a trick, thought Rosie. Neither, it seemed, did simple Tippler. 'Why are they *all* too fertile?' he asked.

Throwing Hazel a warning glance, Nora said, 'Shut up, Tippler. Nobody can understand a word you're saying.'

'He's called Moondog,' said Zav to his father.

'Itsh shertainly different.'

'Different?' Nora was outraged. 'It's demented. I always thought you were daft, Zav, and this confirms it. Can you seriously see me standing at that front door and yelling "Moondog Hankey, come in and get your tea"? That's only supposing Mr Cahn allows us to see our own grandchild.'

'I thought I was "Danny".' Zav's manager seemed genuinely upset.

This cut no ice with Nora. 'You were. But you're not any more. And I've noticed you trying to slip the odd "Nora" in. That stops! You need teaching respect.'

The air was now rent by a long blast on an expensive motor horn. This immediately brought Hamish to his feet. With a Scot's war cry of 'Kids!' the chauffeur made hastily for the lobby door.

Zav had never been one for leaving unfinished business: 'His mother chose the name.'

'Just answer me one question,' rapped out his own mother. 'She *is* white, isn't she? She's not a Red Indian?'

'No, Mother.' Zav could rap them out too. 'She's blacker than the chimney-back, she's forty-five, and she's got two heads. Of *course* she's white. Her father's a big industrialist.'

'Oh my God,' snapped Nora. 'He's been breeding with capitalists! How could you let this happen?' The last part was directed at Danny Cahn.

'Me? He's a grown man.'

'Until it comes to carting him off to America. He stops being a grown man then; he turns into your own private evacuee. I'm surprised you've not got him with a luggage label round his neck. When are you off – is the plane already on the tarmac? You'll forgive me for asking, I know I'm only his mother.'

Danny had taken enough. 'We're going to America because things have reached a stage in England where, if you're not the Beatles, you're nothing. You might just as well not be in the race.'

This was altogether too simple for Nora. 'And they've never heard of the Beatles in America? All that about them topping the charts there is just rumours? You must think I was born yesterday.'

'As a matter of fact, I have a very high regard for you. Now that Zav's going solo we can take his career in a brand-new direction. But the best way of doing that is in the States.'

Nora marched up to Danny's chair and put her face close up to his own. 'Prove to me that it'll work.'

Danny did not flinch. 'I can't. Nothing's that cut and dried in showbusiness.'

Nora's temper tacked off in another direction. 'It's a nice thing when an only son cares less about his mother's feelings than he does about a bloody monkey.' She turned to Rosie: 'Did you know that Joe Fingers has been getting fresh with Mrs Molyneux? I bet you didn't know that Zav's been onto the American cultural attaché about him. High-level stuff. Chimpanzee? You'd have thought they were talking about Maria Callas!'

Hamish reappeared. 'I don't think it was kids at all, I think it was your reporters. They want to know if they could have everybody outside for a bit of a family photo.' He pronounced it 'photy'.

'Why am I the kind of woman who gets her jobs done early in the day?' Mrs Hankey wondered aloud. 'I'd love to go to that front door with a full chamber pot and cause a bit of a splash of me own.'

'Come in the parlour for a minute,' Zav muttered to Rosie.

'That's right, slope off!' But the fight was going out of Nora Hankey. This didn't stop her throwing in one last ploy – she was managing to make herself look an old woman.

As Rosie and Zav went down the lobby, Trixie followed them. The little terrier always liked to be where the latest action was. Zav halted at the parlour door. 'You go in first and shut the blind,' he said. 'I don't want them snatching pictures through the windows.'

But the blind was already drawn. Muted daylight filtering through the pleated white paper added a dreamlike quality to the room. 'This is where it all started.' Zav was now over the threshold and looking around. 'The skiffle group, and then the first guitar from Johnny Roadhouse's, and Elvis singing "Heartbreak Hotel" on the Dansette. . .'

'And Mrs Jelly banging on the wall,' remembered Rosie.

'She did worse than that, she once sent for the police. That was the weekend Mongoose claimed to be a whizz at electricity and the amp blew a socket off the wall.' Zav smiled fondly at the memory. 'That Mongoose really was a head-case.'

This reminded Rosie to feel in her cardigan pocket. 'Biddie gave me something to give to you.' Gingerly, she brought out the battered St Bruno tin.

'Why the face?' asked Zav.

'You'll see.'

But Zav was still preoccupied with people from the past. 'I'm curious to know what the Hankeys are going to do without me. Some crap management tried rushing them into the De Montfort Hall at Leicester on Saturday night. But Mongoose didn't show up. The other two claimed he was under stress. Talk about trying to put me on a guilt trip!'

'That's why Biddie sent you that. Mind your hands; open it on a flat surface.'

As he placed the tin on the sloping drawing board, Rosie

218

realised that she must have left her portfolio at Biddie Costigan's. Oh well, she could always go back later. The lid came off the tin, Zav let out a low whistle, and speaking in a voice to match, he nodded towards the blind. 'Why do the press always miss out on the biggest stories? Who'd have guessed he was on smack.'

'What's smack?'

'Heroin. This surprise package explains about twenty mysteries. No wonder he was always out of cash. And that's what all the jumping around must have been about, and the sweating. Poor sod, poor little sod. There was only ever one spotlight – and I was always the one in it.'

'It's for your time capsule,' explained Rosie. 'But he's got another needle now. Biddie says you're not to blame yourself. It's been going on for ages.'

Mindful of the reporters outside, so still keeping his voice low, Zav said, 'I never wanted to believe the shiny eyes were anything more than pills. That brown powder's a destroyer. Rosie, promise me something.' There was still a minute quantity of the heroin inside a little plastic bag, next to the bent spoon. 'If you ever meet anybody with a block and tackle like this one, promise me you'll run a mile.'

'Where would I meet anybody like that?'

'Promise me.' Zav was insistent. 'One way or another they take you to hell with them. I want to hear you promise out loud.'

'Okay, I promise.' It was only to shut him up. 'Listen, I've got a job at Granada. It's nothing spectacular.'

'You should be getting proper training. If I had my time over again I'd study classical music.' Performers can grab hold of any conversation and turn it back to themselves. 'I could take their techniques and apply them to what I do. It's too late for me but why don't you let me pay for you to go on a photographic course? You could get something in London.'

Rosie examined her thoughts on the subject aloud: 'I'd never be funny about taking money from you because, if I had it and you needed it. . .well, you know. But I've got to stay in Manchester. I've got a reason.'

'He'd better be good to you.' The dark side of Zav was

showing. 'I'm rich enough to hire somebody to do him over.' He focused on the parlour as though he was trying to photograph it with his brain. 'I might write a song about this room. I could call it "Forty Days".'

'Why?'

'Once we've established American residence, that's how much we'll be allowed each year in England. Forty days.' Zav did not look happy.

Rosie sought to help him with, 'You've been away before...'

'This is different. This isn't going away, it's leaving for good.' He picked up Trixie and she licked his nose. 'Can you find me a nice photo of this old fleabag?' Somebody began knocking on the window. 'Oh my God! This is the fame I thought I wanted. I don't blame those poor bastards out on the pavement, they're only doing their job. At the beginning I fed them all they asked for. Once you join that club, the only way you leave it is in a coffin. Come on, let's go back to the kitchen.'

Their journey was accompanied by loud banging on the front door and a plea through the letterbox for 'Just one quick picture.'

Although it was still daylight, the curtains were now drawn in the kitchen and the overhead light was on. 'One got over the yard wall,' explained Mrs Hankey. 'But your dad and Hamish showed him the way out.' Tippler had his arms round Hazel who was crying. 'He's found out about her operation. So you don't get all your brains from me, after all.' Poor gummy Tippler looked as though he too had been shedding tears. 'Your father's eyes have always been too near his bladder.'

Mrs Hankey suddenly rounded on Danny Cahn: 'I blame you. You've robbed us of a son. You've had a grandchild murdered. How much more have you got in mind?' Her face crumpled. She wasn't weeping but the facial muscles looked as though they'd suddenly lost their way. 'Take no notice of me, Dan. I'm just striking out and you're nearest. No, it's not your fault. That bloody song they keep playing on the wireless is right. The times most certainly are a-changing.'

Throughout Rosie's childhood, Hovis the bread manufac-
turers had promoted their wares with an advertisement which
showed a woman on a front doorstep waving goodbye to a
youth who was carrying a small greaseproof-paper parcel.
The mother had proud tears in her eyes, the parcel
presumably contained sandwiches, the illustration was
captioned His First Day at Work.

It wasn't like that, the morning Rosie started work at
Granada. Mrs Hankey didn't even ask whether the television
studio had a canteen. All she said was, 'If your monthlies are
due, you'd better slip a couple of whatsits in your handbag.'

As Rosie stood waiting at the bus stop, Bernadette came
round Gledhill's corner. She was now in the sixth form so she
had dispensed with her schoolbag and was carrying her books
in a shabby canvas holdall. Senior girls at Pendleton High
School were allowed to wear clothes of their own choice, but
Bernadette was still in a gymslip. It was at least a size too small
for her. Here was somebody else who was doing it the hard
way. What's more, Bernadette looked as though she had been
crying.

'Hay fever,' she explained. But Rosie was not convinced.
Bernadette was half sobbing as she said, 'That frock of yours
turned out well. Black and white suits you. I think I'd like a
Jackie Kennedy dress, too.' And now she was crying
helplessly.

'What's up?' asked Rosie. There was no reply. 'If you got
some cheap material off the market, I'd run one up for you.'

'Would he notice?' snuffled Bernadette. 'I don't stand a
chance.'

'What're you talking about?'

'Zav. Those bloody newspapers have been keeping the
story going like a serial. I've just been in the bottom shop. The
Daily Mirror have got hold of a picture of the baby today.'

Bernadette's passion for Zav went back so many years that
Rosie had ceased to remember it. It had stopped being real
for her. But not for the girl from down by the tip, who now
sniffled, 'Anyway, I'd look awful in a short skirt. Who'd want
to draw attention to legs like tree trunks?'

'Perhaps you could wear a Jackie Kennedy as a tunic, over slacks?' suggested Rosie.

'I bet that American girl of Zav's doesn't have to disguise her bottom half. The papers call her a beautiful hippie.' Bernadette looked away from Rosie. 'You must think I'm daft.'

'No I don't. I couldn't. At least you fell for flesh and blood. All I had for years was a crush on an idea in my head.'

A man and a woman had now joined the queue so Bernadette hastily blew her nose. 'Have you tried phoning him again?' she asked Rosie.

'I've been haunting the box all weekend. No reply.'

'Screw love!' said the woman who had just joined the queue. For a minute Rosie thought she was talking to them, but she wasn't. The remark was addressed to her companion. 'These days we're only allowed to speak through our solicitors. I'm going for all I can get. I don't care if he's left without a roof over his head.'

'You were a picture-book couple,' sighed the man.

'Is that what it comes to?' whispered Bernadette. 'Do we go through all this agony to end up like that?'

The woman hadn't finished. '*And* he's going for restitution of conjugal rights.' At that moment the double-decker bus for town lumbered into view.

'Fares please.' The conductor had grabbed hold of the two girls before they'd so much as had a chance to mount the stairs.

Rosie never enjoyed paying on the platform. It never felt safe. To speed things up she said, 'One to town and a half to Pendleton High.'

'Don't patronise me,' hissed Bernadette. The bus was swaying as they climbed up to the top deck. 'Here, take this.' It was her fare. 'I'm sorry for being snappy. We didn't get much sleep last night.'

The back seat was empty so they sank into it. A woman in front of them was saying to another one, who looked like her sister, 'I'm giving him beef sausage tonight – as a punishment.'

Rosie began to wonder whether Bernadette was right. Did

all loving relationships end in hatred? No. They were the new generation – they would do things differently. 'Why didn't you get much sleep?' she asked.

'Mongoose rolled in blind drunk with the police roaring after him. He kept throwing Zav's name around like a swearword. There's going to be trouble there.'

'What sort of trouble?'

'First he grabbed hold of my best lipstick and wrote "Revenge is sweet" on a window. And then he smashed the window with a hammer. I think he was drugged up. His eyes were all glittery. Biddie cried and Sailor bolted. It was awful.' She didn't allow herself as much as a breath's pause before a more important thought rose to the surface. 'I've got to get over Zav, haven't I?'

'I think so. They flew to New York yesterday, he and Danny. Yes, I definitely think it would be for the best.' Would a cold slap of truth help Bernadette to come to terms with the idea? Rosie decided to take a calculated risk: 'Last week he asked me to marry him.' This sudden announcement had been a mistake. She could tell that by Bernadette's face.

'And you turned him down?' Anger was mounting. 'You turned him down for a filthy bugger who does rude drawings on table tops?'

Rosie was horrified. 'Shh.' The two women on the seat in front were already turning round to stare.

Bernadette didn't care. 'I suppose he wasn't good enough for a broken-down toff like you.'

'That's not fair.'

'What's *fair* got to do with anything?' snarled Bernadette. In one moment she had turned back into the girl who had wanted to force Rosie's head down the lavatory pan, all those years ago, in that rank-smelling building in the school yard. 'My fat legs aren't fair. But I'm stuck with them. And I'm stuck with red hair and blobby freckles.'

'But you're clever.'

'Who gives a shit? You're the really clever one. You think of yourself as Little Miss Abandoned. Abandoned? You've got the lot. Looks, background, proposals – you're the girl who's got it made.'

And still Rosie's Quaker upbringing was urging her to try to make peace. 'When all I'm going to do this morning is push a brush around?'

'Yes. At Granada Television. The one place in Manchester where everybody wants to work. Poor cow, my heart bleeds, I'm really sorry for you!' The bus was already passing the motor-car showrooms which meant that Bernadette should be making a move for downstairs. As she picked up her canvas bag and got to her feet, the muscular redhead threw her final round of fury at Rosie. 'Well you can fuck off,' she shouted. 'You and Zav and Old Mother Hankey. I'm with Mongoose – if I can ever do you a bad turn, I will.' Splat. Rosie could hardly believe what had happened; but it had. The departing Bernadette had spat right in her face.

As she took her handkerchief to the mess, the woman who was going to punish her husband with beef sausage said to her, 'Was it over a man? You be warned by one who knows –they're none of them worth it.'

'I'd rather find that out for myself, thank you.' Even as she said it, Rosie could hear that she was sounding like a rich bitch from Teapot Hall.

'You've still got spit on your collar.' The woman was obviously the kind who went in for the last word.

Rosie was content to let her have it. Thoughts of the Bernadette of her childhood were rising up to mock her. The real Bernadette had been the one she had first encountered. The hatred had never gone away, and it must have been brooding and growing inside her. She'd certainly had them all nicely kidded – poor Mrs Hankey was the one Rosie was really sorry for. Nora had a lot of dreams invested in Mongoose's sister. She's bad, thought Rosie, it's as simple as that. She always was and she always will be. Bad Bernadette Barrett. *And* she says 'fuck' on buses.

This last thought was so prim that it suddenly set her laughing. Right out loud. Morning sunlight was shining down on the Toytown battlements of Pendleton church and she'd been mistaken for a girl who'd got it made. Perhaps it was the truth. Perhaps she had got it made. She'd certainly got a job and an invitation to ring an intriguing man. The rest, she supposed, would be up to herself.

That first morning at Granada went remarkably well. It had turned into the kind of day when even the Sellotape came off the roll easily. There was a lot more to the job than she expected. Rosie found herself mounting drawings that were going to be used as captions in a trailer, she made coffee for sixteen friendly people, she was even allowed to block in some lettering on a rough design of Max McGoldrick's.

Everybody was on first-name terms and Max wasn't a bit like the standard idea of a boss. 'Outside phone calls are okay with me,' he said. 'As long as they're only local ones. The switchboard will ask you whether it's personal, but all you have to say is no.'

Encouraged by this, Rosie waited until everybody else was at the other end of the airy studio, and then she lifted up the phone and asked the operator to get her the Rusholme number.

It rang for a long time and then, 'Hello?' His voice was deep and something already seemed to be amusing him.

'It's the girl from Vesuvius,' she said. This much she'd had planned.

'Ho ho,' he said teasingly 'It's for me,' he called out to somebody. 'That girl's finally got through to me. . .Hello?'

But Rosie didn't answer. At the other end, in the background, she could hear someone laughing raucously. And that someone was a woman. Very quietly she put down the receiver. That was that. It was over.

Five minutes later she really was pushing the promised brush. Another half an hour and Max announced, 'Lunch! Back at two o'clock. The canteen's easy to find. If you just go down the outside steps you'll see it signposted.'

But when she got outside Rosie was suddenly gripped by unexpected shyness. The people streaming towards the canteen building were all in twos and threes and she was one on her own. There was no law that said she had to eat on the premises. Instead, she walked across the car park, past the lodge gates, and began making her way towards the city centre. The touring version of *West Side Story* was back at the Opera House – for the umpteenth time.

Rosie paused to look at the photographs outside the theatre. Were these the people who were actually in it? she wondered. Or had the pictures been taken when the show first took to the road? The posters were already up for the next production, which was to be a season of opera. A man, tucking a pair of tickets into a wallet, emerged from the shadowy interior of the theatre. But it wasn't just any man. It was Him. And he was smiling.

'Do you want to come to *Carmen* with me, girl from Vesuvius?'

Rosie even surprised herself by smacking him hard across the face. But he was as quick as she was. Instantly, he had seized her hand and kissed it. Not on the back, but on the palm. She could actually feel the outline of his lips against her skin. The feeling was so intense that she could have drawn their very shape. And the feeling was doing something else to her. Something quite new and unexpected. Inside her head Rosie could hear Mrs Hankey's voice. It was talking about butterflies stirring in unexpected places.

8

'My name is Gabriel Bonarto.' The theatre poster behind his head said, *The Original Production With Specially Augmented Orchestra.*

'You let a woman laugh at me on your phone.' Rosie felt obliged to offer some explanation for having struck him across the face.

But the beam of Gabriel's attention had now been turned onto somebody behind her. 'Hello,' he said nicely to whoever it was.

'Hello,' replied the unseen figure. There was something odd about this voice. Rosie wondered whether she should turn round and have a look. Nothing on earth would have stopped her. First she looked round and then she was obliged to look down because the person holding his hand out to Gabriel was a small boy, with a squashed face and bright boot-button eyes. He was a mongol.

'Do you know him?' she asked Gabriel.

'I didn't,' he was shaking the boy's hand gravely, 'but I do now.'

'Nice day,' piped the child.

'Those are the best smiles in the world.' Gabriel spoke seriously. 'They don't smile to get.' And now he smiled himself. 'Hello,' he said back.

A woman panted up and grabbed hold of the child. 'I'm so sorry,' she apologised. 'He takes these sudden unaccountable fancies to people.'

'Perhaps he knew me in another life.' The handsome foreigner's reply came easily. And, God, he *was* handsome. Animal and aristocratic in one breath.

'Nice day,' repeated the little boy.

'It's a very nice day,' smiled Gabriel. And as he said it, his eyes were on Rosie. It was a good job he couldn't see into her mind because she was already visualising him as the father of her own children. And that bit from the Book of Ruth was echoing through her head like a tape recorder on fast forward. Her own breathless childhood voice was reciting, 'Whither thou goest I shall go. Thy country shall be as my country. . .' He was here. They had finally met one another. At long last she was in the show which is life; and it had indeed got a fully augmented orchestra playing in the background.

'I'm Peter,' said the little boy. 'Peter.' He enunciated it again, carefully.

'Yes, and you've played gooseberry for long enough.' His mother was obviously enjoying smiling at Gabriel. And for the first time since her twin went out of her life, Rosie felt the tiniest prick of jealousy.

'He always knows who he likes,' added the woman.

'Me too.' But the mother wasn't getting the attention he had given the child; once more Gabriel sought for Rosie with his eyes. They were bright navy blue and a less enraptured girl could not have been blamed for thinking that the thick eyelashes were wasted on a man. Not Rosie; she could happily have gazed into all that amused wickedness for the rest of her lunch hour. She was already wishing the mother and son a thousand miles away. Or was that awful, and would God punish her for being selfish? Was Gabriel going to disappear again as tantalisingly as he had materialised?

It was the child who broke this heady silence. 'Goodbye,' he said.

'I'm afraid you'll have to shake hands with him again.' The harassed mother was beginning to look embarrassed.

Gabriel wasn't. He crouched down, put out his hand and said to Peter, 'Always say hello if you see me out and about.'

The boy nodded solemnly; now his attention was caught by somebody leading a golden retriever on a leash and he went off to talk to that. The mother followed. She was obviously a woman who wore a permanent air of half-apology.

'It must be awful for her,' said Rosie.

'Or wonderful. You saw how easily he could love.' The

voice had no accent but it wasn't quite an Englishman's English. This didn't show in the choice of words, rather in the way Gabriel chose to emphasise them. 'What were we talking *about*?'

So she was meant to do the remembering, was she? Rosie tried to flare back up with 'That woman laughing at me on your telephone.' Only it came out in a miserable and slightly ashamed voice. It seemed so petty after the open-heartedness of the mongol child.

'You are jealous.' Did he mean this as a question or a statement? 'The woman who laughed is the one who would be really jealous,' he continued. 'Jealous if she saw me with you.'

'Then what are we doing talking to one another?'

'I cannot be held responsible for my friend's sexual preferences. She would fancy you herself. She is a lesbian.'

'So she's not your girlfriend?' Rosie could feel a beam spreading from one ear to the other. 'I thought she was.'

Gabriel shook his head. He too was beaming and goodness how those eyes sparkled. 'She has simply been painting my room, for money. Am I permitted to know your name?'

'I'm Rosie.' All constraint had gone.

'I shall call you Rose,' he announced firmly. 'The English are so odd about diminutives. Look how they call a handkerchief a hankie.'

Not only had the battle of the sexes begun, he already seemed to be teasing her for being English. 'Where are you from?' she asked him.

'From everywhere. I'm supposed to be Italian and Irish. But my mother sometimes tells me a story that would make me half-American.'

'My mother's in America. At least I think so. She ran away with a soldier when I was little.' It was the first time Rosie had admitted this, aloud, in years.

'That sounds romantic but I bet it was painful for you. We *are* going to be lovers, aren't we?' Whatever he was, there obviously wasn't so much as one drop of reserved English blood. 'I asked you a question, Rose.'

'I'm wondering whether to tell you something.'

'What?'

'Nothing.' Except it wasn't nothing. It was everything. So, greatly daring, she decided to say it. 'I knew you'd turn up one day. I've been waiting for you since I was eight years old.'

Yes, she would permit him to buy her lunch. As Rosie answered that question she realised that Gabriel's English wasn't so much foreign as formal. It made him sound much less like mischief than he really was. Why did time suddenly seem to be going faster and where had these winged feet come from? In moments, it seemed, they were already at Vesuvius. Her appetite had vanished amidst these swirls of excitement so she settled for ravioli which she hoped she'd be able to swallow without effort.

The pale golden light, streaming down into the basement through the window where she had once registered his brogues, was suddenly *her* sunlight. This thought was overtaken by a bigger one: it was their sunlight. *Theirs.* And Gabriel wasn't just a frustrating glimpse of feet; he was a full set of limbs and they were of beautiful quality. He was real and alive and laughing and getting her extra Parmesan cheese. Ravioli might be the reality but, from the moment he walked out of the shadows of the Opera House, Rosie had felt as though she was finally being fed by the gods. And if these were pagan thoughts for a girl with a Quaker up-bringing, she didn't care. In one single moment she had seen the whole point of spring and become a part of it. The long wait was over.

Lunch was over, all too quickly, too. But, by the time she was drinking her cappuccino and he was downing a double espresso, Gabriel was already asking whether he could see her that evening. Formality again took over. He proposed calling to collect her. Could he have the address? Rosie was suddenly remembering the magazine article where Celeste, the astrologer, had talked about Venus's eventual 'gift of love'.

The working afternoon seemed to last forever – and then some. Could Max McGoldrick tell that he had hired one person and was being served by quite another? I really *am*

230

Cinderella, she thought, only there are no ugly sisters. Except there were. Not sisters exactly; Bernadette and her brother. The portfolio was still where she'd left it, in Biddie's shanty. And Rosie really needed to get it back. I love his hands, she thought. And when he'd kissed her goodbye, outside the Granada car park lodge, she had loved the smell of expensive soap. It had smelled of lemons and leather. How had these two workaday ingredients been conjured into a scent that was so subtly dangerous?

Rosie pushed aside this thought and luxuriated in the memory of the look in his eyes. There had been danger there too, *wonderful* danger. One of the designers in the graphics studio kept a portable wireless permanently switched on. It was tuned to Radio Luxembourg. That afternoon, every love song seemed to have been written especially for Rosie. A cover version of a John Lennon song was replaced by a commercial for Odorono; and then Zav's voice came from the radio. He was singing 'You Turned My Chaos Into Love'.

Rosie had never really listened to the words of this before. Zav wrote so many songs and 'You Turned My Chaos Into Love' had been dashed off, overnight, to replace another track on an album. Now she found herself following the lyric as though it was graven in stone – and applying every sentiment to herself and Gabriel Bonarto. There was one line she couldn't apply; it was a mysterious reference to a photograph that changed the singer's life. She supposed she could change this to 'drawing on a table top' – except the drawing hadn't been seen in San Francisco and the singer's photograph had. Dear God! Zav must be singing about the bandstand picture!

The song was about herself. And here she was applying it to somebody else. Now Zav was proclaiming the idea of somebody having seen him through the years and Rosie's head was suffused with glowing thoughts of Gabriel Bonarto. And if that was awful she was too happy to care.

When evening finally came Mrs Hankey wasn't happy. Not happy at all. As she held the big willow-pattern meat dish under a stream of water coming from the brass tap in the back scullery, she said, 'I'm not running a hotel here. You can't just come in cancelling meals as the mood takes you.'

'I've never done it before. It's the first time anybody's ever asked me out.'

'Shall you be going out with *all* the men at Granada?' Mrs Hankey began drying the platter, angrily, on a hessian towel.

'He's not from the studios.'

'Where did you find him then?'

Quakerly honesty always having stood her in good stead, Rosie automatically told the truth. 'We picked one another up in the street, at lunchtime.'

'You *what*? Oh no. . .' Mrs Hankey shook her head. 'No way. This stops before it starts. Picked him up in the street? Your father would have a fit.' With this she marched through into the kitchen and placed the platter on the dresser. It was never touched by meat, it was a sacred ornament.

'But he's coming here at seven o'clock,' said Rosie, desperately. It was already a quarter to seven.

'Well he'll find me on the doorstep.'

'What's his name?' asked Hazel, who was in the rocking chair reading a glossy publication called *Grand Prix Special*.

Rosie was delighted to be given the chance of saying it out loud: 'Gabriel Bonarto.'

'Sounds like an ice cream man,' snorted Mrs Hankey. 'I'll soon put raspberry on his cornet. When I've finished with him he'll be glad to slink back to Ancoats.' This was the district where the Manchester Italian community lived.

'He's not from Ancoats. He says he's from everywhere.'

'In my experience that means either a sailor or a commercial traveller. You seem to forget I'm in a position of trust, Rosemary.'

Rosie suddenly saw red. 'So it's all right for Hazel to get pregnant but I'm not allowed out for so much as an Indian dinner?'

'There you are!' Mrs Hankey rounded triumphantly on her daughter. 'That's the position you've put me in.'

Hazel yawned. 'Has he got wheels?' she asked Rosie.

Rosie considered this. 'I think he might have. He wears very good-quality shoes.'

The back door rattled open and Tippler came in from the yard. He was holding a dripping lavatory brush triumphantly in the air. 'That's the Dolly Vardon unblocked,' he announced with satisfaction. 'If I've told you girls once I've told you twenty times, that drain won't take unmentionables.' Tippler threw something which didn't bear looking at onto the back of the fire. 'It's probably been there for weeks.'

'Get that brush outside,' stormed Mrs Hankey. 'A gentleman's coming here to be inspected.'

Rosie supposed that this was one better than Gabriel being rejected, on the step, by her landlady. The fire was already spitting protestingly as she looked round the room. Mondays always meant steamed-up windows and an overhead rack of newly done ironing. Still, it was clean ironing. Rosie did not consider herself a snob. Anyway, this isn't really my background, she thought. It's just somewhere I was shoved.

'Find your father's teeth,' said Mrs Hankey to Hazel. 'I think he put them in that old toy teapot.'

Lavatory brushes, false teeth – what next? 'I am not a snob.' Rosie was repeating it inside her head, like an exercise in self-hypnosis.

As Tippler came back from the yard again, beaming gummily, his wife said to him, 'Are you better in a fight with your dentures in or out?'

The former pugilist looked alarmed. 'Are we expecting trouble?'

'Milady here's invited it,' sniffed his wife. 'You might be obliged to see this dago off the premises. She's found herself a commercial traveller.'

'I haven't,' protested Rosie.

'Then what is he?'

'I don't know. But he's lovely,' she added loyally.

'You see how the land lies,' nodded Mrs Hankey to her husband. 'Any trouble, I'll tip you the wink and you be ready to give him the bum's rush.'

'Wouldn't a cup of tea and a bit of question and answer be a better idea?' asked Tippler. And Rosie felt ashamed of having entertained stuck-up thoughts.

Rat-tat-tat. Bark, bark, bark. Gabriel was early.

'He's not working class,' said Mrs Hankey. 'Nobody working class would have used the knocker that loud on a first visit.'

'I'm sure I did when I went to your mother's,' pointed out Tippler reasonably.

'Yes, and I'm sure I remember what you had in mind. No, Hazel, you *don't* go to the front door. I'll be the one who judges whether he's fit to let over the doorstep.'

Mrs Hankey walked out, closing the door behind her and leaving Trixie sniffing at the crack; a light growl was emerging from somewhere deep within the little dog's body. It was just loud enough to blur the conversation taking place at the far end of the lobby.

'Don't worry,' said Tippler to Rosie, 'I won't hit him very hard.' He was, however, winking as he said it.

'If he's got good shoes,' pronounced Hazel, 'he's probably got money. Shoes and luggage, they're the acid test.'

Trixie had stopped her noise and pricked up her pointed ears, so Rosie could just about hear the indecipherable rumble of Mrs Hankey's voice laying down the law in the distance. And now the storm seemed to be rolling back towards the kitchen door. It opened. And there, incredibly, was Gabriel Bonarto, gleaming with health and vitality and dressed in a suede jacket and a dark shirt and light corduroy hipster trousers. It was incredible because – for years – he'd been part of a dream. And when it turned into reality, he'd belonged to the one little bit of secret life that Rosie had ever owned. And now her dream made flesh was here – here amidst the rag rugs and the drying washing of the Hankeys' back kitchen.

'Yes please,' said Hazel, not quite enough under her breath.

'I'm a bit worried about his car outside.' Mrs Hankey was talking to Tippler. 'It's only got a cloth top.'

'What is it?' breathed Hazel eagerly.

234

'A Morgan,' said Gabriel. Rosie was relieved to see that Hazel was only getting about the same amount of attention as he had given to the mother of the mongol child.

'Is it in British racing green?' Hazel had reached for the hairbrush.

'I thought they all were,' he said politely. 'I'm not very into possessions.'

It was the first time Rosie had ever heard anybody use the new American expression 'into'. She found this much more impressive than the idea of a racing car waiting at the kerb.

'The more you have the less you are,' nodded Mrs Hankey.

'Stalin.' Gabriel had recognised the quotation. He was looking with genuine fascination at the crown and anchor on the back of Tippler's hand. 'How do you do. I'm Gabriel. And that is beautiful work.' It didn't come out as though he was trying to curry favour, the interest was obviously genuine.

Tippler glowed, he wasn't used to being taken notice of. 'Not many people would have spotted that little one,' he said with respect.

'Not the striptease, Tippler, *please*.' Mrs Hankey had her best Teapot Hall tones on, in the presence of company.

'This little tattoo,' Tippler tapped the back of his hand, 'is a class piece. It was done by Spitting Sam in Hong Kong – that colouring's twenty-four years old.'

'I keep thinking about getting one. Hello.' He had finally acknowledged Rosie. But his smile was worth the wait. It was a smile that said, 'Don't worry about me, I know this has to be got through.'

'Don't get a tattoo,' cried Hazel. 'You'd spoil yourself.'

Rosie was watching Trixie. At least the little terrier hadn't flown at his ankles; but she kept walking round the newcomer and studying him, with her bright eyes, from every angle. If the dog was reserving judgement, Mrs Hankey now proceeded to play both judge and jury. 'How old are you?'

'Twenty-seven.'

Nora Hankey nodded over her shoulder at Rosie. 'She's seventeen. Bit of a gap, isn't there? What do you do?'

'I'm a philosopher.'

'I meant what do you do for a living.'

'I teach philosophy. I'm a university lecturer. Only I'm having a year's sabbatical.'

Mrs Hankey marched across to Gabriel, rose up on tiptoe so that she came to just under his nose, and said: 'How's your wife?'

'I haven't got a wife.'

And he hadn't. Anybody could see that by his reaction. He was amused, but there was considerable respect for Nora Hankey in this amusement.

'Well, I don't know what to say,' mused Nora. 'Do you?' she asked Tippler. Nobody in the household, for one moment, expected him to reply – it was just part of her standard routine.

But he did reply. 'The sooner they're off, the sooner I can get these bloody teeth out.'

Mrs Hankey closed her eyes in a pained manner, opened them again, and said to Gabriel, 'I expect she's already told you that she comes from a very different background to this. . .?'

'No, she hasn't.'

'More credit to her. But she does. You'll know the expression *in loco parentis*?'

He's not got fancy manners, he's just naturally polite, thought Rosie, as Gabriel nodded and said, 'It's generally used to describe somebody who has taken on the role of the parent.'

'That's me.' Nora was getting quite self-important. 'Now I could get onto her daddy in London about this here Indian dinner; I'm going to put you both on trust, instead.' This was the moment that Trixie chose to roll over onto her back, at Gabriel's feet, and to jiggle her paws in the air. The visitor was plainly meant to scratch her stomach.

'Oh give over,' said Tippler, quite sternly, to his wife. 'The dog says he's all right. What more do you want? If you get a tattoo. . .' he had now turned his attention to Gabriel '. . .you want to get a class piece like this.' Off came the shirt, Tippler flexed his shoulder blades – the Union Jack was flapping like something at a victory parade.

'Where to?' he asked. It was the first time a man had ever held open a car door for Rosie.

'Weren't we supposed to be going to the Koh-i-noor?' She was a girl with a boyfriend and he had a car! In the years since she left Teapot Hall, Rosie could count the number of times she'd been in a motor car on the fingers of one hand.

Lily Jelly was out on her front step, taking everything in. 'You want to watch yourself in that passion wagon,' she called out. This was followed by a dirty laugh. Getting into a Morgan was a bit like climbing under the yard gate, and once in the bucket seat she felt dangerously near to the ground.

'Do you like Indian food?' asked Gabriel.

'Oh yes,' Rosie replied enthusiastically. The truth was that she liked the spicy idea but had never tasted the reality.

The car shot from the kerb like a rocket out of a bottle. 'I'm sure you don't mind speed,' he smiled.

'Except when it comes in tablet form.' Rosie was quite pleased with this reply. It would show him that she too had a little bit of sophistication stashed away.

'Well, well, well,' was all he said. But he looked amused.

Soon they were heading towards the top of Bank Lane. 'Could we possibly make a detour?' asked Rosie. 'Next left after the Co-op. I've got to collect a portfolio.' The car swung round the bend and descended the slope with all the ease of a carriage on a roller coaster.

'This is the life!' yelled Gabriel, as smooth tarmacadam gave way to the bouncing rubble road which led across the tip. The evenings were already getting longer and the dying sunlight played on a mountain of empty tin cans, topped off with the chassis of an old perambulator.

'Why are there always hundreds of discarded wireless valves in these places?' shouted Gabriel. 'Those and tea leaves.'

He'd noticed the tea leaves too, just like she always did herself. This idle thought was actually making Rosie glow with the happiness of something shared. Perhaps it was true, perhaps love did make you go a bit mad. Greatly daring, she cried out, 'Why did you write "Absolute commitment offered and expected" on that table?'

'Because you were the most beautiful thing I'd ever seen. But it wasn't something I'd ever meant to *shout* at you.'

'Sorry,' she shouted back, above the roar of the engine.

'No, be glad. Be gloriously glad. I am.'

'Slow down,' she said.

'Why? Do you want me to rephrase it in a polite English way?'

'Never! Just slow the car down – this is it, we're here.' Smoke was rising from the makeshift chimney on Biddie's shanty. Sailor the greyhound was sitting shivering on the step. 'I'm sorry I burst out with my question like that,' said Rosie miserably. 'It's just that I wanted to know. I suppose I should have waited for candlelight or something. . .'

Her protests were drowned out with a kiss. As she felt the sensual imprint of his mouth and breathed in the scent of clean skin, Rosie soared to somewhere she had never known existed. Yet common sense was tugging her heels back to the ground and reminding her that Biddie would have heard the car stopping. 'We're here,' she repeated. 'She'll be expecting us to go in.'

Gabriel looked out of the car window. 'That house is straight out of "Hansel and Gretel",' he said happily.

'The lady who lives here isn't a wicked witch. But she is a gypsy – well, sort of. Why are you crossing yourself?'

'Against the evil eye. I've met gypsies before!' Rosie couldn't tell whether he was joking or not. 'And aren't greyhounds supposed to be muzzled?' continued Gabriel.

He's a bit nervous and he's not afraid to show it, thought Rosie. This made her feel even more fondly disposed towards him. Gabriel wasn't just sexy gloss in a fast car, he was human.

Biddie appeared on the top step, slinging more tea leaves into the breeze from a little aluminium teapot. 'Now there is a face I like,' said Gabriel.

Rosie suddenly found herself overcome by a fierce urge. She needed to touch him again. Greatly daring, she put out her hand and stroked his thigh, which was still stretched

238

under the steering wheel. And that corduroy-covered muscle was just like a magnet – it didn't seem to want to let her go. Her hand luxuriated up and down the velvet pile and she couldn't bring herself to pull it away. This was awful, whatever was she thinking of? And with Biddie standing there, with a teapot!

'Evening,' called down the old woman.

'Come in and say hello,' urged Rosie.

'I'll have to adjust myself first.' He put his hand into a trouser pocket, thrust his body up in the seat and twisted awkwardly – in a way she'd never seen before. 'It's the Italian blood,' he said cheerfully. 'Easily roused, you'll have to watch out for that.'

Rosie didn't really understand, though she'd gathered that it must be something mysterious and masculine – like shaving. Getting out of the car seemed as big a performance as getting in. Not to Gabriel, he was out in one lean hop and already extending his hand to Biddie. 'Gabriel Bonarto,' he said confidently. All fear of greyhounds seemed to have vanished.

'She's only seventeen.' Little Biddie, with the advantage of being on the step, was looking him straight in the eye. 'Seventeen and a virgin. I trust you'll remember your Catholic duty.'

'How can you be so sure I'm a Catholic?' he smiled.

'I can see the holy medal through your silk shirt.'

'I can't,' said Rosie, puzzled.

'You don't have the same kind of eyes I've got. Come in the pair of you, the kettle's just boiled. Grab hold of Sailor, Rosie. There's a bitch on heat over Agecroft way and the poor old scone still fancies his chances.'

And the next thing would be strong tea with sterilised milk; whatever must Gabriel be thinking? But he seemed enchanted by the inside of the converted railway carriage. 'The Infant of Prague!' he exclaimed, as he caught sight of a gaudily painted plaster statuette standing on a pink plastic wall bracket. 'Of course it's a somewhat dubious devotion. . .'

239

'It's God when he was little,' said Biddie sternly. 'And you'd do well to remember it. Where do you come from?'

Gabriel obviously realised that 'everywhere' would be no sort of answer for somebody as perceptive as Biddie. 'I was born in America.'

Biddie narrowed her eyes. 'There's Irish blood somewhere. . .', she reached for the steaming kettle.

'You're amazing.' Gabriel spoke in wonder. 'And you're quite right. My mother's just gone back to live outside Dublin.'

Biddie began to pour the boiling water. 'I'm not amazing, I'm just me. Oh dear. . .' This was addressed to Rosie. 'He's not a bad lad but you might have chosen one who was a bit easier. Where that one's concerned, it's going to be a permanent tug of war between God and the devil.'

Did Gabriel realise that his hand had gone, involuntarily, towards the holy medal underneath his shirt? In an attempt to stem her own goose pimples, Rosie decided to try to change the subject. 'I've come for my portfolio.'

'Oh.'

Rosie didn't like the sound of this 'Oh' at all. What was it meant to mean?

'Well it's still here of course. . .' Biddie's voice trailed away. 'You'd better see for yourself.' She rolled across the cabin, bent down and pulled the folder from underneath one of the bunk-beds.

'Is something wrong?' asked Rosie.

'You'll see when you open it. Mind what you're doing.'

Rosie undid the tapes; as she pulled back the marbled cardboard cover a cloud of coarse confetti fluttered to the ground. Only it wasn't confetti; every single design and photograph had been ripped into tiny pieces. Rosie's feelings were close to physical pain.

'Bernadette,' sighed Biddie. 'And Mongoose helped her. Rosie's gone and got herself into a blood feud.' Biddie mouthed these words carefully, for the foreigner.

He took the announcement calmly. 'Blood feuds I understand. My family is surrounded by them.'

'I guessed that,' said Biddie, matter-of-factly. 'But it's the first one we've had round here for a while. Anybody fancy an arrowroot biscuit?'

Mugs of strong tea and biscuits straight from the packet rendered everything much more sociable and ordinary. Biddie seemed to realise that they were anxious to be off – that the evening belonged to two people rather than three and a greyhound – and soon she was back on the top step, holding Sailor by his collar and waving them off.

'I can't decide whether she's a very good or a very wicked woman,' laughed Gabriel, as the car began its return journey across the refuse dump.

'She's good,' Rosie assured him. 'It's just that her mind is on bigger things than tidying up.'

'But Catholic and a soothsayer. . .' Gabriel was already shaking his head in amazement when – *crash* – something hit the windshield. 'What the. . .'

'It was a stone. Just drive on,' cried Rosie urgently. 'Please.' She had already seen the malevolent figure in a bob hat diving triumphantly behind the mountain of rusting tin cans.

'But somebody threw a stone.' Gabriel had slowed down but he hadn't stopped.

'Yes. Somebody famous called Mongoose. If you don't want your name in the papers, just drive on.'

'Only for you,' said Gabriel. He looked furious and his hands were white on the wheel. 'But I'll get the little bastard sooner or later.' *Smack*. Another stone glanced off the car. And this time Gabriel screeched to a halt. He was out of the car in seconds. 'Come on,' he called, 'chuck another! Let's see where you are.'

The voice which echoed back sounded sad. 'The row's not with you.'

'Oh yes it is,' cried Gabriel. 'If it concerns Rose, it concerns me.' He was outside the car, she was still in it; but she didn't feel at all alone. For the first time in Rosie Tattersall's life, someone was looking after her. Loyalty stirred within her memory. . .Zav had also tried to look after her. But Zav hadn't been what she wanted. And the word 'want' was suddenly taking on a new meaning. Her very

241

being was crying out, 'I want you, Gabriel Bonarto.' This abandoned thought was fuelled solely by instinct. She didn't really know what the words meant. But they were something to do with those mysterious inner butterflies – and they were to do with setting them free.

In Manchester, in 1964, Indian restaurants were few and far between. This made them mysterious. The oldest one in the city was the Koh-i-noor; situated on a first floor, it boasted potted palms and chandeliers, and its windows were framed with Oriental fretwork borders. The restaurant had been in business since before the war, which had given ill-informed tongues plenty of time to wag.

'Why do you keep looking at all the women's feet?' asked Gabriel.

'Shush, they'll hear.' The place smelt like nothing Rosie had ever savoured before. The aromas were so Eastern and exotic that they seemed to reach to her eyeballs, and she was scared they were going to start to water.

Gabriel lowered his voice, mock conspiratorially: 'What's so special about the women's feet?'

Rosie whispered back, 'Mrs Jelly says that Indian restaurants are "right cow shops". And everybody knows that prostitutes wear a little gold chain round one ankle.' Even as she said this, Rosie realised that 'everybody' had been the girls at Pendleton High and at the Junior Art School.

The look Gabriel gave her was brimming with mischief. 'I must try and remember that,' he said solemnly. 'What would you like to eat?'

For all Rosie understood it, the menu might just as well have been written in Swahili. 'I'll have what you're having,' she said brightly – mentally congratulating herself on a bit of quick thinking. A lot of conferring now went on with an Indian waiter who addressed Gabriel by his christian name but also called him 'sir'. Goodness but it was nice to be with somebody who knew his way around.

'They could always make you something mild,' suggested Gabriel.

The cheek of it! 'What's the point of coming to an Indian restaurant and having something mild? I'll be happy with whatever you order.' Oxford Street looked quite different from this angle. People below were already queuing under the brightly lit cinema canopies to see *Ferry 'Cross the Mersey* and Jane Fonda and Rod Taylor in *Sunday in New York*.

Gabriel nodded down towards the first queue. 'We could go and see that, if you like.'

'Gerry and the Pacemakers?' cried Rosie indignantly. 'No thank you! They belong to Brian Epstein. He's the main reason Zav had to go to America.'

Light had obviously taken little time to dawn on Gabriel. 'So that's who the remarkable Mrs Hankey is? She's Zav's mother.'

'Yes, and it was Bert Mongoose who lobbed that stone at your car.' As Gabriel had seemed content to accept the stone throwing as a feud, this was the first real explanation she had offered.

'Well we *are* moving with the times,' he said. Was Gabriel laughing at her? If he was she didn't care. He was there and she was with him, and that was all that mattered.

As if he was with her inside this thought, Gabriel reached over and took Rosie's hand. 'Do you get very bored with questions about Zav and the Hankeys?'

'A bit bored.' She was more concerned about her eyes – they were beginning to feel itchy.

'Zav's better than the rest of the group by a long chalk,' said Gabriel. 'I think he's hugely talented.' And that was that. No further questions, no oohing and aahing – just a considered opinion. If this was what academics were like, it made a refreshing change.

'Could you tell me something?' she asked. 'At the risk of sounding dumb, what *is* philosophy?'

'Everything,' he replied. And he all but smacked his lips with satisfaction. Under any other circumstances, Rosie would have found this reply infuriating; but Gabriel's lips were so beautifully sculpted that she wanted to kiss them. 'How does blood get into lips and make them red?' she asked, just for something to say.

'You seem to think you've got yourself a walking encyclopaedia.' Leaning across the table, he drowned out her protests with a kiss. In that moment Rosie finally understood what was meant by the phrase 'senses reeling'.

'Don't,' she whispered urgently. 'My hands want to reach out and go all over you. . .' What had she said? 'I'm sorry. I don't know where that came from. It must have sounded like talking dirty.'

'It sounded beautiful to me.' There was no mocking left in him. His face was as honest and as open as a child's.

For the next few minutes they just looked at one another. Rosie would never have believed it possible that conversation could be replaced in this heady manner. But it *was* possible. Whole volumes seemed to be being spoken in tender glances and deep gazes. She was only recalled to everyday life by her contact lenses – she was suddenly becoming very conscious of them. Her eyes were beginning to be really sore and she only hoped they weren't bloodshot. Another discomfort had added itself to the situation; these lingering looks were affecting her in the butterfly place and she felt almost damp.

The food finally arrived. It was like a selection of stews in silver dishes. Odd-coloured stews; one was orange and one was nearly green. The yellow rice seemed to have a laurel leaf on top of it, and the Indian bread looked like burnt potato cakes. The waiter just placed the whole lot on the table and then padded away.

As Gabriel reached for a spoon and began doling rice onto the plates, Rosie was reminded of her father and of the oak-panelled dining room at Teapot Hall. Before the room started to be used by the Quakers as storage space for their peace campaign, the Tattersall family had always had Sunday lunch there. And Clifford had sat at the head of the table and carved and doled. Watching Gabriel with that spoon, Rosie was struck by the thought that her clock had been stopped for years, and that time itself was starting up again.

'Enough rice?' asked Gabriel.

'For now.' She began to help herself to the lumpy

mysterious slops in the silver bowls. Gabriel did the same. Why was he waiting so pointedly and not starting? Did Catholics expect you to say grace or something? And then she recalled that women were meant to be the first ones to lift up the fork. Such niceties had got forgotten in the Hankeys' back kitchen.

Rosie took a mouthful and went straight into a state of disbelief. Nothing on earth could be meant to be as hot as this, nothing! Nevertheless, conscious of the fact that it was a long time since she had dined in polite society, she ploughed on with the food. The curries weren't just hot, the spices seemed to be burning their way into her tongue. The eyes that were already sore started to stream; and now Rosie really did fear for her contact lenses. But life had already begun to teach her that everything comes at a price; if loving Gabriel meant eating glowing coals, she would eat them.

'Everything okay?' he asked anxiously.

'It's just a little bit hot,' was the most she ventured. With this she reached for the water jug and began to pour herself a glass.

'That's not supposed to be a very good idea. Let me get you some lager.'

Lager would take time. 'No, this will be fine.' Rosie took a big gulp. The fire in her mouth turned into an inferno. 'Jesus!' she cried. And this was supplication, not swearing.

'Is this the first time you've ever had curry?'

Did she detect a note of little-boy mischief? 'I *may* have had it before,' was her careful answer.

'They're quite fiery here.'

Rosie tried gasping outwards, but this only seemed to fan the flames. And something else was happening: she was starting to itch. As she scratched her arm she looked in disbelief at a series of rising weals. These long white stripes could have been made by whiplashes. 'Look what's coming up,' she cried in disbelief.

'Good heavens, it's like stigmata!' But Gabriel was obviously concerned. 'Do you often get this?'

Rosie shook her head. 'Never.' By now, both her eyes and her nose were pouring. 'I only started to itch when I smelt the curry smell. It began the minute we came up the stairs.'

'There's nothing wrong with the food here or I wouldn't have brought you. You're obviously allergic to something. We'd better get you to a chemist.'

Even in the midst of her discomfort, Rosie liked what he said. After years of being the last person to be considered, there was great luxury in his concern. 'There's an all-night Boots at the top of Oxford Street,' she ventured.

Waiters had begun to hover worriedly. Their Indian concern seemed almost feminine, but it was kindly meant. With a lot of anxious tutting they proposed putting cloths, soaked in vinegar, onto the weals. These were now swelling up like something out of a horror film.

'No.' Gabriel was already, decisively, on his feet. 'We'll see what the chemist says. But, we might have to go to the outpatients department at the infirmary.'

The owner waved aside Gabriel's attempt at payment. He was a kindly man but he seemed anxious to cover his restaurant's good name with 'Too quick for food poisoning. Too quick for that.' He was still calling this after them as they made their way downstairs.

The fresh air didn't make things any better. Rosie's eyes started to feel as though they were closing up. 'Don't scratch,' said Gabriel, 'you'll only make things worse.' All very well for him, thought Rosie. Her elbows were now under attack and she felt like clawing them to the bone.

In the chemist's there was a short queue which was held up by a drunk at the counter. The dispenser was refusing to sell him kaolin and morphine mixture.

'Thomas would have had more luck,' said Gabriel under his breath.

'Thomas who?' She had actually managed to draw blood where she had scratched inside the crook of her arm. 'I'm sorry, I just couldn't help it.'

'Never mind.'

Was that never mind about 'Thomas' or about the blood? The weird marks on her arms were now so prominent that Rosie began to wonder whether she would be scarred for life. Eventually they reached the head of the queue and Gabriel explained Rosie's predicament to the dispenser.

'I can't look closely while you're waving it about, madam. Ah, thought so, that's urticaria.'

'Will it be permanent?' whispered Rosie.

The man in the white coat shook his head and smiled. 'You're not driving, are you? Or operating machinery? That's fine then; a couple of antihistamine tablets should do the trick. The sooner the better I'd say. You can take them here, with a glass of water. Some people find antihistamine makes them drowsy.'

Had the whites of her eyes turned blood-red? That's how it felt. It was no use, she was going to have to ask. 'Have you anything I could possibly put my contact lenses in?'

Gabriel looked as startled as she had expected, but the dispenser seemed helpfully disposed. 'We'll give you two little pill bottles filled with distilled water. I'll get the girl to label them Left and Right.'

'Whatever have I found myself?' sighed Gabriel. But he was looking at her with – there was no other word for it – he was looking at her with love.

Rosie still slept in the attic at Saracen Street, but these days she slept alone – unless you counted Trixie. First thing in the morning, the ginger terrier always played alarm clock by giving Rosie's face a shower of little licks. Not today: instead she was diving on and off the bed. This was Trixie's heavy-duty alarm service. She only went into this routine when the girl under the sheets had refused to stir at first summons, or when some special excitement was afoot.

'It's okay, I'm awake,' mumbled Rosie. She reached out for the old tin Donald Duck alarm clock, which had long ago lost its bell. Rosie hadn't got her lenses in, so she had to hold the clock at arm's length before she could see the shadowy outline of its fingers. Seven o'clock. 'Are you out of your mind, Trixie? Come back in and I'll let you play teddies.'

That wasn't what the dog wanted. She wanted Rosie to get up and go downstairs. She seemed to be flashing this message to her by telepathy. I don't just feel half-awake, thought Rosie, I feel drugged. The outline of the staircase now flashed across the screen of her mind; was this how dogs communicated with one another? she wondered. But the dog wasn't causing this dazed, anaesthetised feeling. It just wouldn't go away. . .and then she remembered the tablets she'd taken in the all-night chemist's. In ten minutes they'd managed to turn her into a zombie in lead boots.

But had they done their job? The itching had stopped but was she still marked? Again Rosie held out an arm and peered sleepily. It was just like that bit in the Old Testament where the man's flesh was whole again '. . .like unto the flesh of a little child'. What was his name? Naaman. And he had a chariot. Rosie settled back under the covers, she really didn't see any need to get up this early. The words of the Bible story started to drift across her mind. 'So Naaman went forth with his horses and his chariots. . .' Gabriel had a chariot too. Well, a green racing car – Rosie yawned – that's how she'd got home. She remembered him leading her to the front door, she remembered Nora Hankey asking whether she was drunk, and then. . .? Nothing. What had happened after that? Where was the rest? Absolutely nothing was coming back.

This did make Rosie sit up. Automatically, her hand went out for her contact lens case. She always kept it on the upturned orange-box which served as a bedside table. Not there. Somehow, something about two pill bottles came into this – but she couldn't be sure how. Her brain wouldn't think straight and her mouth felt as though it was lined with grey flannel. There was always a carafe of water on the orange-box, with a tumbler over it; the Hankey household was a strange combination of gentility and rough-and-tumble. As she groped for the carafe she managed to knock it flying. Nothing broke but there was water everywhere, and the tumbler had rolled as far as the skirting board. Well, that was it, she would have to get up.

Swinging her legs out of bed, Rosie padded blindly towards the chest of drawers. The top one came open with a lot of asthmatic creaking and Rosie felt inside for her old spectacle case. She hadn't worn glasses in ages. Here they were. Had her face grown? Her specs no longer seemed to sit comfortably on the bridge of her nose.

Rosie looked in the mirror and saw the girl she used to be. 'You must have a very nice nature,' she said to Trixie. 'I'd have run a mile from me.' Had she really gone through life looking like that? Why had she never argued her way into better frames? Oh well, that was how she was going to have to go downstairs. Not that anybody there would mind – they'd had years of it. She didn't have to invite Trixie to come with her. The terrier was already scuttling ahead.

Odd that the dog should want to be up and about. Zav had always maintained that the little animal had to be where the action was. And nothing interesting ever happened at the Hankeys' at seven o'clock in the morning.

Rosie pushed open the kitchen door to be greeted by, 'Well, if it isn't specky four-eyes!' Nora Hankey was sitting at the kitchen table, scissoring the rind off streaky bacon. 'I must say you look a comic turn in that patched old nightgown.'

It was shrunken winceyette. 'Nobody's going to see me,' yawned Rosie.

'Good morning,' said a masculine voice which certainly didn't belong to Tippler. Still yawning, Rosie looked around, puzzled.

'I'm in here.' By the scullery sink, stripped to the waist, a bar of soap in his hand, his muscular body gleaming with water, stood Gabriel Bonarto.

Rosie's first instinct was to snatch off her awful glasses; but this was checked by the fact that she wanted to get a good look at his body. The broad tanned shoulders, the smooth sculptured chest, the symmetrical nipples, like dark unblinking cat's eyes – all of these brought Michelangelo's drawings to mind. She'd often wondered what he would look like naked, and here was the breathing reality. He wasn't too hairy, she was glad of that; it was as though somebody had taken a soft pencil and drawn a few deft strokes, in a line that went down from his navel and disappeared into the top of his corduroy pants.

'A sight for sore eyes, eh?' said Mrs Hankey, reaching for the frying pan.

'But what are you *doing* here?' gasped Rosie.

'Wouldn't go.' Mrs Hankey lit the gas stove with a wax taper; the black-leaded range was never used at breakfast time. 'Gabriel insisted on staying to see you were all right. He's a brave lad, I'll grant him that. I'm the one who thought he'd got you drunk. I wanted to send for the police.'

Now Rosie did remove her glasses. 'Where did you sleep?' she asked Gabriel.

Nora answered for him: 'On that cold Rexine sofa in the front room. Talk about "Greater love hath no man. . ."' But Rosie could see that Gabriel Bonarto had gone up several notches in Mrs Hankey's estimation. She was even offering him two eggs.

'Those tablets knocked you right out,' said Gabriel. 'I practically had to carry you in.' You've got one beautiful pair of arms, thought Rosie. They must have been wrapped right round me and I never knew.

'*And* he made us get the doctor,' Mrs Hankey sniffed. 'It was a West Indian on night duty. He said you'll live, but you've got to go to the hospital for allergy tests. They'll be sending you a letter.'

'Are you okay?' asked Gabriel.

'I'm fine,' was what she said aloud. But what she thought was, As okay as anybody in a nightdress that could belong to Little Orphan Annie! Even with her specs off, he looked *gleaming*. It was no use, she was going to have to put them back on again. Not just gleaming, he looked brand-new. That was the moment she caught the faintest whiff of clean male body. This did things to her mind which left her feeling very publicly exposed.

Lard was beginning to spit in the frying pan. 'Tippler's gone upstairs to find him one of Zav's old shirts. That wicked husband of mine won four quid off Gabriel last night. The pair of them were up playing cards till all hours.'

Tippler himself now appeared, carrying a blue denim workshirt. 'Will this do?' he asked.

Rosie wanted to say, 'Not that one,' but she didn't. It was the shirt Zav had been wearing, under his suede jerkin, the day he proposed to her. He was also wearing it on the cover of his last album. Some stray sense of the fitness of things told her that the garment was too *Zav* – that Gabriel was the last person who should be wearing it. And another instinct was telling Rosie that Zav would resent the speed with which the Hankey family had accepted her new admirer. So far, the singer had only been handling the idea of some shadowy man in Rosie's life. But there was nothing shadowy about the figure who was now cloaking his muscles in borrowed denim. Gabriel was flesh, he was energy, and he was very much here. No, Zav Hankey was not going to like that. How wide was the Atlantic ocean, and was that wide enough?

That same morning Rosie went to work by car. Rain was coming down in stair-rods; and as Gabriel drove them past Gledhill's pharmacy, the car went through a huge puddle, which caused a wave of water to rise up and drench a lone figure waiting at the bus stop.

'Sorry,' he called, above the roar of the engine.

'Don't be!' shouted Rosie. 'That was Bernadette Barrett.' And immediately she felt mean. Since yesterday morning, everything in her own life was gloriously altered. And poor Bernadette was still standing on thick legs, letting the express buses go past because the fares were a penny dearer.

These days Bernadette Barrett was noticeable by her absence; she no longer came to Saracen Street to do her homework. Questioned about this, Rosie fought shy of offering any real explanation. She just said that strong words had been exchanged on a bus. She certainly didn't tell Mrs Hankey that they had been about Zav. The last thing she wanted her landlady to know about was the singer's proposal of marriage. And she still regarded Bernadette's passion for Zav as a secret – albeit one imparted in the dead days of mutual confidences.

Nora Hankey did not press for more information. Instead, in her own good time, she put on a pair of old shoes, suitable for crossing a public refuse dump, and made her way to the shanty.

She returned looking older. 'Mongoose tried to touch me for five pounds,' she said in wonder. 'He behaved as though we *owed* it to him. And Bernadette's turned very bitter.'

'How much did she tell you?' ventured Rosie.

'Enough,' was all the reply she got. And then Mrs Hankey added, 'I'm sure I'd no desire to play the bridegroom's mother in a powder-blue two-piece. I'm more worried about those Barretts. They're suddenly made of hatred. I was left with the distinct feeling I was seeing the beginning of something, not the end.'

Even armed with this information, Rosie was always meaning to go down and visit Biddie. Not for one moment did she doubt that she would be welcome; but Bernadette and Mongoose had suddenly turned into a corporate enemy called The Barretts, and it was impossible to calculate when they would be out. Besides, other summer excitements always seemed to take precedence over a trip beneath the dank railway arch.

The green Morgan sports car soon became a regular feature in Rosie's life. It would pick her up at one o'clock and whisk her off to lunch. It was outside the studio gates again, at the end of the working day. Gabriel's time away from Rosie was spent in the John Rylands Reference Library, on Deansgate. What he did there remained something of a mystery. He would talk vaguely of 'research', and say he was superstitious about discussing 'work in progress'. By now she had gathered that his stay in Manchester would be a limited one, that he was on a year's leave of absence from the philosophy department of University College in London.

Half of her was impressed. But this was overshadowed by the worrying half. If Gabriel had a whole life in London, where would she fit into this scheme of things? Yet Gabriel's attitude seemed to be as simple as her own – they had found one another and that was that. Rosie couldn't help wondering whether he would see things in the same light in the autumn when he would be obliged to head south.

For the moment she was discovering a whole new Manchester: a world of Hallé concerts at the Free Trade Hall, and private views at the Whitworth Gallery, and experimental plays at the Library Theatre. Immigrants and foreigners have always known how to make the best use of

252

Manchester, and Rosie was getting the benefit of this. The restaurants Gabriel squired her into were a whole world tour in themselves. But never again did they attempt an Indian meal. Rosie's original hospital appointment for allergy tests had clashed with a heavy run of work in the Granada graphics department, so it had to be cancelled. She had never got round to making another; she'd heard that there was a risk of the tests making you temporarily ill. And nothing was going to be allowed to interfere with her time with Gabriel.

He was proving to be a man of many surprises. One of his favourite pleasures was visiting the Hankeys. Once Gabriel set foot over the doorstep of number seven, Rosie would have a job to get him out of the house. It was Mrs Hankey who had an explanation for this. 'He's an only child,' she would say. 'He's never had the chance to muck in before. Somewhere rough-and-tumble's a bit of a novelty for him.'

In the traditional Lancashire manner, it was understood that Rosie and Gabriel could use the front parlour for 'courting' purposes. But this was the one place where Gabriel resisted the opportunity to hold Rosie close. The car, shop doorways, Light Oaks Park – these were their kissing grounds. The front parlour always seemed to have the same effect on the Italian as a bucket of cold water.

'I'm too much on trust here,' he would mutter. 'It's too like a mating rite – it unnerves me.'

Kissing was as far as it went. Rosie and Gabriel had got that to a fine art. As he held her close, she would try to slide her hand under his shirt – so as to be able to touch his skin. But he always broke away. 'Too many people have told me you're seventeen and a virgin. Even Tippler's reminded me of that.'

'Perhaps I don't want to be a virgin.' It was dusk and they were by the bandstand. The only music playing was inside Rosie's head, and an old drake was hissing in the bamboo bushes, behind the railings of the duck pond. There was nothing *wrong* with Gabriel. She could feel that when he pressed up against her. But she wanted to reach out and touch what she could feel – and this was an intimacy he wouldn't allow. She wanted his hands to stay on her breasts, but as her nipples swelled, his tantalising fingers always parted company with them.

'Why?' she would ask, miserably. 'And why do I even have to ask you?'

He would only shake his head and say, 'Too many people trust me.'

As the weather got warmer, so did Rosie's yearnings. Sometimes they frightened her; how much of her mother was in herself? One summer night, in the deep shadows of the brick and wooden park shelter, things went further than usual. Hands had travelled urgently, buttons were fumbled undone – a bra strap had fallen over Rosie's shoulder. All attentions had stayed above the waist.

Suddenly she said, 'I want to touch you *there*.'

'No.' The word came out like a gunshot. She should just have done it. Except he would probably have pushed her hand away.

This is ridiculous, she thought. It's all the wrong way round. Girls are the ones who are supposed to stop boys. His sharp 'No' had ruined the magical flow of the chemistry between them. Rosie decided to try to explain. 'Half of me's curious,' she confessed in a murmur. 'But I really think that the devil in me keeps on wanting to do it because you're so against the idea.'

No answer.

'I thought people were meant to talk about these things,' she said miserably. In broad daylight she would never have dared to add, 'It's just that when you're pressed up against me it feels so big. And it beats to match your heart.' She wished she hadn't started this. Her voice began to trail away as she added, 'It would be like touching your secrets.'

As Rosie's voice faltered, Gabriel's came through the darkness with fierce clarity: 'If that's what you want, you'll have to marry me.'

'No.' The vehemence of this answer surprised even herself. Perhaps it had come out this fiercely because she had been thinking about her mother. Rosie just wanted to love and be loved. She didn't want to take Gabriel prisoner.

And she had suddenly realised that this was how she viewed marriage. Memories of Connie and Clifford began to flood back; she remembered the stories of hot passion in the cold-storage warehouse, and she remembered the ugly ending – Connie clacking off into the night on her white high heels, leading Christopher by the hand. But Rosie couldn't bring herself to explain all of this to Gabriel. It would involve digging up the painful past, and she didn't want to have to tell him that nobody had wanted her.

It was Gabriel who broke the silence. 'If you won't marry me, we'd better call it a day.'

'Couldn't we just love one another?' How had this thought managed to come out as whining? she wondered.

Gabriel had moved from the shadows into a patch of moonlight. As he buttoned up his shirt, his knuckle caught on the gold and platinum crucifix which lived on a fine chain around his neck. 'Ouch! You seem to forget I'm a Catholic.'

Rosie tried to think of something to say but all she could manage was, 'Don't leave.'

'Just as a matter of interest, why *don't* you want to marry me?' He could have been addressing her from the North Pole.

'It's not you. It's anybody.'

The ice cap marginally melted. 'Sometimes you sound about ten. I'm rich. Did you know that?' She had guessed something of the sort but it didn't make any difference. Gabriel hadn't finished. 'I feel like shaking you. But if I did that, I'd have to touch you. And if I touched you, we'd only find ourselves back at square one.' His handsome face looked woebegone. 'And don't get the idea that I'm a good Catholic because I'm not.'

He certainly wasn't a Catholic on Sundays. He didn't go to Mass – he always took Rosie to Blackpool instead. His love for this gaudy seaside resort never ceased to puzzle her. 'It's like an outdoor version of the Hankeys,' was all the explanation he would offer.

They never really *talked*. She hadn't even showed him Teapot Hall. But that was for a reason that left her feeling ashamed. These days the house was full of nurses.

Bernadette Barrett had always said that men found nurses, in black stockings, absolutely irresistible – and Rosie didn't want any competition. Mind you, if the nurses could get him going and she could grab the opportunity. . .No, getting him going wasn't the problem – the trouble lay in getting him to go the whole way. And if I'm meant to be ashamed of that, thought Rosie, well I'm not!

By now, Rosie had visited Gabriel's bed-sitting room in Rusholme. 'Off-beat' was an expression that was just coming into popular use. It certainly described the red-brick rooming house. It stood on its own, behind a high wall which hid a garden full of rampant golden rod. The flowers, in their turn, half concealed dozens of empty wine bottles.

'Welcome to the place where the university meets light prostitution,' Gabriel would say as he pushed open the front door. This was brown and chipped and somebody had daubed the words *Liberty Hall* in white paint under the rusty iron knocker. It didn't lead you to expect a stair carpet and you didn't get one.

It always seemed to be raining when they went there. And somebody up in the attic was forever practising the trumpet. Gabriel mostly took Rosie back to the house to change his clothes – and he never seemed anxious to linger. Could this have been because the first-floor room was dominated by a big divan bed?

Rosie was beginning to feel so much the would-be seducer that she actually began to have a mental picture of herself, dressed up in top hat and tails, like an Edwardian stage-door Johnny. She sometimes felt as though she should have been carrying a bouquet and twirling a fine set of mustachios.

At a more realistically feminine level, she had been to see the doctor. It was a consultation which Rosie did not care to dwell upon. Old Dr Dootson had been more embarrassed than she had been. Afflicted with deafness, if anything it seemed as though he was shouting his questions across the generation gap. Was she a virgin? Did she use Tampax? As Rosie bawled back the answers, she found herself wondering whether any of the magazine pages outside in the packed waiting room, were still turning. Or were people just sitting there, with their mouths open in astonishment?

'Too young,' he kept shouting. 'Too young! Why don't you take up tennis?'

In for a penny in for a pound. 'Because I want to make love,' roared Rosie. The wall to the waiting room was noted for being paper-thin and she actually heard someone on the other side emit a little mew of shocked horror.

Dr Dootson gave her a note to take to the birth-control clinic. This was so discreetly hidden – next door to the venereal-disease clinic in Salford – that Rosie took a quarter of an hour to find it. She was too embarrassed to ask anybody for directions until she saw a passing policeman. The police, she reasoned, were *paid* to handle awkward situations. As he directed her down a side street he treated her to a sly wink and she seriously considered slapping his face.

Inside the clinic, the examination couch reminded her of being on the dobby-horses at the fairground. There were even stirrups for her feet. As the woman doctor probed and measured, Rosie found it hard to believe that these processes could have anything to do with love.

At the end of this consultation, she was handed something which looked like a small rubber bowler hat. In fact, it was a contraceptive device known as a Dutch cap. Then came a messy lesson in using it – which involved a tube of lubricating jelly with a sinisterly pointed plastic nozzle.

Getting ready for love began to seem as complicated as learning to ice a cake. The whole proceedings had taken place in the glare of remorseless neon tube lighting; when she got outside Rosie felt like holding out her arms to the sunshine. It was natural, it was real. . .She repressed a mild shudder at the thought of the miniature bowler, in its sterile container, in her shoulder bag.

And that was where it stayed. She carried the thing around for weeks until the strap went on her bag and she was obliged to clear out the contents. That's when the device and the tube of lubricant got shoved into the top drawer of the dressing table. Every time she went to get a clean handkerchief, there they were – a mute reminder of her lack of sexual success. Every newspaper interview with every pop star seemed to be about sex; half the songs on the radio were about 'making it'. You could be forgiven for believing that everybody in England was permanently in a state of coitus – everybody except Rosie and Gabriel.

Sometimes she paused and thought seriously about her attitude towards this subject. To the outsider, her useless little pilgrimage to that clinic in the depths of Salford could have seemed cold-blooded. But it wasn't; it really wasn't. A loving heart had applied common sense to a situation which was potentially explosive. Twice more Gabriel said, 'Let's get married.' Twice more she refused. And she had lost count of the number of times he had pulled away from her in the dark saying, 'Let's get some fresh air.'

She was no fonder than the next person of being repetitive but he didn't seem to understand that she had no desire to follow in her parents' footsteps. 'Tell me about *your* parents. Does their marriage work?'

'It did – for a while.'

'So why get married? Tell me some more about them. Tell me about when you were little.'

'Only if you marry me. That way you won't run away when I tell you.'

Rosie saw this as buying into the old order. And she wanted to be part of the new one. A new order which had already declared a sexual revolution – which proclaimed it was useless to get married until you had ascertained sexual compatibility.

'I wouldn't run away,' she assured him. 'I wouldn't leave you if they were in prison for murder.'

But she was beginning to realise that he liked to deal in mystery. His flippant line: 'This is the house where the university meets light prostitution,' was not quite a joke. The first-floor front bedroom was occupied by a woman called Dorothy. She was a prim-looking creature in pink-tinted glasses but her mouth didn't go with the rest of her. It was oddly sensual, and when you looked closely, the eyes behind the lenses were too knowing.

Gabriel claimed that Dorothy did bizarre things, for money, with the male employees of British Rail; and only British Rail. 'She's got the whole Ardwick Depot in the palm of her hand.' But whenever they met Dorothy on the landing, he would always hurry Rosie past. It was as though he was protecting her – when she would really have preferred a whiff of the unusual. For somebody so modern he certainly seemed to have a quaintly old-fashioned streak.

Yet he never tried to protect her from Jo, the lesbian who had painted his bedroom. 'It's just how she's made,' was his explanation. 'And anyway, she doesn't do it for money.'

Jo looked and dressed like a boy. Actually, her hair was much shorter than most men's of that period. Even as she shook hands with Rosie, Jo was emitting a low whistle and saying, 'What a waste!'

For a moment, the girl from Irlams o'th' Height thought that her own virginity must be written all over her – that Gabriel might have told Jo that he and Rosie were not, strictly speaking, lovers. It was only when she registered the undisguised admiration in the other girl's eyes that she realised that Jo fancied her.

Gabriel was not at all shocked by this. He found it amusing. 'The times they are a changing,' he said. And the chances are that a million other people said it in that same moment. It must have been the most overused line of the whole decade.

But they weren't changing quickly enough for Rosie. Inside her head she would catch herself going tap-tap. That awful old pane of glass was still there. Perhaps it's *thinner*, she would try to tell herself. But she didn't want it there at all. And if she believed in any kind of alchemy, it was that love-making could dissolve plate glass.

'You're so good for him,' said Jo. The brawny little physiotherapist was obviously genuinely fond of Gabriel. She treated him as a fellow admirer of women. 'Before you came along, Rosie, he never had any friends. Certainly not girls. I sometimes used to wonder. . .'

Jo didn't finish the sentence. She didn't need to. Rosie had wondered too. But how could he be gay and still have that throbbing thing pressed up against her?

259

'He does seem to have one friend,' she said to Jo. 'Do you by any chance know who Thomas is?'

Jo just smiled and said, 'So you've found out about the obsession with Thomas, have you?'

'Who is he?'

Jo shook her head. 'Get Gabriel to tell you. I don't believe in treading on other people's dreams.'

It had all started weeks ago. April had just turned into May when he took her to an evening harp recital in Manchester Cathedral. This turned out to be boredom on hard seats. Escaping at the interval, they began to wander along the old streets behind the church. Even at night, the area around the Produce Exchange had a smell all its own. Cheese and smoked bacon were on the air and the sun and the moon were in the sky at the same time. The truants from the cathedral paused and kissed and laughed again at the memory of the nervous harpist. And then they turned into a street where tall dark buildings seemed to close in and threaten the passer-by.

'Thomas went to school here,' said Gabriel. He was nodding towards the forbidding pile of the old Manchester Grammar School.

'But it's been closed for ages,' protested Rosie. 'They moved out to Fallowfield before the war. When was this Thomas there?'

'A while ago,' Gabriel spoke vaguely. 'Yes, quite a while ago. I always think of him on this street because this is where he ran away from.'

'Explain,' she begged.

'Too complicated,' he said briskly. 'Let's go and have a drink in the bar of Victoria Station. It's just like my idea of Byzantium.'

Gabriel said many things she didn't understand, so Rosie didn't bother to press the point about Thomas. By now she had learned that the philosopher's mind was as finely honed as his body. And the things she *didn't* understand made him more intriguing and attractive. The main thing she knew about him was that he was hugely kind. There was nothing English about his emotions. He never hesitated to get fierce and he wept openly at sad films. 'That certainly beat Optrex,' he would say, as he blew his nose in happy satisfaction.

For all his laughing and joking, Gabriel was something of an education in himself. He knew which English words began in Greece and which ones came from Ancient Rome. And he wasn't just an academic drone. When the shutter on her camera went haywire, Gabriel took the whole thing apart and put it right without any fuss. If it was a strange moment to make her yearn for him, she didn't care. It did.

The camera went everywhere with them, and so it seemed did Thomas. He wasn't actually there. References to him haunted everything. Rosie learned not to probe. Instead she stored up all the bits of information. She knew for a fact that Thomas went to St Ann's Church – which meant he wasn't Catholic. He had also lived in the Greenheys district: but the house had first been sold and then pulled down.

Was Gabriel slipping in these references as a teasing joke, hoping she would once again try to get him out into the open? If he was, he soon tired of it. Latterly, any mention of Thomas seemed to have slipped out inadvertently. That didn't stop them being there, but even the mildest question would turn him into a clam. The most she got was: 'Just accept that it's something I'm very deeply into. I don't want to discuss him at a casual level.'

'That's not good enough.' It was a Saturday afternoon and they were climbing into the car outside seven Saracen Street. 'It's simply not good enough.'

'It's all you're getting.'

'And that's downright rude.' Rosie clambered back onto the pavement. She was really angry. 'I'll tell you one thing Oxford didn't teach you. It didn't teach you English manners.'

'Don't be so insular.' But he too had got out of the car.

'I am insular. I was born on an island. I'm English.'

'This is ridiculous. . .'

'Yes, it is ridiculous. You have this friend. He haunts everything. You won't even tell me his surname. I'm beginning to get some very peculiar ideas about you, Gabriel Bonarto!'

'What sort of ideas?'

'Are you queer?' It was out. She'd said it.

In moments of stress, Gabriel could hide behind pedantry. 'It all depends on what you mean by queer.'

'I mean what everybody else means. Homosexual.'

'The "o" is short, it's from the Greek.' But he was white with anger. 'Everybody thinks it comes from the Latin for man. But that's not the case.'

'I don't care.'

'It's from the Greek for "the same".' He had been playing for time and trying to control his anger. Now it roared through. 'So you think I'm a *finocchio*?' As he snarled out the word, all his liberal ideas seemed to have gone to the four winds and Rosie found herself confronted by an outraged Italian male – the standard chauvinistic model.

'There's nothing so awful about being gay.' She was suddenly almost afraid of him but she tried to say this airily.

'Not if you *are* gay. And I'm not.'

'Well you're certainly obsessed with another man and. . .' Rosie was not allowed to finish the sentence – Gabriel had grabbed her by the elbows and was attempting to bundle her into the car.

'Get in,' he stormed. She had little choice in the matter. Even as she was considering the merits of a quick escape, he was round the vehicle in five strides and throwing open the door on the driver's side. In a matter of seconds he was not only seated but starting the engine with a flourish. 'How *dare* you call me a *finocchio*?' he shouted over its opening roar.

'I didn't,' she shouted back. 'You called yourself one. And stop this car, I want to get out.'

'If I stop the car you'll *never* find the truth. No. We're going on a journey. You will see what you will see. And then you can apologise.'

Eighty miles is a long way to drive in near silence. 'Where are we going?' Rosie's attempts at striking up a conversation had been chopped off with the barest of answers.

'The Lake District.' Their whole conversation hadn't amounted to much more than that.

After Irlams o'th' Height, Bolton Road is officially known

as the A666. The devil's number, thought Rosie. But that afternoon she learned, for the first time, that it really did lead to Bolton, and that the place wasn't just a Manchester suburb but a black mill town with its own grandiose town hall and its own gloomy war memorial. For all these years it had been just ten miles away, up a gentle incline, and she had never seen it. The people looked rounder and friendlier than they did in Manchester and Rosie would have liked to get out of the car and have a look round. Gabriel was in too much of a huff to be asked favours, he sped the car through the town and on towards the outline of Rivington Pike.

The test of a clear day in Irlams o'th' Height was whether you could see this folly tower, which sat on top of a natural escarpment. Both hill and tower were now just through the window, on their right-hand side. But Gabriel plainly considered that sightseeing was for the sheep. He accelerated the car to ninety miles an hour so that the sign which pointed to Preston flashed past in an angry blur.

Rosie had spent her early childhood with people who dealt in silences. Both her mother and Christopher were capable of keeping up sulks that would last for days. But this wasn't a sulk, it was a fury which seemed to have attached itself to the foot on the accelerator.

As the car scattered a flock of pigeons outside Lancaster, Rosie said, 'If we're not careful we're going to get done for speeding.'

Gabriel just shrugged. And the shrug was so continental that she asked, 'Have you gone back to thinking in Italian?' He had always said he thought in English.

'*Si*,' he replied coldly. She found this almost as alienating as no reply at all.

Brick houses gave way to stone cottages and the trees stopped being the same ones you saw in Light Oaks Park. There were more conifers and they grew so closely together that young saplings looked threatened. Talk about survival of the fittest! Unfamiliar gamebirds winged from the shadowy depths of the woods. What would happen if one of them hit the windscreen of a speeding car? As the Morgan roared to the top of a hill, all morbid imaginings were erased by a view which has inspired poems and paintings by the thousand. The great silvery expanse of Lake Windermere lay beneath them. Rosie recognised it from a Co-op calendar which had once hung inside of the door of Hankeys' kitchen cupboard.

'Just don't quote Wordsworth's "Daffodils",' said Gabriel tersely.

'I wasn't going to.' If this reply came too indignantly, it was because it was a lie. 'Anyway, why shouldn't I quote it if I want to?'

'Because he wrote better lines than that.'

'Such as?'

Gabriel began to recite in ringing tones:

> 'Bliss was it in that dawn to be alive,
> But to be young was very heaven!'

'Oh but it is.' His voice was still ringing. 'Young people, all over the world, are beginning to think like that again.'

'Are they? I'm not.' This came out grumpily because she was trying to disguise the fact that he had made her feel uninformed and out of touch.

'Wordsworth wrote those lines about the French Revolution. Soon there's going to be another revolution – a youth revolution. In a couple of years it will be an offence to be thirty.'

'Well that's going to place you in a sticky position.' The words were out before she realised that they could hurt.

'Thank you for reminding me of it,' he said coldly. 'I would be a fool to expect more from a woman who thinks I'm a *finocchio*.'

Suddenly Rosie was blazing. 'No! You said it, not me. I'd never even heard the bloody word before today. And if it's not true, why are you making such a fuss about it?' Windermere was not all it had first seemed. As the car slowed down to take a bend in the lakeside road, she could have sworn she saw rubber condoms bobbing on water rocked by noisy speedboats.

To judge by the expression on his face, Gabriel's mind was cross-hatched with angry thoughts again. Rosie tried to soothe him with, 'Tell me more about this revolution.'

'No. One thing at a time. I'm taking you to see my boyfriend.'

Between gaps in the pine trees, the water seemed first to stop and then to start again. Was it all the same lake or had a new one begun? Never mind that; who was this 'boyfriend'? Again Gabriel slowed the Morgan, and now he turned it into a car park, within sight of a whitewashed cottage.

'Out,' he said peremptorily.

For an instant Rosie thought of smacking him across the face and hitchhiking home. But curiosity won the day. She would find out the truth and decide about hitchhiking later. There weren't just cars parked, there was a motor coach as well. And the voices around them sounded American. Even the voice of a woman who looked Japanese. 'Fancy Dorothy papering those bedroom walls with old newspaper!' this tourist said to her non-Japanese companion. He was wearing a very expensive-looking Stetson with a formal suit. Rosie dismissed the thought that Gene Autry might have come to England on a sightseeing trip.

Gabriel grabbed hold of Rosie and bundled her towards the entrance of the little house. A plaque on the wall by the door read *Dove Cottage – Home of William Wordsworth*.

'Anybody would think that William Wordsworth was the only author who had lived here,' fumed Gabriel.

'Let go of me,' hissed Rosie.

He didn't. The man on the door eyed them dubiously. 'The tour's just started,' he said.

Gabriel slapped down a pound note. 'Two,' he said. 'And I have no need of the tour, I could almost certainly conduct a better one myself.'

The grip he had on Rosie was beginning to hurt her arm. Just who did the ruthless pig think he was? Had she not been consumed with curiosity, she would have kicked his shins, there and then, and enjoyed telling him where he got off. And she wouldn't have cared if she'd had to *walk* back to Manchester. 'You use knowledge to show off,' she protested. 'And it's despicable.'

'You ain't seen nothing yet!' Was it the sight of all the tourists inside the low-ceilinged cottage that had suddenly caused him to assume this fake American accent? His voice reverted to its normal tones: 'I've never been keen on the guide here. Too tight-arsed by far. Today we're going to find out how much she *really* knows.'

This guide was already in full confident flood: '. . .the cupboards are in fact made of cheap pine, painted with pigs' blood, so as to resemble the more fashionable mahogany of the day.' In her fawn cardigan and baggy tweed skirt, the woman looked so like the traditional idea of a faded spinster that Rosie was startled to see that she also wore an old wedding ring.

In the meantime Gabriel had snarled, 'Waffle. Unadulterated, pigs'-blood waffle.'

All eyes turned on the Italian. 'Do you have a question?' asked the woman sourly.

'I am *made* of questions.' Gabriel's voice rang round the little panelled room in tones as chilly as the stone-flagged floor. 'Why do you never mention Thomas De Quincey?'

The guide's eyes narrowed. 'Excuse me,' she said overpolitely to the other tourists, who parted to make a path which allowed her to walk up to Bonarto. It seemed to Rosie that these two could have crossed swords before. The woman's tones, when she finally spoke, were downright nasty. 'Thomas De Quincey told lies,' was all she said.

'But who was he?' pleaded Rosie, only hoping that the guide would answer the question before they got themselves chucked out.

'He was the English opium eater. He was trouble. Trouble in a big way.' Having dealt with De Quincey to her own satisfaction, the guide cleared her throat importantly. She was plainly intending to resume her standard lecture.

But Gabriel had other ideas. 'This woman. . .' His finger was pointing accusingly at the official expert.

She looked as though she would have liked to have bitten it off. 'How dare you call me a woman?' The outraged female plainly considered herself a lady.

Gabriel was not one whit abashed. 'I dare call you a woman because it's exactly how Our Lord addressed his own mother. I presume you do not rate yourself above the

Queen of Heaven? This *woman* dismissed the greatest writing talent ever to emerge out of Manchester in one word – trouble. Certainly he was trouble, madam. Genius is always disruptive. Thomas De Quincey's dedication to opium was spiritual. . .' The audience suddenly belonged to Gabriel. 'Let me tell you what he had to say about his beloved drug; hear some of the words of his published *Confessions*. "Happiness might now be bought for a penny and carried in the waistcoat pocket; portable ecstasies might be corked up in a pint bottle; and peace of mind could be sent down in gallons by the mail coach."'

Not drugs again! Intuitive fear was stroking Rosie's spine but the rest of Gabriel's audience was held spellbound. 'Those were the words of Thomas De Quincey,' he said. A tapering forefinger was pointing towards a small pencil and pastel portrait hanging on the blood-washed panelling. 'There is the man, and you. . .' the cocksure finger was now pointing at Rosie '. . .you thought I was *sleeping* with him.'

He had gone too far. You weren't supposed to say things like that in the Lake District in 1964. Gabriel had broken his own spell and the crowd began to shuffle and look to the official guide for renewed leadership. He's lost them and he's lost me too, thought Rosie. Lost me forever. I don't understand this opium business and I don't want to understand it. How the hell do I get out of here?

A sign with an arrow pointed up a short set of stairs. The words on the sign read *To Dorothy's Garden*. Scarlet in the face ('*and you thought I was sleeping with him*'), Rosie was up those stairs so quickly that she could have been an arrow herself. The rattling glass and wooden door into the garden was exactly the same as the ones they'd had at Teapot Hall, even down to the handle. She found herself holding onto it for the comfort of the touch of something familiar – in a world that had gone reeling mad. However you looked at opium it was just another drug. She could rarely remember a moment that had been more awful and embarrassing.

But Dorothy Wordsworth had certainly known how to make a garden. It was ordered yet pleasantly overgrown – like a celebration of plenty.

An old man with very clean white hair was looking up into a curiously twisted tree which had leaves like green suede. The man could have been a gardener; his overlarge brown tweed suit looked as though it had been handed down to him by somebody more aristocratic. 'I've lost Tom,' he said.

Not another Tom! But this one was presumably a cat. And the sunlight was cutting the thoughts of ancient opium down to size. But not the thought of Gabriel haranguing that crowd. Just who did he think he was? He might have been named after an angel but that was no excuse for carrying on like Judgement Day. Yet Rosie was forced to admit to herself that his performance had been as passionate as forked lightning. Until he came to the awful part about. . .No, it didn't bear thinking about.

The man who had made the speech now strolled into the garden.

'I'm not speaking to you,' she said. 'Anyway, we've lost Tom.' She decided to concentrate on looking up into the tree.

It was the old man who broke the silence: 'I've still got a bad leg from the last time I went up. Tom's got no fear when he's flying up there. But when he gets to the top, he panics at the thought of coming down.' His voice was neither Lancashire nor Tyneside but somewhere in between.

'I'm just the same myself.' Gabriel attempted to take Rosie's hand.

She pushed it away and thought about the gardener's voice instead. He must be speaking with the local accent. Geography would explain the dialect. After all, they had travelled over eighty miles from Manchester. 'All that way, just for you to show off disgracefully,' she muttered to Gabriel.

'But now you know I'm not a *finocchio*,' he said cheerfully. And throwing his suede jacket to the ground, he began to climb the tree. He had climbed a lot of trees before – you could tell that by the way his feet found the trunk and his arms tested the branches. He was absolutely sure of what he was doing; and the bare, muscular forearms were suddenly striking Rosie as infinitely desirable. As he disappeared up into the velvety leaves, the whole tree began to shimmer and shudder.

'Watch yourself,' Rosie called out anxiously.

'Found him.' The cry of triumph was followed by gentle pleadings with the tomcat. '*Gattino. . .vieni qui, gattino.*' It was the first time she had ever heard him speak Italian. The persuasive words melted the last cold patch in Rosie's heart. But the cat – made of sterner stuff – let out a screech which belonged to the night-time.

'Got you! The little bastard's drawn blood.' The downward descent was not as sure as the bold climb. The cat was obviously refusing to accept Gabriel as its saviour. No sooner did it get a glimpse of the ground than the ginger tom leapt from Gabriel's arms and began to rub up against Rosie's legs.

This sensual massage expedited a plan. A moment before, it had been barely formed; but suddenly it was there – whole – inside her head. And if she wasn't careful, it would soon be accompanied by rustling butterfly wings. Once again it was Gabriel's arms that had done it. The effort of climbing the tree had thrown the muscles into sharp relief, and the veins standing out against them didn't look like a medical textbook, they looked like turquoise on amber.

'As I was saying,' he was a bit short of breath, 'Thomas died a hundred years ago and I'm not a *finocchio.*'

'No, I don't think you are.' Rosie's tones were deadly serious. 'And today's the day you're going to prove it.'

'Who *is* that awful woman in the cottage?' Gabriel asked the old man.

'Her?' He snorted. 'She thinks she's it. Sees herself as a lady of the manor. Gets up socials for the young people – and then she stops them dancing close together. If you ask me, it only makes them worse. They soon learn what the hillsides are for. They're out of the dance and up that back lane before you can say moonlight.'

Gabriel had bent down to stroke the cat, which had suddenly decided to be his friend. This brought him so near to Rosie that she could smell the clean sweat of his recent exertions. It was ten times more erotic than any aftershave lotion and she reached down and touched the back of his neck with fingers that were suddenly made of longing.

'The lane behind this cottage?' asked Gabriel, huskily.

'That's the one,' said the nice old man. And greatly daring, he added shyly, 'The best places are where the bracken meets the rocks.'

9

Where the bracken meets the rocks, where the bracken meets the rocks. . .The hill was as high as Rivington Pike but there wasn't a folly tower on top of it – just themselves. Even higher up, just beneath the clouds, two black and white magpies were circling the great wide sky. At long last, two for joy.

Rosie knew exactly what was going to happen: this was it – this was their time. But the world beneath them wasn't standing still; she could hear a distant phut-phut-phut of a motor launch on the lake below. And that's when she thought of the awful Dutch cap, stowed in the handkerchief drawer, back at Saracen Street. So what! Let it stay there. What had that rubber monument to constraint got to do with glorious freedom? As the pair of them clung together, Rosie realised with absolute certainty that Gabriel's body was finally going to serve up its mysteries. The thought went rippling through her like a fine pencil drawing of the fan-shaped wave made by the motor launch as it divided the waters of the lake.

'Thomas had another house over there. . .' Gabriel had broken away from her and was pointing towards the next promontory.

Rosie took hold of the pointing hand and placed it across Gabriel's own mouth. 'No Thomas,' she said. 'Just us.' And very gently she rubbed her cheek against the hand.

This tiny, loving movement did more for her cause than she could have known. 'You're so beautiful,' murmured Gabriel. 'But are you old enough?' The aching yearning in his voice sounded close to pain. 'God, how I want you. I've wanted you since that first day in Vesuvius.'

'I'm old enough,' Her fingers had turned into a team of explorers. Under the cotton shirt they found the hard swell of his chest and the nubs of his nipples (were these singing like her own were singing?). As her hands went down the outline of his body she could feel how his waist went in at the sides;

271

her fingers moved across until they were actually feathering their way through that intriguing pencil-line of hair beneath his navel.

'Now I take over,' he said. And the hard thing was pressed against her with no restraint. There was still unnecessary cloth between them. . .Oh but his hands were clever. Touch me here, she thought – and he was already on the place. Now touch me there. The thought was soundless but he'd heard it anyway and answered with a caress. Touch me, find me, feel me. . .He was using lips now and a deftly flickering tongue. Her own hands were out of control, they were going everywhere, including *there* – which was suddenly just a part of the glorious whole. Too many clothes, too many clothes.

Rosie paused for breath and, the moment she'd found it, she began to undo his shirt. 'I want to look,' she said. 'I can't help it. I caught one glimpse in Mrs Hankey's back kitchen and it was like seeing God.'

Gabriel was helping her out of her own clothes. Why did knickers have to cut into flesh and leave an ugly mark? Had his own elastic done the same thing? There was no real chance to see. Just another glimpse of the sculpture that was his body. . .and then they were clinging together, as one of her discarded shoes rolled down the slope.

'Go easy,' he breathed. 'Careful. It's too wild, too quickly. Jesus!' This was no curse; he was sending up a great cry of respect to Heaven. And now she seemed to have turned into his mother for he was suckling a breast. Her thoughts did not stay long maternal. His tongue was rallying up responses in the rest of her body. She felt the roughness of his chin as it travelled down her, and then the tender lapping started in her own secret place. Phut-phut-phut-phut went the boat on the lake, but woodpigeons in the gorse were making softer noises.

For a brief moment Rosie opened her eyes. She and her lover were lying in a huge nest of bracken. I wonder if it's leaving a pattern on my bottom, she thought. But this was drenched out by a wilder thought: 'I want you inside me. . .' She had never meant to cry it right out loud.

Rosie was prepared for it to hurt, she'd heard a hundred stories. But Gabriel was so skilled that, as she lay there with

272

her eyes closed, she couldn't tell when fingers and tongue
had ended and the other had taken over. Only, suddenly,
she *could* tell. 'No . . . that's better; it only hurts when you
stab. Oh yes, *slide* it, slide it again. . .' She was nearly
weeping in wonder as she heard herself murmur, 'Oh
Gabriel, I'm getting to somewhere else.'

'It's okay. I'm there with you. Come on, travel, travel,
travel . . .'

So this was it. This was what it was all about. It was
getting lost in time and space with somebody. Every magazine article had led her to expect a hundred complications
where none existed. God himself only knew why she was
choosing to forgive her own mother at this moment; but
that's what was happening. She remembered Connie saying
that the black man had made her feel as though she was
lined with white satin – and Rosie was glad of a phrase that
explained this extraordinary sensation. Only, suddenly,
everything seemed to be turning in and clenching and
tightening up. It was like being on the brink of a great
discovery. That was the moment she heard her own cries
mixed with the sound of Gabriel's frenzied breathing. He
too was riding his way towards something. And in that same
instant she suddenly remembered what Beryl Molyneux had
said.

'No,' shouted Rosie, instinctively. 'Watch out! You
mustn't spurt inside me.'

He pulled out just in time. She watched five arcs of silver
ribbon shoot out of him. You could actually watch the secret
muscle jerking. The only trouble was that she had just
missed getting to that amazing place – and now the silver
ribbons were only slime on her stomach.

Gabriel was kissing her in a new way. Oh but he was
tender and loving and almost alight with gratitude. 'I never
want anybody else again,' he gasped. 'Never. It made me
wish I'd never ever done it before.'

As the pair of them lay back in the bracken their panting
subsided. Gabriel let go of Rosie's hand and began to trace
his fingers through the stuff that had landed on her stomach.
'Just think,' he said, 'there could be a whole army lying

273

there. Millions of them and all boys. In our family we always make boys. How many do you want?'

'Whatever God sends.' What was happening to her? First she'd forgiven her mother and now it seemed that God was back in her life for the first time since that final morning at Quakers. Only this wasn't the God that churches and scripture lessons used to batter people over the head. It was the same God she had sensed for herself in the Quaker silence; a God who felt like everybody she'd ever loved putting their arms around her at the same moment. She was finding this again in the wide sky above her and even in the bracken which had seeds upon its back. And judgemental preachers would not have approved of the fact that she was also rediscovering it in the closeness of Gabriel Bonarto's body.

Rosie suddenly found herself wanting to sing a hymn which they had been forced to learn at Pendleton High. She didn't sing it aloud, just in her head:

'It's in the breeze, the rushing air,
The hills that have for ages stood . . .'

'I think magpies are the devil's servants.' Gabriel had sat up. 'Look how that one's swooping low over my crucifix.' He lifted the cross and chain from out of the ferns and put it back around his neck.

'I never even realised you'd taken it off.'

'Ripped it off, more like. I always do – for that.'

Now Rosie sat up too. 'Why?' She reached for her bra.

There was an awkward pause, and then Gabriel said, 'I wouldn't take it off if we were married.'

'I thought we'd just had the ceremony.' But she was thinking about what he'd said. *I always take it off – for that.* How many other women had there been? The theory of other women was fine; they'd taught him the tricks, honed his technique. But the reality meant that these strangers must have felt him as she'd just felt him; and Rosie found herself hating the idea of their frantic hands on his strong back. He was hers. 'Didn't what we just did *mean* anything to you?'

Gabriel looked much younger and less sure of himself than usual as he said, 'We ought to be married. That way we'd have one another for eternity.' These words made him sound mysteriously alien and Catholic.

'Only Muslims believe there will be sex in Heaven.' It was her father who'd said that, on the night Connie walked out. Odd that the past should cast its shadows on a day when she was meant to be feeling sunlit and changed. The biggest part of the change was that her childhood had lost its power to hurt her. Or had it?

Rosie decided to try an experiment. She wanted to see whether the pane of glass was still inside her head. And even as she thought this, she could have wept with frustration. She didn't even have to go tap- tap – it was still rigidly in place.

Why? Why hadn't it gone? Would she never be free? And then she thought of the tightening and the clenching she had felt inside herself as they made love. Perhaps, when that burst open, everything would be okay. 'It's easier for men,' was all she voiced aloud.

'That's one of the most puzzling things you've ever said.' The phut-phut of the speedboat embroidered another silence. 'Perhaps I'm scared you'll go away,' said Gabriel, quietly.

'Not me,' answered Rosie. 'You're talking to the wrong woman. Did you ever read the story of Ruth and Naomi, in the Bible?' Had she lost her virginity and turned into a scripture lesson? Nevertheless, Rosie began to recite. 'Intreat me not to leave thee and forsake me not . . .'

'I don't know that part. I know the part about where you go, I'll go.'

'And thy country being as my country? And thy people being my people? That's what I believe in, Gabriel. That's what I've always believed in. I just had to wait for you to come along to make it work.'

'So you'll really go wherever I go?' He was leaning on one elbow and studying her intently.

She nodded and wondered whether to put on more clothes or take off her bra again.

'You promise me that?' insisted Gabriel. 'You'll go where I go?'

'I promise.'

He let out a sigh of relief. 'Then we'll soon be going to live in London.' And this time, when they made love, he did not remove the crucifix.

The 'Swinging London' of the mid-Sixties was just a journalist's invention – a kind of litany which went, 'Carnaby Street, Mary Quant, Mods and Rockers and Transcendental Meditation.' These were simply background to a time which provided young people with more money than they'd ever had before. And established middle-aged names found themselves edged out of the way as the young provided one another with everything from fashions to entertainment. If Irlams o'th' Height was a black and white photograph, 1960s London was in Kodacolour. 'And *it* is here,' said Gabriel triumphantly.

'What's it?' asked Rosie – who had been whisked into a new life at lightning speed and had yet to cast off the idea that she was still distinctly provincial.

Gabriel smiled happily. 'It's the feeling of being in absolutely the right place at the right time. Ten years ago it was Paris. Then it went to Liverpool for a few months and turned into music. Now it's in London. It's as though all the creative forces have gathered. And they're showering down like a fireworks display.'

Aristocratic titles were out and back streets were in. Even young Etonians were not above adopting working-class accents. Saracen Street had never handed Rosie its speech patterns but it had certainly qualified her for the times. It was essential to have a back street to rebel against.

Gabriel and Rosie lived in Mayfair. There was so much to *do*. And some of the things were so new that they didn't have names. They were just gatherings of young people glorying in the excitement on the air – and they were called 'happenings'.

Every weekend, to the outrage of their elders, young people simply gathered in Hyde Park and on Primrose Hill in their colourfully dressed thousands. And they were content to listen to free pop concerts, and to blow soap bubbles, and to burn joss-sticks in the open air – and they were content just to *be* – though it is true that the hand-rolled cigarettes, which were passed around with generous disregard for ownership, contained more than tobacco.

If there was one moment which crystallised the times for Rosie it was a sight she saw in Hyde Park on one of those golden Sunday afternoons. The grass was dotted with young people who looked as though they'd raided their dressing-up boxes; it was all Indian prints and collarless striped shirts and skin-tight jeans and battered top hats. A girl in a long paisley kaftan was stumbling after a butterfly when – suddenly – the breeze caught her cotton folds and revealed an ugly built-up surgical boot. In a more conventional gathering this disadvantage would have been on view, for all the world to pity. But the kindly times had offered the laughing flower child the chance to cover it. You could be who you wanted, dress how you wanted, reveal what you wanted. You could redesign yourself. That's what was best about the Sixties.

Rosie's thoughts immediately flew to Poor-Bertha-who-drags-a-leg. Had kindness reached Brindle Heath or were callous children still pointing and throwing stones at the cripple? The hardest thing about leaving Irlams o'th' Height had been saying goodbye to Teapot Hall. Though Rosie had grown into a determined young woman, common sense and reason deserted her on the drive of the old stone house.

You look so sanitised, she thought. It was almost like talking to a person. The Health Authority have cleaned you up and tidied all the romance out of you. But I'll get you back. I will. I promise. And we'll turn the garden back into a great big riot of colour and we'll rip down all these prim notice boards – and we'll be happy together.

And if this was impractical nonsense, Rosie didn't care. She had meant to take one last photograph of the house but uniformed nurses kept straying across her viewfinder. 'I'll just have to remember you as you were,' she said. She actually said it out loud. And as she turned to go she noticed the thing which hurt the most. The tidy-minded Health Authorities had ripped all the birds' nests out of the trees.

You don't just uproot yourself from a Saracen Street without a fuss. But Zav had already done the spade work by proving that flight could lead to prosperity. After days of deep questioning, it was Mrs Hankey who telephoned Rosie's father and said, 'She's managed to get herself a place at Regent Street Polytechnic. It's a photographic course and you'll need to fill in the forms for her student grant. You won't stop her so there's no use in trying. Rosemary's found herself a feller. He's headstrong but so's she. They don't make a bad pair.'

And Clifford, with Quakerly tolerance, had merely hoped that the young couple would find the time to visit him in Teddington. This wasn't a London district where many soap bubbles blew. Clifford returned the signed form by post and remained a stranger.

'Trendy' was the new word. It was applied to music and clothes and even to districts. Mayfair, in the heart of London, was not really part of the youth culture. Yet the young were already aspiring to this expensive district. The new hair-dressers had branches there, record companies had started moving into Berkeley Square, and psychedelically decorated Rolls-Royces were beginning to be seen on Park Lane.

Rosie and Gabriel lived down a narrow turning at the back of this fashionable stretch. Most of the cream-stuccoed houses in Tiddy Street had been turned into offices. But an ancient cousin of the Queen's still put out her own milk bottles, underneath the porticoed canopy of a house at the end. And next door, at number three, Professor Robert Fellowes had converted an inherited property into three flats.

A Conservative Member of Parliament lived in a perma-nent state of noisy disagreement with a boyfriend, on the top floor. Bob Fellowes, who was Gabriel's easy-going boss at University College, occupied the ground floor himself. He was plain and kind and said to be looking for love. Rosie and Gabriel were the sole tenants of the basement.

They even had their own entrance, though this didn't stop Rosie feeling she was living in a London rabbit warren. You went through an iron gate, set in the railings at street level, down a flight of perilous stone steps, across a small flagged courtyard, and came to a fluorescent pink basement door. Mrs Hankey would have died at what lay beyond.

The flat had formerly been occupied by one of Fellowes' daughters who had departed to run a boutique in Fulham. Her memory lingered on in Day-Glo. She had used this fluorescent paint to colour the sitting-room walls in a vibrant shade of lime yellow. The ceiling was midnight-blue with silver stars. For added effect she had sprayed silver clouds onto the throbbing yellow walls and her enthusiasm for the silver spray-can had not stopped at the cast-iron fireplace. 'I feel as though I should be offering to tell fortunes,' was Rosie's first comment. Her second one was, 'We'll either have to do everything to it, or nothing.'

They did nothing. The black and white bedroom remained dominated by a collage of eyes cut from magazines, glued to the wall and varnished over. The bathroom stayed lit by a row of multicoloured electric light bulbs, fastened to a painted wooden batten which looked as though it had been pinched from a fairground. The kitchen was the biggest surprise of all. Plain brown and cream, it didn't seem to have been touched since before the war.

They made coffee there and that was all. 'Either you learn to cook magnificently,' said Gabriel, 'or I'd rather pay for restaurants.'

He proved to be quite capable of hauling her off to Claridge's for breakfast. It was all a far cry from safe Saracen Street. Gabriel was mysterious about money but there was plainly no shortage of it. Within a year the green Morgan had been exchanged for a red Ferrari which he was forever parking outside Italian restaurants; he seemed to count parking fines as a form of supplementary income tax. All this on a university lecturer's salary? When Rosie asked, all she got was: 'Be careful I don't tell you more than you want to know.'

'But oughtn't I to know everything about you?'

'Perhaps I like being mysterious.' He was kind, he was generous, he made love to her like an avenging angel – wild one minute, tender the next. One day she realised it was months since she had last confronted him with an awkward question.

This is not to say that Rosie was entirely happy with the

situation. Thinking women were beginning to assert their rights to self-sufficiency and freedom. But once she'd finished her course, Rosie expected to be earning her own keep – with her camera. For the moment, Gabriel paid all the bills for a lifestyle which effectively cut her off from her fellow students. Her life was him and that was that. Sometimes she caught herself wondering whether 'payment for services rendered' might enter into this deal.

No. When he cried out in his sleep she held him close for nothing. For nothing? She held him close for love. There were girls in her year at the Polytechnic who envied the fact that Rosie seemed to be everything to this mysterious and clever Italian. But these were not the girls who were burning their bras.

Rosie and Gabriel were only one stage removed from living out of suitcases. She could never erase the feeling of marking time, the thought that London was only the trailer for some eventual big picture.

Though Gabriel knew a lot of people, he did not seem to have any close friends. People were certainly drawn to the fast mind and the easy charm, but there was a shy streak in him which seemed to resist anybody offering anything approaching intimacy. All he appeared to want around him were books and ideas and Rosie Tattersall.

It took other Italians to turn Gabriel Bonarto into an altogether more relaxed companion. Was this because he understood their social rules? Or was it because they treated him like a prince? Rosie never ceased to be surprised at the big hello which was always offered to Gabriel in Italian restaurants; there they called him Gabriele. One of his favourites was in Dean Street in Soho; a place full of dazzling white tablecloths, where brandy flames leaped as waiters cooked Florentine specialities on little spirit stoves at the tables. The walls of the restaurant were lined with signed photographs of continental film stars. And the performers themselves were often to be glimpsed, tucked away in semi-private booths, at the back of the room. But it was Gabriel who always got the best table in the place.

'Princess Margaret she not come tonight,' the proprietor

would beam, snatching *Reserved* from between the salt cellars, whilst deferential minions pulled back two gilded chairs.

Rosie had trained herself not to look at the prices in the right-hand column of the menu. If she seemed to be ordering with a view to economy, Gabriel could get cross. She always had to remind herself that, had she been the one with the money, she would have provided just as lavishly for him. And it wasn't as though he didn't get the point of queuing up for fish and chips, because he did.

In that particular Soho restaurant, at the end of the meal, there would always be a big argument over the bill, with Gabriel protesting that it came to nothing like enough. This invariably ended with the proprietor patting Gabriel's cheek affectionately and saying, 'This is just a token charge. The debt was already paid. Your uncles paid it years ago – in Italy.'

And then there was the routine of refusing a cigar to be got through. Gabriel, who hardly ever smoked one, would settle this by slamming down some extra money for a glass of amoretto to be sent to the chef in the kitchen.

Signora Bolla's café, in nearby Old Compton Street, was an altogether more down-to-earth establishment. It had a marble-topped counter and steamed-up windows and a ferociously noisy coffee machine. Rosa Bolla made her own pasta and only served it to people she liked. She was particularly partial to ballet dancers. Rosie was surprised to find that many of the dancers chain-smoked. And the café's owner was quite capable of snatching a cigarette from a famous mouth before she would deign to place food on the table.

With her dyed black hair and lustrous eyes, and a bosom the size of twin domes on an opera house, Signora Bolla looked like an ageing prima donna who had decided to wear a big white apron as a joke. She always had a dog at her heels. Though he was called Umberto he could easily have been related to Trixie Hankey. And he seemed to recognise Rosie on sight. Perhaps this is what endeared her to Signora Bolla –who was forever dragging the girl into the kitchen and attempting to teach her how to cook.

'When these have fallen. . .' she would proclaim as she

patted her great frontage '. . . when these have collapsed, you can always hold a man with a soup ladle. Be sure to beat the stock into the cream, and not the other way round.' 'I not afraid of those Bonartos,' was another of her favourite lines.

'Why should you be afraid of them?' asked Rosie, dipping a finger in the cream and getting her hand slapped for daring to do it. 'What's frightening about Gabriel's family?'

'I only count the good they done,' was the most she ever got out of Rosa. Nevertheless, the big woman tapped the side of her nose significantly.

'Feed him artichokes!' she would cry with abandon. 'They kept my husband stiff for forty years.'

Battered Soho was always a place of pilgrimage for Gabriel. One figure still haunted their lives: Thomas De Quincey. And the nineteenth-century writer had strong connections with this immigrant district, where foreign restaurants were beginning to fight for space with sex shops and striptease joints. Prostitution was still out on the streets in those days, but the girls, with their polite murmurs of, 'Good evening, sir,' never approached a man accompanied by a woman. And these ornaments of the night vanished entirely when narrow and slightly sinister streets gave way to the open space of Soho Square.

That was where the ghost of Thomas De Quincey swooped back into their lives as they sat bathed in moonlight, under the canopy of the open-fronted summerhouse, in the middle of the deserted public gardens.

If this fake-Tudor hut was like something out of a story by Enid Blyton, the tale Gabriel had to tell was entirely factual. 'She propped him up on the steps of one of those houses.'

'Who did?' asked Rosie, curious as to the identity of the woman, but knowing full well that the man could only be spooky Thomas. 'Who propped him up?'

'Ann. That's why I'm always extra-polite to the whores in this area. Ann was a child prostitute.'

'But that's awful.'

'Nevertheless it's how things were, a hundred and fifty years ago. He was only about seventeen himself. Thomas was never one of her clients. They were just stragglers who'd found one another on the streets.'

'I thought he was a Manchester Grammar School boy.' In Rosie's mind this represented the safest respectability on earth. They even wore solemn owls on their blazers.

'He'd run away from school to seek his fortune. Only everything went wrong, and he collapsed with hunger – in this square. Ann propped him up in a doorway and rushed off to Oxford Street and used her last money to buy him a glass of port wine, spiked with reviving spices.'

Gabriel's eyes roved hungrily round the moon-softened buildings which rimmed the square. There were still some shabby porticoed mansions left, and flickering green candlelight was coming up from behind the stained glass of windows set high up in the walls of St Patrick's Church. 'It was two minutes away from here that Thomas first bought the opium. . .' Gabriel seemed to savour the next words, his voice all but caressed them '. . .the dusty brown tincture of opium.'

Was he quoting De Quincey? Rosie had a more important question to ask than that. 'Have you ever tried it?' She dreaded the answer but she had to be absolutely sure that he knew what she was asking. 'Opium. Have you ever had a go with it?'

'No.' The answer was fiercely unequivocal. 'It led Thomas to ecstasies but they brought their own demons. Science has moved on, Rosc. There are newer, cleaner, more clinical substances today. But I do want to be in touch with happiness.' He sounded much younger than his years – like a child longing for Christmas.

Rosie failed to be charmed. She was horrified. 'Happiness? I thought that's what I was for.'

'I want to know God.' Some trick of the moonlight had rendered his face almost luminous. 'Now you know,' he said blankly. 'I've just told you the most truth about myself you'll ever hear.'

She didn't know whether to laugh or cry. 'Nobody can know God,' she protested. 'Not in this life, anyway.' By now she'd settled on her overriding emotion. It was fear.

'Saints have managed to do it. Mystics spend a whole lifetime working at it. Aldous Huxley consumed the extract

283

of a South American cactus and experienced Heaven.' Gabriel rose to his feet and began to move along the flagged path.

If she wanted to ask more, Rosie would be obliged to follow him. She didn't like herself for being so sheeplike but she needed answers. 'You surely wouldn't try anything so stupid?' she asked, as she caught up with him. She hadn't meant it to sound like a schoolmistress's question, but it did.

Gabriel was obviously regretting having told her this much. The face which turned to her was now illuminated by ordinary orange street lighting. This only heightened the fact that it was ablaze with anger. 'What's stupid about the biggest question in life? I have to know for myself whether God exists.'

Some Quaker simplicity deep within Rosie Tattersall found itself outraged. 'And you're proposing to do that with drugs?'

There was a pause and then, 'Only with the right drug.'

His tone was dismissive but Rosie wasn't leaving it at that. 'And where do you propose to find this substance?'

'It exists.'

'That's no answer.'

'People are already using it. They're experimenting with it in America. It's called lysergic acid.'

Lysergic acid diethylamide equalled LSD which equalled something that students were already talking about at the Poly. One girl in Rosie's year claimed to have swallowed a tablet and sat and looked at herself in a mirror – until the reflection revealed the muscles under the skin. And then these fell away to reveal the bones of the girl's own skull. 'You're behind the times,' snapped Rosie, 'you can get it here.' The moment she heard that snap coming into her voice she knew she would be ready, in seconds, to bite off her own tongue. She'd learned snapping at Mrs Hankey's knee and it always led to trouble.

Not this time. Or not yet. 'You can't be sure of the quality here. A man called Owsley makes the best stuff. He's in San Francisco. That's where I'm aiming to find it.' Gabriel began to walk towards the neon signs of Greek Street where a solitary whore was patrolling the corner in a plastic raincoat and very high-heeled shoes. Rosie let him go. But hearing the woman produce a low purr of 'Good evening, sir,' she hurried after him.

'Hands off. That one's mine!' she said to the prostitute.

'Thought I'd struck lucky.' Beneath heavy false lashes the woman had amused eyes. 'At least he's properly washed. Half the ones I get are downright musty. Good evening, Umberto.' This was still a time when all the residents of Soho knew one another, and the small dog from Signora Bolla's restaurant was making his way purposefully along the street.

Gabriel suddenly became himself again. Thoughts of the Almighty were replaced with concern for the scruffy terrier. 'I'm sure he shouldn't be out on his own, after dark.'

'Course he shouldn't.' The Soho businesswoman batted her eyelashes alarmingly. 'But the priest's bitch is on heat. Men have to do what men have to do.' And she winked at Rosie in quite a friendly way.

'But not always?' Rosie's head was still full of Gabriel's talk of chemical routes to Heaven. 'I just hope they don't have to do it always.'

'Every fucking time, dear. Good evening, sir. . .' She had caught sight of a genuine client and Rosie reflected that he did indeed look as though he was going to smell a bit musty. She could only hope that the eyelash lady's other observation about men would not prove to be similarly accurate.

It must have been well over two years since Rosie had last given Bernadette Barrett any serious thought. She knew that the blobby-freckled redhead had won an open scholarship to the London School of Economics because Mrs Hankey had forwarded a cutting from the *Salford City Reporter*. But the rest had been silence. This made it all the more startling when – walking along Regent Street – Rosie thought she caught a glimpse of her erstwhile enemy. When the outline got a few paces closer the legs weren't thick enough for Bernadette.

One thing Rosie did know: she was going to see the real Bernadette quite quickly. She had often noticed that this kind of mistake almost invariably led to a meeting with the genuine person. These ponderings on psychic matters caused her to think about her twin. Yes . . . the faint hum was still there. She wondered whether he'd felt one, inside his own head, at that same moment. Except, if he was still in America, he would probably be fast asleep, or just getting up – depending on which side of the country he was living. There had been no news of Connie and Christopher since the card from Cheyenne, Wyoming. The map had shown that to be bang in the middle of America. So what time would it be there?

Rosie gave up trying to calculate. She was in London and it was early on a summer Saturday afternoon. She looked at her own face in a shop window and tried to imagine it turned into a man's. Her twin must already be shaving. That was an eerie thought. And his little dick, which she'd only ever seen at bathtime, could now be as big as Gabriel's. And if you weren't meant to think things like this about your own brother, she was doing it. And what the hell! Equally, she remembered the young Zav Hankey – naked as one of the Water-Babies – diving into the Hankeys' kitchen on that first bathnight in front of the open fire.

Rosie found herself smiling fondly. She knew where Zav was. He was a great big star in America, forever sending her photographs of his children. Nowadays, Zav owned a house on a cliff out at Big Sur in California – and he still held a unique place in her affections. Odd to think that he'd always been more of a brother to her than Christopher.

Rosie headed out of grandiose Regent Street and into Kingly Street, which was much more crouched and narrow. She was looking for a second-hand camera shop. She had been told they might just be able to supply her with a replacement carrying case for her Rolleiflex. The camera was, as always, over her shoulder; but the case looked on its last legs and was held together with black insulating tape.

The address of the shop had been given to her by a student at Regent Street Polytechnic. Rosie's relationship with her fellow students was not over comfortable. They could not forget that her early photographs of Zav Hankey were world-famous. When the course began, Rosie had not seen why she should admit to them that Zav had got the early bandstand picture for the price of a new film – it could have seemed disloyal. And Danny Cahn had acquired copyrights of the photographs done on tour for a flat fee. As far as the other students were concerned, she was a girl who owned a rich boyfriend and high-earning negatives. These thoughts coloured their reactions to the extent that she would never have dreamed of telling them the financial truth. All in all, it was a bit like being the girl from Teapot Hall who got dumped into a council school – all over again.

The course itself had proved to be something of a disappointment. In technical photographic matters, she had been surprised to find that none of the lecturers were any more proficient than Sid Molyneux. In fact, every passing term had made Rosie more aware of how lucky she had been to have had him as her first teacher. Efficiency had always been a byword with Mr Molyneux. Her college lecturers tended to be much more slap-happy, and far more intent on putting Rosie in touch with her own creative talent. And therein lay the problems.

The pictures she had taken as little more than a child had been totally uninhibited. With growing maturity, that freedom of expression had vanished. The Regent Street Polytechnic had turned Rosie into her own fiercest critic. And she didn't like the work she was producing, she didn't like it at all.

Nevertheless, in the hope of becoming fluent with the camera again, she continued to take pictures. Gabriel unhesitatingly underwrote her meagre grant. Students could get film at discount prices and wherever she went Rosie took shots of anything and everything. She was actually taking one this moment. It was of a group of outer-London teenagers who were plainly heading for nearby Carnaby Street. Would the shot heighten the fact that their outfits were only halfway there? That the kids had yet to be able to afford trendy shoes. She wanted the picture to look as though parents were still clinging onto control of their children's feet. At thirteen she wouldn't have gone through all these thought processes, she would have simply captured the effect she wanted in one uncomplicated click. But now she was twenty and in awe of her own talent of seven years ago.

The camera shop had turned into a unisex boutique called Red, White and New. Wasn't there a law against cutting up Union Jacks? If there was, it was being broken all around her. The national flag seemed to be on everything from bib-and-brace overalls to biscuit tins. Even a year ago this whole area had been throbbing with new fashion ideas. Now it just seemed to have turned into one huge catch-penny.

Would the little Italian provision store across the road have the almond biscuits which were Gabriel's particular favourites? Where *was* the little Italian shop? She had to count along the buildings before she realised that it had been replaced by a vegetarian snack bar called the Banana Trip. It had either been there or on the site of another shop called Uncle Sam's, which sold clothes made out of the Star-Spangled Banner. Loudspeakers outside all these shops were blaring forth different pop tunes. As she walked along the narrow lane the whole atmosphere seemed to have been dyed with commercial air-fresheners which smelt of Eastern incense.

It was as though the grown-ups – the dull, safe, tweed and knitting-pattern grown-ups – were being given notice to quit that side of Regent Street. But Liberty's solid department store was still where it had always been even though the wax dummies in the windows were wearing carefully curled sisal hippie wigs, and carrying bunches of artificial silk flowers which were priced in guineas. The models were draped in yards of traditional Liberty silk which had been reprinted in psychedelic colours – presumably to match the times. The older generation of shops never got it quite right. In fact it was a bit like seeing your own mother stoned on pot.

On the other side of Regent Street, Rosie found herself back in staid Mayfair. Not many signs of the Sixties here, unless you counted a travel agency on Maddox Street which had a poster in its window for overland trips to Kathmandu. Even taxis, with *For Hire* signs lit up, passed through the echoing, deserted streets at speed, as if they knew the area would have nothing to offer them again until Monday morning.

The doorman outside Claridge's Hotel had so little to do

that he raised his cockaded hat to Rosie as she passed. Were the fake gypsy violinists bothering to play their usual sentimental music in the entrance hall? Rosie paused for a moment and tried to hear; but the only noise she could pick up was something which sounded like the distant rumbling of an angry crowd. This furious murmuring was fractured by a man's voice quacking indecipherably through a distant microphone.

'I should avoid Grosvenor Square if I was you,' said the doorman. 'There's another of those demonstrations outside the American Embassy.' He seemed inclined to be chatty. 'They're getting to be a regular menace. Last week we had to sponge ripe tomato off the King of Norway. He'd only nipped over there for cocktails.'

'I can't avoid it. I live just the other side.'

'You could always try going round Oxford Street.'

Rosie smiled politely and continued on her way. Why should he think she should want to avoid it? Was there something about her appearance which marked her down as not the type for youth demonstrations?

She stopped and looked at herself in a full-length mirror in an antique-shop window. Reflected in the mistily silvered glass she saw a girl with long dark hair who was wearing a black and white mini-dress in striped material that looked like deckchair canvas. Well, all of that was certainly in tune with the times. She'd even gone to the trouble of ironing her hair that morning. This was a most dangerous procedure; you spread your tresses over the top of an ordinary ironing board and used a clothes iron to press away any hint of an unfashionable wave. No, it was the willow-pattern-blue eyes and the high cheekbones that made her look aloof and aristocratic and a suitable case for Claridge's commissionaire.

But I'm not posh at all, she thought. I'm Ned Tattersall's granddaughter. And I bet he wouldn't have missed a demo for anything. She offered up a quick prayer of thanks to the Almighty: 'Thank you, God, for good legs because it would be awful to have bad ones with these fashions.' And then she continued walking towards Grosvenor Square.

'Out, out, out!' 'Out, out out . . .' The massed demonstrators' repeated message was punctuated by other less orchestrated cries and shouts, and even by bursts of jeering laughter. Rosie began picking her way between the black police vans as she tried to inch into the body of the crowded square. Automatically, she pulled her camera from its mended case. In any dramatic situation she had grown to regard it as her third eye.

'Excuse me miss, are you press?' The middle-aged special constable was looking Rosie more in the legs than in the face.

'Yes.' She didn't like lying to the officious part-time policeman, but she wanted to get nearer to the official speaker who seemed to be making his noise from down by the embassy.

'Can I see your press card?'

'And can I see your commanding officer? I don't like the way you're undressing me with your eyes.'

The poor little special constable's tunic had a button undone and Rosie found herself wondering whether he'd been mowing his lawn in Chiswick when the call had come for him to help suppress rioting youth. '*And* you're improperly dressed,' she added.

His eyes went straight down to the fly of his trousers and Rosie seized the opportunity of darting into the crowd.

'Come back,' he cried. But somebody chose that moment to knock his peaked hat spinning.

Although Rosie was now in the thick of the mob she found that she could only move where she was jostled. The huge embassy building – modern and white with a gilded American eagle over the glass and steel front doors – took up the whole of the far end of the square. Carried nearer by the crowd, Rosie registered that a van was parked to one side of this entrance. An Indian-looking man was on top of it, haranguing the mob through a crackling portable electric megaphone.

It was all about the iniquities of the American government and the bombing of North Vietnam. Holding her camera above her head, with no idea of what results she'd get, Rosie pressed the shutter. She was fairly sure that the man was Tariq Ali, the revolutionary student leader. And the tall woman – the one next to him on the roof of the van – was she Vanessa Redgrave? Whoever she was, the police hauled her down. Instead of fighting them off she just fell limply into their arms. Passive resistance in the shape of 'going limp' was a relatively new weapon.

The crowd reeked of patchouli oil. If ever there was a smell of the Sixties it was this one. It was very near to the odour of marijuana and the young rubbed it into their skin to confuse the police. Not that they needed much confusing on that sunlit Saturday afternoon. Youth had control of the square. A group of mounted policemen, their horses towering over a long banner which read *LSE Students Against U.S. Intrusion*, were poised helplessly at the corner of stately Upper Brook Street.

Rosie, who loved all animals, decided to worm her way round the hedge which bounded the rowdily jam-packed public gardens in the middle of the square – she wanted to try to get some shots of the horses. Just as she got near enough for it to be worthwhile raising her camera, the mounted police charged the crowd. The London School of Economics banner fell to the ground, a girl tore her way from under it, thrust her hand in her jeans pocket and then threw something under the horses' hooves.

Click went the camera shutter: the girl was Bernadette Barrett and the something she had thrown was a handful of glass marbles. Rosie watched in horror as beautiful horses started losing their balance and crashing to the ground.

It was like a scene in an abattoir. She had rarely felt more angry in her life. How could you make peace by breaking screaming horses' legs? 'She did it,' she shouted at a tumbled policeman. 'She threw marbles and I've got a picture to prove it.'

'You bitch!' roared Bernadette, who was doing anything but go limp as she tried to struggle her way out of two policewomen's control. 'You bloody bitch. I was always out to get you. And when I do, I'll see you double-fucked.'

Bernadette now turned her attention to the policewomen who were trying to drag her into the van. She called them a pair of mauling lesbians and Rosie took more photographs of the scene. But Bernadette hadn't quite finished with her. The redhead's last cry before the van doors clanged shut was: 'One day, Rosie Tattersall, I'll get you – one day I'll piss on your grave.'

Once again the huge crowd, which was swelling and falling and getting itself arrested, caught Rosie in its midst. There was no chance of shooting further pictures, she could only cling onto her camera and go where she was pushed. Just as it was beginning to be frightening – a girl with a man with blood on his face had started screaming uncontrollably – the mob threw Rosie up on a corner. She was finally on the Tiddy Street side of the square.

In the midst of all this noisy youthful passion, it was odd to find herself confronted by a reminder of everyday Mayfair. This came in the shape of a corsetiere's shop window, where the headless wax dummies wore discreet pink tulle frills round their middles. Next door was a shop called Adèle which sold lingerie that could have been fashioned from pure silk cobwebs. When giving directions to their flat, Rosie and Gabriel would always say: 'We're just round the corner from all the pink knickers.' Not that they had many visitors. But they'd got one today.

The woman sitting on the old dustbin at the bottom of the area steps looked absolutely ageless. Thirty? Fifty? It was impossible to tell. Rosie was quick to recognise that the cream linen suit was the work of Sybil Connely, an expensive Irish designer who was rapidly gaining an international reputation. The shoes were definitely Italian, whilst the jaunty shoulder bag was the kind of thing that people brought back from New York.

So far, Rosie had only registered that which was shop-bought; now she took in ash-blonde hair and a pair of bright navy-blue eyes. A voice inside her own head said, 'You are one classy dame.' But it wasn't her own voice; it belonged to somebody she had once heard on the soundtrack of a film.

The vision spoke. 'God knows why the newspapers call this the Summer of Love . . .' The accent was distinctly Irish. 'Grosvenor Square's just like Marrakesh on the night before Ramadan starts. Have you any idea who I am?'

She's enjoying this, thought Rosie; but whoever she is I'm going to like her – that much I do know. Aloud she said, 'I've got the strangest feeling I once saw you in a movie.'

'But never in a snapshot?' The woman sounded disappointed. 'Oh well, they were never a sentimental family. I'm Gabriel's mother.'

'But you can't be,' gasped Rosie. The ironic arch of the woman's eyebrow was already proving her wrong. Gabriel employed just the same trick when he was waiting for somebody to say more. 'I'm sorry,' apologised Rosie. 'It's just that you look too young.'

The woman patted her own cheekbones appreciatively. 'I've just had it hoisted,' she said. 'If you're ever getting it done, go to Los Angeles. The cosmetic surgeons are years ahead there.' Without pausing she added, 'I'd heard you were beautiful and it's no lie.'

Rosie pulled her camera out of its case. 'If you don't mind, I need a photograph of this moment.'

But the woman's professional instincts were even quicker than the girl's. The face she presented to the camera was entirely the picture *she* wanted taking. Gabriel's mother had plainly done a lot of this sort of thing before.

Click. Seeing the woman through the viewfinder confirmed one thing. 'This definitely isn't the first time I've seen you. And it *was* at the pictures.' Rosie lowered the camera and wished that the carrying case was not quite so tatty and mended. 'Oh dear, you've got a mark off the bin on your bottom.'

'It washes.' Gabriel's mother wasn't worried. Then, suddenly, she became downright annoyed. 'Did he tell you *nothing* about me? Nothing about the career and the divorces, and the years with Old Joe? Nothing about the time his bloody family tried to pay the nuns to lock me up?' Irish indignation was now waxing furiously. 'Of course Gabriel would rather have had a mammy who'd boil him an owd pudding!' And just as suddenly she was full of friendly charm again: 'Aren't you going to invite me in? I'm not the kind who'll be upset by a bit of untidiness.'

Rosie unlocked the door. As she followed the unexpected

guest into the basement's living room, something strange happened. She suddenly saw the room – the yellow walls and the silver air-brushed clouds and the star-spangled stencilled ceiling – through Gabriel's mother's eyes.

'Jesus, Mary and Joseph . . .' breathed the visitor. 'It's just like walking into *The Wizard of Oz*. Would there be Munchkins in that cupboard? Or would there be such a thing as a drop of gin – which would be much more to the point!'

'Gin? No. But I think there might still be some chianti in the kitchen,' volunteered Rosie.

'If I never see chianti again, it'll be too soon. Much too reminiscent of those Bonartos. But they were great years in bed. That bastard could play me like a bloody Stradivarius.'

Rosie was dying to say, 'I know exactly what you mean,' but it struck her as too rude for her lover's mother. Rude? Why was she suddenly thinking in Hankey words from her childhood? Perhaps it was because sophistication was standing in front of her in a Sybil Connely suit. Not much change from a thousand pounds there. Still, there was a mark on the bum and the woman hadn't minded that, so perhaps she wouldn't object to a few questions. 'What was the rest of the time like? Out of bed, I mean.' She hadn't expected to blush but she did – it was the first time in years.

The woman smiled and said, 'Your generation didn't invent sex. How the hell d'you think Gabriel got here?' She pulled a packet of Benson and Hedges cigarettes from her shoulder bag. 'Want one?'

Rosie shook her head and marvelled at the thinness of the gold lighter.

Gabriel's mother blew out a cloud of smoke. 'I was certain you'd be sitting round in the half-dark smoking joints. And that's nothing new either. I used to indulge in it, occasionally, with Bob Mitchum in Hollywood. They clapped the poor sweetheart in jail on a narcotics rap. Now there *was* a man. What were you asking me? My years with the Bonartos: old Joe – that was Gabriel's daddy – got stuck in America during the war. Couldn't get back. That's how we met up. At the time, I was being a bit of a film star.' She pronounced this 'fillum star' and proceeded to puff out more angry smoke. 'He must have told you *something* about me?'

Getting no more reply than an awkward pause, she continued with, 'I should have known better than to expect it. Oh yes, that brings it all back in a big way. They volunteer no information. And if you pluck up the courage to ask a direct question, you don't get an answer – you get a bloody demonstration instead. They don't tell you, they *show* you.'

Rosie found herself nodding in agreement as she remembered how she had been swooped up and driven off to Dove Cottage, so that she would understand where Thomas De Quincey fitted into Gabriel's scheme of things.

'You've had some.' The shrewd blonde eyed her knowledgeably. 'I can see that by your face. Why the Americans didn't lock Joe up for the duration of the war is something I have never understood. He'd been a big supporter of Mussolini. Still, I expect the family fixed it. That lot will still be fixing at the gates of Heaven. If they ever get there. Which I doubt.'

At long last Rosie was in a position to ask something she had often wondered: 'Are they the Mafia?'

Gabriel's mother threw back her head and laughed. 'Jesus, I should remember not to do that! It makes the sinews of my neck look old. No. They are not the Mafia. They're much grander and much older. The Bonartos are merchant princes. Not aristocratic, you understand – they despise the aristocracy. They are money. They are power. They're into everything. Everything from olive groves to racing cars. What's more, they're a load of miserable bastards who've probably still got the first farthing they took off the Medicis. They're all of that and worse; but they're also one hell of a classy act.'

That was the moment when Rosie suddenly remembered where she had heard Gabriel's mother described as 'one hell of a classy dame'. Ronald Reagan had said it about her, in an old black and white film, at the Olympia Super-Cinema-De-Luxe, which was down a dingy turning in Irlams o'th' Height. 'You're Colleen Flynn!' she exclaimed in delight. 'And you were always in the most amazingly awful pictures. Oh dear, that was terrible of me.'

'But true.' The former film star was smiling happily. 'I was in some buggers.'

'My brother Chris used to do funny imitations of you.'

'Is he gay? My campy style was always a bit of a favourite with the gay boys.'

'Now I come to think of it, he probably is.' The thought must have been lying, half examined – under the surface – for years. 'He specialised in secrets.'

'Tell me them,' was the prompt rejoinder.

'I couldn't. I'm sworn to secrecy.' Wherever Christopher was, he was now up and awake because the hum inside her head was much stronger than it had been on Regent Street. And nothing would have got her to tell the main secret. The Secret. . .The hum was really whirring.

'I'm glad to see you can keep your mouth shut. It's a great gift. I've got it myself. Of course Gabriel might not be Joe's son at all. It's just as likely he's Orson's.'

'Orson who?'

'Was there ever more than one?' asked Colleen, looking vaguely around. 'Jesus, nothing on offer but rancid chianti. I'm at the Connaught Hotel. Let's slip there. Don't worry about changing your clothes, they're perfect. We'll get them to fix us a jug of dry martinis and have a real good gas. Everybody'll take you for my daughter and I'll love it.'

'Have you got a real daughter?' Rosie was hurriedly running a comb through her hair.

'Only a son.' This was said in tones of darkest dissatisfaction.

In exactly the same moment, Rosie heard the gate in the railings creak open. This was followed by the sound of Gabriel's feet thundering down the area steps.

'Are those his very sexy legs I see through the window?' enquired his mother.

Now he was in the room and addressing Rosie: 'You left the door open again.'

'Only for a minute.'

'A minute is how long it would take somebody to get in.'

'Made of romance!' cooed his mother, infuriatingly. 'Made of it.'

296

'What the hell are you doing here?'

'And full of mother-love,' she beamed. 'Come on, give us a kiss.'

Delight and apprehension seemed mixed in the extravagant hug he gave her. 'How long have you been here?'

'Just long enough to get you worried. My God but you're sexy. Isn't he the most sexy thing?' she asked Rosie. And then she added, reasonably, 'But you'd know. You've been there.'

'Maeve!' roared Gabriel.

'What's maeve?' asked Rosie, puzzled.

'Not what, who. Her!'

'But I thought she was Colleen Flynn.'

'That was just one of my incarnations.' Gabriel's mother fastened one of the buttons of his open denim shirt and then – having plainly decided that it looked better open – undid it again. 'I was born Miss Duffy. Then a queen in the publicity department dreamed up Miss Flynn. Then I was Signora Bonarto and Mrs Heinz. . .'

'I thought you never married Heinz,' said her son indignantly.

'Well I did. But it was never valid in England so it didn't seem worth mentioning. Nowadays I'm the Honourable Mrs Kincaid – it's an Irish title. But you can call me Maeve.' She pronounced it Mave. 'I was named for the Queen of the Fairies. And you're plainly not one of those.' She was addressing her son again. 'Living in a state of sin – just down the road from Chinacraft! He was so beautiful at fifteen, I was sure he was going to be a faggot, but you've butched up quite nicely. And those jeans are too tight,' she added sternly.

So she *is* a bit motherly after all, thought Rosie.

'Mind you, they do say it pays to advertise,' continued Maeve blithely. And Rosie cancelled her previous thought.

'Maeve, you're outrageous!' laughed her son. Though she had managed to embarrass him, he obviously delighted in her. That he loved her there could be no doubt. Rosie was surprised to find that she was not jealous of this; or if she was, it was in an unexpected way. Gabriel was proving himself capable of loving a mother who was unmotherly. Rosie hardly ever gave Connie a passing thought. Yet she would have liked to think about her; but that would have meant dealing with pain. Oh that wretched pane of glass! It had never gone away. But you could live behind it. You could still *be*. She looked out from behind her own thoughts and saw that Gabriel was attempting to bat the mark on his mother's bottom.

'Mr Heinz used to want me to go in for this sort of thing,' said the irrepressible Maeve. 'But I sent him off to the brothels instead. You could do that, in Paris, in those days. In the end I cited a particularly nice tart as correspondent. It only cost me a big bottle of Houbigant's Quelques Fleurs. I expect I'm very different from your own mother,' she said to Rosie.

Quakerly honesty prevailed: 'I wouldn't be too sure of that,' was Rosie's cautious reply.

Before the girl could add any more, Maeve rounded on her son with: 'And how much do you know about *her* mammy? Reams, I wouldn't mind betting. You probably know her bloody size in gloves!'

'As a matter of fact, not much more than Rosie knew about you.'

'What an unnatural pair,' sighed his mother. 'Perhaps it's the generation. In my day, swapping confidences was considered as nice as the cigarette afterwards. Many's the little family snippet that's been passed onto me whilst some gentleman was stoking up his ardour again.'

'Mother, you go too far.'

'At least I don't dabble with the dead. Is he still as struck on that blasted Thomas of his?' she asked Rosie fiercely.

It was Gabriel who answered. 'Leave Thomas out of this.'

'Why? It used to be like "Me and My Shadow". It *does* still go on. One look at his face was enough to see that.' She had turned her attention to Rosie. 'How on earth do you put up with it?'

How to reply? The answer which came out sounded prim and feeble. 'I think Gabriel did a lot of research on De Quincey – while he was in Manchester.'

'Manchester? The danger lies nearer to this basement. The danger lies with that witch he pays all his good money

298

to. The one in Belgravia.' Maeve searched Rosie's face and then said to her son, 'So the child's not been privileged to talk to Thomas yet? She's not missed much. It's a nasty experience.'

'How could I talk to him when he's dead?' demanded Rosie.

'Dead but not lying down. There are ways. They're the devil's ways.' Maeve crossed herself fervently. 'And that son of mine's managed to find them.'

'How?' Rosie couldn't make sense of what she was hearing. 'How can he?'

'I've opened my mouth too wide,' said Maeve. 'I was always a garrulous mare. Let's all go to the Connaught and get very-nicely-thank-you.'

'No.' And Gabriel didn't sound as though he was going to be saying much more.

His mother held out one of her hands and slapped it with the other. 'Maeve was naughty and she admits it. Come on, love. Let's not be at outs.'

'You talk too much,' he said. 'And most of what you say is rubbish. You're the past, Mother. That's all you are. You're ancient history.'

'That was cruel,' cried Rosie.

'But true.' Maeve was speaking realistically. 'Have you seen what's on offer these days, ready-made, for a size twelve? Dresses? I wouldn't use them as a cake-frill! Yes, I'm the past all right; and I'm surprised to find I'm glad to be it. I'm only here because I got caught up in that rumpus in Grosvenor Square. What a tribe *they* were. Cheap Indian scent and hair that looks as though it had been cut with knives and forks. It leaves you wondering what they see in one another. But he isn't bad. . .' this was to Rosie '. . . I'd tell you if he was and he isn't. There's still a child's heart in the middle of all his grown-up pretending.'

It's as though Maeve's using her eyes as a camera, thought Rosie. She doesn't see him often enough and she wants to carry away a firm picture.

'You're almost certainly Orson's,' murmured the middle-aged woman. 'And God knows he was a bag of monkey-tricks.

But I did love him.' With this she gave Rosie a light kiss on the cheek and left without so much as a backward glance at her son.

'You can't let her go like that. . .'

'I just did.' What's more, Gabriel was wearing his 'not speaking' face. Rosie knew better than to try to break through that. Instead, she went over to the bookshelves and found one of the old *Picturegoer* annuals she had brought with her other books from Manchester. She was already fairly sure that there wasn't a picture of Orson Welles in it – and she was right.

Twenty-five minutes seems an eternity when it's one thousand five hundred seconds of angry silence. Enough was enough. Rosie decided to try to alter the atmosphere by talking about herself. 'My mother just ditched me and went off.'

'I know. You told me once before. I'll never ditch you.' If this statement was meant to be reassuring, it failed. It just sounded cold and bald. And then anger rose up with: 'Ditching? I'll tell you about ditching. I'm a world expert on the subject. Maeve may seem all that's sweetness and light to you, but that woman contrived to ditch me on three continents. And Orson Welles was not my father. My father was Joe Bonarto. And he spent hundreds of thousands on lawyers – just on getting me back.'

'Tell me about him. We never *talk*.'

'What's there to say? I loathe small talk. Joe's dead. He was okay. He was nice.'

Rosie could hardly credit what she was seeing. Were those really tears in Gabriel's eyes? It had been a most confusing afternoon. 'If you talk to dead people, do you pay somebody so you can talk to your father?'

'No.' This was rapped out very decisively. 'We did get through to him once, but I didn't like it. I want Joe's soul to rest in peace. Thomas is different. Thomas is a soul who's still wandering.'

'I'm sorry if I seem thick, but how do you talk to them? *How*?' Even as she asked this Rosie remembered what Maeve had said about direct questions leading to demonstrations. She wasn't sure she wanted one of those.

'Grab your hat.' Gabriel was already reaching for his car keys.

'I don't wear one.'

'I was speaking metaphorically.'

'There's no need to patronise me.'

Suddenly he was holding her close. 'You're sure you really want to know?' Before she could answer he changed tack; his voice sounded as though he'd dared himself to say something. 'I always knew you'd been ditched. Always. I knew it before I ever talked to you. You were the most beautiful thing I'd ever seen but it was written all over you. You had such sad eyes.' He wasn't letting her see his own eyes but he couldn't control a loud sniff – and she could feel him fishing in his pocket for his handkerchief. He broke the silence with, 'Takes one to spot one, I suppose,' and he blew his nose. 'At first, I thought it must have been another man who'd dropped you. When I found out we were the same, it seemed almost too good to be true.'

Now she got the chance to look. Yes, his eyes were indeed suspiciously bright. 'Why did you never tell me about being dumped?' she asked.

'Because it's never made me feel very valuable. If we don't talk about things that matter it's because I don't know how. The people who brought me up were just paid to be there.'

She held him closer.

'I did understand about your childhood,' he said in a shaky voice, 'and I wanted to wipe it all out for you. It's just that I'm not very good at it. I don't know how.' There was deep misery in this repeated refrain.

'It's all right,' were the only words she could find. 'Somehow it's all right. We'll manage. We're managing. We're on our way to something and we'll get there in the end.'

'At least we have great orgasms.' This time he blew his nose very triumphantly.

'Amazing ones,' she agreed. 'How many other people can manage it at exactly the same moment? All the girls in my year are dead envious.'

'You never talk about that?' He was horrified.

She wasn't. 'Don't men?' For once Rosie felt firmly in

control of the situation. 'Women talk about that like billy-o. Actually, sex is the only thing I *can* talk to that lot about. Blow your nose again and let's go and surprise your mother at the Connaught.' Having sons must be like this, she thought.

Gabriel blasted this tender thought away with, 'Go and see Maeve? Are you barmy? You see! She's charmed you just like she manages to charm everybody.'

'Well, you love her,' said Rosie indignantly. 'That stands out a mile.'

'Doesn't mean I have to like her.' He was scowling like a character in a cartoon. 'I'm going nowhere near the Connaught.'

'Okay. But let's go somewhere.' He must have been a most endearing little boy. Odd that he should talk about loving without liking – she'd felt the same way about her own brother.

'You wanted to talk to Thomas. You get to talk to Thomas.' The adult was back in control – and already opening his wallet and checking it for cash. Talking to Thomas plainly didn't come cheaply. But they'd managed to talk to one another. They had really talked. And that was something new.

From the outside, the house in Belgrave Square could have been a bigger version of the one in Tiddy Street. Same cream-washed façade, same porticoed front door, but everything was on a much loftier scale. The entrance hall alone was six times bigger than their living room. And somebody had added a mahogany counter – like the reception desk in a hotel. A mysterious flight of white plaster doves was suspended on wires down the centre of the well of a spectacular staircase, which was on a scale that was all but ducal.

If the woman behind the polished wooden counter had been a character in a film, the part would have been played by Joyce Grenfell. She was toothy and eager. Rosie quickly judged that this receptionist was already experienced in Gabriel and his ways. And that whilst she quite liked him, she wouldn't stand for any nonsense.

'If you want another sitting with Phoebe Slater, you can't

have one. She's fully booked. How about an hour with Arnold Tetley?' She ran an efficient finger down a ledger. 'Mrs Musker's giving healing at the moment. But she might just be able to slip you in before she gives her public lecture-demonstration.'

Rosie was more interested in the notice board behind the woman's head. It announced demonstrations of clairvoyance and psychic portrait painting; and whatever could 'flower psychometry' be? These words apart, the whole atmosphere reminded her of the Friends' Meeting House in Manchester. She was, in fact, in the headquarters of the Spiritualist Association of Great Britain.

'You'll settle for Mr Tetley then?' the toothy woman enquired of Gabriel. 'We don't give change for the phone.' This firm rebuff was directed at a woman in a crocheted hat decorated with woollen flowers who was waving a ten-shilling note behind Gabriel's shoulder. Mrs Hankey would have described her as a fanook. Come to think of it, she'd always applied the same word to the Manchester Quakers.

'So that's Arnold Tetley at four thirty; room thirty-seven. You are a full member, aren't you, Mr Bonarto? Three pounds seventeen and sixpence. You'll only have to suffer a short wait. Perhaps you'd like to show your guest our little museum?'

This turned out to be a glass display case, in the middle of a room that was like the lounge of a middle-bracket private hotel at the seaside. Much more cretonne and leatherette than was generally associated with lofty Belgravia. Rosie found herself wondering whether some departed spiritualist had left the organisation these premises in order to annoy his former snobbish neighbours. Except, if you believed in life after death, they presumably *stayed* your neighbours. It was all very confusing . . .

Even more confusing were the contents of the glass case. Rosie's eyes were immediately drawn to a set of photographs labelled *The Mediumship of Jack Webber*. They showed a haggard-looking man, tied to a chair, with gauzy clouds of vapour emanating from both his mouth and his nostrils.

'Ectoplasm,' explained Gabriel airily. 'It can build up into spirit forms.'

'Then why didn't they take the photograph when it had *done* it?'

'Excuse me, do you by any chance have change for the phone?' It was the woman in the home-made hat again, and she was still flapping the ten-shilling note around. Rosie had been rushed out of the flat without so much as being given the chance to grab her bag, but Gabriel began searching, obligingly, through his pockets.

'I saw you looking at the Jack Webber pictures.' The middle-aged woman had a little-girl lisp. 'The best medium for that sort of thing was Helen Duncan. The government had to lock her up during the war. She was getting in touch with soldiers who'd passed over in battle. The War Office were scared she'd start giving away military secrets.'

'Four pennies,' said Gabriel. 'Here you are.'

'But how do we change the ten-shilling note?' wailed the woman dramatically.

'We don't,' said Gabriel.

'Then how can I repay my debt?'

'There will be no need.' And with this he steered Rosie towards an empty sofa in the middle of the room, leaving the woman hovering indecisively.

'I think she only wanted somebody to talk to,' said Rosie. A large bottom had plainly just got up off a discarded newspaper on the sofa. It was called *Psychic News* and you could still see the imprint left by two round buttocks. 'D'you think a human being did that, or a ghost?' enquired Rosie.

'I have to tell you that I take all of this very seriously,' said Gabriel sternly.

'Even the plaster cast of the pixie footprints?' These, too, had been on display in the glass case.

'Perhaps not those,' he conceded. 'This place attracts some very strange people. Lonely ones, too. Look, she's got her money for the phone but she's still flagging that ten-bob note around, desperately.'

'Perhaps she really does want to pay you back.'

As if in confirmation of this the woman lisped out, 'No success yet.'

Yes, she's a fanook, thought Rosie. And so's the sallow

young man who's dressed like nineteen forty-seven, and the girl in the Austrian dirndl with the oversized feet, and that grey man and woman ('spinster' would have described them both). The two fat women – who look as though they ought to be at a nice matinée of Danny La Rue's – are all right. But the Indian boy's as sad as anything. Paul McCartney did right to wonder where all the lonely people belonged. Was it possible that they were all stuck behind their own individual panes of glass?

Still, she thought realistically, I've only ever wanted to be part of this world. I'd certainly no thoughts of getting in touch with the next! Suddenly she felt a flutter of dark apprehension. 'Gabriel? What have you just paid that money *for*? What's going to happen?'

'You'll see in a minute. Would you like a cup of tea? There's a cafeteria in the basement.'

'No.' She could already imagine it. Strip neon lighting and food reformists chewing everything fourteen times before they swallowed. 'No, I'll do without the tea. I don't want to have to get up and go in the middle of Mr Tetley. Does he produce that funny white stuff from his nose, like the photos?'

'They've stopped doing that. It was said to come from every orifice and it could stink alarmingly.' He hesitated for a moment and then honesty plainly took over. 'It also has to be said that ectoplasm went out of fashion when infra-red photography came in. Don't get me wrong, I'm not trying to say that this place is a temple of phoneys because it isn't.'

'But doesn't the whole thing give you the shudders? It does me.'

'There seems to be something in it,' was the most she got out of him. And after that they sat in silence. It was not unlike waiting for the dentist. Rosie straightened out the copy of *Psychic News* and began to read an article about a public meeting in Bristol. Eddie Cochran, the deceased pop singer, had evidently manifested ('via the mediumship of Lily Rossiter') and he had given a full description of the accident which led to his death.

'Zav knew Eddie,' she said. 'He'd be ever so surprised to know that he's met up with Al Jolson on the other side and

305

that nowadays they're both developing new interests in philosophy.'

'You made that bit up,' said Gabriel, but he couldn't suppress a grin.

'I didn't. Look for yourself. . .'

He never got a chance. The woman in the crocheted hat bore down on them yet again. 'Sixpence,' she lisped triumphantly. 'You may keep the change for your courtesy.'

She's absolutely *hungry* for conversation, thought Rosie. It shows so much, it hurts. As if to prove her right the woman enquired overeagerly, 'With whom are you waiting to sit?'

'Arnold Tetley.' Gabriel leaned across and dropped the silver sixpence into a collecting box for the Harry Edwards Sanctuary.

'Mr Tetley leaves a lot to be desired,' said the woman sternly. 'Sometimes he goes into trance and sometimes he doesn't. He can be very vexing. And he is not a gentleman. He has funny personal habits.'

'We'll risk that,' said Gabriel. He wasn't being unpleasant but he did look at his wristwatch. 'Come on, Rose.' He got to his feet, and after she did the same he took her by the arm and walked her towards an archway that led to the foot of the big staircase.

'Mr Tetley scratches his crutch!' The voice calling after them was now quite loud and the woman had begun to sound a little mad.

The receptionist smiled sympathetically at them from behind her counter. 'She's perfectly harmless,' she said. 'She'd do anything for anybody. Room thirty-seven is on the top floor at the back.'

The pattern on the carpet was too cosy for the imposing staircase. 'Three floors up,' said Gabriel, pausing at the first landing. As they continued their climb, the only sounds they could hear were muffled voices coming from behind heavily panelled doors. Rosie was beginning to find it all so eerie that she was glad of the reassuring smell of good wax furniture polish.

Suddenly, from behind one of the doors, she heard somebody begin to laugh merrily. Only the burst of laughter was *too* merry. 'I don't think I can go through with this,' she said to Gabriel. She had frozen in her tracks. 'It's a beautiful day. The sun's shining outside. Why the hell are we putting ourselves through this?'

'You're the only person I'd bring here,' he said.

'You must have brought your mother. How else would she know?'

'She made me bring her. I asked you. There is a difference. You must be able to see that.' His voice faltered. 'I'm trying to let you see more of me. I'm taking a calculated risk. You could run away. But I want you to know who I am – and all of this is part of it. I love you, Rosie.'

He needed loving back. That much she did understand. She held him very close, and on that spooky staircase they kissed as though they were in Hyde Park with a band playing.

'Very nice too. We don't see enough of that round here.' The speaker, a cheerful motherly woman, was descending the staircase carrying a small brown dachshund in her arms. The big diamonds on her knuckles were obviously real. But the unseasonal fur coat was one of the new ones from Beauty Without Cruelty – fur-fabric phantom beaver.

'Will your dog let me stroke him?' asked Rosie eagerly.

'He's so relaxed I think you could swing him round by his tail. He's just been to Mrs Musker for healing.' To Rosie's delight the woman handed her the small animal.

'Can you believe the vet wanted me to have him destroyed? Four sessions with Mrs Musker have turned him into a new person. Just put him down and watch how he manages stairs for himself.'

Rosie was reluctant to let go of the warm little body, but she did as she was told. When it came to descending stairs, the dachshund was a champion. When he got to the landing he sat down and looked up happily at his mistress and her new acquaintances.

'Have you come for healing yourself?' the dog's owner asked Rosie.

'No. We've got a sitting with Mr Tetley.' She was surprised to find that the word 'sitting' hadn't scalded her tongue. In fact it had come out as naturally as if she said it every day.

'He's brilliant,' enthused the woman in the vegetarian fur coat. 'Absolutely spot-on – if you can stand his blunt tongue. Oh my God! Sandy's mistaken the stairpost for a tree! Well, Mrs Musker *was* working on his water-retention problem today, so I suppose it was only to be expected.'

As they left her behind, and climbed higher up the house, the reassurance provided by this realistic woman began to wear thin. Room thirty-seven was at the end of a drab corridor which must once have served as servants' attic bedrooms. The floorboards creaked and Rosie remembered that laughter which had been too merry. What was she letting herself in for?

The door of room thirty-seven was already ajar and Gabriel motioned that she should enter first. 'No,' she said firmly. 'You lead, I'll follow.' The Book of Ruth had already led her into some curious places but this had to be the most threatening one yet.

'Oh God, no. Not you again!' The middle-aged man, eyeing Gabriel up and down, was short and peppery with bright intelligent eyes the colour of snuff. He was dressed in a dark jacket and striped trousers and his neck was too thin for his starched collar. 'I can't pretend I'm pleased to see you.' Arnold Tetley had a marked Lancashire accent. 'Still, they've had your money at reception so you'd better sit down.'

He was indicating a little row of chairs made of tubular steel and canvas. His own armchair, in dark brown moquette, looked as though it had once been part of a three-piece suite.

'Calm down,' the man said to Rosie. 'Nobody's going to bite you.' The grey hair had once been red and he shouldn't have let it get so straggling, but he had a smile of great sweetness. This was switched straight off as he turned back to Gabriele. 'I want one thing strictly understood. You can't just come here ordering up meetings with people who've passed over.'

'I want to speak to Thomas De Quincey,' was Gabriel's equally firm reply.

'It's not how it works. You should know that by now. Mediums are beginning to talk about you, amongst them-selves. Phoebe Slater says she'll never sit with you again. We

308

can only pass on what we're given.' Mr Tetley put a finger between his eyebrows and looked thoughtful. After a moment he said, 'Somebody's encouraging me to continue with you; somebody on the Other Side.' He definitely made it sound like a place that ought to have capital letters. 'Who's Joe? Broken English.'

'His father.' Rosie was impressed.

'Leave him out of it,' said Gabriel.

'How can I when he's here?' The medium took a deep breath and cocked an ear as though he was listening to somebody. And then he said 'Thank you,' to whoever it was. 'Right. . .' All of his attention was beamed on Gabriel. 'Joe says that what we're doing here today is against your own religion. He says that this bothers you. And he thinks it's about time you left it all alone. Where's Firenze?' He had difficulty in saying this last word.

'Florence,' said Gabriel. 'It's Italian for Florence.'

'Well, you're going to find your own truth there.' Mr Tetley was growing in confidence. 'Joe likes this young lady. He says she's "fantastica". "Una in un milione": what does that mean?' he asked Gabriel.

'A lot,' was all he was prepared to reply. Nevertheless Gabriel looked pleased.

'He's translated it for me himself.' Mr Tetley smiled cheerfully at Rosie. 'He says you're one in a million. All right, all right!' he suddenly barked at somebody invisible. 'I'm getting somebody else,' he explained. 'I think this one's a first-time communicator. They're the kind who rush at it and then I have a job getting them. It's no use, he's all jabber. Teddy? No. . .Ed?' The man was concentrating hard with his eyes shut.

'Padding,' murmured Gabriel to Rosie. 'This is how they pad the proper bits out.' She could cheerfully have kicked him.

'Ned!' proclaimed the medium in triumph.

'I don't know any Ned,' protested Gabriel.

'No, but she does – the young lady. By 'eaven, this one's a quick learner. He's managing to show me himself. He's got a flower in his buttonhole, and now he's pulling his lapel back to show me a little glass tube. That's what the flower's sitting in. Oh he *is* pleased to be here. He brings a lovely jolly condition with him. He's pointing up in the sky and showing me a golden teapot. Would that signify?' he asked Rosie anxiously.

Tears began to roll down her face. 'It's Gran'dad Tattersall,' she said. It was the fact that he was 'pleased to be here' which had made her cry.

Gabriel looked worriedly at Rosie. 'We can always go if you want to.'

'Are you mad?'

Mr Tetley was beaming happily. 'Ned says the Eyetie's the only one with a handkerchief – and that it's already been used today. Your gran'dad seems to be a great one for watching over you.'

'I know.' This was no less than the truth. Even at the worst of times, when she'd seemed to belong to nothing and nobody, the *idea* of Gran'dad Tattersall had been like having a friend.

'You're very psychic yourself,' said the medium. 'Did you know that? Who's Nora Pankey?'

'Hankey.'

'Give him a chance. Come to that, give *me* a chance. These things need getting together. He's got a lot of time for this Nora. Says he's sorry now he never left her anything. Oh dear . . .' Mr Tetley was looking at Gabriel straight in the face. 'I don't want to embarrass you but Ned says you're not being straight with her.'

'With whom?'

'Her.' He was nodding at Rosie. 'He wants me to say one word to you, young man. America.'

Gabriel actually went white under his suntan. 'I'll tell her,' he said, frightened. 'It was only ever a question of choosing the moment.'

'See you do tell her. And you. . .' it was Rosie's turn again '. . .you've left a diamond ring somewhere. Whatever you do, get it back. It's going to come in handy.'

'I can buy her diamonds,' said Gabriel huffily.

'Not this ring. It's nothing to do with you. It's family.'

Connie's engagement ring, thought Rosie; the one she gave me the night she walked out. As far as she could remember, it was in an old button box, at the back of a bedroom drawer, upstairs at Mrs Hankey's.

Mr Tetley now assumed a stern expression. 'Gran'dad wants me to tell you something very particularly. He says I won't understand but you will. These are his words: "Glass only melts in fire." It's to do with a pane of glass. But he says he'll always be with you. You've got big tests to go through before you'll see things clearly. Tests of courage.'

Silence fell. It was Gabriel who eventually broke it by saying, 'And I suppose this grandfather hates me?'

'No. And he's laughing at the fact that you spoke up. He says you're an arrogant little bugger but you'll get there in the end.' Suddenly Mr Tetley winced and began to scratch at his crutch. 'I do apologise,' he muttered, 'it's urticaria.'

'I get it too,' said Rosie. 'Haven't you had the tablets?'

'Yes, but they made me feel so dozy that I can't use my gift. Sometimes I could scratch to the bone.'

'Have you tried bathing it in vinegar and water?' asked Rosie.

'Doesn't touch it. Nothing touches it.'

'There's supposed to be a woman downstairs who did wonders for a dachshund,' she put in eagerly.

'Healers have had every opportunity but they've got nowhere with it.' He stopped scratching. 'Listen, I want to ask you something. This isn't clairvoyance, it's curiosity. The only time I've ever seen a gold teapot, like the one I was shown, was on a house in a place called Irlams o'th' Height.'

'That's where I was born. Where are you from?' asked Rosie delightedly. It had stopped being Gabriel's afternoon and turned into her own.

'Swinton. Six bus stops up the road.'

'We used to go there when Silcock's Fair came round,' remembered Rosie happily.

'Well now you're going to America. Isn't she?' The question was addressed to Gabriel.

The Italian was already on his feet. 'I think we've had enough,' he said.

311

'I left my heart in San Francisco.' There was no stopping Mr Tetley.

'Did you?' asked Rosie eagerly.

'No, but I've always been partial to the song. It's that side of America, isn't it?' He too was on his feet and extending a hand to Gabriel. 'When *are* you going to tell her?'

'Just as soon as we get out of this hellhole. And I'm never, ever, coming back.'

'That's how real evidence takes some people,' Mr Tetley explained to Rosie. 'Gran'dad was certainly right about one thing. He *is* an arrogant bugger. But I suppose you ladies go for the light that shines from within him. It's there and it's clear and it's true. There can be no denying that. You're a young man who's on a desperate search for something. Your life's a bloody battlefield – with God at one end and the devil tugging away at the other. May angels guard you, lad.' It was as though he was offering a protective benediction. 'Beware of the dark path. Don't let people make you meddle with magic. Good afternoon.'

'America.' She'd managed to keep the word bottled up until they were outside on the pavement. She hadn't fancied the idea of shouting echoing round that very public staircase. But now she wanted some answers. 'What's all this my gran'dad said about America?'

Gabriel started walking towards the car. 'This will be no use in the States.' He had recently changed it for yet another Italian sports model. 'Fuel injection. It's forbidden in California.'

'Stop skating round the edges,' said Rosie. 'And if you get in that car without answering me, you get in on your own. What's all this about the States?'

'Bob Fellowes is giving me some leave of absence. I've been asked to go out to the University of California at Berkeley.'

'If it's "A Nightingale Sang in Berkeley Square" why do you pronounce it Burkley?' This was just something to say whilst she got her proper questions in order.

'Because that's how *they* pronounce it.'

'So why did we have to have all this secrecy? Why did I have to learn about it like this?'

'That man could have got it all by telepathy. You do realise that, don't you? Stop glaring, Rosie. I didn't tell you because I only know half a story myself. They'll pay me to go out there and they want to talk to me. That's as much as I know.'

'And Bob Fellowes knew about it and I didn't. The bloody landlord knew it first!'

'He also happens to be my boss.'

An oddly assorted couple was walking towards them, a middle-aged Jewish businessman and a strapping young foot soldier. One looked as though he bought his clothes in New York, the other's uniform proclaimed him to be a lance-corporal in the Grenadier Guards. If every picture tells a story, Rosie was fairly certain that she knew the sexual scenario behind this one. In his London days, Danny Cahn had been very fond of guardsmen, who supplemented meagre pay by selling sexual favours.

'Not got a kind word for your old uncle?'

Good heavens, it *was* Danny. It was the grey hair that had made him look like an older version of himself. As though reading her mind, Danny said, 'If I dyed it, I'd look even more of an antique.' He had a job finishing the sentence because Rosie flung her arms round him. The pair of them were laughing with delight. 'How are you, my little one?' He still smelled of Trumper's Essence of Limes.

'Meet Gabriel,' she said proudly.

'Me oh my!' Danny was making no secret of his admiration. 'Mind you, she's always attracted chart-busters. I know somebody whose latest album's just gone platinum – and he's still got a candle in the window for her.' The pop manager was shaking Gabriel enthusiastically by the hand. 'Not that you've anything to worry about. She was always waiting for Mr Right; and from the look of things she did right to wait.'

'Danny Cahn,' said Rosie to Gabriel.

'I guessed.' His smile was relaxed enough to know that he was also waiting to be introduced to the guardsman.

Oh dear, thought Rosie. I just hope Danny knows his name.

It seemed he did. 'This is Raymond. We got chatting in the Bag o' Nails. And then we went and had a cup of tea at Victoria Station. I'm at the Carlton Tower.' Danny still shot his cuffs when he was feeling nervous. 'We're killing time until Hamish goes out. Three times I've rung that bloody suite, but he can't seem to take the hint. I wouldn't care, it's his feelings I'm trying to protect.'

Rosie did not presume to judge what she could not understand. The fashionable attitude towards sex was 'whatever lights your candle'. This was generally translated to mean that you could do what you wanted just so long as nobody else got hurt. In previous years Danny would have been more reticent, but times had changed; the English laws on homosexuality were just about to be altered.

'Mind you, it's still going to be an offence with a member of Her Majesty's armed forces.' Danny's ability to access thoughts had always kept him one jump ahead. 'Oh well, I suppose it'll keep things a bit spicy and forbidden. Why don't we all go and have a proper afternoon tea? The hotel's only just round the corner.'

'I wouldn't want to spoil anything,' said Rosie, dubiously.

'Would I have asked you?'

'No, you wouldn't.' Her delight in seeing him was in no way faked. 'And I couldn't have asked for a nicer surprise.'

As they made their way across the square towards the tower block of the new hotel Danny explained to Gabriel how he fitted into the Hankey scheme of things; that the relationship extended beyond business. The Jew and the Italian shared huge enthusiasm for Nora Hankey. 'I've just bought her a fur coat,' said Danny. 'You can always get them cheaper in summer. I know she'll only keep it in a cupboard. It would be too much to expect her to actually wear it. But she'll enjoy knowing she's got it put away.'

That was when Danny stopped his pavement cabaret and started the questions. By the time they were sitting in the hotel's first-floor lounge – it was modern in red with a lot of white Carrara marble – Danny had already discovered enough about Gabriel to be able to turn the questions into depth charges. A Jewish friend can be an immensely loyal ally

314

and Dan barged straight in where Rosie would have feared to tiptoe. 'So *why* are you going to Berkeley?' he asked.

'So they can look at me and I can look at them.'

'Who's they?'

'The philosophy department at the University of California.'

'And you're hoping they'll come up with a long-term offer?'

'I have to see,' was the most that Gabriel seemed willing to say.

'It's certainly all happening in Berkeley,' nodded Danny.

'More Nobel prize-winners to the square inch than anywhere else on earth,' agreed Gabriel enthusiastically.

'I'm not talking about that. I'm talking about the youth movement, it makes those antics in Grosvenor Square look like the teddy-bears' picnic. I've been to Berkeley so I can tell you what it's like,' he said to Rosie. 'It's Crazyville with bells on.'

'But there's still a lot of good academic work being done there,' protested Gabriel.

'When they're all stoned?' Once again he was feeding Rosie with information. 'You can't move down Telegraph Avenue for dope dealers. They come out at you from holes. It's one huge acid trip.'

She looked Gabriel straight in the eye. 'Is that why you're going? Are you going to look for that special sort of LSD?'

'Oh Gawd!' Danny's eyes went up to the ceiling. Obviously not much struck on the sight of the modern crystal chandelier, he lowered them again and said, 'LSD? I've practically barred the subject from conversation. I'm bringing Nancy Considine over for her first big London gig, and I've had to make her swear – *swear* – that she'll come through customs clean.' Danny was already, automatically, looking round to be sure that they could not be overheard. 'Some of Zav's new lyrics make it pretty obvious that he's been tripping too.'

'That's what I thought.' Gabriel was leaning forward with considerable interest.

'But he's turned against it,' said Dan. 'Thank God! The people who do it are such bloody bores. They drop one tab of the stuff and before you know where you are they want to turn the whole world on.'

'Have you got any?' asked Raymond. This was his first real contribution to the conversation.

'No I have not,' said Danny crossly.

'I didn't even understand some of the words you were using about it,' admitted Rosie.

'Good. I've not got any acid and I'm never proposing to try it. Look what's happened to Brian Epstein. First he tells the press he's done it, and then he acts aggrieved because they won't let him have a rest cure in peace, at that place in Roehampton. LSD kills business acumen. Absolutely kills it.' He finished off quite mildly with, 'So that's why I haven't got any. The only drug I need is life itself.'

The guardsman got to his feet. 'I need a leak. Where's the bogs?'

'Beyond the lifts,' said Danny.

'Are the phones there too?' enquired Gabriel. 'I've got a guilty conscience about Maeve,' he explained to Rosie. 'I think I'll just try her and see that she's all right.'

Danny indicated the top of a staircase with his thumb: 'I think you have to drop down a floor for the phones.' Talk of drugs had obviously displeased him and, as the two men disappeared, he spoke quite sharply to a passing waiter, who had failed to produce tea for three and two bottles of Guinness in a pint glass. There had already been mild ructions because the hotel had been unable to supply the guardsman with his requested 'pint o' mixed'.

'Calm down, Dan, let's enjoy our reunion. It's years since we had a good gossip. What d'you think of Gabriel?'

'Star quality. Stands out a mile. I can always spot it – even in other people's fields. Not much point in asking what you think of Raymond. Are you shocked? Copped me picking up rough trade, haven't you? Yes, that boyfriend of yours is a real star. You can finally be said to be the girl who's got everything.'

'Don't! Bernadette Barrett once said that to me, on the top deck of a bus, and we had a blazing bust-up straight afterwards. Guess what? I saw her today.'

316

'Spare me,' sighed Danny, 'I don't want to know. I get a letter from her brother every single morning of my life. Always the same. I robbed him, if you please.'

'Just letters? Consider yourself lucky. He once tried stoning Gabriel's car.'

'That piddling little Mongoose hates Zav even more than he hates me.'

Rosie was thinking about other things. 'I can't just up and go to Berkeley,' she said worriedly. 'My finals are coming.'

'Don't go then. That's easy. Gabriel's only doing an audition. He *will* get the job though, that's obvious. Did you know that Mongoose has been hanging round outside Mrs Hankey's, with a poster on a stick? *The Family at Number Seven Robbed Me*, that's the pretty message. He's gone bananas. You know that woman who lives opposite? The one with the tubercular hip. They put her out in her wheelchair and he sits on her step talking to her and shouting things across the street. Mrs Hankey has to get the police to move him on, regular as clockwork. He's right out of it, the complete meshuggenah! That's drugs for you, Rosie. Let that be a lesson to you.'

'I don't want a lesson, I want a nice gossip.' But any chance of this was swept aside by a more serious thought. 'I *have* got everything, Danny. I know I've got all the ingredients . . . It's just that I can't seem to get them together.'

'Not another!' he sighed. 'I never knew of a more self-conscious generation. I blame the media. They're forever going on about these wonderful Sixties. Even Harold Macmillan told people they'd never had it so good. It's all hype and it leaves people dissatisfied.' Danny carried on pontificating as he lit a cigarette. 'Nobody ever told me I ought to be enjoying nineteen forty-seven! I just got on with it. And when the good things happened I practically jumped with glee.' Without so much as a heartbeat's pause he added, 'I wonder whether Raymond *will* come back from the toilet? Coin of the realm has not yet changed hands so the chances are he will. *Now* are you shocked?'

'If you want me to be. Yes, I'm shocked. Danny, do let's

gossip like we used to. I never get the chance. Would Hamish be annoyed if he knew what you were up to?'

'Might pretend to be. Might try and use it against me. Want to know what Hamish has become in my life? He's the man who knows where all the bodies are buried.'

'Real bodies?' With Danny anything was possible.

'Not real ones. No, nothing as bad as that, my little one.' As his kind hand gently patted Rosie's, she was surprised to find that she was suddenly – startlingly – near to tears. She never saw *friends* these days; that's what had caused them.

'Know who I love, Rosie? Know who I've always loved?'

'Zav.' This was something which had never been said before.

'Right.' The word was wrapped up in a sigh.

'And he loves you,' she said urgently. It was her turn to take Danny's hand. 'Not like that. But he does love you.'

'If there was even a flicker of interest there . . .' Danny was still speaking quietly. 'I'll tell you this: there'd be no guardsmen from the Bag o'Nails, no Forty-Second Street hustlers, either. I pay for it to keep people at a distance. One look from Zav; one look, that's all it would take . . .'

'But you're being unrealistic,' interrupted Rosie. 'He's one way and you're another.'

'Stories filtered back from that second trip to Hamburg.' Danny was picking his words carefully. 'Perhaps it was his age and perhaps it was the times, I don't know. Yes I do know, I've been over it in my head often enough. I know all right. I know the whole story. It was supposed to have been a very beautiful boy in drag. And Zav was totally deceived. Well . . . to begin with.' Danny waved the story away with an impatient flick of his hand. It was as though he was sorry he'd started it. 'It was probably just talk, and talk's cheap enough.'

'And now he's a father,' put in Rosie, trying to be helpful.

'That never proved anything! Now I'll tell you a bit of real gossip. It's about Darlene. You know, the mother of Zav's children. She's waltzed off into the wild blue yonder. That much I'm sure is true. I'm less certain about the rumours that she's gone and joined up with the Plaster Casters. Those are girls who *really* get themselves talked about.'

'Are they a group?'

'No. They're groupies. The ultimate groupies. Rosie, this conversation is getting bawdy.' The waiter chose just that moment to arrive with a heavily laden tray. 'The Plaster Casters, how shall I put it, they *arouse* pop singers. And then they make plaster casts of their private parts.'

The tray hit the ground with a crash. 'And I thought this was supposed to be a sophisticated international hotel,' said Danny, reproachfully, to the waiter. 'Please pick up the pieces quietly. We're trying to have a solemn family conversation here.' He turned his attention back to Rosie. 'At least Zav will be near you in Berkeley. When he's out at Big Sur he'll only be a hundred miles down the coast.'

'I've already told you, I can't go. I have to do my finals.'

'Which you will because you are thorough. But there's a drop of Jewish blood in you, somewhere; has to be. Where else would you have got those great looks? And I remember something else: I remember you sitting on the bus, on that terrible tour, and telling me how all you believed in was a bit of the Old Testament. "Whither thou goest . . ." You'd follow that brilliant young hunk to the ends of the earth. Am I right? I'm right. Next time I come to San Francisco you'll be across the bay in Berkeley. Won't she?' This was addressed to Gabriel, who had just returned. Danny wasn't really giving away secrets. Gabriel couldn't possibly have heard.

'Won't she what? I think your soldier's just marched off into the street.'

'Story of my life,' sighed Danny. 'Still, as long as there are old fools like me, there'll always be plenty more where he came from. But there aren't plenty more like Rosie. You hear me? And just you see you look after her.' Danny's voice took on tones of great satisfaction as he said, 'She is not without powerful friends in America.' And then it turned gossipy again: 'Any news of your wayward mother, Rosie?'

'Not a dickybird.'

'That could be quite interesting too. America is the most magical country on earth. You can make anything happen there. Anything, anything at all. All you need is one thing.

I think we'll have a bottle of champagne. Yes, Bollinger '204. And bring a glass for yourself, waiter.'

Rosie was only surprised that it had taken Danny this long to notice the hotel servant's good looks.

Danny beamed. 'We're going to drink a toast to courage. That's the one ingredient everybody needs in the United States. But you're going to need it even more, Rosie, if you choose to be the one who's left behind.'

Gabriel's bags were packed, the car was already in storage in Berkeley Square Garage, his passport and his tickets lay on the bed. That abstract idea, '*Gabriel's going to America*', was about to become a reality. They hadn't bothered to order a taxi. You could generally pick one up at the back of Park Lane.

'I've changed my mind,' said Gabriel decisively.

Instantly, Rosie felt a good ton lighter. He wasn't going after all.

'I don't want you to come to the air terminal.'

The weight descended again like an iron door. She hadn't felt as shut out as this since her father dumped her on the doorstep of number seven Saracen Street. Gabriel made things worse by handing her his front door key. 'It's the only spare,' he said. 'You're always locking yourself out and I won't be around to dart back from the department to let you in.'

She suddenly found herself holding him close; he'd done so many things for her, things for which she'd barely said thank you. Okay, they were nothing massive. Except he had given her a whole new life; and all she'd counted was what he *hadn't* done – that lack of conversation and his inability to nurture friendships. 'And now you're going away,' was the only bit of this she said aloud.

'We won't be apart for long.'

'If I just knew *how* long, I'd probably be better at it.'

'It's not as though you weren't invited.'

He was all of her belonging, and he was off. 'You will come back, won't you?'

He didn't answer the question. He just smiled and said,

'Let's go and get a cab. You're coming for a last ride. I want to say goodbye to you in a special place. You grab my carpetbag. I'll bring up Joe's old cases.' They were nineteen-thirties raw hide suitcases, plastered with worn labels for long-vanished Ritz Hotels and for Mena House and Shepheard's in Cairo.

'Goodbye is such a very final word.' They were already outside in the area.

'Blame the English language for that. You'll have to lock the door. I've no key now. Every other language has a word for "until we meet again".'

Immediately, she was filled with childish superstition. 'Well, what language were you thinking in when you just said goodbye?' It was the kind of dangerous superstition that you made up as you went along.

'I was thinking in any language but English. Does that satisfy you?'

It made her feel a little better, but only a little. He had yet to answer the question about coming back. But she didn't dare ask it again, in case the answer was no.

'I love you,' he said.

That had to mean all the yeses on earth. Well, it would with anybody but Gabriel Bonarto. The person Rosie was annoyed with was herself. He's going and I'm not following, she thought. And it goes against everything I believe in. But if I went I'd never get my diploma. Still, what's a piece of paper? The whole thing had been flying around in her brain for weeks, like a steel bullet in a pinball machine in an amusement arcade: Go . . . Stop . . . Go. Stop had won, and that's when the machines always flashed up a message which said *Collect No Points*.

In 1967 the world was much wider than it is today; the idea of somebody visiting California could be equated with a trip to a distant star. Other Mayfair residents might have had more sophisticated views of international travel. But Rosie Tattersall was a girl from Irlams o'th' Height who had been transplanted into London W1. And now she was being left to flower in isolation.

Not tears, she thought in horror. I promised myself there wouldn't be any tears. Remembering she was Ned's granddaughter helped her keep the promise. Of course there'd been a big aircrash the previous day. But that was in Persia. Would danger choose tonight to strike a plane over the Atlantic? This is ridiculous, she thought. And she began to haul the carpetbag up the steps.

'Taxi!' yelled Gabriel who was coming up behind her. He prided himself on having an eagle eye for the orange lights on top of vacant taxi-cabs. He always maintained that this, and the ability to catch a barmaid's eye, were the signs of a real man.

Gabriel insisted on hauling all of the luggage inside the cab and instructed the driver to go to the Pan-American building in Victoria via Great Titchfield Street. 'That's where my companion gets out,' he said.

Companion? Had intimacy ended already? 'And why should I want to get out at that end of Oxford Street? It's nothing but government-surplus stores and branches of the Golden Egg. Anyway, it's the wrong direction for Victoria.'

'I'll explain when we get there. Gloomy-looking day, isn't it?'

'Yes, isn't it?' This last journey, eastbound along Oxford Street, seemed to have turned them into polite strangers with nothing to say to one another. And that was new? Inside Rosie's head, the tragic voice of Edith Piaf began to belt out the song '*Mon Homme*'. When the French lyrics faltered, Billie Holliday took over in English. Billie had just got to the agonising part where her man took her in his arms and made the world all right when the cab stopped with a lurch and the driver said, 'Great Titchfield Street.'

It was nearer than she'd thought but still beyond Oxford Circus. 'Why here?'

'Because this is where Thomas said he'd meet Ann again.'

Thomas and Ann? They sounded like members of a tennis club. And as quickly as that thought came it was replaced by the ghostly images of Thomas De Quincey and his child prostitute. 'Why do they have to enter into this?' she cried. 'What's it got to do with them?'

Gabriel already had the cab door open and was stepping down onto the pavement. 'This won't take long,' he said to the driver. 'And after that it's straight on to the Pan-Am building.'

Reluctantly, Rosie clambered out of the cab. Trust that Thomas to get in on the act! In the three years since their visit to Dove Cottage, the nineteenth-century wraith had turned into somebody a moment away from real. It was as though she was forever just managing to miss him. But there was always the possibility that he would turn up around the next corner. He was neither a smell nor a shadow but something in between. And any minute now it was going to rain. 'Okay,' she said, 'let's get this dreadful goodbye over. But do me a favour, leave De Quincey out of it.'

'I can't. When he went off on his travels this is where he said he'd meet Ann again. And he never found her. Time after time he came looking – but she'd vanished into thin air.'

Gabriel's tones had struck her as a mite too fancy and poetical. 'What's any of this got to do with us?'

'I thought you'd understand.' He said it reproachfully. And then he began to quote: '"When I kissed her at our final farewell, she put her arms about my neck, and wept without speaking a word."'

It was only too easy for Rosie to do the same. He was going. This was it. She tried for words and tears came instead.

'I knew you'd say nothing,' Gabriel whispered happily. 'It's all right, Ann. This time we'll find one another again. This time we'll break the pattern.' Granting Rosie one kiss on the cheek, Gabriel leapt for his taxi. Slamming the door and waving through the window, he looked just like any other twentieth-century traveller en route for an air terminal.

Ann. He'd called her Ann. This was something quite new. And there would be no chance of gaining an explanation for Gabriel's cab had melted into one of the dozens that were streaming along Oxford Street. Rosie rubbed cold arms; she was in the striped deckchair dress again and she thought she felt a first speck of rain on her bare skin. Standing there musing outside Dorothy Perkins wasn't going to get her anywhere. Anyway we need coffee, she thought. This was the moment when it struck her that she was no longer part of a 'we'. She was on her own.

323

Grocers being few and far between in Mayfair, Rosie had long ago settled for doing her bits of shopping in Selfridge's food department. That was where she headed now. That threat of rain was about to become a reality, and she hugged herself in an attempt to prevent goose pimples. And tonight I'll probably be hugging a pillow, she thought gloomily. If love-making with Gabriel was amazing, even the act of sleeping with him was handmade luxury. He was the one who was always first out of bed in the morning. And she never failed to try to hold onto that strong naked body for a few extra moments of warm belonging. Only all of that was in the past. Umbrellas began going up all round her as she increased the speed of her footsteps. One question kept on repeating itself. Why had he called her Ann? Why? Had madness entered into their loving partnership? Ann belonged in a world where post-chaises rattled past shops with bow-fronted windows.

By now Rosie was in the more prosaic surroundings of Selfridge's food hall. 'May I have a pound of ready-ground Kenyan?' she said to the woman behind the coffee counter. Rosie's newly bereft state stabbed her yet again. 'Better make that half a pound,' she said miserably.

'Oh I do understand.' The sympathetic male voice belonged to the person behind her in the queue. 'I'm a sad half-pound person myself.' The speaker was Bob Fellowes, their landlord. He was clutching the string handles of an empty paper carrier bag. This had obviously been used before and kept and straightened out. 'I know all about small pots of Marmite and four-ounce tins of soft cod's roe. Gabriel get off all right?'

Rosie recalled that Fellowes was supposed to be looking for love. She just hoped he wasn't looking to her to provide it. No, the man in the wool gaberdine raincoat was as docile as an ancient golden retriever, and probably one which had suffered the vet's cruellest cut. There was a hopeless 'given-up' quality to him. Yet at one time he must have been quite handsome – in a blond, cricket-pavilion sort of way.

'This wretched brain drain,' he murmured. 'America's getting some of our clevest young men. There could be no standing in Gabriel's way. I had to let him go and see what's on offer. You've got finals, haven't you?'

'Yes. And my grant allows me three months of post-graduate studies.' She began handing over money for the coffee.

'I'll have one of those sample-sized pots of the new freeze-dried decaffeinated,' said Bob Fellowes to the girl behind the counter. This faint request only served to heighten Rosie's misery.

'I'll miss Gabriel,' continued their landlord. 'The trouble is that I was instrumental in hiring him. And it's not my own department. Professor Wolheim's the big cheese. He's just losing another bright young man to Berkeley too. Sluga, he's called. A clever fidget, he's German; I always think of him as stepping backwards onto other people's feet.'

I can do without this academic blether, thought Rosie. Except, what else have I got?

Bob Fellowes picked up a Maxwell House leaflet for reduced British Rail travel. 'I wouldn't blame Gabriel if he didn't bother to come back and serve a term's notice.'

'I would.' There was panic in her voice. 'He's got to come back. All his books are still here.'

'They can be shipped,' said Professor Fellowes airily. 'Was that one and sevenpence ha'penny you said?' He began counting the coins for his purchase. He had his money in a flat leather purse. 'A shipper would clear those bookshelves in no time. But I know Gabriel. I've known him since he came down from Balliol. There's one book he wouldn't trust to anybody's hands but his own. If he's taken that one, he's definitely gone for good.'

'Which book is it?' asked Rosie, even more alarmed. She suspected she already knew. She did know.

Professor Fellowes confirmed it: 'His first edition of *The Confessions of an English Opium Eater*. In truth, it's two articles in a bound volume of the *London Magazine* for eighteen twenty-one. If that's gone, so has Gabriel. I wish I was young enough for the Yankees to want to drain *my* brain,' he added wistfully.

The book wasn't there. There could be no doubt about it. Where it should have been, there was a neat empty gap. Rosie searched along the rest of the shelves just to be sure; but she knew she was searching in vain. Yes, she knew exactly where it should have been because Gabriel had reached for that volume as often as devout Christians seek their Bible, as frequently as Poor-Bertha-who-drags-a-leg had consulted *Napoleon's Book of Dreams*. As if to emphasise its absence, a morocco-bound volume suddenly fell across the empty gap and slapped the next book along. Rosie found this downright eerie.

In this mood, a peremptory knock on the basement door caused her to jump. Cautiously, she peered through the plain net curtains at the window. She could see the three-quarters-profile outline of a young girl in a pregnancy smock, standing waiting in the area. This surely couldn't be another of Gabriel's foibles coming home to roost? Rosie moved across and opened the door.

'Delivery,' said the girl. She was holding a huge sheaf of flowers wrapped in white paper decorated with a black signature. This proclaimed that they had come from a shop called Constance Spry. And the girl wasn't pregnant at all. The smock was 'artistic'.

'Thank you.' Should she give her a shilling for coming?

'They're nice and fresh,' said the girl, 'but if I were you, I'd give them a good drink of hot water.' The post-debutante tones cancelled out all thoughts of a tip. Rosie closed the door and carried the flowers through to the kitchen. Her heart was lighter. Men don't send flowers to girls they're ditching. She could admit it now: it was a thought which had been doing its best to wreck her.

Whatever was she going to put the flowers in? Come to that, what kind were they?

Lilies. White lilies and branches of dark laurel – just like something at an upper-class funeral. Horrified, she tore the card out of its little envelope. *Ann: This time we will meet again. With love from Thomas.*

Had Rosie not had respect for all living things, she could have cheerfully battered the bouquet to bits. She wasn't Ann. She didn't want to be Ann. And she didn't want him to be Thomas De Quincey either. More than ever she needed to discuss this weird development with Gabriel himself. But the taxi would have dropped him off at the terminal by now, and he would already be bouncing along in the airport bus. The first leg of his journey was going to be London to New York. He was planning to spend two nights with an American friend, a man on the *New York Herald Tribune* he'd known up at Oxford.

Which is one friend more than Gabriel made in London, she thought angrily. Rosie filled an old zinc bucket with hot water, unceremoniously dumped the flowers into it, and reviewed her situation.

What had brought her to this dismal moment? A line written in Magic Marker on the top of a table in the Vesuvius coffee bar – *Absolute Commitment Offered and Expected* – that's what had got her here. These words had seemed to reach to some need within her very being. And if the drawing above them had shown her naked, this had been a frank declaration of what she could expect at the summit of her life with Gabriel Bonarto.

Yet they'd managed to make a life. An odd one perhaps, unconventional; but it had been their own. And where was she now? In limbo. The rent would continue to be paid by banker's order. Despite her own protests that she could live on her grant, more money would be credited to her bank account. Her eyes went again to the bucket of lavish flowers.

I'm just an old-fashioned mistress in a modern Day-Glo setting, she thought grimly. No, that's not being fair to Gabriel. I'm the one who banned the subject of marriage. I'm the one who wouldn't chuck everything up to follow him. But I'm me. I'm Rosie Tattersall. And I'm certainly not the reincarnation of some child prostitute from the year eighteen hundred and half-dead-on-a-doorstep.

'I am not Ann.' She actually said it aloud. By now she had stomped into the living room. 'And you're not Thomas De Quincey either.' This was to a photograph she had taken of Gabriel, asleep in bed. The day she took it, morning sunlight had fallen across his naked chest; the sheet which barely covered his groin could have been an artful twist of Renaissance drapery. For two years she had been on the

327

lookout for an antique silver frame for this picture. Would she still be bothered to continue with the search? Or should she slide the glossy print from its temporary clear Perspex frame, and rip it up, and begin a whole new life – on her own?

What sort of life? She couldn't begin to imagine an existence without him. She was still looking at the photo. God, he was beautiful! She wasn't sure whether she was saying it to the picture or to the Almighty. Perhaps both; love-making with Gabriel had continued to restore her belief that Creation was – somehow – an ordered thing.

It didn't seem very ordered today! 'Help me.' It was the nearest thing to a prayer that she'd offered up in weeks. In fact the last time had been when she thanked God for good legs. Still, she'd *said* thank you.

When it came to praying, Rosie had always been brought up to believe that it was better to be absolutely specific, so she added, 'When he rings up, please give me the right words to say.' The praying voice inside her head grew quite conversational as she continued: 'But whatever you think best.' It was, she supposed, a modern version of 'Thy will be done'. She couldn't bring herself to use that. It was too antique and churchified. 'And I have to say something else, God. . .' She needed to dissociate herself from Gabriel's frequent guilt trips. 'If you're not part of what we do in bed, then I'm talking to the wrong person. And please don't let his plane crash. Amen.'

Rosie began to calculate. Two hours of hanging around at London Airport. Eight in the air. Two more to get to this friend's apartment. New York is five hours behind us. . .She gave up. Arithmetic had never been her strong subject. He would ring when he rang.

In the meantime Rosie had to find something to do. Surprised to find that she was quite hungry, she decided to take herself off to a solitary early dinner at Signora Bolla's. But something seemed to be going wrong with time. It was going much more slowly than usual. When she got to Piccadilly Circus it was still only five o'clock so she decided to while away an hour and a half in the News Cinema at the corner of Shaftesbury Avenue. This proved to be a mistake.

The newsreel was full of the Persian air disaster, and one of the cartoons had Bugs Bunny shipwrecked and stranded on a plank in the middle of the ocean.

Had Rosa Bolla ever had an earlier evening customer? Rosie doubted it. The windows of the café weren't even steamed up, and her only company was framed photographs of ballet dancers. There was something very sad about some of them. It was hard to believe that Anton Dolin had once been young. Nowadays his star was as dimmed as the ink on the lavishly signed picture.

'Gabriele gone?' asked the mountainous proprietress. Was it Rosie's imagination, or was there something disapproving in Signora Bolla's attitude tonight?

'Yes, he's gone. Where's Umberto?' In his own way, the dog was a replacement for a head waiter; it was the first time he had failed to greet her at the door.

'I hope you know what you doing,' Rosa Bolla was speaking in her darkest tones. 'Umberto upstairs in flat. I barred that bloody Russian dancer and I think he rang the Sanitary Inspector. We had a visit from the Health. Nothing wrong with the kitchen but Umberto had to be banished. That Sanitary Inspector has no soul.' She slapped the menu down in front of Rosie. 'I more worried about what Gabriele do with his *body*. Them Bonartos got big appetites. Big appetites for everything.'

Rosie had never thought of that. She and Gabriel had been everything to one another for so long that the word 'unfaithful' had vanished from her vocabulary. But it was back now – in a big way. She tried to reassure herself by announcing, 'He's already sent me flowers – waxy white lilies.'

'And what are they meant to mean, death or crucifixion? I just finished making fresh fettucine. Or there are some nice little veal escalopes.'

Rosie's stomach heaved at the thought of cruel veal. But this was not the reason for the sudden disappearance of her appetite. It was a generally accepted fact that Gabriel was outstandingly good-looking and America was full of beautiful girls. A whole procession of Hollywood lookalikes began parading through her head; Faye Dunaway, Candice Bergen,

Jane Fonda. . .and they were all beckoning to Gabriel who was sitting next to his mother and Robert Mitchum. All three were on gilded thrones. 'I think I'll just have a plain omelette,' she said weakly.

'You pregnant?' enquired Rosa Bolla.

'No. And with him away, I won't have to worry about remembering to take the pill.'

'You stop, you get fat.'

'I think you've got that theory the wrong way round.' And what was to say that Bob Fellowes' theory about the book was correct? Not what, who. Gabriel Bonarto, that's who. Or should it be 'whom'? Never mind the English grammar, how many hours *now* before the Italian could ring?

'Poor thing,' said Rosa sympathetically. 'I give you a glass of wine, on the house.' She didn't have a licence so it was always produced in teacups. 'Gabriele's father was terrible unfaithful to his mother. Terrible! And always other film stars.'

Once again that glamorous, utterly unreasonable procession began to file past Rosie's mind's eye. Mia Farrow, Ali McGraw, Raquel Welch. . .No, *not* Raquel Welch – he surely wouldn't go for anybody as obvious as that. I would never have believed I owned this streak of jealousy, she thought helplessly. Just get there, Gabriel, and get to a telephone, and *ring* me.

The call came at seven in the morning when Rosie was woken by the shrilling of the phone bell. She put out a sleepy hand for the cream-coloured receiver; it brought her crackling noises. Then Gabriel's voice said, 'Ann?'

That did it. She was fully awake in a flash. 'I'm not Ann. Get that straight.'

'You're Ann to me. You always have been.'

'Well you've never been Thomas to me. And you're never going to be, not to me.'

'Did you like your flowers, Ann?'

'Have you been drinking? Didn't you hear what I just said? If you're prepared to be Gabriel, I'll talk to you.'

'Okay, okay, I'm Gabriel. I've had one dry martini. I'd

forgotten they keep the gin bottle in the fridge in New York. It's two o'clock in the morning here.'

'How was your flight?' The word 'flight' switched and darted in her mind; in the half-second time lag it took to reach New York, it had already taken on a new significance for her. Gabriel was guilty of running away.

'The flight was fine. They put me next to a woman with a baby. I thought he'd drive me mad but he didn't. He's my new friend now. He's called William.'

'That's nice for you.' Yes, she thought grimly, you won me over once before – on the day we met – by being nice to a child. 'You've run away, haven't you? You took your sacred book with you and you're not coming back.'

'Who says?'

'Bob Fellowes for one. Me for another.' A night's sleep had left her realising that he had never once mentioned returning. 'Come on, let's have the whole story, Gabriel. Are you just going to Berkeley for an interview, or have they already offered you a job?'

An awkward pause from the New York end was followed by, 'Wolheim's got a great department going in London but all I am is somebody who was thrust upon him. My kind of philosophy is just not where they're at at University College.'

She refused to be deflected. 'Have Berkeley offered you a job?'

'Yes. But it's not as simple as that. I have to get out there and see whether I want it. The day after tomorrow I have to fly from one coast of America to the other. I might not want the job . . .'

'You'll want it.' And to think she had slept in one of his old shirts for a bit of belonging comfort. She pulled it straight over her head and flung it across the room. 'Is there anything else you want to tell me?'

'You sound as though you're going away from me. Rose, come back. I need to hear some warmth in your voice.'

'You're the one who went away.' It was cold without the shirt so she pulled up the sheets. 'You told lies.'

'No.' This was very firm.

'Well, you were certainly deceitful.'

331

'Let's just say I dissembled.'

'Save the fancy definitions for the University of California. I'm beginning to think they're welcome to you.' With this she slammed down the phone and hid her head under the blankets.

What had she done to their relationship? She'd prayed to God to be given the right words; she'd begged to be told what questions to ask her lover. Roused from a deep sleep, the questions had certainly seemed to come spontaneously enough . . .

The telephone rang again. Rosie reached out one arm and lifted the receiver into her cocoon of bedclothes. 'Yes?'

'You didn't have a number to call me back on. I thought that you might want to continue with our conversation.'

'I'll continue with our conversation when you've got a whole story to tell me.' She had to sit up to put the phone back. But this time she had no doubts that her words had been divinely inspired.

Her next problem was living with the result. Silence. Thirty-six hours of silence. It'll be a long time before I pray again, she thought wretchedly. But, presumably, Gabriel *would* have to talk to them before he could tell her a whole story. She spent most of her waking hours playing over a mental tape of their last conversation. '*You certainly told lies.*' '*Let's say I dissembled.*' '*Save the fancy definitions for the University of California . . .*'

That was the point at which the tape always went blurred on her. She'd certainly told him where he got off. Could she have given him the impression that everything was over?

In one remembered version she had; and in the other she hadn't. She actually caught herself thinking, The Lord is *not* my shepherd. And then she wondered whether this was blasphemy. And worried that it might have made things even worse.

Rosie was supposed to be working on the final version of her thesis. The text continued to languish where she'd abandoned it, on the floor by the living-room fireplace. The photo-illustrations remained in an accusing pile, on the kitchen table. To get the whole thing together she really needed a tube of rubber fixative. But that would mean going out; and she had become absolutely convinced that the moment she got to the corner of Tiddy Street – and out of earshot – was the moment that the phone would choose to ring.

Eating was awkward: the contents of their store cupboard had always been meagre. Eventually she found herself confronted by a tin of mackerel in mustard sauce, left behind by Fellowes' daughter. There was that and nothing else – unless you counted dried oregano and an old jar of stuffed olives.

By her own calculations, Gabriel's plane should be just about due to take off for California. Rosie risked a trip to Selfridge's. In their food hall her mind went blank. She stood stock still, a crowd milling around her, with absolutely no idea of what she wanted. In the end she settled for a quarter of roast ham, some Russian salad, a packet of ready-made muesli and a pathetically small haggis in a plastic skin. At this point she pulled herself together, made her way to the stationery department, bought a large tube of Cow gum – and wondered whether she was heading for a complete nervous breakdown.

Milk, she'd forgotten milk. Rosie was already halfway down Tiddy Street. She would just have to settle for eating the muesli with water. And then she got annoyed with herself for being so pathetic and remembered that there was a milk machine in North Audley Street: but wasn't retracing your steps supposed to be bad luck? If this carried on, she thought, I'll soon be telling my own fortune by the nicks between the paving stones. If the fourth one's wide, he'll ring me late tonight. She was already doing it!

'I say! Hang on a minute, Miss Tattersall.' It was the girl from the florist's. She was leaning out of a small white van. 'I've just left you a note. We've been trying to deliver to your flat.'

'Not more funeral flowers, I hope.'

'No, red roses. Two dozen of them. They were paid for in California.'

'But he's not there till late today.'

'Wouldn't know about that.' The girl handed down another triangular black and white Constance Spry parcel, with a little envelope pinned to the top right-hand corner. 'Same rules apply as last time. A good long drink. Right up to the neck, if you can manage it.'

At that moment, Rosie could have managed to jump over the tallest chimneypot in Tiddy Street. She had already opened the envelope; the message on the card read *I love you, Rose – Gabriel*. It was a little odd seeing such an intimate sentiment written in a florist's anonymous handwriting. But red roses were a big improvement on the previous morbid offerings – which were still reposing in a bucket in the back kitchen.

As a matter of fact she hadn't got any vases at all, so she went straight to a very grand shop called Thomas Goode and bought a big plain white one in their sale. As she carried this and the flowers back into the flat, the phone was ringing like the bells of Shoreditch.

'Rose?'

'Yes, and I'm holding onto a great big armful of them,' she said happily. 'How have you got to California so quickly?'

'Swapped flights and came yesterday. I had to get things sorted out. I never believed in jet lag before, but it's real all right! I feel as though I'm standing next to myself.'

'Don't make any decisions in that state.' Oh dear, the last thing she wanted to sound was a nagger.

'The decision's made. I'm taking the job.' His voice began to thrill with excitement. 'Oh Rose, this is an *amazing* place. Remember how I used to talk about "it" being in London? Well it's moved to here. You've never seen anything like it. Hyde Park on a Sunday afternoon? That's nothing! You know the San Francisco song, the one about gentle people with flowers in their hair? It's true. It's real. They're here. The streets are packed with them. It's so beautiful.' He made the word 'so' sound about a block long.

'Your roses are beautiful too. Much nicer than those gloomy lilies from Thomas.'

'Thomas likes lilies,' he said sternly. And then his voice began to ring again. 'You will come, won't you? *It* would be no good without you. Do your finals, do the postgrad bit if you have to – but come. Say you'll come.'

An unusual streak of caution conditioned her reply. 'I'll come to you but not to Thomas. It's not as though he's part of your job. The Thomas thing has to stop.'

There was a pause. 'I suppose I could try to leave the whole idea alone.' Gabriel sounded distinctly dubious.

'Not good enough.' Rosie had caught a finger on a thorn; the florist had failed to remove all of them from the stems. She watched blood start to run as she said, 'It's not an idea, it's an obsession. It's spoiling our lives. It has to end.'

A longer pause, then, 'I suppose I could try.'

'Still not good enough.' Her finger needed a plaster but Thomas De Quincey had to be sealed off forever. 'There's one way I'd believe he was over.'

'Tell me.'

'You'd have to burn that book.'

Outrage came down the line. 'Rose! That's a valuable first edition.'

'I don't care. When you can prove to me that you've got rid of it, I'll come to California.'

Suddenly Gabriel was taking far more interest in her thesis than he had ever shown in London. He delivered three whole paragraphs on the subject. 'I'll think about the book,' he added – reluctantly – at the end. 'I *will* think about it.'

'Good. Because until it's gone, there's a ghost standing between us.'

Other people might wonder why Rosie didn't just up and leave him. They wouldn't be people who had spent a loveless childhood. Gabriel was Rosie's only bit of belonging in the whole wide world. And when Mr Tetley had said to her, 'You're very psychic yourself,' he'd put a name to something she had only ever half understood. All the years of being a lodger in other people's lives had taught her to rely on her instincts. These told her that deep down inside – where it really mattered – Gabriel Bonarto was all right. That phrase all right means a great deal more in Lancashire than it does elsewhere.

But Rosie was in London; and never was there a worse

autumn for being divided from a lover in northern California. It was the year of the San Francisco songs. Scott Mackenzie was forever singing the song that Gabriel had mentioned; the one which enjoined you to be sure to wear some flowers in your hair. Then the Flowerpot Men took over with a much more basic message. They simply sang, 'Let's Go to San Francisco'. They chorused of flowers growing so very high, of sunlight blowing your mind up to the sky. As the London leaves changed colour, the disc jockeys dug out one of the previous year's hits; one which talked about all the leaves being brown and the skies being grey, as Mama Cass shook her tambourine in the background. The song was 'California Dreamin' and it suggested that every problem could be solved by heading for the West Coast of the USA. It was *that* autumn.

And all the while Rosie waited for Gabriel to indicate that he had abandoned Thomas. She never, ever, mentioned the opium eater in her letters; she just wrote about delivering her thesis and going to postgraduate seminars, and about trying to find subjects that would interest the picture editors of the new Sunday colour supplements. Gabriel replied on a shower of picture postcards. The messages he wrote on the back were loving and jokey and full of funny things which people had said. But he never wrote the only message she needed to hear.

He came closest with, 'I know – but give me time.' Rosie supposed it was a step in the right direction but she also found herself wondering whether he'd been smoking a lot of grass. LSD she did not worry about. The postcards had made it irritably plain that the super-manufacturer of that drug, Mr Augustus Owsley Stanley the third, had gone missing from Berkeley. And she knew her Gabriel – he would only settle for the best.

The best? She read the postcard about Owsley for the fourth time that weekend, pulled a wry face and switched on the television set. She rarely viewed television, yet oddly enough the set seemed to be on at the hour she judged to be the lowest ebb of the week – a quarter to six on a Sunday evening. This was the time when the BBC transmitted a programme called *Pinky and Perky*. It starred pig puppets with laughing-gas voices. In Rosie's view, Pinky and Perky would be gibbering on every television in hell. Or was it that a quarter to six on the Sabbath was – anyway – a taste of the nether world?

That particular Sunday, at that unhappy hour, the telephone rang. It was Nora Hankey. Down the receiver, Rosie could hear piglet noises coming from Saracen Street. The puppets were obviously jiggling up and down in Irlams o'th' Height too.

'Turn that thing down, Tippler,' said Mrs Hankey. 'The way he's crouched in front of it, you'd think he was watching Ibsen. Are you there, Rosemary?'

'I was just turning mine off.'

'I just thought I'd ring you . . .' Nora let out a deep sigh.

'I'm really glad you did.' This was no less than the truth. 'I'm feeling a bit on my own.'

'I'll soon be very on my own.' Another sigh. 'Has Hazel been in touch yet? She wants you to be bridesmaid.'

'When?'

Next spring. May looks the most likely month.'

'I don't know where I'll be next spring.' Totally unexpected tears began to roll down Rosie's face.

'Rosemary, are you all right? Rosemary . . .?'

'I think it must have been those bloody pigs. They always get to me.'

'Funny you should say that. They get to me too. That's really why I'm phoning. She's marrying a man called Tudor. Says it all really, doesn't it?'

'You mean like Henry Tudor?'

'I mean like Tudor Proctor-Jones. Mrs Proctor-Jones, that'll be a nice name for her to go to bed with, won't it? I'm a bit funny about telling people the next bit. His father's a Tory councillor. It's hurt me more than it did when she got herself pregnant.'

Never really political, Rosie found herself quite enlivened by the news. 'Are they rich? She always said she'd go for rich.'

'They're not without; wholesale butchers. He's like a very small pork chop – even to the ginger whiskers. "Tudor Cutlet" I call him.'

337

And Rosie would have been willing to bet everything she owned that Nora called the poor man that to his face. 'Listen, Mrs Hankey, I never said thank you for sending me my mother's engagement ring. Thanks.'

Nora hadn't finished with Hazel's forthcoming nuptials: 'The wedding's going to be at St Ann's Church.' The 'Hmph' sound which followed was plainly meant to remove any suggestion of approval of such high-flown city-centre junketings. 'Zav's forking out for the lot. But he can't come. He's already got another Scandinavian tour pencilled in. Him not there, you not there, us Hankeys are going to be very thin on the ground. Rosemary?' And now she sounded very stern indeed. 'Not more snivelling?'

'Take no notice of me. I think Sunday must do something to my bio-rhythms. It's just that I didn't know you thought of me as a Hankey.' It was too much. The tears were really rolling. 'I never knew.'

'You sound as though you *need* a hankie. Have you got yourself into trouble?'

'Not that sort of trouble.'

Nora was obviously facing straight up to it. 'You're apart from your man, Rosemary. You're bound to get low without him. Don't forget you're talking to an old sailor's wife. When Tippler was at sea I used to spend weeks waiting for letters. At least you can talk to one another on the phone, these days.'

'No. We should be able to but we can't.' Out it all came. 'The phone's there but we daren't use it, for fear of what we'd say. We're dodging round a tricky subject. And all he sends me are postcards. He sees postcards as safe.' And that's how she was viewing this telephone call. 'I write him long letters. I rip most of them up, so it doesn't look as though I'm sending too many. I write them at night and then, in the morning, I rip them to bits – even when I've already put the stamps on. I'm ashamed of that part. I should steam them off.'

'You're too on your own,' was the Irlams o'th' Height reaction. You've *always* been too on your own. Don't think I didn't understand because I did. But you couldn't be given special attention; I'd me own to consider – I didn't want to make them jealous. But make no mistake, Rosemary, you're

338

one of us. Tried and trusted. What's his bloody phone number? I'll soon sort him out!'

Rosie brushed away her tears. 'Please don't,' she begged in horror.

'Don't tell me what I can and can't do. It's dead easy to get yourself put through to American directory enquiries. It wouldn't be the first time I've done it. They call it "information" over there.'

Nora Hankey was certainly capable of calling Gabriel. The cost would be immaterial – Zav always footed the phone bills. 'You'd never do such a thing, would you?'

'I might.' Her tones changed with, 'Thank God! Them pigs is over. Rosemary, whatever's wrong between you and Gabriel, get it sorted. D'you know, I think I *might* just have a word with him.'

'Please don't.' By now the tears had subsided but she was still in fear of Nora ringing America. The less said now the better; her old landlady loved the stimulus of opposition. 'Give my love to Tippler. Bye.'

Did Nora phone Gabriel? Rosie could never get her to say. But Mrs Hankey had always believed that a good turn revealed was a good turn ruined. It took five days for an airmail letter to travel from Berkeley to London. The following Saturday there was a loud bang on the door at the top of the inside stairs – the staircase which led into the rest of the house.

'He forgot to put "basement flat" on the envelope.' It was Bob Fellowes in rumpled blue and white striped pyjamas, with a beige cardigan over the top of them. 'I hope you haven't been upset by the noise. I got a stray Dalmatian from Battersea Dogs' Home. I thought he would be company.'

A whole letter! Rosie grabbed it hungrily. 'Thank you.' The bulb had gone on the stairs into their own flat. As she piled down to the living room to read the letter she reflected that a Dalmatian would be even better for Professor Fellowes than the retriever she had always thought he'd looked like. Spotted Dalmatians were both sad and a little bit dotty.

My dearest Rose,

You win. It's gone. The book is now in a glass case in a shop window on Telegraph Avenue. The shop is called Karmarama (Centre for Occult Studies) and the *Confessions* are marked 'rare' and underpriced at five hundred dollars. Twice as much as he gave me!

I'm writing rather than telephoning to give myself a chance to get used to the idea, before we talk. But talk we must. We have to plan your trip properly. You haven't even got a passport and you will need to apply for an American visa. You still count as underage so you will have to send the forms to your father for his signature.

I want this trip to make up for the misery I've put you through. I do know that I've done that. You're coming forever but I think the first part should be something of an adventurous holiday. Much as I long to see you, I think you ought to fly to New York; and then you could cross America on a Greyhound bus. That would be a very 'now' thing to do. What's more, as you crossed from state to state, the weather should gradually improve and get warmer – you could both acclimatise and get some great photographs along the way!

She longed for Gabriel but it had to be admitted that this proposed bus journey was as highly desired a Sixties experience as hitting the trail for Kathmandu. Rosie returned to the letter.

I think I should get you a room at the Chelsea Hotel in New York. Just for a couple of nights. That's where it's all supposed to be happening. . .

A dog barked above her and Rosie thought of their London landlord. She had treated the news of this animal very cursorily; in fact she'd failed to react at all. Oh well, that could soon be put right. The rest of the letter was protests of undying love and a bit about his journalist friend Piet De Kuyper, who would be happy to look after her in New York. Did she really want to cross America in a single-decker

340

bus? She could practically hear Gran'dad Tattersall ordering her to say yes. The letter had a postscript. 'Call me, call me soon. I'll be waiting.' And then a PPS. 'Did you know that people call this town Bezerkeley?'

Rosie looked at her watch. Eleven o'clock in the morning meant that it would only be three in California. Too late and too early. Now would be as good a time as any to show more enthusiasm for Bob Fellowes' dog. Perhaps she should go upstairs and ask to be formally introduced. And who was meant to tell Fellowes that their tenancy would soon be coming to an end?

Upstairs was much more grand than the basement. The entrance hall had a squared black and white marble floor, and fancy doors. Panelled rococo ones, like something in an opera. She rapped on one of the pair which led into Professor Fellowes' dining room.

The immediate barking was nearly as theatrical as the doors. By contrast, Professor Fellowes' cry of 'Down, boy!' seemed rather tentative and amateurish.

The door opened. 'I think he wants to go out.' Gabriel's boss was still in his striped pyjamas. When it came to style, the dog outdid him by far. Black spots on a white background and eyes as bright as mercury in a child's puzzle. 'He's already done a little job in the back courtyard, but I think he can feel Hyde Park calling.'

'I just thought I'd come and say hello,' said Rosie. The animal was hurling himself at her so joyfully that she was having a job to keep her balance.

'How kind. He's a little rumbustious this morning. He's just eaten a copy of Kant's *Critique of Pure Reason*. I got him because my sister said that everybody ought to have somebody to love.'

The dog sat down and offered Rosie a paw. 'He's beautiful,' she said. 'And your sister's absolutely right. Everybody really does need somebody to love. That's why I'll soon be off to New York.'

Voiced aloud, it had stopped being a theory. A great flood of excitement went through Rosie and the dog seemed to catch hold of it, for he began to bark merrily and to dance

341

round the room. He was free of Battersea Dogs' Home, Rosie was off to America, winter sunlight was streaming through the window and everybody had somebody to love.

10

Rosie sneezed. Had she, she wondered, brought an English virus to New York? But she wasn't just suffering from good old-fashioned influenza; she was a victim of something much more modern than that. Rosie Tattersall was in a state of deep culture shock.

It was the middle of the night, and she was alone in her awful little room at the top of the Chelsea Hotel. The noise of police sirens rose up – yet again – from the streets below. Time had ceased to have any meaning. Rattle-bang-crash: could it only be another lorry passing along West 23rd Street? It sounded as though the devil himself was taking a night trip through his kingdom.

America had yet to become more than a place of perpetual darkness. Since leaving Tiddy Street she'd already been through two midnights – both of them on the flight. One before they were told to adjust their watches, and another one just after the plane landed. The flight had taken eight hours. Before that, there had been a four-hour delay whilst they waited for the fog to clear at London Airport.

Fog in London and thick snow in New York. The only thing she'd seen on the drive from the airport to the hotel had been a boil on the back of the cabdriver's neck. The rest had been swirling sleet.

Rosie was exhausted. Yet when she lay down she couldn't go to sleep. She hadn't dared to take her clothes off; she just lay on top of the bed. Nothing in her previous experience had prepared her for the Chelsea Hotel It was a far cry from the boarding houses of Ilfracombe! Mind you, she'd been in real hotels before, lots of them – on that tour across England with Zav and the Hankeys. But even that awful room in Cardiff, the one with the purple and orange wallpaper, where she'd got over the effects of Mongoose's pep pills, had been better than this. Come to think of it, she was feeling very similar to

343

the way she'd felt then. Her body was worn out but her mind was racing like somebody who'd been on speed. Rosie supposed this was jet-lag.

The telephone rang. At first she didn't recognise it for what it was. Not brr-brr, just long rings on the bell. And the instrument itself was so old and black and electric-looking that, for a moment, she was scared of touching the receiver in case it emitted shocks.

This was behaving ridiculously. 'Hello?'

'Welcome to America.' It was Gabriel. 'How come you missed Piet De Kuyper at Kennedy?' This was his friend on the *New York Herald Tribune*.

'We were hours late. He wasn't there when I came through the gate so I took a cab.'

'Well he *was* there. Dutch people are very reliable. He'd been there for hours. He thinks you must have slipped through when he went to the john. And then nobody told him that the flight had landed . . .'

'Well I'm very sorry but I was there,' stormed Rosie. Not being used to travel, she did not know that jet lag often seizes hold of an even temper. Hers flared even higher: 'Of course I was there. Ask anybody at Kennedy. Ask that immigration official, the one I nearly came to blows with.'

'Was there trouble?' asked Gabriel anxiously. 'Did you say that you already had funds lodged in the Bank of America?'

'There was trouble all right,' raged Rosie. 'I didn't know you were meant to wait your turn behind the yellow line. I got shouted at. I thought they were going to send me back. And then a giant in a uniform said "Welcome to America." *He* had a gun on his desk!'

She was not best pleased to hear amusement in Gabriel's voice as he asked, 'How long have they stamped your passport for?'

'I never looked. Hang on.' It was underneath the mattress with her currency, her traveller's cheques and Connie's diamond ring. 'Six months. June the something.' Her eyes felt very tired.

'Not bad.' Gabriel sounded impressed. 'You must have been looking particularly beautiful. What's your room like?'

344

'Awful. It's grotty. It's very small and very high up. It reminds me of American films about girls' reformatories. The shower's got tin walls. Can I be at the right Chelsea? I keep expecting a wardress to come through the door and beat me up.'

'It will all seem better in the morning.' Gabriel yawned. 'It's two o'clock here.'

'Time?' she snapped. 'What's that? I never knew before that clocks were something you could fiddle with. Well I did, but it's done my head in.' Her sense of humour began to creep back. 'Gabriel, whatever made you choose this god-awful hotel?'

'It's supposed to be big on atmosphere. Just think, you could be in the same room that Brendan Behan or Dylan Thomas had their DTs in.'

'Well, thanks a bundle!' The laugh which followed this was definitely out of control.

'Rose? Rosie, do stop laughing for a minute.' Gabriel was beginning to sound worried. 'Actually, Piet was a bit bothered about your being there on your own. A lot of Andy Warhol's friends use it. But Piet's upper-class Dutch and they can be very conventional.'

'Gabriel?' The manic laughter had stopped and she was suddenly tired to the point of tears. 'When does real life start again? We seem to have been living in letters and phone calls for months.'

He made a gentle hissing noise down the telephone. The kind of noise that Italians use to calm troubled babies. 'Sss . . . It won't be long, I promise.'

'I've hardly spoken to anybody for ages. Even the woman next to me on the plane was an Arab. She got hysterical when we took off. It took three air hostesses to calm her down. Isn't flying magic? Mr Molyneux always said it was like having an orgasm. It wasn't like that for me so maybe it's just for men. Don't go away for a minute. I just want somebody to talk to.'

'I'm not going anywhere. I'm in bed.'

'With no clothes on. Don't! I can hardly wait.'

'If you're in that mood,' he laughed, 'I *am* worried. Piet's coming to collect you for breakfast at half past eight. Promise me you won't rape him.'

'No,' she said happily. 'I only want you. Just you. You're the only one I've ever wanted. Guess what?' A sudden thought had cheered her. 'At least I've done what I always believed in. At least I've followed you from one country to another.'

In later life, when people heard that Rosie had stayed at the Chelsea at the end of the Sixties, they would beg her to tell them what it was really like. In her account, that drab upstairs bedroom barely figured at all. Instead, she would tell them about the next morning, when she walked down an amazing staircase which was even grander than the one at the Spiritualist Association of Great Britain. It had a highly polished curving banister above leafy cast-iron spindles. A staircase out of *The Sleeping Beauty* – well, out of a quiet corner of that ballet. And the Bonartos couldn't be the Mafia or their name would have got her a better room than that anonymous hellhole where she'd passed a sleepless night. The rooms at the top were plainly reserved for hicks from the sticks.

As she got nearer to ground level, she realised that the big doors on the lower floors led into complete apartments. There were people who lived here the whole time. By now, Rosie was quite frankly nosying. She could hear somebody practising a violin, to a standard that had to be worthy of Carnegie Hall; and through an open doorway she saw a muscular man hurling paint at a vast canvas. She couldn't put a name to him but she recognised the work as something she'd already seen illustrated in the *Observer* colour supplement.

As Rosie got a floor lower, another door opened and an immensely assured black woman walked out of an apartment. The most Rosie could glimpse inside was a huge potted-palm tree, big enough for the jungle. Then somebody else came out: an incredibly doe-eyed half-caste boy, who paused to turn a key in the lock. Holding a supple sable coat over his arm, he began to follow the woman downstairs, always keeping a respectful distance behind her.

346

Descending like an African empress the woman continued to gaze straight ahead as she said, 'What's the weather like outside?'

'Even colder,' he replied.

Without so much as looking at him, she held out her arms. He swathed her in sables. One moment she hadn't got a coat on, the next she looked like a *Vogue* model waiting to be handed a cigarette.

He handed her one and lit it. Each of these movements could have been choreographed. The woman continued down the stairs. Once again the acolyte positioned himself three respectful paces behind.

She's like a black Isadora Duncan, thought Rosie. I've never seen such a straight back in my life. And then she realised who the woman was. Katherine Dunham – who had once been the most famous black dancer in the world. This was the moment that Rosie really knew she'd got to New York. And from somewhere upstairs an unidentified male voice screamed shrilly, 'No wonder you've got no veins left, Bridget!'

Piet De Kuyper was waiting for her in the lobby. Big and blond and blue-eyed, he was dressed like a businessman, but the shoulder-length hair seemed to indicate wilder weekend tendencies. Smiling down at Rosie he said, 'Are you going to be warm enough?'

She was wearing her winter coat – short and black with big scarlet buttons. 'It's all I've got with me,' she said apologetically. 'I didn't expect it to be so cold.'

'In New York, in January?' His eyes were obviously appreciating her red high-heeled, thigh-length Russian boots. But they were kind eyes. 'Borrow these gloves,' he said. 'I'll be fine, I've got deep pockets.' For a man from Amsterdam his voice was quite American.

Pushing your way into gloves that were still warm seemed a little intimate for a first meeting. Suddenly, without warning, Rosie sneezed.

'Oh dear,' he said apprehensively, already moving a half-pace away from her. But he flashed another big smile as he asked, 'So what did you make of your first sight of the New York skyline?'

347

'All I saw was snow. It was coming down like *Scott of the Antarctic*. And all I could see from my bedroom window was a grey building, opposite.'

He held back the lobby door. 'Step outside,' he invited.

When Rosie did, she found that she didn't own a big enough gasp for the moment. The air was icy cold but crystal clear, and the skyline was straight out of *Superman* comics. 'And it goes so far *up*,' she marvelled. 'I knew it was going to be tall but I didn't think anything could go as high as those buildings. And I never expected the tops of them to be so elaborate. It's Byzantium in the sky!'

She cursed herself for having failed to bring her camera downstairs. But would a Rolleiflex have been any use? If Manchester was a black and white photograph, and London was Kodacolour, New York was nothing less than 3D. Three-dimensional and glittering. As she lowered her eyes, she noticed somebody lying on a newspaper on the frozen pavement.

'There's a man there,' she pointed, worriedly. And Piet's brown gloves did nothing for her outfit.

'There's always a man,' he smiled. 'That's New York.'

'But shouldn't we do something about him?'

'You'll get used to it,' he said as he began to steer her by the elbow along West 23rd Street.

Their walk ended with breakfast in a cheerful, chattering diner. Piet told her that they were now on Tenth Avenue. He began to draw a map on a paper table napkin. 'New York's very easy to find your way around. The streets go one way and the avenues the other.'

Another unexpected sneeze burst out of her. 'I do apologise,' she said. He was already handing her another of the paper napkins. 'They're not giving me any warning.' She blew her nose and looked round. Some of the customers were sitting up at the counter and others were seated at Formica tables – like the one they were at. The place was all neon and chrome and displays of artificial ice cream in tall sundae glasses – just like a dated Lana Turner movie. In fact the diner was exactly how Rosie had always visualised the soda fountain where Lana Turner was said to have been discovered.

She was really in America. Another sneeze. Her hand met Piet's as they both reached for napkins. He was looking so apprehensive that she tried to blow her nose very discreetly. All it did was make it tickle more. 'I needn't bother learning New York,' she said. 'I want to get straight on the bus for California.'

'Hey, don't do anything too hastily. That's a tough trip you have ahead of you. You should really rest up for a while. I've got tickets for the Met tonight.'

'Is that a baseball game?'

'No, it's the opera.' He slid into the seat next to his original one. This meant that he was no longer sitting directly opposite her. 'I catch head colds very easily,' he explained. 'Forgive me for moving.'

'Feel free,' she replied airily. Now she was *talking* like Lana Turner. And that was the odd thing about New York. She had expected it to be as modern as tomorrow; yet the skyline, this diner, even the poor tramps out on the cold streets – they were all out of the dated nineteen-forties movies she had seen in her childhood at the Olympia in Irlams o'th' Height.

Nevertheless, she was already finding America to be hugely attractive. In her fatigued state she was operating on instinct; and instinct was telling her that she had finally come to a place that had energy and imagination to match her own. Even as Rosie thought this, she was equally aware that this attraction would always be tempered by a little fear. That this country wasn't quite safe. But she was twenty years old. And at twenty who wants 'safe'?

'This is the best breakfast I've ever eaten,' she said to Piet. 'Everything an English one's cracked up to be, and rarely is.' Even Nora Hankey, in a good temper, couldn't have got the bacon more crispy. Rosie had settled for eggs 'over-easy' just to see what they were – and discovered it meant fried on both sides. As she had always seen egg yolks as accusing yellow eyes, this was something of a revelation. 'And what about all the people?' she said aloud. 'It's amazing to think that their grandparents must have come from the four corners of the earth. And they *chose* to be here.' From the day she left Teapot Hall, Rosie had been a displaced person. And here was a whole country full of willing immigrants. The idea was every bit as satisfying as the crispy bacon.

As she watched passers-by pushing and shoving their way along the street outside she was less enchanted. If I lived in New York, she thought, I'd have to get a pencil-sharpener for my elbows. And nothing would get me used to stepping over tramps on the pavements. And where was this buzzing energy coming from? Was the New York air really like dexedrine? Or was it that she had now broken through sleeplessness and was onto her second wind?

She could almost have sworn that she'd just heard Gran'dad Tattersall saying to her, 'Go West, young woman.' How could she be certain that it was his voice? After all, he'd died before she was born. Once again she thought of the man who had first mentioned this trip, Mr Tetley at the Spiritualist Association of Great Britain, and she decided that she must be having a psychic morning.

'I think I'll get on the bus for California today.' The words weren't out before she was missing Gabriel to an extent which brought her startlingly close to tears. Influenza and jet lag can give rise to dangerously emotional behaviour. What's more, her nose was tickling again. Napkin held high, she opened her mouth to sneeze, but it wouldn't come.

'I think you'd be going too soon,' observed Piet from his safe distance.

'I don't.'

'What about the opera? And at least you ought to see some of the sights.'

'Okay. But I'm getting on that bus first thing tomorrow morning. I hope that doesn't sound rude. Should I ring them and find out when they leave?'

'I already have a schedule.'

'And I can leave tomorrow?'

'This time tomorrow morning.' He grinned confidently, revealing highly polished front teeth, just like Mr Molyneux's. This was the moment when Rosie's threatened sneeze turned into a sudden reality. Piet's smile was replaced by another look of alarm. His furtive looks of Dutch alarm were to haunt their whole day. Piet kept himself a determined two paces away from Rosie. He was like the boy behind Katherine Dunham – only sideways. In the Museum of Modern Art she simply had to blow her nose again; this distanced him still further. Lunch was in a restaurant with a long French name and very wide tables.

But Piet De Kuyper was a dutiful guide; after lunch they set off for a photographic exhibition in a gallery near to the financial district. The trouble with having grown up in the era of films and television is that you've been to places before you get there. This was not the case with Madison Avenue. *Nothing* in her previous experience had prepared her for the height of these buildings. Row after row of windows indicated floors beyond counting. This was New York at its most cut-out and stereoscopic, and the sky was just a strip of blue which was trying to send down some light between the towering buildings.

Rosie shuddered.

'Are you developing a temperature?' he asked, alarmed.

'No. I'm thinking about ticker-tape parades. I've seen them on newsreels. Do they throw them from right up there? What if somebody was in a bad mood and decided to chuck down a telephone directory instead?'

He laughed happily, slung an arm around her, thought better of it – and backed off. By this time she would have felt like a leper had he not also complained to her about a girl who had come to the office with a nasty case of shingles. This strapping Dutchman was as big a hypochondriac as Lily Jelly.

In the late afternoon Piet took her back to the hotel so that she could rest and change. Dutiful? He was indefatigable. By seven o'clock he was back in the lobby in a dinner jacket.

'Is that eau de Cologne I can smell?' asked Rosie, too innocently.

The muscular blond had the grace to blush. Dressed to the nines he had taken the precaution of adding a cloud of protective camphor. Once again Rosie was irresistibly reminded of Lily Jelly. She had to tell herself, quite firmly,

351

that this man had devoted the whole of his day off to her, that she must be costing him a small fortune.

They had a drink in the hotel bar which was called El Quijote and featured an artificial macaw in a dusty cage. It was much darker than bars in London, and a man in horn-rimmed glasses slid up to them at the counter and tried to get them to go upstairs to his apartment. He said that nothing would please him more than to be able to show them an original manuscript by Aleister Crowley; that they would be welcome to partake of a little hashish. That's what he said but his eyes spoke of sex. Piet De Kuyper showed considerable skill in getting rid of him.

'Who's Aleister Crowley?' asked Rosie.

'I neglected to say you're looking stunning.'

She was wearing black and, for the first time in her life, her mother's huge diamond ring. It had seemed the only thing she'd got that was grand enough for a real opera house – anything to draw attention away from her London skirts which looked outrageously short in America.

'Aleister Crowley,' continued Piet, 'was known as the Great Beast. He was a Satanist. Is Gabriel still as obsessed with Thomas De Quincey?'

'No.'

'Good.' He smiled. If Rosie had gone for blonds, it was the kind of smile that would have been very effective.

At the opera she distinguished herself by falling asleep. One minute, singing angels were being lowered onto the stage on wires, the next thing she registered was the fact that a woman was trying to get over her feet. She must have been the kind of woman who got up before the curtain had hit the stage – it was the interval. On Rosie's other side, Piet was now wearing a white silk evening scarf round his nose, like a smog mask. As he pulled this down, guiltily, his wicked blue eyes seemed to be saying, 'But I wouldn't half mind having a go with you.'

God must have sent her answer. It was an unpremeditated sniffle.

America kept its bus stations down amongst the winos. This

section of New York brought the word 'scabrous' to mind. It was all peeling buildings and rusting iron window frames, and cheap liquor stores and black-painted establishments with pornographic connections. Some of the young men hanging round the echoing terminus seemed to have eyes that were much more awake and aware than their listless bodies.

They really ought to have knives between their teeth, thought Rosie. Piet, carrying her suitcases, was still keeping himself at a hygienic distance. It had to be admitted that she was still a little feverish but this coughing fit had only been brought on by the acrid smell of petrol fumes. At the previous evening's opera, the members of the audience had been so well groomed and sophisticated that they could have passed for varnished. Here they were almost aggressively human: all body odour and cheap scented soap, and voices raised in hayseed accents and in a particularly threatening brand of Spanish.

Piet had to raise his own to say, 'Gabriel sent me the money to get you this.' He put down her luggage, fished in his pocket and handed her a booklet of travel tickets. 'Ninety-nine dollars for ninety-nine days,' he said. 'I don't think anybody could stick on the bus for that long. That's how they make their profit. Are you sure you're going to be all right? This kind of travel is pretty basic.'

'I'll be fine.' Her short winter coat was too expensive for this rumbling cavern. And the intricately laced Russian thigh boots were already drawing lewd looks from two men who were neither black nor Chinese but somewhere in between. Bus engines churned and in the distance police sirens continued to raise their unnerving wail.

Piet raised his voice again to say, 'I'm sorry I never invited you to make it. I'm afraid I'm very germ-conscious.'

'I noticed. Make what?' She really didn't know.

'To fuck.' He nodded seriously.

'I'll take those cases,' she said coldly. She was tempted to add: 'And you can fuck off.' But she'd never used the expression before and she was blowed if she was starting in a rancid bus station.

353

'I meant it as a compliment.' Piet sounded genuinely aggrieved.

'I thought you were meant to be Gabriel's best friend?'

'This is nineteen sixty-eight, Rosie,' he said, deadly seriously. 'The least I should have done was *offered*. You are Gabriel's lover, not his property. Fucking is nice. We're all in this revolution together.'

At this stage of her life, all that the word 'revolution' meant was hippie students in Grosvenor Square. 'If you're a rebel, what are you doing in a button-down shirt and an old school tie? I know your sort, Piet De Kuyper – you want the best of both worlds!'

'I'm talking about the sexual revolution.' He put his hand on her arm. 'I'm beginning to think you're ill-equipped for this journey.'

She knocked the hand away, furious with herself for having let it stay there for three seconds. 'I think it's about time you went.'

Piet looked around worriedly. 'You're not very worldly-wise. Perhaps we should put you on a plane for San Francisco instead.'

'*We* should do nothing,' said Rosie haughtily. 'From here on, I'm on my own.' Oh dear, he looked genuinely troubled. 'Look, I'll forget what you said. Just go.'

'I'm not worried about what I said. I'm bothered about your getting there safely. You begin on a bus for Cleveland. We should sort out the baggage and check you in.'

'Anybody knows how to do that.'

Wrong.

But Rosie had no idea of the mistake she was about to make. And she wasn't going to rest content until she had got rid of the one person who could have put her right. 'Go away, Piet,' she said. 'I mean it.'

'We didn't do something else.' He spoke sadly. 'We never saw the Statue of Liberty.'

'You've taken all the liberties I'm allowing.' And if this sounded more like Beryl Molyneux than the dawning of the Age of Aquarius, tough! 'Thanks for your help. I'm sorry if I'm not in tune with your thinking but please do me a favour and scram.' He went. To think that Gabriel had said that the Dutch could be very conventional! Perhaps Piet De Kuyper was simply being conventional in a new way. Rosie reflected that she'd got a lot to learn.

And she had.

Rosie already knew that New York wasn't just a city; it was a state too – but she hadn't expected it to get so leafy so quickly. They'd only been going an hour and a quarter and she'd already seen five white clapboard churches that were straight out of paintings by Grandma Moses.

The bus itself was much fancier than anything she'd ever encountered in England. It even had a proper lavatory, in a little fitted cloakroom halfway up the aisle – more like a train than a motor coach. But where had they stowed the luggage? On the Manchester to London buses it always went underneath the floor, in a cavernous baggage compartment. A steel door opened on the side of the coach and the driver fished the cases out with a hook on the end of a long pole. She supposed the Americans would have improved on this arrangement and brought it more up to date.

In exchange for her big suitcases, Rosie had been given two baggage reclaim tickets. All she had on the vacant seat by her side was a little vanity case. This had been bequeathed to her by Hazel Hankey. It was a relic of Hazel's days as one of Sheelah Wilson's models. Rosie smiled contentedly; she'd certainly come a long way from Manchester. Through the window she spotted a funeral home. It was called La DuBarry. The sign outside read *The Pause Exquisite on the Last Journée of All*. Yes, she was definitely a long way from Irlams o'th' Height.

As Rosie understood it, you could hop off the bus in whatever town you liked, stay a while, and then pick up the next motor coach along. She vaguely supposed that she should have asked more questions in New York City. She didn't even know how many days it took to get to the West Coast. But there was a covered wagon quality to this whole adventure, and all she knew was that every revolution of those wheels was bringing her closer to Gabriel.

'Want something to read?' A figure had loomed up over the back of the seat in front – a scrawny, middle-aged woman. No wedding ring and she shouldn't have worn fawn; too beige herself. In fact the woman was a study in sepia. Even her modesty vest, inside her V-necked frock, looked as though it had been rinsed in tea. She was insisting on handing Rosie a paperback book. It appeared to be an anthology of problem-page letters by somebody called Ann Landers. Rosie began to skim through it and discovered that the answers were much more direct than anything she'd ever seen in England: 'Tell your husband to go and live with the sailor. I bet he finds he's got a boy in every port!'

'Brilliant, isn't she?' The beige woman had now slid into the seat next to Rosie. The offer of the book had plainly been a preamble to captive conversation. 'Really socks it to 'em. I could read her forever.' She had a tight permanent wave and hard, piggy little eyes.

'It's very interesting,' said Rosie politely. Not for the first time, she reflected on the fact that – in the United States – her own voice sounded ridiculously English. 'But I'm not sure that I'd want a whole book of problems.'

'I've got a problem,' sighed the woman; she smelt of stale lavender water. 'I'm going to Chicago to see a top lawyer about it. Where you heading?'

'San Francisco.' The seat covers were plastic and Rosie was already beginning to stick to them.

'Ever been in Chicago?' The smell of garlic sausage was mingled with the lavender water. Without waiting for a reply, the invader continued: 'I used to work there. I slipped on some water that had gotten spilled on the floor of my employers' office. Broke my arm in two places. This wrist used to be double-jointed, but not any more. I'm suing. It could make my fortune. You English?'

'Yes.' And go away, thought Rosie. Oh dear, was she being the worst kind of reserved Englishwoman abroad? She resolved to try harder.

Her new neighbour had already picked up the conversation again with, 'I once had an English neighbour, Mrs Gambalucci. During the war she dug ditches. She was in some women's army where they wore britches. You ever met the Queen?'

'Not personally.' Why was everything coming out as prissy and unfriendly? I'll ask a question, Rosie thought, hoping it would make her seem less stand-offish. 'How do we get at our luggage?'

'Excuse me?' The woman looked distinctly puzzled.

'Our suitcases. When we want to get into them, what do we do? Do we ask the driver?'

'Was you planning on dressing for dinner?' The woman was staring at Rosie in disbelief. 'Lady, you might not care for books of problems but you sure got one of your own. Your baggage ain't on this bus at all. It goes clear to San Francisco on another vehicle.'

If Rosie had been warm before, her temperature now rose even further, and her head began to spin. 'But I've only got what I stand up in.'

'You should've thought of that sooner.'

'Nobody told me.'

'Did y'ask?'

'No. It's nobody's fault but my own. How many days is it to San Francisco?' For the first time since she got on the bus the sneezing threatened to start again.

'Best part of a week I should say.'

Rosie sneezed.

'You sick?'

'Do go and sit in your own seat if it bothers you,' begged Rosie.

'Don't bother me. I been around a lot of Christian Sciencers. Can't go along with all their thinking but I ain't frightened of no splutter.'

'Are you finding the heat very oppressive?' From the baffled way in which the woman was looking at her, Rosie could have been speaking in Swahili. 'Is it hot?'

'Nope.' She leant across and felt Rosie's forehead. 'Jesus H. Christ, the child's burning up! Don't move, sweetheart. I'll be right back.'

As the other passenger returned to her original seat, Rosie began digging in her own coat pockets. Her tickets

357

and her passport were still safe in the left-hand one, currency and traveller's cheques in the other. But everything else – including her mother's big diamond ring – was heading west on some other vehicle. As Connie's ring had lain forgotten, for umpteen years, in a button box at the back of a drawer at Mrs Hankey's, this was an odd moment to start worrying about it. But Rosie was worried. It was really weird. She could see the diamond glistening in her mind's eye; it actually felt as though it was pressing into her brain, like a knuckleduster.

'This is real French.' Her new friend had returned and was already pouring eau de Cologne from a big bottle onto a wad of paper handkerchiefs. This she proceeded to apply to Rosie's forehead. 'I'm Bertha,' she said. 'And you gotta eat.' Out of her coat pocket came a bread roll covered in poppy seeds. Big bits of salami were hanging out of its sides. 'You don't eat, you die. You got money?'

Rosie nodded. It was the name Bertha that had brought tears to her eyes. The other Bertha – the one who dragged a leg – had also been unfailingly kind. Another sneeze exploded out of her and American Bertha went prospecting down the aisles for something called Anacin. 'You got Anacin? We've got a sick girl back there.' It turned out to be the American name for Anadin. The green and yellow box was so familiar yet so different that an exhausted Rosie had to control the urge to have another little weep. Yesterday she had been aware of vague muscle discomfort; this morning, confined in a small space, with barely room to cross her legs, she was suddenly aching so hard that she could have drawn an accurate map of all her own muscles.

Day turned into night and into day again. Every few hours there was something called a 'rest stop'. These lasted forty-five minutes. In bigger places – like Toledo – there were longer halts. That was when American Bertha would haul a feverish Rosie down the steps of the bus, into wayside refreshment rooms, and force her to swallow soup.

Back on the Greyhound, Rosie crossed whole states stuck to the clammy plastic seat. When she went unaccountably cold, the seat changed temperature with her. As she swayed up the aisle to the lavatory she just prayed that her red heels would take the strain without snapping. The influenza had turned into gastritis. Her travelling companion viewed this with enthusiasm. 'Them Christian Sciencers would say that it was only "error" coming away.' Bertha's eau de Cologne continued to cool the patient's forehead; but twenty minutes after each application the smell always seemed to curdle, leaving Rosie feeling as though she was sitting in the middle of a bowl of dying flowers.

Decaying lilac. Death itself must smell like this, she thought. By now she knew everything about American Bertha's life: the demanding mother, the gambling-man she had never been allowed to marry, the grinding years in the offices of a Chicago paper box company. And Bertha knew everything about Rosie. Right down to the amount of money in her coat pockets.

Bertha said she could not pretend to understand traveller's cheques. 'But you've got more than enough, in cash, to get yourself on a plane from Chicago to San Francisco. That much I do know.'

So that was decided upon. Bertha was being picked up by her brother (the one who had a mechanical piano and did amateur conjuring tricks) at the last rest stop before Chicago. She tried to leave Rosie with firm instructions: 'All you have to do is get a cab from the main bus terminal to the airport. If you have to sit around for half a day waiting for a plane it can't be any worse than sitting here. And at least the sweats have stopped.'

'May I take your photograph?' Her Rolleiflex was in Hazel's vanity case.

Before she would allow this, Bertha insisted upon running a comb through her corrugated beige waves. She also applied a coat of colourless lip-salve.

To think I imagined those eyes were piggy, thought Rosie. They were now looking at her through the viewfinder as trustingly as Trixie Hankey's.

'I'll miss you, Rosie – and that's a fact. It's been like looking after a daughter. Tell me when to smile.'

May you have many good reasons to smile in the future,

thought the photographer. And may I be forgiven for misjudging you. 'Okay, now. And another . . . Think about all that money you're going to get from the court case.' The pictures taken, she threw her arms round Bertha. Rosie was surprised to find herself feeling quite sentimental about the odour of decaying blossoms. 'I've got your address in my little book. I'll be sure to send you some prints.'

'And send one of yourself too. Here . . .' Bertha was thrusting something at her. 'This seems a suitable souvenir.' It was Ann Landers' book of problems. 'Watch yourself at that bus terminal. Chicago can be a tough city.'

The bus station was as big and as echoing as the one in New York. Though she'd come a third of the way across America, it was still freezing cold. Rosie felt as though she'd been wearing the same clothes for weeks. As she passed from the petrol-laden atmosphere of the big concrete bays where the buses were parked, and onto an open concourse lined with booking offices and news-stands and rest rooms, she gave her pockets a neurotic pat. Passport and tickets and some loose change in one, traveller's cheques and a wallet of dollars and her special little American address book in the other. The handle of Hazel's vanity case (boldly inscribed *Sheelah Wilson Girls Go Round the World*) was already cutting into her hand; Rosie began to transfer it to the other one.

As she did, two fierce-looking boys in leather motorcycle jackets came running towards her – and knocked her flying. The case sailed out of her hand just as she hit the ground.

A young man in soiled denim who had been coming up behind the motorcyclists helped Rosie to her feet and generally dusted her down.

As she bent down to retrieve the tumbled vanity box, she said 'Thank you . . .' She was talking to the night air. He had already departed at speed. Suddenly there weren't just two boys heading for the main exit. There were three. And they had the look of three people who were very much together.

With a sinking heart, Rosie put her hand back into her pocket. Tickets, passport, some loose dollar bills, some coins . . . so far so good. The rest was awful. In the other pocket, everything else – folding money, cheques, even the little address book – had gone. And the address book was where she'd put the list of American Express cheque numbers – the one you needed to claim for any that got lost or stolen.

Robbed in the Windy City! The only thing to do was telephone Gabriel. But his number was in that same little red book. Panic rose as she rushed for a telephone. And panic did not help her deal with a foreign dialling system. How much were you meant to put in? And did it go in before or afterwards? Somebody had ripped the instructions from the wall of the phone booth.

Dialling 'O' for operator got her nowhere. In the end a soldier told her how to get through to Enquiries. She didn't like the way he was eyeing her long red leather legs.

'You a hooker?' he asked politely.

'No, I'm English. Hello, operator? Do you have a number listed for Gabriel Bonarto in Berkeley, California? It's an address on Virginia Street.'

After some delay the operator put her through to somebody else – who still couldn't help. As she replaced the receiver Rosie went even colder than the rest of Chicago. She knew the name of Gabriel's street but she had never memorised the house number – it was four digits long. Without an address she couldn't even send him a cable. And there would be little point in cabling him at the university. Term was hardly likely to have begun, not in the first week in January.

This was the moment when her eye lighted on a neon sign which said *Travellers' Aid*. They must get a lot of this sort of thing, she thought. How sensible of them to have a special department for it.

The woman behind the counter was black. Some of the students at the Poly had been Afro-Caribbean and Rosie had always found them to be cheerful and kind. Not this woman. As Rosie poured out her story she was faced by an expression of bored indifference.

'You got five dollars?' asked the woman. 'Because if you ain't the cops can arrest you for vagrancy.'

361

Rosie had never felt so far from Lancashire in her life. She began to empty the contents of her pocket onto the counter. They added up to eleven dollars and seventy-five cents. 'I can't get to San Francisco on that. Aren't you supposed to do something?' she asked desperately. 'I mean this *is* the Travellers' Aid.'

'I'm supposed to tell you how to get to where you want to go. You want to go to San Francisco? You get on the bus for St Louis in ten minutes' time.'

The distance from Chicago to St Louis must have been about as far as Land's End to John o' Groats. En route, a flea got inside Rosie's boot and bit her leg. This meant she had to undo about four yards of lacing, and she was horrified to discover that her bitten leg was already criss-crossed with shoelace bruising.

The flu had gone but it had left her feeling as though she'd *walked* this far. She'd always understood that the United States were wide: but *this* wide? On went the journey, on and on and on. Hours and hours of open country and then, just as you got a glimpse of distant buildings – which led you to hope that you were finally reaching somewhere interesting – the road would swerve in the opposite direction and turn back into a ribbon of cold monotony.

Along the way, Rosie had learned that St Louis was really pronounced St Lewis, and not the way that Judy Garland sang it. St Louis bus station was not out of a musical film. It featured more seedy layabouts and petrol fumes and greasy doughnuts. She had long since learned that the great trick in the refreshment rooms was to order coffee. You could sit there forever and they would keep on refilling the cup, at no extra charge.

St Louis was the halt where Rosie ate a sandwich that some rich person had left on a plate. The rest of the time she ate bread rolls and poured a lot of sugar into her coffee; she was terrified of getting down to five dollars because that would make her an official vagrant.

Sheelagh Wilson Girls Go Round the World: Rosie hauled

her unsuitable vanity case onto the bus for Denver. Five different lipsticks, a dozen rolls of film, and not so much as a change of underclothes! Night generally brought its unreasonable share of drunken travellers. By now she had heard a dozen different life stories from the adjoining seat. She had also come to see that America was a country divided into two camps; that if you were young and intelligent it was a case of Them and Us. The opposing cultures were outwardly defined by their style of dress. They – the older people – were drab as peahens and carefully buttoned-up and respectable. Youth was represented by wonderful raggle-taggle gypsies. All Indian prints and peace headbands and the odd guitar strummed at the back of the bus by long-haired youths – openly, defiantly, smoking very thin joints.

Rosie always tried to keep further forward because, on an empty stomach, she was scared of getting stoned – just by breathing in and out. From her small experience of marijuana she knew that getting stoned made time pass much more slowly, and this was the very last thing she needed.

She had nothing in common with Them and her look was all wrong for Us. She was quite sure that by now she must resemble a battered old copy of a front cover of *Queen* magazine; one that had been trampled underfoot, for about a week, at the Marble Arch end of Oxford Street. Not that she'd ever felt as though she belonged in London either. But that personal pane of glass had never seemed thicker than it did on this Greyhound bus.

Rosie had lost count of the number of days she'd been on the road. Night turned into day which deepened into the next night; only sometimes she thought she'd imagined one of the nights – added an extra one in. She knew for a fact that it is *truly* darkest before the dawn. The sky would go absolutely black before the first faint shaft of light appeared from behind the mountains. She supposed she should be enjoying the scenery but all she wanted it to do was hurry up and get past. At Denver they told her to change for Cheyenne, Wyoming.

'For *where*?' she said in disbelief. For many years this town had been filed in her head as the postmark on that last card from Christopher. Even as she thought of her twin, the high-pitched hum started up in her mind. 'Are you still in Cheyenne?' she asked it. All she got back was more of the humming. The twins had never been capable of flashing messages – in words – over long distances.

This was to be the longest hop of the whole journey – around thirty hours. By now Rosie was down to seven dollars and she was firing on sheer determination. When she was little, there had been a man in a sideshow at Blackpool who had fasted for over a month. If he could do it, so could she. And then there was St Anthony of Egypt. Starving on top of a stone column in the middle of the desert had to be marginally worse than doing the same thing on a Greyhound bus in the Rockies, in the moonlight.

Well, it *looked* like the Rockies, anyway. Great open plains with huge stone hills that had been blasted into unlikely shapes by the wind. A high wind was battering against the side of the bus at this very moment. Perhaps it wanted to change the shape of that, too. Rosie spanned her fingers round her own waist. It was definitely smaller than it had been when she left New York. God how she hated these clothes! When she got to California she had every intention of burning them. She raised her camera and took a photograph of a deserted wooden homestead, bleached white by the elements and silvered by the moon.

She could, of course, have pawned her Rolleiflex to raise cash. But she'd got this camera in part-exchange for the one she'd carried away from Teapot Hall. She was blowed if she was leaving her childhood behind her in some American pawnshop!

Connie had been a great one for pawning. Did she want to see her mother again? 'Not in this bedraggled state.' She actually said the words out loud. Lack of food was making her light-headed and occasionally she had a little chat with herself – just to hear an English voice. 'I wouldn't want to meet Connie again at a disadvantage.' Anyway, why should she want to meet her at all? The wicked old cow had pushed her out with less thought than she would have given to putting out empty milk bottles. Could those bales of twigs, blowing across the prairie, be tumbleweed?

Christopher was a different matter. *Hum* . . . Where would he have got with The Secret? In their childhood it had seemed an impossible ambition. But newspaper stories had started to appear which showed her twin to have been ahead of his time. The stories weren't actually about Christopher himself . . . 'That big rock looks as though Roy Rogers ought to be coming round it on Trigger.' She was talking out loud again, and this time she hadn't intended to do it.

The bus ground to a halt. They must have reached a crossroads. Nobody got off this time but somebody was getting on, and proffering a ticket, and laughing in a way that seemed to energise the whole interior of the bus.

The newcomer was a girl in her late twenties. Everything about her was lavishly generous, from the bright red hennaed hair to the Earth Mother proportions of her body. Far from disguising these she had gone out of her way to emphasise them by wearing a vast, high-waisted kaftan. Its fine woollen folds, in magenta and poison green, floated right down to the ground. Never before had Rosie seen so many necklaces on one human being. The girl could have started a shop. There were Indian beads and a gold chain hung with turquoise scarabs, and a whole chime of little silver bells on a purple silk rope; and that was just the top layer. Big she might have been, but she was health, she was energy, and she was making her way down the aisle – towards the empty seat next to Rosie.

'You anti-Semitic?' the girl asked.

'Me? No.'

'Just don't say "Some of my best friends are Jews." That's what they kept saying at the god-awful commune. I just walked out of it. Life is not long enough for dumps like that.' The voice was husky and the seat springs protested as she sat herself down.

'What a wonderful bag,' said Rosie. It was shaped like a huge straw wigwam; a leather thong held the top into a point, and the sides were embroidered with brightly coloured raffia flowers.

'It's my office. If necessary, I could run the whole revolution, single-handed, from out of that bag. Are you planning on smoking dope?'

'No,' said Rosie. She hoped there wasn't going to be a catch to these interesting new developments.

'Good,' said the girl. 'I have just spent three of the worst days of my whole life in a teepee, where the air was blue with smoke. If there's one thing I've had enough of, it's women passing joints around and calling one another *man*.'

'Were they lesbians?' asked Rosie, fascinated.

'No, dear, they were commune members. Three years ago they would have been Flower Children in the Haight-Ashbury. Excuse me for a moment while I write down a good idea.' She opened the bag and fished out a notebook and a wooden pencil box decorated with a hand-painted rainbow.

Flipping back the cover of the notebook, she began to scrawl in lavish handwriting, 'Buy Elvis souvenirs.' Seeming to take it for granted that Rosie would have read these words, she explained, 'I've just decided to fill a closet in my house with them. All the worst examples I can find. In ten years' time they will have enormous value. My name is Miriam Million. I like to keep ahead.'

'I'm Rosemary Tattersall.'

'Okay, Rosemary . . .' Miriam handed her a sheet of paper and one of her pencils. 'Let's play a game. You write down the title of your favourite song. Don't let me see what you're putting. I'll do the same.'

Propping the page on her vanity case, Rosie wrote 'Every Time We Say Goodbye'.

'Sung by?' asked Miriam. She definitely wasn't peeping. 'Put the singer's name down too.'

Rosie added the words 'Ella Fitzgerald'. She just hoped she wasn't going to be found lacking.

'Let's compare,' said Miriam.

They had written exactly the same thing, though Miriam revealed herself as mildly dyslexic – she'd got the 'g' and the

366

'z' the wrong way round. 'How strange,' murmured the Jewish girl lightly. 'I never ever thought of playing that game before. Yet I just *knew* they'd be the same. We are obviously destined to be very great friends. What's your birthsign?'

'Gemini.'

'Me too. Where you heading?'

'Berkeley.'

'Well, fancy that!'

'Tell me something,' said Rosie. 'Why do you sometimes sound a bit English?'

'And the rest of the time like the spirit of New Jersey? Because I spent two years up at Oxford.'

Not *another* one, thought Rosie. Gabriel, Piet De Kuyper and now Miriam Million. It's a wonder there was room left for anybody English.

'What I have to tell you next might shock an English-woman,' confided Miriam. 'I was sent down from Oxford for blowing soap bubbles across the Bodleian Library. That and a few other things – not unconnected with passion. I was very early into soap bubbles. I *do* like to keep ahead. The next thing I want to know is when do we stop for dinner. I'm buying.'

'No,' said Rosie involuntarily. God, how she would have loved to have just said thank you, but she couldn't accept because she had no way of buying back. 'I'm on a diet,' she explained hastily.

Miriam treated her to a very shrewd look. 'Never tell me another lie, Rosemary. You're starving. And it is going to be my very great pleasure to buy you dinner.'

The soup could have been made by angels. The chicken sandwiches were like manna from Heaven. 'And it's so extraordinary that you're on your way to Berkeley, too,' marvelled Rosie. They were now at the coffee stage and her spirits were entirely restored.

'Extraordinary?' boomed Miriam. 'I wouldn't mind betting that every Greyhound bus, from every corner of America, is carrying somebody heading for Berkeley. It's the modern equivalent of running away to sea. Middle-class

367

parents go white at the very mention of the name. Psychedelic substances, my dear. And a campus full of students baying for peace. And that bastard of a Governor Reagan threatening to send in the National Guard. It will be tear gas next, you mark my words.' Miriam's eyes were huge and amber and they had not been strangers to pain. 'But Berkeley has magic.' She was brightening up. 'The morning light is amazing. The days begin as so new that it almost hurts. Do you know your W. B. Yeats?' Without the least trace of embarrassment Miriam began to quote:

> 'That is no country for old men. The young
> In one another's arms, birds in the trees. . .

'Get to Berkeley and you'll understand the Renaissance – it's a *strolling* place. Or it would be if it wasn't for the university Regents and that Grade-B movie star of a State Governor.'

'If you're dyslexic,' said Rosie, 'how did you manage to get into Oxford?'

'They perceived my genius. I was a special case.' It wasn't swank, it was a simple statement of fact. 'Besides, any dumb klutz can spell!'

'My boyfriend was at Oxford. He's a philosopher.' For the first time in her life Rosie was beginning to feel seriously undereducated.

'My old man was a palaeontologist. We are now divorced. I made a grave mistake, Rosemary. I married "out". Five thousand years of Jewish suffering I would have understood. Catholic guilt was beyond my comprehension.'

'Mine's a Catholic too. What's a palaeontologist?'

'The apartment was dotted with little souvenirs of the Ice Age.' Miriam seemed to think that this explained. 'I got sick of falling over boulders. Now I live on my own.'

'What do you do for a living?' asked Rosie, taking a picture of her new friend who was waving a huge sugar shaker around.

'You should get them to ban this stuff,' said Miriam to a pretty girl who was wiping up. 'White sugar? White death

368

more like.' Turning to Rosie she continued with: 'I don't have a job. I'm writing my PhD thesis. We're old money. My family are in pharmaceuticals. I'm the only person I know who is related to Valium on one side and Librium on the other.'

Miriam certainly had a genius for one thing – friendliness. 'Rosemary,' she declared, once they were back on the bus, 'I'm going to stake you as far as Berkeley. I know you'll pay me back. I always know when I'm going to be great friends with somebody. It's just to be hoped our children don't fall in love with one another. Professor Conroy – he was the Catholic husband – Martin Conroy has left me very much against mixed marriages. His mother called me "a common kike". And it's a good job that Irish yenta didn't understand Yiddish.'

Miriam was the kind of person who took over. She liked to know your history, your interests, your ambitions – and how she could further them. If she was loving and giving, she was also almost indecently curious. 'You mean to say that your mother could be in Cheyenne and you're not proposing to do anything about it?'

'She ditched me.'

'She is your mother, Rosemary. Would you mind if I called you "Rosemarie"? Saying the other feels like sucking a tennis ball. Rosemarie, a girl has *duties* towards her mother. God knows I go through tortures with mine. One hour of her on the telephone is enough to send me heading for the shrink. But she is my *mother*. I look forward to meeting yours. What did you say she was called – nowadays?

'Mrs Mason Pollitt. And you won't be meeting her.'

'We'll see about that,' said Miriam firmly. She was already making a note on her pad. 'The place I live in is called Normandy Village. It's on the north side of campus. Maybe I should see if I can get you an apartment there. It's a copy of something old and French. Could have been designed by Walt Disney – on mescalin.' She pre-empted Rosie's next question with, 'That's a drug, my dear. It's a very sensual ride. But if I were you, I'd steer clear of all that. I can't pretend I haven't done it because I have. Last year I partook of LSD, turned into a reed pipe – and *blew* right over the campus. The experience convinced me that anybody who gets into psychedelic drugs is a loser. And if we're going to keep ahead, we don't want that.'

There were such huge amounts of caring concern in Miriam's lectures that Rosie was surprised to find that she didn't resent them at all. It was years since she'd had a friend.

'Yes, I'm a Jersey girl,' she rattled on, 'so I'm in a position to be realistic about northern California. Sometimes I look around my little fake French village and think, Very nice, my dears: but you have all eaten of the fruit of the lotus. Everybody's there to paint the great picture or write the great novel. But they're going to do it *tomorrow*. And tomorrow never comes. A lot of them have gone old and grey just thinking about the great ideas they brought out to the West Coast. Of course, Viva's different from the rest. Viva's very different.'

'Who's that?'

'My neighbour. Viva Rapport. I can never decide whether she's a good woman or a demon. Black braids with grey streaks in them –piled up on top of her head. Talks French a lot. Comes from Birmingham, Alabama. Viva spent years in Europe. She was even at the Abbey of Theleme, in Sicily, with Aleister Crowley.'

That name again. 'Is she into black magic?'

'Do you propose wasting a whole roll of film on me? Viva always maintains she isn't on the dark path. But I don't know – I just don't know. She's a very hot astrologer. She's also into hypnosis in a big way. She *calls* herself an occultist. Who am I to judge her?' Miriam paused, thought about something, and then came out with it. 'She does funny things on Friday nights. Seven young men come to call on her. Always the same seven; you never saw such beauties. Even the Korean one has sex appeal.'

'And what happens?' Rosie was changing film. There were only two rolls left in the vanity case.

'Viva's apartment is across the courtyard from my house. I hear chanting. She's clever to keep it to just guys. Chicks would talk.'

So there really was a world where people said 'guys' and 'chicks'. Rosie had always thought of this language as verbal toupees used by ageing comedians. The fact that there were real people who used it was almost as fascinating as all this talk of occult rituals.

'It can't be sex magic with seven guys and just Viva.' Miriam was still speaking in reflective tones. 'Well, if it is, good luck to her; she must be sixty if she's a day! Friday evenings always leave me wondering whether she'd do anything bad. Would you say that I was an inquisitive kind of person?'

'Yes.'

'And do you think I should have my nose fixed?' Miriam tilted a profile for inspection.

'Maybe. Yes, yes, I think you should.'

'Thank you for your honesty, Rosemarie. The cosmetic surgeon already charged my father three thousand bucks. Hey! I don't strike you as the kind of person who would try to pass for non-Jewish, do I?' The big eyes were full of worried concern.

'Miriam, you're as Jewish as matzos.'

'It's pronounced "motzas". Driver?' Miriam was calling down the aisle. 'Tell me something, driver. When do we get to eat again?' She obviously hadn't got to be that size by accident.

For days the bus had offered Rosie little more than short spells of shabby dozing; now it granted her several hours of deep sleep. She awoke restored. It was as though her whole mind had been turned around to an extent where she could view this cross-country trip as a latter-day version of the *Pickwick Papers*. Even the name of the refreshment room in Cheyenne had an olde-worlde ring to it. It was called the Post House.

'Chilli,' said Miriam. As Rosie came up to join her, the girl in the kaftan was already sitting up at the counter, where she was drawing many curious looks. 'A bowl of chilli is definitely part of the great American experience. I already ordered for us. Did you find the phone book?'

371

'It's fastened to the wall.'

'Was your mother listed? Look me in the eyes, Rosemarie. Was she listed?'

'No. Not her and not Mason Pollitt.' Were her own speech patterns changing? That hadn't sounded quite English. 'Most people just call me Rosie.'

'I have never wanted to be "most people." Maybe we should try to locate an *old* directory. That way we could call the number and maybe trace them. Thanks.' This gratitude was being expressed to a boy behind the counter. He was placing two steaming bowls in front of them. The glistening slop of chilli beans was as bright as his tomato-coloured waistcoat.

Miriam began spooning down the mixture with every sign of relish. 'My mother would die if she could see me eating this. She thinks I still keep strict kosher.'

'Miriam, I don't think I want to find mine.' Rosie's eyes were itching. Perhaps she'd had her contact lenses in for too long. She had certainly taken them out from time to time on the bus, and a difficult job it had been. 'Why should I *want* to find her?' And why was this pungent food bringing back vague memories of hurrying along Oxford Street in Manchester?

Miriam's voice took on maddening tones of patience as she said, 'You are my friend, Rosemarie; that's already decided. Friends should be there for one another. I'm trying to give you back your roots. Know what my dad did? He's beautiful. When I was little, he insisted on taking me to the Wailing Wall in Jerusalem. Why should I want to go look at some wall?' But Miriam was obviously awed by the memory. 'All I can tell you is this; after I'd touched those stones, I ran and clung to him – and we wept. We were at our roots. And you definitely need some too.' Now she was looking at the English girl in astonishment. 'It's a lovely story, and it's absolutely true, but I never expected it to move you to tears.'

'It didn't. My eyes are running and they won't stop. Oh my God!' It had come back with a bang. The Koh-i-noor restaurant on Oxford Street – her allergy. Huge white water blisters were already rising on the back of her hands. They were much worse than they had been in Manchester.

'And your face,' whispered Miriam in wonder. 'It's swelling like a football.' She emitted a startled shriek and her huge body acted as a sounding board, which sent the noise echoing round the whole Post House.

'I'm allergic to curry,' gasped Rosie. 'Chilli must be the same family.' She was frightened to find that she was beginning to have difficulty in getting her breath.

Out of nowhere, two huge men hoved up behind Miriam.

'I smell pigs,' murmured the Jewish girl.

Pigs meant police, thought Rosie wildly. And I've let myself get down to four dollars and fifty cents. The men were in civilian clothes, right down to old-fashioned trilby hats, which they did not remove. Policemen? They were the size and colouring of sides of beef.

'You screamed, lady. You okay?' asked the one with peculiarly light grey eyes.

'I'm fine,' said Miriam loftily. 'But my travelling companion is a little incommoded.'

'She a doper?' asked the other one. From the smell of his breath Rosie could tell that he was chewing a wintergreen-flavoured Lifesaver. She'd chewed them herself to stave off hunger. But how was she meant to stave off this rising panic?

'I said, is she a doper?' Before Miriam could answer, the chewing one spoke again. This time it was to Rosie. 'You sure look like a junkie. I'm going to have to ask you to let me see your arms. You in the sex industry?'

'How dare you!' All two hundred pounds of Miriam were off the stool and she was quivering with indignation.

'Them boots and that itty-bitty skirt sure look like a hooker to me.' The wintergreen-flavoured cop was running his eyes up and down the inside of Rosie's arms. 'No tracks,' he said in a disappointed voice.

Rosie thought she'd better speak up while she could still talk. 'The only drug I need is called Piriton. It's anti-histamine.'

'You English?' The first policeman had taken over. 'Passport. Let's see your passport and your tickets.' Rosie handed them over. The men put their heads together and she

373

heard one of them muttering, 'The visa is for unlimited visits. Some of them hippies come from wealthy families.'

'Very wealthy families.' Miriam was by no means cowed. 'Powerful families.' She began to invent lavishly: 'My friend's father is the Duke of Teapot Hall.'

'How much money you got on you?' the steely-eyed one asked Rosie.

Her heart sank.

'This much.' Miriam had already thrown open her wigwam bag and now she produced an impressive wad of dollars, held together with a rainbow-shaded elastic band. 'I'm minding both our funds.' Miriam's bit of Oxford education was standing her in good stead – her voice was getting grander with every word.

'Okay,' said the chewer. 'Where you heading?'

By now Miriam was a deep contralto: 'Berkeley, California.'

The policemen exchanged significant glances. 'Back on the bus,' said grey eyes. 'I want you over the state line as fast as that bus can take you.'

'Well it's not what I want,' said Miriam. 'It's not what I want at all. I want you should call me a cab, I want the location of a first-class hotel, and the name and address of a good doctor – preferably Jewish.'

Ill as she felt, Rosie was impressed. Oddly enough, so were the policemen. Miriam had used the voice of genuine authority; and this was something that they plainly respected.

The chewer, however, wasn't prepared to give way without a struggle. 'She may not have track marks but she's sure covered in flea bites.'

'*American* fleas did that to her.' Miriam's tones were of deepest outrage. 'I look to you to redress the balance. Or do I have to hire me a lawyer?'

'Dr Harris is a kike,' said the other cop, almost helpfully. 'I expect he'd be only too pleased to Jew you.'

'Rosemarie,' said Miriam too sweetly. 'You've just met your first pair of American rednecks.' Her voice rose dangerously: 'And if you gentlemen can say *kike*, I sure as hell can describe you as that. Call Dr Harris, get me a cab, and alert that hotel. We've got an emergency on our hands, and I do like to keep ahead.'

Rosie opened sore eyes and looked around her. If this hotel room has a religion, she thought, it must be Scottish Presbyterian. The room was clean and basic with twin beds, oatmeal curtains and a grey carpet. It was also totally unfamiliar. How on earth had she got here? Some vague memory stirred of a man with little hands giving her an injection.

'You feeling better?' In this chaste setting Miriam's colours could have been ripped from a parrot's wing. And Miriam herself seemed tense and caged. From the look of the overflowing ashtray she must have smoked the better part of a whole packet of tipped cigarettes. 'You blacked out at the bus station,' she explained. 'While I think about it, you've got to take your contact lenses out – doctor's orders.'

Rosie rose unsteadily to her feet and crossed the room to look in a square of mirror which was fastened to the wall.

'Your face is a lot better than when we carried you in. It had swollen up like a football. My dear, your eyes! They were Chinese slits. The most interesting part of the whole thing is that we're practically under house arrest. They want us out of town. The way they're carrying on, you'd think we were a couple of travelling hoochie-coochie dancers.'

Rosie opened her Sheelah Wilson case which had some-how found its way onto the pine dressing table. Once she'd located the double-ended bottle of contact lens solution, out came one eyepiece, and then the other. The room turned into a neutral blur. Miriam had become something at the bottom of a hazy kaleidoscope.

'I think you should lie down again.' Miriam spoke firmly. 'You've been out for the count for three hours. I have not been idle. I've been performing on that telephone like Jascha Heifetz. Down at the front desk, they got so worried about the number of long-distance calls I was placing, they made me deposit thirty dollars with them. It goes without saying that we had to pay for the room in advance. Isn't there a movie called *Bad Girls in Cheyenne*?'

'Don't know. I'm very thirsty.'

'Stay right where you are. We have home-made lemonade. We also have beautiful lox sandwiches. Here.' There was the chink of a bottle against glass and then some glug-glug noises. 'Sip first and then eat.'

Rosie accepted the cold tumbler and drank something sharp and sweet. 'What's lox?' She took a cautious bite. It turned out to be smoked salmon.

'Dr Harris's mother brought all this. She's the double of my Aunt Rose. The doctor is my idea of a real dish. Just like Woody Allen – but with a full head of hair.'

'And that's a dish?'

'In a cerebral way, yes. I certainly wouldn't mind making it with him.'

So here was somebody else who regarded sex as exercise. Rosie supposed she was just out of tune with the times and not in a position to be critical.

Miriam continued to rattle on: 'If we were all attracted to the same person, Rosemarie, the world's population would come to a halt. Dr Harris – he told me to call him Lionel – is coming back in a little while. He's doing some detective work for me.' Without so much as pausing for breath she added, 'Gabriel's got a nice voice.'

Rosie nearly choked on her sandwich. 'My Gabriel?'

'He's meeting us off the plane tomorrow. Lie down and rest those eyes. Surely you can chew lying down? Close them. That's better.'

It was easier to do as she was told. 'But how did you find Gabriel?'

'It was no problem. Berkeley I understand. I got onto another philosopher and he went off and found Gabriel – who called me back. You wanna speak to him? I have a number.'

Before Rosie could reply there was a knock on the bedroom door and a short dark blur burst into the room. 'Would your Mrs Mason Pollitt have a faygeleh son?' asked a man's eager voice.

Miriam cleared her throat significantly. 'The patient is now awake.'

'What's a faygeleh?' asked Rosie, interested.

Miriam's reply was very stern. 'It's a word we never, ever use.'

'He just did.'

'Only because he's stressed out. Only because we've given Dr Harris a very hard day.' She stopped sounding reproachful and became realistic. 'What the hell! This is nineteen sixty-eight. Is your brother gay?'

'Probably. Hello, Dr Harris. I'm feeling very much better.'

Rosie felt a cool hand on her forehead. 'You'll live,' he said. 'Have you ever had yourself properly tested for these allergies?'

She hadn't. 'I keep meaning to. But . . .'

'Not good enough. Do it.' The direction of his voice changed and he was obviously addressing Miriam again as he said, 'The Englishwoman and her son have moved to Los Angeles. A patient of mine is trying to get me their number. Leave me yours. I'll call you.'

'Please do. And I owe you. When you come to that convention in San Francisco it will be my pleasure to pay you back.'

'Yes, thank you very much,' put in Rosie.

'Don't thank me, thank your friend. She's a whole lot of beautiful woman.'

'Well thank you kindly,' gurgled Miriam. 'Of course Mama Cass has changed everybody's perceptions of us fuller-figure gals. Do be sure and let us have that number. I'm absolutely determined to reunite Rosemarie with her family.'

'It seems as though your brother had a rough ride in Cheyenne,' said the doctor sympathetically. 'It's not easy for his kind in these parts. He and your mother had to leave town in a hurry.'

The plane touched down at Salt Lake City, collected a lot of gleamingly handsome young men in business suits, and took off again. 'Mormon missionaries,' explained Miriam. 'Did you ever see such short haircuts?'

377

Ping-pong went the automated bell on the public address system. 'Ladies and gentlemen, this is your chief steward speaking. Would you please note that there will be no bar service for approximately forty-five minutes.'

'And the No Smoking signs will stay on too,' sniffed Miriam. 'No hooch, no nicotine, no Coca-Cola. Those Mormons even own the goddamn airspace.' She let out a deep sigh. 'In a way I suppose I envy them. Mormons claim to know where they came from, before they were born; and they know where they're going to when they die. It's supposed to be some planet. I wish I knew where I was going.' The one thing that gets forgotten about the Sixties is the huge amount of soul-searching that went on. Two people had only to sit down for five minutes for the agonising to begin.

'Life,' moaned Miriam Million gently. 'What's it all about? Sometimes I think I'll take myself off to the Esalen Institute at Big Sur.'

'What happens there?'

'Nude encounter groups,' murmured Miriam vaguely. 'And you're encouraged to scream.' Suddenly sounding altogether more animated she said, 'Stand up.'

'Why?'

'I need to look at you. Just get in the aisle. I gotta narrow my eyes.'

It was something to do. And it would be easy. Rosie was already in the gangway seat, Miriam's bulk was in the seat next to the emergency exit; she had specially requested this because it gave her extra leg-room and space in which to dump the wigwam bag.

As Rosie stood in the aisle, the plane gave one of those sudden bumps – the kind that always feels like stopping for traffic lights in the sky. Rosie sat down again, hastily.

'It's okay,' said Miriam. 'I got to see enough. Now you've washed your hair, it looks beautiful. But your clothes are all wrong for Berkeley. Nothing that Mama Million cannot fix.' Miriam reached for her big bag.

Rosie hardly liked to say it: 'Your clothes would be too big for me.'

'This will hold everything together.' Miriam had already fished out a scarlet elasticated belt with a double-snake buckle. 'And one skirt.' It was in black wool. 'There's something a bit inevitable about tie-dye tee shirts but this one isn't too bad.' It was in black and white.

'I'm not going to a funeral,' protested Rosie.

'Hold your criticism. I've not finished yet.' Once again Miriam dipped and proffered. 'One genuine band jacket.' It was straight off the sleeve of the Beatles' *Sergeant Pepper* album. A white uniform jacket, frogged across the front in turquoise satin. 'Very Berkeley,' said its owner, in tones of deepest satisfaction. 'I bought it for my Cousin Fred. A man who already owns an original Disney drawing of Mickey Mouse is gonna miss a band jacket? Get yourself to the john. Get yourself changed. God knows why we didn't do it back in that lousy hotel room. And Rosemarie – remove your brassiere.'

'And let myself lollop?' she gasped.

'You want to be the only girl in Berkeley with bosoms like ice cream cones? Make a political gesture. Free the tits. You'll find it's a great feeling.'

Rosie carried her treasure trove up the aisle and into the lavatory. There was barely room to turn round and the plane had started bumping again. Off came her dress. After a moment's hesitation, off came the bra as well. She was a girl in red boots and white Marks and Spencer's knickers. At least they were clean again – she'd washed and dried them in the bathroom, in Cheyenne.

On went the big tie-dyed top. As she slid into the dark skirt Rosie realised that it was of wonderful-quality cashmere. Wouldn't this be too hot for California? The elasticated belt performed the promised miracle – suddenly the tee shirt just looked raglan-sleeved. Now for the jacket. A label inside the collar said *Property of the United Wyoming Marching Bands*. The sleeves were lined with silky material which was soft to the skin. But raising her arms to struggle into the garment had made Rosie realise that her bust was leading a life of its own. She looked in the mirror. The girl who stared back could have been one of Us – one of the new gypsies. If I'm a fake, she thought, I'm a good-quality one. Miriam's made sure of that.

She could feel the tee shirt brushing against her nipples. How many hours to Gabriel? Suddenly Rosie was filled with a need as strong as hunger had been on the bus. And the vibrations of the plane seemed to have turned erotic – which was only making matters worse. Somebody tapped impatiently on the lavatory door. This really was no condition in which to march between seated ranks of Mormon missionaries. But Rosie did it.

'Will I do?' she asked Miriam.

Her friend was already beaming with approval. 'You finally look real. It's made the boots look as though they're ready to march for freedom. Of course I always knew you were in there – somewhere –struggling to get out. What did you do with the bra?'

'Put it down the thing for used tissues.'

'How do you feel without it? God, I remember how I felt when I threw mine away – liberated as all get-out and horny as hell.'

'That about sums it up,' laughed Rosie. 'Horny as hell and swinging free.'

Across the aisle, a horrified Mormon got to his feet and moved towards some empty seats, nearer the front. Now that Rosie was one of Us she could definitely view him as Them.

'Ladies and gentlemen. We are about to commence our descent into San Francisco. Please fasten your seat belts and extinguish all cigarettes.'

Miriam was eating a salted cracker. 'I'm thinking of writing to the airline,' she said. 'A sparrow couldn't live on their food.'

Filled with excitement, Rosie was thinking back to her childhood. 'All my life, I've wondered about that golden gate. You know, the one they're always singing about in the song "California Here I Come". I always imagined it would be a bit like the gates of Heaven. Are they on every road, as you cross into the state?'

'You're putting me on!' Miriam was looking at her in total disbelief.

Rosie hadn't been joking. But now she stopped to think about it, the idea probably wasn't very realistic. 'I was very young when I dreamed it up,' she explained, embarrassed.

'Stay young!' Miriam's voice was all but singing. 'It's the only way to be. And anyway there *is* a Golden Gate. Only it's a bridge. Look!'

Over the edge of the silver wing of the plane Rosie Tattersall got her first glimpse of San Francisco: tall buildings sparkling in winter sunlight, with whole streets of pretty wooden houses in between the skyscrapers. 'Hansel and Gretel meets Superman,' she cried, thrilled. 'It's so pretty. Nobody ever told me it was going to be as pretty as this.'

'And there's the other bridge, Bay Bridge – the one that leads to Berkeley. And there's the Coit Tower. Hello. . .' called down Miriam. 'I'm back!'

The Coit Tower was a bit like the leaning tower of Pisa but straight up and on a hill. It also looked a lot like a male sex organ. As the plane veered and tilted, its vibrations were getting to Rosie again. And soon she would be in Gabriel's arms; her stomach actually gave a little lurch of excitement.

'That view never fails me,' said Miriam quietly. 'No, the city never fails me.'

Four minutes later, with two dainty bumps, the plane landed.

'Welcome to California.' Miriam was already reaching for the wigwam bag. '*You* are in the minority here,' she called out joyfully to a couple of the business-suited men in the aisle. 'But this is a great place for live and let live.' Turning to her travelling companion she said, 'I have to warn you about something, Rosemarie. I notice you never cuss. People here swear like crazy. I do not like it myself. The only fuckin' thing to do is keep ahead of it.'

The last little leg of their journey was completed in a rattling mini-bus. It transported them across the tarmac and deposited them outside the main airport building.

'Gabriel's meeting us at the gate,' promised Miriam.

From the tarmac they began to make their way into a series of long glass corridors where Scott Mackenzie was singing, through the public address system, that they should be sure to wear some flowers in their hair. She was finally here. And in the whole of her journey across America, Rosie had never seen such sharp divisions between Us and Them. It was the older people who rushed. The long-haired young – in their Indian prints and their silken tatters – just ambled along.

'See what I mean about *strolling*?' said Miriam.

It was all Rosie could do to stop herself from breaking into a canter. She was finally in the same building as Gabriel. Hurry up, Miriam, she thought. But some of the larger girl's long swinging beads seemed to have got caught up in the saffron robes of a member of the Hare Krishna movement; he was trying to sell her a book and the promise of eternal enlightenment.

'How did you get through the barrier?' Miriam asked him. 'Anyway, I already gave. I live in Berkeley.' This was delivered in tones which suggested that the statement was self-explanatory. 'They *always* manage to wriggle through the barrier,' she said Rosie.

'Come to our temple and have a wonderful feast,' the boy persisted. Plainly American, he had shaved his head and adopted singsong Indian tones.

'No thanks,' said Miriam. 'I went once. There's a limit to my affection for lentils.'

'Hare Krishna,' said the boy happily.

'Yeah, Hare Krishna. Peace.' Miriam raised two fingers in the approved peaceful manner.

Couldn't she hurry? But nobody was hurrying. The people roaming through these corridors looked as though they'd borrowed their clothes from dressing-up boxes. Some of them really did have flowers in their hair and Miriam's kaftan had stopped looking unusual. Catching sight of her own reflection in one of the glass walls, Rosie realised that – here – her borrowed band jacket and the floating skirt were as classic as court shoes on Knightsbridge.

'I look just like the real thing,' she marvelled aloud. 'Thank you, Miriam.'

'We're all of us only passing for the real thing, everybody in life,' said Miriam severely. 'Didn't you know that?'

'No I didn't. And could we hurry up a bit?' How on earth would Gabriel fit into all of this? He of the expensive sweaters and the neat suede jackets.

At long last they came within sight of the barrier. Miriam let out a low whistle. 'That, my dear, is what I call a piece of real man-flesh. And any attraction is purely physical.'

The man with the tumbling tinker's curls was wearing dark glasses and a pair of jeans. The rest of him was as bare as his feet. His body was tanned to an almost edible shade of apricot. The cat's-eye nipples were exactly the same shape as Gabriel's. Off came the glasses. God in Heaven, this *was* Gabriel – and his smile was blazing to match the California sunlight outside.

Rosie flew into his arms and got lost in a kiss. It was amazing to be wrapped up in him again but he smelt of some unfamiliar antiseptic soap. Never mind that – as their tongues twined she closed her eyes and daylight gave way to a ride along the Milky Way. She was pressed against rock and she wanted it to melt into her. To melt? She wanted him to thrust, to slide. . .'Gabriel, if we don't watch out we're going to get ourselves arrested.'

'Not here,' he smiled. 'You've reached the foot of the rainbow.'

'I'm so sorry.' Rosie was remembering her manners. 'This is Miriam Million. She saved my life.'

'Thank you.' Still holding onto Rosie he held out a hand to the girl in the kaftan. 'Hi. How do you do?'

'I do very nicely, thank you,' said Miriam levelly. 'We've met before.' And then she looked as though she wished she hadn't said it. 'Take no notice of me,' she added quickly. 'If somebody introduced me to Donald Duck I'd be certain to think I already knew him.'

11

Gabriel and the new arrivals were bouncing along Bay Bridge in an open pick-up truck. Now she was actually on the bridge Rosie realised that she had often seen it before – on television. But she had never realised that there was a lower deck. Traffic bound from San Francisco, for Oakland and Berkeley, had to travel through an open-sided tunnel underneath.

Way below them, on either side, the waters of the bay were giving off a chilly sparkle. 'That island over there is Alcatraz,' shouted Gabriel. Keeping one hand on the wheel, he began to struggle into a denim workshirt which flapped like a flag in the stiff breeze. 'It's stopped being a federal prison. The American Indians keep saying they're going to reclaim it.'

The pick-up truck was nothing like any of Gabriel's previous cars. And Henry Ford would have had a job in recognising it as one of his own; it had been repainted in a psychedelic design. Great tongues of gold and white down one side, black and scarlet and silver on the other – it represented Heaven and Hell. The design even spilled into the interior.

'Who did your paint job?' bawled Miriam.

'Did it myself,' he roared back. 'Got bored and started painting again. There's a limit to how much time you can spend with Mother Fist and her five daughters.' Though he was calling over to Miriam the huge smile was aimed at Rosie.

Who was Mother Fist? Light dawned. She wasn't shocked that he was talking about masturbation; just that he had chosen to do it in front of Miriam. Rosie tried not to be startled – and failed. Then she got annoyed with herself; forty-eight hours with Miriam had already taught her that there was no place for sexual reticence in the new youthful scheme of things.

Now the jeep flashed into a proper tunnel, one lit by

electric lights. 'What's new on campus?' shouted Miriam. Rosie was glad that her friend was keeping the conversation going because this suntanned liberated Gabriel had left her feeling unexpectedly shy.

'Trouble's beginning to build up again. Some windows got smashed on Telegraph Avenue last night.'

'And that's new?' They were into the sunlight again and Miriam's red hair was streaming behind her like a tattered scarlet banner. But had her voice sounded a mite too wry? It had left Rosie wondering whether the Jewish girl had taken against Gabriel.

The last bit of the bridge turned into a road which began to wind its way over mud flats. Huge sculptures made out of driftwood and scrap iron were silhouetted against the bay. Fractured light, reflecting from the million glass windows of distant San Francisco, seemed to form a diamond-studded backdrop.

'Nearly home,' said Miriam. There was no longer any need to shout. 'Look! There's the campanile.' She was pointing towards a white pencil of a bell-tower set amongst dark hilly slopes.

'I'm going up University Avenue,' announced Gabriel. 'Where can we drop you?'

We, thought Rosie; I'm part of a *we* again. Her soul was practically singing. At a more realistic level, were those faraway bells really playing the Beatles' 'Yellow Submarine'? They were.

'Drop me at Hearst and Spruce,' said Miriam. 'I live in Normandy Village.'

'Oh,' said Gabriel. And he suddenly seemed very thoughtful indeed.

After they'd dropped Miriam, the bells in the white granite campanile changed their tune to 'Penny Lane'. But the sign on the corner as they drove uphill said they were on Virginia Street.

Gabriel brought the truck to a halt at the kerb. 'Out you get. This is it.'

'Goodness me, I bet the FBI in Cheyenne would have gone

a lot easier on me if they'd known I was coming to this!' From the outside, the white concrete apartment block looked like something out of a James Bond movie. Gabriel put his key into a wrought-iron gate which opened into a mosaic-lined entrance hall.

This led out into sunlight again. The apartments themselves were apparently behind doors, off landings which looked over white balustrades and down into a formal jungle of a garden-courtyard. There were tall palm trees and giant yuccas, and an abandoned hosepipe was leaking onto ivy – growing over a piece of carefully 'ruined' sculpture. A copy of *Better Homes & Gardens* lay open on a white-painted iron bench.

Gabriel, carrying the vanity case and Rosie's winter coat, looked round all this careful horticulture as though he was seeing it for the first time. He never cared where he lived. 'I'm afraid it's not very Berkeley,' he apologised. 'It's just an apartment I took over from one of my more middle-class colleagues. Are you cold?' Rosie had shivered.

'A bit,' she admitted. 'I expected California to be boiling hot.' The weather was like Manchester on a good day in April. And these flats, for all their swank, were like a poshed-up version of Sutton Dwellings in Salford – with jungle touches.

'Are you disappointed?' For once, Gabriel must have been watching her closely. 'It's only temporary. We can move to wherever you like. Guess what we're standing on? We walk up this staircase; there's an elevator but we're only one flight up.' He already sounded quite American. 'We're standing on the Hayward Fault. It's an underground crack – part of the San Andreas fault system. Just think, there could be an earthquake at any minute.' Grinning wickedly, he put another key into the lock of a white door. Then he said exactly what Rosie had been thinking: 'Let's go to bed and make an earthquake of our own.'

She failed to register any of the geography of the flat. All she could take in – as his arms went round her – was the feeling of coming home. The only place she needed was his body. Her own was already seeming to shimmer against him.

As his excitement rose she caught her first real sniff of *him*. Not soap – just essence of Gabriel.

'We're no different from the other animals, she thought; it's all down to scent. She pulled off the band jacket and let it fall to the floor. He was out of his own shirt in a moment and then he helped her get the tee shirt over her head.

'Liberation!' He was smiling happily at the naked breasts. 'Feed me,' he whispered. 'Oh Rose, I've been so hungry.'

'Do we have beds?'

'How many do you need?' As he took her hand and led her down a corridor, the eyes were teasing. 'How many beds?'

'About a hundred. And then we'll begin again at the beginning. God, how I've missed you.'

He had not forgotten how to tantalise her body into yearning.

'Yes?' he asked.

'Please . . . oh please.'

She was filled. She was complete. Her being had been made whole again for an uninterrupted hour. I am the San Andreas Fault, she thought, and you are the Coit Tower. Then she arched her back as the absurdity of the idea made her begin to laugh with sheer joy.

'It's funny?' he asked, not breaking the rhythm and looking straight into her eyes. 'And is this funny? And this, and this, and this . . .'

'It's beautiful. Oh God it's so beautiful.'

'You want to get there?' His breathing had quickened.

'I couldn't stop it. Oh, oh . . . Gabriel?' A sudden thought was trying to recall her to the ground. 'Gabriel, how thick are these walls?'

'This thick, and this, and this . . . I love you, Rosie.' His voice spasmed to match his body. Their wild cries mingled and then the noise collapsed. The moment they got their breath back they both started to laugh. 'We were so frantic,' he marvelled. 'And the wonderful thing is, we don't have to go anywhere. We can just make it and make it.'

So he too had caught up with that expression, had he? For the moment they just lay close and still. 'Who's that man watching us?' asked Rosie.

The man was on a fluorescent poster on the wall. 'Che Guevara. He's a revolutionary. He got left behind with the fixtures and fittings. It has to be the most popular poster in town. That and the one of astrological love positions. I sent Piet De Kuyper one of those, as a joke.'

Should she tell him about Piet? If she didn't it would only haunt her and Gabriel would think she was brooding over something about himself.

It seemed he was already doing it. 'You have a problem?' he asked.

Out it came. 'Piet De Kuyper apologised for not fucking me.' She wasn't at all used to the word so it came out as very prim and elocuted.

Gabriel started to laugh.

'I thought you'd be furious,' she said indignantly.

'I am,' he howled. And his whole body was rocking with amusement. '"Piet De Kuyper apologised for not . . ."' More laughter took away the final words. Finally he regained his composure. Even so, his face was alight with delighted amusement as he said, 'He was just being *hospitable*, Rose.'

She was not amused. 'Next time I'll accept his invitation.'

'Do that and I'll kill you both.'

And he meant it, too. Rosie let out a little sigh of contentment. 'I've plainly got a lot to learn,' she said. 'Tell me about Berkeley.'

Propping himself up on one elbow, Gabriel began to trace the outline of one of her nipples. 'Anything that's called "Free" or "People's" is politically very okay. Like the Free Clinic, and there's even a Free University – it's two old shops.'

The teasing, feather-light touch was renewing desire. 'If you don't stop that, I'll start eating you,' she warned.

Gabriel rolled over onto his back and for the first time she noticed the white mark where his bathing trunks had been. And then she noticed something else. He was beginning to get a fine dusting of hair between his pectoral muscles.

She ran one of her fingers through it. 'I thought people either got that at puberty or not at all.'

'Shows how little time you've spent in the men's locker

room. Some guys don't start getting hairy chests till they're thirty. The body pelt is the last thing to come.' Both hands were now reaching up for her breasts as she sat astride him. 'It's just that you're seeing it in a different light. I'll tell you something else about Berkeley: we're all marching to a new drum.'

'Are we?' Two could use teasing hands and his nipples were nearly as sensitive as her own. 'How new?'

'Very new. Look how hard and shiny I've got again. There's nothing in Berkeley that says that women can't be on top. Let's see how good *you* are at getting us to the same place at the same time.'

'You want me to be hospitable?'

'Something like that. Ouch! Go easy.'

Whenever they made love, Rosie had no doubts about Gabriel. None at all. In bed he was exactly the man she had always thought he was. Tender, gentle, wild, loving . . . and when he ended up on top again it was because she had encouraged it. It was what she really wanted. As the bells filtered back into her consciousness she realised that they were playing 'All You Need Is Love'. Other people were right, the Beatles had been brushed with the wings of genius.

The first time Rosie saw Telegraph Avenue it struck her as a cross between a street in a cowboy movie and a bustling Arab bazaar. There were even throbbing drums. A row of black men were playing them, on the pavement, at the point where the university campus ended and the counter-culture began. The evening shadows had just started to grow long, and soap bubbles were blowing in the deepening golden light.

'Spare change. Got any spare change?' The skinny barefoot boy could not have been a day over fifteen. His embroidered Indian shirt was thin and he looked like somebody who was a long way from home.

Gabriel slipped the youth a couple of silver coins and said to Rosie, 'The trouble is, if you give to one you find yourself surrounded. These kids have made their way here from every corner of the United States.'

Somebody else was trying to talk to Rosie; a Mexican-looking man had dived out of the doorway of a fruit-juice bar called Orange Julius: 'Hash, grass, acid? Hash, grass, acid.'

Mildly panicked in the midst of this rolling, patchouli-scented crowd, Rosie said to Gabriel, 'What does he want?'

'He's just a dope dealer.'

'Want some Acapulco Gold?' The Mexican had been joined by another young man who could have been his brother. He smiled dreamily at the English girl as he said, 'It's just come over the border. Could help you out with a nice little five-dollar deal?'

'Not today thank you,' replied Rosie. And even as she said it, she realised that she'd sounded just like Lily Jelly getting rid of the Betterware brush salesman.

There was so *much* for sale. Stalls on both sides of the packed street were offering everything from candles and sticks of incense to mysterious fragments of stained-glass window.

'Hare Krishna, Hare Krishna, Krishna Krishna, Hare Hare . . .'

The chanting monks were managing to snake their dancing way through the crowds, their tambours beating and tambourines rattling in competition with the pounding of the black men's drums. All the shops had open doors and every single establishment seemed to be amplifying forth a different pop song.

Rosie paused to look at a tree trunk which was fluttering with thumb-tacked notices. *Crash Pad Available. Night Person Only. Contact Russian Mike at Magenta Bookshop.*

'Nobody need be homeless in Berkeley,' said Gabriel. 'People let the kids crash on their floors – for free.'

'What's a night person?'

'Me. You. Anybody who doesn't want to go to sleep till it's dawn.'

Hand in hand, they continued to make their way through the crowds. Rosie's trained eye had been observing the girls' clothes. As at the airport, a lot of the floating dresses had been made out of Indian bedspreads. But there was another look, one which was much more definitely Berkeley. The aim seemed to be to look as much like a cowboy's grandmother as possible; skirts to the ground, tiny flowered prints, and even little wire spectacles perched on young noses.

'And they're National Health glasses!' she exclaimed.

'No, they're copies of genuine John Lennon's.' Gabriel was pointing to an optician's window where hundreds of pairs of wire frames were winking in the evening sun.

'But Lennon's didn't start off as gold,' protested Rosie. 'Everybody English knows that. He just did what we used to do at school. You pull the brown plastic covering off the wire to show the metal underneath. I once got copped doing it and Miss Swaine gave me a hundred lines. Fancy it turning into a proper fashion!'

The rest of the stalls and the shops were nothing like the commercial 'Swinging London' rip-off. In Berkeley, people seemed to pride themselves on making everything by hand. 'Plastic is a dirty word here,' explained Gabriel.

Rosie had already started to tune in to this. 'I wish I'd brought my camera. And I need to get a film.'

'I don't quite know how to break this to you.' Gabriel paused to lean against another of the notice-board trees. 'You've got to be careful of cameras round here. The blue Meanies can swoop on people who are carrying them.'

'Why should the police be against cameras?'

'Because they don't want anybody taking pictures of themselves. The whole youth revolution is supposed to be about peace but things can get very violent. And the pigs are always trying to disguise themselves as street people.'

Up until now, Rosie's vision of a policeman had always been Dixon of Dock Green crossed with Mr Plod from *Noddy*. She smiled as she tried to imagine how the actor Jack Warner would look in a Beatles wig.

'It's not funny,' said Gabriel sternly.

She remembered the police in Cheyenne. 'I know.'

'People have already got shot. And it's going to get worse before it gets better. They regard us as the most subversive community in the whole of the United States. They're afraid of us – they know we want to change the whole order of things.'

Well you won't do it by getting pompous, she thought.

Rosie was looking at the notices on the tree trunk. 'What does *Chicks: Wanna moonlight in a Beer Garden?* mean?'

Gabriel translated: 'If you haven't got work papers – a green card – you can still get a job as a barmaid. It's strictly illegal but who's worrying about that?'

'Have I got a green card?'

'No.'

'They certainly stapled something into my passport at Kennedy.' She couldn't remember the colour.

'That would be a landing permit.'

'So how do I get one of the green things?'

'You can't.'

Rosie, who had begun walking again, halted.

'Let's get this straight: I'm not allowed to take photographs, I'm not allowed to work – all I can say is we'd better write down that phone number.' She nodded back towards the tree trunk. 'It looks as though I'll be that chick who's moonlighting!'

'We have money, Rose,' he said patiently.

Too patiently. 'I need to earn my own living. I can't just sit around on my arse.'

'Why not?' He took her hand again and smiled wickedly. 'There's one way you could get a card. Marry me. You'd get one automatically. Maeve was in California when I was born. I'm an American citizen.'

'No.' She was actually shouting. 'You always ask me for the wrong reasons.'

He was staying calm. 'What would be the right one?'

'I don't know. But I will when it comes along. If it ever does!' And Rosie continued to make her way through the crowd. In her own mind she was now striding out on her own. Nevertheless she could hear Gabriel – behind her – whistling that football song about never walking alone. The first time he'd asked her to marry him had been to soothe his Catholic guilt. And now he'd trapped her into coming halfway round the world to a place where she wasn't even allowed to have a job. And she *knew* she was being unreasonable – which made her even angrier with herself.

What *would* make her marry him? What would he have to

say? Something as simple as 'I love you so much that nothing else could satisfy me'. She actually felt her anger dissolving at this make-believe proposal. Rosie crossed the road at an intersection called Durant Avenue and nearly got hit by a gaudily decorated bus coming from the wrong direction. Except this was America so it was their right direction. What in God's name had she let herself in for?

As she reached the opposite pavement, one of her own photographs of Zav stared out from the window of a shop that sold nothing but posters.

Still behind her, Gabriel changed his whistling tune to one of Zav's biggest hits, 'Mr Joe Fingers'.

Rosie rounded on him in a fury. 'He was *our* monkey,' she said. 'So just you shut up.'

'Spare change? Got any change to spare?' This time it was a young girl, huddled in a shop doorway, attempting to play a guitar which had a string missing.

'I'm sorry. I'm as broke as you are.'

The girl wasn't playing a real tune, just chords. 'Coming to Berkeley seemed a good idea in Greenville.'

'It seemed a good idea in London too.' Rosie registered the fact that Gabriel was handing the child a coin.

If he offers me one, I'll throw it at him, she thought. Trapped, that's what I am, trapped. Why hadn't he told her about cameras and about not working? This thought was enough to set her hurrying downhill. Well, it wasn't a hill really – just a slight incline. But she was going down it fast.

'Gotta roach?' This boy couldn't have been a day over fourteen and Nora Hankey would have taken a nit comb to his matted ginger locks.

'I don't even know what a roach is.'

'You sure look like a head.'

'I don't know what a head is, either.' By now she wasn't sounding so much prim as desperate. People were using the same words as English in England, but they obviously meant different things.

'You been on bad stuff?' asked the boy sympathetically. 'Glucose sometimes helps bring you down.'

For one moment she actually considered explaining to him

that she was stuck behind a pane of glass. Some words they'd been made to learn at the Church of England junior school began pounding through her head: '*As it was in the beginning, is now, and ever shall be* . . .' 'No!' This word actually escaped her and became part of the noise of Telegraph Avenue.

Not as it ever shall be, she thought fiercely. I'll melt that glass – even if I have to take a fucking blow-torch to it. This was the first time she had ever thought 'fucking', so maybe there was some hope of her picking up Californian ways, after all.

'No what?' It was Gabriel, a foot away and several thoughts behind her.

Rosie pretended to look in a shop window which had a human eye painted on the glass. It seemed to be full of second-hand books by authors with difficult names like Madame Blavatsky and Gurdjieff. Vaguely, she registered a glass case in the middle of the window. *Rare – $500*. Rosie's eyes went into sharp focus. The book in the case was open at a familiar title page. It was Gabriel's first edition of *Confessions of an English Opium Eater*. Except it was no longer Gabriel's.

'What more do you want me to do for you?' He was right behind her. In an instant she had whirled round and was holding him in her arms. 'Forgive me for being a pig.'

'You've joined the police?'

Somebody thrust a handbill at her. Not even bothering to look at it, Rosie said, 'I'm feeling a long way from home.' She was suddenly conscious of owing Gabriel something more generous than that. The words came stumbling out: 'Home is you. That much I do know. It's the one thing I know for certain sure. But all of this . . .' She spread out her hands in bafflement, only to receive another handbill. 'It's all so druggy. And I don't like drugs.'

'It's much more than that.' There was real patience in his words. 'Look, they've put some tables and chairs outside the Café Med. Let's go and sit down and I'll try to explain.'

'Not a lecture,' she pleaded. 'I don't think I could take a learned lecture.' But if he didn't explain, how would she ever understand? 'I don't see the café.'

'Across the street. Half a block down. Near those guys in sandals, the ones with the Jews for Jesus placard.'

As they crossed the road she said, 'I hate my voice when it starts bleating.' Even in the middle of the traffic she got handed two different sheets of different-coloured paper covered in swooping psychedelic lettering. 'They must have to chop down a lot of trees to produce all this!'

The chairs outside the café were of tubular metal and the tin table rattled when you put your elbows on it. 'It's a bit like the one I had to swipe from Vesuvius in Manchester.' Rosie began to examine the handbills. The first was a docket for a complimentary cone of falafels – whatever *they* were! The second was an open letter to Governor Reagan; she really would have to learn the difference between Republicans and Democrats. Rosie felt on safer ground with an advertisement for a stationery store; but she sank back into mid-Atlantic confusion when she came to a bit about 'special black light room'.

How could you have a black light? 'I'm lost here,' she said. 'Absolutely fuddled. Would you please explain it all to me?' Once again she held out her hands to Telegraph Avenue. 'How did all of this happen?'

'I'll try to explain but I don't want to sound patronising.'

'Patronise me. I'm a dope. I admit it.' A girl who looked more like Joan Baez than a waitress came up to take their order.

'Coffee?' asked Gabriel.

'I think I'd rather have a glass of white wine.' Why was the waitress suddenly looking so pained?

'Rosie's just arrived,' explained Gabriel placatingly.

Too placatingly. 'I thought California was supposed to be famous for its wine,' she said.

'Famous for being scab.' The girl began to mop the table. 'Those poor grape-pickers are paid in nickels and dimes.'

'We're all boycotting the wine. Have coffee instead,' urged Gabriel. 'Two caffe latte,' he said to the girl. He scraped his chair nearer and took Rosie's hand. 'This was why I wanted you to come by bus. To gradually get the feel of what's happening. This town is one big melting pot. All these people have found their way here because they know that everything has got to change.'

'Hash, grass, acid. Hash, grass . . .' The words were the same but a different dope dealer was threading his way between the tables.

Rosie nodded towards this angelic-looking youth. 'And the fact that drugs are as readily available as dolly mixtures had nothing to do with it?'

'It had everything to do with it.' Gabriel's face was alight with enthusiasm. 'The drugs are all about changing consciousness. Look, this country's run from the top – by the government. It ought to be ruled by the people. It ought to be ruled from the street.'

'But that would lead to chaos.'

'Precisely. And that's what we'll build on top of. England's William Morris had the right idea. He . . .'

'William Morris who did the wallpapers?' Rosie could hardly believe her ears.

'He did a great deal more than that. He urged people to forget the machines. He told them to go back to the land.'

Somebody handed Rosie another paper flyer: *Have You Seen This Girl?* The photograph looked as though it might have been taken to send to a pen-friend. The child could have been herself, before she got the contact lenses. Rosie began to read aloud: '"Appearance may have changed. Melinda Gruber (aged 14 years) ran away to Berkeley from Greenville, Ga, on New Year's Day. If you have seen her please contact police or her mother, Mrs Heidi Gruber, at Hotel Durant. Melinda has psychological difficulties." And this little girl understood all that complicated revolutionary thinking?'

'No.' Gabriel actually seized on this with joy. 'But she felt the excitement in the air and she wanted to be part of it.'

'Well you've just seen her. She was begging in a doorhole. Shall we call the police?'

'No we shall not. Pigs and parents are the enemy. Surely you can see that?'

'And dope dealers are everybody's friend?' Rosie looked him straight in the eye. 'Have you been on drugs?'

'What century are you living in? Lighten up, Rose. I smoke

a little grass. No more than I did in London.' He took out his wallet and opened it to reveal a flattened joint.

She remembered Mongoose who had also smoked a little grass. Only he'd gone on to pills. And when their magic wore off he'd invested in a shining hypodermic. Before Rosie left England she'd read in a Sunday newspaper that Mongoose was in a psychiatric hospital – on a locked ward. 'Maybe I just met drugs in the wrong way. No, that isn't what I think. I've been around them, I don't like them. And if that's unfashionable – tough!' One question had to be asked. Gabriel was, after all, the man who'd said he wanted to know God. 'What about LSD?'

He became much more serious. 'I've not dropped acid yet. Owsley went missing. His is the best. Acid needs treating with great respect. When he comes back I'll score some and do it.' Now he was full of eagerness. 'I've done mescalin.'

'I hear it's a very sensual ride,' Rosie observed wryly. Still, not being Miss Dumbo made a pleasant change.

'Well, well, well . . .' Gabriel was raising an amused eyebrow. 'I bet your friend Miriam told you that.'

'She also said she could get us an apartment in that village.'

'I wouldn't want you living in Normandy Village,' he said quickly. Too quickly.

'Why not?'

For once Gabriel seemed to be fishing for words. He came up with, 'Bad vibes. It's not the place for you.'

Instinct took over. 'Who do you know there?'

'Me?'

'You.'

'Well . . .' he began. And then he obviously changed his mind. 'You don't want to start living too near to people you know. One of the best attitudes here is the right to the freedom to have your own space.'

Waffle. The other things he'd been saying might have made some sort of sense. Not this. But Rosie knew better than to probe. Time or Miriam would hand her the answer. The Jewish girl had certainly seen Gabriel somewhere before; Rosie had already stored this away as something to be unwrapped at a later date.

The waitress reappeared carrying two tall glasses of milky coffee.

'I bet you're sick of people telling you that you look like Joan Baez?' Gabriel was smiling at the girl.

She was far from immune to his charms. 'Hey, Joan's coming back to Berkeley tomorrow, man – for the big free concert.' She placed the coffee on the insecure table where it immediately slopped. 'Joan Baez, and Country Joe, and that beautiful Zav Hankey.'

The sun was just beginning to go down as Rosie turned the corner of Spruce Street. One minute the sky was blue with white cumulus clouds. The next, it was as though somebody had thrown a switch, which altered the lighting to deep orange, and transformed the clouds into boughs of giant trees in an unlikely shade of sage green. Why wasn't everybody rushing out to gaze at the wonder of it all? The fact of the matter was that they'd seen it all before: this was just another East Bay sunset.

The light tinged everything with gold, which only emphasised the fairy-tale qualities of Normandy Village, and hid the truth of these turrets and arches: they were built of something much less substantial than solid stone – they had been constructed of lath and dental plaster and liberal doses of architectural imagination. But as Rosie walked across the cobblestones and under an old iron lamp suspended from the vaulted ceiling of a high arch, she was enchanted. The pathway led into a magically tangled garden which was surrounded by cottages that could have belonged to Joan of Arc's relations. Winding steps led up the back of the tallest tower to a studded oak door, on a higher level than the other dwellings. 'Apartments' seemed the wrong word. The whole place might have been a fake but that didn't stop it being a glorious one.

Madonna lilies: literally hundreds of these waxy white flowers were growing wild at the foot of the stone staircase. Despite the fact that they would have cost at least a guinea each at Constance Spry in London, Rosie's enchantment was suddenly tinged with apprehension. They were too

Thomas De Quincey. Madonna lilies had never brought her luck.

Up on the higher level, the studded door opened and a woman stepped out. Eyes closed, face held up to the dying sun, she began to breathe deeply in a ritualised manner. Her dark hair was streaked with grey and piled up on top of her head in a corona of plaits. The black dress looked like . . . robes. Her full skirts swept right down to the stone landing, and the deep gold braid round the hem was worked in a design of signs of the zodiac. In ordinary daylight the woman would have looked mildly ridiculous – but this wasn't ordinary daylight.

'Omm . . .' She had begun intoning a curious noise into the cooling air. 'Omm . . .'

'Rosemarie, over here!' Miriam's friendly voice brought everyday reassurance to the proceedings. Rosie's friend was leaning out of the open ground-floor window of one of the cottages, eating a bagel. 'I just weighed myself,' she called out. 'Two hundred and twelve pounds. Oh well, the more to love! The door's not locked. Step inside, I'm on the telephone.'

Rosie crossed the garden and noted that Miriam had paper windmills, on wooden sticks, in her own little flowerbed. The door had a flap for peeping out, covered with an iron grille.

Inside the cottage, Miriam was still on the telephone. At least Rosie presumed it was a telephone – the receiver was shaped like a banana. 'Thank you very much, Dr Harris,' she was saying. 'Sorry. Thank you very much, *Lionel*.'

Rosie wondered whether she should be listening. If it was Dr Harris, the call presumably concerned herself. But he might just have rung up to woo Miriam from a distance. As she began to look round the room, Rosie decided she would be justified in *half* listening.

The living room was like a toyshop; there were glass-fronted cabinets full of fairground kewpie dolls, and shelves crammed with wind-up tin toys. Bright cloth kites hung from the ceiling. And the big stone fireplace housed a large collection of model robots.

As Miriam listened to the quacking telephone, she put

down her bagel and began ripping the paper off a package. Gift paper, tissue paper, the final layer was pulled back to reveal a decanter in the shape of Elvis Presley. His head was the stopper. Miriam pressed a switch on the base; Elvis began to revolve and the room was flooded with the tinkling strains of 'Wooden Heart'.

'I've got that information written down,' said Miriam into the banana. 'We'll try calling her immediately. Please give my best to your mother. Goodbye now.' She plonked the banana into a bowl of plastic fruit.

'I thought plastic wasn't supposed to be okay in Berkeley?' laughed Rosie.

'I collect stuff like this *because* it's awful. It's high kitsch. Isn't Elvis something? Just like a little miniature waxwork. Fuck Elvis, we've located your mother!'

'Where?' Rosie sat down with a bump. The chair was an Early American rocker. 'Where is she?'

'Not as far as you might think. Santa Cruz. It's between here and L.A. Doctor-Sweetheart-Harris gave me the number.' The dial of Miriam's phone was set into an apple and her finger was already at work.

'Hold on. How many miles?' Rosie's stomach was full of butterflies.

'I dunno.' Miriam gave her banana an airy wave. 'A hundred? It's way down the coast road and kind of tacky. Boardwalks, amusements, shooting galleries. Here we go! It's ringing . . . no it isn't. It's the noise you get for disconnected. Was Connie good at paying her bills?'

'Terrible. Put that phone down. Honestly, if you'd ever met her, you wouldn't be going to all this trouble.'

The banana returned to being part of an arrangement of fruit. 'But I can't wait to meet her,' insisted Miriam. 'At least we've got an address. Every detail we learn makes her sound more and more like Rita Hayworth in *Miss Sadie Thompson*. I have this vision of her slopping around in a faded kimono.' Suddenly, she was all contrition: 'That was terrible of me. I should never have said that about somebody's mother.'

'You were probably very accurate. Even in my childhood Connie was well down the road to ruin.'

'She sounds a living collector's item.' 'Wooden Heart' had almost ground to a halt. 'Isn't this music box something else? Of course, Elvis was always bound to be an enormous success. He has the dream American *look*. Rudolf Valentino had it and Tyrone Power and so did Tony Curtis – when he'd just stopped being Bernie Schwartz. Gabriel's got it too. But he's got the classy version and he's got it by the yard.'

A thought – which had been developing since the airport – rose to the surface. It was so awful that Rosie tried to push it away. But the idea refused to budge.

Miriam never missed a trick: 'What's eating you?'

The idea was ridiculous, Miriam weighed two tons – but that didn't stop men finding her attractive. 'You already seemed to know Gabriel . . .'

'Go on.' This was said very levelly.

Too levelly? And Gabriel had seemed set against the idea of an apartment in Normandy Village. Rosie took a deep breath. 'How well did you know him?'

'What you really mean is, did we screw?' Miriam started to shake with laughter. 'I caught one glimpse of him – two glimpses – and I liked what I saw. Wanna know where I spotted him?'

'No.' Rosie couldn't drop the subject quickly enough. 'Forget it.' Her cheeks were beginning to burn. 'Promise me you'll forget I even asked you. Let's never have a single word about it again.' She could feel her own insides curling up with embarrassment.

'Look, I'll tell you.'

Rosie's fingers went to her ears. 'Honestly, I don't need to know.' She did know that the memory of asking that awful question would haunt her for years. That when she thought about it she would want to let out little groans. 'Can we just drop the whole subject? And I'm sorry I started it. I'm really sorry.'

'Okay, okay, it's forgotten.'

'Omm . . .' The weird woman on the steps was at it again.

Turning on a lamp, Miriam nodded towards the twilight outside. 'It's Friday night so Viva's waiting for her beauty chorus.' The lamp was a china Minnie Mouse, lit from inside.

'Let's get behind the drapes and watch,' she said in lowered tones. 'Viva Rapport is wonderfully formal. She has tremendous style. I like observing her because I aim to pinch a few of her tricks – for when I finally join the grown-ups.'

'You mean you aim to use magic?' whispered Rosie. Two young men were making their way towards the foot of Viva's steps. One looked French and the other Oriental. Each, in his own way, was comely. 'Good evening, Mr Lanki,' intoned the figure at the top of the stone staircase. 'Bonsoir, Monsieur Laconique.'

'Sixty-five if she's a day!' breathed Miriam. 'And still entertaining seven guys at one go. Look, here come the rest of the procession. It's like a Coca-Cola advertisement. And look how they worship her. It has to be black magic, nothing else would get people in Berkeley to be punctual. You're sure you don't want me to tell you where I saw Gabriel?'

'Positive.' Anyway it couldn't be at Viva's, for the assembled seven were now filing up the open stairwell. And Gabriel was not one of their number. Now she could admit to herself that she had just wondered . . . So much for instinct! Or so she thought.

Saturday was the day of the free concert and Rosie was refusing to be told that she couldn't carry a camera. 'If Henri Cartier-Bresson could do it, so can I.' The Rolleiflex was hidden inside a brown paper parcel. Only a very close observer would have seen that the rents in the parcel's sides revealed the lens, the viewfinder and the camera's shutter.

'You look like a cartoon of an anarchist with a bomb,' laughed Gabriel. 'Look, that's the philosophy department.' The long low Gothic building could have been a Cambridge college. But a lot of the other campus buildings put Rosie in mind of the 1920s concrete mass of Urmston swimming baths. Newer buildings looked straight out of space movies. The whole collection was set amidst leafy glades, and there were sloping lawns and even a winding stream. Rosie sniffed appreciatively: 'The smell's the best thing. It's like the smell you get when you open an old cedarwood chest.'

'That's the eucalyptus trees. They're supposed to be a tremendous fire hazard.'

'I never expected California to smell so woody.' Rosie hoped she sounded as contented as she felt. 'Even the inside of Miriam's house smells as though somebody's just finished sharpening a dozen pencils.'

'Why don't you take a picture of that girl?' suggested Gabriel. 'There she sits, all on her own on the grass, specs on the end of her nose – music open in front of her – trying to teach herself to play "Blowing in the Wind". All of Berkeley would be in that shot.'

'Yes, but you thought of it, not me. Photographs are something I have to think out for myself. Anyway, with any luck I'll soon be taking pictures of the real Joan Baez.'

'And of Zav. You should have let me try to find him. We could have called Manchester and got the number from his mother.'

'No. If we're meant to get together, we will.' Always quick to tune into places and atmospheres, Rosie was already beginning to think Berkeley-style.

'What's his birthsign?' asked Gabriel.

'Leo. Same as you.'

'Could lead to trouble,' he laughed.

More than you think, thought Rosie. The two men had never met. 'Are all these people students?'

'Students and street people. Once the kids get here they seem to think of campus as their own. And why not?'

'I thought you were meant to be a teacher,' she teased. 'Shouldn't you be against trespassers? Miss Swaine would have been.'

All the light-heartedness went out of Gabriel as he said, 'You're either in this thing or you aren't. Anybody who isn't for the revolution is against it. Where do you stand?'

'Me? I'm just the girl with the hidden camera. Perhaps I'll use it to spread the message round the world.'

She had been joking but Gabriel was serious as he said, 'We're stirring everywhere. I talked to Paris last night, while you were asleep. The French students are all set to burst something big. It's the same in Germany; Cohn-Bendit was here last week and he says it's all coming together in Europe, it's all rising up to the boil.'

The paved walkway was leading them downhill – towards the Sproul Plaza. This huge open concourse was already packed with people. And on a makeshift stage, in front of the university union building, which was like a smaller version of the American Embassy in London, Joan Baez was singing to a rapt audience that all her trials would soon be over.

'Let's sit on the edge of Ludwig's Fountain,' suggested Gabriel. The jets of the fountain had presumably been switched off; they were hidden from view under a huge papier-mâché carnival head in the likeness of a bright pink pig.

'Joan's a local,' whispered Gabriel. 'She's a Bay Area Quaker so I suppose peace comes naturally to her.'

As the song finished the crowd went wild. Through the cheering and the clapping Rosie thought she heard a Scottish voice behind her saying, 'Yon's the lady.'

And why shouldn't there be Scots in Berkeley? That afternoon, the excitement on campus made it seem as though the world's axis was running through the centre of the Sproul Plaza.

A pair of tiny hands stretched round her head from behind and went over her eyes. 'Guess who this is?' Though the voice was gruff it obviously belonged to a small boy.

'No idea.' How had a child got so high up in the air? He had to be sitting on somebody's shoulders. 'Give me a clue.'

'You knew Lily Jelly.'

Rosie was surprised to find that her eyes, behind the small hands, were suddenly filling with tears. 'You've got to be Moondog Hankey.'

Sunlight returned as fingers were lifted off her eyes and Rosie swung round to look at the child who was indeed sitting on a man's shoulders. They belonged to a broadly beaming Hamish. And Moondog Hankey could have been Zav, aged six. But instead of being cropped, the hair was an explosion of wild corkscrew curls. 'Hello,' he laughed. 'Have you got a dog? I have.'

'Zav should be coming on any moment now,' said Hamish

as Joan Baez took her bow. Danny's 'chauffeur' was much changed in appearance. The smart Italian silk suits had been replaced by a grey sweatshirt and blue jeans, there was a design of marijuana leaves printed onto his headband, and he'd let his sideburns grow so bushy that they looked like a pair of telephone receivers.

The crowd refused to let Joan Baez go. 'Okay,' she said. 'One more time. And you've got to sing it with me – we're all in this thing together.' She lifted her fingers in the peace sign and then returned them to her guitar. As she began to pour out the message in her heart, three thousand people joined in.

'I think I want to pee,' said Moondog.

'I know your thinking and I bet you don't, not really.' Hamish was plainly good with him. 'Danny's here,' he added for Rosie's benefit.

She was surprised. 'I wouldn't have thought this was his scene. I mean, it's hardly a commercial venture.'

'That's *why* we're here,' sighed Hamish. 'Too much of this sort of thing. He's in the Durant Hotel, sulking.'

'Can I go on your shoulders for a change?' Moondog asked Rosie.

'Would mine do?' suggested Gabriel.

'It's okay, Gabriel, I'll have him for a minute.' Rosie took the boy and hugged him. He felt so nice and warm and trusting that – for a moment – she came over quite broody.

'You know Tippler, don't you?' the child whispered.

'Yes,' she whispered back.

'D'you like whispering games?'

'Yes.'

Putting his mouth right up to her ear he hissed, 'D'you think I'm too young to get a tattoo like Tippler's?'

This was an awkward one. But Gabriel, who had amazing hearing, supplied a whispering suggestion: 'You could have decal. They sell them on Telegraph.'

'What's that?' asked Rosie, in ordinary tones – mildly worried ones.

'A transfer,' said Gabriel.

Moondog tried to get the game back to whispering. 'They

wash off.' Gabriel obliged him with a low murmur of, 'We could get a few.'

'Hey,' said Moondog in a lively voice, 'this man's okay.'

Joan Baez disappeared from view, and without any preliminary announcement Zav strolled out onto the platform. He was wearing the Berkeley 'uniform' of open workshirt and jeans, and these days his hair was every bit as explosive as his son's. Only pausing to adjust the microphone, he went straight into 'Mr Joe Fingers'.

Though the song was about a monkey, it was also about the importance of having a loving heart. It always brought Rosie close to tears – especially the line 'And in Chester Zoo he cried.' A lot of their childhood was in that song and here was Moondog – the next generation – with his arms round her neck. What's more, he was getting heavy. 'Would you go to Gabriel for a minute?'

'Sure.'

As the applause for his song died down, Zav fiddled with the microphone again and said through the crackling, 'Where's Moondog? Where's my son?' Shielding his eyes he began to peer into the crowd, mock fiercely. 'This next one's for you.'

'I'm here,' yelled Moondog.

Several other people joined in, yelling, 'He's over there.' 'He's right here.'

Zav's eyes raked the crowd, located Moondog, and registered Rosie. 'Hallelujah!' he yelled as he fell down onto the stage in a fake swoon. Scrambling to his feet, he grabbed the mike and yelled in tones of sheerest joy, 'Hello, Rosie, welcome to America. Come on, let's hear all of you say it. Welcome to America, Rosie.'

And three thousand adoring fans obeyed him. 'Welcome to America, Rosie' rang round the campus loudly enough to cause a flight of birds to take off from the roof of the union building.

'Come on up here, Rosie Tattersall,' he yelled. 'Moondog, bring her up onto the stage!'

A wave of stifling shyness was overcoming her. But

Moondog was already struggling to get out of Gabriel's arms and into Rosie's. 'Come on,' he said. 'Let's go.'

And people were already opening up a pathway for them. 'Yes, come on, Rosie.' 'Let these guys through.'

Gabriel stayed where he was but Hamish automatically turned himself into a minder and eased their journey onto the platform. Rosie was no longer part of the crowd. Instead, she was facing it. Zav flung his arms round her and gave her a smacking great kiss on the cheek. 'Didn't I always tell you she was the most beautiful?' He was talking to Moondog but speaking into the microphone. The crowd's faces were just thousands of pink and tanned blobs. Rosie's eyes located the gaudily disguised fountain and found Gabriel. Even the set of his shoulders showed that he was not best pleased.

Zav was still addressing his audience: 'A lot of people know that Joe Fingers was a real monkey and that he was mine . . .' Immediately, the crowd began to sing:

> 'Joe Fingers, Joe Fingers,
> The King of Teapot Hall.'

Zav silenced this with: 'But he was Rosie's monkey too. She helped rescue him. Rosie's part of all my songs. She was there the night I first saw the Great Omi . . .'

The crowd roared again at the mention of this familiar title.

'And she knew Lily Jelly. Oh how we knew Lily Jelly!' Leaning the microphone towards Rosie he asked, 'What was she like?'

'Awful.' She was startled to hear her own voice echoing back from the eucalyptus grove.

'Was she for peace?'

'Never!'

'Are you for peace?'

'Of course I am.'

'Are we *all* for peace?'

The vast crowd turned into a single thundering 'Yes'. But one person wasn't joining in. He looked ready for war. That person was Gabriel Bonarto.

*

407

Country Joe and the Fish had taken over the platform by the time Rosie found her way back to Ludwig's Fountain – where Gabriel appeared to be engrossed in a deep conversation with Miriam Million.

'I'd never have gone up if I'd known what was going to happen,' said Rosie – who had remembered to be English again.

Miriam turned and smiled at her. 'Want a toke on this?' It was a joint.

'I thought you didn't.'

'It's Gabriel's, not mine. I sometimes have the odd drag on one, when the pigs are around, just to be subversive. They can hardly bust us *all*.'

In the cause of the counter-culture, Rosie took a couple of draws on the thin hand-rolled cigarette; and then another, deeper one. Her lungs protested at this incautious intake of aromatic smoke, and she began to cough violently.

'If you don't cough, you don't get off.' Miriam spoke dreamily.

'I'm not sure that I want to get off. Not that I will. It's wasted on me, nothing ever happens.'

'It's less harmful than alcohol.' Gabriel took the joint from Rosie and drew deeply on it himself. She just hoped she wasn't going to be subjected to the whole lecture. The one about marijuana being a natural product – as opposed to the chemical tranquillisers of the older generation. But the fact that she'd already taken a toke on the joint must have led him to believe that this battle was already won. It wasn't. Having sensed that he had resented Zav's show of affection, she was just trying to be sociable. That was when she started to giggle.

'What's so funny?' asked Miriam.

'I don't know. No, I don't want another go, thank you. You'd just be wasting money – it has no effect on me at all.' Once again she found herself having to control an unaccountable desire to laugh. And then she was struck by a sudden solemn thought: 'They busted me in Cheyenne,' she said, 'but in Berkeley they applauded me.' Why did these words seem charged with significance? 'And why are my eyes so fascinated by the glowing end of that cigarette?'

'And it has no effect on you?' said Miriam.

'Just two tokes?' She had tried to fill her voice with righteous indignation but that – suddenly – was funny as well.

'Three tokes,' Gabriel reminded her. 'And it's sensemilla. It's not just plain grass, it's solid with bud.'

They make such a fuss about it, thought Rosie. But a moment later she couldn't remember what she'd been thinking. 'A thought just fluttered out my head,' she said, surprised. One thing she did remember: 'Zav wants us to go over to the Durant. Danny's there. Goodness me! Whatever was that?'

'What?' asked Miriam.

'My scalp just started to creep and I sort of juddered.'

'She's got a buzz coming on,' sang out Gabriel happily. 'Don't worry about it, Rose. That's part of the aim.'

Her mind immediately tried to imagine what an 'aim' would look like. She saw it as red with wings – like Biddie Costigan's engraving of the Sacred Heart. If this was being stoned it was not altogether unpleasant. She just felt detached and relaxed and glad to be with friends. And then she realised that nobody had said anything for about three minutes. 'No, I don't think I like it,' she decided aloud. 'But I'll stop moaning about people who do.'

'You ought to be heading for the Durant,' said Miriam.

'All of us are invited.' Very fine rain had started to fall and Rosie was aware of each separate speck touching her skin, amazingly aware of it.

'Look!' cried Miriam. 'It's just like the famous Berkeley picture postcard.' A rainbow had formed and one end was coming down behind the white tower – the campanile.

'Rose,' said Gabriel quickly and urgently – he was speaking as though they were on their own. 'I want to give you a present. I'm giving you all of this. The rainbow, the campanile, the eucalyptus trees, the peaceful people – everything that's Berkeley. But if you ever tell anybody, or you ever try to claim it, it won't be yours any more.'

Gabriel dealt in ideas, Zav in audiences. She couldn't help but feel that her lover was setting herself up in competition with her friend.

The Durant Hotel wasn't far from the campus but it was a million miles away from the peace concert. Gabriel had to stop and buy footwear before they could even think of going in. The shoes he chose were Clark's desert boots – exactly the same ones that Miss Parrish sold in Irlams o'th' Height.

'Boots are okay in these times,' explained Miriam. 'But we have to beware of men in shoes.' Rosie wondered whether these words were as portentous as they seemed, or was it the continuing effects of the sensemilla?

The hotel was up a side street. 'I wouldn't be surprised if the building wasn't pre-earthquake,' observed Miriam.

In those days, the reception area at the Durant was dull and drab – rather like Brown's Hotel in London. 'We've come to see Danny Cahn.' Gabriel was addressing a receptionist who, in contrast with the rest of Berkeley, had a startlingly short and neat haircut.

'He's here on a private visit.' The man behind the desk also had a vinegary manner and a sibilant voice. 'He's not interviewing groups.'

'This is Zav Hankey's sister,' said Miriam, icily.

'That makes the fourth "sister" today.'

'And did they all have English accents?' asked Rosie in her grandest tones. Zav Hankey's sister! What next? As she remembered Miriam describing her father as the Duke of Teapot Hall, she suppressed an urge to titter. Marijuana was in control, she wasn't.

'They're all in the bar,' said the receptionist disapprovingly.

'Actually,' said Rosie, 'we're thinking of *forming* a group. We're going to call it Muldoon's Picnic!' Smiling broadly, she began to lead the others towards a small neon sign, in the shape of a cocktail glass. Rosie had already learned that this was the Californian symbol for 'bar'.

Here was another time-capsulated setting for a 1940s' Hollywood movie – right down to the curving art-deco cocktail counter. But Danny Cahn's party were in basket chairs at the far end of the room. Moondog was the first to spot the new arrivals. Using the highly polished floor as a slide, he joined them in a rush. 'Star stole half my burrito,' he announced. 'And now she says she wants to throw up.'

The woebegone elf sitting on Danny Cahn's knee looked as though she really belonged on top of a mushroom with a bluebell on her head. 'I didn't steal it,' she said. 'You can't steal off your own brother.'

'She'll eat anything,' said Moondog.

'Know the feeling,' murmured Miriam.

'Have you ever eaten half a worm?'

'Never *knowingly*.'

'She has.'

The elf had a tiny snub nose and her hair hung to her shoulders in pale golden tendrils. The eyes gazing at Rosie were Hazel Hankey, all over again. Star took one look at Gabriel and held out her arms to be picked up. Danny seemed quite happy to hand her over to the Italian. 'Didn't I say the next time I saw you would be here?' He was in a dark blue silk suit and his only concession to Berkeley was a flowered Liberty shirt with a tie in the same material.

Rosie hugged Danny and she was pleased to find that he still smelt of Trumper's Limes. 'Meet my friend Miriam Million. This is Dan.'

As the pair shook hands, Jewish appraisal met Jewish appraisal. We'd never *dare* add one another up like that, thought Rosie. All the signs indicated mutual approval. Zav didn't look as though he approved of anybody. He was wearing the body language of a caged lion and Rosie sensed that they must have walked in on a scene.

'Have a drink,' said Danny to the newcomers. 'Hamish, fix them up with whatever they want. You want tequila, Zav?'

'When will you learn I don't do alcohol any more? I'll roll a joint in a minute.'

'Like fuck you will! We don't want to spend the rest of the afternoon in a paddy-wagon.' Danny looked round worriedly; the other people in the bar had nothing to do with student unrest. In fact they looked like refugees from the Saturday junketing outside. Country Joe could still be heard singing, in the distance, on campus.

411

'You're a bigger name than he is,' said Danny. 'What's he doing with the star spot?'

'There are no star spots in free concerts. You just turn up and do it.'

'You make it sound as though you're still working the ballrooms round Manchester.'

'At least I was happy then. I didn't have people telling me off for doing something for nothing. I'm sick of this rat race. I want out.'

'It's the same every time he gets a whiff of this bloody counter-culture,' sighed Danny. 'I could write the next bit for him. All he wants to do is get back to his own stretch of land where he'll grow illegal crops.'

'I'm sick of everything having a price on it. Even *smiles* have a price on them, in your world.'

Danny stopped being a friendly uncle. First his mouth set itself into a straight line and then he opened it and gave forth in a way which brooked no arguments. 'Berkeley may look very hand-spun and home-fed, but there are huge commercial influences at work underneath. All you have to do is walk down Telegraph and look at it through eyes like mine. You've just done a free concert. That means – even as we speak – the record stores will be shifting a whole load of your new album.'

'That's not why I did it.'

'No, but it's why I let you. And before you flare up, we've got a contract.'

'My mother was right.' Zav was still capable of going scarlet in the face. 'You're nothing but a bloody puppet master.'

'Who was clever enough to turn you into a millionaire.' Danny remained firm and calm. 'I'm the one who's managed to save you from yourself, Zav. And I'm not going to stand by and let you turn yourself into a martyr for crackpot causes. Those kids who flood into this town on a Saturday aren't just buying records, we had extra posters shipped in for today. They look as though they're being sold by hippies but they're not – they're being sold by me. And every one that changes hands is money in the bank. Royalties for you, royalties for Rosie . . .'

'Hang on a minute,' she said firmly. 'I don't get royalties on those pictures.'

'Don't you? So you don't. Slip o' the tongue. Still, it was a great opportunity for you.'

'She ought to get royalties,' roared Zav.

'If you'll just hold your noise, she's going to get something else. I look after those who look after me, and I've just had a great idea. What I . . .'

'Is the row over?' Moondog had wandered back from the other end of the room, where he'd been changing ashtrays around on all the tables. 'They never stop having fights but they don't last long.'

'Yes, and you're getting a bit too forward for my liking.' Nevertheless Zav picked up his son and gave him a big hug. You could see they were both descended from Tippler. In fact the whole noisy argument was like something that could have taken place in the back kitchen at Saracen Street.

But they were in the bar of the Durant Hotel and Danny Cahn was being approached by a middle-aged woman with dyed black hair. She was very 'lipstick and high heels'. This was how Berkeley described women whose look differed from their own.

'Pardon me for interrupting,' the intruder said to Danny.

'My name is Heidi Gruber and I'm looking for my daughter, Melinda.'

'I'm afraid I don't follow you, madam.' And then Danny saw that the woman was holding out a handbill. It was the one about the missing girl from Greenville, Ga.

'I've been here a week. I leave tomorrow. I've stopped asking people on the streets, they're too sassy by half. I only ask respectable people now.' She had dust on her mascara. 'We gave that girl everything.'

Inside Rosie's head Paul McCartney began to sing 'She's Leaving Home'. Was she still stoned? The woman looked a lot like Connie had done at the time when *she* upped and went.

'No,' Danny shook his head. 'I haven't seen her. Not that I've done more than walk to the corner. But my friends live here . . .' As he handed the flyer to Rosie the woman flashed her a disapproving look. She was obviously not impressed by the borrowed band jacket – all Rosie had to wear until she

413

could collect her luggage from the Greyhound bus station on Monday. Rosie looked at the picture, and again she saw herself as she was in the days when she too had been forced to wear glasses. If the Connies of this world could walk out on children, why shouldn't the children walk out on them?

'The little bitch only did it because I'm seeing a lot of this new gentleman. But we're not allowed to be modern! Oh no, they have to have it all for themselves.'

Rosie knew that kind of bitterness – remembered it – it could lead to smacked legs. 'No,' she said, 'I've not seen her.' And immediately she began to worry that she'd done the wrong thing.

'You Zav Hankey?' asked the woman.

'Guilty.' Non-commercial or not, Zav threw her a professional smile.

'You'll never be in the same league as Tony Martin.' As the woman turned to walk away, Star was inadvertently blocking her path. 'Scat!' The mother spat the word out, and Rosie felt much better about having lied.

'Of course Gruber is a German name,' murmured Miriam, thoughtfully. And she and Danny exchanged the merest flicker of a glance.

'So what is it you're proposing to do for Rosie?' Zav asked his manager.

'I presume she didn't just take the famous pictures of you? There are surely others?'

It was Rosie who answered: 'Hundreds. I must have started when he was about ten. There's all the childhood stuff and there are loads of early pictures of Zav and the Hankeys. I've even got some of the skiffle group playing in the back yard – next to the mangle.'

'So who owns the copyrights?' asked Danny.

'Strictly speaking, Zav.' Rosie had learned about things like this during her time at the Poly. 'He asked me to do them and he always bought the films and paid for Kodak paper.'

'No,' said Zav. 'You're wrong. Those were just production costs.' He too had learned along the way. 'You never got anything for taking them. The copyrights and still yours.'

'Then she's sitting on a fortune,' smiled Danny. 'If we'd

414

been working out of England, I'd have thought of it sooner. I'll have no trouble in finding a publisher for a good photobiography.'

'Yes, and I'll make sure she gets a proper deal this time,' put in Zav.

'This calls for champagne,' said Danny. 'And I'm told that the Californian kind is quite acceptable.'

'*No*,' roared Gabriel, Miriam, Rosie and Zav – in one voice.

'If you wanna roll a joint,' Miriam was talking to the singer, 'why don't we all go back to my place? There's something I want you to do for me, Zav. You live down at Big Sur. Right?'

'Right. Just outside Carmel.'

'How far is that from Santa Cruz?'

'No great distance.'

'If I give you an address, could you see if you can find Rosie's mother?'

'You want me to shoot her for you?' he asked the friend of his childhood.

'You just find out whether she's there,' said Miriam, briskly. 'Do that and leave the rest to me.'

Being a passenger in Miriam's open-topped sports car was an alarming experience; it was a bit like being at the centre of a fireworks display – one that had got out of control. All around them, in the streams of San Francisco traffic, people had been shouting and yelling and tooting their horns. And the normally equable Miriam had retaliated with the ball of her hand on her own hooter, and with repeated cries of 'Up your kazoo!' Nevertheless, they had rescued Rosie's luggage from the bus station. And once they got back to Berkeley, Rosie had even dared to venture into the Bank of America, where she drew out some of the money that Gabriel had deposited in her new account.

Dared? Now that she was going to be earning money from a book, she had just felt as though she was borrowing against her own future earnings. She had stopped feeling kept. 'Though God alone knows how I'll get Gabriel to take it back,' she said to Miriam, who was privy to these scruples. 'Listen, I don't want to walk out of the bank with all this cash in my hand. Let's settle up here. How much do I owe you?'

'Nothing.'

'Oh come on!'

'Okay, if you insist, you can pay for the flight. But the rest was my pleasure.'

'So how much was the flight?'

'I don't remember. No, not that much. Nothing like as much as that. Take half back. Old Mrs Harris got us a deal with a travel agent who was one of their patients.'

Only somebody who has been bereft of friends and absolutely strapped for cash would understand the pleasure that Rosie was getting from being able to repay this debt.

The luggage was still strapped to the back of Miriam's yellow MG, which was parked on Bancroft Way. It was lunchtime so the food carts near the entrance to the campus were doing brisk business. '*Berkeley Barb*! Get your *Barb*.' The girl attempting to sell them a newspaper was Melinda Gruber. And she was looking altogether more cheerful. 'Hey! I saw you at the concert with Zav Hankey, man.'

The whole morning had been punctuated with comments like this. Rosie longed to get out of the all-too-recognisable band jacket. 'Yes, Melinda, and *we* ran into your mother on Saturday.' She hadn't meant to sound severe but that's how it came out.

'Isn't she a trip? Jesus! A whole gang of us trailed her for days. The hunter, hunted! Mom had no idea. She flew out last night. I got word from some kids who were spare-changing, down at Oakland Airport. Wanna buy a *Barb*? I'm on commission.'

Miriam was already handing over some coins. 'Here,' she thrust the gaudy newspaper at Rosie, 'you've not really got here till you've seen this.'

'See you around,' said Melinda. 'You too, Rosie.' She must have remembered the name from the concert.

'Yes, see you.' This small social exchange left Rosie with a pleasant glow. Berkeley suddenly felt like a village; one where everybody was young. What's more, Miriam had been right about nobody pinching the luggage. It was still where they'd left it, strapped to the back of the open-topped car.

'Stealing is not considered cool,' said Miriam as they climbed in. No question of opening doors: they just swung their legs over the top and they were ready for off. The crowd began to scatter as Miriam roared down Bancroft Way. Slowing down for a moment, she reached out to grab a copy of another newspaper, presumably a free one, called the *Daily Cal*. Miriam scanned the front-page headline. 'So he's back,' she said.

But Rosie was deep in the *Barb*. 'It's a bit like *Oz*.' This was an English 'underground' publication. But no page of English small advertisements would have held her riveted like this one was doing. Silently, she read to herself: *'Become an ordained Minister with the title of Dr or Rev in the Padua Order. Legal in any state. You can perform marriages. Send $20.00.' 'Chick will pose alone or with husband. Box 22.' 'George presents discreet, endowed, handsome, screened male models.'* 'Miriam! They have their size, in inches, after their names. And here's a somebody who says she's a foxy, preoperative transsexual "seeking assistance". But she's got seven inches in brackets, too. What's all of this got to do with the revolution? Come to that, what *is* the revolution?' Everybody talked about this intangible thing but nobody had succeeded in explaining it to Rosie's satisfaction.

'It's something that's still coming together. The old ones have fucked up the planet. We've got to put things right.'

'And these creepy adverts will help?'

'They pay for the serious part of the paper.'

Rosie persisted: 'But why call it a revolution? I'm beginning to think it's like the Emperor's new clothes.'

'When the campus cops are already tunnelling under the tennis courts? When they've got tear gas stored down there? Well take a look at that! We seem to have our own handsome screened male model waiting for us. And from the look of those Levis, he's not short of a few inches, either.' Zav Hankey was sitting on one of the concrete stumps, outside Normandy Village, with a Frisbee in his hand.

'Where are the children?' asked Rosie eagerly, as she climbed out of the car.

Plainly this was not the correct opening line. 'Don't you start,' he groaned. 'I've had to promise I'll spend tomorrow flying kites with Moondog – to make up for not bringing him. He's got a big crush on you.'

'Let's go and sit in the garden.' Miriam was already clattering across the cobbles in her wooden-soled health sandals. Their leather tops were jade green, they matched today's kaftan.

As the trio passed under the arch, Zav seemed to feel some urgent need to explain his own presence. 'I've been snooping in your mother's footsteps,' he said to Rosie.

'And?' Miriam plainly regarded herself as Head Detective.

'Amaryllis Valley wasn't a street at all. It turned out to be a trailer park. That's caravans,' he translated for Rosie's benefit. 'And the bird had flown.'

'Did you get a forwarding address?' Miriam was wrestling some deckchairs out of a big wooden cupboard on the stone front porch.

'All I got was a load of abuse. In fact I had to settle a couple of Connie's small debts before I could get out of that hellhole alive. It's the first time I've ever found myself looking down a gun.'

'That bad, eh?' grunted Miriam. She was no better with deckchairs than she was with motor cars.

'Here, let me.' Zav turned a difficult job into nothing. In a couple of moments there were three chairs awaiting occupants.

The last thing Rosie wanted to do was sit down. The others did, she stayed on her feet. 'Was there anything said about Christopher?' Even as she was saying these words the hum was going off inside her head. What's more, it was much more vigorous than it had been in years. Could that mean that he was nearer?

'No, nothing about him.' Zav waved away a cloud of insects. 'Two wayward ladies was all that was mentioned.'

The high-pitched whine refused to go away. 'I'd like to see Chris. Just to know he's all right.' Reluctantly, she admitted, 'I've a feeling he's not far away.'

'I bought tea,' said Miriam. 'Anybody like tea? If he's gay

and he was in California, he's bound to have headed for San Francisco. Maybe I should get the word out on North Beach?'

'If his mother's followed him to San Francisco, perhaps we should be looking for her in the Tenderloin.' Zav had gone a bit pink.

Miriam managed to sound both shocked and thrilled: 'You mean she's a hooker?'

Zav was looking sideways at Rosie, as though he was considering how much more she could take. 'The neighbours just said that Connie entertained a lot of gentlemen – after dark.'

'I'll boil some water.' Miriam headed into the house.

'I wouldn't mind betting those neighbours said a lot more than that.' Rosie had been trying to work out Connie's age. 'People were already calling her names when I was still a little girl. Zav, how could she be on the game? She's well into her forties.'

'Apparently she had a lot of black visitors.'

'That's her all right.' (Rosie was remembering: *He made me feel as though I was lined with white satin.*) 'At this late date, the poor old thing's probably down to paying *them.*'

'She's got no money. I raided her mailbox. It was nothing but bills. Bills and a threatening letter from some people called the Alfresco Furnishing Company. She was behind with her payments on a barbecue set. There was one other thing.' His hand went to the breast pocket of his shirt. 'This.' It seemed to be a printed postcard.

'Indian or China?' Miriam's head had come round the door. 'What's that?' she asked too brightly, nodding towards the postcard. 'Okay, I'm a snoop. I admit it. I apologise. But don't keep us in suspense. What have you found?'

Zav began to read aloud. '"Don't miss this month's reunion, girls. The shipment of Bisto has arrived – also Typhoo Tips."'

'Drugs?' mouthed Miriam.

'Groceries,' said Zav. 'It's some association of British GI Brides. Hey! Give me that back.'

'Why?' asked Miriam. 'Have you any intention of going to that meeting? Because I most certainly have.'

'You'd have a job. It's over and done with.'

Miriam refused to be squashed. 'There's an address on this card. It belongs to Mrs Brenda Mellon – honorary secretary. Maybe I should write her. What am I saying? You're the one who should be writing, Rosemarie. She could lead you to Christopher.' Miriam's voice was sweetly wheedling. Then it became genuinely concerned. 'If the pair of them have split up, it's just to be hoped he's okay.'

'You could do worse than advertise for him in the *Barb*.' Zav indicated the newspapers that Rosie had dropped onto her chair.

She lifted them up and sat down. 'How do we know he isn't already advertising? "Hunky English Stud Offers Services."' She dropped the papers onto the ground. 'Christopher was never an *easy* person.'

Immediately Miriam rushed to his defence: 'Can you wonder? It's a miracle you've turned out as well as you have. I should definitely advertise if I was you. You could be missing out on an enchanting relationship. China or Indian?'

As they settled for Indian tea, and Miriam drifted back into the house to make it, Rosie wondered whether Connie was a woman who craved Typhoo Tips. Had it been Gordon's gin, her daughter could have come up with a definite answer. And why should she advertise for a mother who'd never so much as sent her a Christmas card? 'Zav, let's change the subject. Did Danny *really* not know that I don't get royalties?'

'It wouldn't surprise me. We know him as good-old-cosy Dan. In reality he's turned into the head of a huge corporation. No, I don't think it had occurred to him.' Zav pulled out a leather pouch. 'Anyway, he's certainly out to make amends. He's talking to a publisher this week.' He began to crumble dried green marijuana leaves onto a single cigarette paper decorated with a design of Egyptian pyramids. 'Where *are* those old negatives? Are they still at Saracen Street?'

'No, they're with everything else – bobbing on the high seas. The shippers came and packed up the lot in the middle of December. They said it would take the boxes six weeks to get here.'

420

Zav finished rolling the joint one-handed, licked the gummed edge and sealed it down. 'Did you insure?'

'Minimally. We've not really got anything that's all that valuable.'

'You thought you hadn't. You're going to make a mint out of that book.' Zav leaned across and picked up the *Daily Cal*. 'So he's back,' he said.

It was the second time she'd heard that today. 'Who? Who's back?'

'Owsley. Augustus Owsley Stanley the third. But everybody calls him Bear. Bear, the drug manufacturer extraordinaire.' Zav lit the joint, inhaled, and then let out a cloud of blue smoke. 'The stuff he makes is nothing like this. His is strictly chemical. He won't have come back for nothing. By this time next week Bear will have half this town flying beyond the stars.'

421

12

Days in Berkeley turned into weeks, which began to drift into months. And all the while the coloured tablets sat on a saucer in the refrigerator. Blue ones and green ones and a couple of red ones – each decorated with a cartoon face. There they sat, staring up at her, every time she opened the door to take out the milk.

'It's not a drug you do on your own,' was what Gabriel had said when he first brought them home.

'Well it's not one you're going to do with me.'

'But would you want me to do something as intimate as that with somebody else?' The saucer could have held communion wafers; Gabriel's attitude towards LSD was sacramental. 'Would you want me to go on the most important journey of my life with anybody but you?'

If they had this conversation once, they had it twenty times. She felt as though she was living with a blackmailer and a time bomb.

Her own supply of National Health contraceptive pills ran out, and Miriam recommended a gynaecologist on Shattuck Avenue. The woman doctor's office was lined with framed photographs of babies; hundreds and hundreds of them. Even the memory of these pictures made Rosie feel guilty about getting the prescription dispensed. Nevertheless she began to walk towards Telegraph Avenue, where she had already spotted a pharmacy.

An even higher concentration of street kids than usual seemed to be gathered on a set of concrete steps which led down into a semi-basement – where secretive-looking venetian blinds covered the windows. 'She's okay, she's just coming down.' 'Maybe we should get glucose?' 'No, just keep telling her you love her.' The figure at the centre of all this attention was propped up at the bottom of the steps, against a flaking wall. It was Melinda Gruber.

Because they'd arrived in Berkeley at the same time, and because she'd lied to the girl's mother, Rosie felt she couldn't just pass this scene by without seeing whether she could help. 'Is she okay?' she asked hesitantly.

The boy with his arms round Melinda had ratty hair and a fringed suede jacket. One glance at Rosie's own outfit (a short dress in cream Indian cheesecloth) had obviously convinced him that she was on the right side because he said, 'She's been on a heavy trip, man. We're just waiting for the Free Clinic to open.'

'Will they be able to give her something?'

'Ain't for her.' His long-lashed eyes were an amazing shade of green. 'Two of us guys have got a nasty discharge. There's supposed to be a lot of gonorrhoea around. We're waiting to get checked out.'

Though Melinda's eyes looked oddly glazed the smile she gave Rosie was beatific. 'Hi,' she breathed. 'God, it's beautiful. It's so incredibly beautiful.'

'She's never tripped before,' explained the boy. His teeth were surprisingly chipped for California.

Melinda was still speaking dreamily to Rosie: 'You're not really *in* this thing, 'You ought to come inside, to where I am. It is *so* beautiful.' She sounded very Southern as she repeated the word: '*Bayootiful*!'

It didn't look beautiful to Rosie. A life sitting on concrete looked downright squalid – all discarded styrofoam cups and half-eaten slices of pizza. But she remained riveted to the spot by the thought that Melinda had perceived that she wasn't 'in' it. In this stoned state, had the child actually been able to see her pane of glass? Whilst she couldn't ask Melinda that, she wondered whether it would be patronising to offer her a bit of money?

The fringe-jacket boy solved the problem: 'Got any spare change?'

Two dollars lighter, Rosie walked up to the corner and turned onto Telegraph Avenue. If she'd just plonked somebody down here, somebody from Irlams o'th' Height, what would they have made of the 'head' shops? *We Do Not Sell Drugs* said the sign on one window. No, but the head shop sold everything that went with them: cigarette papers in a dozen different colourful designs, and wooden pipes, and stone ones, and an Arab hookah with four tubes leading from the hubble-bubble part. And right out on open display, the shop even had special containers for drug smuggling – Coca-Cola cans with false bottoms, and fake aerosols with hidden compartments. The classical music blaring from the incense-laden interior was from the ballet *Scheherazade*.

Dogs danced round your heels on Telegraph Avenue; but these were hippie dogs with their own street fashions – collars with bells on them and grubby spotted neckerchiefs. If a dog fight broke out, word would spread like sheet lightning so that the owners were speedily alerted. The new kingdom had almost come and animals were beginning to be accorded extra respect.

The many bookshops bore witness to the fact that the real work of the university was still going on. Gabriel's rare first edition had vanished from the glass case in the middle of Karmarama's window; but they had a whole pile of copies of *Confessions of an English Opium Eater* – in paperback. With startling clarity Rosie suddenly realised that Gabriel did not collect rare bindings; he collected ideas. He probably knew the words of that book by heart. And if he didn't, he had never promised her that he wouldn't buy another copy.

At the pharmacy she was made to wait. Why? It wasn't as though they were making the birth pills in the back. This caused her to think about Mr Molyneux. And thoughts of him reminded her that the boxes from England – including the one that contained all her negatives – had yet to turn up. In her mind's eye she began to review those early pictures of Zav.

Zav. Oh dear. He had taken to just arriving. And, somehow, he was managing to turn Rosie into a conspirator – on two levels. Zav's argument with Danny Cahn escalated to a point where even the magazine *Rolling Stone* had published a piece about it. As his last album went gold and began to head for platinum, the singer himself was holed up on his farm – refusing to tour, or give interviews, or do anything to promote a career that he was coming to despise.

'You're the only one I can talk to,' he would say to Rosie on his frequent forays into Berkeley. 'You're the only one who remembers the real me.' And then he would add, 'I'd better get off before Gabriel gets back.'

The first time that happened she should just have said 'why?' But she didn't. She was scared of what she might unleash. It would have taken an East Bay therapist to describe what Zav could do to the atmosphere in that apartment: he filled it with unresolved psychosexual tension. This supremely confident man had only to get within two feet of Rosie and he started stammering and blushing and knocking things over. He was as much in love with her as ever.

If Gabriel heard that the singer had been seen out and about in Berkeley he would head straight for home. By the time he got there Zav was always gone. And then the questioning would start. 'You can't blame me for getting suspicious. It wouldn't be very flattering if I didn't. After he's sneaked in here you can practically smell the excess testosterone!'

'There's nothing in it,' protested Rosie. 'There never has been.'

'No, but he'd like there to be. I thought I was going to like him but he's too keen on sneaking in by the back door. One wrong move, that's all he's got to make. Just one . . .'

'Gabriel, I grew up with him.'

'Which means that the whole thing's got very deep roots.'

'They made me an honorary Hankey. And that meant a lot to me. They were there for me when I needed them!' All of her lonely childhood was in these defences. 'Zav's in a mess. I can't just tell him to get lost.'

'You swear he never tries anything?'

'I swear it.' There was only one way to end these scenes and it wasn't always in the bedroom. She must have proved her love for Gabriel on every flat surface in that anonymous apartment. Mrs Smith, the black maid, once let herself in with her own key and narrowly missed having to step over them – on the hall carpet.

Mrs Smith did not wear a cap and apron. The word

425

'maid' was just American for charlady. She was huge, and heavily corseted – under a white nylon coat-dress. Mrs Smith was also slightly distant, with an overdeveloped sense of the fitness of things. This meant that she disapproved of Rosie doing so much as a hand's turn.

'Couldn't I just slip out for oven cleaner for you?'

'The kind I like comes from a special shop. You wouldn't be safe there. Them boys is crazy.'

It was Miriam who supplied the explanation. 'She must go to the Black Panthers' supermarket. They opened it to raise funds. Whites aren't welcome.'

'I hardly ever see any black people on campus.'

'They're all across in Oakland. Or down on the flatlands –in the ghetto. You can't expect her to be a smiling black mammy. They've come a long way since *Gone With the Wind*. Black people are in the middle of a revolution of their own. Listen, I got this in the mail and I'm a bit nervous about showing you. I wrote to that association of GI brides. Here.'

The letter was on two sheets of cheap pink paper, with nosegays of flowers printed in the top left-hand corner. The handwriting was the same English copperplate that Rosie's had once been, before the art school changed it. The words managed to look as though they had been stabbed onto the paper.

Dear Miss Million,
I am in receipt of your letter of this week and I don't quite know where to begin. Far be it from me to call anybody but Connie Pollitt is her own worst enemy. She has run out of people to borrow from and moved on. We too would like an address for her. One of our ladies would also like her husband back.

The sender had obviously had second thoughts about the next paragraph because she had crossed out a whole sentence and begun again with:

Trying to help you is a bit complicated. Connie was Mrs Pollitt when she came to the States and she has also been married to a Mr Goldoni but not for long. He was the one who died on her. If she can be believed. This is a woman who once tried telling a plumber that her real name was 'Lady Tattersall'. In fact she puts on names like other women pull on stockings. It's a sad case but that child of hers must have been a heavy cross for her to bear.

'I hope she's not talking about me,' said Rosie, indignantly. 'No, it's got to be your brother. Read on.'

The pair of them often spoke of trying their luck in San Francisco. Connie can be very charming in mixed company but she can no longer hold her drink. The language is shocking! There have been times when she has made me ashamed of coming from Manchester.

If you find her, please tell her she can keep the mauve trouser suit. Who knows, a daughter might be just the thing to straighten the woman out. Enough men have certainly tried and failed.

Yours faithfully
Brenda Mellon (Mrs)

Rosie attempted a laugh but it emerged as a feeble thing. 'I'm just trying to imagine Connie's bottom in a mauve trouser suit. She must be a sight for sore eyes!'

'Maybe we should just drop the whole idea.' Miriam sounded both embarrassed and guilty.

'And maybe we shouldn't. Look at this bit about Christopher. It makes him sound as though he's in a wheelchair. I just can't drop it, Miriam, not now.'

Miriam looked approving. 'I'm glad you're the one who said it. Let's do what Zav said. Let's advertise.'

'I can't see her coming running. She'd probably think we were debt collectors.'

'There *is* one other way.' For once the normally enthusiastic Miriam seemed filled with hesitancy. 'It's a bit spooky,' she said, 'but it's worth a try. We could go and consult Viva.'

*

A light breeze was whirling the windmills in Miriam's flowerbed. Seen from the top of Viva's steps, Normandy Village looked quite different. It was as though the spring sunlight was determined to highlight everything that was gimcrack and shabby, as though it wanted to tell you that the antiquity was only sprayed on.

Miriam lifted the iron knocker on the door of the tower and rapped hard. 'She's just a little bit deaf,' she explained. 'You'll find she enunciates all her words very carefully. I always feel as though she's trying to hypnotise me into doing the same thing.' Miriam banged again.

'Go away, Mr Lanki,' called a voice from inside. 'And please be good enough to stop telephoning. You are not welcome on your own.'

'Viva? It's me. Am I welcome?'

The door swung open. Viva was in a plain black dress today, but the many piled-up plaits were still reminiscent of Medusa. 'Dear child, I owe you an onion.' This was said in tones of deepest self-reproach. As she beckoned the two girls across the threshold, Rosie reflected that this was just the way that Hansel and Gretel had ended up inside the oven.

Viva's living room was enormous, with very high ceilings and a mysterious little minstrels' gallery – reminiscent of Teapot Hall. But that wasn't the only thing out of Rosie's childhood. The room was whitewashed and in one alcove, above a pretty Regency console table, hung a framed Victorian print.

'The Piper of Dreams!' she exclaimed with joy. 'I haven't seen him in years.'

Viva lit a joss-stick. 'So that's his name! There was no title on the back. It just says "Medici Society, London, England", I bought him in a garage sale.'

'If I'm ever dying,' said Miriam to Rosie, 'just murmur the words "garage sale" to me. I'll be back on my feet in seconds.'

Viva carried the smoking joss-stick across the room and placed it in a small brass holder, in front of an enormous gilded Buddha. 'This end of the room represents Light,' she said impressively. On either side of the golden figure were paintings of Jesus Christ and the Virgin Mary. The elaborate wall lamps were in the shape of carved and gilded angels, holding torches.

'But Light would make no sense without Darkness.' Viva was pointing towards the opposite wall where similar electrified wall brackets were in the shape of figures that were half man and half goat. In between them hung two sinister-looking framed photographs of men with burning eyes. 'My old friend Crowley and MacGregor Mathers,' explained the woman in the dress that was as black as that wall. 'They once did battle on the astral plane.'

Miriam tried to return things to sociable with, 'And this is my friend Rosie Tattersall. She's English.'

'I know. And she has Gemini written all over her. If you are English, dear child, you may be interested in that photograph.' She was pointing towards an elegant jumble of silver frames, on top of an old Austrian wedding chest. 'No, not that picture; that's Queen Marie of Romania. The smaller signed one, next to it. Know who she is? It's E. Nesbit.'

'The woman who wrote *The Railway Children*?' asked Rosie delightedly.

'She also wrote many other children's books of a much more magical nature. Did you know that she was a member of the Secret Order of the Golden Dawn? I can sense your fear vibration from here. Nothing to be afraid of. She was just another seeker after Truth.'

'Do you still use that pendulum to locate missing objects?' asked Miriam.

'Of course.'

Miriam, who had been motioned into a carved chair, leaned forward. 'Could you find a missing person with it?'

'Motives. I would need to know your motives.'

Miriam unfolded the whole story. By the end of it Viva Rapport was already searching the bookcases, which covered one entire high wall, for maps of California. 'It's a good thing you didn't come last week,' she said in her impressive, elocuting tones. 'Last week, we were still the dark side of the moon.'

'Would that have made a difference?' asked Rosie who was now on a wooden stool of carved snakes. She had just realised that Viva's black dress was made of rayon – it seemed a bit mundane for a high priestess.

'Every difference. The dark side of the moon is no time for occult experiment. Here is a map of the whole bay area. Have you anything on your person that belonged to your mother?'

'Nothing. Sorry.'

'It could have helped.' Viva had turned all of her attention onto Rosie. 'I wonder . . .?' She gazed straight into her eyes. 'Like finds like. That's one of the great natural rules. I've a feeling you could be very psychic yourself. Hand me that canister, Miriam – the one with the eye painted on it. And treat it with respect,' she added in commanding tones. 'You are handling living energy.' Off came the lid and Viva took out several objects in glass and wood and stone, hanging on the ends of pieces of fine waxed string. 'These are beautifully charged.' Viva was fingering one which looked like a tiny, turnip-shaped, wooden spinning top. 'No, a crystal one I think.' It could have been the stopper from a decanter. 'Let's take this and the map over to the refectory table.'

This was another piece of highly polished furniture which had to be worth a fortune. Viva spread out the map of the Bay Area. 'You are going to be the one to do it,' she said to Rosie. 'After all, you are literally *infused* with the question. Take the string by the end and allow the pendulum to drop. Now repeat after me: "I seek my mother. And may all the *good* that is *good* go into this experiment."'

Rosie couldn't help wondering whether Viva ever did experiments concerning all the bad that was bad. Nevertheless, she repeated the words as instructed.

Nothing happened. Not at first. And then it began to feel as though the thread was actually growing out of her own fingers, that her nerve-endings had somehow extended themselves into the vibrating waxed string.

The crystal weight began to swing.

'Not going widdershins,' murmured Viva. 'So far so good. Lift it over San Francisco.'

430

That didn't work. The thing had taken on a life of its own and it seemed determined to swing in a much wider arc. It was actually pulling her hand in the direction of Alcatraz. 'She can't be there. Gabriel said it was shut.' Inexorably, it was taking her further across the bay and bringing her towards those mud flats, where the big sculptures were, on the Berkeley side. The swings slowed down and reduced and reduced and reduced. But still they circled.

'Stay calm, just breathe deeply,' exhorted Viva. 'I'm going to fold the map back. There should be a detailed section of this side of the bay.'

There was. With no hesitation whatsoever, the glass pendant began circling an area south of Dwight Way.

'But that can't be,' said Miriam. 'Nobody white lives there. That's the ghetto.'

'No.' Viva was disagreeing. 'It seems to me to be in that run-down part of the flatlands – just on the edge. Let's get a really detailed street map. One that shows every block.'

'No.' Rosie hadn't known she could sound so adamant. 'I don't like it. And if you don't mind, I want to wash my hands. Can we go to your house?' She found herself turning to Miriam. It felt as though this strange room had sucked out some of her energy and she didn't even want to use Viva's sink. She wanted to leave no part of herself here. Not even dirty water.

'Very definitely psychic,' breathed Viva. 'I would say that Mother is as good as found. Miriam, may we regard this experiment as a fair exchange for that onion?'

Gabriel only needed five hours' sleep. Cream linen curtains being no barrier against sunlight, by seven in the morning the shower was generally running and the bland off-white apartment was filled with the smell of fresh coffee and the sound of his expensive radio tuned to some European station.

'We're listening to the future,' he would say. 'Paris is already nine hours ahead of us.' And Paris was where it was all thrumming. The French student movement had taken to the streets and was threatening to bring down General de

Gaulle's government. The barricades were up in the Latin Quarter and revolutionary songs were ringing round the Arc de Triomphe. The radio station was spilling it all out in a torrent of furious French.

'There's a mass sit-in at the campus at Nanterre,' translated Gabriel. 'Daniel Cohn-Bendit's in the thick of that one.'

'Danny?' Rosie remembered him as an attractive excitable Jewish boy who had climbed through a window for Miriam when she accidentally locked herself out. 'When Danny was in Berkeley he was always using Miriam's phone.'

'Yes, and you're always round there, too.' Gabriel looked serious. 'What's more, Zav brought you onto the stage at that peace concert. The pigs are bound to have noticed. They're watching all of us, all the time.' This was an idea he seemed to relish. 'When does your visa run out?' Gabriel began twiddling the knob on the radio. 'I'm trying to get London.'

'They gave me six months. I got here on January the fourteenth.'

Heard in California, the BBC newsreader's voice sounded like Peter Sellers giving an overly-British character performance: 'The Home Secretary is expected to make a statement in the House of Commons, this evening, about the situation at the Hornsey School of Art where protesting students are continuing to stage a sit-in . . .' The transmission was obliterated by crackling noises and the sound of long-distance static.

'Probably the pigs, blocking the airwaves,' said Gabriel. Everyone in Berkeley was beginning to get very paranoid. In fact, that particular May, 'paranoid' was the word of the month.

Rosie poured herself some coffee. She did not wake up as easily as Gabriel. 'When I was at the Poly, Hornsey was always considered very avant-garde,' she yawned. 'I don't even know how you get there. It's somewhere at the end of a bus route. Milk? Where's the milk?'

'Still in the icebox. If the revolution's already got to somewhere at the end of a bus route, things in London must be really gathering pace. Listen, your visa: we'll drive over to Canada for a day, dressed very straight. You can come back into the States again and get your passport stamped as a tourist. People are doing it all the time.'

'Dressed straight? Your hair's a revolution in itself!' Rosie had finally moved across to get her milk. The gaudy little tablets were still on their saucer in the refrigerator. 'Gabriel? Can we chuck these out?'

'Yes.'

A miracle: and full awake she would never have dared to ask him.

Gabriel took hold of the china saucer. 'I'm not sure how stable this chemical is. I've ordered some more.'

'Why?' His last statement had brought her to full consciousness. And it was just too early for her to be equipped to cope.

Gabriel was firing on all cylinders. 'Why? Because now's the time to do it. You've only to listen to that radio. Look, Rose, if you don't want to drop acid, that's fine with me. In fact I've already made other arrangements.'

It all sounded remarkably cut and dried. All she said was, 'Oh.'

'You have to be very careful where you do it. And you have to choose your company.' Gabriel had his university lecturer voice on. He was very much Professor Bonarto – they handed out these titles much more freely in America. 'There are two schools of thought on the subject of LSD. Timothy Leary takes the attitude I just outlined. The Merry Pranksters are the ones who think you should do it in the middle of the mainstream of life.'

If she was going to stop him doing it, she would have to get her head together and take some interest. 'Who are the Merry Pranksters?'

'Remember that bus that nearly knocked you over on the day you arrived? The one covered in rainbows. That was the Pranksters.'

'And you're off to join them?' The remnants of sleep in her brain were like unwanted wisps of cotton wool.

'No. I've arranged to do it with a friend of mine.' He

433

wasn't often pompous, but when he was he made a meal of it. 'We'll do it in an appropriate setting, with the right objects in the room, the right music. Nothing must be discordant. Nothing must jar.'

'That's funny, I've seen people take it on benches, at bus stops, on Shattuck Avenue.'

Gabriel refused to be riled. 'That is the other method of thinking.'

But Rosie *was* riled. She was furious. 'One day I'll make a tape recording of you droning on like this. I'm not one of your students. And just who is this friend of yours?'

'She's a mature person with metaphysical interests. Actually, Viva is a neighbour of Miriam's.'

'Viva! I might have known it. So that's where Miriam saw you before. Well, you're not one of her Friday-night boys. Did you know she counts in the sacred seven every Friday night?'

He remained grave. 'Viva experiments in many fields. I've only ever been to her for therapy.'

Rosie's next question was a fierce one. 'And do you keep your clothes on?'

Gabriel sounded almost human again as he admitted, 'I just loosen anything that's tight. And she always insists I go to the bathroom first.'

'What the hell kind of therapy is this?' roared Rosie

'I'm not about to have a row with you. I've got a lecture to prepare. I think I'll go down and do it at the department.'

'Oh no you don't. You don't slide off as easily as that. That woman is twice as old as time; she exerts a weird fascination over young men . . .'

'She has always been a great seeker of knowledge.'

'Yes, and she's looked in some funny places. Did you know she was once great mates with Aleister Crowley? Nice to think you're getting the Great Beast's leavings! I thought you were supposed to be a Catholic?'

'There can be no light without darkness,' said Gabriel.

'Yes, and it's a bloody good idea to cling onto the light. My God, she *has* got you under her spell. And you're proposing to drop acid with this withered antique?'

434

'On Wednesday night.' He had the grace to look embarrassed as he added, 'We're both particularly well aspected by Venus on that night. It's supposed to be astrologically propitious.'

'If you screw her, that's it. You won't see my heels for dust.'

'I should be obliged if you would stop thinking with your clitoris,' said Gabriel. With this he picked up a file, headed for the front door and walked out.

She was ready to rip down the curtains. Oh he was a Balliol man all right! 'Effortless Superiority', that was their motto. Rosie began to roar into the empty air: 'Stupid, pompous, self-satisfied . . .' Even as she was yelling, her eyes took in the two dozen white roses he had brought home yesterday from the florists on University Avenue. And the funny knitted rabbit that she'd fallen in love with, on Telegraph, when she first arrived. Gabriel had made some excuse and dived back and bought it for her. He wasn't all bad. The childlike desire to please her was all that was good. And she wouldn't have wanted a man who did exactly as he was told. There could be no light without darkness. 'Christ! it's even getting to me.' She actually said this out loud. And just as somebody was knocking at the door!

Two hippies with ginger beards and winking spectacles were standing outside on the landing. Gabriel must have slammed right past them. In Berkeley even the postmen wore hair to their shoulders and Jesus sandals. But these men were delivering something altogether more solid than the mail. Five wooden boxes. The same ones she had last seen in Tiddy Street, in London. Only there'd been six of them then.

Panic rose. 'Is that all you've got for us?'

One of the men consulted a form attached to a clipboard: 'Five. Five was all that arrived at the depot.'

'But there should be one more. A much smaller one.' A much more valuable one.

The man with the clipboard assumed a knowing expression. 'Did it have anything *subversive* in it?' This was another big Berkeley word.

'No. Just negatives and prints and some old cameras.'
And every single thing I need for Zav's book, she thought
wretchedly.

'Could have got stopped at customs. You might be due for
a visit from the pigs. Sign here.'

*The Berkeley Co-op Is Based on the Principles of the Original
Co-operative Society – Formed in Rochdale, Lancashire,
England, in 1844.* The sign hung above the row of cash
registers at the check-out.

Miriam was already pushing her own trolley into the
sunlight. Rosie, coming up behind her, ceased trundling for
a moment and lifted up a pack of lamb chops. 'They're a bit
fatty,' she said, dubiously.

Miriam quashed this with: 'The Co-op here is so right on
that they guarantee to put the worst side on top. That way,
when you get home, you get a nice surprise. Did you ever
look at meat when you were on LSD?' she asked, appalled at
the very memory. 'I keep forgetting, you've never done it.
On acid, one glance at raw meat is enough to show you every
last gasp of the dying animal. Rosemarie, are you okay?'

'Acid' was the word she hadn't needed. Though the
image of breathing raw meat had not helped either.

'Oh God,' said Miriam, only half comprehending.
'I should have kept my mouth shut. It turned me vegetarian for
months but I gradually slid back. It's a lovely day. Let's sit
down on the benches.' These faced the Co-op car park.
Even though it was late in May, a man dressed as Father
Christmas was shaking a tin collecting box for the Free
Clinic. 'And you look beautiful in that.' Miriam was nodding
towards Rosie's dress which was in blue Indian gauze,
spattered with penny-sized mirrored sequins. 'Beautiful but
preoccupied.' Miriam spread the skirts of her own kaftan.
Today's was yellow, and her hair was newly hennaed to the
same shade as Father Christmas's unlikely red beard.

'I've got a lot on my mind.' It had stopped being
Wednesday and become Vivaday. Vivanight too!

'You're still defuzzing those?' Miriam was pointing
towards Rosie's long suntanned legs.

'*And* I'm still shaving under my arms.'

'I do that too,' admitted Miriam, guiltily. Such practices were considered distinctly 'lipstick and high heels'.

Rosie let out a deep sigh.

'Please don't do that,' said Miriam. 'I'm only talking so much to try and cheer you up. Lost boxes can be found. If necessary, I will take on the government – single-handed.'

'It's not just the box.'

'Then what is it? What's on your mind?'

'I'm trying to imagine what Viva looks like with no clothes on.'

'You've got to be joking.'

'As a matter of fact, I was never more serious in my life. Can we leave it at that?' To tell more might be disloyal to Gabriel; Rosie had spent so much of her life on other people's territory, desperately trying not to tread on their toes, that she had lost sight of the fact that she had rights of her own. 'What are you doing tonight? I think I'm going to be in dire need of company.'

'Where will Gabriel be?'

'Out.' The word sounded as though it belonged to an adolescent who was just about to slam through the front door. Rosie couldn't bring herself to tell Miriam that he would be up a stone staircase, flying to the moon – with an antique hell-hag. 'And I can't come to you. You'd have to come to me.'

'Count it as done.'

The whole story would have risen to the surface, there and then, had Miriam not been spotted by a tall sallow girl who was now bearing down on them. 'Oh God,' breathed Miriam, 'Patti Spinoza. A human being with the mind of a committee!' The girl had hair like heather and it was failing to surrender to a white peace headband. Miriam's voice went even lower. 'Bit of yours and a bit of mine: Jewish *and* a Quaker. Hello, Patti.' Her tones rose up and became determinedly bright. 'How long have you been back? Patti's been doing a postgraduate year at the London School of Economics,' she explained to Rosie.

'I felt terrible about coming back. Terrible.' The girl's

voice was as intense as her looks. She had stabby eyes. 'We'd been occupying the building for weeks.'

'This is my friend Rosemarie. She was at Regent Street Poly.'

'One could wish they were more politically active,' was the burning reaction.

Rosie was left with the definite feeling that whatever she said would prove to be too diluted for Patti. 'We were listening to it all on the BBC this morning,' she ventured.

'The BBC? Don't give me the BBC! Five thousand people can be demonstrating in Grosvenor Square and the BBC call it five hundred. Their newsdesk is manned by Fascists. I though everybody knew that. Did you ever know anybody at the LSE?'

'Only a girl called Bernadette Barrett.'

'*Only?*' cried Patti, who was clutching a portable pinball machine. 'You cannot apply the word *only* to one of the most vivid voices of the whole revolution. It's like saying "*Only* Jerry Rubin."' Even Rosie knew that he was Mr Big, that he was Trotsky in Levis. But she wasn't prepared for the tone of Patti's next question. 'How do you know Bernadette anyway?' It was a cross between accusing and disbelieving.

'We come from the same place. We grew up together.' This was the line she always used to cover her relationship with Zav. But the last thing Rosie wanted to claim was similar intimacy with Bernadette Barrett. 'We lost touch.' She said it quite firmly. She *just* resisted the temptation to throw in a line about police horses with broken legs.

Patti Spinoza was already bristling ahead with: 'What's your name?'

'Rosie Tattersall.'

'I'll write her I met you. Did you know her phone in London is being tapped?'

'I *love* the pinball machine.' Miriam was obviously trying to lighten up the conversation.

'What? Oh this. I got it for two bucks. I just came from a garage sale.'

'A garage sale,' breathed Miriam. 'Patti, you gotta tell me. *Where?*'

The intelligent eyes narrowed. 'Later on this week I'm going to need two hundred envelopes addressing.'

'You got them. It's done. Where's the garage sale?'

Patti turned her attention to Rosie. 'I wouldn't like you to think I approve of the violent streak in Bernadette. That side of her frightens me. But Christ, she burns like a flame . . .'

'The garage sale?' screamed Miriam.

'Keep going right down Cedar until you come to . . .' Patti went into one of those lengthy pieces of American direction – all blocks and intersections – the kind that Rosie always found so puzzling.

'Right down there?' said Miriam dubiously. 'You're so *brave*, Patti. It can get very heavy down there.'

'They may be black but they are our brothers.' She held up two fingers. 'Peace.' She tapped the side of her forehead as though she was putting her next words into a file. 'Rosie Tattersall, I'll remember that. And I'll call you about the envelopes, Miriam.' With this she stomped into the Co-op on a pair of hairy legs that were as politically okay as the works of Chairman Mao.

'But it was a beautiful pinball machine,' said Miriam thoughtfully. 'What the hell! If the neighbourhood looks too tough we can head straight back to Dwight Way.'

'Where are we going?' asked Rosie. She was already following Miriam's example and piling brown paper sacks of shopping into the back of the open car.

'To the ghetto, my dear. You're always saying you don't see black people in Berkeley. You will this morning.'

The houses at the Co-op end of Cedar Street were like Rosie's idea of tea planters' bungalows. Down in the distance, sunlight was sparkling on the waters of the bay. As the ocean got nearer, the size of the houses began to shrink. They were still wooden-framed with front porches, but if things carried on diminishing at this rate the smart little sports car would soon be travelling between rows of timber shanties.

'We are not over-welcome round here,' admitted Miriam. 'And when you look where we've hidden them, you can understand why.'

Rosie remembered Mrs Smith and the Black Panther supermarket and '*Them boys is crazy.*' The recent death of Martin Luther King had caused surprisingly little stir on campus, although youths from Berkeley High had rampaged across the town, smashing windows and threatening to fire their own school building. The Black Panther leader, Eldridge Cleaver, was the man who had restored calm. This young politician had actually tried to run for President on the Peace and Freedom ticket, even though he was under-age. One Panther was reported as saying: 'If Eldridge is elected we will paint the White House black and then burn it down.'

Miriam must also have been pondering on this situation because she said, as they turned into an even more tumble-down street, 'We have to remember that Patti got a real bargain.' One of the houses was startlingly neat with a glass case on legs in the middle of the front garden. This display case contained a huge open Bible. 'Just like they have in every room in the Holiday Inn,' said Miriam, who was slowing down the car. 'It's got to be that house on the other side. The one with all the people in the garden.' She stopped sounding nervous and brightened a little. 'I think I just spotted another white face. Any trouble and I'll tell them I know Eldridge. I do too. I once offered to give his car a push, when he broke down on Spruce. He was *not* unattractive. Rosie, climb out of the car as though you're used to doing this sort of thing.' Apprehension had plainly returned.

It was called a garage sale but there was no garage; just a concrete pathway leading up to a clear plastic car-port attached to a tacky brown-shingled cottage. The goods on sale had been laid out on a garden bench, which had been pulled across the cracked path. Silence fell as curious eyes turned on the girl in the floating yellow and the one in spangled blue.

As the pair passed beneath the skeleton branches of a dead tree, Rosie caught the sound of glass wind-chimes, tinkling from the gable end. And in that same instant the word 'honkeys' arose out of the beginnings of some muffled conversation. Why that word? Why the whispering? Why the stares? These people were hearing the same sounds she was hearing, feeling the same sun on their skin. This dainty White Liberal thought was wiped away by closer sight of the goods on sale. They managed to make Rosie feel ashamed. The items were so *poor*. Empty stone jars and old wooden spoons, and one plastic baby shoe – with the button missing. Whoever would want that?

But Miriam had seen something she did want. Propped against the leg of the bench was a portrait of Elvis Presley. Painted in oils on a black velvet ground, it was framed in strips of multicoloured mirror glass. 'How much?' she asked the old black man who seemed to be in charge. He certainly had a child's tin cash box in one hand.

'Two dollars,' he croaked.

'Now just a minute!' This new voice was threatening and nasty. It belonged to the solitary white woman. Rosie hadn't really liked to stare at her before this. Now she saw a mass of overdyed blue-black hair and a black satin tracksuit, unzipped low enough to reveal an indignantly heaving cleavage. 'I'd already decided to have that picture. Elvis is mine.'

'Hello, Mother,' said Rosie weakly.

Squinting into the sunlight, Connie peered shortsightedly at her daughter. 'Say that again,' she gasped in a voice of total disbelief. But she'd recognised her all right. Rosie could tell that by the way Connie's mouth had fallen open; the false teeth were a new addition. And she could tell by the way that Connie transferred her horrified gaze back to Miriam. She wasn't just playing for time, she was sizing up the strength of Rosie's support.

'Well bugger me!' Connie collapsed onto the bench in the middle of the assorted jumble, and the single baby shoe tumbled to the ground. 'You got a shot of anything, Webster?'

The old man felt in his pocket and produced a flat halfpint bottle of pink wine. As Connie unscrewed the top and raised it to her lips, her daughter read the words on the label: *Sweet Rosie O'Grady – Beware of Imitations*.

Absolutely silently, Connie returned both bottle and top

to their owner. 'Come where nobody can hear us,' she said sternly to Rosie, 'I want a word with you.'

Grabbing her daughter by the wrist, she led her towards the porch of the house where off-white towels hung on a string washing line. The path was uneven and Connie's high-heeled gold mules made an angry clacking noise as they travelled. 'Well thanks a million!' she snapped. Previously she had sounded quite American, though the words 'bugger me' had come over as purest Irlams o'th' Height. Now Connie changed her tones to fake Celia Johnson; the style was a straight pinch from *Brief Encounter*. 'Thanks a million for showing me up in front of the neighbours. It's your choice of company I'm talking about. You do realise what that redheaded woman *is*, don't you? You do know she's a J?'

'What's a jay?'

'She's Jewish. She's a Yid. It would be a different matter if you'd brought her here at night.'

'I don't believe what I'm hearing.'

'You only have to look at the pushy way she tried to snatch my Elvis!'

Was Connie using these accusations to cover her own confusion? Whatever she was doing, Rosie was furious with her. 'You are talking about my *friend*. That girl has done a hundred times more for me than you ever did.'

'What chance did you give me?' Connie had stopped hissing and begun to bellow. 'You chose to stay with your father.' Now she was addressing everybody in the garden. 'She chose to stay where the money was. She chose servants and a huge house and we were left to fend for ourselves like refugees.'

'Not one word of that is true. And you know it.' Rosie was surprised by her own calm. 'You settled for Christopher because he was a boy. How is he?'

For the briefest of moments Connie's eyes flickered – panicked – round the garden. 'We split,' she said nervously. Then gaining courage she boasted: 'We got rid of that cissy-boy way back in Cheyenne.'

'Who's we?'

'My sister and I.' Connie could have been the Queen of England referring to herself and Princess Margaret.

Rosie lowered her own voice. 'You haven't got a sister.'

'You don't know everything, In fact you don't know diddley-crap. If I want to call another lady my sister, she's my sister. I sure don't need permission from you, Miss Rich Bitch.' *Brief Encounter* had given way to *Annie Get Your Gun*. 'Where's my good diamond ring?' The second-hand wafts of Sweet Rosie O'Grady were far from pleasant. 'What are you all staring at?' she yelled at her black neighbours. 'The last thing I gave this ungrateful kid was a diamond as big as a pea. An *heirloom*!' roared Connie, as though the very word would put up her own value.

'You can have it back. I'll bring it,' said Rosie. And that's the last you'll ever see of me, she thought.

More waves of Sweet Rosie O'Grady accompanied: 'I wouldn't take it back if you was to go down on your bended knees. That ring belonged to those limp-dick Tattersalls. You can keep your fucking diamond.'

In an odd way, Rosie found herself admiring this attitude. Even though Connie was proving to be a figure from a nightmare, she still had her own rickety standards. 'Where *is* Christopher?' she asked her mother.

'Dead.'

Rosie ran this idea through her own head; the high-pitched whine came back in answer. 'No he isn't.' She could say this with absolute certainty.

Once again Connie's eyes betrayed panic. Teetering desperately across the path she grabbed hold of the picture of Elvis. 'Put this down to me, Webster,' she said sweetly to the man with the cashbox. I'll pay you in food stamps. For your friend,' she cooed, as she thrust the picture at Rosie.

Rosie thrust it straight back. 'I wouldn't let her accept it. Not after what you just said about Jews.' Even as she was speaking, Rosie remembered how good her mother had been at setting traps.

'You hear that?' roared Connie to the assembled company. 'Our junk ain't good enough for her.' Rounding on Rosie she snarled, 'Why don't you just go back to where you came from?'

443

Rosie was suddenly struck by deep hurt. 'Aren't you even interested in knowing how I got here?' she stammered.

'Not even that much.' Connie snapped her fingers. 'Just get back in that fancy sports car and drive yourselves out of my life.' The big liquid eyes were still beautiful. And as she gazed at her daughter in the spangled Indian dress she sighed, and then she said, 'I'll give you one bit of parting advice. Never wear sequins in daylight. It ain't ladylike.'

Rosie had never had any great dreams invested in finding Connie, but the idea of no mother was better than the reality of this one. A high wind was blowing in from the ocean and night had fallen. Not just dusk, real black night. And Gabriel was with Viva Rapport.

In the spare bedroom of the apartment on Virginia Street, Rosie was unpacking the last of the five boxes. She and Miriam had already stowed the heavy winter clothes into one of the fitted closets. The final packing case was like a small jumble sale in itself. The shippers had wrapped each item in pages of last November's *Evening Standard*. Rosie would never have believed that advertisements for Madame Tussaud's and Swan and Edgar could have far-flung magic – but they did. A pile of picture frames was wrapped – each one separately – in corrugated paper.

Miriam began to unparcel them. 'Gabriel with no clothes on! And whose house is this?' The silver-framed photograph was of Teapot Hall.

'Mine. Well it once was. I'm going to get it back.' The response was as automatic as that of a dog sitting up and begging at the sight of chocolate. 'At least I used to think that way.'

'Don't let anything stop you,' urged Miriam. 'We all need big dreams to keep us ahead.'

'That's the house Connie stormed out of. She was wearing two lots of furs at the same time. Big dreams? I'm having big nightmares at the moment. What have the shippers done with the box with all the negatives in it? I called the customs people and they say they cleared all six.'

'It could have gone to one of the other Berkeleys. Let me

handle it. Anything to make up for encouraging you to find your mother! There's a Berkeley in Alameda County, and they go on happening right down to West Virginia.'

America was so wide. But the universe was wider. And the cosmos was the widest of the lot. That – presumably – was where Gabriel was whirling. 'I'd like to go straight down to Viva's apartment and make one huge scene,' said Rosie, through gritted teeth.

'When they're on acid?' Miriam looked alarmed. 'That really wouldn't be such a good idea.'

The English girl pulled a pair of long green- and white-ringed football socks from the box. Very heavily elasticated, they belonged to Gabriel. 'Guess what? In my Swinging London days I used to wear these with a mini-skirt. They looked like fake woollen boots. Miriam, what did acid *do* for you?'

Miriam dropped back onto her haunches. 'For the first half-hour, nothing. So I sat down at my typewriter and began to tap out a letter. Suddenly, the words came zinging up at me in 3D. It was just like the beginning of a movie. And then everything started to go *WOW*! and *PAM*! and *SMASH*! – like a comic. Colours were amazing. You could actually see them breathing.'

'Sounds like Walt Disney's *Fantasia* to me. So why's Gabriel treating it like a religion?'

Miriam looked up from studying another framed photograph; it was of Trixie. 'Try explaining acid to somebody who's not done it and you end up sounding crazy. It takes so *long*.' She made the word sound like a week and then emphasised the image with, 'I was smoking a cigarette, and in the time it took for a bit of ash to fall off the end and hit the ashtray I lived through seven whole days. Waking, sleeping, every single event. God knows what that stuff does to your brain!' The wind outside was making death-rattle noises in the eucalyptus.

'In those days they used to put the acid on a sugar lump. Just one cube picked me up and took me over great seas to a set of islands. I actually knew what it was to *be* land. And to be water.' Miriam began to laugh. 'I told you you'd think

I was mad.' Now she became thoughtful again. 'When it was beautiful I belonged to everything and everybody; but then it all went wrong. I suddenly understood what desolation was made of. And I was trapped in a grubby web of it, for years. Whole years. I really did live through them. At the end of it all, I looked at the clock and it just seemed impossible to believe that the entire experience had only taken eight hours.'

'Maybe I should try it.'

'I wouldn't wish that desolation on Adolf Hitler,' said Miriam. 'Yes I would. And on all those other war criminals. I'm just trying to decide whether I'd wish it on your mother. She does *not* lack style. Anything else you'd like me to tell you? Now I *do* like this lady.' It was a framed photo of Nora Hankey opening the black-leaded oven door.

'Just fill me in on one thing. What kind of therapy does Viva hand out?' Rosie had yet to tell her friend the complete story.

'Hypnosis. She's very keen on taking people back into their childhoods. And then she regresses them into former lives. I suppose it's okay if you believe in reincarnation. You got anything to eat?'

'Yes, I used those chops to make us a Lancashire hotpot.' She nodded towards the picture in Rosie's hand. 'It's Zav's mother's recipe.'

So tripping on acid took eight hours, did it? Rosie carried the football socks over to Gabriel's chest of drawers. The top one refused to slide open. She pulled harder on the handle and the drawer came out so quickly that she was left with it dangling from her hand. The contents had spewed all over the bedroom floor: socks, more socks, a brand-new jock strap and an equally new paperback edition of *Confessions of an English Opium Eater*.

As the wind died down, a grey dawn broke through the open curtains and Rosie decided to get out of bed. This solitary, anxious, fitful dozing was proving to be more exhausting than no sleep at all.

Miriam had returned to Normandy Village at midnight,

446

and telephoned to say that candlelight was still flickering behind the windows of Viva's tower. What time was it now? Rosie's watch showed five o'clock. How much longer was he going to take to come home?

Coffee? No. There was still a bitter taste in her mouth from the last lot. Rosie padded into the bathroom to clean her teeth, and then she climbed into a pair of Levis and pulled on a white tee shirt. Fresh air, that's what she needed. But she didn't want to leave the building in case he returned. Still, there was nothing to stop her going up onto the flat roof of Casino Point – that was the official name of their soulless apartment block.

To reach the sun deck she had to climb a set of ill-lit concrete steps and push open a fire door. The morning light was grey and the distant waters of the ocean were the colour of pewter. There were no walls to the edge of the roof. It would be easy to just walk off it – into space. The idea gave Rosie a sickly swimming sensation which was located somewhere between her legs. Distant San Francisco was so hidden in mist that it was hard to believe that it existed. But Berkeley was as sharply defined as a steel engraving. Or as a list of problems written with a hard pencil: Normandy Village, the ghetto, and faraway quaysides where a missing packing case might or might not be located.

Just to test her own courage, Rosie moved nearer to the edge of the roof. The surface beneath her bare feet was covered in fine shale which was damp with the early-morning dew. It really would be fatally easy to slip. Peering down into Virginia Street she noticed a man watching the building.

He looked *wrong*. His dark hair had a neatly shaped outline and he was wearing a lightweight business suit. In Berkeley the conventional was the unconventional. A sleek black car began cruising up Virginia Street. When it reached the man it stopped, and just such another besuited figure got out. The pair of them appeared to be conferring on the pavement; the driver started pointing down the street.

That's when Rosie noticed Gabriel. He was strolling uphill. When she glanced back at the car, both men had climbed into it and the vehicle was already moving away.

447

Heading for the wooden shedlike building which covered the top of the stairs, Rosie lost all fear of the slippery gravel. If she fell now she would fall pointing inwards. He was back in one piece; that was all that mattered. Leaving a trail of damp footprints on the concrete steps, she reached their own landing just as Gabriel got out of the lift.

'You're up early,' he said politely. His chin was dark with early-morning stubble.

Had Viva felt that stubble against her face, against her body? 'You're home late.'

His eyes were shining. 'It was amazing. Absolutely amazing.'

Rosie's next words were out before she'd even considered what she was saying: 'Did you sleep with her?'

'No,' he smiled, 'we did things that were much more fantastic than that.'

'What things?'

He shook his head. 'It would be like trying to describe colours to somebody who was born blind. God, I'm tired.' They were through the door and he was already heading for the bedroom. 'I could sleep for a week.'

'You can't just come in and fling yourself down and crash out.'

'Watch me!' Lying on the bed he was every bit as relaxed as a cat. 'I'll tell you one thing, jealousy is ridiculous. So is pride. I am you and you are me. We're part of a whole. We're all in this together.'

'Not that old song!' She hadn't meant to sound scornful. 'It's just that I'm getting a bit sick of that well-worn sentiment.'

'Nevertheless Owsley's acid proved it to be entirely accurate. Love you, Rose.' He was asleep with the speed of a trouble-free child.

Well I don't love you, she thought. But she did. Why else would she have crept close and snuggled up to him? And who but a woman in love would have checked that he was really sleeping before she allowed herself to sniff his skin? She couldn't smell Viva's perfume but there was a distinct whiff of joss-sticks. '*We did things that were much more*

448

fantastic than that.' What things? She ceased snuggling and rolled away from him. '*I am you and you are me* . . .' It was all so puzzling.

And things remained puzzling. When Gabriel finally awoke, early in the evening, he refused to shave. 'A man's beard is part of the life force,' he said. 'I didn't realise that before. Why should I try to stem it?'

Rosie was trying to put life back onto a practical footing. 'You do realise that you failed to give a lecture? They rang up from the department. I covered for you, I said you'd eaten something.'

'Food of the gods, that's what I've eaten.'

'You sound like that middle-aged bore, Timothy Leary.'

'But he's *right*. "Turn on, tune in, and drop out." I can't wait for us to drop acid together, Rose. And saying that is the ultimate compliment.' Once again his face was shining with enthusiasm.

'If it's so big a deal, why did you choose to do it with somebody else?'

'Because you refused me.'

If there was a reply to this, Rosie didn't know it. And she was in the wrong town to be able to view the matter dispassionately. Months ago, she had come to realise that Berkeley had its own attitudes, its own standards, and that a lot of these were drug-influenced. Even Miriam, forever meaning to write her thesis as she waited for the next great love to come along, had been influenced by the feeling on the air. Not that Miriam was beyond self-criticism: 'We're all of us doing it with a safety net; nearly everybody here. Who do you know who couldn't call home for the return half of the ticket?'

'Me. I couldn't do that. I'm stuck here. And I seem to be the only person on the West Coast who's got a horror of drugs.'

'More *say* they do them than really do.'

By this time Gabriel was having his acid delivered to the front door. Hell's Angels, acting as couriers, would arrive with a small polystyrene container in one black-gloved hand, whilst the other one was held out for cash.

449

Now that he had embraced the counter-culture at its most sacramental level, Gabriel finally got round to making a whole lot of friends. Some of them were academics, others were his own students: and they weren't just 'all boys together'. You could tell that by the drawings. Gabriel was drawing again in a big way.

Like a husband who doesn't sleep with his mistress in the marriage bed, Gabriel had taken to meeting these friends away from Casino Point. Rosie just tried to be glad that Viva Rapport was not one of their number. Gabriel seemed to be forever heading off for the botanical gardens – this was a favourite place for tripping. Another was a barren hillside called El Diabolo.

Rosie could always tell when he'd been on acid because his voice would change to an overly-cool mumble. And he would start to draw. These huge drawings far outshone anything he had ever done on a Manchester table top, or on the sides of his automobile. You couldn't call them porno-graphic, they were too lyrical for that. But one naked figure ran into the next which flowed on into a third who was caressing a fourth which was conjoined with a fifth. It was 'I am you and you are me' taken to the tenth degree.

'Being faithful is vanity,' he said. 'And vanity is madness.'

'So are you unfaithful?'

'No. But only because it would make you unhappy. If you'd just turn on, you'd see that we should be sleeping with the whole world. To think I used to be jealous of Zav!' The soft lead pencil continued to glide across the page. No, these pictures were not of lust, they were of love and they were strangely beautiful. But Rosie had not followed one man all the way to California to share him with the whole world.

If anything reassured her, it was one line he kept on repeating, like a mantra. She knew that they were the words of Juliana of Norwich, the English mystic. *'And all shall be well, and all shall be well, and all manner of thing shall be well.'* These fourteenth-century words sometimes seemed to be the only thing that was holding their relationship together.

Somebody was trailing Rosie. It felt just like that song which

Arthur Askey, the comedian, had sung on the radio in her childhood – 'Don't Look Now But I Think You're Being Followed'. Rosie allowed herself a quick glance over her shoulder and thought she caught sight of one of the men she had seen from the roof. Yes, it *was* him and now he was pretending to look in the window of Barry Drake's restaurant. And, come to think of it, she had also glimpsed him earlier – in the little post office on the other side of campus. She hadn't really registered him then because he was camouflaged in standard blue denim. As she returned her attention to picking her way through the crowds on Telegraph, a totally unexpected but much more familiar figure was making his way towards her. It was Bob Fellowes, their London landlord.

'My dear Rosie,' he beamed with delight, 'you look so much *cleaner* than the rest.'

Yet it was he who was drawing the curious glances. Dressed for California in a green Aertex shirt and baggy khaki shorts, he looked like a fugitive from a pre-war rubber plantation. Such naked knobbly knees!

Nevertheless, Fellowes was the one who thought everybody else was odd. 'Whatever do they *see* in one another?' he asked. This was exactly the same thing that Gabriel's mother had said when she fled from Grosvenor Square, which only went to prove that the generation gap was more than a theory.

Rosie attempted to bridge it with, 'How's your Dalmatian?'

'In kennels. I'm only here for a week. Two lectures and they flew me over first class! The idea made me feel quite the prima donna. But my goodness me, those customs and immigration people soon cut one down to size. How long are you allowed to stay, Rosie?'

Her visa was due to expire the following week. 'Until June the fourteenth. But I've been told about a dodgy way of getting it extended. You drive into Canada for the day.'

Bob Fellowes made some tut-tutting noises. 'And you used to be such an upright little creature. I hear worse things about Gabriel. I hear he's gone absolutely native. More drugs than Coleridge and De Quincey put together. He's causing quite a stir in the philosophy department. Did you know that he invited the Hare Krishna monks into one of his lectures?' Fellowes had always been a dripping tap of gossip. 'Oh yes, he enjoined them to chant his students into ecstasies. And I expect you know that he also delivered a philosophical lecture on the subject of char-broiled hamburgers?' Fellowes bent down to stroke a sniffing bulldog which had a gold ring through one ear. 'What a remarkably insanitary place this is.'

Even though the gutter was filled with rubbish, Rosie was startled to find herself angered by the outsider's comment. 'There might be a lot that's wrong with Berkeley,' she said, 'but there's also a great deal that's right. People *care* about one another here. They look after one another.'

'Gabriel's not got security of tenure.' The Englishman seemed to be enjoying being severe. 'He's going the right way to get himself the sack.' Now the real reason for all this niggling came out: 'He's stopped taking me seriously. It's like talking to a brick wall. I can't seem to get through to him.'

'Neither can I. Do watch out for your poor white legs in this sunshine. We're all very worried about the hole in the ozone layer.' Berkeley was preoccupied with ecology and pollution a whole decade ahead of the rest of the world. 'That dreadful ultra-violet could turn your legs bright red.' How *dare* he attack Berkeley? 'It could even frizzle those little ginger hairs.'

'You've changed, Rosemary.' He said it sadly.

Echoing one of Fellowes' own words, the inevitable Telegraph cry of 'Spare change, got any spare change?' rose up on the air.

'They really need a Welfare State,' sighed the English academic.

'Perhaps we're trying to build one of our own,' she replied. 'Good morning.' Rosie resumed her downhill stroll. '*Perhaps we're trying to build one of our own.*' She had never realised that she felt as much a part of the place as all that. But Berkeley had magic, it wove you into itself; under other circumstances she knew she could have been very happy here.

'Grass?' A dope dealer, one of the familiar Mexican brothers, had emerged from the doorway of a candle shop. 'Wanna score some grass?'

'No thanks.'

'You get to try before you buy. Wanna smoke a loose joint?'

'No.' And she didn't want to get busted by the pigs for just talking to him, either.

'It's for free,' the boy persisted. 'Still not wanna try?'

A new voice said, 'You need any help?' She had quite forgotten the man who had been following her. If he *was* a policeman he certainly had kind eyes. They were brown, with comically curly eyelashes. Nice muscular body too. Whatever was she thinking of! She only hoped that none of it was written on her face. 'I'm fine, thank you.'

'Just making sure you're okay.'

He fancies me, she thought. But that's not what this is about. Before she could ask the man a direct question, he nodded politely and vanished into the surging throng of blue denim. Perhaps he was somebody who was just being kind; except why was he suddenly dressed as a different person from the one she'd seen spying on Gabriel? Still, he'd managed to get rid of the dope dealer. If the whole town wasn't kept afloat on drugs the place would have been idyllic. Somebody seemed to agree with her; on the side of the Bank of America they had sprayed the words *Smack Kills*. Poor Mongoose! Thoughts of him took her mind to Irlams o'th' Height and to the real reason for her morning outing. She was trying to find a wedding present for Hazel Hankey. Rosie's eyes raked the shops and the stalls. An embroidered Indian wall-hanging? An illustrated edition of the *Kamasutra*? Or what about one of those decorative fragments of stained glass? These were no longer mysterious: nowadays she knew that people held them up against the light and gazed into their luminous depths – as an aid to tripping.

No, all of this was too counter-cultural for the future Mrs

Proctor-Jones. That visa had to be renewed: she would buy Hazel's wedding present in Canada.

'Gabriel, we could drive there and back in four days. It's supposed to be a beautiful trip. You go right through the redwoods.' They were talking in the empty laundry room, in the basement of Casino Point.

'When does it expire?' Gabriel stripped off his jeans and shoved them into the washing machine with the rest of the laundry. This left him naked.

'The fourteenth. Next Friday.'

'You coming in the sauna?' The wooden cabin was right to the tumble dryer. Gabriel opened his hand and revealed something which looked like a tiny, translucent turquoise bead. 'I'm just going to do one microdot in there. I never tripped in a sauna before.'

And this was the first time he had ever proposed using LSD in front of her. 'Do you hear what I'm saying?' she asked him.

'Yeah. Bobby Kennedy's been shot, he's hanging between life and death, and all you're worried about is getting hold of a scrap of paper. Fuck scraps of paper! That's what I say.'

The handsome beard was exactly the same colour as his pubic hair. And sex was a panacea that was retreating from their lives. Gabriel was very proud Italian about it; the most he seemed prepared to say on the embarrassing subject was that he sometimes had difficulty in getting his head and his body together. It frightened Rosie. She had heard stories of people getting burned out on acid. Were these attacks of sluggish impotence some kind of warning signal?

'We really should talk about sex,' she said. Greatly daring, she reached out and stroked his arm. It wouldn't have been daring at one time, it would have been the most natural thing on earth.

Gabriel had already flushed angrily. 'Please don't do my head in when I'm just about to trip.'

'If we don't talk about it, we'll never get things right.'

'I thought we were talking about visas.' Glaring at her, he

454

delved into the washing machine, fished out one of the towels and tied it protectively round his middle.

'Gabriel, that towel's grubby.' The feeling of rejection was even grubbier. It wasn't as though she'd been making a pass at him. She had simply done what the magazine article on impotence had suggested; she'd reached out and touched.

Gabriel was off on another tack: 'Borders and boundaries are purely man-made. Isn't this a beautiful colour?' Microdots were something new. He placed the turquoise bead on his tongue and as it began to melt he continued speaking – though in restricted tones. 'I can't take all this,' he said. 'I'm about to have a few hours' holiday from care.'

Rosie, as usual, took her problems down the hill to Normandy Village. For once, Miriam's door was not on the latch. And when she finally answered Rosie's knock, her eyes were red from crying. 'Bobby died. They just announced it on the radio. Want to go on campus? I need to be with people.'

'I'm people.'

'You are. You're the best. But we should be with all of us. Oh God there will be weeping in this town.' Miriam's own tears were falling again. 'When he came here he brought such *hope*. God rot the fucking Palestinian who did it! I'm going to have a tree planted in Bobby's name, in Israel. And I'm going to ask them to put it where it can look accusingly into Jordan.' Miriam suddenly seemed to have been struck by a cheering thought: 'Maybe they have trees with poison leaves?'

'I have to go to Canada,' said Rosie. 'And Gabriel's too out of it to help me. Can I use your phone? I need to ring Oakland Airport.'

'Forget that. We'll drive.'

'It takes days.'

'We have days. Would Tuesday be soon enough? We'll be like female draft-dodgers. You and me on the road again! Would you say that Canada was ready for us?'

'Sign here.' The hippies from the shipping agents had

455

returned; it was Saturday morning. 'We've got your box. They opened this one at customs. That's why it came in later.'

But was everything still in it? Relieved to see the packing case but filled with new anxieties, Rosie carried the box down the hall. The apartment might have been as drab as a butter bean but it boasted two bathrooms. Well, one and a half, really. The one with just a sink and a shower had no window so she had already converted it into a temporary dark room.

Rosie switched on the light and dumped the box onto a cheap trestle table from Cost Plus. The customs authorities hadn't even bothered to nail the lid back properly. It was only fastened down with heavy-duty adhesive tape. Scissors soon got it open.

Cameras, boxes of negatives, trays of slides – everything was there. Rosie pulled an elastic band from around an old yellow Kodak box which dated back to the days of Mr Molyneux and the dark room at Gledhill's. Originally, the box had held photographic paper, now it should contain old prints. And it did. Zav by the bandstand. Zav on the bus. The Great Omi at Belle Vue Circus. Joe Fingers eating a banana, Lily Jelly on her front step.

Rosie finally appreciated the true value of these pictures. She hadn't just got prints and negatives of Zav's early career –the title *Early Hankey* was already forming in her mind – she had also got a photographic record of the subject matter of all of his most famous songs.

As she delved deeper into the box she came upon old family snapshots. Connie in a square-shouldered cocktail dress, eating a maid of honour at that awful hotel in Ilfracombe. And Clifford looking remarkably young in woollen bathing trunks. To think that his generation complained about bikinis! Tight wet wool was infinitely more revealing. But it was the picture of Connie which really fascinated her. There was something familiar about the face.

And then it dawned on her. Around the cheekbones and the mouth, the face in the picture looked like Rosie's own passport photograph. This was not a thrilling thought. The girl looked into the mirror above the sink. Was she, too, destined to end up with big false teeth and a blowsy outline?

I need to compare the pictures, she thought. I know where I am with photography. Carrying the little snapshot into the living room, she pulled her passport out of a drawer and flipped it open. The resemblance was not quite as marked as she had imagined; it was mostly in the cut of the cheekbone. And there had to be *some* resemblance . . . Rosie flicked the page and looked at her visa. *Valid until June 4th*.

That couldn't be right, she'd come into America on January the fourteenth. She'd always thought they'd given her six months. But they hadn't. There, in rubber stamping, it said so: *Valid until June 4th*.

As panic engulfed her, the phone began to ring. Did she dare answer it? Telling herself that this was ridiculous, Rosie crossed the room and picked it up. Nevertheless, when she said 'Hello', it was in a disguised voice with a fake American accent.

'Hiya.' The expression was purest Irlams o'th' Height. It was Zav. 'I've got a problem.'

'*You've* got a problem?' In three garbled sentences she explained her own.

'Calm down,' he said. 'These things can be fixed. Danny's fixing them all the time.'

'The pictures are here.' It had ceased to seem to be any cause for excitement.

'That means Danny will see you as very hot. He'll look after you. He would anyway. Did you know my album's gone to number one?' The idea did not seem to thrill him. 'No interviews, no concert tour. God knows how it's done it.'

'You sound awful.'

'I'm a prisoner of success. And if that sounds a high-class problem it doesn't make it easier to handle. Danny wants a new album – fast. And that's not how I do it.' The singer sounded as though he'd lost all his zest. 'Dan's on his way out to the coast. He's got an interest in that big event over at San Jose. It's supposed to be "alternative" but he's put up some kind of financial guarantee. I'm supposed to be impressed. Did you hear me spit? Look, he's bound to call

457

you . . .' Zav's voice trailed off. 'I don't quite know how to put this. Don't let him use you. He might try and get you to influence me.'

'He couldn't.'

'He could and he will.' Animation came back into his voice with: 'Listen, I've got to take Moondog and Star to the airport.'

'Where are they going?'

'Would you believe Irlams o'th' Height? I offered to take them myself but Moondog just loves being the cabin crew's pet.'

Rosie was struck by a sharp thought: 'Zav, I couldn't even leave this country if I wanted to. I'm stuck here. I'm an illegal immigrant.'

Rosie felt very alone in the apartment and in her crisis. Like many another person in a tricky situation she reached for the morning paper and looked at her stars. If the forecast was propitious she would believe in it; if it was gloomy, well, these newspaper horoscopes were too generalised to be of much use.

As it was late in the month of May, her own birthsign had reached the top of the column. 'Gemini: You are badly aspected by the planet Mars which could lead to major disruptions of a life-changing nature. Mercury is no longer retrograde and this should open the floodgates of communication. This will be a weekend of ringing telephones . . .'

The phone bell was already going as Rosie ploughed through the final words: 'A pleasing aspect between Uranus and Mercury could lead to sparkling revelations. Are your energy levels up to this red-letter Saturday?' For the moment, the illegal immigrant felt too shattered to do much more than reach for the telephone.

It was a wrong number – somebody wanting Cody's Bookstore. Slamming down the receiver Rosie reached for her address book. Perhaps Danny Cahn's New York office would be able to tell her where he was to be found in California. But would there be anybody there on a Saturday morning? The phone rang again. She picked it up and said, 'I'm still not Cody's Bookstore.'

'I should hope you aren't. My little one sounds more than a bit rattled.'

She could hardly believe her ears. It was Danny. 'That has to be telepathy. I was just looking you up.' And that was the moment she burst into tears. 'I'm sorry,' she sobbed. 'I don't know where these tears came from. Oh Dan . . .'

'Okay,' he said briskly. 'Close your eyes. I'm there. I'm in the room with you. I've got my arms right round you. You're safe, you're safe, you're safe.' He actually began to sing a funny little song with foreign words.

'Oh Dan,' she sniffed, 'nothing's fair. You would have made a lovely father.'

'What a terrible thought,' he spluttered indignantly. 'Now then, tell.'

So she told. And at the end of it she felt considerably better. 'Oh and I've got all the negatives from England as well,' she added at the end.

'Splendid. As for the rest, there's nothing wrong that can't be put right. Now listen, we need to have a serious talk. I'm at the Mark. Come over and have dinner tonight. First we'll talk and then we'll go out and paint San Francisco red.'

The Mark was the Mark Hopkins Hotel. 'What time?'

'Seven o'clock. Just ask me for me at the desk.'

Everything had begun to feel better. She would wear her new dress, the one she had bought in the middle of a student riot from the Indian civil servant. Some of the bigger shops on Telegraph were subdivided into bazaars. The Indian owned a stall in one of these. As students yelled and shouted outside, he had stood in front of his rack of dresses, wearing a black jacket and striped trousers – just like an old-fashioned English floorwalker. 'How is London?' he asked. 'Does the number eleven bus still go along Victoria Street? That's where my office was. I was a senior clerk in the civil service.' Even a hurled brick, which shattered the front window of the shop, failed to stem his questions. Were there still ABC tearooms in the West End? Had work started on the new motorway to Brighton? And then he turned back into a trader, and as people around him trampled on shards of broken glass he swore that he had a dress that could have been designed with Rosie in mind.

At first she had her doubts. It was a bit too like one of Miriam's kaftans and she didn't want to seem a copycat. But Rosie had taken to wearing cream cheesecloth, and this dress was in yards and yards of it, finely pleated. It floated full-length to the ground and the high yoke was embroidered with a bold red and green design of apples and pears.

Rosie always believed in christening a new dress by taking it to an event. This one had been hanging in her closet for eventless weeks. Now it was going to get an airing. Her spirits were definitely rising and the telephone was ringing again.

'Is that you, Rosie?' The woman's voice was Irish. 'It's Maeve, it's Gabriel's mother. Could I speak to him?'

This being Saturday, Gabriel was out somewhere – roaming free. The previous evening, the Hell's Angels had made a late-night delivery so the chances were that he would be roaming in the direction of the botanical gardens with his druggy friends. 'I'm sorry. He's not here.'

'And if he's anything like his father was, you'll have no idea when he's coming back.' The voice became wheedling. 'I'm in San Francisco. I'm going to a big wedding reception in Pacific Heights this afternoon. Would the pair of you take pity on a poor owd soul tonight? Would you show her the town?'

How the hell could she answer for Gabriel? If he was doing what she suspected, he would be a limp rag by sunset. And then there was her date with Danny . . .

Maeve had obviously misread this tiny pause. 'I know you young people dress very oddly,' she said politely. 'I'd be expecting that. Actually, these days, parents quite like their children in gaudy tatters. It proves that the family is with it.'

Hastily, Rosie began to invent: 'I can't swear to it, but I think that Gabriel's doing something – to do with his work – tonight. I'm coming over to the city but . . .'

'Spare me the buts. Any chance of the two of us meeting up? I'm at the Fairmont on Nob Hill.'

'I'll be on Nob Hill too. I've got a business meeting at the Mark.' And it has to be admitted that she quite enjoyed being able to say this. 'Perhaps we could all meet up afterwards?'

'Would there be a spare feller?' asked Maeve hopefully.

She had forgotten Maeve's high spirits. 'There's only one man I'm afraid, Danny Cahn, and he's gay.'

But Maeve could even turn this to her own advantage. 'All the more reason for hauling out the glad rags. Gay guys always appreciate them. Rosie, how *is* that son of mine?'

I shouldn't be pausing again, she thought. I should be answering quickly. 'Okay. Yes, he's okay.'

'That's not what I've heard. Call me from the Mark when your meeting's over and we'll take it from there.' Curiosity crept into her voice. 'Would that be *the* Danny Cahn?'

Remembering Gabriel's mother's film-star past, Rosie replied, 'He'll probably ask me whether you're *the* Colleen Flynn.'

'I'm still the Honourable Mrs Kincaid. I've just sent the poor owd bugger off to Switzerland for Professor Niehans's cell therapy. They say it strengthens the love tube. Call me tonight.' No goodbye, she had already gone.

What shoes should she wear with the dress? Oddly enough, those hateful scarlet boots, the ones that had travelled right across America, might be just the thing. But were they in need of repair? As Rosie walked towards the bedroom she heard the door click open.

'Is that you, Gabriel?'

'Who else? Or do you have a secret lover?' His high spirits sounded curiously like his own mother's. 'We got all the way to the gardens when I realised that I'd left the gear in the icebox.' If he was matter-of-fact about the drugs so was most of the rest of the town.

'Forget it for today. Your mother's turned up in the city.'

His smile was replaced by a glare. 'That's got nothing to do with me.'

'But she wants to see you.'

'Well, want must be her master. I remember boarding schools where I wanted to see her. And that was in the holidays.' He slammed off into the kitchen. Click: the fridge door was being opened. Slam: it was shut. Another click was obviously the front door. A loud bang proved it. And all the time Rosie was thinking an uncomfortable thought. You had to pick your moment with Gabriel these days, and he was so set against families that she'd never even told him that her own mother was lurking in the ghetto.

Danny's suite at the Mark Hopkins was an upmarket version of the apartment at Casino Point: similar pale walls, heavier cream linen curtains, thick carpets in the same shade as the top of the milk. The only real colour was in a huge bowl of fruit and a mountainous arrangement of green orchids.

'The hotel management provided those,' growled Dan. 'And if they knew the state my career was in, they would have saved their dollars. That fucking Zav isn't just resting on his laurels, he's trying to set fire to them.'

The photographs had provoked a happier reaction. Rosie began to tidy them back into a neat pile on the smoked-glass coffee table. 'Could we just talk about my visa?'

Danny had other preoccupations. He dismissed Rosie's question with: 'I'm better at pulling strings in New York. Stay illegal for a few days more. In Berkeley you'll only be one amongst hundreds.' He went straight back to the subject of Zav. 'Want to know his latest stunt? He's only gone and announced his retirement. See for yourself.' Danny smacked a hand against a copy of the *San Francisco Chronicle*. 'The little sod's certainly learned well. Called Reuter's himself and issued a short sharp press statement.' Danny whipped out a pair of spectacles – she'd never seen him in them before – and read aloud, '"The world of pop music is governed by faceless men who are only interested in profit." That's what he thinks about me. And then there's a lot of idealistic guff about youth and the planet.'

'But if he's retiring why would he want to send the children home?'

'He's sent them home because I threatened to bring his mother over here. She's the only person who could have talked some sense into him. With them to look after, she'll be stuck in Lancashire.' And then Danny seemed to relent: 'I'm not being a hundred per cent fair. He's worried about

Moondog, doesn't think he's having a real life. He thinks Saracen Street will toughen him up. The kid loves Tippler and Tippler's been seeing a lot of the doctor. There's so much that's *good* in Zav. But he's stopped being businesslike.' Danny's forefinger jabbed towards the photographs on the coffee table. 'Your book will make money. And what he's doing could be turned to advantage. I could make plenty out of his wanting to be left alone. I could turn him into pop music's own Greta Garbo. But to do that I have to talk to him.' Danny removed his spectacles and looked Rosie straight in the eye. 'You help me and I'll help you.' One look at her face must have shown him that she was hurt. 'I'll help you anyway, I'll help you, I'll help you. Try and get him to talk to me,' he said miserably. 'You might not believe it but I miss him.'

Even the telephone had a muted beige buzz. 'Hello?' bawled Danny. 'The Honourable Mrs who?'

There had been no chance to explain. 'We're going to meet her, later.'

'She's already downstairs. Who is she?'

'Colleen Flynn.'

'My God! Alive? I knew an old queen who used to do imitations of her.'

'I knew a young one,' remembered Rosie.

'Hang on a moment, operator.' Danny suddenly seemed altogether more cheerful. 'Do we ask her to step up?' he said to Rosie.

'Why don't we go down?'

'Please ask the lady to go to the lower bar and have a drink.' He replaced the receiver. 'What was the fake Irish song she sang in that Hollywood musical about the Blarney Stone? I remember, "Pin on Your Shamrock, We're Going on the Town".'

By the time they got downstairs, Maeve had the bar staff running round her like the male chorus in one of her old Hollywood movies. She had already been provided with a dry martini and a silver tray of green olives. And two waiters in white bum-freezer jackets were now competing to light her cigarette.

'I'm so glad you didn't suggest the Top of the Mark,' she said to Danny before they'd even been introduced. 'Half the wedding guests have probably migrated there.'

Maeve was still dressed for a wedding in a yellow and white suit that looked like a diagram in a geometry textbook. 'Ungaro.' She named the designer in the way that other people would have said 'How do you do?' Maeve looked in splendid shape, though the blonde hair had been subtly greyed. 'I'm not drunk,' she confided, 'but I was well enough gone at the reception to remind Nancy Reagan who she really is. Where's that bloody son of mine?'

Rosie hardly liked to tell her that Gabriel was sitting gazing into zonked space at Casino Point.

'Did he send me a message? Or are we back to "Motherhood is only a biological function"? I'm hearing terrible stories about him.'

'Who from?' asked Rosie, startled.

'I have my spies. I love the dress. And the boots. They make you look just like a Russian doll. Where are we going to eat?'

Danny, ordering drinks, looked as though he would have liked to dine off the waiters. And as every third man in San Francisco was said to be gay, that might not have been an impossibility. But one customer in that bar wasn't gay. He was very straight indeed. And he hadn't meant to let himself get caught staring at Rosie.

It was the man with the muscles and the comically curly eyelashes, the one who'd come to her aid on Telegraph. Tonight he was back in a dark silk suit, just as he'd been when she'd first spotted him – trailing Gabriel.

'Where are we going to eat?' cried Maeve again. And she and Danny went into competition as to who was the most unspoiled by money and success. It was all suggestions of homely little Italian places on North Beach and much was made of the joys of Chinese food in San Francisco.

Chinatown won.

'I feel just like a tourist.' Maeve knocked back another glass of rice wine and cracked open a fortune cookie. She unrolled the piece of paper from inside. 'Would you believe

464

that this cheating fecker's in Chinese? It's made me feel deprived. Let's go on somewhere.' Maeve treated a stranger at a nearby table to a dazzling smile and a conspiratorial wink.

Only it wasn't a real stranger. It was the man in the dark silk suit. Before Rosie could start asking questions, Danny began producing credit cards and attempting to pay even though the bill hadn't been presented. He was, as always, a wonderfully lavish host.

The cabaret in the first navy-blue-velvet-lined nightclub was a singer called Ethel Ennis whom Maeve remembered as having been with Benny Goodman. 'But what I really want to see in San Francisco is Carol Doda's tits,' she said. 'They're the talk of the town. They're said to be solid silicone.'

Carol Doda was appearing at a nightclub called the Condor. They lowered her – blonde, naked, and revolving – through a hole in the ceiling. 'My God,' breathed Maeve, 'her bozooms are as solid as puddin' basins. Could we go to Finocchio's too, Dan? One of the boys there used to have birdseed in his bra. He always said it gave him a more feminine wobble.'

Finocchio's on Broadway was a temple of female impersonation. The audience there was a bit 'coach party'. And you had to queue to get in. But Danny made himself known to a woman in a puzzling winter coat who was in charge of a cash register by the entrance.

'Would you think that's Mrs Finocchio?' Maeve whispered to Rosie.

'*Finocchio* means fennel,' she replied. And then she wished she hadn't started. 'It's what they used to throw on the bonfires, when they roasted gays.'

'Nobody's known more difficult queens than I have,' breathed Maeve. 'But I must say I'd draw the line at roasting.'

Dan reappeared. 'We've got that table with Reserved on it, by the stage.' But Dan, whose eyes were never still, was already looking back towards the cash register.

A man was talking to 'Mrs Finocchio'. It was *that* man. He of the curly eyelashes.

As they moved towards their table, musicians were already playing a very showbusiness overture. The place reminded

Rosie of one of the more spectacular working men's clubs in Manchester – all flocked wallpaper and rose-tinted lights. As they settled at their table, Maeve made a very film-starry beckoning gesture with one finger. The person she was summoning was the man.

'It's no good, I have to ask him,' she said. He approached the table. 'Would you be Gino's son?'

'Yes, ma'am. I'm Gino too.'

'Gino junior,' smiled Maeve. 'That's nice. Your father looked after me for years. And would you be guarding Miss Rosie's interests?'

'That's about the size of it.'

'Sit down, Gino junior. This is Mr Cahn.' For a man who had already eaten, Danny was suddenly looking remarkably hungry. Maeve gave the impresario's hand a cheerful slap. 'This is serious family business. Gino, how is my son? No lies. It's me. I knew your father. Jesus, I think I even *slept* with your father. How is Gabriel?'

'Not good.'

'So it's true about all the drugs? With his daddy it was the drink. Even in Hollywood I hated those feckin' dope peddlers.' She fished in her handbag. 'Here's my card. Ireland's only eight hours away. I'd come any time. Go back to your table, Gino, there's a good boy.'

'A pleasure meeting you, ma'am.'

'The pleasure was mutual. Bend down.' She kissed him on the cheek. 'Give that to your dad.'

As Gino junior moved away to a nearby table Rosie could contain herself no longer. 'Who is he?' she exploded.

Maeve looked amazed. 'You've got to be kidding. He works for the family. All I can say is they must approve of you.' Maeve now looked at Rosie more closely. 'You really *didn't* know what he was there for. My dear, they're the most useful people on earth. They fetch, they carry, and they watch out for you. Just a minute . . .' Maeve rose and began weaving her way through the tables.

'Star quality is something that never dies.' Danny was watching her in admiration. 'Stars are monsters, the wickedest people on earth. But in some ways they're innocents – they've all stayed children. Rosie, do your best for me, with Zav, won't you?'

'Please don't ask me to influence him.'

'I'm doing just that.'

Maeve had begun to weave her way back. She was brandishing a visiting card. 'No point in having a dog and barking yourself,' she said. 'Here's Gino junior's number. Any emergency, anything at all, just you call him.'

The lights went down and a man's voice over a loud-speaker said, 'Ladies and gentlemen, it's cabaret time at Finocchio's.' Velvet curtains swished back and a chorus of Carmen Mirandas filled the little stage, singing 'South American Way'.

'They can't be men!' gasped Rosie. 'They're fabulous.' This wasn't a word she used often but she was watching female impersonation of the highest order.

'I don't think it's as good as the Carousel in Paris,' said Maeve.

'Or those places in Thailand,' nodded Danny.

'Shh.' It was quite good enough for Rosie. She found it amazing. But as the leading Carmen Miranda gave her place in the spotlight to a glittering Alice Faye, she caught herself thinking that there was a quality of 'yesterday' to the whole show. That was before a fake Barbra Streisand appeared. And then there was a real man who stuck swords into a make-believe girl in a basket.

As the applause died away, a pair of mauve satin curtains parted and Rosie let out an audible gasp. But it wasn't the gasp that was causing Danny and Maeve to stare at her. The 'girl' singing in the spotlight was her own double.

> 'When I have a brand new hair-do,
> And my eyelashes all in curl,
> I float like the clouds on air do,
> I enjoy being a girl.'

You always did, Christopher, she thought. You always did. You always dressed up in my clothes. You always said you were going to be a girl. That had been The Secret. Inside

Rosie's head the high-pitched whine had started to whirr like an orchestra tuning up. This could only mean one thing. Her twin brother had spotted her in the audience.

'No you can't go backstage and see anybody,' said the woman on the cash register. 'They don't do interviews.' She had plainly spotted Rosie's camera.

'Let's get outside,' murmured Maeve. 'Danny can see me back to the hotel. Gino junior will cope. That's what he's there for.'

'They don't see nobody,' repeated the woman.

'Of course they don't,' said Maeve. 'And it was a lovely show. And thank you very much for having us.' Her knuckles were already urging Rosie through the plate-glass door.

'But Gino's disappeared,' the girl protested.

'Precisely.' They began to descend the steep steps to the street. 'He knows you want to see your brother. He'll make sure it happens. Let's go and have a look at the pictures outside.' Hooting, tooting Broadway was coming up to meet them. 'My goodness me.' Maeve had paused in front of the glass display case at the bottom of the stairs. '"Taylor Tattersall – Britain's Misleading Lady". The resemblance is remarkable!'

'We can't just leave Rosie here,' protested Danny.

'If the child managed to find her way across the United States of America, she can surely kill five minutes on a slope in San Francisco. This is a private moment, Dan. We have to leave her to it. Call a taxi. *Taxi!*' A Yellow Cab had already slid to a halt. 'Goodnight, love.' She gave Rosie a champagne kiss. 'Just you trust Gino.'

It was the only thing to do. As the taxi began to sail downhill Rosie turned and looked at the photographs again. The counter-culture had left no mark on these pretend ladies – unless you counted a bunch of paper flowers in a wig of black Chinese hair. The performers all looked very lipstick and high heels. But the picture of Christopher could have been a *Harper's Bazaar* cover. There wasn't the faintest hint of overstated female impersonation. As he had done on the stage, Christopher looked just like a real woman.

'Hi.'

Rosie spun round. It was Patti Spinoza, the girl with the right on attitudes and the hairy legs. She was with a whole crowd of Berkeley women, the kind of revolutionaries who always seemed to run in packs. 'How you doing?' Patti asked Rosie.

For once the English girl felt that she had an answer that was up to Pattie's highly radical standards. 'As a matter of fact I'm an illegal immigrant.'

'Far out!' Patti seemed impressed. 'Bernadette will definitely approve of that. Anything that fucks up the system!' She raised two fingers in the peace sign and Rosie reflected that this had never stopped making her feel uncomfortable. It looked too like something else. 'Rosie, there's a very straight-looking guy trying to get your attention.' Patti was back at her most stern. In Berkeley terms, 'straight-looking' meant anybody dressed conventionally. 'Do you want we should hang around?'

'He's a friend of mine.' Gino had come down the nightclub staircase.

'In wing-tip shoes?' Happy to be outraged again, Patti began to lead her party downhill. As they went Rosie was reminded of a Sunday-school concert she had once seen, where a lot of girls, dressed as soldiers in the French Revolution, had worn false moustaches and crepe paper hats. 'Any news?' she asked Gino.

'There's only two ways they can leave the building. They either come down this marble staircase or down those wooden steps at the side.'

'Did you manage to talk to him?'

'I shouldn't think Billy Graham could get into that dressing room. The only thing to do is wait.'

Gino didn't seem inclined to go. What on earth were they meant to talk about? 'What do you do for a living?' she asked. She already knew but she wanted his version of it. Her question had sounded ridiculously like somebody at an English cocktail party.

'This and that. I'm a Frascati. And the Frascatis have always worked for the Bonartos.'

469

'But what do you actually do?'

Again he repeated, 'This and that. The family have big American interests. Mostly I'm on Gabriel's case.'

So Gabriel was a 'case', was he? 'And what does that involve?'

There was a moment's pause before he answered. 'Sometimes we throw a Frisbee around.' And then he seemed to feel compelled to add, 'I don't have nothing to do with getting heavy dope. Gabriel is one beautiful guy, he should get off that shit.'

Would whatever she said be reported back? And to whom? Rosie decided that silence was the best policy.

'Wanna know something?' The Italian looked awkward. 'Gabriel always had money so it don't mean a thing. All he cares about is you.'

'Well he's got a funny way of showing it.' This was out before she could stop herself.

'He's a Bonarto.'

Yes, and I'm a Tattersall, thought Rosie. And I'm waiting for another one whom I haven't seen for twelve years – more than half a lifetime. '*The English Sensation ... Taylor Tattersall*'. She had forgotten how jealous she had been, as a child, of the fact that her twin had a middle name. Gran'ma Tattersall had been a Taylor. Whatever would that prim side of the family have made of the idea of their name ringing round a drag cabaret? 'Taylor' was certainly a cleverly androgynous Christian name. Enough of this family stuff, she really ought to be thinking of something else to say to Gino. But he had melted away.

The crowds on Broadway had begun to thin out too. Most of the customers and some of the waiters had left Finocchio's. And now, one by one, the female impersonators began to emerge. Barbara Streisand was bald. And as the leading Carmen Miranda hurried down the marble steps, he just looked like any pretty hippie boy from the Haight Ashbury.

Hurry up, Christopher, she thought, and immediately she heard the whine inside her head. Without even thinking about what she was doing Rosie tried a trick from childhood days with her twin. She imagined a picture of herself, standing in front of this glass display case. An image flashed back of a pair of cork-soled sandals coming down a wooden staircase.

Clack-clack-clack. She could actually *hear* them. And it wasn't inside her head. Rosie looked towards the steps at the side of the building. And there he was.

Was 'he' the right word? The descending figure could have been herself, in tight jeans and an embroidered cheesecloth top.

'I've got exactly that same shirt,' she said to him in amazement.

He nodded towards her own dress. 'And I tried that on last week. Did you get it from that Indian on Telegraph?' He sounded exactly like Jackie Kennedy. The long hair was not a wig, it was his own.

'We're like peas in a pod.' Why was she whispering?

'No we're not.' His voice was still capable of freezing her. 'You're real. That's why I always hated you. But I'm getting there. I'm well on the way.' His beautiful hands pulled the floating top in at the waist, and she saw that he had living, breathing breasts.

'Scared?' he asked. 'Spooked out? Want to run away? I always told you I'd grow up to be a lady.'

'All over?' She had to ask it. 'Are you a lady all over?'

'Fuck off back where you came from! Surgery costs money.'

'But how did you get the bust? Is it like Carol Doda's?'

'No it is not. I got it with hormones. It's so easy for you,' he snarled. Only it was a woman's snarl. 'Yours just grew. I take tablets. They're made from the urine of pregnant mares. Pretty thought, isn't it?'

'I think it's a very brave thought.'

'And don't patronise me.'

As he said it, she could hear her own voice, snapping at Gabriel. 'Chris, can we go and get some coffee?'

'Why?'

'Because I want to talk to you.' She was actually angry with him. She'd never dared to be that before. 'I'm your sister.'

471

'No. Connie's my sister. She's been my sister ever since we left Cheyenne. Let's walk downhill. There's a shop with a mirror. I want to compare us. I want to see how real I've gotten.'

Two passing sailors let out a loud whistle and moved in on the identical twins. 'Oh you beautiful dolls. It's fantasy time,' said one of them in fevered admiration.

'More fantasy than you'll ever know,' laughed Taylor Tattersall. And linking arms with his sister he began to lead her down the slope, in the direction of the Embarcadero.

'They were totally deceived.' Rosie was laughing too.

'Everybody is *always* totally deceived.'

Rosie paused. She hoped he wouldn't let go of her arm, and he didn't. 'Chris, I'll never call you "he" again.'

'Who's Chris? The name is Taylor.' But Taylor was still smiling.

'You're beautiful, Taylor.'

'So are you, baby.'

'And every bit as much a woman as I am.'

'It's amazing what you can stow away under a big piece of surgical tape. I've developed a bladder like cast iron.'

'Can the surgery be done?'

'It *will* be done. It's just a question of where and how. Anyway they can't operate on the brain, and I was always a woman inside my own head. How's Poor-Bertha-who-drags-a-leg?' The reminiscences had begun, and they continued until the pair came to a soda fountain – all neon and fluorescent lighting – on a corner near to the foundations of the TransAmerica Pyramid which was just beginning to be built.

As they sat up at the counter, under that harsh overhead light, Rosie cautiously checked Taylor's face for any kind of five o'clock shadow.

Her new sister was ahead of her: 'Electrolysis took care of that. How does it feel to be out with somebody as unusual as a unicorn? Be honest, that's exactly what you were thinking, wasn't it? I can still read your mind.'

'And I can still read yours.' She knew that Taylor wasn't quite as friendly as she appeared on the surface. That she was still full of guarded resentments and reservations. But Rosie also knew that Taylor wanted to be rid of these – once and for all. And Rosie felt that she had to explain that she understood. 'In Manchester, under the Central Reference Library, there's a theatre. I once went to see *Uncle Vanya* there. And there's a bit at the end of the first act where two women, who've been very wary of one another, make up their quarrel. One of them says, "We shall sing and dance and be as sisters." When I saw that play, you know who I thought of? I thought of you. I never told The Secret. All those years and I never told a living soul.'

The unchecked tears which ran down both their faces were following *exactly* the same pattern.

The next morning Rosie slept late. And she slept well. It was as though someone had taken a smoothing iron to one of the crumpled corners of her life. She was finally tugged reluctantly awake with: 'Rose? Rose, I *think* there's a woman on the phone who says she's your mother.' Gabriel wore the dazed look of somebody who was still coming down from an acid trip. 'She *said* she was your mother.' This seemed to be more for his own benefit than for Rosie's. 'I'm sure she said that.'

Rosie reached for the bedside telephone: 'Hello?'

'Well aren't you the dirty stop-out!' Connie was full of tacky good cheer. 'Your sister's been up for hours. Mind you, she was always easier to get up than you were – even as a little boy.'

Rosie was finding this bouncy babble a bit hard to take. 'Good morning, Connie.'

'What morning? You've missed it. Have you got your engagement book handy?' Her mother had suddenly gone all high society. 'Could you do lunch tomorrow? At my club.'

Whatever club could that be? Rosie had a vision of some bleached grey timber shack, with men shooting bottles off the front porch. But Connie cancelled this out with, 'It's the Berkeley City Club on Durant Avenue.' The place was known as the spirit of respectability. 'And Rosemary, could you be sure and bring that old diamond ring of mine? I've got a proposition to put to you.' Connie's voice rose abruptly. 'Just you let go of my arm, Taylor Tattersall. You strike me and I swear I'll call the cops.'

'Rosie?' Taylor's throaty voice had replaced their mother's. 'I promise you this wasn't my idea. She is the world's number one opportunist. If she ever gets to Heaven she'll be the first to hustle the Virgin Mary for a spare safety-pin!'

'You were brought up a fucking Christian,' roared Connie in the background. There was a bit of clonking and then she had obviously regained control of the telephone because Rosie heard her cooing, 'Shall we say one o'clock at the club?' The voice was purest Lady Mountbatten.

'How weird,' said Rosie to Gabriel as she put down the phone. 'My own mother's pretending to be posh, for my benefit.'

He was pulling on a sweater. As his head came through the polo collar he said, 'How was Maeve?'

'Fine,' was all Rosie was prepared to say on that subject. He'd taken no trouble, he didn't deserve any more.

'And that was really your mother?'

'Yes, and I've found my brother too, only soon she's going to be my sister. It's easier to say *she*.'

'I always told you families were too complicated,' grinned Gabriel. And that was that. He was already heading for the door.

'Where are you going?'

'Out.'

'Sometimes you make *me* feel like your mother. The way you slam off out is worse than any teenager. Are you going to play Frisbee with Gino Frascati?'

Gabriel came right back into the room. 'Since when did you know Gino?'

'Since Maeve introduced us.'

'Never spy on me, Rose,' he said warningly.

'Gino was spying on me.'

'He's paid to do that. You wouldn't understand. Back home in Italy they're only afraid of one thing. Kidnappers.

474

Okay, go ahead and laugh. But all the big families are afraid for their children.'

'Well the state you're in, the kidnappers would only have to tempt you with sweeties with cartoon faces on them!'

'Not while the Frascati brothers are around.'

'So why does he dog *my* footsteps?'

'Because you are my little family.' It didn't sound ridiculous said with Italian intensity, it sounded glorious. 'The Frascatis know that if somebody snatched you, I'd hand over everything I own. And now may I go to my appointment?' he asked in a coldly formal voice. 'I've got a session booked with Viva for two o'clock.'

Viva again. Rosie listened to his footsteps heading for the lift. He was a man who gave with one hand and slapped with the other. As she got out of bed she noticed that he'd left three clean socks on top of his chest of drawers. They were all odd ones. Perhaps their partners had been put away with the last load of washing. She opened his sock drawer and *Confessions of an English Opium Eater* stared up at her. Perhaps she should try reading it again? Rosie opened the book and began looking for hidden answers.

'Am I dressed right for the Berkeley City Club?'

'How would I know?' Miriam was wearing nothing at all. Lying on a daybed and leafing through a new edition of the *Barb* she looked like a living painting by Matisse. It was a hot day and hang-ups about nudity were much frowned on in the counter-culture. 'But I'd never let my own brother see me like this,' she said sternly. 'So perhaps I'm not that modern after all. Or maybe I'm just Jewish. You look very sweet, Rosemarie. Did you *intend* to look like Princess Anne? The Berkeley City Club is supposed to be full of faculty wives. There'll probably be a lot of other ladies in navy and white. I doubt their skirts will be that short.' Miriam yawned and stretched. 'I'm thinking of dyeing my hair green. All of it. And then I could say to all the young men, "Keep off the grass!" What young men?' she asked herself disconsolately.

'Please don't go into a big Berkeley moan,' said Rosie

firmly. 'I could name six men you've refused to go out with. And all because of that bloody thesis – the one you never get down to writing.' For somebody who'd been friendless for years, there was great luxury in being able to be absolutely honest with Miriam. 'One day, I swear, I'll write it for you myself.'

Miriam was allowed to be equally candid. 'Princess Anne would have prettier manners. Or is some problem eating you?'

'Well, there's my mother . . .'

'That's not a problem, it's a drama. And you're loving it.'

'Okay.' Rosie took a deep breath. 'How could we find out what Viva and Gabriel get up to?'

'We could eavesdrop. It wouldn't be very nice of us but we could do it.'

'How could you eavesdrop on somebody in a tower?'

'Do I waddle?' Miriam was crossing the room.

'No. Bits of you stir when you walk, but you're really very nice and solid.'

'Here!' Miriam was holding up an iron key. It was very similar to the one to the front door of Teapot Hall. 'Professor Klosterboer doesn't like the janitor so he gave it to me to keep, while he's in Europe.'

'And?'

'She thinks she could write my thesis! *And* he lives in the other tower apartment. If we were really bold girls, we'd seduce a doctor, borrow his stethoscope and put it to the wall.'

'Or a glass tumbler. Zav's mother always said that Lily Jelly used to listen in on us with a glass pressed against the wall.' But she couldn't really visualise herself as a latter-day Lily Jelly. 'No. Forget it. Whereabouts on Durant is the Berkeley City Club?'

'A block past the Free Clinic. You'll find it hard to believe they're in the same town. It's one of the great women's clubs of America. If you really wanted to be dressed right, you should be wearing stern corsets.'

'They'll be lucky if Connie's got knickers on,' rejoined Rosie. And with this she headed for the door.

As she walked through the garden, Rosie saw something she hadn't noticed on her way in, and she could hardly believe her eyes. American forget-me-nots came in red, white and blue.

'Whatever would Shakespeare have made of those?' The voice was deep contralto, a brown hem hung above monkish sandals which contained long bony toes. It was Viva. 'Whatever would he have made of such hybrid freaks?'

'I don't know,' said Rosie. And she said it very blankly indeed.

'How I love my Will!' Presumably, Viva was still talking about Shakespeare. And now she began to quote aloud:

> 'Weaving spiders, come not here;
> Hence, you long-legged spinners, hence;
> Beetles black approach not near;
> Worm nor snail, do no offence.'

'You offend me,' said Rosie. 'And if that's rude, I don't care. All your mumbo-jumbo sounds ridiculous in daylight.'

'Since when was *A Midsummer Night's Dream* mumbo-jumbo?' cried Viva. 'Those were just some nice words that I learned when I was young and happy. You'll be old yourself one day.' Viva was angry.

'Well I just hope I don't make the mistake of trying to cast spells over young men. What is it you're trying to do to Gabriel?'

'I'm trying to help him. A little astrology, a bit of regression therapy ... Tell me something, what was the hour of your birth? Gabriel got me to draw up your chart, but it's impossible to be specific without the exact hour.'

'He did *what*?' Rosie was outraged. She saw this as a huge invasion of privacy.

'He thought you once mentioned something about five o'clock in the morning.'

In fact, he had asked her point-blank. And she had answered with an old family story. The one about Connie saying that the hardest work she'd ever done had been just before dawn.

'You must not hate me.' Viva spoke reproachfully. 'I'm just a stepping stone. I never knew anybody on such a search for truth as Gabriel.'

So Viva had cast a chart for her, had she? That meant – if there was anything in astrology – the old crone now knew every single detail about Rosie. This was not to be borne. 'You're a wicked woman,' she shouted.

'You're wrong,' said Viva. And she said it with absolute certainty. 'I'm getting on in years, I probably strike you as a bit absurd, but I am not wicked. If I'd wanted to be wicked I could have taken everything this world has to offer. I don't take, I give.'

'At a price.'

Viva spread out a set of fingers that were as bony as her toes. 'I ask for enough to keep a roof over my head. Even a fox must have its hole. And please don't march off in high dudgeon – please. Whenever I look at your Gabriel's chart, I look at yours as well. They're both charged with pain. But the agony will melt, and you're the one who will bring it about. Your natal chart is wonderfully well aspected by Uranus.'

'I'm afraid that planet has always sounded a bit rude to me.'

Viva refused to be deflected. 'Uranus is the planet of the eleventh-hour miracle.'

'And what hour would you say we were at now?' asked Rosie.

'I'd say you were at the ninth hour.'

'Wasn't that when Jesus Christ said, "Oh my God, why hast thou forsaken me?"'

'The gods have not forsaken you.'

A Quaker upbringing had not gone away: 'There's only one God.'

'That, my dear,' tinkled Viva, 'is a matter of opinion.' She was back in control of the situation. Or she thought she was.

From the outside, Berkeley City Club looked like a Moorish convent. There was even an iron grille over the huge front doors. When Rosie pressed the bell, a small door within a

478

big one buzzed open and she stepped into a world that was curiously like an English country house. Except, when you looked more closely, all the beams and the carved stonework turned out to be made of pre-cast concrete. On second thoughts, it was more like a quiet corner in that magnate's castle in the film *Citizen Kane*. The club was a prime example of the architecture of Julia Morgan – a name connected with all that was thought of as most worthy in the East Bay. How on earth had Connie wormed her way onto the membership list of this establishment?

'I'm looking for Mrs . . .' Mrs who? Taylor was using Tattersall so she tried that. 'Mrs Tattersall.'

'She went up to the bar. It's on the first floor.'

Did Rosie detect slight hostility in the receptionist's tones? A huge Ming vase stood on the half-landing and the staircarpet was real Persian. The whole place was impressively hushed. As she reached the first floor she saw that leaded windows looked down into a palm-filled courtyard. There was even an open-air ballroom floor, partly covered with a striped canvas awning. Yet as Rosie looked around, she noticed that some of the lampshades were not quite as grand as their iron, mock medieval stands. And a voice jabbering in the distance was not grand at all – though it was trying to be. The voice belonged to her mother.

'See those big bowls of potpourri, Taylor? We had the same thing at Teapot Hall – only bigger.'

The man behind the bar counter looked like a Pullman car attendant. He was so black his face could have been polished with the back of a spoon, and he was wearing a red jacket. Taylor, on one of the stools, was in a navy and white spotted dress. But Connie . . . Dear God, she must have hung onto that battered mink stole – the one dripping with little tails – since the night she left Irlams o'th' Height.

'Have you heard of Teapot Hall?' she was saying to the barman. 'It's about the same size as Woburn Abbey but *we* never allowed trippers.' Lady Mountbatten slurred on her sherry, at eleven o'clock in the morning!

Taylor had already picked up on Rosie's presence. 'Hi,' she smiled. But Rosie could sense that her twin was curling up inside, just as much as she was herself, at their mother's performance.

'Did you bring it?' Connie had swung round and was eyeing Rosie's knuckles.

'Yes.' She opened her handbag.

'Name your poison.' Connie had gone back to being grandiose.

'Tomato juice will be fine.'

'They always have to have the same thing,' sighed Connie for the barman's benefit. 'Okay, Rosemary, let's see it. And I'll have another of those sherries,' she added over her shoulder.

Rosie hesitated for a moment – but only a moment – before she handed over the ring.

'And a small gin.' Connie was still throwing orders over her shoulder. 'There's nothing like a drop of gin for soaking diamonds. It brings back all their sparkle.' Connie rolled the ring between her podgy little fingers. 'This is something I never expected to see again. He first put it on my finger in the cold-store warehouse. They were in a big panic that day, there'd been a power cut. How much do you want for it?'

'I wasn't thinking of selling.'

'Well I was thinking of buying. On the instalment plan, of course. I could raise capital on this stone. Cliff gave me nothing but the best,' she swanked. 'The chances are that Gran's dad got this ring from Ollivant and Botsford.'

This last word was accompanied by a dainty burp.

'He didn't. He diddled it out of old man Muirhead.' This was information she had gained in her childhood, straight after Connie left. Rosie accepted a tomato juice from the barman. 'What do you need capital for?' She had forgotten how reproachful her mother could look. Perhaps 'diddling' was too lower class for the Berkeley City Club.

'What *for*? I'd have thought you would have known what for. Your sister is in urgent need of a vagina.'

The man behind the counter narrowly missed dropping his bottle of Worcestershire Sauce.

'I gotta go to the can,' announced Connie. Lady Mountbatten had suddenly become Tugboat Annie. She had also become acquisitive. As she made to leave the room, Connie was already sliding the diamond ring onto one of her own fingers.

'This honestly wasn't my idea,' said Taylor. Without even consulting one another the twins had begun gathering up the glasses. They carried them over to the relative privacy of a table under a high window.

'If you ladies need anything, just press the bell,' said the barman. And with this he picked up a newspaper and disappeared.

'How the hell did she get into this place?' asked Rosie, in baffled wonder.

'We came to Berkeley with Mr Schwartz. Connie was on the wagon at the time and she snitched him off an old GI bride. The first month was all very respectable.' Taylor smiled at the memory. 'He set us up in the North Berkeley Hills. And there were charge accounts, and club member-ships, and a pedigree poodle. I kept waiting for Connie to go on a bender but she didn't.' Taylor stopped smiling and seemed to be remembering something painful.

After a moment she continued with, 'One morning he walked in on me, unexpectedly, in the shower. He'd no idea I'd got a three-piece suite down there. His face! And the same day, the cops came round to ask Connie about a bit of shoplifting. She'd been putting the stuff *back*, for Christ's sake! All she was doing was keeping her hand in. Well, that did it; Connie hit the bottle, Mr Schwartz left town, and that's when we started rolling downhill. I've still got the dog,' she added. 'He was all I really cared about.'

Their mother returned from the cloakroom.

'Your skirt's caught up at the back,' said Taylor.

Connie tugged at lime-green chiffon. 'Where did the barman go? He was cute.'

'She's still very partial to black men,' sighed Taylor.

Connie bellowed back, 'Have twins and *then* tell me that size doesn't matter.'

Two women in cotton dresses crossed the threshold of the bar. They were not the corseted dragons that Miriam had predicted. They looked nice and kind and very clean.

One of them reminded Rosie of her old headmistress, Miss Swaine. 'Pardon me but could you tell us where the Hawaiian dancing classes are this morning?' she asked.

'Having twins is no picnic,' moaned Connie who had failed to register the arrival of the club members. 'Can you imagine going to the toilet and doing a watermelon? Well, having twins is doing a watermelon twice.'

The newcomers disappeared abruptly. Connie slid off the diamond ring and dropped it into the gin. 'You a lesbian?' she asked Rosie.

'Me? No.'

'I always wondered whether it cut both ways. First time I saw you again was with a freaky woman. For all I know, you might want to drive a Sherman tank. So, you gotta boy-friend?'

Rosie nodded.

'Some tame Anglo? I'd rather go to bed with white rats!'

'No, he's Italian.'

'Now you're talking! They're bewdiful. Absolutely bewdiful. Artists de la bedroom.' She stopped rhapsodising and became more realistic. 'That Catholic guilt's a bit hard to take. You have any experience of that?'

'A bit,' admitted Rosie. 'He's not very *practising* these days.'

'They all revert to type at the end. They all start shouting for a priest. Look at Mr Goldoni. He was my best hubby. We had a wunnerful scene round the deathbed. Wunnerful. Rosary beads, confession, the lot. "Father," I said – that's what you call the priests, Father – "Father, I was years ahead of you. I'm the one who's been forgiving Mr Goldoni's sins since the first month we married." Taylor, go behind that counter and get your mother a slug of sherry.'

'He said to touch the bell,' protested Rosie.

'A slug of sherry, Taylor. Now I want you to listen to your old mother, Rosemary. The Amontillado, Taylor. Thank you. Now Rosie, any problems with that spaghetti merchant of yours, just you remember to *forgive* him!'

Connie downed her new glass of sherry in one gulp. 'Forgiveness? They love it. And you gotta be lavish about it.

There were occasions when I forgave Mr Goldoni for doing practically nothing – he just enjoyed it so much. Remember that and you won't go far wrong with an Eyetie. Listen, one good turn deserves another. How much do you want for that ring?'

It was still lying in the glass of gin. Rosie needed to ask Taylor an awful question – but not in front of Connie. Yet it was too complicated to flash to her twin as a mental message. She had to know if they were alike in one important area. 'Taylor? Do you know anything about a pane of glass?'

'Do I know anything about a pane of glass? I was *born* behind one. I've been trying to get rid of it all my life.' Taylor patted her crutch. 'Once I get rid of this mistake, that glass is gonna vanish the way mist lifts off San Francisco.'

'You really think so?'

'I know it. It's the one thought that's brought me this far.'

'Have the ring. Have it with my love.' Rosie suppressed the thought that doing a good turn might do something for her own pane of glass.

Connie fished the ring from the gin. It was definitely shining more brightly. 'Well, that's a problem solved,' she said. And raising the glass she downed its contents.

'Guess what? I got the sack.' Gabriel had come home, unexpectedly, in the middle of the morning. For a man who'd just been fired he seemed remarkably cheerful. 'All the more time to carry on with my experiments.'

More acid? More Viva? Before Rosie had time to ask, he had picked up his green plastic Frisbee and headed for the door. By now she knew better than to ask where he was going. She'd had enough of the word 'Out'.

This is only half a life, she thought. No, it's only a quarter – it's not a life at all. At least she had her work again. She crossed the corridor to the dark room where the last of the Zav prints had been drying. These were reprints of the pictures taken in Cardiff. There was Mongoose waving a joint at the camera. Did that make the picture actionable? Could he sue for defamation of character? Hardly.

According to the last letter from Mrs Hankey, Bernadette's brother was now a registered heroin addict. Yet he looked so young and gleaming and cheeky in the photograph. The thick English joint just looked a bit of bravado.

Rosie knew all the arguments about the differences between hard drugs and soft drugs but she was sick and tired of the whole subject. As far as she was concerned her lover's prime relationship was no longer with herself. It was with LSD. With acid and with Viva Rapport. What *did* they do together? A month had passed since Miriam had produced the key to Professor Klosterboer's apartment. He would soon be returning from Europe and she had never made use of that opportunity of listening in. Cowardice? No. Well, perhaps . . . The phrase 'listeners never hear any good of themselves' had frequently rung round her brain.

Was that the bell? It was. She opened the door to find Taylor standing on the outside landing. Her twin had an airline bag over one shoulder and she was carrying a surprisingly masculine canvas holdall. Not that there was any reason for Taylor to overstate her case by being in perpetual buttons and bows.

'I hope you didn't mind me coming here?' She looked as though she had been crying.

'Why should I mind?' Come to think of it, Taylor had always steered clear of visiting Casino Point. 'Where are you going?'

'I've been. Baltimore. I thought I'd come back with a date fixed for the operation. Jesus, I even thought I might come back with it done. They've suspended their gender-reassignment programme.'

'I'm sorry, I don't understand.'

'They've stopped making cunts in Baltimore. It used to be the biggest centre for sex changes in the States. Now they've run a survey. They say it doesn't improve anybody's mental health, or their career, or their general well-being.' Taylor flung her bags onto the living-room floor. 'What do they know? They're just men with knives. It's desperate creatures like me who've convinced them they're demi-gods. Can I use your toilet? My plaster's giving me agony.' Taylor picked up the airline bag again.

'The bathroom's across the hall.'

'You got scissors?'

Rosie was struck by a sudden horrific thought. 'Taylor, you're not thinking of trying to do it yourself?'

'No,' came the muffled answer. Her twin had already found her way to the lavatory. 'But I could knife those doctors at the Johns Hopkins Institute. What gives them the right to say I've got to stay in this state?' Taylor let out a terrible scream. 'It's okay,' she called out reassuringly. 'That was just the plaster coming off. Oh the blessed relief!'

Even from where she stood, Rosie could hear the tinkling noise of water hitting water.

'Just put the scissors round the door,' called Taylor. 'Don't look. I can't bear anybody looking at it. I even tuck it between my legs in the bathtub. That's how much I disbelieve in it.'

Rosie passed the darkroom scissors round the door of the second bathroom and went to put on the coffee. By the time its smell had brought the world back to reality, Taylor had returned. Out of the corner of her eye Rosie couldn't help but see that a new barricade of sticking plaster must have been constructed beneath Taylor's tight mini-skirt. The legs were every bit as good as Rosie's own. The feet, the hands – there was no difference. It was almost impossible to believe in the existence of that despised remnant of masculinity. 'Taylor, we've got to do something for you.' It could have been Miriam Million speaking. 'Could you get it done in England?'

'Yes, but they insist on years of psychiatry. And their waiting lists are supposed to be miles long. Know what's in this flight bag? Ten thousand bucks. That's what we got for Gran'ma's ring. We daren't put it into the bank, there are too many debts.'

'Here.' Rosie already knew that her sister liked her coffee the same way as she did herself – black with one spoonful of brown sugar.

'Thanks. Some transsexuals have managed to get it done down in Mexico. It's all very hush-hush. Some of those butchers are like back-street abortionists.'

Rosie was horrified. 'You can't let just anybody start hacking at your body.'

'I know, I know. I need to get a good one. The best doctor in the world is supposed to be in Morocco. But I don't know how to find him.' Despair took over as she repeated, 'I just don't know how to find him. He did that English one who married into the aristocracy.'

'April Ashley?' Rosie recalled a sex-change saga that had once been serialised in Tippler's *News of the World*.

'She's beautiful,' said Taylor fervently. 'I already called International Directory but they don't have her number listed. Isn't he to dream about?' She had reached for one of Rosie's pictures of Zav. 'I'd go through ten operations for a guy like that.'

Rosie's phone bell was ringing in the living room and she leaned over to answer on the kitchen extension. 'Hello?'

'If you've got the pictures ready, I can give you the address of the publisher. That way he'll get them faster.' It was Danny calling from New York.

'Any news on my visa?' She had been waiting for this for nearly a month. There had been no shortage of talk about a book contract but the subject of the expired visa was one that always got pushed aside.

Rosie found herself listening to an awkward pause. This was followed by, 'The thing is, I've already had a bit of a run-in with the immigration people. I brought the Tidy Flamingos over from London, and the replacement drummer's papers weren't in order. I can't get away with too much too often. Just give me time to mend a couple of bridges.'

'Okay.' Along the way Rosie Tattersall had learned how to deal with Danny Cahn. 'But those pictures don't go in the post till I get something. I need the name of the doctor who did April Ashley's operation.'

'He's a man in Marrakesh. I only know because he did somebody from the Carousel as well. You want I should call Paris? It's done. I'll ring you back in ten minutes.'

And he did. Name of the doctor, address of the clinic, telephone number – the lot. 'And *now* will you post those prints?' Danny began to dictate another address.

Rosie wrote it down. 'Count it as done,' she said soothingly. Dan's style was catching.

Whilst they had been waiting for his call, the pictures had already been packed into photographic envelopes. 'Come on, we're going to the post office. All I need is to address them.'

But Taylor wasn't letting go of the pad. Her eyes were shining. The Holy Grail could never have been held more reverently. 'Just the words of the address are like a magic spell,' she said. 'It's like having a passport to being the real me.' Her eyes filled with tears. 'To think you did it. God, I used to hate you! I was vile. But that wasn't me it was *him*.'

Rosie wondered whether she should be crying too. 'Be a bit careful of using the word "passport" around me,' she said ruefully. 'You do realise they could deport me?'

It was almost a mistake to say 'thank you' to the middle-aged woman behind the counter of the little post office on Euclid Avenue. As she stamped your parcel she would always reply, wearily, 'There's no need to thank me, I am only doing my job.' Today she added, 'No more, no less – just my job.'

By contrast, Taylor's thanks were in every shade of joy known to man, woman or transsexual. That's when she wasn't crying with happiness, or laughing at herself for doing it. She had the Moroccan address folded up in a pocket. Every now and then, as they began to cross the campus, she would take it out and just pause and gaze at it, in amazed wonder.

Rosie could actually *feel* Taylor's euphoria. 'It's amazing how that telepathic thing we've got has lasted, isn't it?'

'I'm supposed to be quite psychic,' smiled Taylor.

'Me too. At least that's what a medium in London said.' She remembered something else: 'He was the person who told me I was to be sure to bring the diamond ring to America. Taylor, can you *read* people?' It wasn't a question she would have asked anybody else.

But Taylor knew exactly what she meant. 'You mean the first glance will always tell you more about somebody than five years of living next door would? Of course I do that. I've

487

always done it. When I was little I thought everybody did it. Does it ever let you down?'

Rosie thought of Bernadette Barrett. 'I get in trouble when I go against my instincts. Sometimes common sense and just being around somebody makes me think, No, you've got to be wrong this time. They're not awful, they're lovely. And sooner or later they always turn round and stab me. I was once wrong about a woman on a Greyhound bus but I wasn't well at the time. What do you make of *him*? That guy over there. Quickly, tell me what you can read.' Over on the grass, two young men were deeply occupied in throwing a green plastic Frisbee around.

'The one with the muscles or the Greek statue?'

'He's Italian actually. Yes, that one.'

Taylor answered unhesitatingly: 'Spoiled. But good and kind underneath. And lost, dreadfully lost. I feel as though I want to weep with him. Huge sex appeal but whatever happened to his sex drive?'

'Drugs have got it.' She hoped Taylor wouldn't ask her anything more about Gabriel. 'You're much better at it than I am, you're more specific.'

'The other one's quite cute,' said Taylor. 'Bit too much like a willing dog. I've had johns like that. They always want to be somebody's slave.'

They continued walking towards the Sproull Plaza. Johns? Wasn't that what American prostitutes called their clients?

'Yes,' said Taylor – though Rosie had not asked the question aloud.

'But how could you oblige them? I mean . . .'

'In this in-between state? Men are fools. They always begin by thinking they want to screw you. What you have to do is turn them round to an alternative. But you gotta make it sound exotic: "Oh Charlie, I've got a *much* naughtier idea than that." I only ever did it when we were broke. Real broke. *Hungry* broke.'

'And none of them ever knew?'

Taylor paused and gave her sister a sparkling smile: 'Those that did paid extra – for the privilege.'

Down on the Sproull Plaza, Holy Hubert was bawling his head off. This spiky-haired evangelist was such a lunchtime fixture that the fountain on the Plaza had been named after his dog. It was called Ludwig's Fountain because the black mongrel always stood ankle-deep in the waters of the fountain's basin.

'This town is turning into the new Gomorrah,' proclaimed Hubert.

'Promises, promises!' Taylor shouted back. She could even shout like a woman. And Rosie had noticed that when her former brother spoke, he pitched his voice in such a way as to retract the faint suggestion of Adam's apple in his throat. The illusion of femininity was total. And until she'd walked through the streets with Taylor, she'd had no idea of how many men got off on the idea of bedding a pair of twins. You could see it in their eyes. And the looks they gave Taylor were exactly the same as the ones she got herself.

But the twins weren't drawing glances at the moment. Zav Hankey was. He was walking towards them with his mouth hanging open in astonishment.

'What are you doing in Berkeley?' asked Rosie.

'Who's *that*?' was all he replied. But the words were charged with excitement.

'I'm Rosie's twin,' said Taylor. 'With *all* that implies,' she added wickedly.

'But you can't be.'

'Oh but I can.' Taylor was skilled at handling men; Taylor knew how to *fascinate* them.

Reluctantly, Zav transferred his gaze back to Rosie. 'If I'd met her in the street, I'd never have known it wasn't you.' The voice belonged to a man who was suddenly confronting amazing possibilities.

Rosie remembered what Danny had told her, years before, about Zav and the female impersonator in Hamburg. *'He didn't know. Well, not at first.'*

But Taylor was leaving him in no doubt. 'I used to be Christopher. Now I'm Taylor. And soon I'll be off to Marrakesh for the final snip.'

She could have been one of the Knights Templar talking

about the Holy Land. Hadn't their sexuality been a bit questionable, too? But this wasn't just sexuality – it was a matter of gender.

Zav seemed not one whit perturbed. 'I've just bought an old Ford Thunderbird. The best mechanic for them is here in Berkeley so I brought it over to be fixed.' He dragged his eyes off Taylor and allowed Rosie a smile. 'I've been calling you but you were always busy.' For the first time in his life Zav was speaking to her as though she was just his sister. It was as though years of yearning had evaporated. The whole core of his attention was now directed towards a new alternative.

This had to be the sexual revolution taken just about as far as it could go. And Rosie felt a sad sense of loss. But that was mean, it was being a dog in a manger. 'So what do we all want to do?' she asked them.

'Please!' murmured Taylor reproachfully. She seemed in as much of a trance as Zav.

He took charge. 'I was thinking of going to see *Fantasia* while I was waiting.' It had been playing non-stop, at a cinema at the bottom of Telegraph Avenue, for four years.

Taylor was sparkling again. She really *was* a sequin in sunlight. '*Fantasia*? The air's bright blue in that moviehouse. You only have to breathe in to get stoned. You go straight off to Never-Never Land.'

'That sounds kind of nice,' smiled Zav.

'Okay,' said Taylor happily. 'Let's go.'

But Rosie didn't want to breathe in and get stoned. 'You two go.'

Zav came back almost too quickly with, 'You're sure?'

'Don't forget your things are at my house,' Rosie reminded her twin. The words 'my house' for an apartment had sounded very American. 'Have fun.'

'Try stopping us,' sparkled Taylor. 'Catch you later.'

As the pair of them melted into the downhill crowd, Rosie couldn't be sure but she thought that Taylor had already taken hold of Zav's hand. Oh dear, whatever would Mrs Hankey make of all this? Ludwig, the dog, let out a sudden anguished howl.

Gabriel stayed out all night. No warning, no telephone call during the evening; he simply went off with his gang of acid-heads and returned well after dawn. What's more, he was smashed. Not just a bit dazed and coming down. No, he was still flying like an eagle. Or perhaps it was seven eagles because he kept saying, 'I've got seven thought processes going on in my head, at one and the same time.' After a while he attempted to clarify this with: 'It's like juggling with seven golden balls. If I want to, I can throw one thought up higher than the rest but all seven are going on concurrently.'

One of these thoughts must have turned round and bitten him because – suddenly – he began to mutter to himself in Italian. No longer inexperienced in such matters, Rosie made a strong solution of glucose and hot water and forced him to drink it. This was a potion which generally managed to tether him back to the ground.

'It's that new stuff,' he grumbled, 'that shit acid they're making in Walnut Creek. Sorry.' He wasn't apologising to Rosie. He was speaking to the cup.

How much more of this am I meant to take? she wondered. Through the open window she could hear noises that suggested the beginnings of a real-life Sunday morning: a lawnmower sputtering from somewhere down below, and the thwack of a rubber ball bouncing through children's laughter. A distant bell could only be tolling for early Mass on Holy Hill. Rosie remembered the Roman Catholic church next to Teapot Hall. And then all the other churches they used to pass, the God-boxes of Broad Street, on the way to Quakers. She had never looked forward to Meeting for Worship, but once it was over there had always been a tremendous sense of release. If Gabriel escaped with drugs perhaps she needed to be able to escape into something of her own.

'That glucose really works,' he said. 'I'm nearly down. At least I think I am. You haven't by any chance repainted this room with sparkling silver stuff?' he asked innocently.

'No, Gabriel, I haven't.' She could have been talking to a six-year-old, a nice wayward child. 'Do you want coffee?'

'I have to get to Viva's.'

Not so nice. 'At nine o'clock on a Sunday morning?' She was suddenly filled with the kind of anger that causes people to reach for knives.

'I have an appointment.' He went into his routine of stretching like a cat. 'I made it for early because I didn't think you'd be up.'

'I've been up half the night.' If the coffee pot hit his stupid head it would make a very satisfactory bang. But it was still a beautiful head, she couldn't deny that. And perhaps she shouldn't judge Viva too harshly. In her time, Rosie had cast her own spells; she had done a drawing of the man of her dreams and willed him to appear.

And here he was. Unemployed, burned out on acid, and all but impotent. How could you leave somebody in that state? But if she was going to go, it had better be soon. Where? Where would she go? She couldn't even begin to imagine a life without him. And what would she use to go with? When would they pay the advance on Zav's photo-biography? She hadn't even signed the contract. But it was here. It had been sitting on the desk since yesterday. She would sign it and then she would post it. Whether she sent it or whether she stayed, at least that would be doing something in her own right.

Gabriel had stopped stretching. 'Got to get moving. Mustn't miss my session.' He lurched for the door on legs that looked rubbery.

Rosie barred his way. 'You can't go out in that state. And if that woman has any conscience, she'll never agree to hypnotise you. Not whilst you're all doped-up.'

'You don't understand our experiments.'

'I understand that you've lost all respect for your own brain. It used to be faster than anybody's I'd ever met. And now you've gone and fried it.'

'Gotta go,' he insisted stubbornly.

'At least promise me you won't take the car?'

'Drove here,' he muttered. 'Why shouldn't I drive there?' Then he spoke quite clearly: 'Can I get past you please?'

Just because he'd said 'please' she automatically moved to

one side, and even as she did it she could have kicked herself for her own weakness. 'There comes a point when I have to start thinking about self-preservation,' she said to him.

'Why?' he smiled. 'Why, when I am you and you are me?'

Her reflexes weren't quick enough. Her kick only hit the door which he had left open as he darted out. The kick slammed it shut. Now her toe hurt and she felt half-drugged herself, from lack of sleep. Wild thoughts were coming in on her like a rain of arrows. These thoughts were not specific, they were more like test samples of emotions: panic, fear, and brief visions of leaving the country on an aeroplane. Perhaps a shower would calm her down.

It didn't. Rosie dried herself and reached for the aerosol of deodorant. That was when she remembered that she'd thrown it away, in the cause of protecting the ozone layer. Mrs Smith, the maid, must have tidied the new roll-on stick into the bathroom cupboard.

Yes she had. Only what was this? An old tin soap box sat on the glass shelf. It hadn't been there last night. Gabriel must have brought it in with him. Somehow she knew, even before she looked inside, that it would not contain a bar of Lifebuoy. The tin box contained exactly the same thing as Mongoose's tin box had contained, all those years ago – the barrel and the needle of a hypodermic, a clear plastic bag of brown powder, and a blackened spoon.

Every tile in the bathroom seemed to be pressing in on Rosie and she felt so nauseous that the only thing to do was put her finger down her throat so that she would be properly sick. She wanted to be sick and she wanted out. She had pitted herself against LSD and against Viva Rapport. 'But I'm not going to be a heroine for heroin.' As she said this aloud, she realised that she had just uttered something approaching a pun. And Rosie had always hated puns.

What's more, if she went . . . No, *when* she went, she knew she would be in grave danger of hating herself. Once and for all she had to know exactly what she was leaving. She needed to fill in some missing details.

She walked across to the living room, reached for the nasty, lightweight cream telephone and dialled Miriam's number. Two rings and it was answered. 'You up, Miriam?'

'Since hours ago.'

'Have you still got that professor's key? The one to the apartment next to Viva's.'

'I even managed to get hold of a stethoscope. Another garage sale! I thought I'd keep ahead. I've been expecting this call.'

'Has Gabriel just gone up there?'

'Yup. He seemed to be having a bit of a problem with the steps. Actually, he was talking to them.'

Rosie took a deep breath. 'I may have had enough, Miriam.'

The answer that came back was spoken in a deadly level voice. 'He is your man, Rosemarie.'

And that was when Rosie finally allowed herself to weep. 'I know. I do know,' she sobbed. 'But how many allowances am I meant to make? Anyway, you got rid of your husband.'

'Blow your nose and come on down. We'll play Sherlock Holmes and Dr Wilson.'

'Watson.'

'Whoever. Just get yourself here.'

As Rosie walked down Virginia Street, sunlight was playing on dozens of little fountains. In reality they were water sprinklers, set into the lawns of solid, white-painted houses. But they still made for a lot of miniature rainbows. Too many rainbows and too much chasing after them. This whole West Coast dream was a fake, an illusion. Words sometimes lodged themselves in Rosie's brain and refused to go away. This morning the word was 'chimera'. Didn't it mean something that was forever beckoning yet impossible to reach? Even if it didn't, that was how Rosie felt about Berkeley. And about the so-called revolution. And most of all, it was what she thought of her chances of a whole life with Gabriel Bonarto.

A disconsolate figure was sitting on a fire hydrant. It was Melinda Gruber.

'Hi,' the child said. Even that one word came out as Southern. 'I'm just waiting for this guy. I'm beginning to think he went in the front door and straight out the back.'

'How you doing, Melinda?'

'Me? I dunno. Yes I do.' She let out a deep sigh. 'Suddenly it ain't bayootiful any more.'

Professor Klosterboer's apartment was not precisely the twin to Viva's but it was very similar in basic design. And their living rooms were divided from one another only by a lath and plaster wall.

'Keep your voice down,' murmured Miriam. 'This whole tower is like a giant listening trumpet. I'm not even sure we'll need these.' She was clutching a heavy glass tumbler and an antique stethoscope, labelled *John Bell and Croyden, Wigmore Street, London W1*. It looked old enough to have been left behind by Edward the Seventh, on one of his visits to San Francisco.

'I got it for fifty cents,' whispered Miriam. Her voice grew slightly more natural as she looked round the apartment. 'God, isn't there something tragic about old bachelors who live on their own?' Her sweeping gesture embraced an array of strictly utilitarian furniture, a bottle of cough medicine on the mantelpiece and a discarded sock-suspender by the telephone. 'I don't think he has sex any more,' she added sadly.

'I know the feeling,' said Rosie. From the next apartment she could hear the indistinct rise and fall of Viva's fluting tones.

Putting her finger warningly to her lips, Miriam placed the open end of the tumbler against the wall and pressed her ear up against the glass base. 'She's asking him if he's quite comfortable.'

'I've a terrible feeling we're going to hear more than we should.'

Miriam removed the glass. 'Okay. We'll give up right now.'

'No. Give me that stethoscope.' Could there be very old germs on the pieces that had just gone into her ears? Experimentally, she placed the listening part against Miriam's heart. It was banging away like a piston engine. Miriam's stomach chose that moment to rumble and Rosie nearly jumped out of her skin. 'You're very wild in there.'

'Try it against the wall.'

It wasn't the same as a telephone but you could definitely hear. Right through the wall you could make out exactly what Viva was saying: '. . . and nothing can harm you. You are blissfully happy and blissfully relaxed. Relaxed and happy, happy and relaxed.' The hypnotic drone ceased and the next word, 'Gabriel?' was quite sharp. 'I'm taking you back to your fifth birthday. You are five years old. What town are you living in?'

'Hotels. We always live in hotels.'

It was the voice of a small boy. Rosie nearly let go of the stethoscope in amazement. But Viva was talking again: 'Did you get any birthday presents?'

'Chicago. We're in Chicago.'

'Did you get any presents?'

'Orson sent a big conjuring set.'

'Would you like to tell me anything else about Orson?' asked Viva greedily.

'Did you know he sawed Rita Hayworth in half? For the soldiers. It's only a trick,' the solemn little voice assured her.

'Are you having a party today, Gabriel?'

'No. Just room service. Maeve and me always have room service. I'm in Chicago,' he repeated, as though he feared he hadn't been understood.

'Okay, Gabriel, I want you to start breathing deeply again. In and out, in and out. Each deep breath is taking you deeper and deeper into trance. Relaxed and happy, happy and relaxed. Now you are three years old . . . two years old . . . You are now one. And another deep contented breath takes you into your mother's womb.'

Viva's voice droned on: 'You are going back in time. Back and back and back. Back to a previous life. Deep breaths, deep breaths. Latch onto that different life as you feel it flooding in . . . and *speak* to me.'

'Good day to you.' It didn't sound much like Gabriel at all. This new personality's voice was lighter than the Italian's usual one – it sounded like the voice of a man who was very thin.

Viva went straight in with: 'To whom am I speaking?'

'To Thomas. You are speaking to Thomas De Quincey.'

'And how are you today, Thomas?'

'Full of debt and constipation.'

'How old are you, Thomas?'

No reply.

'Are you still looking for Ann?'

This question set Rosie thinking that the pair in the next room must have travelled along this route before.

'Remind me a little bit about Ann,' urged Viva.

Another pause and then: 'When I kissed her at our final farewell, she put her arms about my neck, and wept without speaking a word. I hoped to return in a week at farthest, and I agreed with her that on the fifth night from that, and every night afterwards, she should wait for me at six o'clock, near the bottom of Great Titchfield Street – to prevent our missing each other in the great Mediterranean of Oxford Street.'

Miriam was obviously deeply impressed. 'What wonderful antique-sounding words.'

'Yes, but they're not his own.' Rosie let the stethoscope fall to her waist. 'He's quoting directly from *Confessions of an English Opium Eater*. Whether he knows it or not, he's just reciting something that's already written down.'

Nevertheless, Miriam remained awed. 'I wonder whether Viva knows he's doing that?'

'I don't know and I don't care. I only came to America because I thought that fixation was over.'

'Would you mind if I listened to a little bit more?' Miriam, who had always had beautiful manners, seemed more worried about intruding on Rosie's privacy than on Gabriel's.

'Feel free.' That foxy Thomas was much more deeply rooted in their lives than she had ever realised.

'I don't believe it.' Miriam's ear was still pressed to the glass. 'You've got to listen to this.'

Rosie placed the sounding piece of the stethoscope back against the wall. The tinny male voice on the side was intoning, 'I was buried for a thousand years, in stone coffins, with mummies and sphinxes, in narrow chambers at the heart of eternal pyramids. I was kissed, with cancerous kisses, by crocodiles; and laid, confounded with all unutterable slimy things, amongst reeds and Nilotic mud.'

'Who is he *now*?' gasped Miriam.

'Still De Quincey. And it's still from the book. He's talking about the effects of drugs.' Rosie had abandoned all pretence of lowering her voice. 'I can suddenly see something that I ought to have seen years ago. Gabriel is possessed. I don't care whether all this Thomas stuff is real or imaginary. It's just drugs, drugs, drugs – in that life as much as this. I can't win. I don't stand a chance. And I need some peace.'

Miriam turned into a monument to contrition. 'I entered into this whole thing too light-heartedly. But who was to know . . .? I'm sorry. I'm really sorry. What kind of peace can we get for you?'

Rosie was weeping like a bewildered child. 'The sort of peace there used to be when I was little – in the silence. At Quaker meetings.'

Another set of church bells had begun ringing in the distance. 'There are Quakers here,' said Miriam quietly. 'They're on Vine Street at Shattuck. It's only five minutes away.'

'And I'm meant to limp right back to the point where I started? Beaten?'

'It's as good a way as I can think of.'

'I can't go on like this, Miriam. I can't.'

'Then go and see what your silence has to offer you.' Miriam fingered the glass tumbler distastefully. 'I'm going to throw this in the trash,' she said. 'After what it's just been through, I wouldn't want anybody to drink out of it.'

The Berkeley Friends' Meeting House was a single-storey, brown wooden building. Solid and not at all a shack, its stern edges were softened by creepers and by plants and flowering shrubs, which grew right up to the edge of the concrete steps. The people making their way into the building could have been Friends from Mount Street in Manchester – in semi-fancy dress. There were some elderly

Californian fanooks (how long was it since she had last thought of that word?), all sunburned skin and well-washed cotton. And there was a liberal spattering of girls in trailing Telegraph Avenue garments, and of long-haired young men in standard revolutionary denim.

It was the eyes that Rosie had forgotten. Quakers have a lot of serenity in their eyes. But not all Quakers; and certainly not Patti Spinoza who was standing on the sidewalk and catching hold of people, self-importantly, as they headed for the entrance.

'Rosie? What a surprise! A nice one, of course,' she added in more Quakerly tones. 'I must write and tell Bernadette that I saw you again. She was so pleased to have your address.'

'My address?' Rosie knew she must have sounded stupid, but why on earth should Bernadette Barrett want her address?

'I got Miriam to give it to me. Is this the first time you've been here?'

'Yes.'

'Your first meeting?'

Rosie could tell Patti was all set to take her over. But she had an answer up her sleeve which was guaranteed to put a stop to that. 'Oh no, not my first meeting at all. I'm a birthright Quaker.'

The room used for worship smelled of old woodfires. It was too warm for one today, but there was an open fireplace and not much else of any distinction. Just white walls and a table, and a lot of wooden chairs. And peace. Real peace. One chair at the front was different from the rest. It was upholstered. And even as she noticed it, an old man came in carrying an inflated air cushion and placed it on the seat. As he sat down, he too was entirely familiar – there had been just such another elderly Friend at Mount Street.

She had forgotten the *texture* of the silence, the fact that it had a life of its own. It was like trusting the water to hold you up when you wanted to float. She trusted and was borne up and was held. All those years ago . . . her last meeting had ended with Christopher singing 'I'm Alabammy Bound'.

Silence.

Odd that it wasn't boring. But it wasn't. It was a silence you could belong in. Silence.

A Friend rose to her feet. She looked like one of the well-scrubbed women who had enquired about Hawaiian dancing classes in the bar of the Berkeley City Club. But this was somebody with more important issues on her mind. 'The young people are all living in fear of the Governor sending in the National Guard to control their demonstrations. If they do come here with their weapons, we should be ready for them. We should cut thousands of flowers and give them to the young people – to put down the soldiers' guns. We may not be able to turn their swords into ploughshares but we can do that much.' The woman sat down with a thump.

Silence continued to weave the Friends together. After quite a few minutes the old man in the special chair got up. 'If I have a fear in these troubled times, it is that the students will react violently to the sight of armed troops. Could we just hold the cause of peace in this town in the light?'

So they were still holding things in the light, were they? As a child, Rosie had always imagined this as a bright pinhole in velvety blackness. It began like that and then spread out into a broad golden beam. And that's where you were meant to place your problems. She tried to hold the figure of Gabriel in this glow and her new calm was immediately fractured. 'I'm lost.' She could hear herself talking inside her own head. She wasn't standing up and giving ministry – this was just between herself and the light. 'I tried to do what Ruth said in the Bible. I went where he went. That's what got me here. I've done everything I know and it's not enough. I have to leave him. I have to go home.'

Except home wasn't a place, it was a state of mind. 'And I can't find it. I want out. And I want it now – before my resolution weakens. But I can't leave America because of the visa. And I'm sorry I said I didn't have a safety net . . .' Now she was openly talking to God. 'I did have one, I had the ring. I could have sold that, only now it's given away.' Against all common sense and reason, peace began flooding back into her. And Rosie's mind was unaccountably filled with those words written by Juliana of Norwich: *And all shall be well, and all shall be well, and all manner of thing shall be well.'*

The highways and byways of this thought process had gone on through the silence and through people giving ministry, and she must have been thinking for a long time because the man in the armchair suddenly stood up and shook hands with the woman next to him. Meeting for Worship was at an end.

For people who specialise in sitting in silence, Quakers can also make a lot of noise. Suddenly people were vying with one another to get to their feet and brandish bits of paper and make announcements about peace vigils and crèches for displaced Korean mothers. Under cover of all this, Rosie got to her own feet and slipped out.

Another escapee, a young man who was already smoking a cigarette on the steps outside, smiled at her and said, 'Aren't you Professor Bonarto's lady? I'm one of his students. We're really going to miss him. He was the best.'

It was an uphill climb to Casino Point. Along the way, she passed a modern wooden church with people pouring out of it. And that was the moment Rosie got the old sense of release: the reward she'd always seemed to get in her childhood, on the way home from Mount Street as her father's car drove them past all the emptying God-boxes of Pendleton.

When she put her key into the front door of the apartment, the telephone was already ringing. It stopped just before she got to it, and then it started up again. The whirr inside her head told her that this could only be Taylor. 'Hi, Taylor. You'll never guess where I've just been!'

'And you'll never guess where I am. I'm down at Big Sur. Zav and I are just going off to have lunch in Carmel.'

'All your things are still here.'

'I've got new things now.' Taylor sounded like somebody living in a dream.

'You can't have got a new ten thousand dollars,' her twin protested indignantly. 'I wrapped the flight bag in plastic and put it at the bottom of the fridge. It's in that big drawer that's meant for salad.'

'I'm in love, Rosie.'

'I know.' Without even thinking about it, she had known for days.

'We called Marrakesh.' Taylor's voice was practically singing. 'My own doctor has to send him a report but it looks as though I'm just weeks off surgery. There's only one fly in the ointment; we're dodging reporters. Can't talk. We've got a table at Nepenthe's for twelve thirty. I'll call you again later. Hang on, Zav wants a word . . .'

'Rosie? Good morning. I love you. But I love Taylor more. Is that okay?'

'Don't ask me. Ask your mother!' The whole idea was so unusual that she couldn't think of anything else to say. Except: 'Be happy.'

'Happy? I didn't know what the word meant before this.' He sounded exultant. 'And the new songs I'm writing are going like a bomb.'

Well, that's one in the eye for astrology, thought Rosie as she replaced the receiver. One twin shining with happiness and the other surrounded by problems. Except Connie's watermelons hadn't arrived together. There had been thirty minutes' difference between them. Presumably, in half an hour, a lot could alter in the heavens.

Something was altering on earth. The Sunday quiet was being shattered by loud bangings at the front door and cries of, 'Police. Open up. Come on, open up!'

What could Gabriel have done now? She'd warned him not to take that car. 'Hang on,' she called out, 'I'm coming.' She opened the door. There were two of them and both were in uniform. 'What's happened? Is he okay?'

'Are you Rosemary Tattersall?'

'Yes.'

'Get your passport. We're taking you downtown.'

At least she wasn't in a cell. They'd dumped her in a windowless office. Apart from the wooden desk and a steel chair, it had the look of a storeroom. Big cardboard boxes labelled *Live Gas Cylinders – Handle With Care* were piled up to the ceiling. A notice board on the wall had an old 'Wanted' poster on it – the same kind as in Western movies. But the man in the photograph wasn't a cowboy, he was Ken Kesey of the Merry Pranksters. Somebody had drawn a balloon to his mouth which circled the scrawled words, 'It's nicer on the Milky Way!'

One of the policemen who had brought her downtown pushed open the door. He was carrying a paper cup full of slopping coffee. 'You take sugar?' He had the shortest haircut she'd ever seen in California. Big and blond, he looked like an ageing version of one of those actors in surfing movies. 'The guys from immigration have a way to come.' The sugar was in paper sachets. 'You mind stirring it with a pencil?'

Rosie shook her head. 'What's going to happen to me?'

'Your passport says you've overstayed your welcome. You're going to be deported, lady.'

'Just like that? No trial, no nothing?'

'Just like that. You've not had your phone call yet. You're allowed to make one phone call.'

Miriam? No, she'd said she was going out to brunch. Zav would presumably be sitting at some restaurant table, the name of which she had already forgotten. You could never reach Danny on a Sunday, he always vanished to somewhere called Fire Island . . .

'Brits generally call their consulate.' The policeman was trying to be helpful. 'Not that they could do much to assist you.'

Gabriel? Sad to think he came so low down on the list but you could never guarantee what state he'd be in. And she certainly didn't want the police escorting him back to Casino Point – not with heroin on the premises.

'I've been in England,' the policeman was offering her a filter cigarette, 'in the service. I was at a place called Burtonwood. Ever hear of it?'

'Oh I've heard of it,' she replied darkly, as she waved away the proffered Lucky Strike. The American air base at Burtonwood could have been said to have changed the whole course of her life.

503

The policeman seemed to be remembering the place with affection: 'We used to go for nights out in Liverpool. It didn't do to meet your girlfriend at the station. The hookers used to try and beat them up. Used to call them "lousy free fucks". If you'll pardon the French,' he added politely.

'It's a word I *have* heard.' Who could she telephone? Who?

'Those Lancashire women were really tough.' He gave equal weight to every syllable of the county. 'You ever hear of somebody called Bernadette Barrett?'

Rosie was flabbergasted. 'How on earth did you know her?'

'Me? I don't. But she was the one who sent us the information about you. She wrote a letter. You carry matches?'

She still had some in her handbag, from Finnochio's. She had taken them as a souvenir. 'I fully expected you to take everything off me,' she said. 'I mean to say, I could set fire to the place.' The matches were tucked in a tight pocket in the silk lining of the bag.

'So you've heard all the stories about us, on Telegraph, eh? What was you expecting, a strip search? No, you're immigration's baby not ours.'

She was still having difficulty removing the matches. Something else was wedged in with them. The two items finally came out together, matches and a visiting card. Gino's visiting card.

She actually thanked God in words in her head: 'Thank you very much, God,' she said. Aloud she announced, 'Now I know who I need to call.' But would Gino be there on a Sunday afternoon?

13

Irlams o'th' Height was beginning to catch up with the Sixties. A notice in the window of the dry-cleaner's on the corner of Claremont Road proclaimed *Mini-skirts Cleaned Here – Twopence Per Inch*. Round the next corner, in Saracen Street, Mrs Hankey had barely an inch of space to spare, but she still found room for Rosie.

'As long as you don't mind sleeping in the attic. Moondog can come down a floor and go in with Star. It'll be easier to keep an eye on him, in the back room.' Mrs Hankey had aged ten years in two. 'I've got something to tell you. Tippler's in bed in the front parlour; he can't manage stairs any more. In fact there's not much he can manage.' Could those really be tears in the stern eyes? 'He's not got long. That's why Zav sent the kids over. That little lad idolises his gran'dad, absolutely idolises him.'

'What's wrong with Tippler?' asked Rosie. She was still dazed from the night flight.

'Years of smoking bloody Woodbines, that's what's wrong.' Tears had been replaced by anger. 'I feel like wheeling his bed into one of their shareholders' meetings. I'd like those bloody profiteers to hear the sound of that cough. It's cancer.' They never quite said the word aloud in Irlams o'th' Height, they mouthed it instead: 'cancer'.

Rosie felt as though something was eating at her soul. Her body was back in Lancashire but her mind was still in California. Goodness only knows what she would have done without the help of Gino, and the Bonartos' American lawyer. Whilst she had remained in that awful office with the gas cylinders, they had collected all her belongings from Casino Point, persuaded the immigration authorities to allow her to leave the United States without a deportation stamp in her passport – there had been no question of Rosie being allowed to remain – and got her onto a flight for

505

London, first class. Throughout all of this Gabriel had remained vanished.

'But he's never stopped ringing up,' said Mrs Hankey. 'He doesn't seem to have any sense of day and night.' At that moment the telephone began to ring again. 'Moondog! See who it is.'

The familiar taste of tea with sterilised milk had revived Rosie a little. But she wasn't sure she was up to talking to Gabriel. In fact she knew she wasn't; and she just hoped it wasn't him.

It was. 'Say I'm not here,' she hissed at Moondog.

'She says she's not here.'

Rosie took the phone from him. 'Gabriel? I'm jet-lagged and I'm absolutely surrounded.' As Mrs Hankey began ushering the children into the scullery, Rosie tried to signal that this would be unnecessary. 'You let this happen to me, Gabriel. Or maybe I wasn't firm enough and I let it happen to myself. But it has happened. And there's no chance of them allowing me in again for months. Anyway I don't care. I'm not coming back to live with you and a fridge full of drugs.'

'You keep 'em in the refrigerator?' An interested Moondog had strayed back into the kitchen. Mrs Hankey extended a long Olive Oyl arm and pulled him back into the scullery. The door slammed shut.

There was the usual transatlantic delay of a second before Gabriel's voice came back with: 'Okay, I'll come there.' He sounded about as grown-up as the child she could hear protesting on the other side of the door.

'Gabriel, this isn't Berkeley. You couldn't lurch round here with glazed eyes. You'd soon find yourself locked up. I've just got one word to say to you. Heroin.'

'Are you mad? This line could be tapped. Look, I don't want to get other people into trouble . . .' His voice broke off and then he started again with, 'I'd do anything for you, Rosie, anything.'

'What other people? Dope dealers? And I know your anything. It just involves reaching for your cheque book. I'm not for sale. You began by having me for nothing and it didn't mean a thing to you.'

'It meant everything.'

'No. You don't even need me. If you're having an affair with anybody, it's with an idea – it's with Thomas De Quincey.'

'Leave him out of it.'

'Fine. But that means I'm leaving you out of it too. I don't know where you end and he begins. And I've stopped caring, Gabriel.' She was too tired to do more than repeat herself: 'I've just stopped caring.' With this she replaced the receiver.

Only it wasn't true. She hadn't stopped caring at all. Love takes no account of common sense or bad experience. Against all odds Rosemary Tattersall still loved Gabriel Bonarto as much as she had ever done. She had simply run out of the strength to cope with him.

'Can we come in?' called Moondog through the door.

'Course you can.' Real life had to start again. The Berkeley dream was over.

Rosie grieved yet Rosie prospered. There is a great difference between being hard and being strong; and the American experience had bred a streak of self-preservation that she would never live to regret. The first person to come up against this was Danny Cahn.

'Dan? Can you hear me?' The international operator had landed her with a poor connection. 'Listen, the one thing that got left behind in California was that contract. I never got round to posting it. I'm on Mrs Hankey's telephone, the operator's advising duration and charge, so this has to be snappy. I need a new copy of the contract and it's got to have a new clause in it. I have to be able to approve the finished book. Before, I didn't care. But things have changed. That book has to be absolutely right because I'm all set to make my career work properly.'

'You sound like a robot.'

'No, I just sound like the new me. I've already sold a set of my Berkeley pictures to the *Observer* colour supplement. And they've commissioned me to do a big spread on the Manchester club scene. Zav wouldn't recognise the place.

The whole town's clubbing it. I want to be sure you're hearing me, Dan. No clause, no contract.'

She got what she wanted.

Rosie's victory was symptomatic of a time when liberated women had stopped burning brassieres and started building bank balances. Tenderness had not vanished from her life. Like passion, it was now directed into her work. When man landed on the moon, Rosie was inspired to take one of the most famous pictures of her entire career. The moment the news of the successful Apollo Mission was announced, people rushed out into the streets in excitement. And Rosie snatched a photograph of two little girls pointing a Box Brownie camera at the moon.

She developed and printed this picture in Mr Molyneux's darkroom at Gledhill's the chemists. The darkroom alchemy was magical as ever. Under the red light's glow, beneath the surface of the washing waters, the print started to form itself on the sensitised paper.

'If you ever needed any proof that your talent's back,' breathed Mr Molyneux, 'you've got it there. We taught you well, me and Freddie Click-Click.'

'Whatever happened to Freddie Click-Click?' It was years since Rosie had thought of the television personality who had handed the basic skills of photography to a whole generation of young viewers.

'Last I read about him he was supposed to have gone into a monastery. But that was yonks ago. While we're here, shall we print up that little register-office wedding?'

She had never ceased to be Mr Molyneux's assistant. It was a fair swap for the use of processing facilities. Besides, it suited her very well – it stopped her getting big-headed and kept her real. Sid Molyneux already had the wedding negatives out. 'Didn't you shoot off a roll yourself, Rosie?'

'Yes. I've already printed up the contacts. One shot might just have something.' She handed him a sheet of tiny black and white prints. One of them was ringed round with a yellow wax-pencil circle.

Sid put a jeweller's spy-glass into his eye and peered. 'My God! It's to be hoped that the bridegroom never gets to see

508

this. She didn't want to marry him! And it's all there in her eyes. Now why did you catch that and I didn't?' he marvelled. 'Oh well, some take wedding groups and some make Art!' He hadn't changed. He was still as likeable and enthusiastic as he had been in her childhood.

For all her growing fame, Rosie thought nothing of doing quite humble jobs for Sid. On Saturday afternoons she was generally to be found rearranging brides' wedding veils and chivvying giggling bridesmaids to form themselves into graceful groups.

'Could we have you all under the baptistry window?' she asked. This was soon after her return from America. They were in the grounds of Worsley parish church. Worsley considered itself a cut above the surrounding districts. 'Three bridesmaids, is that right?'

'Three bridesmaids and a matron of honour. I was wondering when you'd recognise me, Rosie. I'm just back from my own honeymoon.' It was Hazel Hankey. Only these days she owned a shortie mink jacket and was called Mrs Proctor-Jones – a woman who was no longer on speaking terms with her own mother.

'Tudor!' she called out importantly. A handsome little ginger goblin came running, top hat in hand. 'And hands off, he's mine!' Hazel said to Rosie. The tails of the man's hired morning coat nearly touched the ground. His wife must have seen Rosie looking at them. 'He's usually beautifully turned out,' she said sadly. 'And I don't just mean Austin Reed.'

Rosie resumed her official role: 'Hazel, could I get you to mingle in with the bridesmaids?'

Sheelah Wilson had never taught Hazel how to mingle. The matron of honour managed to turn the other girls into a supporting cast. 'I want you to come and see my home,' she called to Rosie as Mr Molyneux moved in to take the picture. 'We're having a bit of a Hippie Night, next Friday. Why don't you come?'

The letters from Miriam were a constant source of pleasure. 'And she doesn't mind what she puts on the back of a postcard,' marvelled Mrs Hankey. 'She's certainly

509

completing our postwoman's education.' Miriam was in the throes of a new romance and – in typical Berkeley fashion – details of each succeeding caress were committed to paper. Miriam scorned commercial stationery (save the trees) and scribbled her notes on anything that came to hand, frequently on the back of paper flyers from Telegraph Avenue.

It was from these that Rosie learned that the dream of the revolution was escalating into a violent reality. One handbill even detailed a defence against tear gas: 'Separate the white of an egg from the yolk. Using a small paintbrush, apply egg-white in circles around eyelids and on sensitive skin under eyes.'

A whole lot of the handbills were concerned with something called People's Park. This was a vacant lot at the back of Telegraph Avenue. Strictly speaking, the site belonged to the university who had pulled down a warren of old rooming houses – the former homes of tribes of young people who had been drawn to Berkeley by the counter-culture. They retaliated by building a garden on the flattened land. And that was the cue for the long-anticipated pandemonium to break out. *Beware the Helicopter!* screamed one of the handbills. *The pigs are using telephoto lenses to gather evidence against us from the sky.* Miriam's letters told of tear gas, of flying bullets, and of Governor Reagan having the Riot Act read to tens of thousands of unheeding protesters.

Just the sight of all that psychedelic printing was enough to transport Rosie's mind back to California; this evening she was meant to clothe her body in hippie fancy dress, in the cause of Hazel's party.

'That daughter of mine's nothing but a bloody snob.' Mrs Hankey was devouring the printed side of the handbills with relish. 'I was born too soon. I'd have been in my element in all this. Trust our Hazel to go and turn the whole idea into a fund-raiser for the Young Conservatives. I don't know why you're even bothering going.'

'Guilt. I never got round to sending her a wedding present.'

'She's already got everything that opens and shuts. Present? You could try giving her a hammer and a sickle. They might just remind her that she's a traitor to her own class. Now Hazel's hooked that Tory midget, do you know what her next ambition is? She wants to be Queen of Ellesmere Park.'

Ellesmere Park, in Eccles, was a Victorian housing development; an estate of private roads edged with grandiose, turn-of-the-century houses, behind sooty private hedges, up tarmacadam drives. By the end of the Sixties, many of these had become white elephants on the property market, and not a few had been converted into flats. It was the later houses, the more manageable 1930s' villas on the edge of the park, that had come to be more sought after. Hazel Proctor-Jones lived in one of these. Double-fronted with Tudor touches, it didn't have a street number on its five-barred gate, it had a name – Mainwaring.

'Pronounced "Mannering",' said Hazel, as she took Rosie's coat. 'There's really an admission charge tonight but I'm waiving it in your case. Love the dress!' It was the cheesecloth kaftan, the one embroidered with apples and pears. Hazel herself – all lipstick and high heels – was wearing a peace headband round heavily lacquered blonde curls, and a sequined cocktail top in shades of the rainbow. This, over denim jeans which looked as though they'd been specially ripped for the occasion. 'Come through into the period room,' she said.

'The what?' gulped Rosie.

'It's where I show off my antiques.'

The room was furnished in reproduction Queen Anne. Even the logs in the fireplace were artificial. But the biggest fakes of all were the 'hippies'. Men in Beatles wigs from joke shops and girls hung in yards of plastic Poppit beads. The stereo was blaring out 'Let's Go to San Francisco'. Rosie couldn't decide whether she wanted to weep or shout.

'Tudor went all the way to Moss Side and bought some cannabis grass,' said Hazel, proudly. 'The only trouble is, we don't really know how to get it inside the cigarettes.'

'Have you got skins?' asked Rosie. She hadn't meant her voice to sound weary but it did.

'Do you mean Rizla papers?' They were sitting in a blue Wedgwood bowl with some Twiglets. The grass was lying on

511

top, in a clear plastic bag. 'The man said it was good stuff,' Hazel assured her.

'The man *always* says it's good stuff.' It was nothing like sensemilla. No buds, just chopped-up leafy bits. Rosie began to roll the American way. It involved less fuss than the English ritual of sticking the papers together.

'Who'd like a joint cigarette?' called Hazel importantly.

'Aren't we meant to pass just one around?' Tudor was smiling ingratiatingly at Rosie. The white tee shirt, with Golden Gate Bridge on it, was a mistake. It was very tight round the middle where the curve of his little tummy went down into his navel.

Hazel hadn't liked that smile. Her tight expression made it obvious that Tudor was meant to have eyes only for her. Plainly convinced that her husband was irresistible to all other women, she sent him off to the kitchen to collect a bowl of avocado dip.

'Is that the correct food?' she asked Rosie, earnestly. 'I couldn't decide what hippies would eat.'

Rosie remembered the kids on the steps of the Free Clinic with their slices of somebody else's discarded pizza. 'Whatever's going. They eat whatever's going.'

'I'm a bit annoyed with God,' said Hazel – she could have been talking about the Allied Dairies. 'He's arranged the television programmes very inconsiderately. There's a big hippie documentary on tonight. If it had just been last night, I'd have been all clued up. It's called *Revolution*. It's about that place you were in – Berkeley.' In the Lancashire accent of her childhood, Hazel would have pronounced the name of the town correctly. These days she was very careful to make it sound like Berkeley Square. She was obviously terrified of being taken for anything less than a lady.

Rosie handed the first joint to a young man who had been sitting waiting eagerly on the floor. 'What time's the documentary on?' she asked Hazel.

'Now.'

'If you want to me to roll some more of these, would you mind if I do them while I watch it?'

'The telly's in the lounge. You're in luck, we've just gone over to colour.'

Smoke was already rising from the joint. Rosie only hoped that the smell wouldn't make her cry with nostalgia. Joints on campus, joints at Miriam's, quick tokes outside the Durant Hotel . . . This joint smelt wrong. The odour was familiar but it had nothing to do with California. It dated right back to her childhood. Poor-Bertha-who-drags-a-leg had always been troubled with her chest. The man on the floor, inhaling reverently, wasn't smoking grass at all. He was smoking Potter's Herbal Asthma Mix. Oh well, at least the Proctor-Joneses had been privy to one genuine hippie experience – they'd managed to get themselves ripped off by a dope dealer.

'Good stuff this,' said the young man on the floor.

Hazel led Rosie through into the lounge. The older generation seemed to have settled themselves here. They had made no attempt at fancy dress and, as Hazel switched on the set, one woman said quite pointedly, 'We could have stopped at home and watched television.'

Under these circumstances Rosie didn't like to ask her hostess to turn up the volume so she just concentrated on the picture.

Was that Cody's Bookstore? Yes, it was. The police seemed to be trying to round up an angry mob on Telegraph. Blazing canisters were flying – quite slowly – through the air; and then there were shots of people rubbing their eyes. One of them was one of the Mexican brothers, the guys who always said 'Hash, grass, acid.' Now the film cut to a huge mob down a side street. A home-made notice proclaimed this to be *People's Park*.

The camera isolated a stray dog, a whippet in a spotted neckerchief, looking around unhappily and shivering with fright. A policeman landed out at two demonstrators with his night stick and then cold-bloodedly kicked the little animal. Immediately, a man thumped the kicker – really socked him one. The man was Gabriel Bonarto. The camera stayed on him as he picked up the stray and started running. Police and soldiers floored the pair of them. But the dog was still licking Gabriel's face as they were manhandled into a riot van.

'You bastard,' she said to Gabriel on the screen. But what she really meant was, 'I know exactly why I still love you.'

513

*

'God only knows what that postwoman made of *this* one!' Mrs Hankey was handing Rosie the mail. The picture postcard had a naked Carol Doda on the front and a cryptic message, in Miriam's handwriting, on the back: 'Pigs busted Gabriel. He has broken bail and vanished. Any ideas?'

The only thing she could think of was a telephone call to Gino. But the card had arrived in the second post, which would make it three in the morning in San Francisco. She would have to contain her impatience.

The best way Rosie knew of killing time involved filling the camera with one film and her pockets with more. She still kept her photographic supplies in the front room, in the meter cupboard. But the parlour was now Tippler's domain.

'Is he awake?' she asked Nora.

'The doctor's stepped up the dose of those happy-daft pills. The poor soul's mind is in twilight. Aren't you going to open your proper letter? Isn't it a pity we don't know anybody who collects foreign stamps?' The stamps on this particular envelope had Arabic writing on them.

Tippler was, as predicated, half-awake and half-asleep.

'May I sit on your bed?' asked Rosie.

'Have we docked yet?' he asked weakly. 'Is this Famagusta?'

'No, but I've got a letter from Marrakesh.'

'You want to watch out for them Arab bints, Sid.' And then he was overcome by a fit of coughing. These days Tippler was nothing but skin and bone in striped pyjamas. As the coughing subsided he wheezed, 'All Arab bints are after is your piastres. Don't go drinking that arak, Sid. It gets in the system. Just one glass of water, tomorrow morning, and you'll find yourself blind drunk again. Drunk on watch!' Suddenly he sat bolt upright. 'This isn't the port I thought it was,' he said sternly.

'Isn't it?' She had long since learned that it was easier to go along with the flow of his imaginings. 'Where are we?'

'Durban.' He lay back and dozed off again.

By now Rosie had opened the envelope and begun to unfold a sheet of wonderfully thin writing paper. Whilst thick

514

writing paper was generally supposed to be posh, this had a crackling elegance of its own.

In bed in the clinic

November 23rd, 1968

Twin,
Dear, dear, dear twin – because you are the one who made it possible.

Taylor sounded almost as light-headed as Tippler.

After a lot of delays the operation is finally done. At long last I'm me. And if there are marks on the page it is because I am crying. But they are happy tears. I've been a woman since Wednesday.

The operation itself was nothing. Just a jab in the arm and I woke up heavily bandaged. Actually, I was strapped to the bed but I didn't care. It was done. The pain since then has been the kind of agony I never knew existed. They keep poking things up me to prevent the walls of the new vagina from healing together. I expect to be here another ten days and then I'm going to Italy. No point in replying to the clinic. I will write again from Milan.

Want to know the bad news? Zav and I have split up. But that is a story I don't want to put in a letter. It will surprise you! More tears are hitting the page and these are *not* happy ones. Still a bit weak and very sore but I would have gone through this ten times over if I had to.

Love you

Taylor

Tippler stirred restlessly and then he opened his eyes. 'Hello, Rosie,' he smiled. 'Fancy you being on board.'

She tucked his sheets in, took some film from the gas meter

cupboard and headed back into the kitchen to get her camera. 'I'm going off to take some pictures of The Height,' she said to Mrs Hankey. 'Whilst it's still there.'

The whole village was buzzing with talk of demolition that would make way for a wider road. Gledhill's side of The Height was scheduled to be entirely demolished, and the man who owned the off-licence had opened his mail one morning to discover that compulsory purchase orders had been made on both his shop and his house. It was the beginning of the end of Irlams o'th' Height.

Teapot Hall would not be affected by any of this. The Health Authority had worked their own vandalism there. Even the golden teapot had been removed from the top of the tower, which now had an inappropriately flat roof. On the one occasion that Rosie had walked up the drive, uniformed nurses had glared at her as though *she* was the interloper. The dream of living there again had died. Or had it? All minds have unreasonable corners and that was the bit of Rosie Tattersall which was still hoping against hope . . .

She began walking along Bolton Road. How could anybody allow such a complete nineteenth-century village to be destroyed? And all in the cause of the motor car. One was slowing down at the side of her, at this very moment. And the bespectacled woman behind the wheel was winding down the window.

'Rosie? It is Rosemary, isn't it?'

The woman couldn't be who Rosie thought she was. Not driving a car. And never in fur-backed gauntlets. But it was: it was Poor-Bertha-who-drags-a-leg.

'The chariot is courtesy of the National Health,' Bertha explained confidently. 'I had five separate operations before they finally handed me this. I can't offer you a lift, Rosie, I'm not supposed to carry passengers. It's all specially modified and adapted.' She still talked without pausing for breath. 'I hear you've been to America. Did you see Christopher? I've never stopped thinking of him as my little boy.'

'You were the first person he asked about. Only . . .'

'Only what?'

Rosie had forgotten how easily Bertha could look

perturbed. She took a deep breath: 'Only he's had an operation. He's a lady now.'

'Thank God,' breathed Bertha. Tears began to roll from under her bifocals. 'It's what the poor little thing always wanted.' She took out a clean handkerchief and blew her nose loudly. 'If I tell you something, will you promise not to laugh? When he was little and he got me on my own, I always had to call him Jennifer. He was *never* a lad, never. And I'll tell you something else: Jennifer was a much nicer person than Christopher. Does he go under that name now?'

'No. Taylor. Taylor Tattersall.'

'I'm not sure I approve of that,' sniffed Bertha. 'Fancy going to all that trouble and then naming yourself after a man who sits threading needles. Have you got such a thing as a photo of him . . . er . . . her?'

'Not on me. But all you've got to do is look at me and you're seeing Taylor.'

'It's the best news I've heard in years,' enthused Bertha. 'It beats *Cinderella* into a cocked hat. What about you, Rosie? Has your Prince Charming come along yet?'

The telephone receiver was sticky, Moondog must have got jam on it. 'Hello? Can you hear me?' Could that echoing chipmunk at the other end really be a man? 'May I speak to Gino Frascati?'

The line went clearer: 'Gino's not here.'

'I need to know about Gabriel Bonarto.'

'Gabriele is not here, either.'

It was like talking to an Italian-American brick wall. Perhaps her own name might help. 'This is Rosie Tattersall.'

'Hi, Rosie. This is Rocco.'

He was the other Frascati. The one she'd first seen, with Gino, from that early-morning rooftop. He had also been very helpful in getting her out of America. 'Rocco, what's happening? Where are they?'

'In Italy. Things got ugly here. Gabriele was busted in the riots. And the police found that student's heroin in the apartment.'

'What student?'

517

'Gabriele took it off some guy he taught. He'd been helping him to cold turkey. But the pigs thought the smack was his.'

Me too, she thought. Me too. 'What happened?'

'We got him out.'

In the past the Frascati brothers had always treated her like a revered sister: today she was sensing reserve. 'Is he okay?'

'The family are having him looked after.'

'Would you tell him that I'm still at Mrs Hankey's?' Should she explain that she hadn't known the true ownership of the heroin? No. Too complicated. 'Just tell him that I'm still at Saracen Street.'

'It's hard to get messages to him in there.'

'In where?' But the line had already gone dead. And when the international operator rang the number for her again, nobody answered.

Early in his career, Zav had bought number seven Saracen Street off the landlord and given it to his parents. These days there was a bathroom above the scullery. But nobody had ever found the answer to the creaking floorboards in the lobby. Heard from the kitchen, they always sounded as though somebody was going to walk into the room and say something awful. And this morning Mrs Hankey did: 'That was Lily Jelly knocking. She says that when Tippler finally goes, if we take off a door she'll lay him out on it. I don't know what year she thinks she's living in! Did you phone Dr Bentley again?'

'He's on his way.'

'I'm so tired I don't know what I'm doing. I suppose it was good of Hazel to have Star. Meself, I think it was anything to avoid a deathbed.' Fatigue gave way to anger: 'Zav should be here. I don't *care* about a comeback concert in Rio – he should be on the spot.'

In the front room, Zav was more than adequately represented by his son. Moondog was sitting on a little stool by the big bed with a 'Rupert' book on his knee. 'Tippler's rattly breathing started again but it's stopped now.'

Mrs Hankey's mouth tightened and then she said, 'I wish you'd gone to your Auntie Hazel's with Star.'

'No.' He was just as stubborn as his father had been at that age.

His grandmother did not spare him. 'You do know what's going to happen, Moondog, don't you?'

'He's going to die. And I said I'd stop with him.' The child's American accent had all but vanished. Nowadays he was to all intents and purposes a Lancashire boy.

'You *can't* stop with him. You're too little.'

It was the first time Rosie had ever heard Mrs Hankey sound defeated. But this was the first deathbed the girl had ever attended. It was beginning to go dark. Should she suggest putting on a light?

Suddenly, Tippler tried to sit up.

'Watch him or he'll topple over again,' cried Mrs Hankey. The figure in the bed was skeletal and as disjointed as an unstrung marionette. As they settled him back on the pillows Rosie reflected that nothing had changed since the days when medieval painters portrayed approaching death.

Tippler let out a terrible scream. 'Christ!' he gasped. 'It hurts.' And then he began to plead. 'Make it stop. Make it stop hurting, Nora.'

'The doctor's coming,' she said, tears rolling down her face. 'Hang on, love. He's coming. Dear God,' she asked the room at large, 'how much more is he meant to go through? If you kept an animal in that state, they'd lock you up.'

Rosie did something she'd never done in her whole life; she took hold of Mrs Hankey's hand. The gas fire was making popping noises as cold February rain hit the glass of the parlour windows and made them rattle in their frames. On the mantelpiece, Rosie noticed an old photograph with a corner missing, tucked inside a framed picture of Zav. The torn photograph was of Trixie. How long was it since the foxy little dog had died? Four years, five? And why had nobody ever got round to asking Rosie to make a new print? She supposed she could do it when she eventually made some prints of Tippler the ones that would soon, inevitably, be requested – and forever treasured. The rain was really pelting down now and somebody was banging impatiently on the front door.

'That'll be him.' Nora was already heading for the lobby.

519

'Put the little table lamp on, Moondog. There's no need for a funeral parlour before we get there.'

The doctor was all bluff attentive cleanliness, in a crombie overcoat. 'This one's a fighter,' he said as he removed the stethoscope from Tippler's chest.

'He used to fight for money.' There was no energy behind Nora's words. 'He had the finest physique for miles around, and look at him now.'

Tippler let out another scream.

'All right, lad,' said the doctor. Somehow these Lancashire words sounded patronising, spoken as they were in middle-class tones.

'Do something!' stormed Nora Hankey. The energy was back.

Dr Bentley busied himself with his bag. 'I'm going to give him an injection. It will definitely stop the pain but it might render him a bit confused.'

'He was never a candidate for the *Brains Trust*,' sighed Nora as she watched the doctor bend over to administer the jab.

He straightened up. 'That should see him through. Mr Hankey might seem to rally for a bit but I'm afraid it won't last.'

Nora seemed to have been struck by a sudden thought: 'Dr Bentley, would you please tell this little boy that he shouldn't be in the room – not when it happens.'

'I promised,' said Moondog stubbornly. 'Tippler didn't make me. It was me own idea.'

'He's been very good with his gran'dad,' sighed Mrs Hankey. 'Very good indeed. They were very close.'

Rosie noticed that her landlady was already using the past tense.

'Wouldn't you like to go and sit in the kitchen with this young lady?' the doctor asked the boy.

'No.'

Dr Bentley made a 'Hmph' sound, picked up his bag, and then he added, 'Mind you, these days, they've already seen everything on television. I'll see myself out. Phone me after it happens, I'll need to sign the death certificate.' With this he was gone.

'Well, this *is* nice.'

The people round the bed nearly jumped out of their skins. The voice belonged to Tippler.

And it was Tippler at his most genial. 'All get in a line,' he said. 'We're going to play British Bulldogs.' He sat up in bed – apparently in full control of his limbs again – and peered at them closely. 'We *can't* play British Bulldogs,' he said accusingly, 'not with *girls*.' And now he registered Moondog. 'Hello, Zav.' His voice had gone happy. 'Don't tell your mother I give you that money for guitar strings or she'll leather the pair of us.' Suddenly he began to sing, robustly:

'Will your anchor hold in the storms of life,
When the clouds unfold . . .'

'Oh my God!' said Mrs Hankey. She was laughing, even though tears were rolling down her face. 'I never knew he had a bloody hymn in him. What on earth's that doctor given him?'

'Men, in a few moments we will be docking at Mombasa.' Tippler was imitating somebody of the old-fashioned officer class. 'At first the women will strike you as coal-black. After a few days they will get lighter. Soon they will be merely coffee-coloured. But how would your mothers view them as wives?' The voice turned back into Tippler's own. 'Hello, Nora.' He smiled very sweetly. 'I'm afraid the answer's got to be "No can do". The old man's just warned us against jig-a-jig-a-jig. But we could always slip behind the bandstand,' he added brightly.

'He'll be singing Zav's greatest hits next,' laughed his wife.

Tippler suddenly gasped, 'Give us a drink!'

Rosie held a glass of Lucozade to his lips. He filled his mouth and spat the contents onto the bedspread. 'Get that gum shield back in,' he said. 'There goes the bell. I'm not beaten yet.' He began to shadow-box wildly at the air. And then his hands fell to his sides and his face was filled with puzzled delight. Delight wasn't a strong enough word: he was filled with joy. 'Mam? Have I got to come in now? Is me tea ready?'

521

In that instant, Tippler Hankey was gone and a corpse collapsed towards the edge of the bed.

All Nora Hankey said was: 'Get the kiddie out, fast.'

The body was at the Co-op funeral parlour but the row over it was raging in the Hankeys' back kitchen. 'Burned without so much as a prayer said over it?' screeched Hazel.

'I'm a Freethinker,' said the new widow. 'Always have been. We'll just have a reading from Bertrand Russell and then the coffin can roll away.'

'And what do you think Little Mummy and Little Daddy will have to say about that?' This was Hazel's way of referring to her husband's parents.

'I'm afraid I'm not in the business of obliging pork butchers.' Mrs Hankey fired her next salvo: 'I don't want any wreaths either.'

'So which charity do I tell them to send the money to?'

'You don't. Why should Tippler's death force people to put their hands in their pockets?'

'Because it's *usual*,' snapped Hazel.

'Conventional, you mean. You weren't *always* this conventional, Hazel. Does your husband know you once had an abortion?'

'Of course he doesn't.'

'Well you leave the funeral arrangements to me or I might just be tempted to tell him.' For all her fire, Mrs Hankey looked exhausted. 'Rosemary, can you see who that is at the front door?'

As Rosie creak-creaked down the dark lobby she could hear a taxi's meter pinging outside, and then the sound of the vehicle moving off. More rain was hitting the glass of the fanlight over the door, and just as she undid the lock the street lights went on outside. They illuminated the figure of Zav Hankey. 'The plane was delayed at Chicago,' he said.

'Where's your luggage?' He was carrying only a shoulder bag.

'I travel light. Always did.' Rosie wondered why he was still standing in the street – like a stranger. Zav lowered his voice:

'Have you had reporters here? I mean, have they been asking awkward questions about me and Taylor?'

'No.'

He let out a sigh of relief. And only now did he step inside. 'I'm a bit cut-up about me dad so do me a favour, Rosie, don't ask me to explain about Taylor. Let her tell you the story.'

'Who is it?' called Mrs Hankey from the kitchen. 'Is it Lily Jelly?'

'No, it's the man who made her world-famous,' called back her son.

'About bloody time too!' The kitchen door was flung open. 'Well come on, haven't you got a kiss for your mother?'

Zav held her close. All the confidence seemed to have vanished out of him. When he finally spoke he sounded very young and bewildered. 'I know it sounds daft but I don't want to go into the kitchen.'

'Well you can't just stand there like a plum,' she said in surprisingly kindly tones.

'It feels funny,' Zav was still lingering in the lobby. 'I don't like it. It doesn't feel like our house any more. I keep thinking I'll hear him clear his throat and then it'd be all right.' Suddenly he started to weep, just as Moondog had been weeping, on and off for days. 'Mam?' He sounded no older than his own son. 'Mam, I want me dad.'

At most funerals the mourners could tell the life story of the person in the coffin. This wasn't the case at Tippler Hankey's funeral. 'It's just like a pathetic jumble sale.' Tippler's widow, in the front pew, was looking back over her shoulder and round the small chapel of Agecroft Crematorium. 'Where are the fighters? Where are the old sailors?' The event seemed to be charging her with false energy. 'Still, why should they be here?' she asked philosophically. 'Tippler never made much effort to go to theirs.'

It wasn't a large congregation. Behind the Hankeys and Rosie, dotted around the pitch-pine pews sat Lily Jelly, and Sid Molyneux and his wife, and Bertha, and Hazel's parents-in-law. Beyond them there were just a couple of old men who looked as though they'd feel a lot happier when the pubs opened; and then, right at the back, Biddie Costigan and the only surprise mourner – Bernadette Barrett.

The service was being conducted by a man whom the undertakers had summoned up for Mrs Hankey. Middle-aged, in a grey tweed suit, he belonged to some Humanist organisation, but if Rosie had been told that he was a Quaker, she would have had little difficulty in believing it.

'Would you all please rise?'

One of the most basic coffins the Co-op could ever have been called upon to provide was already on the runners, in front of the little wooden doors which presumably led to the flames. Hazel had defied her mother and sent a wreath. It was sitting on top of the unvarnished casket. Rosie could even read the message on the card: *Until we can say the words 'Cun I dancu' again. All my love – Hazel.* 'Cun I dancu' was 'Shall we dance' in Esperanto. How many years was it since Mrs Hankey had stopped trying to interest them in that language? Yet, without telling anybody else, Hazel and her father must have clung onto this one phrase from their past.

Mrs Hankey had been absolutely adamant that she wanted nothing mawkish about Tippler's farewell. In the event, the man from the Humanist Society did not read from Bertrand Russell. Instead, he told the story of H.G. Wells watching his own wife's coffin being consumed by the flames: '. . . one sheet of flame of amazing beauty.' Rosie was startled to find herself impressed. But she couldn't help thinking that it all seemed too antiseptic for tattooed Tippler, that he really deserved a grand finale with a bit more drama to it.

And he got it.

Zav rose to his feet, pushed his way into the aisle and turned to face the congregation. 'I always thought the coffin rolled away at crematoriums,' he said. 'But I'm told that they just close the curtains here. Well I'm not letting those curtains close on me dad without a song. I respect me mother's feelings in this matter. But when I was little, Tippler used to sing me something he learned at school. And now I'd like to sing it to him.'

Clasping his hands behind his back, Zav began to sing fearlessly:

'Will your anchor hold in the storm of life,
When the clouds unfold their wings of strife?
When the strong tides lift, and the cables strain,
Will your anchor drift, or firm remain?'

The whole atmosphere had changed and the congregation seized on this change with relief. Most of them had been educated at church schools so they knew what to sing in response to this verse. And they sang it. They belted back a chorus which said they had an anchor that kept the soul, steadfast and sure while the billows roll; fastened to the rock that cannot move, grounded firm and deep in the Saviour's love.

'And I thought I'd managed to keep religion out of this,' sobbed Mrs Hankey. Rosie couldn't decide whether her landlady was sobbing with fury or because the curtains had finally closed on Tippler's coffin.

Ordinary piped crematorium music began to ripple through the air, an attendant opened the bottom door, and the inhabitants of the front pew shuffled out and led the rest of the mourners into the winter drizzle. The purple ink on a card above a roped-off area of paving stones was already beginning to run. The dripping words said *Reserved for Floral Tributes for George McGinty Hankey*. There were none. Presumably, Hazel's wreath was going up in flames with the body. Or did they pile up the coffins and burn up a few at a time? This thought of Rosie's was interrupted by a loud angry voice.

'You!' Zav had rushed towards Bernadette Barrett. 'I don't know how you've got the nerve to show your face here. Not after what you put Rosie through. Well, you can sod off! And if you ever show your face again . . .' He was scarlet with fury. 'I've never hit a woman in my life but there's always a first time.'

White and afraid, Bernadette began to run through the rain, down the gravelled path between the tombstones. Rosie was left standing next to Biddie Costigan. The old woman from the railway carriage was, as always, carrying the remains of a sliced loaf wrapped in greaseproof paper. 'That wasn't Bernadette's *real* punishment,' she said sadly. 'No, her real punishment is that she's doomed to go through the rest of this life as herself. Mind you, that's leaving no room for miracles. We should always leave room for the eleventh-hour miracle.'

'I hope so,' said Rosie. 'Oh I do hope so.' And she wasn't thinking about Bernadette Barrett.

Winter gave way to spring but life at Saracen Street grew thinner. The children had returned to California. The house became the province of two women, Mrs Hankey and Rosie, each isolated in her own loneliness. By the time the next spring arrived, Irlams o'th' Height seemed to have been taken over by men with measuring tapes and theodolites – those objects that look like telescopes and generally herald the arrival of bulldozers. The Sixties were over.

Rosie was making a systematic photographic record of the village. She took pictures of Kidd's fish-and-chip shop (already closed) and Morton's temperance bar. It was hard to tell that the Olympia had ever been a cinema de luxe. These days it housed a showroom for television sets. But soon it would be levelled to the ground; the spot where Roy Rogers had thundered across the prairie would simply be a bit of anonymous road between Liverpool and Manchester. Wherever she positioned her camera, people always made the same comment: 'Soon be gone, soon be gone.'

Industrial fog was becoming a thing of the past, but let there be even a suggestion of mist and Rosie would be off out with her camera. She wanted a dreamlike quality to these photographs. Fine rain could capture it too. Today, a shower had turned into a downpour. Rosie couldn't find the protective hood for her lens in the camera bag, so she turned up her coat collar and headed for home.

These days you had to jiggle the key in the lock of the front door to get it open. Tippler would have fixed it in minutes. A lot of little jobs had gone neglected since his death.

As Rosie began her creak down the lobby she suddenly caught a whiff of patchouli, the scent of the dead Sixties. But from the living room – incredibly – she could hear a voice that was very much alive.

'I do like to keep ahead, Mrs Hankey.' It couldn't be but it was – it was Miriam. There she sat, in Tippler's old chair, wearing a kaftan covered in moons and stars, happily drinking the inevitable tea with sterilised milk.

Registering Rosie's arrival, Mrs Hankey pointed towards Miriam's dress. 'You should have seen Lily Jelly's face when she copped that frock! She thought she was missing out on something. She thought Miriam was knocking on doors, giving away free samples.'

'My weight is now two hundred and thirty pounds,' beamed Miriam. 'Even more to love!'

And to hug. 'Miriam, you're like the sun coming out!'

'I'll leave you girls to it,' smiled Mrs Hankey. It was obvious that Miriam had cheered her up, too. 'I've got to slip to the Height Co-op. I'm blowed if they're pulling it down before I collect me divi.'

'That's a dividend,' Rosie explained to Miriam. 'At the end of the year you get a bit back on each purchase.' By now Mrs Hankey was out in the lobby, getting into her coat.

'Co-ops I understand,' said Miriam. 'I bring hot news.'

'You're going to get married?' Letters and postcards had already suggested this as a Seventies possibility.

'Not me. Gabriel.'

'What?' Rosie had to grab hold of the mahogany dresser to steady herself.

'He's going to become a bride of Christ.'

'That's nuns.'

'As you may have noticed, I am *not* a Christian. But I presume a monk is a male nun?'

Gabriel as a monk would make perfect sense. Rosie remembered all that talk about wanting to know God. Mind you, she thought, I'd rather God had him than another woman. 'How did you find all this out? And what are you doing here?'

'I got it from somebody in the philosophy department.' Miriam reached for her wigwam bag, an item Rosie had never expected to see propped up against a table leg in Saracen Street. 'I have all the details written down. Gabriel is still flirting with the idea. He has yet to make his final commitment. Those Berkeley philosophers gave me chapter and

527

verse – they're such gossips! As for myself, my new lover has taken off for a commune in the Orkneys. I am in hot pursuit. He needs dragging into the Seventies.' She was rattling on as though they'd last seen one another yesterday. 'I plan on losing sixty pounds for this new decade. I shall wear regular clothes. Everybody else is going into these maxi-dresses. I an to flash a bit of calf.'

'You're the last person I would ever have expected to turn up . . .'

'I just did. Stop opening and closing your mouth like a goldfish, Rosemarie. We have plans to make.'

'I can't go to the Orkneys. I'm in the middle of . . .'

'Shut up. If you're in shock, drink my tea. It tastes of chemistry. You're not going to the Orkneys, you're going to Italy. Oh God!' she exclaimed. 'Not more goldfish imitations. Look, I'll give you the easy version, designed for little kids.' Miriam began to tick off explanations on her fingers. 'I am here because my mother gave me a trip. She discovered my new guy is Jewish. And his father is rich – old money – so she sees this trip as an investment. Are you receiving me, Rosemarie, because the next bit concerns you. If you don't get to Italy, pronto, Gabriel will be walled up for life.'

'I don't think they do that any more.'

'Three.' Miriam was still ticking off on her fingers. 'Remember that Gino guy? The one who was so good about getting you onto the plane? And what a weekend *that* was.' Miriam smiled at the memory. 'I still see him around. He was at the Stones concert at the Cow Palace and he says you ought to go.'

'So why didn't he call me?'

'Because Gabriel forbade it. Guilt, my dear, terrible guilt. You can surely rise above that? I must say I thought my arrival would be a lovely surprise but . . .'

'It is. It is.'

'Well don't take your coat off. We're going to Manchester. Do you have money?'

'Yes.'

'From what I remember of England, Thomas Cook was always the best travel agent.'

528

Mrs Hankey's head came round the door. 'Right, girls, I'm off. Are you sure you won't stop the night?' she asked Miriam.

'Thank you but no. Love is calling me north of the border. And this is the kind of day when both Rosemarie and I have to keep ahead. I know what a huge influence you've always been in her life, Mrs Hankey. Do tell her that she ought to go to Italy.'

Did she want to see Gabriel? Did she really want to open the old wounds? And how was Rosie to know that he would want to see her? The arguments had raged all Friday afternoon. Now it was Sunday, and as the plane for Milan took off from Manchester Airport, Rosie remembered the two assertions which had persuaded her into Thomas Cook's. 'You haven't really talked to Gabriel for years, in California you were only coping with the effects of drugs. Well, now the drugs are over.' This had come from Miriam. But it was Nora Hankey who had finally clinched the argument with, 'If it meant getting Tippler back for just five minutes, I'd take on the Pope himself!'

That was when the phone calls started. Mrs Hankey was due for a telephone bill and a half. For a start, there had been twenty minutes with Gino – at peak rate – when he had turned himself into an unlikely agony aunt, begging Rosie to give Gabriel one final chance. 'He's very serious about the monastery. Too serious. It's just like another drug. Those monks must be really excited at the idea of getting a Bonarto. When Gabriele takes a vow of poverty, just think of how much the monastery stands to gain.' All Italians are not good Catholics.

The next phone call had been to Italy. Not to Gabriel; Taylor was modelling in Milan, and she added her voice to the chorus that was urging Rosie to get herself on a flight into the sunlight.

So here she was, in a window seat, on an aeroplane which belonged to Alitalia. A bell pinged and then a lot of crackling Italian jabber came over the public address system. This was followed by: 'Good afternoon, ladies and gentlemen. This is your captain speaking.' He had a strong accent. 'If you care to look over to your left, you will see that we are passing over the white cliffs of Dover. As we approach the coast of Europe we will be changing our altitude. This is because we are anticipating some turbulence. Please fasten your seat-belts.'

You are anticipating some turbulence, thought Rosie. God knows what I'm anticipating! All she had was a rough idea of the outline of the shape of her day. The plane was due to land at Milan in time for an early lunch. Taylor was going to meet her at the barrier. Two hours in Milan and then another plane for Pisa. And after that, a bus ride across Tuscany – to Florence.

I'd got him out of my system, she thought. Not true. Anyway, she might not be allowed to see him. According to Gino this was entirely possible. The worst thought of all was a bit mixed-up. It was based on a distant memory of a black and white film which had starred either Charles Boyer or Don Ameche. She just remembered him as some Continental. And when his girlfriend tracked him down to a monastery, a big fat Abbot said to her, 'The man you knew as the Comte de Paris is no more; today he is just a simple monk called Brother Pierre.'

Rosie was fairly sure that the girl had been Greer Garson. As children, she and Christopher had always re-enacted the movies they'd seen and the pair of them had gone round repeating this scene for days. Naturally, Christopher had assumed the Greer Garson role.

The plane began to bump alarmingly. Nevertheless, determined Italian stewardesses managed to stagger down the aisle with the luncheon trays. 'No thank you,' said Rosie. 'I'm lunching in Italy.' And that was when she felt her first stab of excitement.

Despite the fact that they had flown above a storm, the plane landed on time. As Rosie gathered together her belongings and made her way down the steps and into the airport building, something unnerving began to happen. People were pausing and turning round and staring at her. Why? She was dressed for May in her new cream coat with olive-green stockings and shoes. The outfit had been a mite too eye-catching for Irlams o'th' Height, but she had never expected it to stop the traffic in Milan.

Behind his desk, the Italian immigration official was giving her passport more than a cursory glance. Had the American authorities stamped it with some secret code sign which indicated that she had been as good as deported from the States? The passport was returned to her with a great big friendly grin.

They must have got the luggage off the plane very quickly because, in a matter of minutes, it was travelling round the carousel. She was treated to more curious stares as she waded in to retrieve her bag. And the customs officials waved Rosie through with the kind of beaming smiles she would have expected them to have reserved for Gina Lollobrigida. She could already see a crowd of people waiting for passengers to arrive off the Manchester flight. One of them was in just such another cream coat as her own, but Rosie's was a copy and this one was a Fontana original. It was worn by Taylor.

She looked so new. Rosie would never forget her first sight of her sister after the operation. New. Brand-new. And much more affectionate than she'd ever been in the past. It was all 'Welcome to Italy', accompanied by warm hugs and even a kiss.

'You look amazing,' said Rosie. 'You make me feel like a country cousin.'

'Can I carry anything? Want to see me at my best? Follow me!' Now the crowds were really staring as Taylor led Rosie to the bookstall. 'Look!' Taylor's photograph was on three of the magazine covers. One of them wasn't even Italian, it was a German magazine called *Quick*. 'I could do without that one,' said Taylor, 'that was *not* a modelling job – and it's a bit full of gory details. Still, at least they haven't dug up Zav.' For a moment, the bright newness seemed dimmed. But she smiled again as somebody pointed a camera in their direction and a flashbulb went off. 'Paparazzi,' she explained. 'They're everywhere. I'm afraid you're going to have a hard time of it.'

'Me? Why?'

'You've only got to look at us. You can't tell who's who. Let's find a mirror and really compare.' There was one at the back of a showcase filled with highly desirable knitwear. 'My God!' gasped Taylor. 'I can think of fashion photographers who'd pay us a fortune to work together. Cone on, we've got to find the Ladies.'

'Do you need to go?'

'I need to show you what the surgeon did. Before the operation I was *almost* tempted to ask you to photograph your own – so he could copy it.'

'We can't both go in one cubicle,' protested Rosie.

'You paid for these alterations to my body. I'm dying for you to see them.'

Rosie found herself pushed through a door. As Taylor locked it, a light came on. She hoisted her skirt and started tugging down her white cotton knickers. 'Have a good look and tell me what you think.'

Nobody would ever have known it wasn't genuine. 'I think it's a bit neater than mine,' ventured Rosie.

'But not too neat?' asked Taylor anxiously. 'I once saw one done in England – it looked just like ruched blinds.'

'Yours is exactly like the real thing. Honestly, you could take your clothes off anywhere.'

Taylor let out a huge sigh of relief and sat down on the seat. '*And* it works,' she said. 'Might as well go, while we're here.'

Since they were on the subject, Rosie dared to ask: 'Is it okay for the other?'

'Very okay. And yes, I *can* have orgasms. Sensational orgasms!'

A pair of nuns gawped at the sight of the identical twins emerging from the same cubicle. 'Lunch,' said the new woman. 'There isn't time to go into Milano, we'll have it here.'

Airport food in Italy was much better than in England or America. As Rosie devoured artichoke hearts in a smooth lemon dressing, she noticed that even the cutlery was beautifully designed. That was the moment she realised that she had arrived in the land of style.

'How's Mrs Hankey?' asked Taylor, fishing in her handbag. She put on one pair of dark glasses and handed Rosie another. 'I can never decide whether these make people stare more or less. Still, I love being famous.'

'Mrs Hankey's suddenly gone very old. Taylor . . .' Rosie

hesitated and then plunged in with: 'Zav said you'd tell me the whole story.'

'About me and him? You won't like it. When push came to shove he didn't want me to have the surgery. It was the in-between state that he found so fascinating.'

'Zav?' Rosie could hardly believe what she was hearing.

'Zav,' replied her twin, in the tones of one who'd been further and seen more. 'I don't know why I was surprised, but I was. Half the transsexuals on earth have surgery in the cause of a man who is really interested in the one bit they want to get rid of. Don't get me wrong, these boyfriends wouldn't go to bed with another *man*. Not with a guy with muscles. I told Zav that a proper man was exactly what he ought to try. And then the real row broke out.' Taylor removed her dark glasses and looked thoughtful. 'They want the best of both worlds and they don't want anybody calling them gay. I've got another theory about Zav. It was obvious he was obsessed with the idea of you. While I was in that state, he wasn't being unfaithful to the idea. You were still the only woman in his life.'

'And now you're a woman.'

'No.' The fierceness of this reply was startling. 'I've got over that idea. I'm just the best that can be done under the circumstances. I'm a post-operative transsexual. Women operate on a twenty-eight-day cycle – no doctor on earth could make me do that. But I can *live* like this. You wouldn't understand.'

'You forget that I can see inside your head.' Rosie was already sensing a new serenity.

'If you're so clever, tell me what I've got for you in the left-luggage place.'

An iron barrier came down inside Rosie's mind. 'You're blocking me off,' she laughed. 'You're doing it on purpose.'

'Clothes! Beautiful Italian dresses. They're always giving me things so I brought some to the airport for you. Without you I wouldn't have the clothes, or the fame, or anything. Not if you hadn't given me that ring. You should have seen Gabriel's face when I went back to collect the money from your refrigerator. He was tripping and he thought I was you.'

Obviously reading Rosie's mind she added, 'No, dear, I didn't let him lay a finger on me. But what a dish! Still, you deserve him. And if I never said thanks for the ring I'm saying it now. *Grazie, grazie, mille grazie.*' Against all odds Taylor had managed to put a great distance between herself and the charmless small boy she had once been – the unhappy child who had stabbed a doll because it was the wrong gender.

Another flight, on a smaller plane, ended in a sunlit busride from Pisa to Florence. The countryside was gentle and rolling, and the trees on the crests of the hills were shaped like lollipops. All the windows of the bus were wide open and the breeze was causing their canvas curtains, striped in orange and yellow, to fly above the passengers' heads – like Renaissance pennants.

Only now did Rosie take out the brown Manila envelope which contained Miriam's present of a guide to Florence together with her notes on Gabriel's alleged whereabouts in that city. According to Miriam – though you always had to allow for dyslexia – he was supposed to be at a monastery called San Miniato al Monte. The guidebook was not blessed with an index but it was full of photographs of great art treasures and a drab text told Rosie: 'Although Florence is amply served by taxi-cabs, most parts of this compact city can easily be reached on foot by the tourist.'

'Firenze!' exclaimed somebody behind her. Even the Italian word for Florence sounded like another fluttering banner.

And there it lay, down below them, glittering in the afternoon sun. Domes and inlaid marble towers, and ancient bridges across a winding band of olive-green river. As umber and golden Renaissance buildings began to rise up on either side of the bus, Rosie felt as though she was flying through the pages of one of her favourite childhood books – Arthur Mee's *One Thousand Everlasting Things*.

Rosie's luggage was on the empty seat at her side, just a small suitcase and her camera bag and Taylor's presents, which had been handed over in a selection of almost dauntingly elegant carrier bags. The bus dropped them behind a huge square which was full of outdoor cafés and dominated by a somewhat tacky version of the Marble Arch, with a neon advertisement for Cinzano stretched across its middle.

Though Rosie didn't know it, three o'clock on a Sunday afternoon was the perfect time to arrive in Florence. The streets were almost deserted and she soon left the other people from the airport coach behind her. Turning a corner, she walked into yet another illustration from that childhood book. She actually knew the name of the vast, castellated, apricot stone building – it was the Palazzo Vecchio. And *everybody* knew the name of the statue in front of it – Michelangelo's *David*.

Well, I never imagined there'd be just me and David alone on a Sunday afternoon, she thought. He wasn't wearing a fig-leaf and he was – to say the least of it – discreetly endowed. The traveller smiled to herself as she remembered Mrs Hankey saying, all those years ago, 'We don't dwell on dickies in this household.' And that was the moment that she heard the flute.

As Rosie turned in the direction of the sound, she saw another gigantic marble figure which had to be Neptune. But sitting cross-legged at the base of the statue was a small boy wearing britches and a floppy felt hat with a feather in it. A tin box at his feet contained a few coins and he was obviously hoping for more. This was the boy who was making the music. The painting of the Piper of Dreams had come to life.

You've always been there when I needed you, she thought. You were on the wall at Teapot Hall, and you turned up in the headmistress's study on that awful first day at the church school. And you were there again – in yet another frame – at Viva's in California. And now you're here and you're real. As she opened her handbag to find some money, a couple of uniformed policemen walked up to the child musician. They were obviously telling him to move on, but this was a thoroughly amicable conversation, with the men and the boy laughing and joking. One policeman even dropped a coin into the tin.

At that precise moment Rosie suddenly realised something

amazing. *Her pane of glass had gone.* She had always thought it would take a person or an event to shift it. But no – it had taken a place. Italy had melted Rosie's glass. And she finally felt that, whatever else happened here, she had as much right in the sunlight as everybody else.

The hotel was in an old palazzo which faced the river. There was a white linen cover over the red carpet on the marble steps that led up from the street. And at the reception desk there was a lot of hissed muttering of 'Taylor Tattersall' and many curious glances at her passport. 'You have perhaps another name? An *artistic* name?' queried the receptionist.

'No, that's my sister.'

'Of *course*, signorina.' Though he was gravely handsome, she had the uncanny feeling that he was suppressing a longing to wink at her. A bell-hop carried Rosie's luggage up a broad staircase with a marble plaque on the wall which said in gilt lettering that King Umberto had once stayed here.

And how on earth did I manage to read that? wondered Rosie. Except it was easy: Italian seemed to be bits of Latin and bits of French – all melted together. It was the first time in her life she had ever been consciously grateful for the brief time she had spent at Pendleton High School.

The porter flung open one set of doors and then a second pair. The large bedroom was in semi-darkness with wooden shutters across the window. He soon had these rattled back. Through the glass doors onto a balcony she could see that the far river bank was dotted with men with fishing lines. Behind them arose the façades of more grandiose houses, set against the backdrop of a green hillside. And on top of the hill was another inlaid marble building with a high pediment. 'San Miniato al Monte,' explained the porter, already holding out his hand for a tip.

He could not have been expecting as much as Rosie gave him. If the porter's thanks were profuse, they were nothing like as fervent as her own to her Maker. She had arrived safely, and Gabriel was just the other side of the River Arno.

Rosie needed to look her very best. Showers in strange

bathrooms always filled her with panicked visions of being boiled alive, but the Italians seemed to have anticipated this: the controls were simplicity itself. And the soap in the recess inside the marble shower cabinet smelt just like Danny Cahn's enviable cologne – it was scented with limes. Even the hair-dryer had one of those new styling nozzles which only hairdressers had in England. Ten minutes with this and a brush left Rosie looking as though she had just stepped out of Sassoon's. She only hoped she could buy one of these attachments for herself, and she wouldn't mind owning this big white towelling dressing gown – the hotel had left it hanging behind the bathroom door.

Anxious as she was to find a way of getting to Gabriel, Rosie passed into the bedroom and flipped open a Florentine tooled-leather blotter on the writing desk – just to see whether any further treats lay inside. Writing paper, envelopes, and a little booklet entitled *Florence – Crucible of the Renaissance*. As she turned a page she saw an illustration that was just like the view out of the window. It was a photograph of San Miniato al Monte. Underneath was a bit of history dating back to AD 1063 and a list of opening hours and church services. On Sunday afternoons there was a Mass at five thirty. Three-quarters of an hour away. Having come this far, Rosie would willingly have swum the river to get there but she supposed a taxi would be a more sensible idea. Only what should she wear? All the photographs she had ever seen of film stars visiting the Vatican had shown them in long sleeves with their hair covered. Maybe there would be something suitable in one of Taylor's carrier bags.

Pure silk folds up small. It was just like one of those conjuring tricks where the illusionist produces more and more silken objects from small containers. Taylor had provided her with enough clothes for the entire summer. And the glossy red carrier bag which Rosie had cursed for banging against her leg was full of handmade shoes and gloves.

The plainest of the dresses was in dark grey. And when she shook it out – yes – it had three-quarter sleeves. Rosie had only to add a pair of white gloves to be well covered. And over her hair she could tie a white silk scarf of her own. When she passed the ends round her neck, and fastened them at the back, the whole effect was purest Grace Kelly. Probably all to the good – you couldn't get more Catholic than Princess Grace!

That was the moment Rosie remembered something worrying. Taylor had said, 'The Italians are wonderful about transsexuals. I'm welcomed with open arms everywhere but Rome.' What if the priests or the monks, or whatever they were, mistook her for her celebrated sister? What if they slung her out? For safety's sake, Rosie added the big pair of dark glasses.

All of this had been accomplished with great bravado, apprehension only returned as she walked down the hotel's wide staircase. But Italy continued to smile upon her: the concierge summoned a porter who found a taxi immediately, and the driver even spoke English.

'Ponte Vecchio.' His stabbing finger was indicating a bridge which was two away from the one they were crossing. Rosie immediately thought of the radio programme *House-wives' Choice* and of Joan Hammond singing 'O My Beloved Father'. The line from the song that she was particularly remembering was: 'I'll go to Ponte Vecchio to buy a wedding ring.'

As if reading her thoughts, the driver said, 'All the little jewellers' shops are on the bridge.' Pale old umber stone buildings, actually on the bridge itself.

Whey did she suddenly want to weep? Certainly not because she was unhappy. It was just that the whole place was so magically beautiful. And not museum-beautiful – it looked *used*. Used and a bit battered, but oh so goldenly magnificent. Now they were on the other side of the river and the car was already beginning to climb above terracotta rooftops. Within minutes they had swung through some iron gates and the taxi was scrunching to a halt on pebbled gravel. 'San Miniato,' said the driver.

As she got out to pay him, Rosie let out an audible gasp. The whole of Florence lay beneath her; from up here it looked like a toy city that could have belonged to an infant Medici.

'You interested in astrology?' quizzed the driver. 'All the signs of the zodiac are inside San Miniato.'

Trust Gabriel to have found a monastery like that! White-robed monks were wandering across the silver gravel. Some of them had stopped to talk to knots of tourists with cameras. For once, Rosie had not brought her own. And everybody else seemed so relaxed with one another that she was left feeling like a Quaker interloper.

Just what was she doing here? It wasn't as though she had a specific plan. In her mind she formed the words, 'I've come to case the joint.' She followed a family of Americans down some steps and into a garden. 'And I'll go to the service,' was the next specific thought. 'And I'll just see what it's all about.' Mass was due to start in ten minutes' time.

The garden proved to be a graveyard. The tombs were like miniature churches with altars visible inside. A pathway led her into an airy glass and stone arcade which was filled with more tombs. Some of them were half smothered with cut flowers in marble vases, but there was one which looked downright dusty and unloved. The only words inscribed on the stone were *Edith and Kathleen O'Rourke, R.I.P.* How on earth had two Irishwomen got here?

Rosie remembered having heard that Catholics are meant to pray for the repose of the souls of their dead, so she said a quick one for poor old abandoned Kathleen and Edith. 'I hope they're okay, wherever they are. And please God would you mind helping me? Because God only knows what I'm doing here! And if that was taking your name in vain – I'm sorry. Amen.'

As she turned to leave, her eyes lighted on the biggest tomb of all. Flights of marble angels surrounded a door into a small chapel with a prie-dieu in front of the altar. You couldn't get to this praying stool because there was a glass panel in the way. The pane of glass was inscribed with one word – *Bonarto*.

'You melted the other one,' she said to God. 'Do you think you could have a go with this? That's if I'm not too late.'

A bell which sounded a little bit cracked had begun to ring from the higher level. Was she, she wondered, just a little bit cracked herself? Sightseers were getting ready to turn themselves into worshippers and Rosie followed them out of the cool of the arcade, across the garden, up the steps and into the church.

Once again, those unexpected tears came into her eyes. For the first time in her life Rosie was glad that she had not brought her camera. She didn't want to freeze the image; she wanted it to wander through her brain like the incense she was smelling. The interior of the church could have been a Byzantine guildhall. It was all height and raftered splendour and inlaid marble and mosaic surfaces glittering with Florentine gold. The end of the climb to Heaven must be like walking into San Miniato.

Women in black lace mantillas were dipping their fingers in a holy water stoup, and then touching their children's fingers with their own. Everybody except Rosie was blessing themselves with the sign of the cross. And then they began streaming across the mosaic floor towards a chapel which seemed to be behind an elaborate altar.

Rosie followed the crowd down more stone steps and into a gloomy crypt. There was a wooden horseshoe of empty seats behind a coffin-shaped altar, but the worshippers were taking their places opposite this. Some electric lights went on and the gloom was fractured by incredibly slender white columns reaching up to a vaulted ceiling. A bell rang, and everybody got to their feet as the monks began to file in and take their places in the seats behind the altar.

From behind her dark glasses, Rosie's photographer's eye was admiring the way that the white robes exactly complemented the architecture. But her heart had taken in something else. It was leaping and thrilling and near to despair. The last monk in the line was Gabriel Bonarto.

She was right at the back; he had not seen her. And he continued to fail to notice her throughout the entire service. The ritual proceedings were a complete mystery to Rosie. There was a tricky moment when something white and circular got held above a golden chalice and everybody else fell forward – leaving Rosie sitting bolt upright.

All this way to find that her lover had turned into God's boyfriend! 'I call that pinching.' Once again she was having an internal conversation with the Almighty. 'You've got a whole beauty chorus there. What did you need Gabriel for? If there's any more kneeling to you in this service, I'm not going to do it. You can count me out.' As she thought of an old hymn, she added, 'And your mercies don't "aye endure". You let me come all this way to find you've swiped him.'

Her heart was coming out with all of this but her mind was already assembling thoughts which were more reasonable. The monks were all dressed the same, but did this mean that they had all taken their final vows?

At the end of the Mass, they filed out as formally as they had arrived. Rosie climbed the stone steps and crossed the vast floor of the church again. Enchantment had vanished. What was the point of building things to the greater glory of God when he already owned everything?

And you can have too much of sunlight, she thought as she got outside. I had too much of it in California. But I *want* Gabriel. I want him as much as I did the first time I saw him in the Vesuvius coffee bar.

For several minutes she stood looking down at Florence. Its beauty was undiminished. Behind her, she could hear a group of people speaking in English. Two women in American-English and a man using the language she spoke herself. It was the boss priest – the one who had taken the service.

As he waved goodbye to the American tourists Rosie found it hard to decide whether he was a young man who looked old or an old man who looked young. There was something timeless about him. 'Good afternoon,' she ventured boldly.

'Good afternoon.'

Did she sense reserve? Had he noticed her sitting bolt upright when all the rest were slumped forward? 'I'm not a Catholic,' she explained defiantly.

'That's not your fault.'

And I can do without the sympathy, she thought. 'May I see Gabriel Bonarto?'

'I'm afraid that's impossible.'

'Well, I need to talk to somebody about him.'

'And who are you?'

'My name is Rosie Tattersall.' Was that amusement she could see in his eyes?

'You may come and see me tomorrow afternoon at one fifteen. Just ask for the prior.' Having delivered this autocratic pronouncement, the monk floated off on feet that barely touched the ground. But inside his sandals, his long bony toes looked every bit as sinister as Viva Rapport's.

The night sounds were minimal, the hotel bed was comfortable, yet sleep was evading her. *'You may come and see me tomorrow afternoon at one fifteen.'* Why couldn't he have talked to her there and then? And what had that amused smile been about? Mrs Hankey had always *said* that Roman Catholicism was a religion of fear!

As Rosie hovered between sleep and wakefulness, the face of the prior seemed to be hanging inside her mind like a glowing mask. The was something familiar about this old-young visage; not familiar in the way of seeing people every day, outside Stott's the greengrocer's – more like a face from an old newsreel.

Rosie drifted off into an exhausting doze filled with dreams of Gabriel being walled, brick by brick, into a monk's cell. 'I can get erections again, Rose,' he murmured, 'but I don't think we can make love through this gap.' A tiny Jesus was watching the proceedings from a crucifix, hanging on the wall. He looked surprisingly like the Duke of Edinburgh. And then his face changed into that young-old face of the prior before everything shaded into darkness.

Rosie was brought back to consciousness by a loud banging on the bedroom door. Sunlight was trying to find its way through the slats of the wooden shutters and her watch showed it to be half past ten. Rosie stumbled out of bed. The person knocking was a chambermaid: '*Scusi*, you leave today?'

'No. Not today.' With no idea of what was going to happen, Rosie had reserved the accommodation for three nights. The maid followed her back into the room, flung back the shutters and opened the glass doors onto the balcony, which was covered in terracotta urns overflowing

542

with spring flowers. As the maid smiled and vanished, Rosie reached for her dressing gown and stepped outside.

'Well at least I've found you,' she said aloud. She was talking to the city of Florence. Enchantment had not died in the night. The fishermen had vanished and workaday Monday had brought a lot of spluttering motor scooters out onto the street. Amidst all this glowing antiquity they seemed curiously impudent and jolly. 'Jolly' had been a great word in the days of Rosie's childhood, and now it seemed to have gone out of fashion. What should she wear today? Coffee would help to make up her mind. She picked up the telephone and asked for room service.

An hour later, wearing a yellow linen dress of her own and a pair of grey suede shoes from out of Taylor's carrier bag, Rosie walked down into the street and began to wander. Oh dear, these little peg heels were not at all the thing for marble pavements. Was that really a marionette shop? It was. And if she wanted to negotiate this bend in the road, she was going to have to cross cobblestones. Though Rosie had been earning real money for quite a while, she had always been too busy working to think about it. If the shoes were unsuitable, there was nothing to stop her buying another pair.

As she started looking for a shoe shop her eyes lighted on a sign which said *Appartamento d'Affitto*. I could even come and live in Italy, she thought. On my own. Photographers can live anywhere. I could get a flat and I could get a dog. Why had she never got one in California? Because she'd never felt settled, that was why. Yes, I could be a spinster with a little dog. Except she was getting admiring glances from practically every man who passed her. The young ones were so classically handsome and they wore such tight jeans that, had one leg been yellow and the other orange, they could have walked straight off fourteenth-century canvases. Or out of a production of *Kiss Me Kate*.

I could even take a lover, thought this new adventurous Rosie. Except I don't want a lover because I've already got one. Or at least I had one. I need to know what's *happened* to him. Hurry up, one fifteen.

Finding sensible shoes took half an hour. As a matter of

fact they were highly elegant shoes – grey kid moccasins. And somebody pinched her bottom as she walked out of the shop. Her feet were now taking her across one of the bridges to the San Miniato side of the river. In an attempt to kill more time she sat down outside a workmen's cafe and drank two bottles of Coca-Cola – all because she didn't know the Italian for lemonade. And the man gave her so little change that she suspected him of having rooked her. I shall learn Italian, she thought; maybe the dog will help me. In truth she had meant this seriously, but as Rosie realised the absurdity of the idea she began to laugh out loud. The laughter gave way to a tug of apprehension. It was now five minutes to one.

The last stretch of road up to the monastery proved to be a dusty haul. But she didn't have to seek out the prior. He was already standing on the steps of a little stone pavilion to one side of the church.

'Come into the office,' he said.

It was cool and shadowy inside the stone building. The chairs were antique, the desk belonged in a museum, but the camera that sat on top of it was the very latest Rolleiflex. And in that moment Rosie realised who the priest was. She did know him. 'You're Freddie Click-Click!' she exclaimed incredulously.

'I was,' he laughed. 'I most certainly was.'

She was finally face to face with the man who had taught photography on television in her childhood. Rosie found herself blushing with pleasure. 'I owe you a huge debt of gratitude. I still do half the things you taught us. As a matter of fact, I grew up to be a photographer.'

'I know.' He was still smiling. 'I know a lot about you. You see, I'm not just the prior here, I'm also Gabriele's spiritual director.'

'What's that? No, begin at the beginning. Explain this place to me.' Freddie Click-Click was somebody she had no hesitation in questioning.

'What can I tell you? We have twelve monks. And then two American student monks, and an elderly abbot who lives with us in pension.'

'Where does Gabriel fit into all of this?'

'He has been living here under obedience.'

'Don't understand.' She knew instinctively that it was all right to talk to him like this.

'Do sit down. I am breaking no confidences when I tell you that Gabriele arrived here in a confused state. Legend has it that St Miniato swam across the river with his own head in his hand. Gabriele arrived in much the same condition. It was of course the drugs. The poor man had tried to take short cuts to a greater awareness of God.'

'Don't I know it!'

'He was filled with the idea that he had a vocation for our kind of life.'

All she dared ask was: 'And?'

'He has about as much vocation as that chair. He is a good man, but Gabriele as a monk?' The former Freddie Click-Click began to giggle in a most endearing manner. He turned back into a composed prior with: 'I must say that your arrival is the best news we've had in months. Do you still love him?' He could have been asking whether she used Kodak film.

But this made it easy to simply answer, 'Yes.' And then she asked, 'Is being under obedience like being certified? Is he locked in?'

The prior brushed this aside with, 'He waits at table, sometimes he keeps the door, he makes up the numbers in the choir. If he wants to go out, I consult with his family. After we spoke yesterday, I telephoned his uncles. I've never heard such cries of joy in my life.'

'About me?' she asked, astonished.

'Yes, about you. Of course the Bonartos already knew you'd arrived in Italy. Never feel you have to fear them, Rosie. It's centuries since the Bonartos were people to be feared.'

One thing had to be clearly stated. 'I can't cope with Gabriel on drugs.'

'That's over. And, by the grace of God, I don't think you will find that he needs them again.'

'There's one other thing I can't cope with – Thomas De Quincey.'

'San Miniato has given Gabriele the space to come to terms

with the differences between reality and phantoms. These days he can even *joke* about De Quincey.'

'Joke?' This was amazing news. 'Thomas was always sacred territory.'

'Not any more.' Somebody was knocking on the glass of the door to the courtyard. 'Turn round,' said the monk.

'Me?'

'You.'

The figure silhouetted against the toy city of Florence was Gabriel Bonarto. Today he was not in a monk's habit, he was just in jeans and an old blue jersey that she remembered from Berkeley.

'All yours,' said good Freddie Click-Click. 'Sort it out between yourselves.'

It was Gabriel who opened the door and Rosie who flew into his arms. Their embrace was as valid and as full of belonging as the silence of a Quaker meeting. 'You came,' he said eventually. 'You make me feel so ashamed. But you had the strength to come.'

'Don't be ashamed.'

'I am.'

One thing about last night's dream had been right. She could feel that his body was back in working order. This thought was interrupted by a discreet cough. 'I wonder if you would excuse me?' asked the English prior. 'I have to organise some flowers for a dressmaker friend of mine. It's the feast of St Rita and they will make her so happy.' In a moment he was floating away and, today, the toes inside the sandals just looked like any old toes.

'Who's St Rita?' she asked Gabriel.

'The patron saint of dressmakers. This world and the next are wonderfully mixed up at San Miniato. I'm so full of guilt . . .'

'Don't be. Maybe you had to come this far to turn into you. The real you.' She had no worries on this score because she could see in his face that he had matured into the person who had always been waiting inside. But this guilt of his was not to be borne. And that was the moment when the only useful advice that Connie had ever given her came flooding back.

She could actually hear her mother saying: 'You have to forgive Italians. You have to forgive them *lavishly*.'

Rosie took a deep breath: 'Gabriel, I forgive you. The bad times are over. They're done with. Your only penance is that you've got to accept it. And if you apologise again I'll kick you.'

'You have a heart the size of Italy,' he said. And his smile was in competition with the sunlight.

'I love Italy,' she smiled back, 'love it. It's as though it's always been waiting for me.'

'And guess what we have waiting, down in the town? A car. The prior borrowed it for me, from an antique dealer, for the day.'

They laughed their way down the hillside where flowers were growing out of rocky walls. And they talked their way past the first two bridges. The one they finally crossed was the Ponte Vecchio. There weren't just jewellers' shops on the bridge, there was also a bronze monument to the greatest jeweller of the Renaissance – Benvenuto Cellini. And people had thrown red roses into the sparkling waters in the copper basin of his memorial fountain.

But Gabriel wasn't looking at these, he was gazing into the window of one of the old stone shops. 'Dare I ask you? Shall we buy one?'

Rosie began to laugh and cry in the same moment. 'Gabriel, it's just like Joan Hammond on *Housewives' Choice*. We've come to Ponte Vecchio to buy a wedding ring. Oh yes.' Italy had swept all her doubts away. 'Let's buy one. Please let's buy one.'

And that wasn't all they did. They collected the little car – a white Fiat – and Gabriel drove them out of the town and into the countryside where rolling fields were edged with the tall cypress trees of Tuscany. 'I want to show you somewhere,' he said.

'What kind of somewhere?'

'Somewhere that's mine . . . ours. I inherited it when I was fourteen. Castello degli Angeli.'

The road curved and then dipped, and as they came to a break in an old rubble wall he slowed the car down to a halt.

Far beneath them, down in a valley, she saw a house. It was a house that was entirely familiar to her. Only the version she knew and loved was in Irlams o'th' Height – where its tower was lopped off and its weathervane removed. But this tower was intact. And instead of a teapot, a golden angel was spreading his wings towards the Tuscan sun.

'Castello degli Angeli,' said Gabriel. Rosie Tattersall had finally found her way home.